THE VIRGIN
IN THE GARDEN

THE VIRGIN
IN THE GARDEN

A. S. Byatt

Vintage International

VINTAGE BOOKS
A DIVISION OF RANDOM HOUSE, INC.
NEW YORK

FIRST VINTAGE INTERNATIONAL EDITION, JANUARY 1992

Copyright © 1978 by A. S. Byatt

All rights reserved under International and Pan-American Copyright
Conventions. Published in the United States by Vintage Books, a division of
Random House, Inc., New York. Originally published in Great Britain
by Chatto and Windus, London, in 1978. First published in the United States
by Alfred A. Knopf, Inc., in 1979.

The author wishes to thank *The Times* for permission to reprint 'Dawn of the
Year' in Part II. Grateful acknowledgment is also made to Princeton University
Press for permission to reprint an excerpt from *The Collected Works of
C.G. Jung*, trans. R.F.C. Hull, Bollingen Series XX. Vol. 12: *Psychology and
Alchemy* copyright 1953, © 1968 by Princeton University Press.
Excerpts reprinted by permission of Princeton University Press and
Routledge & Kegan Paul.

Library of Congress Cataloging-in-Publication Data
Byatt, A. S. (Antonia Susan), 1936—
The virgin in the garden / A. S. Byatt. — 1st Vintage
International ed.
p.   cm.
Originally published in Great Britain by Chatto and Windus in 1978.
ISBN 0-679-73829-0 (pbk.)
I. Title.
PR6052.Y2V57   1992
823'.914—dc20   91-50495
CIP

Manufactured in the United States of America
79B86

PACIFIC UNIVERSITY
LIBRARY

CONTENTS

THE VIRGIN IN THE GARDEN

For my son

Charles Byatt

July 19th 1961 – July 22nd 1972

PROLOGUE

The National Portrait Gallery: 1968

She had invited Alexander, whether on the spur of the moment or with malice aforethought he did not know, to come and hear Flora Robson do Queen Elizabeth at the National Portrait Gallery. He had meant to say no, but had said yes, and now stood outside that building contemplating its sooty designation. She had also, for good measure, invited everyone else present at a very ill-assorted dinner party: only Daniel, beside himself, had accepted. There had been a young painter there who had declared that the words National and Portrait were in themselves enough to put him off, thanks. It was not, this decided person declared, his scene. It was Alexander's scene, Frederica had firmly said, and Alexander had demurred, although he had always had a fondness for the place. Anyway, he had come.

He considered those words, once powerful, at present defunct, national and portrait. They were both to do with identity: the identity of a culture (place, language and history), the identity of an individual human being as an object for mimetic representation. Both mattered, or had mattered, to Alexander. He found himself, nevertheless, aesthetically amused by his surroundings. There was the black circling curve of railings to which was tied a repeating series of pale reproductions of the Darnley portrait of Elizabeth Tudor, faded coral, gold, white, arrogance, watchfulness, announcing "People, Past and Present".

On the way he had passed several recruiting posters for the First World War, pointing accusatory fingers at him, and a shop called "I was Lord Kitchener's Valet", full of reproduced bric-à-brac of the British Empire, backed not by bugles calling but by the universal clang and moan of amplified electric guitar. On a Shaftesbury Avenue hoarding he had seen a monstrous image of a rear view of a brawny worker, naked to the waist and from there enclosed in tight-buttoned red, white and blue breeches. "I'm Backing Britain" was scrawled across this person's bulging backside.

Above him, on the steps of the National Gallery were the peripatetic folk with the new ancient faces. Jesus boots, kaftans, sporadic bursts of song or tinkling breaking a tranquillised hush.

Alexander went in. She was not there, as he might have known. The Gallery had changed since his last, not recent, visit. It had lost some of its buff and mahogany Victorian solidity and had acquired a stagey

richness, darkly bright alcoves for Tudor icons on the stairway, not, he
thought, unpleasing. He went up to look for the Darnley portrait,
which had been removed for the performance, so he was left to sit on a
bench contemplating an alternative Gloriana, raddled, white-leaded,
bestriding the counties of England in thunderstorm and sun, painted an
inch thick, horse-hair topped and hennaed, heavy with quilted silk,
propped and constricted by whalebone.

The crowd flowed between him and the paintings. It seemed to have
overflowed from the steps of the National Gallery, variously uniformed,
uniformly various. Grimy thonged feet under, silky, fluffy, matted
beards over, sari and saffron robe. Military jackets from Vietnam and
the Crimea, barely sprouted moustaches and poultry-thin necks popping
out of gilded collars above tarnished epaulettes. Rubber-hard girls in
silver tights and silver boots, with silver skirts bouncing on compact
rumps. Limp girls in black velvet dangling meshed-metal purses, with
paper flowers in the coils and curtains of their artificial hair. Several
George Sands, Mesdemoiselles Sacripant, in trousers, frilled shirts, and
velvet berets. Shuffling, sexless people in drooping garments made from
the ill-printed Indian bedspreads that had gathered dust in the seaside
attics of Alexander's childhood. Some carried brand-new Benares
begging bowls. Like cows they clattered new shiny bells round their
necks. Alexander had seen these for sale in dozens of street-stalls. The
vendors had little placards saying that the bells symbolised inwardness.

Under English macintoshes, English tweed, English cashmere,
American tourists edged doggedly forward, wired from plastic knobs in
the ears to the inward murmur of the boxed soundguides. It was no
doubt whispering about the iconic and yet realistic qualities of these
English Renaissance images, barbaric and crude two centuries after the
solid and airy glories of the High Renaissance, yet a style that was
beginning to know what it was. A secular style, a new beginning after
the iconoclastic excesses under young Edward VI, when angels, Mothers
and Children had flared and crackled in the streets, immolated to a logical
absolute God who disliked images.

Alexander thought, surveying Thomas Cromwell and the mock-
soldiers, about the nature of modern parody. It seemed to him who did
not understand or like it, undirected and aimless: they imitated anything
and everything out of an unmanageable combination of aesthetic
curiosity, mocking destructiveness and affectionate nostalgia, the desire
to be anything and anywhere other than here and now. Did these
soldiers loathe or secretly desire warfare? Or did they not know? Was
it all a considered "statement", as the painter would have said, about
accommodated and unaccommodated man? Or was it just a hysterical

continuation of childhood dressing-up? Alexander himself had considerable knowledge about the history of clothing, could place a shift of seam or change of cut in relation to tradition and the individual talent almost as well as he could a verse-form or a vocabulary. He watched his own clothes and his own poetry in the light of these delicate shifts of subdued innovation. But he was apprehensive that at this time there was no real life in either.

He was nevertheless, at fifty, in well-cut olive gabardine, cream silk shirt and gold chrysanthemum tie, a handsome man.

He went out again, against his better judgment, to look for Frederica. He leaned over the balcony above the stairwell. Directly below him, in front of a portrait of the late King, his Queen, and two princesses in vermilion lipstick, drooping skirts and sling-back shoes, all dwarfed entirely by the huge canvasful of pale green good taste and glitter of chandeliers and silver teapots in a drawing-room in Windsor, Frederica was engaged in a feinting, weaving dance, round a quilted triangular stool, with an unknown man. This man was large, and, foreshortened from above, consisted of a wide expanse of glossy black PVC raincoat, crisping out round a bulky body, and a heavy mass of straight blond hair, with a sheen like cool butter.

This man reached across the stool and caught her wrist: she reached up, spoke in his ear, kissed him under it, and twisted away. He reached after her as she moved off, and ran the flat of one large hand down her spine, over her tail, cupping it, resting there. It was a gesture of complete, and public, intimacy. He then shouldered his way out through the crowd, not looking back. Frederica laughed, and came on up. Alexander retreated.

"Ah, *there* you are. Have you seen Daniel? I'm amazed he thought fit to come."

Alexander did not answer, since he could see Daniel coming along the landing, a fat man in black cords and black turtleneck sweater. He came heavily up to them and nodded.

"Well met," she said. "We three. Were you given gifts on the way in?"

"No," said Daniel.

She extended her hands. In one was a greenish square of mirror glass, possibly a tiny bathroom tile. In the other was a crushed strawberry cloakroom ticket with 69 on one side and LOVE stamped on the other in mauve ink.

"Pressed on me by a platinum blonde Pocahontas and a cowboy in a green eyeshade. Is it a joke, or an earnest message?"

"Both," said Alexander. "All our earnest messages are couched as

jokes and we take our jokes deadly seriously. We frame them and cover
our gallery walls with them. The great British Sense of Humour,
cross-fertilised by American self-consciousness, the Latin absurd and
the Oriental finger-snap or educative blow on the ear. Your messages
say what they say – and they indicate that what they say is absurd – and
they add, moreover, that the absurdity is due to a further profundity.
And so *ad infinitum*."

"My dear," said Frederica, "that reminds me. Did you know you are
now an established O level set text? Do they have to ask your permission?"

"Don't," said Alexander, wincing.

She held out the glass. "What shall I do with it?"

"Carry it. Like a type of vanity. Or a just possible alternative – a type
of self-knowledge."

She held it to one eye. "You can't *see* much in it."

"Put it in your pocket," said Daniel, "since you took it from them."

"That was good manners, English good manners."

"Good manners means you pocket it gracefully."

"Yes," said Frederica.

The long gallery, in which they took their seats for the recital was full
of a different kind of people. Alexander amused himself by counting
powerful women: there was Dame Sybil Thorndike, graciously accepting a throne-like chair from Dr Roy Strong, at that time Director of the
Gallery, and an iconographer, possibly even an idolater, of the Virgin
Queen. There was Dame Helen Gardner, head up, face benignly severe,
Merton Professor of Renaissance Literature in the University of Oxford.
There was Lady Longford, biographer of Queen Victoria, and in the
background he thought, he hoped, he discerned the large, contem-
platively vague figure of Dr Frances Yates, whose writings on the
images of Elizabeth Tudor as Virgo-Astraea had, as it turned out,
signally changed the whole shape of his own life. There also was Lady
Antonia Fraser, accompanied by a dumpy woman in a raincoat, and
wearing a St Laurent skirt, a pair of high soft suede boots and a jerkin
and hat which were derived remotely and through endless shifts of
urban elegance from the buckskins of cowboys, Indians or trappers. She
was considering the Darnley portrait, which hung above the dais, with
a firmly courteous if critical gaze. Her sympathies were presumably
elsewhere, although she had a look, he thought fancifully, of a modern
Belphoebe in those garments, sunny hair and the accoutrements of a
huntress. If she was Belphoebe, Frederica, in a kind of brief knitted
corselet of dark grey wool with a glitter in it, and boots with a metallic

sheen, was Britomart, her hair itself cut into a kind of bronze helmet, more space-age, maybe, than Renaissance. He turned his attention to the Darnley portrait, his favourite.

There she stood, a clear powerful image, in her airy dress of creamy stiff silk, embroidered with golden fronds, laced with coral tassels, lightly looped with pearls. She stood and stared with the stillness and energy of a young girl. The frozen lassitude of the long white hands exhibited their fineness: they dangled, or gripped, it was hard to tell which, a circular feathery fan whose harsh whirl of darker colours suggested a passion, a fury of movement suppressed in the figure. There were other ambiguities in the portrait, the longer one stared, doublenesses that went beyond the obvious one of woman and ruler. The bright-blanched face was young and arrogant. Or it was chalky, bleak, bony, any age at all, the black eyes under heavy lids knowing and distant.

Her portraits had been treated as icons and as witches' dolls: men had died for meddling with them in various ways, such as stabbing, burning, piercing with hog's bristles, embedding in poison.

She herself had been afraid, but had not lost her head.

It was so clear, thought Alexander, that there had been someone real there to be portrayed. But she was like Shakespeare, a figure whose over-abundant energy attracts dubiously mixed emotions, idolatry and iconoclasm, love and fear, and the accompanying need to diminish and reduce their strangeness and ordinariness by reductive myths and pointless "explanations". Shakespeare did not write Shakespeare: Shakespeare was not Shakespeare: he was Marlowe or Bacon or de Vere or Queen Elizabeth herself. Elizabeth was not Elizabeth the Virgin Queen: she was a whore, of Babylon or London, a clandestine mother, a man, Shakespeare. He had once, with delight, read a book with a laudatory preface by Erle Stanley Gardner that "proved" that Shakespeare's plays were the secret fruit of the Queen's marriage to England, the result of a double vow, to celibacy (at 15) and to literature (at 45). Arguments advanced in favour of her authorship of Shakespeare were the likelihood that she might be well enough educated to possess the necessary very large vocabulary (variously estimated at 15,000 or 21,000 words) and the necessary Negative Capability. This Negative Capability was exemplified in her capacity to hold military, marital and economic decisions in endless unresolved suspense. She had, of course, concealed her authorship to ensure fair criticism of her work, and because she feared she might be charged with neglecting her duty as a sovereign.

Alexander smiled secretly. If Shakespeare, like Homer, must be proved to be a woman, people, including many of his own contemporaries, had always found it necessary to prove that Queen Elizabeth was really a

man. As a boy he had been excited by that idea. More, much more, than
by the secret hustling away of Leicester's putative bastard. Thews and
sinews buckled under whalebone, male muscles, and other things,
buried and hidden in rustling silk. Later still he had come to associate
this arcane pleasure with Spenser's Dame Nature, who "hath both kinds
in one", "nor needeth other none". A satisfactory state of affairs. To
imagine.

The actors entered, recited, were applauded. Dame Flora, plain in
plain black, recited the Queen's own lyric

> My Care is like my shaddowe in the Sunne
> followes one fliinge, flies when I pursue it . . .

There were rich descriptions of her coronation and generosity to the
commonalty. There was the Tilbury speech. Alexander was quietly
moved.

Frederica was not. She found Dame Flora's rendering too softly
feminine: she was perhaps predisposed to be critical. The stiff Petrarchan
antitheses were delivered with a liquid Victorian painfulness and the
rich, plaintive, sincere voice stumbled over the most ferocious and
famous assertion: I know I have the body of a weak and feeble woman
but I have the heart and stomach of a king. This was all woman,
Frederica thought crossly, ordinary woman, like peering into the Royal
kitchenette at Buckingham Palace to be reassured that robes and furred
gowns hide a wife and housewife. Turn this queen out of her kingdom
in her petticoats and handy-dandy, which is the actress, which is the
queen? And the grand, fierce cadences of the great prose given human
pauses and "natural" flow. "I take no such pleasure in it that I should
much wish it, nor conceive such horror in death that I should greatly
fear it; and yet I say not, but if the stroke were coming perchance flesh
and blood would be moved with it and seek to shun it . . ." Frederica
wondered what they had sounded like, the speeches, whether they had
been as sonorously perfect as she imagined them, or more broken,
halting, nervous, written up maybe and polished for posterity, of which
she herself was part.

Actor and actress recited a poem she, Frederica, had not known,
A Song betweene the Queen's Majestie and Englande.

> Come over the born Bessy
> Come over the born Bessy
> Swete Bessey come over to me;
> And I will thee take
> And my deare Lady make
> Before all other that ever I see . . .

I am thy lover faire
Hath chose thee to mine heir
And my name is merry Englonde . . .

Memory tugged. Come over the born, Bessy. Frederica got excited.
When the performance was over she tugged in turn at Alexander's
sleeve.

"That poem, that's *Lear*. Look, where he stands and glares. Wantest
thou eyes at trial, madam? Come o'er the bourn, Bessy. That's Edgar.
And the fool: her boat hath a leak. And she dare not speak, why she
cannot come over to thee. My footnotes always said that meant syphilis.
Surely that was risky, surely that was sacrilege or something?"

"It was about the end of her reign, when they were afraid the kingdom
would be divided, *Lear*. Decay of powers. And of merry Englonde."

"She said, when she talked to the archivist in the Tower, she said, I
am Richard II, know ye not that?"

"I know," said Alexander. "I know."

"So you do, it was in your play, I probably learned it from there."

"Probably," said Alexander, possessed by terrible sadness. He wished,
he thought, that he had never written that play. To be here, now, with
the Darnley Portrait, was like being in a room with a woman you had
once been led to assault, unsuccessfully, with whom no other relation
was now possible.

"If I had the chance to do that again now, I'd do it quite differently,
quite."

"You always could do it again."

"Oh no." Alexander had a strongly linear sense of time. Chances did
not come round again, they went, and stayed, past. He had sometimes
thought of more modern, more artificial ways of rendering that matter,
the virgin and the garden, now and England, without undue sentiment
or heavy irony. But he would not try.

"It was good the first time, though," Frederica was saying. "In the
first place. All the singing and dancing. Funny, the fifties. Everybody
thinks of it as a kind of no-time, an unreal time, just now. But we were
there, it was rather beautiful, the Play, and the Coronation and all that."

"A false beginning," said Alexander.

"All the beginning there was," she said. "My beginning, anyway.
That was what did happen."

"I must go," said Daniel. "I must go."

They turned to him in distress. He hadn't said anything, had he
enjoyed it? What did he think?

Nothing, really, said Daniel. To tell the truth, he was so tired, he'd sunk into a kind of peaceful coma, he'd heard almost nothing, he was sorry. He must go now. He had to see someone.

Someone was a woman whose son had been damaged in a smash. He had been a beautiful boy, and still was, a walking unreal figure of a beautiful boy, a wax doll inhabited alternately by a screaming daemon and a primitive organism that ate and bulged and slept, amoeba-like. His father had been unable to bear it and had left. The woman had been a good teacher, and now was not, had had friends, and now did not, had had a pleasant body, and now did not. She was afraid, and angry, and exhausted and would not for a moment leave what was and was not her boy. She wanted Daniel to come with her to Court about the damages: the grounds she gave were that someone might laugh at her boy, and she would go berserk. Daniel had said he would come: it was tiring, waiting in court corridors for the case to be heard. He had come today to hear other voices than her repetitive desperate shrilling and the boy's occasional snort. But he had not managed to listen. He shook his head, and repeated that he must go.

They walked companionably out together, the three of them. Daniel said with an effort, "I preferred your play", and Alexander said, "No, no", still brooding on the irreversibility of art and time. They cut through to Piccadilly Circus, and Eros poised over the hunched and lolling and weaving junkies. Daniel suddenly announced that he was going into the Underground, he had to get somewhere. Frederica said, "Stay and have tea" and Daniel began slowly to descend with heavy steps, into the warm and smelly dark. "Let's have tea, in Fortnum's, that would be amusing," said Frederica to Alexander. He meant to say no, but said yes.

1. *That Far Field*

In 1952 history took a grip on the world of Alexander Wedderburn's imagination. When the King died Alexander's play was in fact largely finished, although later he had perpetual difficulty in establishing, in other people's minds, the true chronological order of his own choice of themes and the accident of death. His play was frequently misrepresented as a pageant, commissioned for the Festival which celebrated the handing-over of Long Royston Hall to the still insubstantial new North Yorkshire University. The Festival itself was certainly timed to coincide with the spontaneous outbursts of national cultural fervour in parks and gardens all over the country in celebration of the Coronation. If Alexander's play had not existed, it would have been necessary to invent it. Fortunately, it was to hand.

In the beginning he had been innocently obsessed with the renovation of the language, and of verse drama in particular. This was in the air. There were Eliot, and Fry. As an undergraduate at Oxford Alexander had decided that the problem was Shakespeare, who had been in one sense so much too much that he had made it almost impossible to write good dramatic verse after him. Either the playwright was distractedly obsessed with innovation for its own sake, or he wrote watery imitation Shakespeare, involuntarily. It had come to Alexander that a thing to do might be to take a run, as it were, at Shakespeare, head on. To write a historical drama, like Shakespeare's own, but in modern verse, and confront the time, the place, and the man. Later, for some private reasons and some aesthetic reasons, he had come to leave Shakespeare out and to concentrate on the Queen. He was aiming at a vigorous realism, and had great trouble with a natural warp in the work itself towards pastiche and parody. The writing took him several years, on and off, years of loving research, formal experiment, despair, visions. He was at the time Second English Master at Blesford Ride School, in the North Riding, and realised, almost involuntarily, tinkering with his verse whilst invigilating a biology examination, that the thing was finished, it had come to an end. He could do no more. He did not know what to do without the hope, the obsession, the glassy cage of singing rhythms and moving forms inside which he had walked about. He put the text of the play in a drawer, left it a month, during which the King died, and then took it to Matthew Crowe.

Partly because he had finished the play, he felt a great sense of loss and aimlessness when the King died. He took a group of Middle School boys to hear the Crier proclaim the accession on the steps of Calverley Minster. "The King is dead: long live the Queen." And the trumpet sounded, thin and clear. The boys shuffled solemnly, expecting to feel something. This death marked a period to the first brief part of their existence, that must have seemed eternal: rationing, the end of a war, utility. Alexander remembered the King, prodding bomb rubble, on newsreels. A disembodied voice, on the radio, announcing war. Nervous and pastoral. He imagined a nation, attempting to imagine this known figure, dead alone in his bed, and failing in the attempt. That was what kings were for. His personal grief was both ludicrous and natural.

It was Matthew Crowe who gave Alexander's play literally a local habitation, and a cultural and financial reality. Crowe owned and lived in Long Royston, architecturally a relation, further north, of Hardwick Hall, though without the spread of glass and the weight of towers: it was a large building made both for living in and for display, but with slightly more emphasis on the living. Alexander was already indebted to Crowe, a natural entrepreneur and patron of the arts. It was Crowe who had engineered a short run at the Arts Theatre for Alexander's first play, *The Buskers*, of which Alexander was now slightly ashamed, since his new hopes of bold realism reinforced his belief that plays about plays and plays about actors were one of the signs of general debility in the theatre. It was Crowe who provided the grandest and liveliest part of Alexander's social life, outside Blesford Ride. He was a strenuous believer in local culture, local loyalties, local talent, and, although he had had a brief career as a West End director as a young man, now spent his time putting on festivals and play-cycles in churches, music-halls, village barns. He was, and said he preferred to be, a huge fish in a reasonably small pond. He was very rich. He rarely went South.

When he had read the play, he invited Alexander to dinner, declared great enthusiasm for the work, and over coffee and brandy by his study fire, told Alexander some political secrets and made some revelations. Crowe enjoyed politics, secrets and revelations. He leaned forward into the firelight out of his high-enfolding leather chair and described briskly and gleefully to Alexander the machinations and inner workings of the powerful bodies who were labouring to devise the New University. There was the very strong Adult Education Movement, which had first proposed the University, the ladies' teacher training college, St Hilda's, the theological college, St Chad's, which were to be incorporated into it, and Cambridge University, the original sponsor of the extension lectures for adults. Crowe spoke intimately to Alexander of the Bishop,

the Minister, the man from the Treasury, the graspings and com-
promises, and Alexander, who had little political sense, failed frequently
to admire the true brilliance of some concession or manoeuvre or piece
of timing. Crowe spoke of the long business of syllabus-planning; the
attempts to make this peculiarly local, peculiarly for adult students, or,
like Keele, the only then existing exemplar, founded a few years earlier,
to make the students acquire all kinds of knowledge before specialising,
to make them become, as the Renaissance ideal had required, complete
men. Crowe spoke of his own part in this: the tactical revelation, at the
right moment of impasse, of his intention to make over Long Royston,
house and grounds, on condition that he had a right to live in his own
corner of it in perpetuity.

The point was, Alexander must see, that all this was most timely; the
inauguration of an Appeal, the announcement of the Gift, the Royal
Charter, in Coronation Year, all could coincide, and be celebrated,
amongst other things, by a performance of Alexander's wholly appropriate play in summer evenings on the terrace of Long Royston itself. It
was a play ideally suited to raise the countryside – in the sense of providing work, cultural employ, for armies of local people. There must be a
cast of thousands – with a bit of tinkering – and musicians, and scene-
builders, and costume-designers and sewing-ladies – all the people of the
locality. It was not a pageant, Alexander said. No, said Crowe, it was a
work of art, which would with luck have the good fortune to have
justice done to it. He would himself be in his element, setting it up.
Alexander should see.

The speed of the setting-up left Alexander a little dazed. He was
summoned shortly to meet the Festival Committee, again at Long
Royston: this consisted of the Bishop's Chaplain, the man from the
Treasury, Miss Mott from the Extension courses, Councillor Barker of
Calverley, Crowe, of course, and Benjamin Lodge, the director from
London. Alexander's play had further solidified and proliferated:
everyone present had his or her own duplicated script. Everyone present
congratulated Alexander on the brilliance and topicality of his work.
Crowe presided benignly: the Committee discussed dates, costs,
publicity, supporting events, possible casting, sanitary arrangements.
Alexander was never sure at what point, or by whom, it had been
formally decided that his play would be put on: he was faintly troubled
by Lodge, who once or twice spoke of "this pageant" and said it would
need cutting. Crowe, clever enough to notice these doubts, held back
both Lodge and Alexander to have a drink, elicited compliments from
Lodge for Alexander's verse, and from Alexander for Lodge's excellently
stark production of the Wakefield plays, which he had seen, and had

indeed greatly admired. Lodge was a heavy, taciturn man in a monstrous mustard-coloured sweater, whose black hair was thinning, and was compensated for by a huge, bushy-soft beard. Crowe himself, in his sixties, had a crimson cherub-face, something, still, of an unfinished boyish look. He had wide pale blue eyes, a little curled sensual mouth, and a tonsure of finely-floating silver hair. He was a little rounded by age, still this side of portly. Whilst Lodge and Alexander were still glowing, presumably, with fine malt whisky and a sense of achievement, Crowe whisked Alexander away, declaring that he would drive him home to Blesford Ride.

Crowe drove an elderly Bentley, rather fast. He took Alexander across country, between drystone walls and rough fields, the edges of the moor, down into Blesford Vale, up the long school drive, lined with limes. He stopped the car just outside the school's red Gothic arch.

"You should be pleased with this day's work. And with yourself."

"I am. I am. I hope you are. I can never thank . . ."

"You're worried by Ben, I can see. Don't be. He won't make a pageant out of it. For one thing, I shan't let him, and for another, he's no fool. Just likes to be sure he's doing creative work of his own. Likes to slap your text about a bit, until he feels it's got his mark on it. You noticed that, of course. But you can trust me to keep an eye. You can. And you must keep your own eye. Will they let you have time off this awful place?"

He cocked his head up at the clumsy, louring archway.

"My ancestor's godawful Folly. How long d'you mean to stay in this place?"

"Oh I don't know. I like teaching. I suppose I'd like to think of writing full-time."

"Well, go and find yourself a first-rate school. With a first-rate Head of Department. That man's remarkable, but he's a horror."

"Oh, I'm easy-going. And he's a first-rate man in his way. We do very well."

"You amaze me," said Crowe. "And what will he say to this enter- prise?"

"I dread to think. He's not keen on verse drama."

"Or on me," said Crowe. "Or on me, I assure you. Or, it is said, on the University, at least as it's projected at present."

"I'll talk to him."

"Brave man."

"Well, I must, mustn't I?"

"I wouldn't," said Crowe. "I'd quit. But I know you won't. Have a good talk."

The Bentley swung away in a spurt of gravel. Alexander wandered, still dazed, into the school.

The school cloisters, across a lawn under the arch, were thick and red, with Perpendicular arches somehow made squat. They were peopled by rough neo-Gothic stone figures, impartially selected from some universal Pantheon: Apollo and Dionysos and Pallas Athene, Isis and Osiris, Baldur and Thor, horned Moses, Arthur of Britain, St Cuthbert, Amidha Buddha and William Shakespeare.

Blesford Ride School was public, progressive and non-discriminatory. It had been founded in 1880 by Matthew Crowe, the present Crowe's great-grandfather, who had made a fortune in linsey-woolsey and was a distinguished amateur comparative mythologist. He had built the school largely to ensure that his six sons should be educated neither at home nor in any contact with believed Christianity. Agnosticism was laid down in the Founder's Charter which expressly forbade the building of any "chapel, retreat, quiet Room or other apology for ecclesiastical institution". The cloisters and Pantheon did not count, since they were Art. During this Crowe's lifetime the school had flared briefly with pure eccentricity, which possibly explained why two of the six sons had become itinerant preachers and one a prison governor. Of the other three, one inherited the wool business, one taught classics in the school, and became an archivist, President of the Blesford Historical and Topographical Society. One died young. Matthew Crowe, who had been sent to Eton and Oxford, was descended from the archivist, whose eldest brother had died without issue.

Blesford Ride was never more than moderately successful. Geographically it was somewhat desolate, up in the Yorkshire Moors miles from anywhere except the minor Minster town of Calverley, which was neither as civilised as York nor as grandly self-contained as Durham, and dwarfed by both. Historically, it had been tactless. Eccentric when conformity was a powerful force, the school had grown more conformist and cautious, owing to financial difficulty and milder leadership, at a time when its original oddity might have given it a certain cachet. Now it was recommended to parents who did not want their sons to have to join an Officers' Training Corps; who were against fagging; who had been frightened in sensitive childhood by roasting boys' flesh in *Tom Brown's Schooldays*; who were not above gentle mockery of Flag and Empire; who lived locally. It was equally recommended to parents who disliked dirt, sandals, cigarettes, alcohol, sexual licence or vehement sexual instruction, do as you please, learn as you go, and intellectualism. It was inhabited largely by middle class children whose frugal and conscientious parents had hoped and believed they might pass the 11 + and had felt unable, in the event, to expose them to the howling hordes in the local Secondary Modern. There were Founder's Bursaries for non-ecclesiastical minority groups: Jews, epileptics, orphans, woollen-workers' children, bright boys from overgrown families. The school was theoretically run by a Parliament of boys and teachers selected by a complex system of proportional representation devised by a recent head-master. The staff were of three kinds: bright young men who came in search of academic and moral freedom, stayed briefly, and left for Dartington, Charterhouse or journalism; bright young men who came, somehow never went away, and grew imperceptibly older; and Bill Potter, who had been there for nearly twenty years. The school was a reasonably usual liberal school: all things to all men, middle of the road, minor.

Bill Potter was Alexander's Head of Department. He was generally agreed to be a first-rate teacher, inspired, dogged and ferocious. He was respected by University Selection boards, and feared by the headmaster. Although he had been offered a House, he refused to do anything but teach, and lived still in the red-brick semi he had brought his wife to – one of an isolated line of small houses put up for married teachers at the edge of the furthest rugger field, the Far Field. This was called Masters' Row. Alexander now set out to call on Bill Potter, not without mis-giving.

Bill was in many ways a reincarnation of the original spirit of Blesford Ride. He proclaimed the weighty agnostic morals of Sidgwick, George Eliot and the first Matthew Crowe. He worked ferociously at his own version of Ruskin's and Morris's popular culture, with a dour respect for real workers and their lives and interests more akin to Tawney's work in the Potteries. The vigour behind what local cultural life existed in 1953 was in large part his. He gave University Extension lectures to which people travelled miles in all weathers, in vans and country buses, from moorland villages, seaside resorts, wool towns and steelworks. He ran a Settlement in Blesford Church Hall, and was a power behind the continuation of the Literary and Philosophical Society in Calverley. He could make people do things, themselves, that were durable and worth doing. The Settlement dramatised, and put on a series of Lawrence's Tales with a grimly manic perfectionism recognisably his. The Lit. and Phil. had accumulated and catalogued its own series of "papers" on local literature and culture, from a study of rhyming games by a singing teacher, through a study of the symbolism of the drawings of the patients in Mount Pleasant Mental Home done by a menopausal amateur painter who had spent time there, to scholarly essays on the sources used by

Mrs Gaskell in *Sylvia's Lovers*. There were informed amateur studies of speech patterns, and researched interviews with writers who lived and worked in the North, done by shopkeepers, teachers, business men's wives. Bill's distinction was to stamp the work not as pupil-work but as Work worth doing, and to give the collection, and the community that collected it, a sense of identity. He was a slave-driver, but also a listener: he could give an inarticulate woman the right hints about the direction in which her clumsy sentences might be twisted to make a pleasantly idiosyncratic style. All this without neglecting the Blesford Ride boys, whom he drove through exams, harassed, taunted and stretched.

He had made a not very vigorous attempt, when Alexander first arrived, to draw him into all this local work. But Alexander, reasonably good with boys, had less touch with adults. And even then he considered himself an embryonic metropolitan professional writer, and recognised with a mixture of arrogance and humility that he was unable to add anything to the energies of this communal, provincial, amateur striving. If he had wanted to, he would have had trouble, since his literary priorities bore little relation to Bill's. Bill accepted his lack of apparent enthusiasm surprisingly equably. Bill was bad at delegating power or authority, and Alexander, who saw himself as poet first and school-teacher second, wanted neither. Bill inspired fanatical devotion in most good pupils and some bad ones. Alexander, despite his spectacular good looks and enthusiasm for the subject, did not. He was genuinely shy and unassuming, and perhaps finally for this reason Bill seemed to like him.

Nevertheless, he was not sanguine about Bill's probable reactions to play and festival. Bill would be particularly displeased by Crowe's initiatives in the matter. Crowe, an easy charmer, had tried to draw Bill, whose energies he had recognised, into his circle, not without one startling success. They had collaborated on the Lit. and Phil.'s 1951 *Beggar's Opera*, where both had seen that their talents were complement-ary, and Crowe had added gloss, pace, colour and lavish music to Bill's social fury, textual accuracy and skill with actors. All the same, Alexander had sensed at the time, Bill would in some ways rather have done a tinnier, clumsier, more personal version in the Blesford Church Hall. He was in good and bad ways a purist, and beyond that had a basic, almost animal objection to Matthew himself which Alexander only slowly recognised. Crowe's upbringing, Crowe's money, the whisky and leather which attracted Alexander himself, excluded Crowe as automatically from serious consideration in Bill's world as a black skin or a thick accent would have excluded other men in others'. Bill would not take kindly to Crowe's cultural uprising.

Nevertheless, as Alexander crossed the school grounds in the dusk, the solitary joy that had been waiting all day invaded him. Across the gardens in front of the school, behind long glass-houses, later to be full of economic and delicious tomatoes, was a heavy, studded door onto a long mossy path between high walls. This ran down to a footbridge over the mainline railway; over this was the Far Field. Behind the wall on the left was the Masters' Garden, protected by a band of glittering triangles of glass set in cement, watery, bottle-green, glacial. Inside, this forbidden place was tidy, square and dull, with a rather small cedar tree and a paved hump at one end, supporting a sundial. It was reminiscent of those war memorial sunning-places for the elderly. Here, last summer, Alexander had played the lead in the staff production of *The Lady's Not for Burning*, a mildly bacchanalian occasion. That seemed very long ago.

He came out of the mouth of the lane onto the cast-iron bridge. Under it, behind high embankments, the railway wound its way along the edge of the Field, providing in a long loop, also, the curve of the horizon. Along the edge of the embankment ran a heavy steel mesh fence behind which trains rushed north and south, showering billowing steam onto the field and the few rhododendrons on the embankment, and clouds of fine, hot, pricking grit onto the boys in the jumping-pits at the edge of the path, leaving black smears on leaves and skin.

Alexander stopped and put his hands on the rail of the bridge. He felt flatly happy. He felt complete. He had the strange thought that he was as intelligent as he needed to be: he could take in whatever came. This was something to do with the fact that the play was now one thing and he himself another, deprived, but at liberty. He had habitually seen these fenced fields and the school itself as imprisoning. When he first came he wrote to old Oxford friends mocking its ugliness, northernness, narrowness. Then he stopped mocking, afraid that to talk at all was to admit that the place constrained him, too. Occasionally he had said to people at Blesford Ride itself: I am writing a play: and they had said: oh yes: or, what about?: but it had felt at such moments thin and hectic, a fever of the mind. Now it was being carried around, reproduced, read. And now he was separate from his work, he was separate also from Blesford Ride. And separate, could take a benign, curious interest in it. He stared down at the grimy field with arrogant pleasure in the fact that it was as it was and he saw it.

The failing evening light thickened shadows and outlines, blackened the mesh of the fence, extinguished the remnants of colour in the muddy grass. He felt under him the tremble and hum of the bridge which heralded a passing train. He stared with gleeful curiosity. It came black and sinuous, then thundering and plunging towards and under him, working pistons, hammering wheels, enveloping him in spat sparks and

acrid steam, banging away into the real distance. He came down: the
earth was still shuddering, as though the thing had a wake in soil like
vessels in water. Long strips of vapour spread raggedly, vanishing, at
the edges, into the grey coming of dark. Someone was standing beside
the Bilge Pond.

The Biology Pond had always been known as the Bilge Pond. It had
been dug out when the school was founded, and was now untended and
decayed. It was a circular pond, stone-rimmed, set into the grass under
the embankment. There were one or two water lilies and some duckweed, a rickety flagstone for newly transmuted frogs to sit on. The
surface was silky black and the depth was difficult to determine, since
the bottom was covered with a sediment of fine black mud. Boys had
earlier cultivated water-life there, but now used the school's well-
endowed Field Research Station higher in the moors. There was an
unsubstantiated rumour that the Bilge Pond was full of leeches which
had propagated there since its beginning. No one put his feet in, in case
these possibly mythical creatures should fasten to his ankles.
    The figure beside the pond was bent awkwardly over it, stirring with a
long stick. As Alexander came nearer, he saw that this figure was Marcus
Potter.
    Marcus was Bill's youngest child and his only son. He had a free place
at the school, and was officially due to take A levels in two years' time.
Nobody knew much about him. There was a general desire to treat him
"normally", which meant in practice never singling him out, and leaving
him as far as possible to his own devices. Alexander occasionally heard
himself addressing the boy in an unnaturally colourless tone, and knew
he was not the only one to do so. But this was possibly because Marcus,
unlike Bill, was an unnaturally colourless person.
    Bill could be seen to believe that Marcus was uncommonly gifted.
There was little conventional evidence for this: he was working at
Geography, History and Economics, and his work was described as
satisfactory and uninspired. "Satisfactory" covers a wide range of
performances, between the excellent and the almost inadequate. In
Alexander's classes, for instance, Potter habitually left sentences unfinished and was surprised when this was pointed out to him. In class he
seemed silent and strained, and Alexander had entertained the idea that
he was one of those who put so much initial effort into the process of
attention that they fail in practice to hear anything, frozen into an
attitude of concentration.
    As a small boy, however, he had had the uncanny gift of being able to
do instant mathematics. He had also been discovered to have perfect

pitch. When he was fourteen the mathematical ability had mysteriously left him. The perfect pitch remained, but the boy showed no great interest in music. He sang in the choir and played the viola in an accurate expressionless way. Bill's colleagues were aware that he himself, almost entirely unmusical, was touchingly proud of his son's gifts, which he persisted in regarding as evidence of a capacity, in due course, for an even more phenomenal academic success than those already achieved, more conventionally, by his two elder sisters.

Alexander had had a brief period of intense interest in Marcus. A year ago he had produced a school *Hamlet* in which Marcus had been a chilling and extraordinary Ophelia. The boy's acting had something of the same quality as his maths and his music: something simply transmitted, like mediumship. His Ophelia was docile, remote, almost automatically graceful: the songs and mad speech were a hesitant, disintegrating parody of these qualities. He had not made a sexually attractive girl, although he had made a vulnerable one, and a bodily credible one. He had given the flirtation and the bawdy the gawkiness of extreme uncertainty about how these forms of talk should be conducted, which was exactly how Alexander thought the part should, or anyway could, be played. He had produced these moods and manners from Alexander's smallest hints, though he had always waited for direction of some kind, never adding anything of his own volition except an apparently faultless instinct for the rhythm of the language, the fall of the lines. Boys before the age of self-consciousness are lovely to direct and could give, as Alexander well knew, depths they were unconscious of to lines they didn't understand. But Marcus had achieved something extraordinary that had moved Alexander, and indeed frightened him, though apparently no one else. No other performance of Ophelia had ever made it so clear that the play's events simply cracked and smashed the innocent consciousness.

Bill had sat through that production, for all its three nights, grinning with pride and a sense of achievement. Alexander hoped to be allowed to use Marcus in the new play – he had an idea for him – and hoped further that if this came off he would be able to catch Bill's interest for the play in general.

As Alexander crossed the grass, Marcus dropped on all fours and laid his face on the paved margin of the Bilge Pond. Alexander veered away and made noises, coughing, shuffling, to indicate his presence. The boy sprang up and stood shaking. There was mud on his face.

He adjusted his spectacles, moony National Health, which had been driven to one side by his extravagant manoeuvre. He was an undergrown boy, thin, with a long pale face and a lot of fine falling, colourless, dusky blond hair. He wore flannels and a faded blue tweed jacket, too small for him.

"Are you all right?" said Alexander.

Marcus stared.

"I was going to see your father. Are you going home? Are you all right?"

"No."

Alexander could not think of a further question.

"Everything shook. The earth."

"That was the train. It always happens."

"Not like that. It doesn't matter. I'm O.K. now."

There was something unattractive about Marcus Potter. Alexander knew he should probe further, and did not wish to.

"I'm O.K.," the boy repeated, in one of his more dutiful, robotic tones. Alexander was quite clever enough to know that the boy wanted this statement setting aside. But he said only, "May I walk home with you?"

Marcus nodded. They set off in silence for the little row of lights in the houses at the edge of the field.

Marcus Potter had grown up on these playing fields. During holidays he was often their only inhabitant. They lay about him in his infancy and he lay in their mud and tussocks, making them Passchendaele and Ypres and the Somme, trenches, dugouts, No-Man's land.

He had played a game called spreading himself. This began with a deliberate extension of his field of vision, until by some sleight of perception he was looking out at once from the four field-corners, the high ends of the goal-posts, the running wire top of the fence. It was not any sense of containing the things he saw. Rather, he surveyed them, from no vantage point, or all at once. He located with impossible simultaneity a berberis stenophylla low on the left, the muddy centre of the field, the Bilge Pond away on the right.

He was quite little when he became good at this game, and quite little when it went beyond his control. Sometimes, for immeasurable instants he lost any sense of where he really was, of where the spread mind had its origin. He had to teach himself to find his body by fixing the mind to precise things, by shrinking the attention until it was momentarily located in one solid object, a half-moon of white paint gripping blanched grass, the softly bright chained cricket rectangle, the soft black pond-water. From such points he could in some spyglass way search out the crouching cold body, and with luck leap the mind across to it.

He learned early to be grateful for geometry, which afforded grip and passage where knots of turves and cakes of mud did not. Broken chalk lines, the demarcation of winter games crossing summer ones, circles, parallel tramlines, fixed points, mapping out the surging, swimming mud, held it under, were lines to creep along, a network of salvation.

There had been some years when he had neither played the game nor thought about it. Lately he had started again with a new compulsiveness, although he did not like it. It was like masturbation, something that came on him suddenly, all the more urgently because he had just decided not to do it, and had therefore relaxed. And then he would think he would do it, just do it, quickly, and start life again immediately after.

This time he had thought he would get across the field without it. He would walk on the lines and get across that way, on them. The sudden train had shaken him out of himself with none of the preliminary visual and bodily manoeuvres that were necessary to comfort and maybe survival.

He was now bitterly cold. He could not remember with any exactitude what had happened. It always left him bitterly cold.

He dragged his feet along the grass, still trying to pursue the safe white lines.

They went under the tall white rugger posts which as a tiny boy he had believed to be a high jump for superior beings. They opened the wicket gate and went up the garden path.

2. *In the Lion's Den*

Alexander had been frequently told he had a standing invitation to walk into the Potters' house. They would, they said, turn him out unscrupulously if he wasn't wanted. They never had turned him out, and he had never felt quite wanted, but always as though he was interrupting some closed and peremptory family process. He was afraid of homes and families, and treated them with exaggerated respect. His own parents kept a small hotel in Weymouth in and out of which he, an only child, had wandered at his own times, never at least accused of treating his home as a hotel, since that was what it was.

The back door opened into the kitchen, where Winifred stood at the sink. She held out her arms to Marcus, who avoided them, and invited Alexander to supper, which they were just, she said, going to have. It would easily stretch to one more. Alexander would find them all in the sitting room.

She rose rigid and uncurving through layers of lisle stocking, grey skirt, limp flowered overall, to a heavy crown of greying blonde plaited hair, its severity mitigated by a fuzz of flying split ends which gathered a haze of light about it. She looked like a Victorian image of an exhausted Scandinavian goddess, and had the straight Danish nose and close eyes of many indigenous North Yorkshire people. She had, too, a judging expression, but Alexander could not remember her saying anything that was not primarily conciliatory. She said, in fact, very little. Her accent was pronouncedly Yorkshire. Alexander had known her for at least a year before he had discovered she had a Leeds degree, in English.

Bill and his daughters sat in silence. Their sitting room was the kind of room in which Alexander imagined most Englishmen lived, although he had been into very few like it. It was small and contained too much furniture: a three-piece suite upholstered in rust, uncut moquette, a large curvilinear radiogram, a fireplace with liverish tiles and rounded square corners, a walnut bureau with griping animal claws, very vaguely Directoire, two pouffes, two standard lamps, two nests of little tables. French windows opened onto the back garden plot, between linen curtains with a Jacobean design in tones of rust and sage and blood. The carpet, a little threadbare, had some oriental tree on it, with vague birdshapes roosting in curling branches, obscured by age.

Silver-framed on the radiogram were photographs of all the children, aged more or less five. The two girls held hands, in velvet dresses with lace collars, and frowned. Marcus was alone in space, dwarfed by a huge, unrelated, beady-eyed teddy-bear.

"Alexander," said Bill. "A surprise. Take a chair."

"Have half the sofa," said Frederica, who was extended on it. She was clothed in crumpled school uniform, maroon and white, Blesford Girls' Grammar. Her fingers were ink-stained to the knuckles. Her ankle-socks were not clean.

Alexander took a chair.

Bill said to his son, "How did you come out in your History Test?"

"Fifty-two."

"Where were you?"

"I don't know. Eighth or ninth."

"It's not your main subject, of course."

"No."

"Show Alexander the cats," said Frederica to Stephanie, sharp.

Stephanie was crouched over a small table with a pile of exercise books. She uncurled herself and stretched. She was a mild, soft, blonde girl with large breasts, elegant legs, and a rather too tightly rolled pageboy hairstyle. She had just taken a double First at Cambridge and was now teaching at her old school, Blesford Grammar.

"My daughter Stephanie," said Bill, "has a Samaritan compulsion. We could all be said to suffer for it. She likes to salvage things. Living, half-dead, preferably against odds. Very much against odds in this case, I'd say. Are they dead yet, Stephanie?"

"No. If they get through tonight, they've got a reasonable chance."

"You propose to sit up all night."

"I suppose so."

"May I see?" said Alexander, very politely. He would much rather not see. Stephanie pushed the large packing-case beside her chair a few inches in his direction. He leaned over, rapidly, his hair brushing hers, which smelled clean and lively. She was always the same, it seemed, wholesome, moving and speaking economically, creating an atmosphere of slight bodily and mental laziness, alternately comforting and exasperating to others.

In the case were three premature kittens, whose bulging heads feebly bumped and nuzzled each other. Their eyes were seamed with dark yellow crusts. Now and then one opened a pink mouth, showing fishbone fine teeth. They were slick, damp, reptilian, trailing tiny hairless feet.

Stephanie scooped one up; it lay curled in her hand like a foetus.

"I rub them with a flannel, for warmth," she said, soft. "And feed them very often, with a dropper."

She reached for the dropper from a saucer in the hearth, pushed back the soft skin from the helpless jaw with a little finger that looked almost brutal, inserted the dropper, squeezed.

"It's easy to choke them this way, that's the trouble." The creature spluttered, gave a miniature heave, flopped into inertia. "That went down, anyway."

"Where did you get them?"

"From the Vicarage. The cat there died. It was appalling really." Her voice didn't change but went on softly stating. "I was having tea with Miss Wells and the curate banged on the door and said the char's little girl was screaming and screaming in the kitchen. So I went down, and there was the cat . . . there wasn't anything to do . . . she just kept gasping and twisting and gasping and twisting and died."

"Must you?" said Bill.

Marcus, as far from the kittens as he could be, put his hands between his knees and began to work out a kind of mathematical pattern using knuckles and fingertips.

"There were these, and three born dead. The little girl was in a bad state. I suspect she started it off – picked the poor beast up wrongly. She was quite hysterical. So I said I'd save these, if I could. Getting up all night is a bore."

The thing in her hand produced a shrill whispering sound, without the force to be a shriek.

Frederica said in her harsh voice, "I didn't know cats died in childbed. I thought they just popped out. I thought it was only heroines of novels."

"Something got twisted inside the cat."

"Poor old thing. What will you do with these?"

"Find them homes, I suppose. If they live."

"Homes," said Frederica, making the word thick with irony. "*Homes. If* they survive."

"If they do," Stephanie agreed calmly.

Alexander stood up, slightly sickened by all this brooding and birth-smell, and opened his mouth to explain why he had come. Bill, who had been gathering his forces for speech, started to talk at the same moment. It was a habit of his. Alexander, nevertheless put out, as he always was, closed his mouth and studied Bill. He was a small, thin man, with the lengthy face, hands and feet of someone designed to be taller. He wore flannels, a blue and white checked shirt, open at the neck, a gingery Harris Tweed jacket with leather elbow-patches. His thinning hair had once, presumably, been the same horse-chestnut as Frederica's and was now fading, with silver flakes like ash on a dying fire. Several long strands floated over a bald crown. His nose was sharp and his eyes a very pale blue: in childhood both Potter girls had given the angry Pied Piper their father's face, the eyes glittering "like a candle flame where salt is sprinkled". There was usually an atmosphere of smothered conflagration about Bill – not visible flame, but the uneasy smouldering in the heart of a straw stack, the cracking at the base of a bonfire which might suddenly flare, flare and fall in.

"You can tell me," he said, driving over Alexander's conversational opening, jerking his abrupt head in the direction of his son. "How's he thought to be getting on?"

"Quite well." Alexander was embarrassed. "That is, as far as I know. He works hard, you know."

"I know. I know. No, I don't know. Nobody tells me anything. Nobody says anything to me. Least of all him."

Alexander looked covertly at Marcus, who seemed simply not to be listening. He decided that this appearance was genuine, however unlikely.

"If I ask," said Bill. "If I ask, as, being his father, I'm likely to do, I meet – general evasiveness. Nobody will swear to it he's doing as well as he should. Nobody will offer any useful criticism. Nothing. You'd think the boy didn't exist. You'd think he was invisible."

"I only teach his subsidiary English, and I'm quite satisfied . . ." Alexander began, wondering, as he spoke, what "quite satisfied" in this context meant. The awful thing was that the boy partly was – voluntarily Alexander was sure – invisible.

"Satisfied. Quite satisfied. Now tell me, as a teacher, as an English specialist, as a man of letters, what *exactly* you take 'quite satisfied' to mean . . ."

"Supper," said Winifred magisterially in the doorway, as though electrically summoned to their common rescue. The girls rose. Marcus slipped out.

The dining room was both tiny and imitation baronial. It was almost filled by oak and leather: gate-legged table with ponderous, gouty, bulging legs, leather-backed chairs studded with brassy knobs. The walls were papered with imitation raw plasterwork. Over the head of the table hung a very small framed print of Uccello's *Hunt at Night*. The very scale of this print led Frederica to suppose until middle life that the thing itself was huge, spanning a whole wall: its real modesty somehow outraged and enchanted her.

The table was spread with a plastic cloth which imitated, with unnatural cunning, white rosy damask on one side and pink-spotted gingham on the other. Winifred belonged to that generation of wartime housewives to whom plastic, any plastic, was a labour saving miracle, and colour, any colour, indisputably liberating and cheering. Today the damask side was laid with the Potters' heavy ornate wedding-silver, with plastic mats imitating woven rushes, with limp seersucker napkins, obscurely tartan, pulled through silver rings far too wide for them, relics of the ceremony of a solid way of life, weddings, christenings, that the Potters had left partially behind without aspiring to anything more graceful. In the middle of the table were jars: piccallili, H.P. Sauce, mustard pickle, chutney, ketchup.

Frederica and Stephanie, who were both in love with Alexander, were worried about the impression he would have formed of all this. Alexander was informal with a difference, cavalry twill, hacking jacket, suede boots, gold Viyella shirt. His beauty was casual – long soft brown hair falling slightly across a thoughtful brow, everything long and fine and clean-cut and groomed, but delicately so, with no hint of the hearty or plummy. They were afraid he must almost certainly think them vulgar. They would have liked to appear differently before him. Their embarrassment was, however, complicated by the moral certainty that it would be vulgar and wrong in Alexander to hold any views at all about the Potters' external circumstances. It would equally be vulgar and wrong in the Potters to care at all what views he might form. Finally, the inner life and rectitude were all-important, and not to know that was most vulgar of all – they thought – an anomaly of views that ran right through the Potter character, uniting them all.

Bill, his shirtsleeves rolled up on his pale-veined arms, carved cold mutton, dispensed hot cauliflower and boiled potatoes, and continued to quiz and hector Alexander on his son's intellectual habits. Obsessive single-mindedness was another strain in the Potter character. According to Bill, Marcus had read no books except Biggles. He demanded to know how unnatural this was. At Marcus's age Bill had read everything: Kipling, Dickens, Scott, Morris, Macaulay, Carlyle, the lot. Indeed, the Congregational minister had taken *Jude the Obscure* from Bill at just Marcus's age and invited Bill's family and friends to watch him make a burnt-offering of it.

"In the chapel boiler. Opened the little round door into the burning fiery furnace and poked in poor Jude, with tongs. At arms' length. Sermon on evil thoughts and the arrogance of the half-educated. Meaning me."

"What did you do?"

"Retaliated in kind. Holocaust. Swept up every missionary pamphlet, Johnny's pennies bringing eternal joy to the miserable starving heathen, gratitude of lepers for the Word of God and all that rot, when *real* rot was their problem, not a need for trousers and monogamy and blessed are the meek, who are *not* blessed. I hadn't the guts to say a sermon, but I wrote one, God help me, in my best handwriting, and pinned it on the noticeboard, saying *auto da fé* meant act of faith, which although half-educated I knew, and this was mine, and in my book they were damned for false logic, false values and soppy prose. And for burning Jude before I'd even got to the end."

Alexander laughed uneasily. "I'm surprised your parents didn't cast you off."

"Oh, they did, they did. Of course they did. I walked out of there with a black tin trunk of books and a few clothes the next day, and I've never seen 'em since. Win took the girls, once, but *I'd* not be let darken their doorstep, even if I'd go, which I won't. No, I took to commercial travelling. Men's Surgical and Supportive Underwear. Got into Cambridge from Working Men's Institutes and night schools. Finished Jude. Learned my lesson. What you've scraped for and fought for, you value."

Alexander was impressed by this and was about to say so when Frederica said:

"It's funny then that you burn our books."

"I do not burn books."

"Literature you don't like, you do. You censor what we read."

Bill made a gobbling noise.

"Censor. Who wrote to that dried-up old virgin when you were fool enough to get *Lady Chatterley* confiscated at school? And told her for good measure that it was wicked not to stock *The Rainbow* and *Women in Love* in your school library?"

"I didn't ask you to. In fact, I wish you wouldn't."

"The moronic woman replied, I believe, that she had purchased six copies of a work called *The Glorious Moment or How a Baby is Born*. She seemed to consider this some countervailing proof of liberal-mindedness."

"She's shy," said Stephanie. "She means well."

Frederica appeared to be enraged. She glared wildly from side to side, apparently in some uncertainty about whether to attack Bill or *How a Baby is Born*.

"All right, it's a pretty useless book. Full of diagrams you can get out of any Tampax box anyway. And a lot of stuff about supreme bliss and deep loving trust, and opening the virgin treasure – honestly, what a daft metaphor, there's nothing *in* there. And I don't like her little religious talks on it either, I don't want my biology contaminating with her religious rhapsodising, no thank you. She doesn't *know* anything."

"But you object when I complain that she sees fit to deprive you of real books and real experience."

Frederica turned on him.

"You *sent* us to the horrible Grammar School and then you won't leave us to deal with it in our own way. You make my life impossible, if you want to know, by always writing letters to the Wells about sex and freedom and literature and all that. If you want to know what I really think, I really think *Women in Love* is just as corrupting and damaging to all our tender young blossomings as *The Glorious Moment or How a Baby is Born*. If I thought I'd really got to live the sort of life that book holds up for my admiration I'd drown myself in the Bilge Pond *now*. I don't want the immemorial magnificence of mystic palpable real otherness, you can keep it. If you've got it. I hope to God Lawrence is lying, tho' I don't know how you expect me to tell, tho' you do make me read him. And you do burn books."

"I do not burn books."

"You do. You burned all my *Girls' Crystals* and all those Georgette Heyers I borrowed from that almost-friend I once had, and those weren't even *mine*."

"Ah, yes," said Bill, with sharp retrospective delight. "So I did. Those weren't books."

"They were harmless. I liked them."

"They were prurient fantasy. And vulgar. And untruthful, if that word means anything."

"I think you could trust me to recognise fantasy when I meet it. A little fantasy never hurt anyone. And it gave me something to talk to other girls about."

Bill began to speak about literary truth. Alexander looked at his watch, surreptitiously. Winifred wondered, as she often wondered, why Bill found it compulsively necessary to quarrel so disastrously, to argue, for him so crudely, with the one child who had inherited his indiscriminate and gleefully analytic greed for the printed word.

She remembered the episode of the *Girls' Crystals*. Bill – it was never known by what inspiration he had been guided to snoop – had found them stowed away in a box under Frederica's bed. He had carried them out, blazing with wrath and delight, and had incinerated them in the pierced dustbin in which he burned garden rubbish. Crystal after Crystal disintegrated and darkened; ragged scraps of crisping black tissue and pale flames rose and danced on the summer sky. Bill stirred with an iron rod, as though officiating at a rite. Frederica danced round him on the grass, tossing her arms and screaming with highly articulate fury.

Winifred was alarmed by this one of her children. Frederica seemed sometimes possessed by a demon; her end of term reports characterised her style and even handwriting as "aggressive". Winifred believed it. Stephanie, milder and lazier, was said to be cleverer. Marcus was, Winifred trusted, peaceful and self-contained. These two she admired for meeting wrath with her own stoic patience. Frederica was always so embattled.

Over coffee, Alexander at last managed to introduce the topic of his play. He began roundabout, with a preamble on Crowe and his plans for the new University, to which Bill took instant exception. Bill knew very well, he told Alexander, about the negotiations that had been going on. He had been in at the beginning when there'd been a real hope for something new, something that really had grown straight out of the grass-roots of adult education where it had begun. But he'd lost patience, what with Vice-Chancellors mucking up his syllabus till it was no different from any existing universities' courses, what with Crowe sticking his nose in where it wasn't wanted, and what with the Bishop adding redundant frills and furbelows and theological colleges. All they were going to get was a prettified imitation Oxbridge, with pastiche ceremonial and the older local houses done up with brass knockers and horrible sky-blue Festival of Britain paint for patronising dons. No thank you, he said. *His* work would have to go on outside all that fuss and flutter as it had always gone on. As for Crowe he was like an old spider, he'd sit in towers casting out webs for cultural flies and get made Vice-Chancellor, let Alexander mark his words. And the new Renaissance man wasn't needed thank you – literacy, numeracy, experience at first-hand and articulacy would do fine.

Alexander said there was to be a Festival, and that he himself had actually written a play and would like Bill's opinion of it. It was to be put on at the Festival. He was lucky. He mentioned Crowe's plans for the cultural enlivening of the whole locality. He said, dubiously, that he knew Bill would be needed. He said he hoped to be able to give some time, in the summer term, to working on the play, but that this would depend on Bill. By now the euphoria and independence he had felt with Crowe, and on the railway bridge, had left him. He spoke soberly, even apologetically. Bill heard him out, rolling a home-made cigarette in a rubber-and-metal machine, fiddling with raw wisps of gummy dark tobacco, licking his lips, and the fine edge of the cigarette paper, with precision.

"What is it then? A sort of cultural pageant?"

"No no."

"A blue print for a new Renaissance."

"No. A play. An historical play. A verse drama. About the queen." He hesitated. "I wanted to call it *A Lady Time Surprised*. After that portrait. But we decided on *Astraea*, because it's easy to say. And I took a lot of the machinery from Frances Yates on Queen Elizabeth as Virgo-Astraea."

He could see Bill thinking all this was pretentious and academic in the wrong way.

"Well," said Bill, "you'd better let me read this work. Is there a spare copy?"

Alexander produced one of Crowe's cyclostyled scripts. He realised, with a slight shock, that it had simply never crossed Bill's mind that he might have written a good play. Bill's tone was that of the schoolmaster, encouraging hard work, but honourably withholding the enthusiasm he was ultimately not going to be able to offer.

Frederica said, "Are we going to be able to act in it? Are we local culture ourselves? I am going to be an actress."

"Oh," said Alexander. "There will of course be auditions. A great many. For everyone. Including the schools. Although I did myself want to suggest that Marcus – if he were willing – should be specially considered for a part. I wanted to know what he – and you – thought."

"I thought he showed real talent in *Hamlet*," said Bill.

"So did I," said Alexander. "So did I. And there is an ideal part for him."

"Edward VI, I bet," said the irrepressible Frederica. "He could do that. Lucky old so and so."

"No," said Marcus. "Thank you."

"I really think," said Bill, "you could manage, even with your work . . ."

"No."

"At least give us a reason."

"I can't blunder about without specs."

"You did in Ophelia."

"I can't act. I won't, I don't want to act. I can't."

"We could discuss it later," said Alexander, meaning, away from Bill.

"No," said Marcus firmly, but on a rising note.

The door bell rang. Frederica bounded to it, and came back to announce portentously:

"A curate has come to call. He wants to see Stephanie."

She made the announcement seem an absurd anachronism, a strayed episode from mocking Charlotte Brontë, Elizabeth Gaskell or Mrs Humphrey Ward. Curates did not call on the Potters. Nobody called, exactly. And curates, who might still call elsewhere, certainly never came there.

"Don't leave him standing, it's rude," said Winifred. "Let him in."

The curate came in, and stood in the doorway. He was a large man, tall, fat, hirsute, with coarse springing black hair, dense brows, and a heavy chin shaded by the stubble of an energetic beard. His black garments hung loosely from powerful shoulders; his neck was heavy and muscular above the dog-collar.

Stephanie introduced him, nervously. Daniel Orton, Mr Ellenby's curate, from St Bartholomew's at Blesford. Daniel Orton took in the assembled company and asked, in a rotund voice which might just possibly have been a routine clerical attempt to set them at their ease, if he might sit down. His voice was strongly Yorkshire – a southern industrial Yorkshire, less inflected and singing than Winifred's northern one.

"If this is a pastoral visit," said Bill, "I should say immediately you're in the wrong house. No churchgoers here."

The curate did not react to this. He stated simply that he had come for a few moments' speech with Stephanie, with Miss Potter. If he might. He had promised little Julie at the Vicarage that he'd drop in and see how the kittens were doing. He sat down, on the other half of Frederica's sofa, seeming by instinct already to have located the box. He looked in.

"They're not doing badly," said Stephanie. "It's early to tell."

"It's clear that child blames herself," said Daniel Orton. "I hope you rear them."

"Please don't raise her hopes – please don't rely too much on me. They're not only motherless, they're premature. It's a lunatic task, really."

"No, quite right, always tell th' truth. I wanted to come here – I didn't have time to say to you, on my own account – you did a marvellous job wi' that child. I wanted to tell you so."

A curious trace of clerical unction flickered amongst the flat Yorkshire sounds. Bill said, rapid and repressive, "We've already heard quite a lot about the cat episode. Thank you."

Daniel's big dark head turned slightly in the direction of this interjection, assessing it apparently. He turned back to Stephanie.

"I wondered if I could interest you in a bit of my work. You were kind enough to express an interest in the way I run my work. I have to be pushy in my job or I get nowhere at all, and there's something I've got a feeling you're the right person to help with. Just an inkling. I wondered . . ."

"Another time, perhaps," said Stephanie, crimson, looking at her knees, almost inaudible.

"Maybe I interrupted something," said Daniel. "If so, I'm sorry."

Alexander looked at his watch, at the Potters, at the curate.

"You have some very fine wall-paintings in your church, Mr Orton. I've seen nothing to equal them in England. The Mouth of Hell over the nave – and that very *English* laily worm – are particularly fine. Even faded, a real burning fiery furnace. Very lovely. Pity you've not got a more informative guidebook and a bit less rhapsodic. Wife of a previous vicar was the author, I believe."

"I don't know. I've not read the Guide Book. And I've no judgment of what's particularly fine. No doubt you're right."

"You've come to the wrong place," said Bill, "if you want anyone in this house to help with your work. As far as I'm concerned, the institution you represent purveys lies and false values and I wish to have nothing to do with it."

"Well, that's clear," said Daniel.

"I live in a culture whose institutions and unconsidered moral responses are constructed in terms of an ideology based on a historical story for whose accuracy there is *no* respectable evidence, and the preachments of a life-denying bigot, St Paul. But we all put up with it.

We are all Polite to the church. We never ask, if we swept it right away, what truths might we discover." Bill glowered. He was saying what he said often, but did not often have the chance to say to clergymen.

"I'm not asking you to come to Church. I came to ask Miss Potter to help wi' a project I've got on."

"You ought to be asking me to come to Church, that's the point. If you've *got* any beliefs. The thing's not only dead, it's flabby."

"I have my beliefs," said Daniel Orton, gripping his large knees with his heavy hands.

"Oh I know. One God, maker of heaven and earth and so on. Up to the communion of saints, the forgiveness of sins, the resurrection of the dead and the life everlasting. Do you *really*? In Heaven and Hell? What we believe matters."

"I believe in Heaven and Hell."

"Cities of gold, cherubim and seraphim, trumpets sounding, rivers of pearl, fiery pit, claws and leather wings, the primrose path to the everlasting bonfire and all that? Or what? Some clever modern version in which your own character is your own hell in perpetuity? I'm very interested in modern churchmen."

"More than I am, it seems," said Daniel. "Why?"

"Because our communal life is a lie because it is *haunted*, tho' most of those haunted are unconscious of it, by the sick and rotten images you purvey. A corpse on two planks. Some exciting untrue images of fire and apple trees."

"Why are you attacking me?"

"There is more truth in *King Lear* as far as I know than in all the gospels put together. I want people to have life and have it abundantly, Mr Orton. You're in the way."

"I see," said Daniel. "I've not read *King Lear*. It wasn't set for Higher when I did it. I'll repair the omission. Now I'll go home, if you don't mind. I'm not the debating kind of churchman, nor yet the preacher. And you are making me a bit cross."

"You can't *say* that, Daddy," said Stephanie suddenly. "He practises what you preach. I've seen what he does – in hospitals and places – where for all your talk – about experience – you don't go. He *knows King Lear*, even if he hasn't read it."

"I bet I know my Bible better."

"I bet you do," said Stephanie. "But whether that's a point in your favour or his, I'll leave him to say. Please forgive us, Mr Orton."

"So you'll talk to me at some more sensible time," said Daniel to Stephanie. He, like the Potters, was obsessively single-minded.

"I promise nothing."

"But you'll talk."

"I admire your work very much, Mr Orton," stiffly.

"Right. Now I'll go."

Alexander looked at his watch again and announced that he was going too. They came out together onto the bare street and stood for a moment in a more or less companionable silence.

"The man must be mad," said Daniel Orton. "I hadn't done any-thing."

"The irony is that he's a believer and popular preacher born out of his time. In revolt against his upbringing."

"Ay. Well, so am I, the other way. I ought to sympathise. I can't say I do. It's not of much importance. I'm not much of a preacher myself. Words, words."

"Words are his work."

"Let him stick to it, then. He lacks grace." There was no clue in his tone as to whether he meant this criticism to be theological, aesthetic, or in some quite different area. He offered Alexander a large hand and walked away, by no means gracefully, sturdy and rolling towards the town. Alexander set off in a great hurry in the other direction. Like all people over-anxious to keep an appointment without the terrors of being early, he had made himself late. He began to run.

3. The Castle Mound

On the outskirts of Blesford, where pre-fabs and ragged allotments pushed out into real fields, Alexander, still running, came to the Castle Mound. The Castle, which had briefly housed the defeated Richard II, was now a stone shell encircling mown humps and hillocks with the ambivalently bursting appearance of grave-mounds: iron labels indicated the sites of dried well, vanished defences, foundations of bedchambers.

Outside this trim anonymity was a piece of wasteland, once an Officers' Training Camp, where there was a semi-circle of battered Nissen huts on splitting tarmac; through long cracks in the surface willow-herb and groundsel poked weak, tenacious stems. There was no flagpole in the concrete slot: no cars in the designated car park: the place appeared, not recently, to have undergone a successful siege. The huts let out, through dangling doors, a strong smell of stale urine. In one, a long row of basins and urinals had been deliberately shattered and fouled. The regulars, Alexander saw, were there. A circle of grubby boys lifted their heads from the cupped glow of matches as he passed. In a doorway a gaggle of girls whispered and shrilled, leaning together, arm in arm. The largest, skinny and provocative, thirteen maybe, stared boldly. She wore a drooping flowered dress in artificial silk, and a startling red latticed snood. A cigarette stub glowed and faded in one corner of her pointed mouth. Alexander made a rushed and incompetent gesture of salutation. He imagined they knew very well why he, why anyone, went there.

Over a wire fence he saw her, walking briskly away from him across the only field, through thistles and cowpats. She had her hands thrust deeply into the pockets of a raincoat, whose blue skirts stood out in a stiff cone above tiny ankles and feet. Her head, gallant in a red cotton square, was down. He was terribly moved; he went after her; under the trees of the little wood, over the stile, he caught up with her and kissed her.

"My love," said Alexander. "My love."

"Look," she said in a rush, "I really can't stay, I've left Thomas sleeping, I shouldn't take such risks, I must go home . . ."

"Darling," said Alexander. "I was late. I get so afraid of being early and losing my nerve, I make myself late . . ."

"Yes, well, it's as well one of us isn't. Isn't afraid, I mean."

She took his hand, however. Both were trembling. The euphoria of the early evening returned.

"A good day?" she enquired, dry and nervous.

"A wonderful day. Jenny, listen, Jenny . . ." He told her about the play.

She listened in silence. He heard his own voice fade. "Jenny?"

"I'm very glad. Well, of course I'm glad."

She was trying to edge her hand away. Alexander was entranced by this small resistance. The trouble was, or the delight was, that he was entirely entranced by her. If she was irritated, which she frequently was, her stopped-off movements of wrath filled him with intense pleasure. If she looked furiously away he stared with intense pleasure at her ear and the muscle of her neck. His feelings were insanely simple and persistent. Once, when he had tried to explain them, she had got very angry indeed.

Now, he saw he must do something. He tugged at her wrist: her hand was back in her pocket.

"You aren't pleased. I'm sorry I was late."

"That's immaterial. I expected you to be late. I expect I'm selfish. If the play's a success – which it will be – I shall see less and less of you. If it's enough of a success you'll go away altogether. I would, if I were you, I . . ."

"Don't be silly. I might make a bit of money. If I had a bit of money, I'd get a car."

"You always talk as though a car would transfigure everything."

"It would make a difference."

"Not much."

"We could get away –"

"Where to? For how long? There's no point in any of all this."

"Jenny – you could have a part in the, in my play." They had had the car conversation so many times. "Then we should see each other every day. It would be what it was in the beginning."

"Would it?" she said, stopping, however, and leaning against him, so that he felt dizzy. "We live in a perpetual beginning anyway. We might just as well stop."

"We love each other. We agreed, we must take what little we can . . ."

That was where it always came to.

It was her husband, Geoffrey Parry, the German master, who had asked shyly if Alexander could find her a part in *The Lady's Not for Burning*. He had hoped, he said, it might prove therapeutic for post-natal depression. Alexander had taken in Mrs Parry only vaguely, plodding across the school lawns gracelessly bulbous as tiny women, in his experience, tended to be. He had courteously heard her read, in his rooms, over a glass of sherry, a whirlwind Cleopatra, a chanting and lyrical Jennet, almost overpowering in so small a space. He had cast her as Jennet, naturally. Talent was sparse at Blesford Ride. Geoffrey had thanked him.

In rehearsal he had come to dislike her. She knew her own part, the rehearsal schedule, and everybody else's part, after the first two days. She suggested cuts, changes in moves, possibly useful curtain music. She prompted without being asked, and offered suggestions to other actors on how to speak their lines. She made Alexander nervous and the rest of the cast uncoordinated and insecure. One day, practising with Alexander in the music-holes, airless poky places under the stage, she corrected his grammar, queried his casting, and corrected his quotations in the same sentence. He told her, mildly, not to treat everything as a matter of life and death.

She stood back, swayed, sprung at him, and aimed a wild blow at his face. He stepped backwards, fell over the gilt music-stand, hit his head on the piano and crashed to the floor. Blood trickled where the piano had wounded the base of his skull and where Jenny's nails had ripped his cheek. She, so furiously launched, came down on top of him, babbling that it was a matter of life and death, to her it was, her life and death, the baby smelled and was boring and the boys smelled worse and were more boring and everyone in the boring place was obsessed by the appalling boys. She struggled to her knees between Alexander's outspread legs in the dust, pushing crossly at falling locks of long black hair.

"I see life is just a regression. The nearest we ever come in this place to what I once thought was real conversation is when we play at students playing at actors playing at medieval witches and soldiers. Flimsy whimsy. So I get bossy and insufferable and you get patronising, and gently point it out."

She aimed another blow at him, which he parried, simply covering his face with his arm, smiling at her.

"When I was a student I was fool enough to suppose life opened up once you got out of university. But what I've got is complete closure. No talk, no thought, no hope. You can't imagine how it is."

Alexander had become, perhaps unavoidably, the major confidant of a string of energetic young married women, bored, lonely and unemployed in a small male community. He thought he knew very well how it was, but had no intention of saying so to her. Instead, he pulled her down on top of him, folded his arms round her, and kissed her.

Staff plays only took place every two or three years. This was because the community took time to recover from upheavals invariably caused by the unaccustomed combination of drink, drama and undress. Alexander, usually an amused observer, felt at first tarnished by the conventional development of the flirtation that followed, with visits to the Ladies' Dressing Room and its atmosphere of timid, burlesque licentiousness. He did not like to disappoint. He hooked his leading lady into her gowns, adjusted décolletés, put a cheek, lips, against little round breasts, when no one was apparently looking. But his embarrassment had to give way before her shining recklessness: he responded as a good actor responds to another's great and unselfish performance. He said, as they stood, waiting to go on, on the First Night, "You know I love you," and watched her confusion, heat and hope improve her performance as he had supposed it would. He meant, he intended, to take her to bed when it was over.

That was almost a year ago. A year of snatched brief meetings, of pre-arranged phone calls, of hiding and running, of letters and lies. The letters had run beside his play; phrases from the letters had run into his play. The letters had discussed, with wit, with gentleness, with salacity, with impatience, with quotations, with four-lettered words and increasingly elaborated details the moment when a bed would be available and they would lie in it. It was almost, he thought, now, as if the letters were the truth. So much joint imagination had been expended on the act that it was as though they did, innocently, carnally know each other.

The Castle Wood, at the root of the Mound, was beleaguered by new building and cramped. They had quickly discovered where they could sit in it without exposing themselves. Their hiding-places almost always showed signs of other recent occupation. There were times, when the initial recklessness persisted, when they found these amusing, when their love transmuted depressed leaves and lipsticked tissues into new matter of interest. Once Jenny unearthed a used sheath in a half-empty can of baked beans. "Ersatz domestic bliss," she remarked, primly, as Alexander chucked it over the neighbouring bushes, and Alexander said, "A non-fertility rite, take it all in all, what with boiled beans and intercepted seed," and they had both laughed a great deal.

He whipped away a torn newspaper and arranged her in a hollow, back against a tree. With his left arm round her, he began to undo her clothes with his right. She put a hand on his thigh.

"I always imagine rows of grinning boys will bob up out of the brambles. This wood always feels full of boys. Nosing things out . . ."

"You're obsessed by boys."

"I know. It's awful. It never occurred to me I was going to loathe them. Poor little Thomas will grow up into one. I'm not having him on a scholarship at the School and ostracised like little Potter . . ."

"Is he?"

He had undone macintosh and cardigan. He turned these back, and started on the skirt.

"Yes, he is. He's never with anyone. I think there's something wrong with him. I saw him the other day running up and down like a rabbit, in all directions, for no reason, all alone in Far Field. Then lying down."

Alexander laid bare her throat and breast. He made a folded frame of her clothing: she sat, still as a statue; he sighed and laid his face on hers. She shivered.

"Alexander – do you *like* boys?"

"Hush."

"No, but do you?"

"Are you suspecting me of being queer? All wives suspect all un-married masters of being queer." He moved his face contentedly against the skin he'd bared. "No, I like them to teach, not to touch. I've never wanted to make a grab at one, or anything."

He thought, his head comfortable on her breast, that he'd never been quite overwhelmed by desire to touch anyone. There had never been an occasion when he couldn't almost as well *not* have touched. What he wanted, what he really wanted . . . could not be said. He said instead, "Why am I so happy? When I should feel unbearably frustrated."

"Yes. You should. Why don't you?"

"If I had a place – a bed – you don't think I'd hesitate . . ."

"I don't know if you would or not. It doesn't look as if I'm ever going to find out."

These expressions of aggression and discontent were also a ritual bent of their dialogue. She sat quite still. Alexander turned his attention to her thighs. He touched the cool and solid flesh between the slippery, straining stocking and the gripping rim of the roll-on. He ran delicate finger-tips over bumps of suspenders, ridges of elastic. He moved spread fingers inside the cutting edge of the pants to the warm creases and wiry hairs, the soft. She sighed, leaned back, put a hand on him. Don't move, don't move a muscle, he begged her in his head, fluttering his silent fingers. Bodies in clothes amazed him, the criss-crossing layers, the varieties of smooth, solid, tugging, fluid . . . There must be as many ways of making love as there are people: what he liked was a slow intensification as close as possible to immobility. It would have been perfectly possible to take her there in the wood. Under a coat or blanket the risks of action, in terms of discovery, were hardly greater than the risks of what they were now doing. He believed his reluctance to be aesthetic. Forcing her, amongst twisted and knotted clothing, smashed twigs, adhesive beech mast, different kinds of damp. So rudely forced. It was odd that although he suspected the lady would be willing he persistently thought in terms of forcing. No doubt he was a little odd. He must live with himself. He continued to flutter her with his hands to keep her still and open, and thought, as he often thought in this position, of T. S. Eliot. The inviolable voice. Philomel by the barbarous king so rudely forced. And still she cried and still the world pursues. The tenses. It was all very well struggling with Shakespeare, but the other voice was nearer and more insidious. He had a moment of panic. He would never have a voice of his own. There was a line he had thought was his, or at least his with a clever modern-Renaissance echo of Ovid, which he must change, he must remember to change, the damned cadence was certainly Eliot's . . .

Jennifer spoke a run of words into his thought.

"Darling Alexander, I've got to, I simply must, go back to Thomas, and my bottom's gone numb, too –"

He remarked that his own hip was dead or dying and his supporting wrist very painful. He looked at Jenny. There were large tears in her eyes. Silently he took out his handkerchief and gently wiped them up.

"Is anything wrong?"

"No. Only everything. I love you."

"I love you."

He tidied her, shutting away the white breasts, primly buttoning shirt, cardigan, raincoat, twisting a stocking-seam, brushing down skirts. They took out diaries, arranged to meet again, promised to write. Then, as she did always, she set out almost at a run, not looking back. He always gave her fifteen minutes start.

He sat back in the dead leaves composing a sentence of a yet-unwritten letter that would somehow weave the frailties of numb and cramped bodies into the sense he had of infinite golden time and space. She left such warmth behind her. He felt possessed by her. He smiled.

When he was a little boy, alone on Weymouth sands he had always had, or possibly been, so intense was her foamy presence, an imaginary girlfriend out of the sea, white and gold and clean and shining like Ellie in *The Water Babies*. Some memory of this presence was behind his Elizabeth. Possibly he had wanted to be a woman. This felt like some rather remote observation about someone else. If it was right then it ought to have added some sort of energy, or force, to his play. Which was what mattered. He must check that pseudo-Eliot-pseudo-Ovidian line.

After the proper time he got up and strolled deliberately back to the Castle Mound. The male and female gangs had now amalgamated and were cooking things in cans over a twiggy bonfire. The girl in the scarlet snood was splayed backwards over the knees of the largest and grubbiest boy, her dress rucked up over her thighs. The three smaller girls were sitting crosslegged, staring intently, their observation obviously an essential part of whatever was going on. As Alexander came out of the dark they switched their stares to him. The girl in the snood, wriggling with a movement as deliberate as a three-year-old's automatic exposure of round belly and drooping pants to any male, arched her little crutch at him, quivering, waved a languid hand and made a loud, vulgar noise. Alexander felt the blood rise to his face and move under his hair. Worsted in some primitive test of audacity, he looked away, and hurried on.

4. *Women in Love*

The sisters sat by Stephanie's electric fire in nightclothes. Stephanie was dripping, injecting milk into the increasingly bedraggled but still living kittens. She wore striped Marks and Spencer's boys' pyjamas, rather

large, inside which her rounded body seemed formless and elusively
bulky. Frederica affected a long white nightdress with full sleeves, and
a yoke of broderie anglaise threaded with black ribbon. She liked to
imagine this garment falling about her in folds of fine white lawn. It
was in fact made of nylon, the only available kind of nightdress,
except for vulgar shiny rayon, in Blesford or Calverley. It did not fall,
it clung to Frederica's stick-like and knobby limbs, and she disliked its
slippery feel. She was always too easily seduced, when buying clothes,
by some Platonic ideal garment possibly, though not necessarily, also
envisaged by the makers of the cheap imitations she could afford to buy.
She would have had a Yorkshire sense of quality in cloth if she'd had the
money to go with it. Lacking money, she refused to be shrewd about
the second-rate.

They talked about Alexander, and about their lives. There was no
rivalry, only a curious complicity, about their love for him, probably
because both in different ways were convinced that the love was hopeless. In Frederica's case, the hopelessness was believed to be strictly
temporary: she could not expect him to notice the glories of her mind
and body just yet, since both of them were clouded by the repulsively
constricting uniform, conventions and intellectual horizons of Blesford
Girls' Grammar. It is harder to know why Stephanie was so sure her
love was hopeless. Alexander had watched her grow from girl to woman
over five years and had never really *seen* her, so there was no reason to
suppose he would suddenly do so. Her idea of him, which she enjoyed,
was an idea of a man untouched, remote and pristine. This was part of a
symbolic view of Alexander held by both sisters, elaborated in talk,
which was in itself another reason why they were so equable about
sharing their passion. He stood for things they had not got, desired,
and feared they would not have: art, as opposed to criticism of it, male
mobility as opposed to female provincial rootedness, savoir-faire, the
possibility of metropolitan glamour to come. He spent holidays, long
ones, abroad: he had friends who were actors and dons in London and
Oxford: unlike the other masters, he took flight for civilisation at the
end of each term. Marriage was observably bad for masters, and worse
for masters' wives. If they loved him, they feared the awful effect on
him of loving them, or anyone. The talk was an intensified version of
earlier talk.

"He looked lovely tonight."

"He dealt with the shouting so gracefully. He always does."

"He won't have to much longer. He'll go. He'll go, Steph, and leave
us darkling."

"I suppose so. I suppose he stayed so long, to be quiet, and finish the writing."

"He talks to you about the writing. He doesn't to me. I annoy him. I don't mean to. I wish I didn't."

"Perhaps his play is *really* good."

"Can you imagine what it might feel like, to be *really* good, and know it?"

"No. No, I can't. Terrifying."

"I mean, Steph, Shakespeare must have *known* he was different from other men . . ."

"He isn't Shakespeare."

"You don't know."

"I was only offering an opinion. Perhaps Shakespeare didn't know."

"He must've." Privately, Frederica thought it a terrible strain to live with the knowledge that you were possessed of the force and scope of Frederica Potter, especially before you'd decided exactly where to apply this force. Alexander's undoubted superiority didn't seem to be essentially one of force. On the other hand . . .

"Your curate was very fierce, Steph."

"Not my curate. But frighteningly fierce, yes. You should see him *work*."

"I can't see why most people just sit about so. I shan't."

"No, you won't."

"Why don't you go away from here, Steph? *You* could."

"I suppose I will. I'm just taking a little time to think."

She bent her head over the kittens again, unwilling to contemplate that question.

"Go to bed, Frederica. I've got to be up all night, I need to doze a bit, go to bed, do."

5. Daniel

When Daniel let himself into the Vicarage, it was dark outside, and there were no lights in the body of the house. It was not late, but the Vicar's wife was sparing with heat and light, and the square Victorian stairwell was a mounting column of chill shadow. Daniel, who knew where he was, silently padded between the hazards of the coat-stand and the black oak chest, avoided the uncertainties of threadbare and fraying islands of Turkish runners, and made for the Vicar's study.

Here were the ghosts of riches. A very heavy leather-topped desk, a pair of cut-glass, silver-lidded inkwells, a dark leather wing chair, walls of hide-bound books, behind glass. The Afghan carpet was threadbare in places, its black and gold shimmer worn away, where people trod, to an unreflecting sackcloth. The room was passionately cleaned, but there was a pervasive smell of narcissi, the lightly rich scent of freesia. In a shallow black china dish, with a faint silver sheen on the glaze, floated palely an artistic arrangement of cropped flower heads: cups of crimson and purple anemones, green-tipped snowdrops, as well as the papery narcissi and pale gold freesia, shadows of colour mirrored on the water.

They were put there by Miss Wells, daily, the Vicar's devoted lodger, Stephanie's senior colleague. Daniel disturbed her offering, reaching for the desk-light. He remembered that his mother had said it was dangerous to have flowers in a room at night. When his father had been lying dead she had shifted all the flower vases nightly into the scullery, packed them into the chipped, blood-red earthenware sink. They breathed out some poisonous gas, she said, the nurses in the hospital had told her. Daniel dismissed this memory. He reached for the Vicar's library ladder and surveyed the bookshelves.

The complete Shakespeare, tooled in black and gold, was on the top shelf. The glass door was locked. Daniel surveyed the other doors. No key. Heavily he descended the ladder, searched the surface of the desk in the feeble circle of light, opened a silver box, tobacco-scented, a wooden coffer full of paper-clips and economy labels. He began, like a thief in the night, to rifle through the desk drawers, turning over little caches of coins, rubber bands, old woven Palm Sunday crosses. In a drawer within a drawer, worked by a secret spring in an upper pigeonhole, he found what he was looking for: the collection of keys on a gilt keyring which operated various household arcana, from the safe to the sewing-machine. He mounted his small ladder again, breathing heavily, swung back the door, and, after some peering at gilded letters in the gloom, reached down *King Lear*. The concave trough of pages was deep with dust: Daniel blew out a fine cloud of it, watched it disperse and fall, spoiled a handkerchief with black smudges. He closed case, drawer, desk, study softly behind him, and went on upwards.

His room was on the first floor. It was vast and cavernous, with a high moulded ceiling, bulging with swags of dust-darkened roses and white plaster apples stained onion-skin gold by creeping damp; there were two high windows still hung with the Ellenby's war-time blackout curtains, black and gold cotton-rayon twist, with a raised pattern of large gold links. This room, inhabited by all Mr Ellenby's curates, was described as a bed-sitting room: it had a hard little divan in one corner

and a curtained alcove in which was a washbasin and a Baby Belling
stove on which Daniel was expected to make himself cups of Nescafé
and cook his own evening meal. (Breakfast and lunch he was expected
to eat with the Ellenbys.) It was at once over- and underfurnished, both
cluttered and bleak, like a furniture store. There was a real sense in
which it was a furniture store: Mrs Ellenby's natural course was to
relegate to the bed-sitting room pieces of furniture which had no present
function but were too good to throw out. Daniel was surrounded by
two wardrobes, three chests of drawers, an ottoman, a wash hand stand,
two coffee tables, three armchairs, a writing table, a roll-topped bureau,
three standard lamps, a bookcase with glass doors, a pouffe, and three
tiny whatnots. There was also a pile of stacking chairs in tubular steel
and mock leather. Some of these pieces were oak, some walnut, some
mahogany, some whitewood. The upholstery was dark blood red or an
indeterminate dun. On the walls were Dürer's Praying Hands, Van
Gogh's sunflowers, and a large photograph of two lacy altar boys and a
brass vase of lilies in a very long shaft of sunlight. The floor was covered
with mottled smoke-grey linoleum, islanded with carpet pieces: a
crimson Jacobean patch, a peg rug with a white ship on ultramarine
waves, a florid Wilton with a splashy impressionistic pattern of splayed
marguerites and tumbling ears of corn.

Daniel pushed a shilling into the gas meter, and lit his fire, an old
Sunbeam which roared and spat in uneasy bursts; two of the radiants
were damaged. He pushed behind his little curtain and washed, quickly,
to the waist, frowning. He folded his black clothes, put on pyjamas and
a shapeless speckled sweater and got into bed.

The bedside light had a shade made of woven ribbons of crimson
plastic; its bulb was economically dim; the effect was grim and hectic.
Daniel leaned out sideways to let the red light spread on the pages and
began, awkwardly, to read *King Lear*.

He read slowly and carefully, concentrating. He did not like his room,
but he had made no attempt to change it, or mitigate its gloom. That
would have been a waste of energy, and he was increasingly controlled
and automatically subtle about the disposition of energy, his own or
anyone else's. If he had not had good eyes and a capacity to ignore
physical discomfort he would have changed the lamp, or its position.
Since he had decided without thinking that it required no attention he
gave it none.

He was not a great reader. He was slow, and had always been slow. He
had been a pale, heavy little boy, who had felt his fat as something he
was under, weighing on him. Just before his conversion, when he was
fifteen, he had read that fat was fuel, to be burned into energy; this had

moved him; had shifted his sense of the relation of the inner Daniel to the outer; had indeed made it seem for almost the first time possible that the two were intimately related. He now frequently used the idea of fuel, humorously, against himself, in the pulpit. Being fat entailed, at some level, acting fat. Acting fat, both for the child and the man, had been a question of bearing. One could carry oneself with the assumption of placid good temper; the Billy Bunter alternative, playing the fool, was sometimes thrust upon one, and was now a professional hazard.

When his father was alive he had known there was power under the fat. His father was an engine-driver. Daniel grew up in Sheffield, in a little row of blackened smoky houses with closed yards and slate-roofed bogs. Engine-drivers were respected, a cut above the other workers in the street. The Ortons' curtains were crisper, their doorsill whiter, their brass shinier than other men's. Ted Orton was huge and noisy. When he came in through the front door he brought the clatter and heat and thrust of his engine with him. He irritated his fussocky wife by falling over things, displacing ornaments, eating loudly. He liked crude jokes – would suddenly whip a hot teaspoon out of a scalding cup of tea and sting Daniel's hand with it, would discover, grossly, half-crowns and florins in his helpings of Spotted Dick, perform a lengthy and excruciating mime of the shattering of his teeth, and give the coin to Daniel. At home, he glared and shouted, bidding Daniel to jump to it, get a move on, stir himself. Daniel opposed his flickering wrath by moving with unnaturally stately deliberation; he thought he was afraid of his father; he cast his eyes down and his fat face was heavy and neutral; but secretly the eddying violence, the constant requirements excited him.

Away from home, Ted's clumsy vitality became a smoother power, an engine which had left the station and exchanged its choked preliminary puffing for the voracious smooth flow of a long run. He liked to take Daniel round the engine sheds, up the track, in his cab. He scrutinised Daniel's work, suddenly firing at him strings of words to spell, or a long mental arithmetic problem. He promised him a stamp album and a trip to the seaside if he passed the 11+.

Daniel did pass, not spectacularly. He still had the stamp album. The trip to the seaside never materialised. Ted was knocked down by an errant string of crude ore trucks on a gradient only a week later. There was a further week when he lay, monumentally broken, in the hospital. Then he died. Daniel was not taken to see him. First he was told that when Dad recovered consciousness he could visit, then that it was all over. He was curiously angry with his father, he now saw, for going in this untidy and evasive way, seeming to promise, as he had never done before, something that he could not perform. Daniel was not taken to the funeral, but left to "play" with another boy in the street. His mother did not speak to him of what had happened.

Later, he used to tell people that he could not remember the time of his father's death. This was a deliberate half-truth. He closed his large face, he behaved, as he understood it, "normally", he survived. There were days when, falling asleep, sitting inactive in a chair, some mechanism took him back to the moment of the first telephone call, as though he were perpetually trapped in that moment, as though time brought him now only back and back to that point. He felt that he was being required to know, in some unimaginable way, what had really happened, and that he could not, really, know, and so was forever open to being made to try again. He never spoke of this.

He still had the stamp album, empty pages of minute squares, translucent, unopened envelopes of gummed hinges. He had neither thrown it out, nor looked at it again.

He had supposed that he and his mother must be drawn closer to each other: sentimentally, he had seen himself as the little man of the house, as an orphan, offering and requiring comfort. In fact his mother soured, rapidly and ungracefully, and spent much of her time complaining over the back gate about the inadequacy of her pension, scratching and scraping, sore bones. Daniel was mentioned as a burden. Mrs Orton was a little woman who had been sharp and fragile; she was now padded with spare fat, on shoulders, ribs, hips, cheeks, in which her nose and chin, her delicate fingers and small eyes were sketched reminiscences of a narrower state. Her only intense pleasure in life had been flirtation, her ripe days the days of teasing and vacillation and power before marriage. Ted had subdued her; she had proliferated placatory objects, little cakes, doilies, antimacassars, polished spoons and brass bells, with which she would fidget, adjusting, polishing, whilst he talked, looking modestly away from him. In her widowhood, many of these objects vanished; although the curtains were still spotless, Daniel came insensibly to think of his home as dingy. Mrs Orton substituted the pleasures of gossip for the pleasures of flirtation: as she had once giggled with other girls over the discomfiture of suitors and rivals, so she now helped to weave an endless web of speculation, criticism, rumour about the doings of the neighbours. She changed shoes for slippers and fed Daniel out of tins.

Daniel was lonely – so lonely that he dared not think of it. At school he became silent and unremarkable. He made efforts with his homework and never had any grasped understanding of what he was doing, of any underlying rational structure of geometry, or grammar. Because he always just passed his tests nobody enquired whether he knew what he was doing. He did not expect to know. If he had been better, some teacher might have tried to inspire him. If he had been worse he might have attracted some remedial attention. As it was, he went on. He was good enough, just, to go unremarked.

When he was fifteen, imprisoned in coiled, rounding tyres of flesh, he was sent with a motley crew of schoolboy delegates to a Sheffield Civics Week, an inexorable festival of speeches and shows, ranging from rock strata to the steam-sterilising of milk bottles, from the record of Earl Waltheof's Hall in the Domesday book to the smelting of steel, from the procedural forms of the Corporation to a rhythmic performance by the Isis Players of the Skinners' Play from the York Mystery Cycle.

Among the speakers, for no ascertainable reason, was a Father from a local Anglican community, St Michael and All Angels. The Community was High, and adhered strictly to vows of poverty, chastity and obedience. It had experimented with worker priests, had sent men to work in mills and cohabit in hostels with groups of released prisoners. The Father was billed to speak on Openings for the Ambitious.

He spoke late on a heavy afternoon to a huge, captive, sluggish and aimlessly irritable audience in the cavernous and pillared gloom of the Sheffield City Hall. He rose neatly, as it were from underground, and stood, precisely, gaunt in his pillar of black skirts, flanked by the formally inanimate bronze fascist sphinxes couched on either side of the stage.

What he then said was, and had remained, Daniel's only experience of communal passion.

The Father was an orator, communicating, without obvious tricks or flourishes, some imperative biological urgency. He stood still for a moment, sounding their shifting listlessness, and then, with dry, slicing speech, set about the destruction of the grey coils of torpor and with-drawal in the Hall. In the beginning, he told them only of what he did, his work in the world; drily he created for them meanness, narrowness, pain, mental confusion, horror. He was decorous, not harrowing, sharp, not pleading. He fixed no one's eye, imposed no obligation to respond and yet held the attention with a nervously controlled authority. He seemed single, spoke to himself in what was clearly his own voice, making no concessions to the supposed youth or tenderness or stupidity of his audience. And yet he had an extraordinary multiple presence. As he spoke, he inhabited other bodies. From moment to moment his body shifted slightly with what he contemplated while the dry voice informed. A lip drooped in paralysis, set stony with fear and horror, pain held his hands momentarily, vacancy peered uncertainly out of his eye at a shapeless world, though the harsh voice never faltered.

He said that it seemed odd, that when so much was clear, was admitted, so few answered. That when Christ had said how men should live, so few even considered living so. He said bleakly, his face somehow stripped, that what was required was that people should use their lives. Very few people, he said, knew what they were really capable of. Most were afraid to find out. And afraid that circumstances might nevertheless force them to know. Better – he spread his hand, flickering, straining fingers – better to walk out and face it, purposefully, for a good reason. It was hard for a man to know he had only one life, could do only so much and no more. But such knowledge, like all knowledge, was really power. To know one's limitations and then to act, and act again, was power, and engendered more power. A man must *use* his life, must think how to use it. The raised, spread hands were somehow taking in, receiving at the fingertips the electric silence of a listening charged with energy. He turned his hands over and down, a Magian gesture, told them that there were two or three in the room, maybe, who would settle for not less than everything, would turn all their power one way, work for God, with God. He did not want half-crowns, he wanted lives. Christ came that they might have life more abundantly. Not happiness, life.

It was not what he said, though he was by now eloquent, enfolding them in a mesmeric incantation of common sense and pure reason. He was alive, certainly, and not only Daniel but all the others stirred and reached out for the knowledge he proffered at the ends of his branching fingers. He looked out over their heads at the pale suspended electric globes on their bronze chains in the dusk, and they, like one creature, followed and were held by his bright eye: if he had walked down, they would have reached and strained for him to lay his hands on them.

Take, he told them, take what is there, what is real, the chance to do one thing well. There is one Way, one Truth, one Life. The rest is a dream.

He quoted:

> The best lack all conviction, while the worst
> Are full of passionate intensity.

He said: we can change that. Any one of us, all of us, can change that.

Daniel was no judge of phrases. Many he could not, later, remember, and those he did remember had lost their grace and thrust, seemed, even, banal or flamboyant. But he remembered forever, after the man had drawn in, from a final gesture of threat, incitation or embrace, the voluble arms and circling energy – he remembered the eddying passion in the hall, the sense that it was possible to speak the unspoken, the loosed power. Boys stood in knots, disputing and urgent. There was a kind of glee abroad that all had been moved, that the strangeness could be shared and perpetuated. Daniel stood too and talked excitedly too, enfranchised from the solitude of his fat and silence. The next day he went to see his local Vicar, and his Headmaster, in order to find out what qualifications he would need to enter the Church. He was even pleased to find that he would need to spend an extra year at school, picking up School Certificate Latin – resistance and difficulty sharpened his sense of power. He had a purpose and his eyes were bright with it.

Theological College taught him a lot about what it was that he had seen on that dim afternoon. He had remained doggedly faithful to the requirement that he had then known was being made of him. But as his training proceeded he defined it more clearly to himself. What was needed, he came to see, was someone practical, someone completely committed to *practical* solutions. He used this word to himself in a sense perhaps uniquely his own. As it became clear to him that he was neither a reflective man nor a scholarly man, that he was interested neither in his own nor anyone else's motivation, nor in early heresies and liturgical forms, he reiterated to himself that there was need for someone wholly committed to being practical. To be practical was to deal directly with pain, poverty, horror, quite directly. To drag back to a place where they were measured by human standards those forced out of human pro-portions of body, or understanding, or social relations, by the forces of evil. He needed qualifications, to be employed to do this. The rest was simply impedimenta, to be dealt with.

He had enough practical cunning to conceal from those in authority his lack of interest in prayer-meetings, or communal self-examinations. He believed, but did not bother to say, that the state of his, and his fellow-students' souls, should properly receive less attention than the work they had to do. He was both innocent and subversive, but he looked fat and respectful, and was put down by those above him as willing, but slow. The Blesford curacy, when it came, was as good a place as any for an apprentice practical man. He was looking, not for a cause, but for a job, and no one therefore noticed that he was a fanatic. If Mr Ellenby was beginning to have an ide. of this, Daniel himself still had none – he was working out what his work was, and how best to do it.

He usually spent solitary evenings writing up his work, correlating information about work to be done, people to be seen in the parish, in long columns of square black handwriting in coloured folders. He believed in records, in case he missed, or forgot anything important. He believed in making a network of help – using the lonely to visit the housebound, the bereaved to visit the very ill. People were moved, amazingly, to be practical by his own solid assumption that it was possible for them, required of them. He just had to be clever about who should be asked to do what. Once or twice he had made errors. Mrs Oakeshott had offered to mind Mrs Haydock's autistic son and had run from the house in terror and complained to Mr Ellenby about spiritual blackmail. He had been asked to apologise. He had apologised. It occurred to him, now, that Stephanie Potter showed most of the qualities required for dealing with Malcolm Haydock. She had been admirably calm, practical, imperturbable and reasoning over the death of the cat. If she was not Christian, she was conscientious. He could only ask, and he should ask.

He shifted in his hard little bed and addressed himself to *King Lear*. It seemed important to have read it. He was not quite sure why. He had been driven to it by a kind of wrath and a more obscure desire to deal with the Potters, particularly Stephanie. He did not know, as he read, exactly what he was reading for, and so read for the story, to see what happened to Edgar and Cordelia, whom he took to be hero and heroine, admiring, without awe, Shakespeare's cleverness in creating so hugely real an old man, so maddening, so injured, so inevitably broken and cracked. He did not see, what Bill Potter *anima naturaliter theologica* automatically saw, the black and violent anti-theology of the play, not because he supposed it to be about redemption, but because he knew, at a point where he asked no questions, that the world was like that. *King Lear* was true. He noted down various phrases for sermons. Age is unnecessary. These are unsightly tricks. Return you to my sister. It was plainer to read, much plainer and more forceful than he remembered from School Certificate Shakespeare. He wished he could achieve such plainness. There was a kind of clerical slurring to what he said which he disliked, knowing that it set him wrongly apart, without knowing how to deal with it.

As he came to the end, he realised he had learned something about pain. His body was strained and stiff. He felt stirred and apprehensive – something to do with the reading, more with Stephanie Potter. He remembered how she had cleared away, after the death of the cat, so fastidious and practical with her blood-stained hands, how she had rubbed and wrapped the kittens, had held the weeping child lightly against her own body, to comfort her. A ferociously sentimental old lady had said to him, that week, of her daughter's new baby, "Oh, I could *squeeze* 'im, I could just *squeeze* 'im." He recognized in himself the desire to squeeze Stephanie. Whilst her father preached to him, he had imagined, with extraordinary clarity, that he might lean forward and take hold of her round, lazy ankle and grip, grip till the bones shifted.

6. Picture-palace

At weekends, Marcus courted vacancy. He had an inviolable place, where no one came, the café of the Blesford Gaumont. Going to the flicks was forbidden at school and discouraged by Bill, except on carefully selected occasions. *Snow White* had been judged to be a creative experience, when he was little, and had loosed him into horror, vast and shapeshifting, like the illusions which beset the newly separated soul, according to the Tibetan Book of the Dead, swelling and gulfing monsters, deep romantic chasms, white cataracts, roaring slabs of rock, spinning blades of light, clawing crumbling cliffs and creatures, blood red, slimy green, black. Frederica said it was smashing. Marcus was smashed. Even so little, he had tried to unmake the illusion by twisting his head to stare at the clear cone of light wavering and streaming from the high projector. But for the small boy, encompassed and whelmed by racket, reason was no protection. The phantasmagoria rushed into his skull when he closed his eyes at night.

Bill did not let him see *Bambi* or *Dumbo*, which were judged sentimental.

It was not forbidden pleasures that tempted Marcus now. He hurried past the exterior blandishments of chrome-framed stills depicting smooth lovers leaning at impossible angles into each others' bodies, or a boy hero, delicately dabbed on white skin with scarlet gore, riding a pirate poop through frozen, lacy, ivory peaks of boiling tide, or unnaturally glossy dogs and deer ambling amiably across unnaturally verdant forests into vibrant rose horizons. Marcus never went to see films. What he liked was the centre of this closed citadel, whose outer walls were blank and blind, whose doors were barred on the inside.

To get there, you climbed stairs, dark at midday, winding upwards and inwards, your feet soundless, printless, on shallow treads carpeted in thick crimson, curved round by a balustrade of twisting gilded ivy crowned with a swelling dark-rose plush handrail. The stairs were softly lit by peachy light from frosted flesh-pink florets on gilded cups, which cast a warm life on the glossy faces on the wall, dark enchantresses in black lace with scarlet nails and long jewelled cigarette-holders, soft pale stars with swelling breasts cradled in white swansdown, pouting lips and silvery hair waved into evenly rippling ridges, little girls with sunny fleeces of tight gold curls, crowned with floral coronets.

In the middle of the crimson plain of the landing was a softly plashing fountain, dropping from a flat cup held in the hand of a very 1930s translucent greenish glass nymph, featureless face, regularly fluted gown, posed toes and fingers, high little knobbed paps, the water running shallow over a pool of mirror glass, splashing on bronze water lily leaves, lit from below, rose and viridian. You went on up, into deeper quiet, and the gate of the café was across the second landing.

The gates were bronze and plate-glass, thick-curtained inside. You pushed, and were in a palely lit underworld, with some small natural light diffused through heavy, creamy ruched curtains, reinforced by clusters of dusky pink light bulbs, organised long buds on brassy curving stalks, thrusting out from pillars tiled with bronze mirror-glass. The carpet was dense with roses, pink and cream, the size of cabbages. The little chairs were gilt. Between pillars you saw the Soda Fountain, bronze-mirror-backed, with faintly hissing urns and rows of goblets. Two girls in little white caps and aprons sat on high stools, leaned on their elbows, chatted quietly. Their clientele was intermittent. Marcus was frequently alone there for hours.

He bought himself milk shakes, dark pink, salmon pink, brown, bright yellow, crowned with slowly bursting foam. A milk shake took a long time to sip, if you were economical, and while you were sucking, or seemed to be, no one disturbed you, you could sit quiet and safe. From the unseen depths below sounds rose intermittently; faint strains of music, bursts of gunfire and distant tumult. At symphonic climaxes the whole place vibrated gently and then swayed back into thick silence. Marcus kept still and avoided thought.

He had various techniques for avoiding thought. One was a soundless humming, a set of variations on a deliberately restricted number of notes in the middle range. Another was the analogous construction of rhythmic sequences with tapping and clutching of knuckles and thumb-nails. Another was a kind of mathematical mapping of the Café and Soda Fountain. He would plot heights of pillars and distances between them, numbers of pink bulbs and creamy carpet roses, radii of light, spun from table to table, off the refracted glitter on the mirror work and gilt, which slowly homogenised the whole place into an ordered cube of ribbons and threads of soft, crossing light, bronze, cream, dark pink, pale pink, with something of the flexuous complexity of Arab tilework. This technique was more vulnerable, if more satisfactory than others, since the slowly constructed cocoon could be suddenly ripped by an unexpected movement of the waitresses, who tended to be represented in the patterning by ovoid black spaces.

He was therefore not pleased to hear, as he sipped his sweet roseate drink, a voice above him asking if he would mind terribly if he was joined.

He started and gulped. The other swept out a chair.

"I see we had the same idea. Peace and quiet. Coincidence. I like coincidences, don't you?"

Marcus made an indeterminate gesture with his head. He had managed to recognise the intruder, who was Lucas Simmonds, the Junior Science man at the school. Simmonds must have been rising thirty, though he looked some years younger, clean, fresh, pink, with brown curls and rather large brown eyes. His shoulders, under heathery tweed, were square and his bottom was slightly heavy for his neat torso. His shirt was very clean indeed, his flannels only slightly less so. He smiled a frank smile at Marcus, who looked away.

Marcus attended a general science class given by Simmonds to extend the cultural range of A Level candidates. This course was desultory at best, easily deflected by the brighter boys who liked to confuse Simmonds with awkward questions, which was easy, since he seemed to be a slow thinker, all too ready to give up if his planned proceedings were interrupted. He was, however, curiously immune to teasing, and would simply abandon trying to teach and attempt cheerfully and inadequately to respond to what was said, no matter how absurd. Quite bright boys thought they were scoring off him. Very bright boys believed he was simply not clever enough to see what they were aiming at. Marcus thought the real explanation was at once too simple and too insulting for boys to grasp. Simmonds simply did not care whether they learned anything or not. People should be able to recognise indifference, Marcus considered. He himself respected it. Throughout the general science class he sat quietly amid the uproar, drawing. He drew, on pieces of graph paper, a pattern of spirals moving through concentric diamonds. The point of this exercise was to avoid, yet indicate and deal with, the point at the centre where all the lines converged on infinity. One way of doing this was to draw the lines almost invisibly pale, so that the preformed network of the graph paper supported and restrained their vanishing. Once Simmonds had come up behind him and looked down on the current pattern for some time, nodding and smiling silently. Marcus remembered this. He did not like to be overlooked.

"You're sure I'm not intruding? What do you recommend? I see you're having a milk shake. I'm partial to those myself. Waitress —

another milk shake – whatever my friend here has got, the pink. And a doughnut. Two doughnuts? No? One doughnut then, but perhaps *two* milk shakes more, yes. Thanks."

Marcus had one and a half frothy pink glasses in front of him. They were not things you could bolt.

"Funny we should meet. I came in here quite on the spur of the moment, never been in before in my life, but you were a bit on my mind, so to speak, so I take it as meant, one of those coincidences that are meant. Do you believe in those? Never mind. You were on my mind because you keep cropping up at staff meetings. Not happy in your work, they wonder. Not happy in yourself. Baffled, they seem to be. Wedderburn says you won't act in his play. Don't look so worried. Nobody really sees why you should."

Marcus made a strangled sound.

"No need to look so betwattled. I expect I'm butting in where I'm not wanted. Just thought I might help."

"Thanks."

"Not at all."

"I'm all right, thanks. I just can't act. If that's what they're on about."

"Oh, but you can. I saw *Hamlet*, you know."

"I don't want to. I don't like it."

"I could see you didn't. Very moving, very unhappy. Oh yes."

Simmonds took a long pull on his milk shake, puffing one or two minuscule raspberry bubbles into the air as he did so. Marcus, fastidious, wiped one off the back of his left hand. He remembered Ophelia.

All those nights, stripping the wrecked garlands and crumpled white dress from his body, the wrong body, he had been in such trouble, his hands not his hands, the only words in his head her chilly plaints, his hair not his hair, prickling ghoststruck under the mat of long blonde hair he lifted off, nightly. Her breaking song he heard from some lost part of himself crying to get out, to come back in, which? It was like being "spread" only without the sense of thin air and extended space – out of himself, but only to be cabined and confined in strange clothes and clogging skin of greasepaint, rubber breasts and her shroud wound and knotted round his limbs. He had heard singing and screaming and had never known if he had sung or screamed afterwards.

"Alarming thing, acting," said Simmonds. "Culture excuses all, in modern eyes, but earlier folk knew better. Those old Puritans knew very well you could get taken over, the *soma*, that is, the physico-chemical body, they knew it could be devil's work. Dangerous to tinker with consciousness unless you're very sure what you're doing. Some people have closed consciousness, of course, come to no harm. Some revel in power over others, exhibitionists and mesmerists and so on. Not you."

Marcus did not very much understand most of this, although Simmonds's phrase "taken over" did uncannily express the sense of his Ophelia-experience, which he was determined never to repeat.

"Very struck by your performance, I was," said Simmonds. "More like a medium than an actor. A vehicle for another consciousness. I'm by way of being a student of consciousness myself – in a scientific way. I think we're not adventurous enough. I don't mean all that arty-crafty spiritualism, you must understand, crystal balls and so on, and séances and mumbo-jumbo left over from the garbage of old rites. Equally I don't mean the pure laboratory stuff where you never get beyond counting coloured pips blindfold on playing cards, or bending the law of averages through a few degrees. No, we ought to start with people who can be *seen* to have special gifts of consciousness – that might extend the limits of human power. Which is why I'm interested in you, young Potter, very interested indeed."

"I don't," said Marcus. "Lots of people could act Ophelia."

"I know that. But you have other gifts, have you not? A perfect pitch? A capacity for solving mathematical problems without the usual contortions of ratiocination?"

Marcus stared silently. He never spoke of these things.

"Have I spoken out of turn? You do well to be cautious with such gifts. In the wrong hands they can prove terrible. Like the capacity to let other forces inhabit your body. Powers for good or evil. Maybe I should explain my position."

One of the uncomfortable properties of this dialogue, heavily weighted as it was to one side, was that it appeared to be arousing contradictory emotions in Simmonds. On the one hand he was extraordinarily cheerful, wreathed in smiles and winks of boyish goodwill. On the other, he was clearly unduly agitated: he was sweating, and kept mopping his brow, pink as the raspberry milk shake, with a crumpled paper napkin. Marcus neither invited nor forbade him to "explain his position". Indeed, he was incapable of either. So Simmonds went on.

"I'm a religious man, I suppose you might say, in a scientific way. I'm interested in the laws of organisation of the universe. Big organisations, big organisms, planets and galaxies, little organisations, little organisms, Lucas Simmonds, Marcus Potter, mice and microbes. Yes. We don't begin and end with our bodies. All through history men have had techniques for getting beyond the physico-chemical *soma*. Good and bad. Prayer and dance, science and sex. Well and ill used. Some people find it easier than others. Now, in the beginning God formed, or informed, do you see – FORM, IN FORM – the inert mass of things. If you are not informed by God, you can be informed by lesser, or worse things, or both."

"I don't see."

"I know. I am telling you."

"I don't believe in God."

"I know. That's of no importance, old chap, if G. believes in you. I've been watching you for some considerable time and it's my considered opinion that He does. As an inlet for force or form."

"No."

"Tell me how you did the mathematics?"

"I can't do it any more."

"Since when?"

"Since I – told – someone – how it was done."

"Aha. You betrayed your vision. The old prophets were punished for that."

"Listen. It *wasn't* a vision. It wasn't a religious thing. It was a kind of trick."

"You have no concept of what a religious thing might be. However, be that as it may. Why can't you do it now?"

"I don't want to say."

"You don't want anything. I've been watching you, I *know*. Have you ever thought, it might be to do with that? A power, a gift, you turned your back on."

Marcus had not thought that. He had, as has been said, sedulously avoided thought. It was possibly true that his general sense of having no place in the world, no hope, no solidity, as well as the recurrence of odd and disturbing tricks of his constitution, like the "spreading", might well date from his loss of the maths. Simmonds took on the double appearance of mind-reading mage and interfering maniac.

"Please – as a scientific experiment – try to remember."

"Look – it was very scary. I'm trying to forget."

"I won't hurt you. I only want to know. Not to do anything to you."

His father had brought a professor of mathematics. Marcus had been put through his tricks. They – father and professor – had been very excited. He began to speak.

"I thought for ages anyone could do it. I thought it was the normal way of seeing. The normal way of seeing a problem, that is. I don't know how anyone can see what is in anyone else's head. I don't know how or why they should try –"

"Don't get excited. Just tell me. It's of no importance if I don't fully understand."

"It might help."

Marcus was coming to share Simmonds's view of himself as someone urgently in need of help.

"Well – I used to see – to imagine – a place. A kind of garden. And the forms, the mathematical *forms*, were about in the landscape and you would let the problem loose in the landscape and it would wander amongst the forms – leaving luminous trails. And then I saw the answer."

"Can you tell me what the landscape garden looked like?"

"No, no."

This was where he had broken down, last time. Under their eyes, greedy and proud. This was the vanishing point where it had all gone, a cone or triangle of black descending, a cone or triangle of black rising, his mind the pressure point at the meeting of these ambivalent solids or planes. He had crashed face down on the table in a dead faint. He had embarrassed his father. He had been put to bed and told to take it easy. After that he had never done it again; had known categorically that he could not do it again.

"When I did try to tell, I fainted. And after that I couldn't, ever again, I couldn't . . ."

"Of course. That is usual, with such gifts. Tell me now. It can do no harm now."

"You see – it was important to see only obliquely - out of the edge of the eye – in the head – the *kind* of thing it was, the area it was in, but never to look directly, to look away on purpose, and wait for it to rise to form. When you'd waited, and it was *there* in its idea, you could draw the figure or even say words to go with it. But it mustn't be fixed, or held down, or it . . . It was important to *wait* and they, the people asking, were pressing on me, how could I be patient, how could I, so I tried to fix, to fix, to fix . . . and it was no good."

"I understand. In part. What were the forms like?"

"*Forms*," said Marcus, incomprehensibly, as though this was self-evident. "They changed shape. They weren't exactly solid or not. Plane geometry, and surfaces floating sort of, and things not exactly like trees or flowers. Or you might walk in a field without thickness amongst series after series of planes – all dimensions – shifting. Not real landscape. In the head. But not like other things in the head, like if I try and remember Ramsgate or Robin Hood's Bay. *Bits* were landscape—any old field or wood – bits not at all . . . Oh, I can't."

Simmonds frowned, puzzled, put out authoritative hands to clasp Marcus's wrists and withdrew them abruptly. He murmured, "Fascinating. Fascinating."

Marcus remembered now those lost and shining fields for which he had not grieved because he had been too afraid to imagine them sufficiently to think of loss. He remembered, not with words, but as a floating shadow, how sensuously delightful the place had been, how clear and clean, how bright, airy and open.

"I *think*," Lucas Simmonds was saying, "I think my stab in the dark was right. You do have direct access to the thought forms, the patterns, that inform and control us. What you need, and I can provide, indeed, by a providential coincidence have come here to offer to provide, is the spiritual discipline to make all that safe and evolving. In late years we've too much concentrated attention on *soma* at the expense of *psyche*. Bodily control, physical control, of ourselves, our world, our universe, we are gaining in large measure. Consider the microscope, telescope, radio-telescope, cyclotron, bevotron. Pitch and frequency, colour and light. Thinking machines a man cannot emulate though he can design. And we, where are we? We have lost what primitive techniques we once had for communicating with the consciousness that Informs us. You are peculiarly gifted. You could – with support, with intelligent experimental planning – develop new techniques. How about it?"

Marcus intensely disliked loud sounds and bright lights. He had not been told, then, that asthmatics can pick up higher frequencies of sound than the average man, but he was to be told, and to believe it. Now for a moment he felt his head suspended on wires, with fine, fine metal rods piercing it painfully through its orifices, crossing and grinding with a cruel music in the skull, extending to infinity. He shook his head to shake away the vision and the long rods moved with it, pressing sharp on the yielding matter and cavities of his mind.

He didn't want Simmonds. Simmonds would not restore the fair fields.

"Of course you appreciate that it's hard not to utter gobbledegook, astral bodies, auras and ectoplasms – I don't mean all that *stuff* – I mean your ways of taking in the universe, Potter."

"Sir, I can't. I want leaving alone."

"But you told me, and you haven't blacked out, now."

"No."

"You feel better."

"No. No. No."

"I think you'll find it will make sense. I think coincidence will bring us together again. In the meantime, I've said my say. I'll pay your bill, don't move." Simmonds stood up. He smiled cheerily. "There are no real accidents, in God's universe, remember."

"I don't believe in God. All this stuff doesn't make any sense to me."

Simmonds's pink face creased in pain and then snapped out again, like expanded elastic, into a smiling blandness.

"When something happens that does make sense of what I've said – as I've no doubt, no doubt, it will – come to me. That's all I ask. Remember I'm there. The rest will be taken care of."

7. *Prospero*

In March, black and gusty, Matthew Crowe set about to inform and enliven the local community. The Festival was to be his *magnum opus*. He meant to call into being music and flowers, midnight shout and revelry, dancing tipsy and solemn, a realisation of a Royal Progress, with incidental mock-chivalric tourney and goose fair, besides the staging of Alexander's *Astraea*. He moved with unbelievable vigour up and down across North Yorkshire, from cathedral close to fishing village, from officers' messes to workingmen's clubs in mining villages, prodigal with ideas, promises and cash. Alexander, when he could be spared, went with him, fascinated by what amounted to a genius for organisation. He himself stood on platforms looking handsome and reserved whilst Crowe spun out his eloquence over local bodies large and small, Mothers' Unions, Townswomen's Guilds, Sewing Circles and Garden Groups. There was something in his manner as absolute as that of Lord Beaverbrook requiring women at war to hurl aluminium, zinc baths and iron railings onto scrap mountains for national munitions, or Savonarola calling the ladies of Florence to repent, save their souls, and cast their false hair and jewels into his bonfire. Crowe worked up his Yorkshire bodies to perform prodigious labours, requiring those same grim energies which, already figments of nostalgia, they had expended on knitting abb wool into comforters or digging for victory. He too required clothes and jewels – any bits of glittering paste or bright or glossy cloth, to be pooled, remade, refurbished to furnish queens and fine ladies. He required skills – real embroidery on kirtles and farthingales which would, he declared, be works of art and museum pieces in their own time. He wanted the country combed for real old English receipts: frumenty, verjuice, boar's heads, salmagundy. He wanted everyone, this spring, to make the land remember its old sweetness and loveliness, to make the too-much loved earth more lovely with the real old flowers, the sweet-smelling ones, lavender, wallflowers, ladslove, clove gilliflower and matted pink.

He wooed the men too, pursuing the territorial army, the Young Farmers, builders, bakers, Boy Scouts, asking for horses, candy stalls, wagons, palanquins, pavilions. He encouraged the rejuvenation of church monuments, the regilding of rows of dead Elizabethan infants in the Minster, the purchase of bulletproof glass cases to display ancient hidden chalices. He passed through little coastal towns where men had been driven from cottages and villas by the tempests, raging winds and pouring tides of that terrible January and February. He prodded sympathetically at slimy carpets and rotted wallpaper and gave out cash for their renovation. The colours of the Festival of Britain sprouted incongruously, then, amongst the old slate, grey and white: cottage walls, garage doors, imitation American ranch fences were palely bright in sky blue, acid primrose, occasional harsh heliotrope. Later in the year, Crowe told Alexander, he would see to it that mock Tudor houses in suburbs of Calverley and Blesford would be decked with mock Tudor scented hedges and bunting with mock Tudor roses and odds and sods on.

"Colour and light and movement and sounds and sweet airs, why the hell not," he said to Alexander. "The land's sick for it and I mean to go out in a burst of fireworks and a froth of pleasure, leaving behind me one or two enduring monuments, small things and not entirely my own, but touched with my touch, a University, my dear, and your lovely play and a brightened up garden or market square here and there. Then I shall break my rod, if not drown my books, and rest from my labours in my little turret and survey the brand-new students in their little black gowns wandering between my yew hedges in an ornamental manner. I'm afraid there's been some controversy about the gowns – démodé for a *new* place, a democratic place – but I believe grace, and a little humouring of my last whims, will prevail."

He said also, "What it wanted was a Master Plan. To involve a lot of time and a lot of space and a lot of people. I appeal equally to high ideals and base passions. Real culture – sewing as well as glue, barley sugar as well as candy floss, old words, new words, going gracefully together. Also vulgar competition, dear boy. The Best Elizabethan Feast, the Best Old Elizabethan Garden, the best New Elizabethan Garden, the best Village Pageant. And we hold deliberately exhaustive and long-drawn-out auditions for all the musical events and dancing displays and most of all for your play. Like the worst film tycoons we will comb the country for undiscovered talent, peer down the gymslip of every schoolgirl, get the little boys saying they'll put girdles round the earth and the big ones doing Caliban . . . We'll draw everyone in . . ."

He sat there, small, cherubic, red and shining, his silvery hair floating delicately above his pointed ears, his plump arms circling and circling, miming the drawing-in of everyone. He poured more scotch for Alexander, who had, these days, drunk perpetually a little too much scotch for comfort, and proposed a toast.

"The Golden Age, Alexander. Redeunt Saturnia Regna. It is all boiling and bubbling. I hope and trust and believe."

Local Festival Committees were set up in towns and villages. Alexander put a great deal of despised charm into persuading Bill Potter to chair the Blesford one, which also included Felicity Wells from the Grammar School and the Vicar, Mr Ellenby. Bill's contempt for these two persons, combined with his wrathful fear that Crowe was taking over his austere cultural groups with promises of gilded cakes and ale, pulled him both ways. Finally he agreed to join, with a somewhat Trotskyite intention of subverting Crowe's frivolous values, with Crowe's money, from within Crowe's structure. He would see that information was purveyed about the Tudor police state and judicial barbarities, about starving and plague-ridden armies: he would have a torture and execution exhibition in Blesford Ride that would be popular and a highly serious lecture by a political historian that would not, but would be well attended, on the swell of Crowe's tide of interest and the boys' morbid curiosity.

The Festival Committees visited schools and colleges, eliciting exact and solid support. It was in this way that Alexander found himself filing on to the platform of Blesford Girls' Grammar School behind the Vicar, in an incongruous line that included a grinning Crowe, a very gracious Headmistress, and the distressed Miss Wells, only too aware that Bill was next to her and alert for any indication of pusillanimous morals. Felicity Wells was scheduled to speak. She had trouble with her chair leg and a potted hydrangea. She made the error of prefacing her description of the new Renaissance with a long and complex analysis of the old one, as it had affected Calverley in particular. She was led by some demon to digress at peculiar length on the damage wrought by the New Model Army, who, quartered in the nave of Calverley Minster, had burned up a unique roodscreen to keep warm. She was a diminutive woman with thinning pewter-coloured hair, pulled into a wispy bun round one of those doughnuts of meshed horsehair held in by large black pins like miniature croquet hoops. Under this hair her naturally olive skin looked like polished old wood, and her eyes were surprised and black over a large nose and mouth. She had tiny hands, which she frequently raised, in a gesture of amazed enthusiasm, palms out, beside her ears. This gesture made her look a little like an intricate Victorian mechanical doll or monkey.

She was aware that Bill was flexing his muscles beside her, the facial ones into a joyful sneer, the bodily ones, quite possibly, as a preface to rising to make an unscheduled speech. Both his daughters, who were present, were stiff with fear that he would do this. Stephanie, amongst a decorous row of minor members of staff, and by an accident of fate exactly behind Alexander, her knees cramped almost against his buttocks, knew that Miss Wells was going on too long, and felt protective. Miss Wells was, Stephanie believed, without malice, and never displayed anger or impatience. In Stephanie's view, this entitled her to reciprocal tolerance. Miss Wells was now bravely compounding her tactlessness by explaining what a good thing it was that Cromwell's project for a new University at Calverley had never come to anything since she herself, like T. S. Eliot, Royalist, Anglican and Conservative, would much rather see it come to be in this new atmosphere of revival of ancient truths and forms, under the auspices of . . . Bill made a loud snorting noise. Crowe smiled and smiled, out of tact, amusement at Bill, pleasure in power. Stephanie looked at Alexander, and Alexander looked uneasily out into the Hall.

Facing them, cross-legged on the floor, were several rows of little girls, intermediate girls, larger girls. Over the heads of these from under the balustrade of the gallery, the Lower and Upper VI examined the platform party, restlessly crossing and uncrossing rows of varied legs in lisle stockings, folding arms awkwardly or suggestively over tiny pointed breasts and generous ripe breasts whose globes distended the box-pleats of their gym tunics. Alexander found them, massed so, appalling. When he had come into the hall he had heard the shushing and rustle that fell like a curtain on the shrill piping and twittering of all these female creatures. These noises alarmed him, whereas the thump and guffawing undertow of boys was reassuring. He crossed and recrossed his own legs, aware of snaky lines of small female eyes on his exposed ankles and trousered knees. When he caught sight of Frederica, bolt upright in the shadow of a pillar that supported the balcony, he felt himself blushing with weakness, Artegall in the house of Radegund, Hercules stared out by Omphale.

Stephanie, sitting behind him, her hands relaxed in her decorous lap, trying to suppress the useless concern for the foolhardy Felicity, to avoid the eddies of feeling emanating from the whirlpools of violent emotion in the places where her father and sister were sitting, thought of Alexander, and tried to see the Hall through his eyes. Much like other school halls: windows too high to see through, and dusty, with long loops of cord and ratchets, dangerously botched-looking gallery, boards with brief gilded lists of Merit, Oxbridge scholarships, her own name last and freshest. A plaster copy of the Venus de Milo, halfway along the Hall.

A large part of her history was here. When you were little you sat in front of the Venus, with her blind and horrible empty eyes staring out behind you. When you reached puberty, more or less, you sat, more or less, beside and below her, and had an upward view of her bulky waist and huge swathed hips above your head, and the stumps of her sliced arms. When you got to the top of the school you saw her staring out, away from you, from behind, ponderous and hefty-buttocked. Her texture was polished old cheese, the colour of Cheddar with a coat of thick varnish, which for many years had borne little relation to the marble it imitated and now seemed, seen critically, to be corpse-colour, opaque and turgid. From eleven to eighteen her vague feelings had focused, every morning, on that sightless block. Here, now, she looked down on it, but it still bulked large.

She looked at Alexander's combed hair, so very much alive, and thought weakly that she must have come back here from Cambridge because she loved him, she wanted to be with him. What she loved him for was a kind of secretive grace he had, a shyness, which made her imagine that if he ever did notice her it would be possible for them to share a life that was private, understood, economical with language. She did not know what he wanted, and had wondered if he was queer. One usually knew about those who were, or anyway one's body surmised. She wondered if he ever thought of her at all. Other men did. If he did not, why did he not? Why was she invisible for him? Maybe she loved him because she did not know.

Alexander too wondered why he did not think of her. Whenever he saw her, he wondered that, and never thought further. Whenever he spoke to her, as he had, briefly, about his play, he had meant to do so again, and never made the opportunity. She was golden and reassuring and quick and understanding; and maybe he was afraid of those things, as they led to things he was certainly afraid of; though she was not, he thought, menacing, as Frederica, who suddenly rose into his vision, was. She was directing all her attention at him, crude and unsmiling. That girl, he thought, should have been heavily spanked in childhood. As Bill rose to speak, whether spontaneously or in the order of things was uncertain, he reflected that she quite probably had been. He dropped his eyes before her single-minded glare.

Bill was scoring debating points. He was speaking of the opportunity to exhibit the *real* history of Calverley and its environs: press-gangs and rick-burning, spinning jenny and hunger marches. He felt he should just point out, in passing, that the real damage to Calverley Minster had not been done by the New Model Army, which had conducted itself with reasonable decorum, but by the iconoclastic excesses of the supporters of the secular Virgin and her puritanical young brother. Stephanie tried not to listen. It did no good, no good at all, listening to Bill. Though as his voice rasped eloquently on she thought her fantasy of a silent entente with Alexander was to do not with Alexander but with Bill, and that her decision to come back and teach in this mediocre and stifling place was to do with Bill, that she had clanged the gates of the Cambridge gardens behind her so the noise would resonate in Bill's ears.

She was here as an extreme act of passive defiance. The one thing Bill did not want was that she should "throw herself away" on Blesford Girls' Grammar. So here she was. In his house, asserting her independence by refusing to leave it, refusing to inhabit his ambition for her, which would be a worse prison than his house. He had been a careful tutor, and she had, by nature and through art, the gifts he desired for her, and because the ambition was his, not hers, she would not use them. She was doing as he preached and practised, an honest job in a place where the rewards of an honest job were sparse and hard to come by. She was maddening him. He wanted her to be a Fellow of Somerville, the literary editor of a worthy weekly, a provincial professor. If he had not wanted it, she might have. Now, she would not. She was, she thought, sorry for Frederica, who was blown differently by these contrary hot and cold winds of morality and ambition. She became sorrier as Miss Wells came to the list of those girls who had been pre-selected to attend auditions for *Astraea* at Blesford Ride. Frederica's glare became a scowl of desperate anxiety. She had never wanted anything so much as she wanted to be on that list.

Lists are a form of power. Frederica spent much of her school-time studying the forms of the exercise of power. Control of pace of feet, of numbers of girls abreast, of socks, knickers, stockings, size and colour of gingham checks. Inclusion, exclusion, prominence, failure, were regulated and embodied in public lists. Lists of Posture Prizes, Conduct Marks, Tennis Teams, Debating Team, School Cert credits, Form Orders, in subjects and overall. Frederica hated the lists, and created wild energies with the hatred. But she had to be first, in every case where she had not decided not to be reckoned with at all. She knew the teachers did not like her, but justice required that she come first on any academic list, and it was the duty of those who made the lists to represent, whilst they made them, abstract justice, incarnate and undefiled.

She believed she should also come first on all dramatic lists, but was aware that it was harder to construct these on clear principles of abstract rectitude. She had nevertheless no idea how horrible she was to have in any drama class, or play-reading. It was impossible for a teacher to distribute parts without becoming aware of Frederica's desperate concentration, fingers, toes, eyes, mouth, strained with eagerness. If she was cast, she read aloud with throbbing *brio*, embarrassing other girls, who felt that classroom conditions required muted tones, as a matter of good manners. If she was not cast, she glowered and concentrated and muttered over her desk, only too transparently producing a corrected counter-reading of everything in her head.

An odd aspect of this obsession was that the parts she ostentatiously desired were dictated more by sex than by number of lines: rather Goneril than Lear, rather Miranda than Prospero. Her readings of women were tremulous or ringing with feeling. Her men, though there are more, and more passionate men in Shakespeare, were paradoxically less alarming to her involuntary audiences.

The worst was *St Joan*. Miss Wells did not know, she told Stephanie, how she had survived *St Joan*. There were times, she said, when she had seriously feared that Frederica would rise and strike her for casting some other girl as Joan in the Trial Scene or the epilogue. There were times when, having cast Frederica, she wished to leave the room rather than endure the stress and embarrassment of the passion put into the performance.

Miss Wells rose now to read out the crucial List, twenty or so names long, and Frederica screwed herself round in agony on her chair and cast a desperate glance at Alexander, who pretended, obviously, not to have seen. Stephanie was mildly irritated both with Miss Wells and with Frederica. There had been a determined attempt to exclude Frederica from the list, on the ground, advanced by Miss Wells, that she was an academic high-flyer who could not afford to take so much time from her studies, and on the ground, advanced by the headmistress, that Frederica put herself too much forward, and that other girls should be allowed to shine. Stephanie knew that Frederica's name was on the list because she herself had argued with unusual firmness that it was unjust that it should not be, and had known, whilst arguing, that she asked for so little, and was so useful, that the others would do as she asked. When Frederica's name was read out Frederica drew in a long breath, un-gripped her hands from her chair seat, cast a triumphant and possessive look over Alexander, and visibly lost interest in the proceedings, as though that name was the only name. Stephanie felt a moment of pure rage. And then a guilty fear: for after this small success, what could be hoped? And Frederica's face was ablaze with arrogant and silly hope.

The Blesford girls were driven to the boys' school in a hired bus.
They wore berets with stitched golden roses and portcullises. They wore
striped ties. They looked remarkably like each other. They stood in a
tight flock in the drive as other buses drove in and deposited other little
gaggles. Many wore ankle socks, but above these their uniform made
them look portly and matronly. Girls in those days, even not in uniform,
tended towards this state, partly at least because the types of beauty
presented for their imitation in glossy papers and films were on the whole
women, not girls, hatted, gloved, mysteriously veiled or painted with
the ripeness of experience. Experience, paint, and veiling they could not
proffer; the matronly was all that was left. They all stared suspiciously
at each other. Boys ran past, between classes: some whistled. Miss Wells
made useless little rushes at some of these boys, and was detained by
Frederica, who said that she would take them to the Hall, where the
stage was, and the auditions must be. Once she began striding through
the cloisters the other girls, the other schools, fell into a crocodile
behind her, so that she strode into the Hall, banging its swing doors,
like a commander of troops. They were shuffling troops, who hung
back, and bunched in the way out.

Inside, the atmosphere was different: liberty could almost be smelled.
Lodge was sprawled in an armchair, one leg hooked over the arm, in a
huge and filthy sweater. He was smoking. Alexander was leaning
classically against the proscenium arch, one leg across the other at an
elegant angle she was later to note in Hilliard's decorous lover behind
the delicate pale roses. Crowe was on the move, shepherding the girls
into chairs, shouting orders to some invisible being about floods, so
that the stage, and Alexander, were gradually and warmly illuminated
with rosy-gold light.

They had prepared auditions. Perdita, Helena, Imogen, the Duchess
of Malfi. Frederica had practised for hours before the mirror, uncertain
between Helena and the Duchess. Stephanie, overhearing these out-
pourings, had with courage offered to play audience, and with greater
courage begged Frederica to be a little less expressive, to let the verse
speak for itself. Frederica had cursed Stephanie – shouted at her that
she couldn't speak, *she* didn't know, she underplayed herself and
everything else.

Lodge divided the girls into small groups and, unexpectedly, told
them they must now run, and dance. They must shed hats and coats,
sweep across the hall and on to the stage, form circles, skip, jump.
Alexander moved across to the piano and began to play Thomas Bull.
The girls began to run, and Lodge shouted "Faster". Long plaits
bounced on Prefects' badges, soft bunches brushed flushing cheeks.

"Now, leap," cried Lodge, laughing. He and Crowe were writing copious notes. "Leap *high*, spring up, stretch yourselves right out."

Frederica was without bodily grace. During all her rehearsals before the mirror, no matter how her voice swooped and sobbed, her arms had been rigid along her rigid trunk. She had no idea what to do with them. She had held out a hand in the Duchess's plea to her timid suitor and had reminded herself of a clockwork tin drummer she and Stephanie had had when they were little. Woodenly, now, crashing down heavily on wood, she thrust furiously up in a straight line, heavy-footed amongst the thicket of tossing arms and feat toes. Alexander, at the piano, moved like a wave of the sea, with rippling shoulder muscles and flowing hair and fingers. Frederica's face grew dusky with unavailing effort and humiliation. She stumped, as soon as she was decently able, off the platform, and sat scowling in the shadows.

Now they were limbered up, Lodge declared, he would hear their speeches. He read out their names, the Gillians, Susans, Judiths and Patricias who now, because of the dancing, were paradoxically loosed from their drilled similarity and came up, one after the other, blinking from the rosy light into the dark, and recited Perdita's flower speech, Helena's love for the bright particular star, Imogen's trouble over Milford Haven, the Duchess's proposal to her steward. Perditas predominated. O Proserpina! For the flowers now that frighted thou let'st fall From Dis's wagon. In Yorkshire, in tinkling china tones from the expensive convent, faltering, gushing, an incantation endlessly delightful, however frequently renewed. When Frederica came it was Crowe who asked her what she would do, and Crowe who told Alexander to read in for her, as he had for others, the necessary few lines of Antonio's part. Frederica's voice shook as she announced herself. Alexander, standing opposite her, was moved with unaccustomed gentleness towards her.

"Steady, Frederica. Take your time. It's not the end of the earth."

"No?" she said, with a dimmed flash of the old contradictory passion.

"No," said Alexander. He smiled. It was the first smile of real warmth, for herself, she had ever had from him, teacherly and considerate. She was irritated, as well as excited, by this thought.

Alexander said his piece.

> Conceive not I am so stupid but I aim
> Whereto your favours tend: but he's a fool
> That, being a-cold, would thrust his hands i'th'fire
> To warm them.

Blindly, Frederica began on the answering declaration: she had meant

it to be prettily, though nobly, tentative, but Alexander's presence and
her wrath over the fiasco of the dancing had added to it qualities she
could not quite control; a touch of impatient aggression, a touch of the
pure will to have what she desired, which had taken her so far, and
sustained her. She did not move: but because Alexander was Alexander
she trembled in her rigidity.

> The misery of us that are born great!
> We are forced to woo, because none dare woo us;
> And as a tyrant doubles with his words
> And fearfully equivocates, so we
> Are forc'd to express our violent passions
> In riddles and in dreams, and leave the path
> Of simple virtue, which was never made
> To seem the thing it is not. Go, go brag
> You have left me heartless; mine is in your bosom:
> I hope 'twill multiply love there. You do tremble:
> Make not your heart so dead a piece of flesh
> To fear, more than to love me. Sir, be confident:
> What is't distracts you? This is flesh and blood, sir;
> 'Tis not the figure cut in alabaster
> Kneels at my husband's tomb . . .

Towards the end of the speech she took one involuntary step towards
him, aware that she was doing it wrong, roaring too much, asking for
support, coming to an embarrassed halt. "Thank you," Crowe said,
unexpressive, when she had finished, and she got down, somehow.
Alexander pushed back his hair and mopped his brow with a very white
handkerchief.

There was a pause, and coming and going and comparing of notes,
between the three men, and then Crowe announced that they would like
to hear ten of the girls read again, a poem. He read out these names, the
no doubt penultimate List. Frederica's name was not amongst them.
She experienced a moment of simple incredulity. They must have
forgotten. The ten, nervous and shining, made their way back to the
stage and Lodge uncoiled himself from the chair and went up to one
of them, a tall, cleanly-carved pig-tailed girl from the Convent, named
Anthea Warburton. Would she mind, he enquired, if he undid her hair.
And the others, would they . . .? The Convent's chaperoning nun
rustled but did not protest. Lodge wound expert fingers up one glossy
snake of pale hair: Miss Warburton, brisker altogether, her eyes cast
modestly down, undid the other. Lodge shook her hair about her face.
She stared at him, coolly questioning, through its cloud, and Frederica

realised with pain that the chosen had one thing in common. They were all pretty. Very pretty. Frederica had never before been made to know so clearly her own limitations, or the large variety of qualifications in the world. There would, she saw, be singing and dancing under the trees in the gardens at Blesford Ride, and laughter and verse. But she would not be part of it. Well, she had no intention of making an audience for anyone else's performance. She would get up and go. She got up, and went.

Matthew Crowe caught her arm in the Pantheon.

"Where are you going?"

"Home."

"Why?"

"There was no point in staying."

"Why not?"

"It was clearly," said Frederica venomously, "a *beauty contest.*" She had a sudden soothing vision of scanty bathing suits, high spiked heels, satin sashes supported on jutting bosoms.

"A play is a spectacle," said Matthew Crowe.

"I see that."

"What we are mostly looking for is attendant nymphs and graces. For a masque performed before the Queen. I don't see you in that category."

"No." Then, "I don't see why you couldn't have said it was – that – you wanted."

"It wasn't all. Serving wenches, crowd."

"I see. Well, now I shall go home."

She tried to step past him. They were standing between the statues of Baldur the Beautiful, his limbs relaxing in granite death, in conscious or unconscious imitation of Michelangelo's Dying Slave, a meticulously Gothic piece of mistletoe protruding from his left nipple, and Pallas Athene, stonily swathed in a granite chiton, clutching the horripilant Gorgon head.

"I shouldn't go. Your audition gave me a rather amusing idea. It was rather good in itself, actually. What gave you the idea of making her so aggressive?"

"Well, she had to be. She was her wicked brothers' sister. She was a great prince. She was greedy. She clutched at apricots. She was used to having her own way. Actually, to tell you the truth, I meant it to come out more – well, less – more pleading. I got cross about the dancing. I can't dance. I felt awful. I was flustered. I can do it better than that. Tho' when I was doing it, I saw, you *could* play it on the edge of being – overpowering. It would make sense."

"Indeed. Very clever."

"Thank you." She drank in praise like a reviving plant. Crowe leaned on the gorgon's writhing stone serpents and said, "Let me look at your face." He ran a finger down her sharp nose. "I really think it might be worth your while coming back."

"Why?"

"Well, speaking of type-casting . . . as we were . . . we might be able to wangle at least an understudy of the first act . . ."

This was a much worse exhibition of the power-game than lists. This was the fairy-tale shift of fortune, the Noel Streatfeild children's tale in which rude girls like herself had their pretensions depressed and were then allowed, after all, to pass GO. She touched her sandy hair and stared at the tiny impresario. It was like a fairy-tale because he enjoyed engineering fairy-tales. He lived in a world where such engineering was the pattern of art; and life, and power, imitated art.

"Ah," she said, "ah thank you – I've never wanted anything so much, never. If you only *could* – I'd be –"

"Mind, I promise nothing," he said. And then, "You didn't talk to your dad about the Duchess?"

"Entirely my own work. I promise."

He laughed. "Come back. Come back."

She swept eagerly after him.

8. *Ode on a Grecian Urn*

Stephanie sat in a chill brown classroom, whitened over with chalk dust, and taught the *Ode on a Grecian Urn* to those girls who had not gone to Blesford Ride. Good teaching is a mystery and takes many forms. Stephanie's idea of good teaching was simple and limited: it was the induced, shared, contemplation of a work, an object, an artefact. It was not the encouragement of self-expression, self-analysis, or what were to be called interpersonal relations. Indeed, she saw a good reading of the *Ode on a Grecian Urn* as a welcome chance to avoid these activities.

She had never had trouble with discipline, although she never raised her voice. She exacted quietness, biologically and morally. Girls came in from outside, buzzing, crashing, laughing. Barbara, Gillian, Zelda, Valerie, Susan, Juliet, Grace. Valerie had a disfiguring boil and Barbara an acute curse pain. Zelda's father was dying, this month or next, and Juliet had been shocked by a strange boy who had thrust his fist up her skirt and crooked an elbow around her throat in a Blesford ginnel. Gillian was very clever and required a key, mnemonics and an analytic blueprint of the Grecian Urn for exam purposes. Susan was in love with Stephanie whom she tried to please by straining her attention. Grace wanted only to have a florist's shop, was held at school in a vice of parental ambition, biding her time.

Stephanie's mind was clear of all this information, and she required that their minds should become so. She made them keep still, by keeping unnaturally still herself, as tamers of wild birds and animals keep still, she had read in childhood, so that the creatures became either mesmerised or fearless or both, she was not sure which.

She required also that her mind at least should be clear of the curious clutter of mnemonics that represented the poem at ordinary times, when the attention was not concentrated upon it. In her case: a partial visual memory of its shape on the page, composed, in fact, of several super-imposed patterns from different editions, the gestalt clear, but shifting in size: a sense of the movement of the rhythm of the language which was biological, not verbal or visual, and not to be retrieved without calling whole strings of words to the mind's eye and ear again: some words, the very abstract ones, form, thought, eternity, beauty, truth, the very concrete ones, unheard, sweeter, green, marble, warm, cold, desolate. A run of grammatical and punctuational pointers: the lift of frozen unanswered questions in the first stanza, the apparently un-disciplined rush of repeated epithets in the third. Visual images, neither seen, in the mind's eye, nor unseen. White forms of arrested movement under dark formal boughs. Trouble with how to "see" the trodden weed. John Keats on his death-bed, requesting the removal of books, even of Shakespeare. Herself at Cambridge, looking out through glass library walls into green boughs, committing to memory, what? Asking what, why?

She read the poem out quietly, as expressionless as possible, a ditty with no tone. And then again. The ideal was to come to it with a mind momentarily open and empty, as though for the first time. They must all hear the words equally, not pounce, or tear, or manipulate. She asked them chilly, "Well?" prolonging the difficult moment when they must just stare, finding speech difficult and judgment unavoidable.

She sat there, looking into inner emptiness, waiting for the thing to rise into form and saw nothing, nothing and then involuntarily flying specks and airy clumps of froth or foam on a strongly running grey sea. Foam not pure white, brown and gold-stained here and there, blowing together, centripetal, a form cocooned in crusts and swathes of adhesive matter. Not relevant, her judgment said, the other poem, damn it, the foam of perilous seas. The thing had a remembered look, not pleasant, and she grimaced, as she saw it. Venus de Milo. Venus Anadyomene. The foam-born, foam from the castrated genitals of Kronos. Not a bad image, if you wanted one, of the coming to form from shapelessness, but not what she had meant to call up.

"Well," she said to the girls, "well, what do you *see*?"

They began to talk about when Keats required his reader to see an urn and when a landscape, what colours he called up and what he left to choice, and moved from there to the nature of the difficulty of seeing what is formed to be "seen" by language alone, marble men and maidens, the heifer and altar, a burning forehead and a parching tongue, cold pastoral.

> Heard melodies are sweet but those unheard
> Are sweeter,

said Stephanie. Clever Gillian commented that the word desolate was the centre of the poem, almost allowing one to be taken out of it, like the word forlorn in the *Nightingale*. They talked about beauty is truth, truth beauty. They talked, as Stephanie had meant them to, about a verbal *thing*, made of words so sensual and words not sensual at all, like beauty and truth. She talked about what it could mean, that the urn should "tease us out of thought As doth eternity." It is a funeral urn, said Zelda. That is not enough to say, said Susan, staring at Stephanie.

Things moved in the classroom, amongst eight closed minds, one urn, eight urns, nine urns, half realised, unreal, white figures whose faces and limbs could be sensed but not precisely described, bright white, the dark, the words, moving, in ones, in groups, in clusters, in and out of whatever cells held their separate and communal visual, aural or intellectual memories. Stephanie talked them out of the vocabulary she was supposed to be teaching them and left them with none, darkling. Gillian, who was enjoying the process, reflected that words could be quickly enough snatched back, when the occasion required it. Stephanie reflected that this poem was the poem she most cared for, saying ambivalently that you could not do, and need not attempt, what it required you to do, see the unseen, realise the unreal, speak what was not, and that yet it did it so that unheard melodies seemed infinitely preferable to any one might ever hope to hear. Human beings, she had thought, even as a very small child faced with *The Lady of Shalott*, might so easily never have hit on the accidental idea of making unreal verbal forms, they might have just lived, and dreamed, and tried to tell the truth. She had kept asking Bill, *why* did he write it, and the answers had been so many and so voluble and so irrelevant to the central problem, that she closed her mind to them, even whilst effortlessly committing them to memory for future use, as Gillian now must and would.

The bell rang. They came out blinking, like owls into the bright daylight. Stephanie, gathering her books, allowed herself to wonder whether the irrelevant flying foam she had seen had come from the Nightingale, or from her own intellect, making Freudian associations all too tidily between marble maidens, the Venus and the subconscious knowledge she had of the nature of that foam. It was not very nice foam.

Afterwards she tried to get out of the school quickly. She wanted to think. She passed through the staffroom, and thought about teaching. One could say: I teach: and smell ink, and dampish serge, and floor-polish. In the staffroom too many dirty gaudy utility chairs, peacock, lemon, tomato and a thick smell of tea. Window frames, too high, opening on no vista. One could say: I teach: and listen to unheard melodies and see white figures running under dark boughs. Miss Wells, returned from Blesford, rose from a chair and offered a posy of prim-roses. An identical posy dangled from her own purple knitted cardigan. Stephanie bent her nose to their pale honey and wine, pinned them to her coat, and put that on, a gesture of grateful adornment, a prelude to departure.

"Lovely," she said. "I must fly. How did the auditions go?" She had not wanted to be trapped to be told.

"He made them all dance, and undid their hair."

"Not Frederica!"

"She didn't dance very well. They liked my sweet Mary. There were one or two lovely Perditas. Frederica did a very *aggressive* audition, dear. And I fear they only wanted nymphs and maidens. But they kept her. When I left, they had her on stage, saying some lyric of Elizabeth's own. They were laughing. And arguing. 'A muscle-bound lion's cub' I heard Mr Crowe say. She looked so cross."

"Oh dear." Stephanie could bear no more. "I really must fly. I've got the bike. I *am* grateful for the flowers, you do such lovely flowers."

Susan, desperate, lurked amongst the lockers, waiting for Miss Potter's passage to the bike shed. She had prepared a very intelligent question about the Urn that required in her view a long and con-scientious answer. When Miss Potter got on her bike, Susan would rush out, and, perfectly naturally, get on her own, and at about the crater, would catch up, and for about ten or fifteen minutes they would, they must, ride along side by side, and speak, just the two of them, as had never happened.

The crater was a waste dip encroaching on tennis lawns and the school drive. Blesford's only bomb, partially exploding, had thrown the earth up fairly harmlessly there, breaking a few windows, leaving a ridged whirlpool and decadence of mud which had generated grass and willow herbs and had not been reclaimed. It had become a kind of War Memorial, and little girls used it as a theatre for imaginary dramas.

Stephanie Potter, knowing Felicity Wells had counted on tea, guilty but determined, strode past. The smooth pale hair was tied under a grass-green scarf; the primroses were now pinned to a rather dashing voluminous coat, also green, shaped a little like an artist's smock, with full sleeves caught in tight cuffs.

Susan darted to the cycle shed and eased her machine out of its concrete rut.

Miss Potter rode past briskly, pedalling firmly, flowing gold and green.

Susan mounted, shoved, swayed, set off.

Stephanie descended into the declivity of the path that crossed the crater, in bumps and starts, braking.

Into the crater from the other side, ponderously manoeuvring, came a large black figure on a massive black bicycle. As though, Susan thought, also braking, he had simply risen up from the sooty laurels the other side of the crater. Which he had, indeed. He came heavily on, bore down on Miss Potter in a rut, clashed their handlebars, like horned beasts engaging each other. Clumsy, thought Susan, which it had not been, exactly.

Stephanie hopped a few steps, entangled, caught her calf painfully on the edge of a pedal, stopped to rub it. Susan saw a long oily streak on the smooth stocking. She wondered whether she herself was now obliged to go past, turn back, or very obviously hang about.

Daniel, head down, manipulated handlebars and interlocked brake-blocks with ferocity. He had reckoned he might get ten minutes. With luck. It would have to do. He had planned the encounter with his usual care, calculating that she must be more or less in that place at that time. Better here than fail to pull off some more apparently casual bump in Blesford. But now he could not speak. So he ground metal and rubber.

She stared at him, out of her struggle with green cloth, oil, chain. Black hair all over, black raincoat, black trousers, black shoes. Huge shoulders and belly. Dog-collar. Cycle clips. So much of him. She did not speak.

He wrenched his mount away, by main force, and said baldly: "I was waiting for you."

"So I see."

"I want to talk to you."

She was rubbing her leg: he ignored that.

"I was in a bit of a hurry. Perhaps some other time."

"It's important."

"There isn't anything wrong?" Her bland and lovely brow creased in anxiety.

"No, no. Just that I-I myself – I wanted to talk to you." He repeated rather crossly, as though she should have known, "It's important."

He could only keep saying exactly what he meant. He had wanted so little in his life. What he had wanted he had got. If he could get her to stay with him just ten minutes, he knew it, she would begin to see the necessity. He knew already, without having to work it out, that she found it very hard to say no.

"You could spare a few minutes," he told her.

"Oh, a few minutes." As though he had been demanding hours. "A few minutes. I suppose I could. Would you like a cup of coffee in the new coffee bar? That's near."

It was not what he would have chosen, but he could be graceful.

"Thank you, yes. I'm sorry I scratched your paint."

"It's not fresh enough to matter. The chain-guard's more of a problem. We should make the coffee bar."

The peering literary child watched them bump off uncertainly together, through the dusky bushes, the fat dark back and heavy piston legs obscuring her view of the captured green and gold. She was shaken by disappointment and rage, as though dark had descended. She thought irritably, oh let it go, it's only Blesford Grammar and a crush on a teacher, it's only the bomb crater, and I'm only very young. As though she knew that at some future time age might make other grass and other people more real, more durable. As though other unseen colours must necessarily be brighter than the vanishing gold and green.

Blesford's new Coffee Bar, an early northern exemplar, was underground, an experimental conversion of the basement of the Spinning Wheel tea-shop. It had a new expresso machine, a few booths with peg-board screens, candles in bottles on the table, and posters depicting Italian beauty spots: Sicily, Pompeii, the Spanish Steps. The lighting was gentian-coloured, which made the froth on the cappuccino look like phosphorescent ink.

Daniel eased his dark bulk down the wooden ladder, hunching his shoulders, reminding Stephanie briefly of Alderman Ptolemy Tortoise in Beatrix Potter. They sat in a corner booth on rexine tumps: Daniel's creaked ominously under his weight. They faced each other with blue lips, teeth glinting hyacinthine, the caverns of their mouths grape-purple. Stephanie's hair and the primroses were without colour, and metallic.

The dim light flowed into the folds of Daniel's shadowy clothing, sank into his hair and heavy brows and shaded chin, making him seem warmer, fluid, less portentously substantial. Unaware himself of this he remarked that the lighting was in his view cheerless, and ordered coffee.

He wondered if he should just say: I believe you should marry me. Or, which was more exact and more modest: I believe I should marry you. He was distracted, rare in him, by the fact that she had become glittering and blue. Being a man who usually said what he meant was a disadvantage here, where what he meant was extreme and unprepared for, and might even sound silly. He tried:

"I felt we ought to talk."

"What about?"

"Well, a great many things. But it wasn't 'what about' I was thinking of. Just that we – that you and I – ought to be talking to each other. It seemed important."

She maintained a courteous silence, as though waiting for him to say something to which there was an answer. He blundered on.

"I wanted to get to know you. I don't usually – I mean, only for work – this is for myself."

She said, "Don't."

"Don't?"

"I – I don't like people to say things like that to me."

"Why not?"

"Oh dear. Because so many people do. That's something you should understand."

He did not: he had never addressed a girl out of personal need before: but he was thinking quickly. He was suddenly, despondently aware of her as a woman of whom much was demanded, by family, work, chance acquaintances, and no doubt other men. What was unique for him was not for her. It was his turn to be silent.

"I don't know you," said Stephanie.

"That's what I'm asking you to do."

"I know. But you make it seem so – *much*. And I feel, I feel it's nothing to do with me. Please try to understand."

There was something wrong and nervously patronising about her gentleness, a response already mechanical with use. He was enraged by this: he glowered. She looked nervously at him and saw this. She said, "Oh dear."

"Well," he said, "that's that. Shall we go?"

"Oh dear," she said again.

"Oh dear," he agreed, ferociously, and waved at the waitress. He felt suffocated.

"Don't go. I shall feel bad. I only meant –"

She could not say what she only meant, and he could not say that he didn't care if she did feel bad. So they sat. Finally, with a crude social effort, she asked about his work. Felicity Wells, living in the Vicarage, had developed an apprehensive admiration for Daniel's bulldozing pastoral methods, and his use of time, although she was worried about his theology. Stephanie had listened to Miss Wells's talk, and had responded to something wholly reasonable and yet usually impracticable in Daniel's moral behaviour.

"The work'd be easier if folk weren't so scared of each other," Daniel said gloomily. "People get all meshed and mashed in conventions. Don't speak if you aren't spoken to, charity's a dirty word, don't put on people, don't get put on. Scrunching their guts away from inside with loneliness and pointlessness, but they'd not cross a road to say a word to anyone else in the same mess. Mostly my job's just asking, politely if possible, a bit rudely if not, making it look official, like a committee, *requesting* this and that. What I do is invent an alternative set of non-operative conventions. Ones that say you've got to speak out how it is, *find* out how it is."

"Conventions," she said, "have their uses. They keep people safe – from hurt, from taking on what they can't bear. Or they can make a slow, bearable way of getting into – bits of life. You can't always rush people to extremes. In case people can't stand them."

"Extremes *exist*," said furious Daniel. "Take Miss Phelps. Pelvis smashed, no chance she'll walk again, day after day in a hospital bed, in pain, looking at the likely end, trying not to. Take Miss Whicher. Lives two doors away from Miss P., doesn't know her, or anyone else, serves me tea in rosebud cups, cup after cup, *ever* so dainty, oh Mr Orton, I feel my life is slipping away to no purpose, no one really needs me, so I say, go and see Miss Phelps. And the carry-on, the carry-on."

He imitated, for Stephanie, Miss Whicher's layered caveats. One might be thought *pushing*, or *do-gooding*, or might turn out to have no interests in common, or find it all too *painful* and make it *worse*, or say the *wrong thing*, and they would be so conscious they weren't really *friends*, not *naturally*, as it were ... Stephanie was amazed at his power of mimicry, amorphous and indignant in the blue dark. She had thought of him as always and essentially the same, a man on one note, a line heading one way.

"The Vicar," said Daniel, who did not normally utter complaints, "bothers about intruding. He smiles and says, lovely roses someone brought you, Miss Phelps. Better weather we're getting, Miss Phelps. Not, no more walking, Miss Phelps, how will you manage, nor yet, there is someone still there inside you, Miss Phelps, you can speak, we are both here and not finished yet. He doesn't say that."

"You have to say that so it sounds right, if you say it at all. You can't generate everyone's energy, all on your own."

"I can't see what else I can try to do." He grinned grimly. "Vicar doesn't like me. I disturb things."

"You like disturbing things. You're right, of course." This admission led her to ask, involuntarily and unnaturally politely, "Is there anything I could do?"

"I did have an idea." He risked a joke. "Apart from talking to me. There's Mrs Haydock."

"Mrs Haydock?"

"Brontë Buildings, Branwick Estate. Must be about thirty. Husband walked out. As happens. Two kids, a scared girl, autistic boy, six, nine. That boy's a smasher. Quiet, quiet, not a word, never has spoken one, everything systematically pulled apart – crushed, bashed, ground, ripped. Not people, ever. Only things. Sometimes he hums. They say he can hum quite complicated things. I wouldn't know, I'm not musical, I can sing the responses and that. He stares a lot. Not stupid, not *at* you, not away from you. In another dimension, he stares. She won't have him put away. She loves him. I'd say that might be a difficult decision, if you take a good look at the other kid, the girl, not a mousehole to call her own or hide her head. But there is no decision, she loves him, she gives her life to him."

"You haven't tried to make her give him up?"

"Thought about it. Yes, I did think. Because of the little one, little Pat. But I think it's possible Mrs Haydock'd just come to pieces without him. Having made him her life. Funny thing, the variety of lives, you can't know *what* accident won't set yours in some very simple terrible deep channel for the rest of its run. To have such a child, or a daft parent. Love. God. Anyway, I decided –"

"You decided –"

"If she had a day, even an afternoon, off a week, to take little Pat out, not to have him, if she had someone reliable to mind him, who'd come, regular, so she could *count* on it. Things would change for all of them. She'd never ask. She'd take persuading. But if someone *offered*. Can you imagine being her?"

"I should be scared," said Stephanie Potter.

"And don't you think Mrs Haydock isn't? And Pat?"

"And such responsibility . . ."

"We must all take some."

"Daniel – Mr Orton – why me?"

"I just always thought you were the right one. You could hold it for her. You could do it. I think if you went, you'd see I was right."

She was suddenly afraid of him. He dealt absolutely, in areas where one neither thought nor lived, normally. Where one hoped to avoid living. He saw the world *in extremis* and was right. She tried to imagine the life he had made for himself and could not. She did not want to have to. He dealt in what had properly daunted Keats who had abandoned surgery for poetry but knew that poetry had no answer to pain.

"You'd get blood out of a stone," she said. "If you and I understand that I'm only offering once or twice – till I see if I can manage – I'll try. I can only try."

She smiled briefly, more animated than he had seen her yet. She added proudly, "But if I do agree, I am reliable. I can say that."

"You don't have to. Some things I do know about people and some I don't. That kind of thing, I do."

9. *Meat*

Marcus spent inordinate lengths of time in the bathroom. Each week, Winifred thought, he added half an hour or more. He ran water, in inexplicable rushes, between long silences. Sometimes she saw Bill creeping across the landing in socks, brown toes, arched knees, profile of a scowl, to take account of this, to peer and listen. Once or twice he beat with frantic fists in the panel of the door, requiring answers, exits, explanations, which Marcus did not oblige with. Winifred tried not to react. To either of them. In Bill's case this was because to endemic wrath any behaviour at all was simply provocation. About Marcus, she felt superstitiously that if she averted her attention from him, her eyes, her anxiety, her love, there was a chance he might get by. Might go unnoticed, either by Fate or his father. So she observed him, in her dressing-table mirror, slip out of the bathroom in one of Bill's lulls, and gave no sign. Peace and quiet were her priorities. At all costs, peace and quiet. For this boy, above all.

She remembered clearly not only his birth but what she believed to have been the moment of his conception. He was born at the time of Munich, in the unreal lull before the unimaginable storm. He must have been conceived in that house, in that bed, one night when Bill had come home from a WEA lecture on Shakespeare, beery and contentious, to lecture her on acceptable and unacceptable reconcilings in the Last

Plays. He disliked *A Winter's Tale*. Partly because it was said to have christian overtones, primarily because it was strictly improbable, he had said, thumping about the bedroom, odour of effort rising from his relaxing stockinged feet. A man does not lose his wife for twenty years and get back an animated statue and profess joy in a deception as though it was a miracle, not so easily. This was Shakespeare's real failure at the primitive level of plausibility of plot, Bill said. And what about Hermione, Winifred said mildly. All the years of her womanhood gone, and her two children, one dead, one vanished, and no feelings required but gratitude and joy. His class, Bill said, had tried to tell him that the statue represented a resolution of the pains of life in Art and he had said, some things could not be so resolved. Prospero was a more complex, a better solution. Less easily slipped into, the circle of recon- ciliation, more consistently artificial. He must have got round to loving his daughters by the last plays, Winifred had said, there were so many the same, and Bill, in his underpants by now, had grinned, and said there was no evidence about daughters.

It hadn't been because he or she had wanted a son – though the elaborately feminine names of their daughters, both versions of names for a son, had been his choice. It had been because the daughters they had were for once miraculously quiet, and because of the WEA beer, and because he was talking to her, which he was usually too tired, or too busy, or too dogged by bills and babies, to do. Or too angry.

She had married him because he was the man she most admired. Just, passionate, prodigious with effort, discriminating. She had been most afraid of living like her mother, too many children, too little money, mastered by a house and husband which were peremptory moral imperatives and steady physical wreckers. Winifred had been her mother's confidante about every detail of blood, polish and indignation: she was the eldest. She knew about childbirth and male "selfishness" after it, about black lead, white stone on doorsteps, laundry blue, starch and scrubbing. Her mother had made efforts, ambivalently, to let her out: had not stood in the way of the Grammar School education, which had led to Winifred learning that one could, indeed should, marry for passion and conversation, not for bleeding or black lead. Bill had lent her *Lady Chatterley* and preached about freedom: he was in flight from a more harshly defined version of the house, man, woman, she herself meant to step beyond.

By 1938 she had learned that it is not possible to create the opposite of what one has always known, simply because the opposite is believed to be desired. Human beings need what they already know, even horrors. The unknown is hard to get at, because it is unknown. Paradoxically,

Winifred had decided, two people are closer before they have lived together or even slept together or talked for very long – what they do say is more their own saying, makes less concessions to habit, or quirks of temperament, or previous failures to get through. She had talked to Bill in those days, making him in her own image, it was true, but she had talked more truthfully, and if she had, it was possible that this was also his case. He was now constantly enraged by cooking, cleaning, crying daughters. But she knew he was not like this at work: he was patient, persistent, forbearing. And she discovered in herself a fatal and steady need for tasks and reprobation. Maybe rage and patience were all that could be left.

In the beginning she had been violent in bed. Not demanding, no, nor insistent, but wild and tough, ready to bite and lick and smell and touch and taste and battle. Conventions closed on her imperceptibly, one by one. She could not be bothered to take off her nightdress. Or shift from the horizontal to the vertical. Or kiss his mouth. And his feet irritated her. She opened her eyes once in the dark and realised that someone, not exactly herself, had been sneering inside her at Bill's insensitivity to her pain and fatigue when he was doing what would, after all, have delighted her a year before. She supposed this might be usual, but had no friends whom she could ask. And she would never talk to her daughters, she vowed, as her mother had talked to her, never. She would be quiet. Quiet spread over more and more areas where hope had been.

So that evening in 1938, when Bill had actually, because of the beer, spoken to her about Shakespeare, and when Frederica had not, for once, woken screaming, she was wearily grateful, no more, for speech, and stayed on her back, murmuring about Hermione. And Bill hoisted himself up and moved purposefully up and down, and she felt as she now habitually felt at best, mild claustrophobia and a mild peripheral possibility of pleasure, not worth straining for. When Bill sighed, and shook himself, and rolled back to his side of the bed, she felt suddenly dark and cavernous inside, chill and a little dizzy, and had listened as though changes were happening, like electric currents, which a perception fine enough might note. She believed steadily afterwards that she had indeed noticed the moment of conception. The tepid, largely accidental beginning of Marcus, her son.

The child and the war swelled inevitably together. Bill, predicting Armageddon, cultural annihilation, and evil in jack-boots stalking English lanes, chose to blame some unspecified inadvertence of Winifred's for the untimely birth. Younger masters left the school to volunteer. Bill, discommoded, fumed and spent more and more time

out of the home. Winifred, heavy and frightened, pushed the perambulator around Blesford, Frederica gingery, furious, imperious under
its hood, Stephanie dangling plump legs under its handle, staring too
solemnly from under a sunbonnet. Fear is infectious. Stephanie was
learning fear. Winifred was not enough of an actress, and had also not
enough physical strength, to communicate assurance or reassurance.
She stared over her daughters' heads, nerving herself for everything,
pushing the pram, facing Bill, the birth of the baby, bombs, gas,
occupation. She had fantasies of small bodies spitted on bayonets, of
cots, and flesh, crushed in thundering rubble. The baby should not have
been conceived, but since it was there must now be protected. If
possible. That was all.

He was born, swiftly and entirely painlessly, one bright afternoon in
July, so fast that for days she felt unreal, as though there were some
ordeal still to come. "It's a boy," they said, and she answered politely
"That's what I wanted", although she had never seriously considered
the possibility that the child was not a girl. She raised herself, with her
unexpended strength, and saw him, still attached by the cord, pulsing
livid and slate-blue. His dark eyes blinked unseeing against the flooding
sunlight. He was tiny, delicate, enraged, an exact replica of Bill in a
spasm of fury, wavering impotent crimson fists over a creased bald pate
streaked with damp gingery strands. Nothing at all of her. What had
lived in her, stirred, turned, what she had held and protected, turned
out to be Bill's rage, simply. A boy. She lay back very calmly on the
pillows and waited for them to take him away.

Bill flared in and out of the hospital, volatile with unpredictable joy.
He made the nurses unwrap the boy and display on the white muslin
the comparatively vast genitals, crimson-dark. He named him, without
hesitation. He had wanted to be called Marcus himself, as a boy, he
said. She lay still and watched him poke his finger into the small, cold
clutch of his son. She almost felt she had lost someone.

Three nights later, in the dark, something terrible happened. They
brought the baby to be fed, under green-shaded light, a virtually weightless scrap, trailing damp ends of flannelette sheet and stiff hospital
nightgown. She shifted the lolling head, the gaunt, disappointed face
in the crook of her arm and knew that he was fragile and that she loved
him. She knew the need to hold him close, and close to the need, the
fear of crushing him. Babies' flesh is chilly where it is not hot and damp
with striving. This baby was uniformly still, and chilly. She sat on her
rubber sheet possessed by terrible love, in fear, although he had only
just come, of the moment when they would take him away. As she
had known when he began, so she knew now that the whole pattern

of her future was changed, he was best, first and worst: she was already making dispositions. He fed, neatly, quietly, collapsed into sleep. Already she assumed that the violence of these new feelings was dangerous to him, or at least burdensome: it must be dissimulated. They came and took him away. She waited all night in rigid apprehension and immobile delight for the moment when they would bring him back. And so something began.

Bill roared in the kitchen "Get out of that bathroom, boy. There are other people with biological needs in this house." The walls were thin, the piercing voice pierced. Bill had made such classic errors. Every toy bought six months before the boy could deal with it. Every teacher told – with the unfortunate support of the mathematical strangeness – every teacher admonished that the boy was a genius. Most of all Bill had wanted to share Marcus's early reading. He himself had scratted in the thin dust of evangelical tracts. Marcus should have imaginative worlds which Bill would enter with him. What do you feel, what do you picture in your mind's eye, what moves you? The slow boy looked into space. And did sums. Which were not his heritage, and, in that innumerate family, not shared, nor marvelled over.

In the face of the blast of Bill's love she could only keep quiet. Convert energy to inertia. Undo, unmake. Perhaps she did the wrong thing. It was not a very satisfactory thing to do.

She heard a cautious click of the bathroom door. She followed him into his boy's room, with its bench, engines of war, models, neatly aligned. He was looking out of the window. He had not looked much like his father since those first moments in the air. He looked like her, more than the daughters did. Stolid, mild, large, plain. She wanted to touch him and did not.

"Are you doing anything, Marcus?"

He shook his head.

"I'm going shopping in Blesford. Would you come and carry?"

"O.K. I'll get my jacket."

She did not say: when we get back he might be better about the bathroom. Marcus gave no sign of knowing that was involved. They communicated, if they communicated, without speech. Sometimes she wondered if she ought to shout out: Marcus, you are strange, there is something really *wrong*, Marcus, speak to me. But she did not say such things. He relied upon her not to say such things. Or so she believed.

Masters' Row, backing on to the Far Field, was at the front a row of isolated suburban houses on a country road, at least in 1953, turning between fields with hawthorn hedges or drystone walls. In those days too, Masters' Row had its own bus-stop, a tarmac bay with a galvanized shelter and cast-iron sign. By 1970 the whole road had been developed, widened and straightened with orange glass and concrete lamps along its sleek and mottled black length. Uprooted hedgerows and levelled fields were thickly planted with tiny ranch houses, miniature drives, dwarf white plastic fences. The Masters' Row houses, then, seemed besieged and impoverished. In 1953, it was still possible for the Potters to see themselves as country-dwellers, of a kind. They took regular walks along cart-tracks, away from the school grounds, through meadows, and fields of oats and barley, to a sewage works. On these walks Winifred told the children names of plants: harebell, stitchwort, toadflax, St. John's wort, eggs and bacon, vetch, trefoil. The girls chanted these names after her. Marcus, who had hay fever, sneezed and shook, his eyelids glossy and swollen round his lashes, his sinuses drilled boxes of pain, his palate raw and puffy.

The sewage works was like a closed fort, iron-railed, windowless concrete boxes, artificial grass mounds. There was a human silence. All the sound was the discreetly humming wires, the scratching of rotor arms on deserted round tubs of gravel. The girls tended to veer away from the place as though it was, or must be, unhealthy. Marcus liked it, to a certain extent. It had no feathery grasses and it had the order of a well-kept cemetery, the mown neatness, the humps, the noiselessness. He felt that they should stop and look at it, since it was their declared goal. But they never did. Recycled water, recycled liquid wastes, Lucas Simmonds had once told a class, were purer than spring water, quite sterile. Marcus thought, at that moment, about the quiet business of their own sewage works.

Trips into Blesford, by bus, like the walks to the sewage works, were for Marcus an order of repeated information and pain. He had gone to school the other way, many more miles, to the prep school attached to the Minster choir school in Calverley. Blesford was shops and the hospital. When they went there, Winifred told him its scanty history, as on the sewage walk she told him botany. It had been a mediaeval market town, of which there were still some relics, beleaguered by identikit square glass and pebble dash concretions. The shell of the old castle still stood on a minimal grassy hump, and was reached by a flight of steps and an iron handrail. There was a market-place with striped stalls and down by the railway on Wednesdays a cattle market, where for a few hours the stones smelled of straw, dung, urine and panic before it was all hosed away. There were old names: Beastfair, Finkle Street, Slutwell Lane, Grindergate. The bus circled the periphery of these narrow roads, past functional red-brick buildings with asphalted yards: Blesford Main Post Office, Blesford Hospital, Blesford Bus Station.

Marcus had spent many weeks in the hospital, either with his worst attacks of asthma, or undergoing inconclusive searches for the asthma's cause. "They" believed he might contain a "focus of infection", of which the asthma might be a secondary effect. He had been x-rayed, skin-tested, weighed and measured. His tonsils and adenoids had been hopefully removed. He had learned things, mostly about the nature of vision.

He had once heard Alexander and his father talking about the effects of consumption on art: hectic brilliance and speed, Alexander had said. Years later he himself was to speculate about the relationship between oxygen and insight. At the time he was roused enough to remark to himself that asthma was not like that. It was not energising. What it did was stretch time and perception so that everything was slow and sharp and clear.

When he was not ill, the hospital was a neutral retreat. Cavernous, dark red, smelling of carbolic and flowers, nurses passing and repassing, starch, bits of boiled metal.

When he was ill, space and time were both biological and abstract. Every rib was defined and located by pain, every cold breath, laboriously and noisily drawn in, laboriously and noisily expelled, impressed its duration on his consciousness. He had developed the characteristic crouch of the asthmatic, bowed spine, hunched shoulders, hanging rib-cage, the weight of the body on rigid arms and tensed knuckles. An anthropoid cage for pain and struggle. From this crouching stillness he perceived more sharply strictly limited things. Colours, outlines, people, trolleys, vases. A coiling inner design of grating, whistling air moving the stops of an intolerably sensitive organ. Everything, inner and outer, precisely defined in black outline against an encroaching haze.

There was an extreme point where pain refined vision to mathematics. He would see a two-dimensional map, grey-black-white, of linear relations: curtains, furniture-corners, bed, chair, fingers plucking up triangles of blanket. This was related to the inner map of blocked, narrowing, imagined passages for air. Twice, losing consciousness, he had seen the same last thing, just before. Once had been when he struggled with the pad of ether, for the tonsils, and once an attack so severe he had fainted. (He fainted relatively frequently, and hated it.)

What he saw was turning geometry, spinning graph paper with the squares decreasing in size on some almost definable geometric principle, and simultaneously rotating, so that somewhere in the centre, on the periphery of the field of vision, was the vanishing point, infinity.

So that geometry was close to, and opposed to, the suffering animal.

It intensified with pain, and yet the attention could, with effort, be deflected from pain to geometry. Geometry was immutable, orderly, and connected with extremity. He did not, in his mind, oppose pain and geometry: what was opposed to both was "normal life" where you took things easy as they came, things shiny, glossy, soft, hard, shifty, touchable, not needing mapping or ordering. When the Blesford bus turned round the hospital, he noted the number of upper and lower windows, their geometric proportions, and crossed his fingers. His mother sat beside him, clutching her handbag, with her own memories. They did not speak to each other.

The Butcher's Shop was not in Beastfair, which contained the new Marks and Spencer, Timothy White's, Etam and some little wool shops. It was an old and flourishing High Class Butchery with green and white tiled walls, and sawdust and blood on its floor. Its proprietor, W. Allenbury, was florid and vigorous, an active man, as butchers seem to be, responsibly engaged in local politics and ready, indeed pressing, to discuss the state of the nation and the nature of the universe with the housewives over whom, in the days of rationing, he had exercised a benign despotism that had somehow never worn off. He was helped by three young men in long blood-stained white aprons, all exceedingly, sometimes indecently, lively. Marcus associated their liveliness with the Potters' Sunday joint. There was a time when they regularly sat down to a roast sirloin, preceded by large squares of Yorkshire pudding, crisp, golden, steamy, sprinkled with salt and hot gravy. Bill and Winifred frequently adjured pale Marcus to take some of the good red juices from under the joint to put a little life and colour into him.

Allenbury's shop window was, in its way, a work of art. It is not possible, with meat, to create the symmetry, the delicate variation of colour and form that a fishmonger can make on marble or ice with a wheel, or an abstract rose, of his proffered goods. But Allenbury's window had a compensating variety. It combined the natural, the man-made, the anthropomorphic and the abstract in a pleasingly eclectic way. It had its own richness.

From a glittering steel bar on elegantly curved hooks hung the chickens, with plump naked breasts and limbs, and softly feathered stretched necks. The ducks, in line, had their webbed cold feet tucked neatly along their sides, gold beaks, black eyes, neck feathers scarlet on white. Beneath them the display counter was lined and fringed with emerald green artificial grass. On this miniature meadow capered various folklorique figures and mythical creatures. A grinning cardboard pig, poised on one trotter, bore on its forelegs a platter of steaming sausages. It was covered, possibly for decency's sake, with a blue and white striped apron, and wore a tall, white, three-dimensional chef's cap, at a rakish angle. A benign and jovial bull's head, all curly hairy strength and weighty life, cut off at the nape, was juxtaposed in a kind of triptych of glossed cardboard with various bright cubes of Oxo and beakers full of hot brown energising liquid. A very young cut-out nursery-rhyme black-and-white calf skipped sportively on daisy-spangled grass under a bright sun and clear blue sky. On the top of a mound of little pies wrapped in cellophane, a chicken, calf and piglet disported themselves in circular dance, representing the English concord and harmony of veal, ham and egg.

On the next layer, white marble below the brilliant green, were enamelled dishes of more recondite goods, alternating in colour and texture. A block of waxy suet, a platter of white, involuted, honey-combed and feathery tripe. Vitals: kidneys both stiff and limp, some wrapped still in their caul of fat, the slippery bluish surface of meat shining through slits in the blanket, the cords dangling: iridescent liver; a monumental ox heart, tubes standing out above it, a huge gash in one side, darkening yellow fat drying on the shoulders. Half a pig's head, boiled, pale and faintly blood-stained, a metal tag clamped to one ear, bleached white bristles round the snout, stiff, salty white eyelashes, a levelled plane at the base.

In front of these, cuts and joints. A Bath chap, sliced and pushed into a regular cone, coated with golden crumbs, glistening in its cellophane wrapper, a neat, impersonal object. Lamb cutlets in neat lines, a repeating pattern, pink flesh, white fat, opalescent bone, parallel lines, identical uneven blocks, achieving a kind of abstract regularity through the repetition. A crown roast, twisted, knotted, circled with curled coronets of snipped white paper on every protruding rib. Rump and flank and shoulder and hand and belly of beef and pork and lamb and veal tidied into long and short, fat and slender rolls, held in networks of knotted strings, punctuated by miniature wooden stakes and skewers.

If all flesh is grass, all flesh at some other extreme is indeed geometry. The consuming human, with his ambivalent teeth, a unique mouthful, herbivore and carnivore, is an artist in the destruction and recon-struction of flesh, with instruments for piercing, prying, tidying, analysis and palatable rearrangement. Man the artist can reconcile under golden skies the jocund pig and the plump and tubular sausage, or he can create, from sweated suet, mangled breast of calf, chopped parsley, bread and beaten eggs an incurving sculptural spiral of delicate pink and white and green and gold.

On each side of the door hung, straining from a hook through the tendon, half a carcase of beef. Marcus walked in with his mother as it were through this creature, which must have been splayed across the doorway that morning, headless neck down, and slowly sliced down the spine with blows of a hatchet. He had seen that done. He saw now the bulging flesh in its stained and clinging muslin coverings, and saw also the cold structure: chain of vertebrae, fan of ribs, taut sheen of inner skin between veiled bone and bone. Beyond this was a row of pale pig corpses and stiffly extended lambs.

The geometrical defence was hard and close to the grain, here. The smaller the cut, the greater the geometrical precision, and with the precision, the possibility of contemplating the thing. If a man might see, or imagine, or think in terms of units like molecules, units like chops might in turn be tolerable, parts of varying and interesting other organisations. Units like half-pig's-heads were not possible. But the earth and the air were full of matter that may once have been part of a half-pig's-head. He couldn't care about everything, nor about nothing. Through his own eyes, half-a-pig's-head was a meaningful and bearable unit.

From behind the wooden block, scored, indented, scooped by chopper and cleaver and saw, dark Grinner greeted them vigorously. Stephanie and Frederica had named him because his expression varied only between the more and less gleeful. Once he had invited Frederica out for a ride on his motor-bike, leaning across the counter, wiping his hands on a damp and bloody dishcloth. Frederica would have gone, but Bill had forbidden it on the grounds that the motor-bike was certainly and the Grinner probably dangerous. "What can I do for you?" he asked Winifred. His hand was buried inside a distended fowl, from which he drew, in a long stream, with a suck and a crack, all the contents: soft pale guts, hard giblets in glistening fat, red-veined golden-skinned clusters of eggs, his manipulation swelling the creature into a gawky parody of life.

"A pound of lamb's liver and a shoulder of veal," said Winifred. The Grinner nodded, swung out a thing like a child's seaside bucket, from which he popped out a glossy pie of frozen livers from the Antipodes, brittle and dark. He tapped it with his big knife.

"Too 'ard. There's some just in from t'slaughterouse, Mrs Potter. I know you appreciate fresh offal. 'Alf a tick, I'll 'ave a look."

To Marcus's sickening eye the fresh liver had a hot and bursting look. The Grinner slapped it compact with his left hand and sliced it, razor-thin, with his right. He then boned the veal, working with speed and precision with the three remaining inches of a long carving-knife

sharpened almost to thin air. He shaved delicately, clearly, and the soft
flesh fell away from the glistening knob, pearly white, bluish-mauve,
rosy, increasingly unreal. Marcus stared. He arranged. He rearranged.
He looked from side to side. The meat surged. He thought: people
come in and out of here all day quite all right, people *do*.

"There," said Winifred. "That'll make us a good meal. Marcus."
Offering him, thinking of the cooking, the transformation into eating.
His pleasure perhaps. Then she saw his face. "Marcus!"

"Mummy," he said. "Oh, Mummy –"

It was not a word he now used.

It was not a word she had ever liked, to be truthful. It reminded
her of bad things, the dead preserved in dusty cerecloths, and moreover
it had a disagreeable gobby sound. She had never told her children
not to use it, nor had ever asked them to call her by her first name.
That was not her way. They had all learned it, from other children,
other women, used it tentatively, and then unlearned it, substituting
Mother when direct address was unavoidable, and nothing, most of
the time.

She took his hand and led him out on to the pavement.

"Marcus, tell me. Marcus, there *is* something . . ."

In their ears, drowning speech, a horn sounded, peremptory, shrill,
unnaturally prolonged. They both started; drawn close in to the
pavement, its coming or previous presence unremarked, was the
gleaming black sportscar of Lucas Simmonds, a brief Triumph on which
he could be seen, in the school quadrangles, lavishing extraordinary
cares. He rolled down a window and beamed up at them innocent and
rosy.

"Mrs Potter. Marcus. Were you by any chance returning to Blesford
Ride? Could I offer you a lift – if Marcus doesn't mind being a little
bit bundled in the back of a vehicle *really* only designed for two?"

Marcus took two steps away, shifting. Winifred thought that he
looked worse than ever, ill almost, likely to faint as he was given to
doing. So she addressed Lucas Simmonds with gratitude, said how
timely his appearance was, to which he replied that he always tried to
oblige in that way, with a slight embarrassed snicker to cover any
oddness in this remark. Lucas Simmonds's car was loud, and swooped
round corners so that Winifred, inside it, had to brace herself and
could not feel any emanations, friendly or hostile, from Marcus coiled
behind her. Lucas talked, mostly inaudibly, with complete banality,
about Blesford traffic. When they got home Marcus said he was carsick
and went to bed.

10. *In the Tower*

Frederica received a letter.

> Dear Frederica,
>   We are still undecided about all the casting of *Astraea*. The committee would like to hear you read again. I wonder, therefore, if you would come up to my room in School on Wednesday, as soon as you can after you get home.
>
>   Yours
>   Alexander Wedderburn.

Frederica wrote several grateful, enthusiastic, intelligent replies. The one she despatched ran:

> Dear Alexander,
>   I shall be very happy,
>   Frederica.

She hoped, but doubted, that he would notice the nuances.

Alexander lived in the red western turret of the school, approached under a Gothic arch and up a spiral stone staircase. He had an oak door to his room, and inside it a green baize door, in imitation of Oxbridge. He had vaguely Perpendicular windows, facing two ways, south, over the lawns and flowerbeds towards the walled gardens and Far Field, west, towards the Castle Mound, and its bit of surrounding country (which included the sewage farm). Over his door was a fretwork contraption with a sliding shutter, obliterating either the possibility that Alexander M. M. Wedderburn, M.A., B.Litt., was IN or the possibility that he was OUT. The staircase was red stone and smelt of Jeyes fluid.

On the Wednesday he looked gloomily out of his southern window and saw her advancing on him, spiked heels pitting the prohibited grass. He had expected school uniform but she was done out like a ballet dancer in mufti, in severely buttoned black and grey, with her hair scraped into a knob, and her sharp nose up, snuffing the air. She was early, at least in the sense that she was earlier than Lodge and Crowe. He felt beleaguered. It had been made clear to him by the discussion after her auditions that he felt some element of positive dislike towards Frederica Potter. It was not only that she was embarrassing, nor even that he had wondered if she had some kind of crush on him: such things were natural and best dealt with by kindly ignorance. But Crowe's pleasure in her performance, his positive insistence on her powers as an actress, coupled with the belligerence of her last appearance, had given Alexander a disproportionate and unreasonable certainty that she was at best a nuisance and at worst dangerous. It was like trying to ignore a boa-constrictor with a crush on you. Well, if not was, would be.

He heard the rapid clatter of her feet. Her knock crashed. He cursed Crowe and opened his inner door.

"It says you are OUT," she accused him.

"I am always forgetting."

He tried to take her coat, but she was prowling about his room, scanning book shelves, pacing distances, getting bearings on the two views. He tried, as far as was consonant with his duties, to keep people out of this room. Certainly she had never been there. He asserted himself.

"Sit down. Give me your coat."

She did as she was told. She had a lot of grey and black woollen skirt and a black bat-winged sweater, with a snarl of stainless steel jewellery on a leather thong, of a kind he particularly disliked, round her neck. She crossed her knees like a Hollywood secretary, and glared at him like an inquisitor. He got behind his desk.

"The others aren't here yet. We are a bit early."

"I am early. You live here."

"Yes."

"Would you tell me what this is about, please, Alexander?"

He ignored the desperate shake in the voice. He said, "Perhaps it's best if I do. The problem is, a difficulty has arisen about the casting of – of the main part. Lodge wants – and Matthew wants – to cast Marina Yeo as the Queen. In fact," he said, disguising he hoped a little bitterness, "they have approached her – she's an old old friend of Matthew's – and she is very keen, I'm told."

She stared and said nothing.

"She's too old," said Alexander. "For the, for my play, as it stands, that's the trouble."

"I saw her in *Hedda Gabler* in Newcastle. And as Cleopatra once. You can play Cleopatra old. I saw that awful film, *The Mortal Moon*, too, where she was Elizabeth. She was O.K. in that."

"That was made some time ago. She is a great actress. Crowe had a bright idea – he wanted to split the part, to – to cast a young girl as Elizabeth in the first act – before her Accession – and let Marina take over and age gracefully from there. I don't want that, myself. It's only fair to say that. I wrote it as one part."

"If I'd done that," she said, "I'd be furious if they tried to split it. It's the wrong *style of thing* . . ."

"It's not a pageant," said Alexander incautiously.

"No."

"Anyway, Crowe was hit by your likeness to – the original – and thought it was just possible to cast you for the first scenes."

"I wouldn't want that," she said, "even if they wanted me, I wouldn't, if you didn't . . . I mean, I care what *you* think, and it's your play. You wrote it."

"That doesn't make it mine, now," he said scrupulously. "It's in Lodge's hands now. He liked you."

What Lodge had attributed to Frederica was "a peculiar dry sexiness", a phrase which had stuck in Alexander's mind because he had never considered her as sexy at all. Blundering, and in his presence she blundered perpetually, excluded sexiness in his eyes.

"Crowe said I might hope for an understudy," she said. "I *was* hoping. But I still don't think you should let them impose *any* splitting on your play if you don't like it. It's *yours*."

"I don't want to stop you hoping . . ."

"I wanted to be in on it. There won't ever be anything like it." She thought of the visions she had alternately cherished and abandoned: fanfare, farthingale, gloss and glimmer of English language, men and maidens and talk and who knew what else, and Alexander. Alexander . . . naturally Alexander. "It's premature to say," she said, "that I won't do it, to split it, they probably won't like me. But I *wouldn't*, I mean it."

She wondered what she was saying. She meant what she said. She saw what he thought. In his place, she would think that. It was his work. But the most important thing was that she, Frederica Potter, should have a part, should have *the* part. So why was she saying all this? Not exactly so that he should say, as he now did, "No, no, you must do your best, the decision is Lodge's . . ." Just that she knew what his interests were, and cared about them, and knew what hers were, and cared more about those, and he did not, but must come to.

She stared round his room. She had always meant, some time, to penetrate this place. It was only partly as she had imagined. It was cool and plain and as modern as possible inside its Victorian-Gothic shell. The walls, in a way that was fashionable in those post-festival years, were all painted in different pastel colours: duck-egg blue, watered grass-green, muted salmon rose, pale sandy gold. The arm-chairs were pale beach, upholstered in olive cord. On the window sill, in black basalt Wedgwood bowls, were white hyacinths and dark crocuses.

On the blue wall, behind Alexander, was a large print of Picasso's *Saltimbanques*, framed in thin strips of light oak. Opposite, on the pink wall, was Picasso's *Boy with a Pipe*, which Frederica did not recognise. On the green wall, over the hearth, was a very large and gleaming photograph, white on black, of a nude woman, sculpted in marble, lying on one side, seen from the back. This, too, she did not recognise. Under this, on the shelf, was a mound or cairn of irregular stones. One or two were polished eggs, agate and alabaster, others were just stones. Those which would not heap were laid out in a tapering row beside those that would.

On the gold wall, fading a little, was a mounted poster announcing *The Buskers* by Alexander Wedderburn. The letters of the title were formed from sprouting twigs or branches, held up by capering and posturing *commedia dell'arte* figures. Brown and green letters, black and white chequered figures.

Frederica read, twice, the information on this poster, vanished days and hours at the Arts Theatre in 1950. Then she read the titles of the books on the shelves nearest her. She was magnetised by print, by lettering, she took sensual pleasure in reading anything at all, instructions about Harpic and fire alarms, lists, or, as now, the titles of books. *Notes Towards a Definition of Culture. A la Recherche du Temps Perdu. Théâtre Complet de Racine.*

On the door was an empty gown and a tweed jacket.

What was the room not, that she had expected it to be? Something more dramatic, richer, darker. Its decorous airiness was unexpected if pleasing.

"I like your stones."

He stood up nervously and turned them in his hands, cold, susurrant, clashing.

"I bring them up from the Chesil Bank. Where I come from, my place of origin, Dorset."

Another scrap of information; she stored it away, greedily, but could think of nothing to say, about stones, or about Dorset. She was a girl unusually ill-equipped with small talk. The lengthening silence was broken, almost to her relief, by Crowe and Lodge, who strode hurriedly into the room.

They were prepared to be mysterious about their intentions, which embarrassed both Alexander and Frederica, neither of whom chose to describe the discussion that had already taken place. Crowe talked, with meaningful little winks, about a possible understudy, and Lodge said that they had been impressed enough with her previous appearance to be considering her for a speaking part. Could she perhaps recite the Perdita speech for them, as a preliminary.

Frederica said she would rather do something else. She had discovered, she told them grimly, that she was no good at girls. Could she not do Goneril? Lodge laughed aloud at this, and said that girls, not Goneril, were unfortunately what was wanted, and it would be nice to discover, if she didn't mind, how far she could go in the direction of girlhood. Something in the elaborate mock-courtesy of this made Frederica sense that she was being treated specially, was liked, was wanted. They were prepared to bandy words. So she grinned, and said well, they knew by now she was no nymph, and made her way obediently through O Proserpina! For the flowers now that frighted thou let'st fall From Dis's wagon. It was not inspired, Alexander thought, but it was a little more than workmanlike: the breaths and pauses were in viable places, the verse was at least unimpeded in its flow: it sang, almost, even if Frederica did not.

"And now," said Lodge, "if you could study a small speech from Alexander's play . . . Alexander, do you have any particularly suitable bit in mind?"

Alexander said perhaps the Tower speech. Frederica tried to assess his expression as he handed her a script. Patient melancholy. The speech was a soliloquy by the young Princess, thrust into the Tower by Mary Tudor, a moment of history, and fiction, that Frederica had lived often enough, since she had grown up on the heady romantic emotion of Margaret Irwin's *Young Bess*. She supposed Alexander had not, though there was romantic emotion here, all right.

Alexander watched her. There is always something unnerving about watching someone else purposefully, rapidly, going over something one has written. He began to hover, and, almost involuntarily, to offer scraps of useful, or mitigating, or distracting information. She set her face cross and private to read: he did not acknowledge it, but he feared her judgment.

"I take it she did mean it. I shall never marry. The play assumes that those historians are right who believe she really meant to stay single," . . .

"Yes, I see . . ."

"The 'she' she keeps referring to is Anne Boleyn. There is of course no record of her ever having spoken of Anne Boleyn."

"I know that."

"Ah, yes. I might point out that the speech is meant to begin in a hysterical rush, like the descriptions of Anne Boleyn in the tower, laughing and weeping, and then it modulates its tone . . ."

"Yes, yes." Almost impatient. "The sentences are very long. To say."

"It isn't easy," said Alexander. Matthew Crowe said, "Let the poor child concentrate, do." Alexander went and looked out of the window.

The verse was nervous and glittering, adjectival and highly metaphorical. The Princess described the cold wet stone of the tower, the black Thames, the narrow garden plot with a few uncut flowers. Then she wove a long serpentining period out of red and white roses, the Tudor rose, blood, flesh, marble, a spring shut up, a fountain sealed, *ego flos campi*, not to be cut off by the butcher. A thematic sideways curve, ornate and delicately whimsical, about the Princess who lost a golden ball in a fountain and repelled a clammy frog. Marble and the gilded monuments of princes. The periods gave way to flat, uncompromising claims. Elizabeth would not bleed. She would neither be butchered nor marry. She would be a stone that did not bleed, a Princess, *semper eadem* and single. Her virtue her stronghold.

Frederica stood in one window embrasure, looked down at the garden, settled her imagination, and read. The particular difficulties were, as she had intimated, grammatical, and she was good at grammar. Alexander, although he had not told her so, had already heard several potential Elizabeths, all of whom had had trouble with his language. Frederica, contrary to his expectations, had powerful negative virtues. She did not murder his sentences. She had, fortunately, come to the intellectual conclusion that the language was so ornate, florid even, that the best way to speak it was plainly and quietly, let it elaborate itself as it must. Alexander was disproportionately impressed by this approach. He was afraid of vibrant actresses "expressing themselves" athwart his words. He had assumed she would be worse than most. She was not. Possibly not vibrant enough, indeed, to impress Lodge. He found himself hoping Lodge would not think her too dry and monotonous.

What Lodge thought was not clear. He did indeed take her over the peroration again, asking her to give it all she had got, and exacted from her a kind of gruff ferocity he seemed pleased with. He said, do you think you could learn to move more naturally, and Frederica said, of course. Crowe said that he was of the opinion that their little plan was distinctly promising, and Frederica prevented herself from asking what was their little plan. Crowe then offered her a lift to her home: it was clear to her that, with his liking for hints, indiscretions, manipulations, he would tell her about the "little plan" and no doubt about Alexander's opposition to it. Of the three men, Crowe was the one who most certainly liked her, who was on her side. He was also the least appealing: he had only money and power, whereas Lodge, and even more Alexander, were artists, which was obviously more impressive. She was in fact naive enough to suppose that what she felt to be her aesthetic morals in this case coincided with what she more vaguely labelled, inaccurately, her political interests: the man it was necessary to impress was Alexander. The play was his play: she needed his approval of her reading, of their plan. She supposed, wrongly, that the other two were already in favour of the conflation of herself and Marina Yeo into one Queen, and that they had staged this reading to convert Alexander. So she told Crowe that she did not need a lift, she was at home already, had only to walk down the lane and across Far Field. And then, by blatantly not leaving through a door held open for her, she contrived to be left alone with Alexander.

Alexander said, magnanimously, that he admired her reading. She said that it had been a pleasure, despite the strain, because the verse was so exciting, because of the imagery. Alexander said that that speech was the metaphorical centre of the whole play. She liked, she said, the colours. The red and white. He said he had always seen that scene red and white and grey, and Frederica said would he not get green out of doors and he said no, not if it was late enough, you could make stones with artificial light, he hoped. Would she like a glass of sherry after her ordeal? He had, he told her, pouring sherry, taken the red and white from the little poem about Elizabeth the Virgin he had incorporated in his text.

Under a tree I saw a Virgin sit.
The red and white rose quatered in her face.

Quartered had made him think of hanging and drawing there, as well as heraldry, and so the red and white, blood and stone, had grown. Would she sit down on the sofa? Was she interested in the iconography of the idolization of Elizabeth? It had its interests. Elizabeth had acquired many of the traditional attributes of the Queen of Heaven. Rosa mundi, tower of ivory. *Ego flos campi*, said Frederica, and all that bit about the fountain sealed. That, she said, was on their school blazer, "Knowledge is now no more a fountain sealed." Where was that from, then?

Alexander was startled into ribald laughter. *That*, he informed her, was from Tennyson's "Princess" about the feminist academy. The poet was more or less mocking the virginal aspirations of his Princess Ida, the bluestockings and all. Before that, long before that, of course, the fountain sealed came from the Song of Songs, and was highly erotic. A garden enclosed is my sister, my spouse. A spring shut up: a fountain sealed. In *that case*, said quick-witted Frederica, on her second glass of sherry, Tennyson was being emancipated or obscene since he was suggesting that common knowledge, far from being original Sin, was a good thing. Alexander said he feared it was a joke on the part of the Laureate at the expense of the virginal idealists who claimed access to the springs of knowledge: backed up by the fact that their lovely lyrics ran counter to their proclaimed message, being highly erotic or in praise of babies. Now sleeps the crimson petal, now the white, for instance. One of the most suggestive poems in the language. Frederica said that she was glad the Blesford Girls' Grammar blazers were not only hideous but secretly obscene, it made it all seem more tolerable, and she was grateful to him for telling her. It became clear to both of them that they were sitting side by side on a sofa, talking about sex.

They shifted apart, but not far apart. Alexander unwisely poured more sherry. He had forgotten – it was strange how one could forget – how he had worked on Elizabeth's metaphors, winding into her verse the iconography of her cult, the phoenix, the rose, the ermine, the Golden Age, the harvest-queen, Virgo-Astraea, virgin patroness of justice and *foison*. Alone in this room he had worked and worked, and since he had finished the work, no one had remarked on these things. Crowe and Lodge talked about dramatic pointing, contemporary relevance, cutting to speed it up, overall pace, character. No one mentioned those images he had so lovingly, with such an indescribable mixture of voluntary elaboration and involuntary vision, constructed. This girl picked up bits of these, like a superlatively good A-level candidate, which of course she was. But then, he was a teacher. He explained how Elizabeth's motto, *semper eadem*, had in his mind come to be associated with the homogeneity of stone, on the one hand, and the sempiternities of the Golden Age, on the other. Whereas Mary Queen of Scots's motto, *eadem mutata resurgam*, I shall arise, the same transmuted, he felt was Christian and much less rock-like than Elizabeth's pagan reliance on her own eternal identity. It seemed a pity, said Frederica honestly, that a play so much about rock-like identity should be in danger of having a dual protagonist thrust upon it. Alexander said incautiously that he minded this prospect less than he had imagined. There was at least half a chance of his language not being messed about. Frederica was lit up by hope. She said it was marvellous language, invigorating language, people would come to understand . . .

Lovely enchanting language, sugar-cane, honey of roses, whither wilt thou flie?

In the fifties they wrote critical articles on "Blood and Stone Imagery in Wedderburn's *Astraea*."

In the early sixties helpful lists of these images were published in Educational Aids to help weak A-level candidates.

In the seventies the whole thing was dismissed as a petrified final paroxysm of a decadent individualist modernism, full of irrelevant and damaging cultural nostalgia, cluttered, blown. A *cul de sac*, the verse drama revival, as should have been seen in the beginning.

On that day, having deserved, and extorted, partial approval from Alexander, Frederica decided to change the subject. She pointed at the photograph of the woman, an easy transition, and asked him what it was.

It was, he said, Rodin's *Danaide*. He went and stood under it, studying minutely what her distracted gaze had skated over the gloss of.

"Look what a line. Look."

He ran his index finger along the indicated line of recumbent marble spine, under the marble-silky skin, a half-moon from abased nape to rounded buttocks vanishing and shining into the black. An ambiguous gesture, purely instructive, purely sensual. Frederica watched the moving finger and saw the statue.

She was acute enough to realise, despite her excitement over Alexander himself, that she had never been made to look at a visual work of art before. This kind of silent sensual contemplation was usual for him, she saw, and profoundly new to her. She had never, she realised, looked at a picture or a carving or even landscape without some immediate verbal accompaniment or translation. Language was ingrained in her. Bill had done that. He had described her own early words to her, sung them back at her, repeated them admiringly to others in her presence, improved on them unconsciously. He had read and read and read.

But he was completely uninterested in forms not made with language. He was like any other moralising Philistine from his own chapel background when it came to colour or light or sound not made with words. He would not have said so, but he conveyed with every gesture, every judgment, a feeling that these were dispensable luxuries, not moral, at best adjuncts to an essential civilisation based elsewhere.

So, early inured to the knowledge that *Lear* was truer and wiser than anything else, she had never been surprised enough to ask herself why, why a man should want to write out a play and not simply deal at no removes with the grim truths of age, ague, recalcitrant daughters, folly, spite and death. Or why a man should want to write O Western Wind rather than lie in bed with his love or the pleasure and pain of absence. Knowing nothing, she imagined that poem and play were somehow more what they were than those things they were images of.

But watching Alexander's familiar description of the Danaide's spine, she was enough struck by strangeness to marvel that a man might choose to make a marble woman, and another man, or another woman, might prefer to stand and look at that stone, rather than to . . . do anything else. When she got home she would indeed imagine other scenes on that sofa, that finger on her own spine, but she was even canny enough to know that for that time the imaginary relish was enough and more than enough. And so got herself away before he had time to regret any of his gestures, a rare moment of grace, for her.

Alexander was immediately distressed by his own behaviour. He knew very well what it meant to show things, particularly his own things, to people. It was next to giving gifts. He had shown Jennifer the Danaide, had talked to Jennifer about the mystery of stones whilst they turned over his cairn together. Jennifer, unlike Frederica, had been volubly admiring, had achieved an almost immediate familiarity with his things, discriminating stone from stone, finding adjectives for the woman's white despair: she knew it was despair. She had brought additions to his things: the bulbs in the Wedgwood basalt were her gifts, and she had wept, unwrapping them from their white florist's shrouds, because they had had to be bought with Geoffrey's money; nothing was truly hers to give. Alexander ran a finger over these marble men and maidens, and came to rest under *The Boy with a Pipe* who was his private, his secret joke.

The Boy is crowned with blurred and decadent orange-red roses. He sits against a burnt-earth wall on which are depicted pale, white-ribboned bouquets of full-blown flowers. His face is harsh, austere, corrupt, clean, judging. He wears a tight blue jacket and trousers, and sits with his knees apart. Between his thighs his creased clothes indicate complete sexual ambiguity, deep-pleated and firmly bulging: he could be anything, or more probably everything. One hand is between his legs and one holds a neat stubby pipe, awkwardly, pointing in at his body. No visitor had ever commented on these, fairly obvious, characteristics of the Boy to Alexander, nor had they proposed, as had been suggested to other masters of a Gauguin nude or a Lautrec whore, that he be put away. It might have been that he was assimilated by conjunction into the ambience of the Saltimbanques, coloured patches between earth and sky, partaking of both, insubstantial.

Alexander knew, he thought, what this Boy was. He knew also from time to time what he himself was: a man who displayed the Rodin Danaide to fierce girls but kept on his wall, as a mode of knowledge, this Boy. It was not that the Boy was a desirable boy: he was not. What Alexander felt for him approximated most closely to vicious envy.

11. *Play Room*

Softly, in shreds and patches, brightly, in beads and feathers and tinsel, the play invaded the Vicarage.

Last year the Blesford ladies had made petit point hassocks for the pews of St Bartholomew's, embroidering cream and ochre lilies and fishes on a discreet khaki background. So as not to show the dirt.

Ten years ago they had gathered in hand-downs for evacuees, paperbacks for soldiers, knitted wool squares for blankets for bomb victims.

This year they were building farthingales.

In London thousands of small seed pearls and crystals were being sewn into a shimmering work on the Queen's coronation dress of white slipper satin. Emblems of Commonwealth and Empire were being embroidered in coloured silks, roses and thistles, maples and acorns, on the hem of this garment.

Felicity Wells, co-ordinating the artistic efforts in Blesford, saw herself at the spinning centre of endless threads of culture, reknit, reknotted. Baskets stood in vicarage hall and church porch for any bit of stuff, rich or rare, that could be spared. Embroidery classes stitched rays of small plastic pearls into Sir Walter Ralegh's black velvet cloak, silver moons and golden birds and crimson and white roses on kirtles and loosegowns and trains, knots of straw and carnation ribbons on embroidered garters.

We have been starved of colour, said Miss Wells, emptying a carrier bag of new reels of Sylko out on to her carpet, rolling, clattering, glittering, gleaming, all shades and gradations of colours. Gorgeous household-stuffe, she exclaimed to Stephanie, and confessed that she had always desired a whole drawerful, and had had no excuse.

Stephanie had meant to have nothing to do with the play. She had had enough of it with Frederica: in so far as it was Alexander's, it evoked in her a lazy, or reticent, disinclination to put herself forward. If she sat, as she did, and knotted gold cord in the vicarage in the evening, or bicycled over the moors with messages about whalebone and material for ruffs, it was because she could not refuse Felicity.

It had come to be accepted that Daniel, when not at work, sat there too. The ladies stitched and deedy Daniel made tea and washed teacups. Daniel was in a bad way. True, he had been right about Stephanie

Potter and Malcolm Haydock. She had offered her services once, twice, and then regularly, promising alternate Saturdays and Sundays. Mrs Haydock had wept in Daniel's room out of relief, and fear that it would not last, and guilt, to Malcolm, to Stephanie, both of whom seemed, though neither Daniel nor Mrs Haydock saw them at it, to have found a way of surviving their time together. It was a miracle, Mrs Haydock said, considering the damage Malcolm did, the way Miss Potter always had the house neat as a pin when she herself got in, she was quite ashamed really, knowing that when she had care of Malcolm there was always trails of flour and mud and smashed crockery and worse up and down the house any time anyone cared to call. True, Miss Potter might have had to put a pile of broken cups or milk-bottles in the bin, but it was always quiet and neat, Mr Orton, so you could come in without feeling awful, at the work to do, or even at just coming into that racket again. It shamed her really, that Miss Potter should have such a grip on things, such a way with her, it made her wonder if she was doing worse than she needed herself. Daniel said no, she was Malcolm's mother, he knew her, he behaved different with her because of that, and Miss Potter had only to manage one day. All the same, she was a treasure, he was glad of it.

Once or twice he had called at Brontë Buildings, as was surely more or less obligatory, to see how she was getting on. He usually found her and the boy in a state of distant stillness and silence, she with folded hands in a chair, the boy, as was his custom when he wasn't hyperactive, sitting in the corner of the floor knocking his head rhythmically and alternately against the meeting walls. He was daunted to his own surprise, by the quality of the silence and felt some inhibition about disturbing it. He asked her once in a cheery clerical voice how she did it, how she kept the boy so quiet, and she said she did it by keeping quite still and taking her attention away from him. When you did that, she said, he tended to imitate you, so they both got abstracted, for the allotted time. She thought perhaps she ought to try to make contact, or play with him, but she had no skills and no knowledge how to begin. At least he was doing no harm.

No, Daniel agreed, no harm. He came to feel, both there and in Felicity Wells's little room, that consciously or unconsciously she was treating himself in the same way as Malcolm Haydock: imposing silence on him by absenting herself and her attention. She was there, but she gave him no opening to speak to her, presented a smooth soundproof barrier like a plate-glass wall. He did not know, he told himself, why he went on sitting there.

He did, of course, know. She obsessed him, and for this unreasonable state of mind he was ill-prepared. For years he had hardly considered himself except as an instrument of his own purposes. Now, he thought constantly of her, and if, by some vehement act of will, he succeeded in expelling her image from his church or his bedroom he became horribly aware of himself, instead. He tried to see himself as she might see him, and could not. Various certainties disintegrated. He considered his own history and wondered if he was not profoundly unnatural, in some way, not to have been troubled like this before. "Impure thoughts" had not been his problem. Masturbation was a relief to which, wise in his generation, he had always considered he had a right, since it was a quick and practical solution to certain biological urgencies. Before Stephanie, it had not been accompanied, not really, by visual images. Now and then he heard a plaintive echo of his own tough voice expressing the wish that she would be *kind*. This disgusted him.

There was also trouble with God. He had not had, and had not required, a personal relationship with God. He never addressed God, when he prayed, in words of his own. The Church's words were like the church's stones, there. Prayer was to know that there was much more there, much stronger, than himself, to sense the tug and rush of forces behind his perception or comprehension.

The Christ he loved was the Christ who had been aware of the forces upholding sparrows and considering lilies. Also the Christ of devastating common sense who neither equivocated nor stood any nonsense, and exposed the machinery of the soul and of divine justice in witty parables. He did not address this Christ because, although he did not know exactly that it was so, he believed in fact that this Christ was dead.

His beliefs had not mattered compared to the certainties of strength and solidity he had felt, alone with God. Now she got between him and God, so that God became problematic and he himself was aware, as in boyhood, that he was confined in his own fat.

He could have thumped her. Or broken her.

He came to tea because if he was in a room with her she was at least reduced to size, confined to the chair she sat in. That was not, of course, his only reason: If he must desire her in the flesh he preferred the flesh present: he was not one for evading reality. So he sat with her in hot black trousers, and suffered.

Felicity Wells took her own pleasure in their company. She cosseted them and lectured them, watched them with dark, vague, sad eyes. The fact that it was her room, her stage management as it were, suited all three of them.

One day Stephanie came in to find her friend poised on one foot, framed against the last light from her dormer window, at the peak of an uneven stairway composed of a dictionary, a footstool, a coffee table, the bed, and a higher table. She was wearing a vast skirt and overskirt of bluish-green shiny curtaining, which she clasped, in two large knobs, in her two little fists heaved high before her. On her head was a satin cap wired with pearls, and a skewed organdie head-rail.

She was to make one of the loyal crowd at the Coronation of Elizabeth I, of the mourning crowd at her death. "Practical trial of stepping gracefully," she said, smiling down on Stephanie. Behind Stephanie, Daniel loomed. Miss Wells waved, swayed, and crashed to the bed, giggling amongst the billowing cloth, searching with a blind hand for the dislodged hair-piece. Daniel thundered with laughter.

"You are a naughty boy. You startled me. I hope no pins are driven into me. I knew it required practice to mount stairs in a bum-roll. Give me a hand, girl."

Stephanie tugged. Miss Wells's trunk rose upright amongst her skirts: she put up her hands to twist together hair and wire and netting and false hair.

"A treacherous garment," she observed, clicking her teeth in gleeful disapproval, crouching in the wired bum-roll. Stephanie saw her painfully, a little breastless breathless woman whose skin about her low-cut bodice had that crinkling decadent delicacy that precedes wrinkles. Daniel put out huge arms and lifted her easily to her feet. They both laughed. Stephanie took up her hemming.

Miss Wells's room was tiny, decorated, perched in and temporary. Black Victorian bookcases, with machine-cut Gothic beading of the kind that ruined the young Alfred Tennyson, supported a bitty collection of objects. Cut glass candlesticks, tin teacaddy with Gloire de Dijon roses, Japanese silk pincushion, conical Benares brass vase with two peacock feathers, three biscuit barrels (rotund glass, floral china and wicker, wooden keg with brass knobs), Florentine leather sewing bag, scissors with enamelled handles representing a crane stalking, a miniature Spode cup, six sugar-pink grey-tinged Woolworth's tea-cups, a pile of apostle spoons, half a loaf of bread, half a pot of lemon curd, a pile of bills weighed down with a plaster of Paris hand, an ebony and silver crucifix, a crocheted beret, a bundle of lisle stockings, a bottle of ink, a jam-jar of red pencils, pussywillow and a Palm Sunday cross from the Holy Land . . .

Stephanie had learned all these things. She had a blandly, unselectively retentive memory. As a child she had never failed, even against Frederica, to win that game where objects are brought in on a tray under a tea-towel, unveiled and whisked away again. She always remembered the details of the pattern on the tray, as well as the spoons, scissors, clocks, shoelaces, marigolds and glass animals disposed upon it. At night it was difficult to disembarrass herself of the day's accumulated irrelevant knowledge. Remembered objects clogged her thoughts, floated, vivid spectra, before her closed eyes. She had sometimes to call them up deliberately one by one and mentally wipe them out, make her mind's eye a temporary, illusory *tabula rasa* before sleep was possible. Even then, waking next day, she had trouble with an endless conveyor belt of unrelated objects, soliciting precise memory.

Until she started teaching she had not thought there was anything unusual about this. She had supposed everyone was enriched or tormented by some such swarm of useful irrelevant remembered things and information. Education, then, was memory-training and those pupils she discovered with no memories were at a disadvantage. Later, when habits of mind, time and history were to be constructed without the pains of "learning by rote", without mapped categories of sequence, grammatical, temporal or aesthetic, when art and politics were concerned with now and the future, such skills as hers were taken more lightly, or even mocked and discouraged. There are fashions in habits of mind as in habits of gear, and memory-banks went out, a little after the time of this story, a little after the coronation of Elizabeth II, as memory theatres had gone out with the Renaissance, and with memory-banks went works of art that were themselves memory-banks, went tradition and the individual talent, the bible, the pantheon, the different organisations of other languages. In stalls in the Antique Hypermarket or the Furniture Cave you might have seen on japanned or lacquered or brass or inlaid trays a pile of shored fragments like those that cluttered Felicity Wells's surfaces, but you would neither have seen nor remembered their order or disorder in the way Stephanie did in 1953.

In normal times Miss Wells's room was hung with pieces of cloth. Lace over the table, dimity over the bed, red and gold silk, weighted with little gold beads, like milk-bottle covers draped, casually, for warmth and mystery, over the table-lights. But now it was layered and lined and stuffed with rolls and heaps and hanging half-constructed garments of bright and glistering cloths.

Stephanie saw it all double, with wide clarity and narrow sharpness. She saw what things meant to be, and missed no detail of how they, in fact, presented themselves. She could imagine the scale of grandeur envisaged by those who deployed a Maple's Louis Seize suite in a tiny lounge with walls of whipped-up plaster like the frosting on a cream cake. She could see what cleanness and simplicity had been imagined and desired by those who, ignoring existing geometry, converted Victorian kitchens to contemporaneity by tacking flimsy plywood

over solid bourgeois panels, and added tiny hexagonal plastic door-
knobs in "clear bright" modern colours where decent white china
or solid brass had been. She saw, then, the layered glowing mystery,
the gorgeous stuff Felicity Wells saw, and saw further the ambition
to embody, here, now, in the present time and place, the vigour, the
sense of form, the coherence lost, lost, with the English Golden Age.
She saw how the hanging stage-cope on Miss Wells's wardrobe-rail,
and the *Illustrated London News* photograph of the Dean of Westminster
in a cope worn at the coronation of Charles II, brought out for the
coronation of Elizabeth II, and Daniel's dog-collared presence, brought
to Felicity Wells a happy sense of coincidence, superimposition even,
of past grandeur and present business.

She saw, and did not share. She saw too the hammered milk-bottle
tops on the cope, and Daniel's complete lack of interest in ceremony,
Shakespearean, Yeatsian or High Anglican. She saw the chips in the
teacups and the holes in the stockings. It was not her business to fuse
any of these into new wholes. She just saw.

Daniel took the tea-pot down to the Baby Belling on the half-landing
and made tea. When he came back, putting the pot down carefully
in the hearth, kneeling at Stephanie's feet, Miss Wells, enthroned now
in her art silk robes, was lecturing Stephanie on colour symbolism in
Elizabethan dress. Everything she was declaring, had then had its
precise significance, colour could be read. Yellow was joy, though
lemon yellow was jealousy. White was death. Milk-white was innocence.
Black was mourning, orange spite, flesh colour lasciviousness. Red
was defiance, gold avarice, straw plenty. Green was hope, but sea-green
was inconstancy. Violet was religion, and willow was forsaken. Her
own dress she feared betokened inconstancy and was certainly unreliable.

Daniel was sceptical of these mysteries. How, he enquired, did an
Elizabethan tell white from milk-white, or distinguish straw from
yellow from lemon from gold. And why, said Stephanie, did Carlyle
speak of sea-green incorruptible if the thing meant inconstancy. In
those days, Felicity Wells informed them, what was valued was the
true colours. Not hues or shades. Yellow, blue, scarlet, green. Mixed
colours almost always indicated shiftiness or corruption. It made for
a brighter world. Carlyle was a Romantic and saw the sea as a natural
force. With the Elizabethans nature was not the first thing, the first
thing was the mind's truth. Colour was harder for them to achieve.
Stephanie said such certainty and intricacy were beautiful. Daniel
said it seemed a bit daft. Miss Wells laughed at him waggishly and
said that prostitutes wore green for a pretty reason. The pretty reason
was the grass-stains on the girls' gowns when they were tumbled.

Also it was the bridegroom's colour. For lusty spring. She sighed, glanced from Daniel to Stephanie. Lovely words, there were, for green. Popingay, gooseturd, willow. Even the shapes of the clothes, in those days, were full of significance. Early Tudor men and women were so very male and female. Huge shoulders and trunks. Full hips for childbearing, and bosoms you could see and judge. Only it got overblown. Vast peascod doublets and codpieces, farthingales and ruffs one could see neither round nor over so that the clothes were in truth a prison for the body. Or, in the case of women, the clothes showed they were someone's property. Immobilised like hobbled horses by their own finery. Sexual symbols taking over from sexual display. Stuffed and wired. The old queen dyed and painted, with a commode under her farthingale. She blushed with appropriate pedantic earthiness. Daniel encouraged her, asking questions about special Westminster scaffolding for members with stuffed breeches. This irritated Stephanie. Clergymen were always trying to prove they were as animal as the next man. She did not see why.

The dark closed in. The gas fire roared, spat and grew hotter. Daniel looked at Stephanie, at the place where her shirt collar met above her breast, at her glistening nylon calf, under the flow of silk she stitched. He burned. Miss Wells watched him burn.

"Clothes," he said glowering, "are to keep you warm, not gorgeous. King Lear."

Miss Wells told Stephanie she should have heard Daniel using *Lear* in his old age sermon, last Sunday. Stephanie said, not lifting her eyes, she thought he hadn't read *Lear*. It had been pointed out to him, he said, that he ought to have. (He had meant to speak to her about *Lear*. But now could not. It had been a reasonably good sermon: he had talked it out.)

"Unaccommodated man," said Miss Wells, filling the silence. "But as a churchman, you should know that adornment has meaning . . ."

The Cloth, said Daniel, was often enough like an embarrassing smell or skin rash. People had shifted out of railway carriages, when he got in. He wore it because he reckoned if there were rules, then you kept them. But he took no pleasure in it.

This remark had the effect of drawing their female attention to his body, in its bulging and shiny suit. He felt sweat run under his arms and his brow as shiny as his trouser seat. He felt mocked. He said: "I'll be off, now".

Miss Wells raised a finger. "No, no. Stephanie, my dear, you can get about. Offer Daniel a Jaffa cake, please."

She stood up, fetched the biscuit box, the floral one, came and stood close to him, hip against his shoulder, her breast near his face, bending solicitously over him. Her skirts – she was wearing the obligatory layers of stiffened net petticoat – rustled. Her shirt-dress was dark rose-pink. Her falling hair on her gold cheek was curved and full. He was seized with strangled rage.

"No. I won't, thank you."

"Take one, do," said Felicity Wells.

"Go on," she said, uncharacteristically lingering. "Be a devil."

"I'm meant to be getting thinner."

"Just one," she said, with absurd urgency, "can't make any difference."

"To my fat? Oh, yes it can. I can burst out of my only suit. Go away. Take it away."

And still she stood, laughing, proffering.

"Really," he exploded, "really, I said *no*. Really no. For God's sake, Please."

She drooped her head and took an irresolute step away. Miss Wells suddenly moved surprisingly fast, despite the bum-roll. Murmuring "excuse" and "bathroom", she closed herself out of there. Daniel put his head in his hands. He held onto his own hair. He felt her stepping uneasily this way and that. He heard her say, "I don't know why people are so awful about other people's slimming. They seem driven to interfere with it. It's funny."

He heard his own voice. "It's not only slimming. People seem to be driven to interfere with other people's attempts to resist any kind of temptation."

She drew back to the mantelpiece, laying a round arm along it, stealing a look at him. "Oh?"

The gas fire poured out its creaking, dazing red heat. The talk sickened and muddled him. She was all rounds and folds and flutes of warm clean pink and gold. He understood for the first time that to compare a woman to a flower or a fruit was not just ornamentation.

"People like to offer – biscuits and things – as an exercise in power. The woman tempted me and I did eat."

"No, really." Her face deepened to the rose of her dress. "Really that won't do. You can't preach sermons on Jaffa cakes. Apart from dubious theology."

"I'm sorry my style doesn't suit you." He allowed his sense of injury to come through. He did not look at her. She would be immediately sorry. She was such a nice girl. He did not know how much she knew about what was going on. He added nothing, stared sullenly at the carpet, let her own anger embarrass her. If he said nothing at all, did not smile, placate, nor smooth . . .

She floated back across the carpet, stood squarely next to him.

"Daniel. I'm sorry. I didn't mean to be so rude. I don't know why I'm so rude to you . . ."

Don't you, he muttered in his head, don't you just. Or don't you? He continued to stare at the floor. He burned. After a moment, incredibly, she put out a hand and brushed it across his hair.

At this the ruthless Daniel began to tremble. He leaned blindly forward, grasped, pulled her against him, buried his hot and furious face in the pink laps of her skirts. She stiffened, began to tremble herself, then took one steadying step nearer, and her arms closed, light, protective, round his head. He pushed his face against her thighs, rocking them both. He heard her saying, "It's all right, it's all right . . ." He thought, you don't know, you don't know *what* it is. He murmured into the cloth, I want, I want, and withdrew hotly as Miss Wells, yet another example of stage-management and timing as the exercise of power, re-entered the room. Her eyes glittering as she took them in, she chattered away to them for ten relieving, even pleasant, interminable minutes, and then grandly dismissed them.

One flight down, Daniel paused on the landing. "I live here." She nodded, not looking at him. "Come in a moment," he said. He had not known, until he asked, whether he would. She walked in. He noticed that she shut the door behind her soundlessly, releasing the catch slowly in the socket. She stood just inside the door. Daniel turned on, one after another, all the gloomy lights. Then he sat on the bed.

"What can I say now?" he asked, almost angrily.

"You don't have to say anything."

"Oh yes I do." He pushed fist into fist. "You can't go on doing that to me."

"I've said I'm sorry. I had no intention of provoking."

"Oh no, you're nice. You are so very nice. You meant to be nice."

"Don't dislike me for it."

"I don't dislike you." He sighed heavily. "I just – no, what's the use. This talk has got to stop here. You'd better tie up your scarf and go home. You're not stupid, you can see you'd better go home. As for me, I can take good care it doesn't happen again."

"That seems a bit bleak. As though I'd deliberately upset you. Just to dismiss me."

"You know it's not that. Listen. You didn't start this, right? I did. You are just being nice. Because you're sorry for me, because of my job, and other things, fat for instance, so you're nice. You must be nice. Well, I could take advantage of that, and the result'd be horrible. And I'm not using up time and energy on that sort of mess. So I think you should go home. And stay there a bit, please."

"You're so sure you're right. You make such heavy weather . . ."

"No. I'm being practical." He gathered himself and announced bluntly, "I love you. I want to marry you. I want . . . I want. No, it's not heavy weather, but it's me as has got to deal with it. It interferes with my work."

"You can't want to marry me. You . . ."

"That is what I want," said Daniel, with finality, as though no answer could be possible or expected. He half expected her, faced with this bald statement, to get up and go away. He truly half hoped she would. What she surprisingly said was, "People always do."

"Always do what?"

"Want to marry me. It's frightening. Men at Cambridge. People I've only met twice, even only once. A waiter once at a hotel where we had a holiday. One of Daddy's miners. The boy in our Bank. I think I must – it isn't sex appeal, it's always marriage – I think I must just look *comfortable*. It doesn't feel like anything really to do with *me*. They don't any of them know me. I must have a face like they choose for cigarette advertisements, an archetypal wife-face. It's almost humiliating."

He said wrathfully, "I see, I see. A recurring problem you have. A bunch of misguided men. Puts me in my place. All right, I'm sorry, please go home."

She began silently to weep, brushing her eyes with the back of her hand, standing stockstill in his doorway. She brought out:

"They don't say, let's go dancing, let's have a holiday, let's go to bed, or anything but I want to marry you, with a sort of awful reverence. I can't deal with it. I don't understand it."

He stood up and led her to the bed, where he sat her down, and sat beside her.

"I could make you understand. But there's no point. It's not an awful reverence. I just want you. Better to marry than burn, and burning's an appalling waste of time, I can tell you, so I would marry you, only I am able to see it won't do. But don't go away supposing I don't know you. I want you, the way you would be, married to me –"

"Don't be arrogant."

"You've noticed that. Well, I've got most of what I really want. But this – no. I've prayed about it, to be let off –"

"How dare you?"

"What?"

"That's a horrible thought. Discussing me with . . ."

"I don't *discuss* . . ."

"I won't be prayed about. I don't believe in your God. I'm not anything to do with that."

She could not tell why the thought of being prayed about filled her with such rage.

"That's another reason why it's hopeless," said Daniel, equally furious.

"Your Church makes too much out of sex."

"If you mean they spend far too much time lecturing on it, and talk like Freud, as though everything was it, and nothing was anything else, yes, I agree," he said. "But I'm in no position to judge. I simply haven't personally bothered about it before now, simply not."

She turned a dubious, tear-stained face to him.

"I don't think I'm homosexual or anything. Just very busy. If you can believe that. Until this . . ."

Some of his furious energy left him: he dropped his large head and began to shake again. She edged timidly closer.

"I didn't understand."

"I shouldn't roar at you."

"You shouldn't take things so hard."

"That's easy to say."

"I see that."

She put a hand on his knee.

"Oh, Daniel –"

"Leave me alone."

"Daniel –"

He turned then, and cast his arms heavily around her, and bore her over onto his protesting bed, where they lay, she staring over his shoulder at the ceiling, he with his weight, all of it, across her body, his face on her wet face on his pillow. He lay inert. She felt, her body felt, entirely relaxed. He moved a little and the opening of her shirt came into vision. Slowly, painstakingly, he undid the buttons, staring with alarm, amazement and pain at the golden-pale breast and throat. With an invisible fumbling hand he pushed up her skirt and felt her thigh, smooth and warm. He shuddered.

"It's all right," she said, still staring at the ceiling, as she had reassuringly said so many times that evening. "It doesn't matter. It will be all right."

Daniel shifted his mountain belly and pressed his face right into the breast he had laid open. With fingers hesitant or listless, how could he tell, she touched his hair. He heard her, quickly, one, two, kick off her shoes. He undid another few buttons and her belt. For a wild moment he ran his hand round under the breast, inside the dress, holding her beating ribs, her hinted spine. There, under him, in his grasp. He lifted his head and addressed his mouth to hers, which was warm, and opened softly and sweetly, retreating before him. He arranged his weight clumsily on one of his own knees and looked down, knitting his brow, at her expression. She was still staring at the ceiling. He made out, he thought, that her accepting posture was one of despair. She meant to please him, she meant to give him something, she felt he ought to have something, and it seemed to him that she expected nothing for herself from this, there was no corresponding need or fury in her. He thought that this was maybe how she always was, this posture was habitual.

He pulled himself away. "No. You don't know what you want."

"No, Daniel, I do, I do. It's all right." Almost querulous.

"All right. All right. You keep saying, all right. I want more than just all right. Anyway it's not true."

"I should have thought about that. *You* can't, of course, you'd be doing – wrong."

She had in fact thought about that. There is something pleasurable in breaking real taboos, even for moralists like the Potters, maybe especially for moralists like the Potters.

"If I am, that's my affair. You must sit up now. You're going home."

"But why?" She did not move.

"I will not just be given things. Now, sit up. Sit up."

"Don't be rough."

"You must know what you want."

"One doesn't make up one's mind in cold blood, love."

"Oh yes, one does. About many things that really matter. And don't call me love. I am not."

"You are too hard on me," she said, and began to cry again, sitting now hunched on the bed, plucking at disordered garments.

"Please go home now," he said, harshly, looking away, unable to move. Pride, need and policy were now inextricably confused. He didn't know if he was sending her away because she was patronising him, or because to finish it now would be to finish it completely, and unfinished business has its own power, things undone torment the imagination, sometimes pleasurably. Partly, he could simply not take any more.

She was putting on her shoes. When he made no move to get up, she put on her hat and coat too.

"Well," she said, "goodbye."

He shook himself. "No, wait. I'll walk you home. Let's just walk back there quietly together."

She looked as though she would protest, and then said, "All right."

12. Nursery Garden

Marcus supposed that if one was properly mad one was not afraid of being mad. Mad people in films and books seemed to have in common a rock-bottom certainty that they were in the right. His own increasing anxiety about madness could perhaps be taken as a sign that he was sane. And madness in this literary household had overtones of raving, vision and poetry which were nothing to do with what was bothering him.

What was bothering him was spreading fear. More and more things aroused it: things he could no longer do, could no longer bear to see. These things were recognisable because of the little shocks that went with them, shocks of consciousness momentarily disconnected, like stepping down two steps when the body has only allowed for one. It had to do with geometry: careful measurement and sense of scale could prevent it. It had to do with an animal fear of not responding quickly. Like burning oneself, because one's skin, or sense of smell, was not functioning as it should. He was out of touch all ways, animal and geometric both.

Every day something new became problematic and difficult. An early thing was books, always bad and now impossible. Print reared off the pages like snakes striking. His eye got entangled by the anomalous, like the letter g, and the peculiar disparity between its written and printed forms. Reading was unmanageable because he measured frequencies of gs, or sat and stared, mesmerised by one. Any word will look odd, stared at, as though it was incorrect or unreal or not a word. Now all words were like that.

Going downstairs was another area of the problematic. He had never liked it. Now he stood irresolute for long periods at the top of flights, and then slithered down, step by step, both feet on each, hip and flank scraping and measuring the intervals between bannisters.

And the bathroom. When the water rushed into the lavatory pan, burst from the front, sheer fall from the sides, plain trickle at the back, all knocked into a turmoil by the others, and sucked away down, he was afraid, yet had to watch the lines pulling. Also he did not like the plughole, a cartwheel covering an empty tunnel with a circular design.

He delayed going to the lavatory, then delayed leaving it to wash his hands, delayed leaving the basin to dry them, delayed leaving the bathroom because of the stairs.

But he was not mad, and was not quite compelled to behave as his fears dictated. If at school he was joined in the bog by another boy he moved around quite briskly. It was just pleasanter to comply, in private. And his evasive rituals had, he was vaguely aware, their own seductions. Waters, vertigo, figures, rhythms, the letter g, released him from worse imperatives. They conferred the ease of safety. He managed, too, to stop eating meat without taking up a position on vegetables. This was an evasion of a looming imperative that he should give up eating altogether.

What finally threw him was when the light shifted.

He was crossing those playing-fields on a Monday morning, towards the school. He was equidistant from the lines of force exerted by the fading white lines of the pitches. It was a spring day, with cold sun on new grass and evergreens. The polished curves of the railway were lit, and so was the wire grid round the tennis courts, intermittently flashing with shoots of brightness. The sky was empty, blue and pale. The remote sun, a defined, painful, liquid disk, hung somewhere. The laws of perspective were no help with that sun, either what it was, or where. It could be taken in only by looking at where it was not, somewhere to the side of it, stealing a flickering glance at it. It was not gold, it was more white, and very shining. Its multiplied after-images dotted the green fields with indigo circles.

The fields stretched on, even and green, tramped and mown. The Bilge Pond lay to his left, little, black and ordinary. Suddenly the light changed and he stopped.

An essential part of what then happened was his own reluctance to believe it was happening. When he remembered it his body remembered huge strain and oppression, caused by two antithetical fears, working together: the fear of being changed completely, beyond help, and the equally powerful fear that all this was only a fantasy, perversely imposed by his errant consciousness on the real world. And even at this moment, which possibly changed all his life, he heard a cheery inner voice telling him that it was possible, as with books, staircases and bathrooms, not to have to know. Later he thought this was a lying, evasive voice. Later still, he remembered it as a true comforter, its cheerful hollow smallness a guarantee that he had kept his identity, had gone on being himself . . .

The light then changed. He stopped because it was hard to go forward, there was too much in front and all round him, light almost tangibly dense and confoundingly bright. He stopped in parts, his body first, then his attention, so that there was a sickening moment when the inside of the head, the cavern, was striding on beyond the frightened soft eyes and contracting skin.

The light was busy. It could be seen gathering, running and increasing along the lines where it had been first manifest. Wild and linear on the railway tracks, flaming, linking, crossing on the tennis-court mesh, rising in bright intermittent streams of sparks from glossy laurel leaves and shorn blades of grass. It could also be seen moving when no object reflected, refracted or directed it. In loops, eddies, powerful direct streams, turbulence and long lines proceeding without let through stones, trees, earth, himself, what had been a condition of vision turned to an object of vision.

Things were newly defined by it. Objects it met, rocks, stones, trees, goal posts, were outlined darkly and then described in light. Its passage through these things only increased their opacity.

Beyond its linear movements it could be experienced as sheets, or towering advancing fronts, like crested waves miles high, infinite or at least immeasurable, like walls and more and more walls of cold, white flame. It had other motions not measured by measurements available to man, or separable in the experience of man, yet there, so that he had to know he could not know more than that they were there. He was confined by their closeness and ubiquity, stretched and distorted by his stressed, distressed sense of their continuous operation beyond any attention he could fix on them.

So he came to see this as a presence, and a presence with purpose. It was a presence wholly outside his scale, conducting its work with a magnitude and a minuteness at once too grand and too precisely delicate for him to map. Stretched and contracted he sensed it lap round him and through him and for the worst moment he was almost concentrated on its passage through his own consciousness. He was both saved (from bright blinding, from annihilation) and prevented (from losing himself in it) by a geometric figure which held as an image or more in that glare and play of light. He saw intersecting cones, stretching to infinity, containing the pouring and rushing. He saw that he was at the, or a, point of intersection, and that if it could not pass through it would shatter the fragile frame to make a way. He must hold together, but let it go through, like the burning glass with the gathered light of the sun. The rims flared and flared and flared. He said "Oh God." He tried to be and not to be, and most dangerous, to go on.

When he walked it came with him, or was seen to be ahead also. He thought he might die before he got to the school and could not go back because what was behind was steadily increasing its activity. He took a step and a step and a step and the fields of light swayed and roared and came and went and sang.

He arrived in some way at the school and was able to sit down on the low wall of the cloister, opposite horned Moses, a figure who owed something to Michelangelo and more to Rodin's bulky Balzac. Marcus stared into the convex stone eyes and considered.

The turbulence was at some distance: it stopped short of the red brick: the edges of its activity troubled the lawn and the glasshouses. He could not go on or back. As he considered, a figure in white garments stepped radiantly through the films of light as though it inhabited them briskly and easily. Its head curled softly bright in the sun. Marcus, cold now, blinked painfully. It was Lucas Simmonds, heading for the Bilge Lab. He did not believe, how should he, in signs and portents. But this was the third time. In the Odeon, in the Butchery, Simmonds had offered a helping hand. Now he came past. Marcus got up and began exhaustedly to trail after him. There was in any case, the small voice pointed out, absolutely no one else.

The Bilge Lab was part of the old buildings. Physics and Chemistry had a new extension, rectangular, glass-walled, tiled with abstract mosaics. The Bilge Lab was Gothic, with "Biology, Human Physiology and Anatomy" over its door in gold Gothic lettering on a midnight blue ground. The door was arched heavy oak.

He got in. Rows of high empty benches, high stools, curving serpentine brass taps, tiny porcelain basins, gas fittings, green shaded lights. In the window, in the sun, a figure in a white coat with crumpled grey flannels hanging below.

"Sir," he said. Although he felt he was bellowing and winced at the roar, his voice was in fact reedy and faint, slurred like the feet he couldn't drive forward. "Sir . . ."

Simmonds turned round, smiling.

"Hullo, old chap. What's up?"

"Sir . . ."

Slowly clutching the doorknob he came down to the floor and sat clutching the door. It swung unstably. Pure hatred of its shiftiness moved over him.

Lucas Simmonds ran round the benches.

"Take your time. Don't worry. Had a shock? Lie down, that might be best."

He did not touch Marcus. He stood over him, with a grin of concern and gestured at the lino. "Go on. Lie back. Much the best."

Marcus lowered himself gingerly. He arranged his arms, out of some nervous compulsion, neatly alongside his body. Above him, bent over him, Simmonds's bright face beamed and wavered.

"Had a shock," he reiterated. Marcus acquiescently closed his eyes. "A drink might do you good."

He brought a lipped glass laboratory beaker of water, which he put down beside Marcus's head. Awkwardly, rolled over, upon one elbow, tears in his eyes, Marcus sipped. There was a faint chemical taste, and the taint of ether, which always hung over the place.

"Been seeing things?" Simmonds now knelt beside Marcus, peering closely into his face. This casually pressing question increased Marcus's hazy sense of portent and working destiny. Anyone else surely would have asked are you ill? He turned his head from side to side on the lino. "Seeing things?" Simmonds echoed himself, watching, smiling.

"Not *things*."

"Not things. I see. Not things. What?"

Marcus remembered Simmonds going on about the mathematical landscape. Beyond that, his hunted mind casting this way and that to escape Bill's relentless questions.

"What?" Simmonds insisted gently.

He closed his eyes and mouth. He opened them furtively and said, "Light. It was the light." And closed again. Everything he could.

"Light. I see. What kind of light?"

"I can't say. *Too much light*. It was terrible light; *alive*, if you see what I . . ."

"Oh yes," said Simmonds, rapt. "Oh yes, I do indeed. Tell me."

Marcus opened his mouth and was very sick. When he next knew anything he was lying with his head on some sort of cushion and something, Simmonds's raincoat, was tucked over and round him. He was cocooned by incapacity. Simmonds's face reappeared close to his own.

"You are shocked. You must keep still. Just lie there until you feel more like it. Don't worry about a thing. I'll take care of everything."

He had no choice.

"I'll finish what I was doing and we'll go on with our chat when you're more the thing."

Simmonds was striding up and down along the benches, piling up aluminium lunch-boxes and corked jars. He seemed extraordinarily solid, superlatively normal. He whistled a little, gaily, through his teeth. Marcus remembered the dissection of the earthworm. Simmonds had dropped the worms, enough for the whole class, one by one into a beaker of chloroform, where they frothed and paled. Later, Marcus had had to slit and pin back the livid, rolling skin.

This room went back a long way, to the humanising intentions of the school's founders. Here, aided by the study of the development of species, fish, flesh, fowl and frond, the boy should learn to obey the primary commandment: Know Thyself.

A few stuffed birds, an owl, some terns, a dusty group of robins and wrens, were perched on the top shelves of glass-fronted mahogany cupboards. Under these a wired skeleton lay on its side, joints dangling. Boxes of unstrung vertebrae, tarsals and meta-tarsals, chalky, creamy, rattled on desks by generations of boys like so many Jacks, scattered, swept together, returned to the shelf for next time.

A case contained things in bottles – kilner jars like those in which his mother preserved gluts of Victoria plums or unripe fallen apples and pears. Jam-jars, test-tubes. Dozens of foetuses. Tiny creamy-pink rats, blunt-headed, blind-eyed, with minute stumps of feet and tails, all rolled together and surely slightly crumbling like cheese in the surrounding liquid. Larger round-bellied ratlings, cord and placenta attached, flat-headed unborn cats, pallid flesh, unformed eyes closed against the glass wall and the light. Snake embryos, preserved in strings, like beads on a chain, coiled and forever undelivered, bird embryos preserved with the wall of their egg-shell cracked open to show the clenched ball of damp feathers, skinny thighs, flaccid beak. There was an Edwardian monkey embryo, in a mahogany-framed case, a grim homunculus, a brown shrivelled Genius in a bottle.

Parts of creatures were also preserved, to be handed for inspection from boy to boy, a bottle of lungs, of hearts, of eyes. Marcus remembered particularly the skinned cat's head, its black-jelly-dark and lustreless eyes in the cloudy liquid, sunk and horrid. And the white rabbit in his ovoid box, his little paws, still furry and clawed, held apart to frame his pale innards, stained crimson, viridian, cobalt, guts, lungs, heart, over which his rabbit teeth grinned and his long ears drooped, squashed against him by the jar.

There were living things as well: a scuttering white mouse in a treadmill, a tank of water-snails and sticklebacks, a formitory through whose glass walls the dark passages of the ants could be seen, and the ants too, dragging pale pupae from level to level, hurrying and purposeful in mixed light and dark. There was the old experiment with the growth of seeds and photosynthesis. Peas and beans deprived of water, shrivelled and self-contained on cotton-wool. Peas and beans deprived of light poking up, blind and weak, straggling and colourless, their questing points. Warmed peas, cold peas, crowded peas, peas in slanted light and half-light, little blunted energetic tips here; there, already, a bowed uncurling leaf.

Marcus took another tepid sip of water and turned his attention to the comparative neutrality of diagrams. The urino-genital systems of frogs and rabbits, drawn in Indian ink by Lucas Simmonds, were displayed in two-dimensional good taste near the blackboard. Marcus's knowledge was sketchy and Lucas's notation minimal, so that he was quite unable to decide whether certain blunted, wriggling, finger-like shapes were protrusions or pockets, and thus mistook the male for the female rabbit and could see no apparent difference between the frogs.

Directly opposite the master's dais, on which he was now lying, hung, side by side, in all their clinical and resolutely unlovely emancipation, Man and Woman. Both were in quadruplicate, on ancient, unrolled strips of parchment-coloured oilcloth. First, they appeared skeletal, next, a flayed and liverish pattern of muscular pulls and directions, next again, a view through the frame to the internal organs. Last, solid and cheesy, naked, steatopygous and hairless, the surfaces of flesh, the thing itself.

They stood repeated with dangling arms and parted legs, ciphered mouths, possibly smiling, skulls demarcated like battlefields in zones and hillocks. They were pierced like Victorian Sebastians by long black darts on the end of which appeared, in subdued Italic lettering, the names of parts. They had a look of ancient disuse, as though some maybe Edwardian usher had repeatedly indicated and partially obliterated their salient points with a long rule, and they had since fallen into neglect.

Lucas Simmonds returned and knelt beside him.

"How are you doing now?"

Marcus shook his head miserably.

"Tell me about this light."

"Sir – I could be getting ill. It could be the aura of an illness? Or fits, or brain trouble. Sir."

Lucas's mouth-corners turned up quizzically in the middle of his round pink face.

"Do you really think that? Do you really feel that's so?"

"How do I know? I've not been feeling right, exactly, for weeks. I've been . . ."

There was a tabu about describing tabus. He huddled under the raincoat.

"Please go on. I can probably help. Go on."

"Well. I can't concentrate. Not on the right things. Not on work. Too much on the wrong things. I get frightened of things. Not things it makes any sense to . . . treat that way. Silly things. A tap, a window, stairs. I worry for ages. About *things*. I must be sort of ill, I must. And now this."

"We label too many things as illnesses," Simmonds said, paradoxically clinical in his white coat. "Anything unusual. Anything that changes our conventional habits, often very detrimental to our true well-being. Maybe you are being distracted for good reasons. Please go on to tell me about the light."

Marcus closed his eyes. Simmonds gripped Marcus's shoulder with one hand and jumped sharply away again.

"You see, it's something about the playing fields. Always there, I've felt funny. I can get that I don't know where I am, there, I can get that I can't find my – I get spread." Secretively offering the important word as code, or hostage.

"Spread. You mean, out of the body?"

"I don't know what you mean. You could call it that. It's a technical trick. I used to be able to make it happen or not, when I was little. Now it's got out of hand."

"A technical trick. A technique. I like that, that's good. You can do it at will?"

"I don't like doing it. Any more."

Simmonds's smile was enamel-bright.

"And did this technique produce the shock? This light you speak of?"

"Oh, no, no, no. I didn't do anything at all. *It* did it. I mean, that's the one thing I'm sure of. It just happened."

"That's better. Now. Tell me *what* it did?"

"How can I? It was frightful. It crowded me out. I was afraid of being – done away with."

Simmonds wound his hands agitatedly together.

"And you think there's something *wrong* with you, boy?"

"I told you. I was afraid. I couldn't hold together."

"Maybe you weren't intended to. Maybe you were in the presence of a Power."

Marcus found Simmonds's attitude partly reassuring and partly alarming. It was reassuring that someone seemed confident of recognising and docketing phenomena he had feared only he was aware of at all. It was alarming because Simmonds seemed to have intentions, plans, a vision, in which he was by no means sure he wished to share.

"Photisms," said Simmonds. "There's a technical term for it, Potter. Photisms. Experiences of floods of light and glory which frequently accompany moments of revelation. The phenomenon is known."

"Photisms," Marcus repeated dubiously. He decided to sit up.

"The explanation of the phenomenon is of course open to scientific doubt. But it is a known experience, recorded and discussed."

"Oh."

"For God's sake," shouted Simmonds, greatly excited, "does it not occur to you that what you saw may have been more or less what Saul saw on the way to Damascus. What the shepherds saw in the fields at night. They were sore afraid, *sore* afraid, and so should you be, it's no joke. You have to be trained, you see, to withstand, to respond to, things like that. Which you are not."

"I told you, I don't believe in God."

"And I told you that was of no importance if He believed in you. Did you say anything aloud, when you saw the photisms?"

"I said, oh God."

"Precisely."

"Look here, everyone, people, say that, all the time. It doesn't mean anything."

"Nothing 'doesn't mean anything'. All words are said for reasons. I knew what you said."

"Anybody might –"

"You are subject to too many coincidences. The most important of which is me. I happen to have the techniques to channel the forces that properly scare you. I've been working on ways of training consciousness. Meditation if you like, but scientific. You came to me. You could run away now but God would engineer another nasty shock, and you'd be back."

"No."

"I say yes. Tell me about the manifestation."

"It did something to my sense of scale."

"Did you see anything?"

"A diagram."

Lucas Simmonds became enthusiastic. He confused Marcus, he produced pencil and paper, he extracted a drawing.

On paper it looked like nothing. But the memory was still faintly dangerous.

"An infinity symbol," said Lucas. Marcus diffidently mentioned that it had seemed to indicate a burning glass. Also, Lucas said, an infinity symbol, a symbol of infinite energy passing through a point. They should, would use the symbol as a mantra, an object of joint contemplation and meditation.

Marcus looked at it silently. It looked diminished, as Lucas interrogated it. The whole thing was becoming diminished, safe to handle, wrapped in Lucas Simmonds's fluent words. Although Simmonds was paradoxically trying to unwrap it. With speech, it all receded, seeming, as it vanished, bright and desirable for the first time.

Simmonds, brightly reasonable, leaned on the teacher's bench and lectured him.

"The Renaissance was when they got Man's relationship with Spirit wrong. They revived the old pagan idea that Man is the Measure of all things, which of course is absurd, and that idea did untold damage. Instead of infinity you had to be content with a circle a man could touch at every point." He drew a crude version of Leonardo's encircled microcosmic man beside Marcus's infinity symbol, and smiled peacefully.

"Conjuring with wrong images. Since then we've been living in an anthropocentric universe with our eyes and ears and minds shut. What's called Religion isn't about inhuman Spirit but about Man and Morals and Progress, which are much less important. And then Science came, which should have given them an inkling, an inkling of the inhuman Powers that Be, but what they did was develop their anthropocentricity into the terrible idea that Man is the Master of all Things. Now that, Potter, is black conjuring, that produced Hiroshima and Satanic mills. Science *could* have been used, of course, to re-establish the ancient knowledge that Man had his place on a Scale of Being as an intermediary between Pure Matter and Pure Spirit. But they talked about the indomitable human spirit and the empty heavens and lost their chances. Including any chance to deal with, or describe, or even recognise experiences of the kind you've just had."

He was sweating again. His facial muscles twitched. Marcus observed these signs with frigid alarm. What attracted him about Lucas was not yet his theories, but his air of assurance, when he had it, his tweedy normality, that quality so ambivalently dear to all the younger Potters. When he was agitated, Marcus was put out. But today his assurance seemed mostly inspired, if the word could be thought appropriate, and included a sense of the shifts of Marcus's moods.

"You suspect the language. Science is O.K., it has technical terms. This doesn't, because Man has neglected spiritual forms for somatic ones. You don't want me to talk about alchemy or auras or even angels I can tell. All those things are misshapen descriptions of things we've got askew. In fact, I believe, I do believe the world is trying to evolve out of matter into spirit . . . Here. I've written it out, actually. In a fumbling way. I'd like you to read it."

He brought out, from his briefcase, a wad of cyclostyled paper. "You might find some profit . . ."

It was blurred, much-handled, soft. Marcus read.

The PATTERN and the PLAN
Written by Lucas Simmonds M.Sc.
To the Greater Glory of the Maker.

To show the Ever more Complex Evolving Plan
and Pattern in which and according to which
IT desires us to Play our Part.

"I think we should work together, profitably. It must be your decision, in so far of course," he laughed, "as no higher Powers take a hand again. The first stage is your reading my book – just to see if you have any comment, to clear the ground. Then I think we might devise a few experiments.

"What shall I do?"

"Do?"

"Now. I feel awful."

"Now. Now I should go to the Nursery and tell Sister you've been sick in the Bilge Lab, and get her to tuck you up in bed. I might come with you, but it's better not to excite comment, we must keep our secrets close . . . Just say you were sick."

"I was sick."

"Exactly so. I look forward to our next meeting."

He did not say when that would be, but by now Marcus doubted no more than Simmonds that it would be taken care of.

13. *In the Humanist's House*

Frederica, entering Long Royston for the first time, did not take to it. She had meant to. It was a step, several steps, up and out of Blesford. Like Everest, climbed that year, it had always been there, but inaccessible. Now, invited by its owner, she walked across its gardens, planted, according to Crowe's instructions, more or less in accordance with Francis Bacon's prescriptions in his essay "Of Gardens". It was a hideous grey spring, that year, but Bacon's April flowers, in walled gardens, were struggling out. Bacon liked the breath of flowers on the air. Frederica breathed in: the double white violet; the wallflower; the stock-gillyflower; the cowslip; flower-delices and lilies of all natures; rosemary flowers; the tulippa; the double piony; the pale daffadil; the French honeysuckle; the cherry-tree in blossom; the dammasin and plum-tree in blossom; the white-thorn in leaf; the lilac-tree. It was all in the guide-book, issued with pretty drawings when the gardens were thrown open at Easter and in June. You may, said Bacon, have *ver perpetuum*, as the place affords. Even in North Yorkshire, though the moorland winds do sorely ruffle. Frederica crunched along the terrace gravel, on which later the play was to be enacted. The breath of flowers is far sweeter in the air than in the hand. Wallflowers are very delightful to be set under a parlour or low chamber window. They were. But those which perfume the air most delightfully, not passed by as the rest, but being trodden upon and crushed, are three: that is, burnet, wild thyme, and watermints. Therefore you are to set whole alleys of them, to have the pleasure, when you walk or tread. Crowe had provided that pleasure. Frederica saw other people walking and treading in pleached alleys planted with these things, known faces, unknown faces, familiar from photographs and posters. The revels are now beginning, she told herself.

When she got in she was less happy. There was a white-coated butler, who took her macintosh and her name: there was Crowe, who said "how lovely" and passed on, there was a young man in a peacock corduroy jacket, studying a carving, half his face hidden behind huge tinted aquamarine lenses. She thought what she felt was social unease – alarm at being unable to impress herself on this knot of highly articulate, loudly fluting, brilliantly mobile creatures. Social unease always made her aggressive. Later, she wondered whether what daunted her was not Long Royston itself.

They were gathered for a preliminary briefing, to consider costumes, and because Crowe thought it would be fun. They sat down to lunch in the Great Hall, under the minstrels' gallery, fifteen at table, the prospective principal actors, the triumvirate and the wardrobe mistresses, the wife of the Dean of Calverley and someone Lodge had inveigled from Covent Garden. Marina Yeo was enthroned between Crowe and Alexander, pronouncing on the power of garments. Frederica, at the other end of the table between the aquamarine young man, who had not taken off his goggles, and Jennifer Parry, who was to play Bess Throckmorton, and just qualified, in this huge cast, as a principal, observed her critically.

"Clothes have terrible power, on the stage," said Miss Yeo. "What one appears to be, there, one *is*, one is at their mercy, always, to some extent. Some actors impart power to their clothes. Ellen Terry's daughter would never have her costumes cleaned. They were stiff with her *mana*. Sybil told me once that when she put on those shimmering beetle-wings that Ellen Terry wore as Lady Macbeth she became *simply absolutely fearless*. They bore her through the part. Do you know,

Alexander, the Oscar Wilde story about those beetle-wings? How he
said – the Queen of Scotland – purchased the banquet – a very frugal
one – in the local shops – and patronised the local weavers – for her
husband's – drab – kilt. But for her own garments – she shopped – in
Byzantium. So it was."

"I shall never forget your Lady Macbeth," said Crowe. "I can still
see your hands, as though you would wring them away . . ."

"I preferred the nightdress in that," said Miss Yeo, "to all those
rather *square* robes I had to cart about . . ."

"You shall have a lovely nightie to die in, in this," Crowe told her.
"Wait till you see. Clothes to the author's own design, a novelty."

"Really," said Miss Yeo, turning total attention on Alexander, who
felt required to woo her. Frederica and Jennifer Parry both watched
him to see how he would deal with this requirement, Jennifer covertly,
and Frederica with an unabashed stare. As she had expected, he dealt
badly, stammering woodenly, obviously insincere, which in fact he was
not. Marina Yeo's face was long and dark-skinned, her hair thick,
smooth and greying, her eyes very dark under deeply sculpted lids. Her
large mouth was invariably described as mobile. Her neck was very
long and had aged like finely knotted wood, without puffiness. She
twisted her face about too much all the time, Frederica decided, composing her own stiffly. Frederica had been much impressed by the rigid
and mask-like quality of portraits of Elizabeth.

"I didn't catch your name," said the creature with the goggles,
turning these on her, lifting his face under the high windows so that
sparks danced in the iridescent lenses. "I believe I know you."

"I doubt it. I'm Frederica Potter."

"Ah. You see I do. Bill Potter's daughter. The second one, the fierce
one."

Frederica drew back, said "How," and recognised his manner.

"You are Edmund Wilkie. How odd. Why are you here?"

"I am Sir Walter Ralegh, love. The local prodigy returning to the
fold to astonish and confound prophecy. Why are you here?"

"I am Elizabeth. Until Marina Yeo is old enough – or young enough
– to do it, to be her. If you see."

"I see precisely. What fun. You will have to learn her mannerisms.
Not difficult, they're very clear-cut." He bent his body towards her in
a very passable imitation of the actress's curvilinear attentive stoop.

"I can't see your face," Frederica protested. "Those glasses are most
off-putting. I don't remember that you had to wear glasses."

"I don't. They're experimental, my own design, an explanation of
the effect of intense colours on mood. I did try those reversing glasses

they put on chickens but I only dare wear them in my own place.
Guaranteed, when you take them off, to produce oceanic feelings of
totality. The top of the world and the bottom identical. Or at least the
top and bottom of the stairs since your senses confound your intellect
and declare that each is the other. Colours are easier in public life. I
have several pairs. Brown, gold, blue, grey smoke, purple smoke,
Bristol crimson and conventional rose-tinted. I'm keeping a long and
detailed record of my moods and reactions. I get my girl to keep a
control record. So far the only thing we're both dead certain about is
that the less you can see me the ruder I am."

"Everybody," said Frederica, "seems very proud of being very rude,
these days."

"True. How right you are. A facile way of appearing witty. By all
means let's be revolutionary and polite. Tell me what you think of your
alter ego, the other Gloriana?"

Edmund Wilkie was Blesford Ride's maverick success. At the school
he had, with extraordinary facility, passed A-levels both in arts subjects
and, subsequently, in sciences. He then left, and went to King's College
Cambridge to become a psychologist, where he was said to be showing
unsurpassed brilliance. He had also risen meteor-like to national fame
as an actor, had written, directed and acted in a review called Midnight
Mushrumps which had had a brief London run and had played a
Marlowe Society Hamlet about which Harold Hobson had written, "The
most intelligent, least bombastic Prince to grace the stage in my
memory". Frederica was very temporarily in love with him, after a
vision of him as Bunthorne, in grass and primrose velvet, in a Blesford
Ride *Patience*. He was the sort of boy schoolmasters secretly hope will
come a cropper, so blithe, so arrogant, so effortless, so ingrate had been
his academic proceedings. They wrote heavily qualified references
which Cambridge ignored.

Gossip columnists were already speculating about whether he would
be a great psychologist, an innovatory don or doctor, a brilliant enter-
tainer, a valuable Shakespearean actor. Alexander had thought he might
properly be called back to do Ralegh, that man of many parts, climber,
poet, mountebank, scientist, atheist, soldier, sailor, historian, prisoner.
Ralegh carried a lot of the play's weight: he was part-chorus as well as
character. Wilkie was to Frederica living proof that escape was possible
from Blesford to metropolitan speed and glamour. Bill's vision of her
future did not include such things: he was cautious about Wilkie,
gloomily testifying that he was sharp-witted and possibly something
more.

Frederica knotted herself into a tangle of polite words about Miss

Yeo, from which it emerged that she found her very fluent, bodily and verbally. She spoiled what politeness she had managed by saying that Marina Yeo reminded her of the Tenniel illustration of Alice as serpent frightening the dove. Wilkie said, "Brainy girls like you think everything can be done from the head."

"There's nothing wrong with brains."

"Don't be touchy, dear I never said there was. I love brains. They're my work."

"They said you were going to be a head-shrinker."

"No, no, no. An academic psychologist. I intend to study the relations between perception and thought. Not libido, dear girl, *thought*. The ultimate narcissism, the brain measuring its own ticks and fluctuations. The roots of knowledge."

"How can it?"

"How can it?"

"How can it know itself? How can it study what itself *is*? It can't get outside itself."

"Machines, Frederica."

"Machines it thought up itself."

"Well – not it. Several discrete brains. But it's a valid point. A closed circle. The brain can't check the brain's conclusions about the brain's conclusions about the brain. No harm in trying, though."

Frederica struggled vertiginously with the image of a brain attempting to contemplate itself. A light approaching a light in a mirror. A puff of smoke, an explosion. Coils of grey matter locked in mortal combat with identical coils of grey matter. Brains were busy, yet one imagined them formless and torpid.

"It would explode," she claimed hopefully.

"Now you are imagining it on an electrical model."

"No. I see snakes of grey matter battling with other snakes of grey matter."

"And fusing? It's interesting, the constancy of imagery about the concept. Always coils – electrical or serpentine – cells – organic or in batteries – and then this fusing or explosion. Followed, in my case, by nothing. A satisfactory empty space of clear light. To which I shall never attain, being too busy, by nature, and not quite bold enough."

Crowe rose to introduce them to each other. Three professionals, men from Stratford and the old Vic, men who had had speaking parts in Olivier's films. Max Baron, tall, slim, worried-looking, playing Leicester, Crispin Reed and Roger Braithwaite, Burleigh and Walsingham. These two were curiously similar, though make-up would no doubt produce metamorphosis, clean-cut, dark-haired, suede-shoed, with gleaming

teeth and rounded voices in which they swapped stories of theatrical
near-disaster. They were heavy men but spoke with a combination of
unction, emphasis and excitability, an alternate rushing and lingering of
delivery, which Frederica could not relate to those two cold watchers,
the careful men of power. Bob Grundy from York Rep, another
professional, destined for Essex, was already growing a beard.

The amateurs began with Thomas Poole, head of English at the
Calverley Teacher Training College, who was Alexander's friend, square,
blond, silent, and was to play the sage and serious poet, Spenser.
Spenser, with Ralegh, formed the chorus. Alexander had spent some
lunatic, embarrassing and unprofitable weeks trying to tackle Shakespeare himself. One night he dreamed he was ceremoniously forced to
his knees and executed by a masked headman of huge size who was
muttering unintelligibly a flow of what Alexander knew, in the dream,
to be the true dark current of English. It was, this figure made clear,
not Shakespeare, but himself, who could not abide the question. He
woke up with sweat cooling in rivulets all over him and thought of
Spenser.

This poet, more remote, more apparently inaccessible, had proved
easier to deal with. The lines Alexander had written for him, a sliding,
shifting mixture of deliberate theft, loving pastiche, and Alexander's
own clarity were, Alexander thought, possibly the best thing he'd done.
The Elizabethan verse ran easily with the parody and the new thing
with its source in the old. Eterne in mutabilitie, as Spenser might,
himself an incorporator of archaisms, have said of the language, and
had said of Adonis; Alexander had incorporated the phrase itself in
Astraea. From where, in due course, it found its way into O-level and
A-level footnotes. Alexander was glad of Thomas Poole who knew the
Faerie Queene and spoke with neutral and musical clarity.

The women, besides Marina Yeo and Frederica, her youthful shadow,
as Crowe put it, were a prim and passionate Calverley teacher type-cast
as Mary Tudor, a mountainous lady from Scarborough Rep, Miss
Annette Turnbull, who was Lady Lennox, and Mrs Marion Bryce, wife
of Canon Bryce of Blesford, who had given up a promising career as
an actress to be a church wife and produced annual nativity and passion
plays, Christopher Fry and Dorothy L. Sayers, in Calverley Minster.
She was dark and bosomy, with liquid, troubled eyes and voice, undeni-
able presence and great emotional flutter and tension. Her part, though
dramatic, was brief, for Alexander hated Mary Queen of Scots and had
made her presence felt largely as an absent menace. There was also
Jenny, who might not have been there had Alexander not particularly
desired it.

She was already distressed by her attempts at conversation over lunch. She and Wilkie had exclaimed suitably over their dramatic married state. Wilkie had enquired if she did a lot of acting.

"Oh no. I've got a small baby. Quite a small baby, anyway. I don't get about much. Do you?"

"I might take it up professionally. One has talent scouts in the dressing room. Quite flattering. Quite lucrative, anyway for a year or two. I think I'll stick to the grey cells."

Frederica had burst in. *She* meant to act, her father was keen on Cambridge, she feared Cambridge was a distraction. Wilkie's aquamarine glitter veered her way. He lit a cigarette in a long black holder, an apparition like a proboscis between the glowing moth eyes. He said seriously that she couldn't do better, at present, than Cambridge, for openings. And she could teach when she was "resting". Better than coffee bars. She would not teach. Frederica roared, anything else but not teach. Those that can't, teach. She meant to be *good*. Even the good rested, Wilkie said drily, but added, quite avuncular, that you couldn't be good, if you didn't grind at it, it was true.

Jenny was alarmed by these brash and brilliant children. At twenty-four she was old, although she could hardly have been more than two years, or less, older than Wilkie, who had done National Service. They were ambitious: they saw themselves wheeling up, up, and over, whereas her horizon was strictly bounded by Geoffrey, Thomas, Blesford Ride and what beyond that but, with luck, little bits of despised teaching? She had been good at acting at Bristol, but it had never occurred to her to try and build on it. She had known that she must solve the problem of marriage and child-bearing first, before she could identify any rational future. She had wanted marriage, without even considering not wanting it, all through her degree, and indeed from before she had even been entered for it. She had no idea at all whether, if she had thought differently, she might have identified herself differently, seen herself brilliant and perhaps become so. She felt dislike, not for Wilkie, who clearly believed he was a genius, but for Frederica, who equally clearly believed herself to be a genius, and expressed this belief comparatively grossly and stridently. That these judgments were a function of sex she was resentfully aware. She had tried to catch Alexander's eye, to be at least sexually comforted, but he was busy wrapping a stole round Miss Yeo's shoulders. She tried to attract Wilkie's attention again, asking him what his research was, what brain processes he studied.

"On – the relations between visual images and languages. The way we form concepts, ultimately. Whether, as some psychologists think, visual images are more primitive, more fundamental than words, or whether you can't think without some sort of precise symbolic language. I want to work with eidetic phenomena – people who think by simply visualising. Certain kinds of mathematical genius – Flinders Petrie for example – think visually – visualise a slide-rule and read the numbers off it. One could study interesting relations between visual memory and conceptual memory and analytic thought . . ."

Frederica, wildly animated, butted in again.

"My brother could do instant mathematics."

"Could he now? And can he still, and how did he do it and what kinds of thing did he do, do you know . . ."

"Well," said Frederica, and began to tell a very garbled version of Marcus's mathematical Fall, which had been interrupted by Crowe's rising. One could surely not become invisible at twenty-four, thought Jennifer.

Crowe led his guests into the library, where various sketches and mock-ups were displayed. Along one table ran a scaled-down recreation of terrace and trees, with various movable bright pavilions and aery throne-rooms that could be wheeled on and off. There was a cardboard White Tower and a Coronation litter in matchsticks and string and gauze. It was like one of those box-within-a-box microcosms, model village or Russian doll, where the model village contains in its precinct a model model village, which in its turn, like the smallest faceless green pear-shape, contains undifferentiated white kernels, houses or emperors too small for human hand to carve or eye to divide. Or like the gardens of Adonis, miniature landscapes of corn, lettuce, fennel, put out at his feast to flower and die, thrown out, like the effigies of Death and Carnival, when the dancing was over, to propitiate the river.

On the table were Alexander's drawings. He had not begun these with the intention of showing them to anyone. They were a product of his obsession at its height. The writing had led him, half-scholarly, half-besotted, to portraits, miniatures, the garments themselves, in the V and A. And then he had taken to drawing his people late at night. It was Crowe, having elicited the information that the drawings existed, who had carried off a sheaf of them. A possible designer had already produced preliminary sketches, thematically linked in colour along lines to be traced in Alexander's text, red and white, green and gold, Tudor roses, rosettes of ribbons. Burleigh and Walsingham red and white, Spenser and Ralegh green and gold, the Queen all of these. But Alexander's love of particularity had revolted. He had intended, partly, a thick and accurate realism, a richness thinned by these blatant schemes. He only showed the drawings to Crowe to explain what was wanted.

Though he knew more than drawing: could place hooks and eyes, tucks, facings and darts. He had always done wardrobe for school plays.

The actors gathered and exclaimed. Alexander had given some of the small figures the faces of their originals, and some those of the actors who were to play them. Ralegh in his black velvet rayed with pearls was Ralegh. Leicester, for all his patchy pale beard, peered under Max Baron's anxious brow. The Queen's costumes were inhabited by shifting faces and figures. Over a ceremonious ruff glared the chalky, beaked worn face of the white and gold Queen who bestrode England in the thunderstorm portrait. Above the pleated night-gown appeared a hybrid face with Marina Yeo's huge mouth and serpentining neck under Elizabeth's high plucked brows and piled wig. Frederica found her own gowns, which pleased her; a white and gold dress to be imprisoned in, a green and gold dress to run in Catherine Parr's orchard. She was put out to see that the face above the dresses, in these drawings, was an empty oval.

Alexander had been secretly self-indulgent with Bess Throckmorton. He had done her in water-coloured imitation of Hilliard, and given her Jenny's nervous eager little face over Jenny's known round breasts inside the true Bess's lacy fan collar. She was holding down billowing coral skirts backed up against a Hilliard white rose-tree on a precisely pricked out carpet of white violets and pied daisies. Only the woman's garments in this idyllic spring scene were troubled by the anomalous gust of wind. Alarmed by his own to him glaring representation of feelings in this picture, he had tried to make it appear more technical by drawing in details of plackets, laces, points, round its margins and had only, to his eye, so accustomed to reading dark conceits, made his meaning more apparent. He gave himself the pleasure of watching Jenny study herself in his palely bright and orderly little wood, looked over her shoulder as she said, "I recognise the woman up against the tree."

"Swisser swatter," cried Wilkie behind them.

"That's in my play," said Alexander. Crowe, behind them again, finished off the Aubrey quotation.

"As the danger and the pleasure at the same time grew higher, she cried out in ecstasy Nay sweet Sir Walter. Which became swisser swatter."

"She proved with child, and they were put in the Tower," said Wilkie. "Lovely petticoats, Mr Wedderburn. I shall enjoy those."

Frederica caught Alexander's arm as he was about to follow Jennifer.

"Caught you," she said, arch through embarrassment. Alexander, with a whole summer of Jennifer before him, felt kindly.

"I'll show you something, Frederica. Look at this."

He took out of a brown paper parcel a long narrow strip of velvet, dark red.

"Something time went past. Matthew found it; he was having the chairs recovered, and found this rolled in the stuffing. Fresh as when they tucked it in, under James I."

He hung it from his hands in the light.

"If you hang velvet the wrong way you lose the sheen. The life goes. This hangs this way. Look." His fingers caressed the brown-bright pelt. "Look how the light changes in this – from silver through blood to black. Carnation – a shade darker than russet – a corruption of incarnate. Dark flesh colour, darker than all the sonneteers' damask roses and cherry lips. The thing itself."

"You do like *things*, Alexander."

"You sound critical. Don't you?"

"No one's ever expected me to. I've got a good Yorkshire respect for a good weight of wool and a decent sharp blade. That's about it."

"Maybe your age. Life thickens as you get older. I doubt if I'd have been so entranced by the objects in this house at your age."

"It's all too much for me. I don't *see* it. I'm the austerity generation. Butter and cream and oranges and lemons are mythological entities for us, you know. Daddy liked it. Utility bread and chairs and dried egg and marge. All these carvings and hangings just make me uneasy."

Alexander said to Crowe, "Here's Frederica saying she has no feeling for your things because of the war."

Crowe raised his silvery brows at her.

"I'm sure that's not true."

"It is. They intimidate me. There's too much."

"Not if you know it. I shall show you my beautiful house and teach you to see detail. We shall start with the plaster-work in the Great Hall. Have you looked at the plaster?"

She had noticed that there was a plaster frieze running round the Great Hall, under the gallery. She had taken in no more than a vague impression of forest trees, naked running figures and animals, in chalky relief. Now, staring obediently at this, she saw that the figures were both vigorous and slightly wooden, an uneasy marriage of the English and the classical. She located a man becoming a stag, a creature whose tortured energy of metamorphosis was something like that of the foliate men in Southwell Minster: stretched sinews, hardening distorted feet, spreading rib-cage, branching horns, creamy-furred dewlap and opening muzzle-mouth under a human brow.

"Actaeon," said well-educated Frederica.

"Right," said Crowe. "This wall depicts the tale of Diana and

Actaeon. The other is about Venus hunting the errant Cupid. Over the hearth, you see, the two goddesses meet, Cupid is tamed and berated and Actaeon is neatly butchered. The whole thing is in my view a continual allegory. Much livelier than most English plaster. Look at the pretty goddesses."

Frederica looked at the pretty goddesses. They appeared and re-appeared in scenes which melted into each other, giving the repeated concrete figures a multiplicity or ubiquity. Diana stood high-breasted, thin, tall, in a circular pool amongst bulrushes with human Actaeon peering behind a boulder. The observer's eye was behind the observing hunter, and could thus see the human muscles on his shoulders and buttocks. In the next scene the irate goddess and a bevy of delicate-muscled maidens overlooked the change from man to beast and then followed the long hunt, dog-feet, girl-feet, horse-hooves flowing like white vertical waves through white flowers and white tree-stems whilst Cupid appeared and reappeared with his toy bow and the goddess leaped, took aim, and reappeared in the next clearing. Towards the hearth a procession of maidens bore the dead weight of the broken body swinging from long poles to where the goddesses, triumphant, in pallid pleats and floral garlands sat throned, hand in hand, above the fireplace.

On the other side of the room, in a style much less fluid and more artificial, Venus awoke in a forest bedchamber, its walls made of ambiva-lently decorative white trees or pillars with foliate heads. She flew off in a dove-drawn chariot, alighted in a tiny walled city on a pastoral hill where peasants and miniature sheep and cows pointed to white wounds to show her son had passed and vanished. Venus was more rounded than Diana and wore her elaborately woven girdle over exiguous garments through the fine lines of which her limbs swelled prettily. Wherever she stood white flowers budded from the earth and fell through the white air in sprigs and posies. Her face had a smiling calm as Diana's had a cold one: together, at the end, amongst formalised wreckage of weeping, bleeding nymphs, victims of Cupid's arrows, and the stiff deer-man laid out for the knife, they were somewhat disturbing. Frederica said so. Crowe said she was right, and that it was his belief that they were an oblique commentary on the attitude of Elizabeth to Johanna Seale, daughter of the house, whose fate had been much like that of Bess Throckmorton. Virginity and venery had destroyed that lady, who had died young, brought to bed of a second son, most unwisely conceived during her imprisonment. There was a loyal icon of the Queen herself over the entrance to the Hall, opposite the god-desses, which was apposite to Alexander's play and might interest Frederica.

Frederica stared up at this altogether more cluttered, less delicate creature, and observed that the queen seemed to be squatting.

"Indeed she does. That's partly an effect of foreshortening. But mostly because her garment is the map of England which necessitates some squashing and extending of the body. You see Land's End fluttering beyond her left knee. And Scotland knotted over her left shoulder. Related to Drayton's Polyolbion frontispiece, of course."

"The cornucopia," Frederica began unguardedly, "seems to be coming out from between her legs from her . . ."

"I take that to be the Thames Estuary. Centre of commerce. This is Elizabeth as Virgo-Astraea. Astraea, last of the immortals, goddess of Justice, ascended to heaven in the iron age and became conflated with the zodiacal Virgo. She acquired Libra's scales, but also Virgo's harvest-attributes, since Virgo and Libra are the signs of harvest."

"I know. I was born under Virgo. August 24th, St Bartholomew."

"An unexpected conjunction of portents."

"I don't believe in all that."

"She was born under Virgo, Elizabeth. It's arguable that Virgo and the Virgin Mary are quite closely related to much nastier savage harvest-deities – Cybele, Diana of Ephesus, Astarte."

"Birkin's Moon."

"But his icons are so *forced* don't you think, when you see this?" Frederica stared dutifully up at Elizabeth-Polyolbion-Virgo-Astraea. Because of its squat position the figure, partly absurd, had a craggy, chthonic, amorphous presence, more primitive than the nymphs and goddesses with their neat spherical breasts. Under its literally landscaped draperies it was heavy and exuberant, castle-crowned. The left hand held a naked sword; the scales of justice depended from the right; the cornucopia rose powerful and huge, a stiff curving horn, a river of plenty, between the monumental knees, spilling to its earth and along the architrave a cascade of plaster flowers and fruit, ears of corn and gilded apples.

This was not the end of Frederica's aesthetic education. All of them were taken, willy-nilly, on a guided tour of the State Bedrooms. These were cosmologically named, Sun, Moon and Planets, opening into each other, each containing a huge curtained bed under an elaborately painted ceiling. These large and draughty rooms had several entrances and exits, leading to closets, corridors and landings. Crowe bustled, somewhere between housekeeper, art historian and slave-driver, his arms heaped with the protective paper that hid the bedspreads, embroidered by the unfortunate Johanna Seale, from the light. In the Moon room these, and the hangings, had silver crescents on blue: Crowe pushed open the shutters and let in a little pale, cold, doubtful sunshine. All the bed-chambers had plasterwork by the imaginative English Master of classical metamorphosis. In the Moon room this depicted the doings of Diana: the deaths of Niobe's children and Hippolytus, the changing of Egeria to a spring of water. The ceiling, as Crowe said, unfortunately dominated things: a baroque innovation, it depicted in strange perspective the descent of Cynthia down the domed heaven to Endymion sleeping in his cave.

Wilkie said, "I wonder how long since anyone made love in those beds? Rather a grand experience, I should think."

"They'd have been very cold at night," said Thomas Poole. "Even with a fire, and all those hangings."

"I should think," said Frederica, "if you bounced on that you'd raise vast puffs of dust. I should think if you shut yourself in those curtains you'd get claustrophobia. I should think with the room being a kind of thoroughfare you'd be quite put off."

"The ceiling was no doubt designed to put you on," said Crowe.

"Not me," said Frederica robustly and personally, who had never exactly been put on to make love to anyone. "All those roundy slabs of pinky-brown flesh, and that awful flat unreal blue, and sickly rosy clouds. That flesh has an awful baked look, or half-baked, you wouldn't want to touch."

Wilkie stared into the trompe-l'œil dome and after a moment took off his glasses. When he turned to Frederica she was startled to see that his eyes, which she had imagined were bright blue like his lenses, were in fact chocolate-brown. He blinked. She blinked. He said:

"It was an Italian artist. That's not English flesh, nor English light. The shadows are too sharp, the light's too thin and intense, those browns and pinks aren't part of our landscape. English eroticism isn't rich blue and terracotta. Or carne cotta. It's sylvan and aqueous. We expect to look through mists into depths. The English Arcadia is brakes and thickets and watery obscurity. Ho for the greenwood and the midnight clearing in *Women in Love*, or Lady Chatterley's naked lover rushing around in the pelting rain in the forest."

"Mystic palpable real otherness," said Frederica, producing her most-mocked quotation, quite aptly. "No thank you."

In the Sun room Mrs Bryce said her feet hurt, sat down on a carved chest and rubbed her arches. Reed and Braithwaite, enjoying themselves, scooped up papers from the resplendent fiery bed. Crowe pointed out the plaster Daphne, amongst the loves of Apollo, the plasterer's master-piece in his view, so very English, sprouting leaves on knobby joints, human veins starting and spreading into leaf veins, the arrested leaping

legs thrust down into roots, the funny little face like an ancient English
elf, not a Greek nymph. Miss Yeo quoted Marvell. Not as a nymph but
for a tree. Reed and Braithwaite chanted about vegetable love and its
vast growth. Crowe got hold of Frederica's elbow and directed her
gaze at the ceiling.

"Better than next door. Jacopo I suspect was not profoundly inspired
by women. But this."

The ceiling depicted the death of Hyacinth. It was in doubtful taste,
if that was the way to describe the curious discomfort that overtook
most who looked at it. The pale gold naked sungod, his golden locks
elaborately dressed on his narrow shoulders knelt with his arms spread
wide in horror or erotic adoration above the limp, idealised, bleeding
brown body of the boy, whose redder blood stained the red sand in
pleasing swirls and was already blossoming at the edges of its pools,
into hyacinths, purply crimson on the scarlet and terra-cotta. The god's
head was poised, contemplating his work, on one side. The lids were
dropped over the eyes, so that he peered through narrow slits, the wide
mouth was stretched and down-drooping, slightly parted in that
ambivalent expression that might be pure pain or pure pleasure, a mask
of extreme feeling, frozen.

Crowe gripped tighter.

"Look at the line – the inner line of Apollo's thighs, and the way they
echo the boy's. Look at the mindlessness of both those faces, and the
line of the head in the blood, the repeated curves –"

"He's dead," said Frederica. It seemed important to establish that he
was dead.

"Death and sexual ecstasy were interchangeable images."

"Still are," said Wilkie. "People do look like that. Dead or ecstatic."

He spoke with authority. Frederica had no wish to ask him how he
knew. Crowe went on.

"Note the different perspective. Next door's world's enclosed in a
regularly lit dome. Here the desert horizon stretches well away beyond
the edges of easy vision – the eye has to travel, it can't rest and take it
in. And in this formless desert the central group is wholly formed,
wholly composed. Look how precisely the flower-petals echo those
glittering droplets of gore on his flank – with the droplet shape reversed
in the flower. The whole thing's a pyramid made up of little segments
going up or down, like these drops – look at Apollo's hair, the apex,
the repeated curls and kinks. My theory is that it's all a deliberate image
of the cycle of generation and regeneration under the sun – the blood
drops into the soil, the flowers spring up . . ."

"Blue flesh," said Wilkie, removing the goggles again. "Allowing for the after-image of these things. A lot of paradoxical cold reds, painted over blues, too."

"He has a cruel mouth," said Frederica.

"He was a cruel god," said Crowe. "His stories are cruel stories. You shall see my little Marsyas, last of all. This god didn't kill the boy, but look how Boreas, who did, over there, echoes his posture. Last of all, note the subsidiary groups of figures. Art historians label 'em nymphs and shepherds but I think that's highly unlikely. My view is that the lot in the right – the ones formally dancing – are the Muses – 'his choir, the Nine' – you know – and those on the left, rather *obscurely* leaping around and gesticulating, are the initiates, the young men who celebrated Hyacinth, or Adonis, or Thammuz or whoever with orgies of self-mutilation and so on. You see the whole thing's an infinity symbol – an elongated 8 on its side if you look – follow the arms and bodies through-crossing through Apollo and Hyacinth in the centre, where their bodies – ah – almost touch. Jacopo was quite a student of arcana and neo-Platonic mysteries. Here we have Apollo as principle of order and disorder, art and destruction. Resurrection and so on. Florid with a hard shape underneath."

"How obscene," said Wilkie to Frederica, who giggled.

Alexander and Jennifer had managed to get left behind beneath the visiting moon. They stood in tacit agreement at opposite sides of the room until the last straggler, who was Thomas Poole, came in, opened his mouth to address Alexander, thought better of it, and hurried on.

Alexander stood inside the window, looking out over herb-garden, kitchen-garden, high walls, to the moor beyond, with its blown, tumbled, sharp-legged sheep.

"Jenny. Come over here."

"You come over here and look at this bed." They stood, side by side, peering solemnly at its convex silk surface. "You are always saying, if only we had a bed. Here is a *monstrous* bed."

Alexander agreed that it was. His hand found hers, in the small of her back. They stood enlaced.

"I should push you," he said, "ever so gently over, and take up your feet, so, and take off your shoes, and let down your hair . . . and then take off everything else – quite quietly . . . and spread you out . . ."

"And stand and stare whilst I shivered in the middle of all this space."

"No, no. I would . . . I would . . ." He could have written it. He could not speak it.

"You would do such things. I know, I know. We've been through all that. But we don't, do we?"

"We shall. There are months ahead –"

"No, no. We must either give up, or –"

"Or –" said Alexander.

"Or get married. Then we could –"

"Married." He contemplated the moving curtains. He realised he supposed Jennifer was not good at marriage. He drew her closer. He was very nervous of being seen. He pulled her rather roughly behind the bed-curtain. He kissed her.

Footsteps clattered. They sprang apart. Alexander pointed up at the ceiling and said the first line which came into his head.

"And thee returning on thy silver wheels."

"Oh yes, Tennyson," said Frederica with a chuckle of irrelevant complicity. "I always used to suppose that was about a statue on castors, not a chariot, silly fool I was. I've been sent to get you both, Mr Crowe wants to lock this wing and take us into his own turret he's going to have when the students come. To see his Marsyas, he says. Personally, not being in the habit of sightseeing, I don't know if I can take any more. Anyway, I'm here."

Crowe's little wing, if not as hugely grand as the staterooms, was still palatial. He gave the cast tea in his study, a panelled dark room, in which only the little Marsyas was directly lit, and that Frederica took at first for a murky and obscure crucifixion. Crowe explained, with glee, that it was Jacopo's subtlest and nastiest work, not, like Raphael's Marsyas, an image of the animal strung up to await the divine flaying that would produce high art, but like Ovid's Marsyas an image of pain on the point of disintegration, the body after flaying but still, for a brief moment, holding its terrible shape. The furry pelt was extended on the ground, the flesh and laced muscles were exposed, and gouts of blood were bursting out under the muscles, so that what had appeared at first glance to have the firmness of marble was running and slippery, bulging, about to burst into formlessness. Carved horn pipes lay cast aside: in the middle distance Apollo smiled his terrible empty smile and struck his lyre.

Crowe put his arm round Frederica's shoulder.

"What do you make of that?"

"I don't like it."

"It is very painful. It is lovely. It is the moment of the birth of the new consciousness. Marsyas cried out to Apollo: *quid me mihi detrahis.* Why do you tear me from myself. And Dante prayed to be so torn. Apollo should deal with him 'si come quando Marsia traesti: Della vagina delle membre sue.' As when thou didst tear Marsyas from the sheath of his members. A metamorphosis, yet again. The shining butterfly of the soul from the pupa of the body. Lava, pupa, imago. An image of art."

"It's repulsive," said Frederica. "I don't want art if it has to be so nasty. Thank you."

"You still feel oppressed by my beautiful house?"

"Oh, more so. But more interested."

"In what way?"

She considered, casting a now cold eye on the hanging satyr.

"Well – before I looked at it, it seemed amazing but unreal. And now I have looked, it seems amazing and too real. But I do want a good long walk in the open air."

Crowe laughed and released her. He said, "You must come and look again. You must familiarise yourself with all this."

14. *Cosmogony*

At Blesford Ride, what most schools would have called the Sanatorium was called the Nursery. It was presided over by a stout Sister in not quite clean starched white, who wore a cap like a winged helmet, a row of scissors and pens across the swell of her breast, and a vigorous greying moustache. Her prescription for most upsets was darkness and starvation, which she called giving the brain and stomach a little rest. Most boys, after an hour or two of privation, more or less miraculously recovered and asked for release. Marcus was often in, with asthma and headaches. He did not ask to be let out.

After the light and the Bilge Lab Marcus tried weakly to erase God and Lucas Simmonds from his consciousness. He did not read Simmonds's pamphlet. He went the other way if he saw Simmonds in school corridors. He sought company before crossing the playing fields, or walked round. He had headaches with lights flashing just behind his head, neither in nor out. He did not throw the pamphlet away, but he kept it in his desk.

One day, in a maths lesson, Marcus looked out and saw light moving on the tops of a row of lime trees on the horizon. He looked again, and saw it gathering and dancing. A bird went up in sunlight and flung sparklings and sprinklings of brilliance in the air. Marcus, greening, thrust a blind hand in his desk, seized the papers, put up his hand, and asked to be excused on account of migraine.

In the Nursery, Sister tissocked her teeth, opened cold sheets on a high iron bed, watched him climb in and pulled down the green blind. The wooden acorn rattled on the sill. The room was in submarine gloom. Marcus drew up his knees to his chin, and did not look at the splinters of white light round the edges of the blind. Sister rustled out, closing him in.

He was visited by brief visions. Light, the glassy hyaline rising like a sea and drowning him. Himself clasping Simmonds's grey flannel knees and howling like an animal. Nothing else he called up seemed substantial or possible.

Sister had put the papers in his bedside locker. He rolled over, let up the blind a cautious half-inch, and began to peruse them.

Marcus had not, as Eliot said of James, a mind so fine that no idea could violate it. In a sense, however, all ideas appeared to him to be of the same weight as each other: he made no judgments about their possible truth or untruth: his response to them was not so much an intellectual as a near-perceptual planning of their coherence or incoherence, as he mapped the squares and possible moves on a chess board. His sense of coherence with verbal structures was also less acute than his response to visual, or mathematical forms. He assumed, without formulating the assumption, that words were crude indicators anyway and their messages only approximations at best. So he skimmed Simmonds's pamphlet as he might, in his youthful eidetic days, have skimmed a picture he was offered of fields or streets or shoals in waterways, simply as a kind of neural reconnaissance to aid memory. If his reading, even in this neutrally cognitive form, was also at fault because he had no knowledge of other texts from which Simmonds had patchworked his theory of the universe, this was counterbalanced by the fact that he was reading Simmonds. He was indeed, in that sense, Simmonds's only reader, though he had no desire, unlike every other person in this story, to prove his skill at reading people.

The Plan and the Pattern was concerned to describe the interrelated wholes, indifferently named organisms or organisations, of which infinity was made up. There were three infinities: the Infinitely Great, the Infinitely Small, the Infinitely Complex. Some sort of weighting of value of things seemed to be attached to degrees of the last Infinity. E.g., "The further we proceed up the Scale of Matter, from minerals to vegetables, from vegetables to animals, from animals to Man and creatures more complex than Man, so it becomes truly manifest that the corpuscles that compose matter, atoms, electrons, protons, neutrons, tend to group themselves in ever more complex ways to form ever more complex compound Bodies.

"In respect of Complexity a living Body is superior to an inanimate Body since an arrangement of cells is more complex than an arrangement of molecules. An ant is therefore superior to the physical Being of the sun.

"On this Planet there is no more complex organism than the human brain.

"The whole Organisation of the Life of the Earth can be regarded as a sensitive film called the Biosphere stretched over the earth's solid surfaces. This with the Lithosphere (the solid earth) the Hydrosphere (the liquid globe) and the Atmosphere (the gaseous envelope) make up the four aspects of this physical globe. I say nothing yet of the Mental Globe.

"The view that the Biosphere should be regarded as a living entity with its own Inner-Togetherness has been advanced by many biologists and geologists since Süss first formulated the theory that was later developed by Vernadsky.

"Such a view is a challenge to our simply stratified view of existence, for it entails no less than a total reversal of our Megalanthropic, Anthropocentic belief that Man is the highest order of Being given to us in sense-perception. If the Biosphere is a living Creature, then we men are parts of its physical organism or organisation, and indeed parts so small as to stand in much the same ratio of size and number as does the single cell and the living body of man.

"If we hypothetically regard Mankind as the brain-cells of the Biosphere the numerical coincidence is indeed striking. It is estimated that in the human brain there are 3,000,000,000 cells which is equal to the expected human population of the earth in 2000 AD. Moreover there are some 10,000,000,000,000 ordinary cells in the body, which figure agrees with a reasonable estimate of the number of metazoan animals on the surface of the Earth . . ."

Marcus felt some vague doubt about Simmonds's hypothetical Scale of Matter, but felt attracted to the idea that his consciousness was only one cell in a vast interconnected system of apprehension. That made both the graph paper vision and the intrusive and excessive light more tolerable. He skipped some more dubiously related figures and analogies between human cells and created birds and beasts and arrived at Lucas Simmonds's theory of Mental Evolution as the successor to the Darwinian kind.

"The physical surface, the outside of matter, evolved to a certain point and produced Man. Scientific observers since Darwin looking for observable mutations that could be said to be evidence of continuing evolutionary processes have been unable to produce anything convincing. This is because the species has now achieved its ultimate physical form and identity. The struggle for existence and the process of development have transferred themselves to the Mental Sphere. Thus the developed Biosphere is in its turn contained inside an even denser layer of Thought. This layer is the Noussphere, the Earth-Mind. It would seem reasonable to suppose that the present Goal of Existence is the transference of Material Energy into Mental Energy. Thus Man, and drawn steadily after him, the whole of the lower creation, will be transfigured into pure Mind. Thus the phenomenon of entropy, the loss of tangential material energy in the terrestrial globe through the giving-off of heat in every new operation of matter, can be seen, not as a threat to our survival, but as a working-out of a higher purpose, a necessary operation in the realisation of a Plan.

"It is reasonable also to suppose that other celestial bodies and organisations available and unavailable to us in sense-perception have nousspheres or entelechies, dimly figured in the Living Creatures of the Apocalypse perhaps, or in the crude representations of angels, archangels and so on, or as C. S. Lewis has intelligently propounded through Science Fiction in the giving of names of pagan Deities however clouded by anthropomorphism to the Souls or Nouspheres of the other planets of our solar system."

When the work came to God Marcus discovered that Simmonds's habit of referring to this by a cipher was not, as he had supposed, facetiousness, but an attempt to de-anthropomorphise the Space-Filling Universal Mind which was represented in the text by G. G was the organiser of all organisations, the Planner of a Pattern which was "actualised" according to certain Laws. Marcus found the descriptions of the operations of G considerably harder to follow than the hypotheses of biospherology.

"All our minds can be seen as aspects or particles of G. G is streaked with all minds' world-lines like the Tulip, or the dawn-sky, but does not depend upon these flickerings for its existence: without G they would not be. It is the goal of Mental Activity, human, subhuman and superhuman, to reach fuller awareness of G.

"The Plan springs directly from G. The Plan is the Idea, the perfect and total Idea of the Maker, towards which the whole creation strives. Pattern is the actualisation in Time and Space of parts of the Plan. The Plan and the Pattern stand to one another as Male and Female principles, the former affirming and potent, the latter denying and actual. The sun must be looked on, not as the mother of the planets, producing these out of her own substance, but as the Father impregnating the unformed planetary material with the Plan, the shining Light, of his own genetic constitution."

There followed several very specific pages of scientific "facts" which Marcus had trouble with. They concerned an analysis of proteins as pattern-carriers; there were many millions of distinct protein-structures present in living organisms but these were only "an almost vanishingly small proportion of the total number of proteins chemically *possible*".

Even a simple protein made up of 20 amino-acids, Simmonds exclaimed, each occurring once, would give about 2,400,000,000,000,000,-000 different compounds, each containing the same amino-acids in identical proportions and differing only in their space relations. He went on to the genetic coding transmitted by sperm (a hundred-millionth of body-weight) and ovum: the development of the complex eye from the small number of undifferentiated protein compounds present in the sperm. Marcus, faced with figures, was troubled by weak links of coherence: his attention was focused again by a peroration on Life as a Cosmic Reconciling Force.

"But how few Men are aware of their true nature or function! Most men are hardly raised above the level of self-awareness of the Species seen in other mammals. A cow is like a machine. She can be only what she is, the actualisation of the pattern, Cow, which irrefragably includes only a rudimentary self-awareness. The grass and the lettuce she converts to her body-matter have of course no self-awareness at all. A Man should struggle to fulfil his potentiality. An ordinary Man may act from deliberate choice perhaps 10,000 times in the course of his life. If we compare this with the 100,000,000,000 involuntary or reflex actions that his organism will have performed during the same period we must be bound to conclude that self-direction is a power that is scarcely ever exercised in Man.

"The highest grade of self-awareness transcends of course any individual or species and is present in any entity able to be aware of the Pattern of life itself: i.e. entities such as biospheres.

"In existence beyond Life, the existence is the Pattern, without interference from denying actuality. In G the existence is the Plan, not actualised in any form of matter. Life is response to an affirming Plan. But existence beyond Life is affirmation itself. The earth is what it affirms and the sun likewise. The difference between one supra-animate level and another consists qualitatively in the degree of freedom that resides in the power to create its own pattern and affirmation rather than receiving the imprint of a higher order.

"It is precisely because the sun is less actualised than the earth that it is freer in respect of affirmation. The galaxy in its turn is freer than the sun, but by far the greater part of its existence remains purely potential".

When Marcus had got through these exhortations, and further similar ones, he pulled down the blind and curled up, knees to chin. He went into a heavy, deliberate dreamless sleep which, like the spreading, was something he had always been able to do. When he woke, Simmonds's writings had settled in a pattern in his mind, a harmless pattern of spheres and informing lines of protista and purposeful light. He decided, on balance, to do nothing. If Simmonds was right, nothing need be done.

This proved to be so. Three days later, slurring his feet through the cloisters, he caught sight of the familiar white hem. The grey legs paced and stopped. Marcus looked up. Simmonds, pinkly severe, beckoned and Marcus followed.

"We meet again," Simmonds stated. "You have read my work."

"Yes."

"So you now have some inkling of the importance of the task that confronts us. We must be very intelligent. Part of our task is to discover the true nature of the task, the modes of consciousness we must explore. I have various pilot schemes in mind. I believe in being eclectic. We will undergo various traditional contemplative exercises. Also we will practise direct transmission of thought. From each to each, and through us maybe to the Noussphere direct. Sit down, boy, and I will explain. The first thing is to learn – which is hard, very hard – to *clear your mind* . . ."

Marcus sat down. He folded his thin hands, one in the other, and bent his head submissively. Lucas's words, increasing in speed and number, fell gratefully, disturbing the unruffled surface of a mental pool only too often clear and empty.

There was no one there to reflect on the irony involved in his protecting himself from vacancy with Simmonds's endless discourse about clearing away the clutter and rubble of dead words and language, in his protecting himself from silence with Simmonds's cheerful flow of talk about the silence they would achieve together.

PART II: A FLOWERY TALE

'Dawn of the Year'

The Times, Monday, April 6th, 1953

The complex cycle of the calendar has brought Easter back to its natural and primeval place in the year; for the Gregorian fifth of April – March 25 of the unreformed chronology – is Old New Year's Day, a feast now habitually held in honour only by Commissioners of Inland Revenue. It emphasizes the meaning of the first bank holiday of the year, which, even though the forecast speaks of cold winds, snow and thunder, marks for the Englishman the moment when he turns his back upon wintry thoughts. Alone among the recurring annual holidays, this makes a clean-cut break with what has gone before, contrasting most markedly with Christmas, which comes as the climax of weeks of mounting preparation. For the townsman at any rate Easter generally means the sudden discovery that the annual miracle of the spring has come upon him unawares. Emerging from city streets where the seasons have for months dragged so sluggishly as to seem unchangeable, he finds in the country that all the signs of rebirth have burst upon him together – the daffodils nodding in the breeze and the primroses glimmering by the roadside, new buds breaking, birds in full song. Life so long apparently suspended in darkness and stagnation is suddenly urgent, buoyant, burgeoning again. The signal has been given, and the human routine changes in time and tune with the revival of nature.

"Old" and "young" – they are terms taken from the measure of human life and inevitably so. There is no pathetic fallacy here for we are part of the order of eternal change that we observe and on which we moralize. There can have been no time, since the human mind became capable of compassing abstract ideas at all, when man did not see in the passing of the seasons an image of himself.

> Whose flowering pride, so fading and so fickle
> Short *Time* shall soon cut down with his consuming sickle.

Assuredly Glaucus the son of Hippolochus beneath the walls of Troy was uttering no original thought in that most lovely simile of the falling of the autumn leaves and their rebirth in the spring, which HOMER bequeathed to VIRGIL from whom DANTE took it over to pass it on to MILTON. The more we pore over the half-deciphered runes of pre-history, the more we are forced to conclude that primitive man, as he saw himself, not merely shared the destiny of the dry husk that fell into the earth, but mysteriously *was* that seed in its mortality and in its potency, and so was also the green shoot springing up again in the dawning of the year. Whole societies have been built upon the conception, for the parallel extends itself beyond and through the life of the individual to the life of the family and of the tribe and of the nation.

In this springtime above all the primeval imagery should have for us its richest meaning; for the Coronation is the nation's feast of mystical renewal. We have passed through a grey and melancholy winter, dark with natural disaster, darkened also in the symbolical-personal orbit wherein our society revolves by the recent loss of a beloved QUEEN. But the spring comes with its annual message that all disasters and losses can be transcended by the unconquerable power of new life. As a nation, as a Commonwealth, we take as our supremely representative person our young QUEEN, and in her inauguration dedicating the future by the ancient forms, we declare our faith that life itself rises out of the shadow of death, that victory is wrested out of the appearances of failure, that the transfiguration of which our nature is capable is not a denial of our temporal evanescence but the revelation of its deepest meaning. It may be

> that all things stedfastnes doe hate
> And changed be: yet being rightly wayd
> They are not changed from their first estate;
> But by their change their being doe dilate:
> And turning to themselves at length againe,
> Doe worke their owne perfection so by fate:
> Then over them change doth not rule and reigne;
> But they raigne over change, and doe their states maintaine.

15. Easter

Easter, in that year of extremes, was freakish, especially in the North. In the north-west there was heavy snow, in places, on Good Friday, and on Easter Monday there were hailstorms. In Calverley and Blesford black sleet alternated with glassy sun.

The play people temporarily vanished. Felicity Wells turned her attention from carnation ribbons to the decoration of the dear little Easter garden in the nave of St Bartholomew's. Alexander bought and rode away in a second-hand silver grey Triumph. He also bought the new gramophone record of T. S. Eliot reading the *Four Quartets*. Frederica managed by furious concentration and an assumption of pupil-to-master virtue to borrow this to play during the school holidays. She then played it repeatedly, in a talismanic manner, until everyone in that unmusical household was driven to a frenzy of irritation by the repeated rhythms.

On Easter Day Stephanie decided to go to church. She found herself a hat, to observe the proprieties, a half-melon of navy velvet with a wisp of veiling. Under this, preceded by a wavering circle of scarlet umbrella, she fought her way across tombstones and wet grass.

She might have come to church anyway without the problem of Daniel. She might have come to please Felicity. She might have come because she liked to take part in the ceremonies of the year. At other Easters she had dyed eggs, cochineal crimson, onion-skin gold, and had travelled to mining villages to see eggs on trestle tables in the upper rooms of pubs, tie-dyed, boiled with ferns and lace doileys, boiled with lurid socks and old club ties, beetroot, wax and gentians. Bill liked the eggs, but never went near Easter in Church. Stephanie had taken both as they came. This year was different. She was angry with Daniel. She had come to take a look at him, there, in the Church. Where he belonged.

He had upset her. He had pushed his consecrated huge face between her knees and trembled. He had declared passion and told her to go home and disregard it. He had involved her in his jumble of tea-party politeness, dead stories and ceremonial: he had made her feel like a professional cock-teaser. When he saw her in Church he would see she was sorry and respectful. When she saw him in Church she would know for certain it was all ridiculous; she could wipe her feet of it, after, in the Church porch.

One of her own Fourth form handed her a prayer-book: she sat down at the back, against a pillar, and watched Miss Wells come in, fluttering chiffon scarves in various pinks, depending from a dish-shaped hat and bursting like bedraggled butterflies out at the neck and between the buttons of her rat-coloured gabardine. The next people to come in were her brother Marcus, and a young man she vaguely recognised, and then placed, as the curious biology chap who had once, at a school Christmas do, repeatedly asked her to dance, and had left large sweaty hand-prints on the back of a pale evening dress. Simmonds bowed and smiled to everyone and then ushered Marcus into a pew, like a hen with a chicken, a chamberlain with a prince.

Stephanie was profoundly shocked to see them both genuflect and cross themselves. What was this? How long had it been going on? Marcus had not seemed to see her, but then he never did.

The organ wheezed, raised itself, crashed. The choir marched and shuffled in, singing with a shrill effect that was damped by the weight of unstirred air in the arches of the roof. With them, a heavy shepherd, came Daniel, in a surplice. These were followed by Mr Ellenby, who was to speak for his Easter offering. Daniel's expression did not match the jubilee of the music. His black brows met across his nose: he looked as though he was about to embark on the commination service. She could pick out his voice, a rough bass, in tune but not harmonious. His exertions seemed directed to making a heavy beat to align other singers. She did not attempt to sing herself.

He did not look, as she had supposed, perhaps feared, he might, silly. Nor did he seem, as she had also imagined he might, to burn with spiritual energy. She had come to see that energy directed: she had come to watch him pray. But he looked as he always did, black, fleshy, solid, with the white cambric a flimsy and extraneous bib. She smiled to herself at this thought. And whilst she was smiling, he saw her. He looked at her and frowned deeper, with the electric rigidity of shock: he turned away. Then slowly, above dog-collar and snowy pleats he flushed red and hot, blood flaming through the dark jowl to cheekbone and brow. She felt caught out in a lapse of taste. More hailstones rattled on stained glass.

They sang, rose, kneeled, chanted, murmured, confessed. Her dislike of Christianity hardened like ice. She realised she had half-hoped to share what was ancient and inherited. Christmas moved her. O Come All Ye Faithful, especially in Latin, left her with real regret at her exclusion from faith and community. The difficult birth in bad weather, the golden angels singing in snow, the word within a word unable to speak a word, this she would have liked to have, feeling excluded from the heat and light in the stable by redundant rationalism. But the dead man walking in the new morning in the garden left her cold. The congregation rendered psalms in that combination of speech and song, grutching and sharp as chalk skidding on blackboard, wailing, toneless, patient, dismal, English. She was repelled.

Perhaps there was something particularly unpleasant about English Easter. It had not been possible to graft Eastern blood rites and dismembered God on to English Spring as it had been possible to bring together Northern celebrations of the winter solstice, moving star, evergreen tree, ox, ass, shining messenger and stone-frozen land. There was a hot, barbaric quality about the lessons for Easter Day which had nothing at all to do with pussy-willow and lemony floss chickens, although it might possibly have related to forgotten druidic atrocities. The lesson from Exodus was about the Paschal lamb and the god who flew over in the night and slaughtered the first-born men and beasts. It gave instructions for smearing blood on doorposts and for slaughtering and broiling the immaculate offering. The second lesson, from Apocalypse, presented Alpha and Omega, first and last, the Son of Man white like wool, white like snow, with flaming eyes like fire and feet like fine brass burned in a furnace. The scarlet and white woolliness of the souls washed in blood had mystified and appalled generations of men, and Englishmen. But it was alien. Birth was a real miracle, Stephanie's cold mind ran on, and resurrection would be a greater one, if believed, but the blood we drink, the shadowy, temporary Form outside the spiced tomb, are neither believed nor needed as the song of the heavens at the Birth is believed and needed. Our Green Knights sprouted new heads on riven shoulders, their startled veins ran new blood, Langland's Christ harrowed Hell like any hero visiting the underworld and returning scatheless. But those were Christmas again. English Easter tried to graft to the imagery of cleansing ritual slaughter the renewal of sap, the bounding of Wordsworthian lambs, the emergence from smooth sealed eggs of fluffy chicks, living gold from stone. But the English mind was secretly horrified by glassy sea, crystal walls, white wool, brass feet and throne of the New Jerusalem where Spring would never come again because there was neither grass nor winter.

Mr Ellenby preached on St Paul. He assured his congregation that if Christ had not risen there would be no Church and they themselves would be condemned to eternal death. If after the manner of men, said Mr Ellenby, adjusting his glasses, licking his dry lips, I have fought with beasts at Ephesus, what advantageth it me, if the dead rise not? Let us eat and drink; for tomorrow we die. A terrible saying, said Mr Ellenby, beating his fist on the stone edge of his pulpit, smiting it, if we were not assured that Christ is alive *now*, that the natural processes, so terrible, were thwarted and changed, a dead heart beat and dead feet walked, decomposition was stayed and reversed, and therefore we rejoice, in fear, because we too live forever. The people nodded and smiled as they nodded and smiled annually, and Stephanie felt every stage of rejection, from embarrassed discourtesy to frozen hate.

After the service Mr Ellenby and Daniel stood at the door and shook each parting parishioner by the hand. She knew by now that she should not have come; that Daniel knew she had come to look at him praying; she tried to linger. She strayed over to Miss Wells's Easter garden, around which a knot of people had gathered, exclaiming at its prettiness.

It was heaped up and landscaped on carefully chosen pieces of local limestone and granite, the interstices padded with wet earth and turfed with strips of moss. The tomb was a squared wigwam of leaning slates: inside it linen handkerchiefs were carefully rolled and disposed as cerecloths. Outside, a pottery angel with a silver wire halo leaned a little uncertainly against a sprig of hawthorn, its hands clasped in prayer or rapture. At the top of the hummock Christ, also porcelain, stood in pale blue and blessed the air with pallid hands. Lower down, Mary Magdalene, darker blue, followed his upwards progress along a spangled trail of snapped heads of primroses and aubretia. Round a little pond, made of mirror glass, stood clumps of spring flowers, snowdrops, wood anemones, aconites, their stems encased in cotton wool in meat paste pots beneath the stones. Scyllas as tall as Christ himself nodded open-mouthed over the stones above him. Stephanie was reminded of the dolls in *Two Bad Mice* who leaned against the dresser and smiled and smiled. The children had placed offerings round the periphery: shells of eggs, thrush, blackbird, plover, a few floss chickens with sharp wire feet. Miss Wells begged Stephanie, as once before, to smell the honey and wine of the primroses: she did so, and there was the smell again, pure honey, pure wine, cold earth.

A new voice reminded her of other problems. Lucas Simmonds inserted his shoulder beside hers and made a way for himself: he thanked Miss Wells, as though she had made it for his benefit, for the little pretty garden, greeted Stephanie and remarked that it had been a very happy service, he thought.

Stephanie had nothing to say. Even more than the china Christ and angel, Lucas Simmonds smiled and smiled. Involuntarily she caught Marcus's eye. As Daniel had blushed, so Marcus paled. His hands were pleating his trouser-leg along his thigh. It was the first time she had seen him, at least apparently voluntarily, with anyone else, she realised, for as far back as she dared remember. It was the first thing, outside daily routines, she had known him *do*, since . . . Ophelia.

"Easter is a time of triumph," said Simmonds. "The Church has never fully understood the universal significance of Easter. Easter, not Christmas as is vulgarly presumed by our practices at least, Easter is the central feast of the true calendar. In it we celebrate – as we so beautifully see here emblematised in this little garden – our unity with the vegetable creation, the grass that is mown and springs up, the harvest that is sown from the gathered seed. In it too we celebrate the eternity of the Spirit, the eternity of the Species, the assurance that we shall not fail. There is something in this Feast for everyman, even those who are not of this Faith, who do not worship according to this rite. A man must worship in the time and place he finds himself in. I have not seen you here before, Miss Potter."

"No. I don't – come here."

"I am glad to see you on this occasion," said Simmonds, as though the church was his. The pontifical tone bore no relation to the painful attempts at small talk she remembered from the Blesford Ride "do".

Stephanie thought she should say something to her brother: as though to meet was natural: which, God knew, there, it was not. Simmonds said, "We must slope off, Marcus. There's work to be done!"

"On Easter Day!" protested Miss Wells.

"God's work," said Simmonds, inclining his head and pushing Marcus out of the church before him. "God's work."

Stephanie looked around the church and saw that she was now almost alone in it, with Felicity. She decided to hurry out.

In the porch, Vicar and Curate waited. Mr Ellenby took her hand in both his, said he was pleased to see her, that he hoped ... voice trailing. Daniel held out a stiff hand, touched hers.

"Good morning," he said. He looked into the church hopefully for another customer.

"Good-bye," he said, on seeing that there was none.

It had stopped raining. She strayed across the churchyard, between grassy hummocks and leaning stones, stopped to look at a bunch of daffodils thrust into a polished urn amongst marble chips. Grass, daffodils, yews, the dead, Marcus.

She wondered if she should possibly be glad Marcus had a friend. He never had had any friends; never brought anyone home. The peculiar grimness of their family life made it possible for this to have gone unremarked, as her own and Frederica's reluctance to invite friends in went unremarked. She herself had had friends. She was popular in her mild way, had gone camping with the Girl Guides. Frederica had passionate relations with girls much older or much younger than herself, which led to disaster, rebuff, or sudden distaste. But their father's unpredictable behaviour precluded bringing friends home. He might, excellent teacher, socratically quiz a young visitor, paying flattering and manipulative attention to that visitor's views and beliefs. He might just as likely be heard screaming through lath partitions that it was intolerable that no thought should be given to his need for silence to work in, or, worse, that mince had been served once too often that week already and the cook could expect to have it thrown at her.

Winifred appeared to believe that what they had was a "family life" more intense and significant than such casual entertaining, if it had even taken place, could aspire to be.

Stephanie thought: I have no idea what Marcus is like with other boys because I have never seen him with one. She thought, even if that man is making a pass at him it's almost arguable it's better than nothing at all.

But she hadn't liked Simmonds's phrase "God's work", no, it had been gnomic, public, complacent. She could have consulted Daniel, and would have done so, if sex had not confused everything. She felt uncharacteristic self-pity. She had not asked Daniel Orton to become crimson and floundering and intense and censorious. She could have co-existed with his Christianity if he'd kept his distance. She liked him and now it was spoiled. This thought and the thought of Marcus's friendless state made her sorry for herself that she was here. Cambridge had wanted to keep her: she could have paced the polished corridors of Newnham or Girton discussing Keats's prosody and the protection of clever debutantes from their sillier selves. She could have married any of five or six or probably more young men, future dons and civil servants, teachers and town clerks, even a minor landowner with a vintage Rolls Royce and an ancient monument in need of a mistress, he said. She had come back to grim bedrock because reality was *enduring* things. But was what Marcus endured, reality? Was she simply burying her one talent in the grimy soil of Blesford?

She had come back, she admitted, partly because of the young men, because she was always so very glad to get out of their beds. She couldn't have kept that up. Nor could she have kept up refusing what they seemed to want or need, on the other hand. She felt used, and that if she was, it was her own fault. If Marcus was having a weird fling she hoped at least it was bringing him some pleasure, however superficially unlikely that seemed.

She found she had walked halfway round the periphery of the church and was now standing against the vestry wall next to a water butt and compost heap, built of dead wreaths and faded bunches of flowers. Walking towards her between the tombs was Daniel, divested of the surplice. He stopped some feet away and asked peremptorily.

"Looking for someone?"

"No. Just walking up and down."

"Why did you come?"

"I don't know. To see what it was like."

"And are you satisfied?"

"Satisfied?"

"*Did* you see what it was like, then?"

"I don't know. I don't know. I didn't like it."

"I don't suppose you expected to."

"I mean, I was so convinced it was all untrue. I was miserable. Christmas means something to me – even if I don't – but all this – Christmas has its own truth."

"Things are either true or not," he said harshly. "Ultimately. Christ-

mas or Easter. Either they happened or they didn't. Either you believe
them, or you don't. They aren't pretty stories or nice metaphors, nor yet
folklore, and you know that. You don't believe a word. You shouldn't
have come here."

"You can't tell everyone not to come just because there are things
they don't believe. You'd have no one left."

"I'll be judge of that. But I'm not telling everyone. I'm telling you.
You oughtn't to have come."

He looked at the earth at his feet, ridged and grassy. His hands were
clasped behind his back.

"If you mean – I came because of you – if I did – I only came – to see
what you believed. To try and understand. Was that bad?"

He hunched his shoulders, as though his neck ached.

"I reckon it wasn't much good. *Did* you understand?"

"No." The ice hung heavy in her. She was a woman who, out of a
usual combination of sensitivity to others' feelings and moral cowardice
would put herself endlessly out in order not to offend sensibilities or
trample down firmly held beliefs. With him, she was not to be like that.
She said waspishly, "No. Truthfully, if I try to take it seriously, I find
the whole thing repellent. A tarted-up blood-sacrifice, a fairy-tale with
no evidence an historian would accept, and a kind of revolting sappiness
covering it over, like sugar. I really feel that."

"Well," he said slowly. His face closed blackly. "You knew you'd
feel that. I could've told you what you've just said. You ought to've
stayed away."

She became angry in turn.

"Is that all you have to say? You don't take me seriously, do you, it
doesn't *matter* to you what I think, we won't discuss it, oh no. You just
behave as though I'm some sort of tempter, as though all this – confusion and embarrassment – is my doing. As though I was a sin of yours.
Well, I'm not. I am –"

"All right. That's fair. I retract. It was all my doing. Because I was
slow. I should've stopped it all before it properly got going but I was
too slow. Such things hadn't happened to me before, as I told you. I
didn't rightly see how things were. Now I do, I'll manage. I'll manage."

"And what can *I* do?"

"Forget all about it. Go home."

He appeared to be deliberating with himself. He said with weighty
kindness, reassuring himself, her, neither of them, "I should be able to
take notice in time, next time. There must be a point where you can
choose things not to happen. If you watch out. There must."

She too was slow. She had used violent words and released violent feelings: any expression of anger, since she always carefully avoided it, terrified and elated her. She had committed double sacrilege, offending his feelings, breaking her own rule of mild behaviour. And he simply condescended to her. Anger filled her, and took the strange form of a desire to touch and disturb him. Morally he was right and she was indefensible. Nevertheless she took a stumbling step across the mown grave-hump, and pulled crossly, urgently at his locked hands. She was visited by a precise memory of his face on her legs. He twisted his hands sharply free.

"If this goes on," he told her, "I s'll have to leave this place altogether. Can't you see that? I don't want to."

"You treat me as though I wasn't there."

"I wish you weren't, now."

"You're as bad as you say I am. You needn't have come out here now. You could have left it as it was."

"I wanted it cleared up," he said, with dubious authority. "I've prayed, and I've thought, and I've come to see I'm paying for having thought I'd not got much in me – much private needs, much sex, and so on. I'm slow. I'm slow. But it oughtn't to do any more damage."

"You are appallingly self-centred and arrogant."

"As you've already told me. Maybe we both are. I've still got a right to ask again – what do you *want* out of this now? Why are you still here?"

"I told you."

"And I said, you shouldn't have come."

At this, she turned, and began to walk rapidly away across the grass.

Daniel, who had in fact premeditated none of what he had said, who had neither prayed, nor thought, as he said he had, who was still slightly winded by the shock of seeing her there at all, nearly growled out a command to her to stop, thought better of it, let her go. He would have liked to shake her till her teeth rattled and then bang her against the yew. Instead he kicked leaves, rusted wires of wreaths on the compost heap, tossing up coffee-coloured dead daffodils, rotting and blotched roses, shrivelled irises, in the rubbish. His serviceable shoes were wet and muddy and spattered with clinging dead petals. Looking back at the gate she saw him there, glum and substantial, grinding dead stalks into the earth.

16. Hypnagogy

Stephanie woke from a liquefying dream to a liquid sound. In the dream she was standing in a bare room, boards and plaster, by a carpenter's table on trestles, explaining to someone just out of vision that the house was well-made, very solidly made. Its window-frames were primed but not painted: the room was daylit, but when she looked out of the window she was looking into a night sky, tossing and agitated, which she slowly understood to be not sky but sea, towering heavily, blackly crested, swaying higher than her house. She went to the window and looked out, and saw, or knew, what perhaps from where she was she could not actually have seen, that the house stood on a sandbank that was already eaten away in a huge curving cantle by the advancing water. Under the window the water was lit, so that she could see the sand breaking in wet wedges, dissipating, running out in swirling currents of grains, like yellowed mist. There was a steady sound of slopping wet sand and slapping water, and an ominous creaking of wood. She woke herself just before the house shifted. The dream, she thought, was somehow the same as the one in which all one's teeth crumble and gape. She resented, also, being made to dream in biblical parables of such crude relevance. The sound, however, persisted, a wet sound, a creaking of wood.

Her room was next to Marcus's room, her bed-head, through the wall, next to his. When the sound did not stop she went out to look; there was a strip of light, under his door. She knocked. He didn't answer. She tried the handle and went in.

He was lying in bed, the reading-lamp still on. The sound was the sound of long, bubbling sobs, mixed with an intermittent creaking of the bed. She whispered his name: he did not answer: she crept nearer.

He was turning his head from side to side. His eyes were closed, screwed up as though against the sun; his brow was wrinkled; his mouth was pulled open. The whole of his face was running wet, and so was part of the pillow. As she watched, more tears burst out under his eyelids and ran down into his open mouth. His hair was wet. On the floor by the bed were papers, spread in a fan, covered with geometrical drawings and crude little pictures of stick-men, trees, buildings, connected by arrows in different colours, or chain-like links. There was also an exercise book with a label: *Hypnagogic Vision*. She did not touch the papers, but put a hand on his shoulder, and when he neither woke nor stopped weeping she sat and stroked his hair, tucking the sheet round his chin. He closed his mouth and the sobbing stopped. He sighed heavily, jerked up his knees and buried his face in the pillow, seeming to compose himself into immobile sleep. After some time she went back to her room.

Two or three nights later she heard the same sound and found him again, tear-soaked in a lit room. The next night she was woken by different sounds, scrabbling, a heavy thump. She listened for sobbing, but there was none. Instead, she heard Marcus's feet padding on his floor, and then heard his window pushed open. She went to her own window, in the dark, and saw, in the dark garden, Marcus's square of light on asphalt and black lawn. Then she saw his shadow move on the light and was afraid he meant to jump, or would fall, from the window. But he padded back again, and the light went out. She heard him going cautiously downstairs. She went back to the window and stared into the dark. After a time she made out, at the garden gate, a still hunched figure, rain-coated, waiting, white-faced in moonlight. She waited and watched. Marcus, carrying his shoes, came in stockinged feet across the flowerbeds, a hump or burden silhouetted on his shoulders. Without waiting, touching or speaking the two figures wheeled away into the dark. She went through into her brother's room. The bed was neatly made, a Biggles book, *Biggles in Moonlight*, beside the bed. Nothing else. No paper, open drawers nor pyjamas cast aside. The fear that he was sleepwalking persisted queerly in her mind. It was apparent to reason that he was not; that there had been a preconceived signal, a meeting, for which he had been ready.

She did not hear him come back, but in the morning, a little ghastly, he was at breakfast. He drank tea and ate nothing. She said nothing.

Lucas Simmonds's invention and generalship had blossomed variously and extravagantly. All moments of Marcus's consciousness, and of his own, were as far as possible docketed and recorded: dreams, visions, periods of meditation, encounters, so that any unexpectedly frequent coincidence could be isolated and concentrated on. They did not know, he observed frequently, where the field of experiment exactly *was*, so they must cast their net as wide as possible, and make the mesh as small and as diverse in design as possible, so that nothing at all that might be a sign or a message should slip through their clutches.

To someone already harassed by a combination of total recall and uncannily glittering or menacing objects-with-meanings, this could have been, and in many ways was, a covert form of torture. Days he had been able to make into ordered geometric webs of cross-referencing, black and white grids of threaded thoughts that were safe to think as pavement cracks were safe to walk on, now became technicoloured phantasmagoria of carpets, bicycles, laurel bushes, weather cocks, policemen, angels, airmen, all of whom, blue-black, gilded, hyacinthine, glossy-spotted green, might have been heavenly messengers, infernal portents, symbols of the divine Pattern which, stared at, would yield to the naked eye, to his, Marcus's, stereoscopic visionary eye, their necessary internal structures or simple messages, pullulating with coded forms, molecular, genetic, thermodynamic, which, like burning bush and God's hinder parts, would speak the keys to eternal truths by which he, Lucas Simmonds, Blesford, Calverley, England, and who knew what else, might be, would be, transfigured and illuminated.

There was, it was true, some form of protection from the horrid brilliance or vanishing deeps of these things and figures in the very fact of having to write them down. Compulsive record-keeping was a partial substitute for the geometric elegances which had protected him from things seen and unseen, before Lucas. Writing about, or even drawing things, neutralised or earthed them in a way Marcus suspected Simmonds could not know, since he suspected that for Simmonds these things had no life or significance before they were set down on paper. Simmonds could draw, professionally, with exquisite scaled detail that made Marcus's crude mnemonics, gesticulating stick-men, mapped sides of beef or washbasin vortices, look like the scrabbling or urgent invocations of some primitive creature long before Lascaux.

There were two or three days when they both saw significance in the movements of flocks of starlings which whizzed and chittered and flowed across the mussel-shell and pearly skies of that changeable Easter. Marcus tried to pattern with dots and hopping Vs the way the creatures came and went. Simmonds produced a Peter Scott-like colourwashed vision of a realistic flock of birds wheeling against a bank of marestail clouds on a vermilion and speedwell sky. They were quite excited by these drawings as a tracing of Marcus's flight-paths, rescaled, slid over Lucas's image to make a complete wheel of Marcus's interlocking funnel pattern. Lucas lent Marcus a book on the social behaviour of the starling. Marcus watched starlings, shimmering and jerking in the Far Field, stretching and snapping elastic worms, and wished to be let off.

At the same time he embarked on a detailed investigation of Marcus's visionary, or psycho-somatic, or spiritual history. This entailed a manner very different from the nervously questing attempts to partake of Marcus's vision. During these investigating sessions they sat on each side of a table. Marcus related what came into his memory, and Lucas wrote it down. In this way he elicited a detailed description of the spreading, the mathematical landscape, Ophelia and the broken wreaths, the forbidden aspects of certain articles of plumbing and architecture, the closing graph-paper cage of ether and asthma.

Marcus did not exactly like Lucas's manner during these interrogations, as he secretly thought of them. Trusting anyone was for him such an unaccustomed experience that he tried to make it total, to accept this one authority as he had rejected all others. There were other reasons for trust, which will be described later. He accepted the marked shifts in Lucas's personality as a probable necessity of the new discipline, or of being close to anyone which he had always avoided. Had he thought about this, which he did not, he might have concluded that he was used to mercurial shifts of shape and temperament from living with Bill. He was in any case no judge of personality, and had no precise words to label the shifts with.

He saw the differences as different faces. The geometrical-meditation Lucas-face was a rounded square, with ruffled pale hair curling and flaming from it cheerily, large eyes, and a variegated and animated mouth, usually open, but not fixed in length or angle. It was a red face, and drops of sweat shone on it. The interrogation face was considerably longer, darker, browner, more fixed, with a pursed blob of mouth, narrowed eyes, slicker darker hair and a general air of contemptuous anger. The first Lucas pleaded to be told what he saw. The second barked imperious gnomic questions, tapped teeth perpetually with a pencil, and answered little more than "hmn" or a faintly Germanic "So" to offered information. This second Lucas occasionally asked about Bill or Winifred, or whether he remembered his birth, or if he had "fantasies" or "experimented with himself." He got, Marcus assumed, little joy of these questions, since Marcus chose not to talk about relationships, presented a blank face of incomprehension when asked about them, and since Lucas himself would not be more explicit about the nature of the fantasies or experiments he wanted to know about, Marcus was able to assume a bland innocence, or ignorance, when the subject arose. This increased the acidity in the tone of interrogatory-Lucas, who appeared to believe Marcus was being wilfully naughty. Occasional skirmishes on this topic usually ended with the resumption of some other, more acceptable Lucas-face, so Marcus provoked and stonewalled them, as he came to understand the game, with increasing skill.

There was a third Lucas – at least a third – whose presence considerably complicated the activities of the other two. This one first appeared when they had been having trouble with a series of shared pictures of mown grass, which could not have happened accidentally – two people in March *do not*, as Lucas excitedly pointed out, *do not* both see fields of hay lying every which way unless it's meant. If not accidental, they were nevertheless resistant to interpretation or development, and finally Lucas declared they were tired and could have tea. Tea-making Lucas, and later coffee and cocoa-making Lucas, were the third face, cheery, normal, cocked attentively for gossip, solicitous and gentle. This Lucas provided huge sticky fruit cakes, cucumber and sardine sandwiches, toasted teacakes and chat to match. Barrow Minor's acne, VE's shocking O Level prospects, the bad moral influence of Edmund Wilkie, the laxness, in these latter days of his incipient fame, of Alexander Wedderburn. Cosseting, gossip and affection, he offered Marcus, honey, milk, apples and nuts, a kind of perpetual smiling beano which later extended into a dormitory feast.

This extension was because of the mastery of time and space. At first, as Lucas took Marcus's days in hand, his nights got worse. If there was something comforting about sharing his troubles about untouchable objects, especially when the sharing was followed by tea and crumpets, he paid for this with nightmares. Some of these he told, like the one in which he had been set spinning, in the centre of space, and flowing from his fingers had been spun threads which made him into a swastika, then into a mechanized cocoon, at the centre of a looser web which both held space together and stifled him. Others, like the one in which he was hanging most painfully wrong way up from a tall steel nail and was about to be able to rise, again and again, and again and again was beaten down by Lucas, he did *not* tell. Lucas said adverse influences were attempting to break through at night as they put the days increasingly under control. Lucas said discipline, self-control, were the answer to almost everything. Marcus must learn to wake himself at regular frequent intervals, to prevent anything, or anyone, controlling his valuable consciousness without his consent. When he woke himself, he must write down what he had been dreaming. Marcus tried this. He woke to find himself wet with tears, and worse, and physically prevented from lifting a finger to write anything. He dreamed of vessels, retorts, beakers, decanters, full of liquids spirituous and volatile, which exploded, smoked and splashed. Lucas got excited again and claimed that he too had dreamed of glass containers, but that they had remained stable and filled up slowly. He said that if they watched at night, as they watched in the day, they could gain control . . . Marcus dreamed of a peacock, shrieking hideously, banging a glass container on a rock like a thrush with a snail. Lucas said that was very hopeful indeed, that was really very hopeful, he was quite sure that the peacock was some kind of alchemical symbol, that maybe the cracking glass was the egg breaking. Marcus said thrushes killed snails and ate them. Lucas said that Marcus was like a snail, he hid in himself and would not look out at the world only he could see, dammit. Marcus said that snails that looked out got eaten even faster than dormant ones. He produced a pale smile after this almost-joke, and Lucas said, "Good old chap, keep your pecker up, and I'll be at your garden gate tonight as sure as eggs is eggs and retorts is retorts, and we'll watch and pray together and come through, you see if we don't."

The first night, Lucas's spattering stones on the window coincided with the explosion in Marcus's head of a tun of dark vinous stuff which clouded everything, when let out, like octopus-ink. He got up in a hurry and rushed blindly out in raincoat and pyjamas, cannoning into his friend, who put out a hand and steadied him. Marcus was mad.

"Don't *do* that. Don't ever make a noise like that again. Don't ever crash like that, or I'll . . . If you can't *think* me awake, or vice versa, the whole thing's no good." Lucas patted his chest, his shoulder, his upper arm, and made soothing and apologetic noises. He walked Marcus back to the school across the dark Far Field, steadying his weaving steps where it was uneven, ushering him, gripping his arm, into the dark channel beyond the railway bridge behind the Masters' Garden. He gabbled excitedly into Marcus's ear that the Far Field was indeed a field of force, he had felt it distinctly himself, he was sure the earth moved.

When they came to the cloistered Pantheon, where there were lights, he let go Marcus abruptly, and passed his hands several times through his hair, pushing it into its sunny aspect. He opened various glass doors with keys and trotted along dark corridors, past the familiar formitories and vermitoriums, finally opening the door into his own little brightly hot bedroom, placed in the opposite turret to Alexander's, furnished not dissimilarly, but set out with Simmonds's own pictures and things. These included several rather well-made photographs of ships at sea, furrows following free, and several others of sea-gulls in ploughed fields, a large dim print of Dali's Christ of St. John of the Cross, in the position over the hearth where Alexander's Danaide crouched, two glass tanks of newts and Canadian pond-weed, and a reproduction of a Tibetan mandala in a museum in Durham. The room smelled sporty, an intrinsic smell of rubber soles, sweaty socks and shirts, damp wool and mud which was so familiar to both of them that neither remarked it, but Marcus was subconsciously reassured by it. In front of the hearth Simmonds had a Swedish woven rag rug in jolly primary colours, scarlet, lemon, Cambridge blue. In his chairs he had rather small hard square cushions in the same colours, but different cloths. They were clearly chosen to match the rug, or vice versa, and the match was unsuccessful enough to trigger off a perceptual disturbance in Marcus, who kept glancing from one to the other in an attempt to find some relationship of balance or tone between them, though they were too similar for any *discordia concors*, if not similar enough to be easy on the eye. This problem was temporarily eliminated when Simmonds, in order to create a homely or intimate atmosphere, switched off all the lights but one, a large table-lamp made from a carboy with a dark honey-coloured shade embellished with swarms of little commas, or organisms, or curved pins, in black, which swirled in aspiring tear-shaped clouds towards the upper rim which they never touched. This lamp made a pool of dark yellow light on the hearth and reduced the cushions to shadows of colour. Simmonds sat in the hearth, where he had a gas-ring, and made cocoa, producing milk from an earthenware cooler, water from a kettle, mugs and spoons. He gave Marcus chocolate digestive biscuits and urged him to keep his strength up. He took off his own macintosh and flannels and was discovered to be in striped pyjamas: he wrapped himself in a manly navy-blue dressing-gown and offered Marcus a blanket to throw round his shoulders. While they drank the cocoa he talked: about the photographs, and his experiences in the Navy, a meandering series of reminiscences about machine-oil, comradeship, discipline in small spaces, the contrasting vastness of the night sky, the majesty of floating icebergs, the horror of seal clubbing, the community of penguins, the force behind the adaptation of organisms to extremes of heat or cold, the human skill involved in inventing hulls of ships to sail under ice. Marcus, drowsed by the fire, the rug wrapped round him, the hot cocoa and the effect of attention, nodded and jerked awake. Simmonds observed this, and was all solicitude. Marcus should curl up in his bed, in his bedroom, just curl up and sleep. He, Simmonds, would watch, would watch him, would wake him if he showed any sign of agitation that might betoken a dream, would record it for him, and in this way they would fulfill their duties, the requirements of their task, and Marcus would be safe and rested. It didn't matter about himself. He would sleep it off later, would pop into bed when he had seen Marcus home. It was the holidays, he had nothing to do, he could afford it. He would get Marcus up at dawn and see him back across Far Field. They would see the dawn come up together, that would be nice, and maybe illuminating, strictly illuminating, in view of the position the Sun held in the Plan, its loose entelechy, the moment of mystery there had always been for Man at the point of his first daily contact with it, so strange and familiar, didn't Marcus think? Marcus did not think, he nodded and swayed, and Lucas took him by the shoulders and propelled him into the bedroom, watching intently as he climbed into the narrow bed and curled his body into its usual knot, in the hole left by Lucas's body, earlier, in the sheets.

Here, he dropped off immediately. Dropped off was an accurate description; he felt himself plummeting pleasantly through feathered dark down and down, in a kind of free fall that he knew, safe in that dark, was a dream suspension which would have no event, no end. Usually, when he found himself in dreams wrong way up he was tormented by intermittent intellectual assessments of his situation, the realisation that he was unprovided with moscan equipment or suckers for roof-walking, that there must be a hard bottom to the well or funnel he was descending so casually. But here he felt safe. When he woke to Lucas's dawn-shaking, he was informed almost grumpily that he had slept so sweetly that Lucas had seen no cause for disturbing him. But that it was to be hoped that they would do better on a subsequent occasion.

As, of course, they did. So well, that Marcus began to suffer seriously from sleeplessness. Like Lucas's other ministrations the providing of warmth, cocoa and bed turned out to exacerbate problems akin to those from which he offered temporary shelter or relief. If the firm grasp of Lucas's hand under his elbow guided him in one piece, neither spread, nor shattered, nor very much afraid, across Far Field; if, concentrating on the intellectually tiring and frequently pointless or obfuscating spiritual exercises, he was no more invaded by seas of light or supersonic trumpets, a series of methodically broken nights, no matter how lovingly accompanied by material sustenance and spiritual cheerfulness, began to act on him like nights in a brainwashing cell. There was a cold, harsh light behind his eyeballs, even in the dark. He saw stars, not celestial, but physiological. He heard rushing winds, not Aeolian, but like radio interference crackling in his proper eardrums. What do you *see*, What do you *see*, the various voices wheedled, sang, threatened, begged, warmly awaited. Nothing, he hoped to be able to answer, and in his soft sleep honourably could. But the soft sleeps were so short.

So it was that Stephanie found him the third time, spreadeagled on the stairs at five in the morning, his face wet as before, his shoes and socks glistening with dew and slivers of grass beneath his pyjama-legs. Her first thought was to get him out of the way of Bill. Her second was that he now was scarecrow thin. She shook his shoulder, gently. He said, no, no, no, no, no, on a rising protest, and began to judder and jerk, all over, so that she had to grab both his armpits to prevent him falling downstairs. He began to mutter:

"Whipping things, in rather orderly wheel-shapes. Going into hard shapes. Ammonites mebbe. Light whizzing round 'n round 'n solidifying into ammonites. Lots of little . . . lots of little . . . little . . . Can I stop?"

"Marcus. Hush. Marcus."

"Wool, oh, white wool, yellow wool, red wool . . ."

She shook him.

"Soft," he said and woke, staring at her without recognising her, sliding down a step.

"*Get up*, Marcus. Or Daddy . . ."

Galvanised, he pulled up his legs, staggered again and came up the stairs. She followed him into his bedroom.

"Marcus – is anything badly wrong? Can I do anything?" His cheeks were all muddy and grubby like those of a small boy who had wept and rubbed his eyes. He stared at her without answering.

"Something *is* wrong," she said. He gathered himself, wrinkled his brow with effort, leaned forward on clenched fists as he had been used to do with the asthma, and informed her in a voice of gentle despair that she knew not the day nor the hour. Then he turned his face away and pitched into a sleep from which she judged it wisest not to wake him.

17. Pastoral

Stephanie went round to the Vicarage. She went straight up the stairs and knocked on Daniel's door before it struck her that a man so busy was unlikely to be in. However, he came and opened the door. He was wearing a huge fisherman's sweater in natural wool over green cord trousers. He looked ruffled, both in appearance and in expression.

"Oh. You, is it? What can I do for you?"

"I wanted your advice. About a religious problem. At least, I think that's what it is."

"You don't have religious problems," he said roughly.

"It isn't my problem. But I think I have to deal with it. And I think something terrible may be going to happen."

"O.K.," said Daniel. "Come in."

His room in daylight was sadder than in the dark, the bleak clutter emphasized, the mystery of heat and shadow gone. He offered her a chair and sat opposite her, his hands on his knees.

"Right," he said. "Tell me."

"It's about my brother. I saw – when I came to church that time, I saw – he was there with that man, Simmonds, from Blesford Ride, the biology man. He was talking about God's work. I thought you might know what was going on."

"What do you think is going on?"

"I don't know. I think it's some sort of religious . . . religious . . . I don't know. I mean, obviously, I wouldn't mind *that*, in itself . . ."

"You would. But you'd not interfere. Go on."

"Anyway, whatever it is is having a terrible effect on Marcus. He's losing weight, and in his sleep he cries continually; I've gone in and watched him. He goes out at night, I'm sure with Simmonds, I've seen him waiting in the dark like a dog, like Lady Chatterley's lover . . . well, I wouldn't mind *that*, either, necessarily, but . . . "

"You wouldn't mind anything on principle. But."

"No, if you'd seen him, you'd not mock me for ineffective liberal views or whatever. He's terrible, and ill. I wouldn't really mind if it was just a homosexual phase – I even thought that might be good for him –"

"Or even not a phase?"

"Don't jeer at me. He's never had a friend, Daniel, he's never had a friend, nor anyone. I came to you because I thought you might know something."

"You put me in a very difficult position . . ."

"Please, forget about you and me. This is too awful."

"I wasn't thinking about that. Don't put words in my mouth. I'm in a difficult position because Lucas Simmonds has already discussed – well – tried to discuss – this matter with me. And I don't feel able to break a confidence."

He watched her blush: and noticed that she looked desperately tired herself: and felt the old, steady, violent, useless love.

"Can't you – in that case – indicate *something* I could do or say? I can't let him go on like this –"

"No. I didn't know how he was. Nothing was said about how he was."

He thought back to the curious confession or statement or prophetic utterance of Lucas Simmonds, who had sat where she was sitting now, talking very fast, not, as she did, looking with puzzled eyes into his own, but babbling and chattering to ceiling and window, hand in trembling hand in his crotch.

He said, "Also, of course, there are people who come to tell you things, who want to have told someone a certain thing, to have talked about it – but can't actually bring themselves to say what the real matter is. Some people are very oblique – partly because they daren't say – partly because they're not prepared to trust anyone who can't guess what they only hint at – partly because they don't know what they *are* on about, and hope if they go on talking it'll become clear to them. They don't care so much if it's clear to me. So in a sense – not being a mind-reader – I'm not as knowledgeable as Mr Simmonds maybe thinks – or hopes – I might be, by now. And I don't know what of what I did gather I've got any right to pass on to you."

"It all sounds sinister."

"I don't know. I don't think it's sex. Or at least – he went out of his way to tell me it wasn't. To tell me he didn't approve of sex. He seems to believe in celibacy. He talked a lot about Purity. He didn't actually name your brother. Only about Others. I mean, he said he had to ensure no harm came to Others. What sort of harm wasn't clear, either."

"Marcus hates you – hates anyone – to touch him. Even as a baby, you couldn't cuddle him. He got asthma."

There was an awkward silence. Daniel remembered Simmonds's garbled discourse, which had touched on dangers to Others from spiritual forces unleashed by invocation, or by impurity, which had asserted plaintively that the Church had the forms to contain such forces, and had complained sullenly that the Church had abandoned living religious Power, for dead shells and empty echoing buildings. There had been digressions on chastity, science, Steps Forward in consciousness, the superior powers of Others, Simmonds's own known inadequacies. To Daniel's attempts to question he had answered always querulously that Daniel knew already all he needed to know, didn't he, he was well-informed, he must watch and pray. At the end, after a good three quarters of an hour of this recurrent, recapitulating speech, he had suddenly thanked Daniel for his wisdom and counsel and left in a hurry. It was possible that his thanks were ironic. It was equally possible that he supposed he had successfully unburdened himself to Daniel.

What to say to Stephanie was another matter.

"I got the impression it was to do with religious exercises – prayers and visions and things. But it seemed to be scientific experiments too. He seemed to be afraid of the effects of the experiments on Others. I honestly don't know if he meant Marcus. I could ask, if you'd like me to. I don't like meddling."

"There seems to be so much scope for unintentional damage. I can't understand it – Marcus has never, *never* shown any sign of interest in religion and all that. I can't see what's got into him."

"Maybe as you said, he needed a friend. Maybe he always did need religion and didn't know it, not with his upbringing, until it was brought to his notice, like. That's been known. It seems odd to me. But I'm not very religious myself."

"*What?*"

"I'm not very –" Daniel said. Then he smiled sheepishly. "Well I'm not, not religious in that way, the real way. I don't see signs or hear voices or experience great peace or all that, nor I shan't."

"I've never met anyone more religious."

"Nay, but you've no idea, if you don't mind me saying so, no idea at all of what the word means, let alone the thing itself."

She bridled, "I was trained to deal with words."

"*Words*," said Daniel, and laughed. "I'm a glorified social worker, only I don't do it for society, which I'm not that bothered about as an entity. I just want to work, flat out. T' Yorkshire work ethic confuses that wi' religion, but it's not, and you know better, and so does Simmonds, for all his guff."

She laughed nervously. "So I came with my religious problem to an irreligious religious man. That's a joke."

"Not really. Th' problem's still there. Can I make you a cup of coffee? Will you stay? I like talking to you."

"I should love coffee. I like talking to you too. If only you weren't so formidable."

He busied himself with powered coffee. "Formidable?"

"How old are you?"

"Twenty-two," said Daniel, a believer in truth. That particular truth left him peculiarly exposed. He was accustomed to be treated, to treat himself, as a man well over thirty.

"Nobody behaves as though you were only that."

"It's my weight. In both senses. Fat and representative function."

He could feel her attention on him: she was thinking that he was young and saw everything, pain, illness, terror of death, horror of bereavement, feeble-mindedness, raving madness, loneliness and metaphysical anguish, all the things most people successfully avoid, much of the time, or suffer, unprepared, on their own account, once or twice. Well, so did doctors. So did Mr Ellenby. So, professionally, *must* Mr Ellenby. He only seemed, he seemed only, concerned with parish politics, precedence and prettiness of altar-piece and bazaar. Mrs Haydock had been there before Daniel came and no one had badgered herself, or anyone, into sitting with Malcolm.

"Why did you go into the Church, Daniel?"

"Because I can't do wi' half-measures. I'm scared of sitting on my backside and doing nothing. I'm scared of relaxing. I need a good shove, I need it to be *required of me* that I don't stop for a minute. I need unthinking discipline."

"You're a born rebel –"

"Doesn't exclude the other, does it? I need forcing. The Church forces you. Do you see?"

"Partly," she said, imaginatively caught by the combination of terror of lassitude and inexhaustible forced energy. She had never seen the church as anything other than a centre of drowsiness, an ossified exo-skeleton containing an organism almost inert, pleasantly ruminating sustenance long champed dry of its vital juices. "But I feel the church isn't the best place, not the liveliest place . . ."

"We'll not go into that again, or you'll be having me in the Town Hall behind a pigeonhole."

He could not see what she objected to, not truly. He knew as well as she did that Mr Ellenby was a lazy snob, and he knew that she knew that charity was enjoined but he could not see how she did not see how the strength of the Church did not lie there. He could not imagine the whole force of her simple disbelief of the Christian stories themselves, though he had been trained to deal with Bill's peremptory theological opposition. Bill would, and could, dispute the who, how, and why of the rolling away of the stone in the garden. Stephanie was simply not prepared to be interested in it, so clear was it to her that the truth of events was not as the New Testament declared it to be. Psychologically acute, Daniel was doctrinally simple: he needed to be: and to him Stephanie's obvious virtues were Christian virtues, her scrupulousness, her gentleness, part of what he valued in Christ, and were derived from Christ, and that was that. You could have good Christians who thought they weren't, and into that category she indisputably and tiresomely came. He had an inkling, nowhere near the full force of distaste she would in fact feel, that she would find this concept distasteful.

"Were you always in the Church, Daniel?"

"Well, no. It began when I was a boy, the only time I've ever been part of a body of people that was moved as one. Terrifying, that, actually. Hitler or the Mirfield Father."

"Tell me."

He told her. As near as he could remember, conscious that the story was, unlike parts of his life, something she would find sympathetic. She did. She was moved. She said so.

"That was what I call religion, too," he said. "That man'd've known by intuition whether this Simmonds was a prophet or a crank, or a vision was a delusion, which is something I've no skill in, it comes natural to me to advise people not to mess in such. So I'm not much use wi' Marcus. I can't say more than keep an eye on him and by all means send him to me if it'll do any good, in your view."

"Thank you," she said. Nothing was changed, but she had the impression that it was, just because Daniel's energies were loose in the field of Marcus's anguish.

"Look here – I've a day to myself – Wednesday next week – all day. I've kept it clear, I'm getting out of here. To be truthful I wanted to go away somewhere – think what to do about – what we've kept off. I thought I'd go for a long seaside walk. I'd like it if you'd come wi' me. Not to argue, you understand, just to walk. We didn't do badly, today."

"No, we didn't."

"Then you'll come."

"I like the sea."

"So you'll come."

She never said no, he reflected. It possibly followed that she never meant yes. She liked to please. She liked him. It was exasperating.

"Yes," she said. "I'll come."

18. *Anadyomene*

They went to Filey because Daniel had spent childhood holidays there. Proposing this place, he explained that he usually didn't go back to places, but then he usually didn't have a private life, so had thought he might. It took them some time to get there: bus to Calverley, train from Calverley to Scarborough, another train from Scarborough to Filey. Most of this journey was sufficiently beset by engine-noise and wheel-rattle for them not to need to speak to each other. Daniel was without his uniform, in the fisherman's sweater and a vast shapeless black duffel coat, hooded and toggled, that he had bought at an army surplus store. It made him look, the enormous man, something like a Brueghel peasant, Stephanie thought, as though he should have had a hod, or an axe, to complete him.

They were almost the only people to get out at the station, which was bright with sunshine and bitterly cold. Daniel had planned the day. They would walk down into the town and out along the sands to the Brigg. They could take a pork pie and a bottle of beer and eat out there. Stephanie, in sensible shoes, but without hat or gloves, shivered. Daniel took notice.

"Ay, there'll be a wind up," he said with satisfaction. "It'll be blowing the sea up, I hope. You should have a hat. I'll buy you one."

She demurred.

"No. I'd like to give you something. I'd like you to be wrapped up well before we get going, so I don't have to worry about getting you back."

They walked into the town past pebble-dashed bungalows, and colour-washed holiday homes, winter-bleached and dormant. They found a dark brown Victorian drapers, with bosomy russet and oatmeal dresses tucked and tied like matronly scarecrows on chrome T shaped stands, behind felt basins and tulle drums, royal blue, petunia pink, greener than any apple.

Inside a beige woman in a beige knitted dress with a crocheted front opened for them cracked shiny white boxes of gloves, wool, leather, "fabric". Stephanie, looking for cheapness and warmth, chose pale blue fair-isle mitts, with pale stars or sunbursts spangled on them. Daniel then insisted on the matching beret, which had a large pale yellow bobble. She pulled it on obediently over brow and ears; the neat roll of yellow hair curved out at the back, shining on her coat collar. How *sweet*, Daniel thought with overwhelming sentiment, and made a discovery. Behind the cliché was something old and fierce and absolute, a primeval passion of taste, Biblical honey. Ezekiel had eaten up the rolls of writing and called them sweet. It was the same, Daniel thought ferociously, with this clean round face under the childlike wool, the shining hair, the gentle, doubtful gaze.

They came into Cargate Hill, which was steep and cobbled and had hand-rails, the land giving a last uncompromising lurch, out and down. Ahead was the grey water, heavy and dark, with narrow lakes of glossy light lying where sunlight struck through racing clouds. His father had always roared out, there it is, there it is, seeing it for the first time, had hurtled towards it roaring, with Daniel on his shoulders, who had at first cried out shrilly with him, and had later felt exposed to inhabitants and settled visitors who might guess he had only just come. Though why that had mattered, at times when he *had* only just come, he was now at a loss to know.

"There it is," he said to Stephanie Potter, and took her arm.

You came out onto the beach through a huge stone arch under the promenade, a cavernous tunnel where the wind rushed and died. Sand piled in dry drifts, heaped against its walls, had its own irregular tide-line on the cobbles. He had plunged down daily through its cold shadow, kicking off rubber beach shoes, a fat boy wriggling fat toes in its cool, and then warmer siftings, coming out onto the sunny shores.

"You could ride ponies up here," he said. "When I was little, you could come right up into't town on your own horse, like, to your own door." He had been a fat baby in a basket seat with leather pommels on a wobbling donkey. He had been a fat boy in long grey shorts with fat calves pinched by stirrup-leathers, half-worried, half-jubilant, as the thin piebald pony strained slowly up, its rough mane jiggling under his eyes. Some of the flesh on him now was the same flesh and some was gone forever. His dad had walked beside him, slapping his behind, saying straighten your back, son, look lively, don't sag. The summer after the accident he had come up once or twice on his own: his mum didn't walk up, and indeed only paid for him to go up, twice. He used to think if his dad would leave him to get on with it he could talk to the horseboys who hung onto his reins. But in the event he never did.

Stephanie wondered why this thought made him look so grim. They came under the arch.

"And the wind like a whetted knife. Me Dad always said that, every time we came through here. Invariably. I think it was the only line of poetry he knew."

"It's a very good line," said Stephanie.

"I wouldn't know," said Daniel, who still appeared unaccountably gloomy.

When they did come out onto the sand, out of the tunnel, the sea-wind hit them like a wet canvas wall to walk into, a deafening, stinging buffeting on their faces.

"Oh," said Stephanie, opening her mouth, swallowing cold salty air. She staggered and laughed. "Oh, Daniel."

A steady noisy fluttering set up in the skirts of her coat. She beat ineffectively at them, put up a mittened hand to the starry beret.

"Come round this side of me," said Daniel. "I'm a good solid wind-break." He stood between her and the stream of air off the sea, under the harbour wall. Dry sand blew and snaked and eddied, rose in a crest and fell inanimate under the wall. The tide was running out; beyond them it had flung its limit-line of glittering black grit, ground dust of mussel shells, tossed strands of bladderwrack. The sands were printed with long dimpling ribs, mirror-images of the water; where the beach dipped, a ruffled sheen of it still winked and shone. Daniel laughed with idiotic pleasure.

"Six miles of sand," he said, waving his thick arms out, embracing it. He buttoned his collar, pulled the black hood over his bristling hair. The wind swung round his head, and little heads of sand lashed furiously at his turn-ups. Here he could put out scarecrow arms and almost be blown, clumsily weightless, along with the weather. He crooked his arm, and offered it to her.

"We'll walk to th'Brigg," he said, showing where the line of rocks and boulders jutted into the sea. "You don't mind the wind."

It was not a question. Her lips and cheeks stung. Her eyes were filmed with cold air and tears. She put her head behind his shoulders and gave an ambiguous nod. They set off, close together, making an erratic, sinuous, tracking path, in wandering mazes, occasionally bumping each other, out of step, occasionally trotting, almost running, as the wind filled their clothes like sails and almost lifted them into flight. Once, separating her head from his shoulder she looked back at the still wide curve of the bay, onto which the receding sea was thrown in white looping skeins, off which the wind-dried surface sand was snatched and tossed. It was all a pother, and yet a smooth shape, a clear shape. When she took her ear away from him it filled with a frozen roar. She put it back.

In this way, after a stretch of time, they came to the end of the sea-wall, where the slipway ran down to the beach, down which the fishing-cobles rolled on rubber wheels, up which pony carts trotted in the summer, bright with 1930s Minnie Mice and Donald Ducks. Beyond the slipway the beach was bounded by the unstable cliffs, whose grassy brows and red muddy walls declined steadily towards sand and water. Perched in this cliff, shored up on girders, was the Marine Café. Daniel indicated it with a sweep of his free arm.

"If it should be open," he boomed, "we could get a cup of coffee and a bun, to fortify us for the next bit."

There were one or two old men with dogs hugging the shelter of the wall and some lugworm diggers by the waterline. It did not seem likely the place would be open. Stephanie felt a strong desire for coffee, hot, wet, sweet. She swallowed. Daniel bounded ahead up the cliff steps, dipping crazily, wooden sills to vanished mud surfaces, and beckoned from the door. It was open. Life was good. She went composedly up, crimson-cheeked, and sat down in the sudden hot quiet with eardrums throbbing and roaring. It was a little time before they could speak. They ordered coffee and toasted buns. The smell of toasting was almost painfully warm and promising.

The Marine Café was a faintly boat-shaped construction, with metal-framed windows and little basket-work tables with tops of ice-green glass. The windows of the sun lounge were smeared and blurred by the salt spray; the emerald table-tops were smeared and blurred by in-discriminate wiping. Outside clouds raced across the sun, streamed in the bright sky. Inside the glass brightened and darkened, muted. It was like being in an aquarium, in some thicker element. When the coffee came, it was hot and not nasty. Daniel wanted to produce a compliment on her bright eyes and rosy cheeks, and dared not.

He said instead, "I used to come here with me dad and mum. They had cups of tea and I had ice-cream in a silver cup. Well, I suppose it wasn't silver, but I called it that."

"Family life," he said. "Family life. It's a funny idea. When we were here in this place – us three – we were supposed to be together, we'd come here for that. And not one o' the three of us had any idea of what to say. Sometimes my dad'd clown about. He couldn't abide to be still. No, he couldn't abide to be still. He had to be doing something. Holidays drove him mad, I sometimes think. My mum sat in a deckchair and I wasn't much use to him. Too fat and slow. I wouldn't climb and run, I never learned to swim. He'd go out in all weathers, he'd plunge up and

down, and we'd watch from th'shore. Silly way of passing time, really.
I reckon he heaved a sigh of relief when we could go home and he could
get back to work and stop thinking up things to do, like, or to amuse
me."

"You can't abide to be still, now."

"No," said Daniel, "I can't. But that came later, that came after he
died."

"I didn't know he was dead."

Daniel looked irritated, as though she should have known that. He
was struggling to tell her what, in view of the position she held in his
thoughts, it was easier and pleasanter to assume she already knew.

"He died before I was eleven."

"I'm sorry. What did he die of?"

"Iron ore trucks. Broke loose and crushed him." He brooded,
separate from her. He saw his father, huge, white, streaming with
water inside the green-lit, sea-smelling, canvas-smelling beach-tent,
towelling his shoulders and trunk, and the vigorous hair, like Daniel's
own. He thought of all that, cracked and smashed, and told Stephanie,
"I didn't grieve. I don't remember grieving. I should've grieved
more."

She put a hand in his direction. He did not take it.

"I'm sure you did grieve, Daniel. Maybe it was too painful to
remember, after."

"He was a good man. A big, kind, ordinary good man. He was
exacting. Always at you, at me, that is, to excel, to do things properly.
I wasn't grateful. I am now, though. I resented it then, I think. I don't
know. I loved him."

How could he make her imagine that dead man? Why, indeed, should
she? He wanted her to have his past. But that wasn't possible.

As for Stephanie, she knew what he wanted, and yet was angry. It is a
frequent irony that those to whom we feel we need to make an offering
of our past feel threatened, or isolated, or diminished by that past. It was
a further irony, in their case, that a small truculence rose in Stephanie as
a result of this. The shadowy engine-driver was not there, after all. But
she was. She was. Daniel should see what was there.

When they came out on the slipway it was colder. The clouds were
piling up in vaporous, slaty banks, curdling and swaying behind the
crumbling red cliffs. There was another huge half-moon of sand to cross
to reach the Brigg. Daniel felt low: he dug his hands in his pockets and
stood squarely, staring out. She tugged his sleeve.

"Come on then. It's going to rain. It's blowing enough of a wind to
satisfy even you."

He looked down at her, shrugged, and took a step. She said something he didn't hear.

"What?" he roared into the wind.

She spoke again, and again he could not hear; the air took her words and mixed them with its own noise. He pulled her closer to him, and they set off across the last segment of sand.

They crossed a shelving ledge of the squeaking, raw-red mud, and then were on firm sand, which was crossed, from time to time, by rapid channels of blood-coloured water, running down, slicing their own neat shores, to the sea. Once they had to jump, where effluent bubbled and hurried, peaty-cream and frothy, from an iron pipe that rose from the mud, and for a little distance blood-red and creamy froth and silver light off sea water mingled and glittered and turned. Then as they moved out into the bay everything was a plane of dazzling sun off watery sand. There were no other footprints, only dark conical miniature volcanoes of wormcasts breaking the glitter. They advanced crabwise, through the whirling air, both seeing a turning combination of earth, air, water, light, through the stung rainbow of their own tears. Their ears ached and hammered: chorales thundered in Daniel's head broken by his heavy breathing. Stephanie, lungs beating and distended, waited for her second wind, amazed that cold salt could so scald. It was hard to see how far they had come or had to go, the sand was so extensive and bright, so that they seemed to be struggling on without progressing, running on the spot. And then her second wind came, she breathed a comfortable breath, and the wind came at them in a flurry and they were practically blown on to the Brigg.

To get on to the Brigg proper it is necessary to scramble over boulders and piled stones, sharp with barnacles and limpets, thick with bubbling brown and soft matted green weeds. They climbed and skidded, arriving in time at the man-made causeway that runs out for some of the way along the spine of the Brigg into the sea, shoring up, solidifying with asphalt and concrete, what is jammed and cracked and grinding and sloping and rocking. They got onto this somehow on all fours, and stood up under the memorial tablet to the Paget family, swept away by a huge wave, their fate carved there as a warning to other men. The salt smell was now organic; briny, iodine, alive, alien. Daniel breathed it in with pleasure. He said, "Do you want to go on? Shall we go out to the end? Or round to the caves?"

"Out," she said, pointing.

"Good." He could hardly wait. "We can get quite a way before it'll be dangerous. Tide's low. Did you know this place was said to have been built by the Enemy of Mankind to lure ships to their doom?"

"I can believe it."

"Or as the first stage in bridging the North Sea. But he got impatient, and it fell about, so he gave up and we have the unfinished ruin."

They began, upright at first, and later, as the path vanished, crouching, squatting, sitting, clutching, to edge out to sea, intent only on their progress. Periwinkles rolled and clattered; Stephanie skinned a wrist on barnacles; fitted fingers into clutchholes in porous light boulder clay; went about and about to avoid patches of that leafage so vivid a green that it is tempting to call it unnatural, except that it grows, flourishes, in tufts and thickets, quite naturally, swept and submerged by the sea. A kind of third wind filled her. She began to enjoy her protesting body, placing fingers and toes, balancing spine and hip and shoulder. As they came out of the shelter of the headland the wind beat differently: less monotonous, less flapping, shrill, sharp, singing, whirring. They came to a high flat place and stopped to look about.

Immediately ahead waves were crashing in over the submerged tip of the rocky projection, flung high and smashed, rolling, circling, converging, splashing. And waves already divided by the end of the headland were crashing in from both sides, waters rising in a precipitous mass, hurled flat on a table of grit, running, trickling, sighing away down holes and channels to where it sucked and swayed invisibly under their feet. There was a weird homogeneity to the world out there. The sky was flung fragments, very blue and bright with flying shreds of cloud involved with tossed and whirling foam, flakes and flecks of white, off-white and cream, and grey and brown, with the birds turning and calling harshly in both elements, white birds, specked brown birds, beaks gold and blooded, hooked, harsh and clean in line.

They stood on wet stone, stupidly obsessed by seeing, passive while a rapid swell rolled in, green-grey, gold-grey, lifting, cresting, whitening, and suddenly towered beside them, stood formed and tall over them for a moment of time, and fell, and dispersed on the rock at their feet, drenching them both, trickling, chuckling, streaming, broken by every stone and strand of weed, running back every which way into the undifferentiated cold mass. The fair-isle beret was soaked. Daniel shook his black head like a dog, and drops of water flew from it, sparkling and glittering in the patch of bright cold sunlight that seemed suddenly to have steadied over them. He looked at Stephanie who was standing, quietly standing, with the wave's last waters running busily over and round her shoes on their way out. Slowly she took off the beret: the yellow hair was picked up and blown by the wind. It was streaked darkly with water, and her macintosh was covered with long, dark pointed stains. She stood there as though mesmerised by the water, her mouth open slightly, smiling secretly, while the wind rippled on in her wet hair and clothes. The sun was so bright now he could hardly see her. A smaller wave failed to hurl itself as high as they were. She again said something he could not hear.

"What," he cried, "what did you say?"

She approached her mouth to his ear. He heard ". . . your language, then. Let there be light, I said." She seemed drunk and chuckling, lit up. "Come on," she said. She began to go out along the rocks, very fast, holding her arms wide to balance herself, half-running, half-striding. He went after her. Another tall wave bowed, jarred, cracked and whispered at her feet. She turned to him a face he had never seen, blindly smiling, wild, white and wet. As she set off again, another wave rose, Daniel seized her, the drenching waters descended, and Daniel took hold of her hair and body. He kissed her. There was a mixture of salt and cold and heat and unbalance. She kissed him back. She kissed him so certainly that they both staggered and Daniel could only right them by tugging her hair and shoving with his knees. This caused her to become pliant and docile, who had been straining and flying.

"You are not going to be drowned," said Daniel, dragging. Between two boulders he gathered her most uncomfortably and kissed her again. She had a look almost of lewd abandon. Daniel was in a state of extremity. He banged her accidentally on the rock, then propped her on his own solid body. The cold sun shone on.

"You will have to marry me."

"No. This is – a romantic moment – we made. It doesn't change anything."

"Yes it does. We made it. We can make a lot more. We can do anything."

"*You* made it happen," she said, pleading.

"I want to live like this."

"You can't. I know. These things – don't last."

"Things I do last."

Tears were rolling down her cheeks, hot on cold sea and cold flesh. She knew, she knew that such things slipped away whilst you tried to recognise them, died whilst you tried to find out how to keep them alive, vanished whilst you tried to heave your life into new forms to accommodate them.

"Have you ever felt like this?" said Daniel, as though the question were conclusive.

"No. But –."

"Nor me."

"Daniel – it almost doesn't mean anything – it's only for here and now."

"No it isn't. I don't want much. But I want to go on like this. I want you. I want you. I want to have you."

"Oh, Daniel."

"And so do you want it. I know what you want."

He did not. But she said, "All right."

They were both taken aback. She repeated it almost irritably, as though if he hadn't heard it it could be retracted. "All right. I said, all right."

Her face was streaming with tears. Daniel retracted an arm.

"No, no. I'm forcing you. You don't have to –"

"You don't understand. I thought you did. The thing is, I've never *wanted anything*, not anything for myself, in my whole life. I don't know how to fit it in with anything else I know. I can't deal with . . ."

If he lost his certainty of purpose now they were both lost. But he said, "Then it's all right. That's the only thing. It will be all right." He stared out over her pale head at the still and hurrying, blown and shining sea and sky.

Much later they had sandwiches and beer in a pub in Hunmanby. They sat side by side on a wooden settle by an open fire and devoured rare red beef, onions and salt pressed into new brown bread. They could hardly eat fast enough: the taste was sharp and strong and entirely delightful. They were unused to being happy. Both were unconsciously preparing themselves for the moment when happiness would crack up.

"What next?" said Daniel, draining his pint.

"Next?"

"Next today, next in a week, next in a month. What shall we do now?"

"What can we do?"

"Get married. Soon. There's no point in anything else."

"How soon?"

"Well, there's banns. Somewhere to live. That's not easy, I earn next to nothing. You don't want to live with the Vicar. Nor do I."

You said, all right, and suddenly everything was unrecognisable. She could not imagine living with Daniel. Or, it was true, without him.

"I must see the term out, I must talk Daddy round. He won't like it."

"Now or ever?"

"Possibly not ever. But he might sort of come round a bit."

"I wouldn't rely on it, myself. I wouldn't wait, myself. But you must do as you think right. Vicar'll want to talk to you."

The Church reared its ugly, sluggish solid head.

"What will he say? He likes me."

"Aye, he likes you. I sh'd think he'll think you'll make a good vicar's wife. Being so clearly on the side of the angels. You don't need to get embattled wi' him."

"You would."

"Yes. But then, I care about such matters. Your point is, you don't. I sh'd think he'll think you'll civilise me. He thinks I'm uncouth."

"Daniel –"

"Hm?"

"In the nineteenth century, I would, I would have made a good vicar's wife. In the twentieth, it's not morally possible."

The bread and meat were comfortable inside him: the fire-warmth was on his sea-wet legs: her thigh was on his.

"You'd make a good wife for me. You need to be doing. So do I. We're alike. We'll get on. It's not as though I was one of the smells and bells kind of churchmen, and all that stuff, is it?"

He put his hand in her lap, over her hand. Desire lunged at them.

"I want, I want, I want," said Daniel in a conversational voice through closed teeth.

"So do I," she said, truthfully.

"There isn't anywhere we could go."

"No. We could stay here. We could book a room, and make up a story, and telephone and tell some lies. People do. All the time. It ought to be easy."

His face took on its heavy, brooding look. "Would you find it easy?"

"No. I'm a rotten liar. I'd worry."

"Aye." He grasped her hand, crunching bones. "There must be a way. There must. People find all sorts of ways."

"Fewer people than you think."

He laughed abruptly. "In my profession you get to know how many people. How many of my kind of people. It seems an awful lot to me. There seem to be an awful lot of people who perpetually find themselves in situations where it's downright difficult not to . . . Perhaps I'm just incompetent. Or not trying hard enough. What shall we do?"

"I don't know."

They walked a lot more, in the event, and came inconclusively back to Blesford on buses and trains. At Blesford bus station he said,

"The best I can offer is powdered coffee in my room."

"Well, I can't offer anything at all."

The Vicarage was dark and empty.

"They're out."

"Aye, it seems so."

They mounted in the dark to Daniel's floor. They closed themselves in. They listened. She said, "Where's Felicity?"

"I don't know."

"Why don't you shut the curtains?"

He did that, and lit the fire, and the coal-scarlet bedside lamp. He turned to her. "Oh God, what now?"

She did not know. They were both afraid of going to bed, not, oddly, because they had any primitive fear of failure in the act, but because they were more mildly, more insidiously, more deeply afraid of embarrassment. They feared the sudden irruption of the inhabitants of the house, or urgent parishioners. Daniel feared the ancient springs of his bed, and the faintly mildewed smell which when he was alone did not bother him. Stephanie feared her own incapacity to deal with Daniel's morality. Sin, which she supposed it was, was a complex business. There must be some sense in which going to bed with her would be wrong, and the urgency of his intention to ignore this wrong excited her. It made the whole business serious and important in a way none of her Cambridge encounters had been, although it now occurred to her that it had suited her to flatten out all the responses of the young men to the automatic and everyday level at which she chose to behave herself. But this plunge into the unknown consequences of Sin alarmed her. She would not want to damage Daniel in his own eyes. She would not want to deal with a tempest of remorse. She held the fair-isle beret in both hands and twisted it nervously round and round in front of her like a fluffy chastity shield.

"At least take your coat off," he said. She arranged it with exaggerated slow neatness on one of his many chairs. The pointless deliberation irritated him. He made a creaking, sidling stride towards her and got his arms round her waist.

She sidestepped.

"What is it?"

"I can't tell if you're going to be sorry."

"I'm not. Not over you."

"But you ought not –"

"It doesn't seem to matter. If it doesn't bother me, I don't see why it should bother you."

"I don't see *why* it doesn't."

"It doesn't bother you," he pointed out. "As an act."

"No. But I – am not –"

He could see what was troubling her but could think of no answer, because the problem seemed to him irrelevant and he had no intention of engaging it, then or ever. The forces and clarity of the day, sea and sky and wind, were being unnecessarily dissipated. He cast about to distract her, and said with low cunning, "Of course. I've never before . . . never in fact . . . *That* worries me."

It did not worry him. He assumed quite wrongly that passion and attention would make up for lack of skill. But it did have the effect of deflecting her attention from his bruised morals to his presumed sexual insecurity.

"That doesn't matter," she said.

The house was silent. Daniel began to turn the bed. She did not try to stop him. When he had done this, she said, "Have you got a towel?"

"A towel?"

"We shall need a towel."

He found one, white with red stripes, and put it on the pillow. He wondered if he should start undressing her, or himself. She said, "If we put the light out, and keep quiet, if they come back, they won't know we're here."

"Aye," he said. "That's so."

So in the dark they undressed, fast, and got into the bed, cramped cold flesh, hot flesh, pale and dark into the narrow bed together.

It was not very successful, a disorganised arhythmic flurry, with both bodies constantly in danger of slipping off the bed, inhibited almost to the last by creaking springs and unanchored, slithering bedclothes. Daniel, overexcited and wild, did not know, half the time, whether he was in or out, coming or going. Stephanie, not habituated to piercing sexual pleasure, made no attempt to exact an orgasm and did not achieve one, a fact of which the floundering Daniel appeared to be unconscious, since he made no attempt either to induce one, to enquire whether one had happened, or to apologise for the apparent deficiency. This she found more comforting than not, because of the lack of embarrassment. They got hot, and wet, a little battered and confused. Daniel groaned and it was over.

He turned away and she sat up, nervously examining his face, heavy and shut. She could not imagine what he felt. She could not tell who he was. Almost she expected him to rouse himself and roar out transports of self-reproach or self-referring ecstasy, either of which would have embarrassed her profoundly.

He opened shrewd eyes and grinned, lazy, amused, still.

"Well" – he said, "That was a beginning, anyway. I reckon that's the main thing. That was a beginning."

She stared down.

"I like to see you there," he said. "That seems right." He put up a heavy arm and pulled the blonde head down on his chest. She lay along

him, growing accustomed to his hard ledges, the heavy rolls of flesh.
He had a huge hand on the small of her back, and one in her hair. She
felt that the limits of their bodies were not quite clear. She heard his
strong racing heart.

"Are you comfortable?"

"Extraordinarily."

"Can you imagine –" She missed the end of the sentence.

"What? Can I imagine what?"

"Can you imagine anyone getting married without really wanting to?
So many must, from looking at them. There seems no sense in it, without
really wanting . . ."

"People might not want to be alone."

"I wouldn't mind."

His certainties alarmed and delighted her in equal proportions. Now,
she sighed, and was asleep.

When they woke, occasional thumps and bangings indicated that there
were now people in the house. They debated in whispers whether to
put the light on, and did not: they did not want Ellenby chatter, or the
hopeful, participant gaze of Felicity Wells. So they lay still and dozy for
another hour or so. When the Ellenbys had made bed-making noises,
and burglar-precautionary noises, bathroom noises and switching off of
last lights, they got up and dressed. They were both very hungry and
needed the lavatory. It was this ultimate embarrassment that finally
decided Stephanie to creep downstairs and home: Daniel pointed out
that she could use the gardener's outdoor closet in comparative security.
It was agreed that he would not come out. So he watched from his
window as she tiptoed across the moonlit lawn, head bent under the
beret, looking up once at his dark bulk in his darkened window. He
lifted his arm in generous salute, a victorious general. His body was
pleasantly warm. His imagination was pleasantly at ease. He did not, he
hoped, underestimate the difficulties of the next advance. But he had
come so far, so far, with daring and love, it was impossible to imagine
he would not go further.

19. Mammon

Some weeks later, when term had begun, when Alexander had returned
in his car and carried off the *Four Quartets*, Stephanie and Frederica had
coffee in the Chattery in Calverley's big department store, Wallish and

Jones. They were sheltering from a downpour and the plate glass window was steamy inside and out. The tables had starched damask cloths. There was a dense silent carpet, rampant with compressed horizontal leafage, jungle lianas and water-lily leaves improbably cross-fertilised with palmate horse-chestnuts, in tropical greens and English autumnal browns and golds, with bright little bunches of berries like drops of blood at geometrically measured intervals. This absorbed, besides all noises from stiletto heels, sensible brogues, clattering claws of lapdogs, the drips from umbrella tips and plastic macs and oiled silk caps and carrier bags. It was hot. The ladies sweltered, discarding layers of clothing. Your voice, if you spoke, did not carry, being absorbed into damp coats and Axminster tufts. It was customary to lower your voice, all the same, whether you were discussing the dreadful price of net curtains or the dreadful after-effects of your hysterectomy. The Potter girls liked it. They had been coming there all their lives.

It was Saturday. Frederica wore, dashing at that date in that place, tight black slacks and her batwing sweater with a little scarf knotted round her neck. She was heavily made up, with grass-green eyelids, black lashes and a plummy mouth. Stephanie was dishevelled and overheated in a coat and skirt. Frederica drank iced coffee de luxe, with two blobs of ice cream, a long spoon and straws. Stephanie had coffee with a pot of cream. She said, "I want to tell you something."

"Go ahead."

"Well." There seemed to be some difficulty. Frederica looked up from her purple-stained straws. Stephanie was crimson, the rosy colour flooding even the tips of her ears and the roots of her hair.

"Out with it."

"I'm going to be. That is, I'm getting married."

"*Married?*"

"I'm going to marry Daniel Orton. Quite soon."

Frederica for a terrible moment glared with outrage. She said the words that came into her head.

"I didn't know."

"We haven't told anyone yet."

"I didn't know," Frederica repeated, on an aggrieved note.

"I can see there are going to be difficulties."

"I should think *so*," Frederica agreed sharply.

"I shall have to tell Daddy."

"He'll hate it. That's for sure."

Frederica stole a glance at her sister, now duskily incarnadine, an absurd colour under the pale hair. A large round tear stood in one eye-corner. Frederica found this repellent.

"Being a Vicar's wife is a full-time career. Fêtes and Mothers' Unions and bosoms to weep on and things. Will you do all that?"

"Some of it, I expect. I don't mind."

"Well, I do see what you mean about difficulties. Oh dear."

Stephanie cried out, "I wish you would say something else. I am *very happy*." She pushed aside, with a swimming gesture, white china, silver-plated cake-forks and paper napkins, buried her face in her arms and sobbed, abandoned.

Frederica was horrified. She summoned a waitress, tapped Stephanie's shoulder, said,

"Of course I'm delighted, two more coffees please, with cream and *quickly*, Stephanie, it's just a shock, I had no idea, nobody had. Are you in love with Daniel Orton?"

"Yes. That's certain."

"How do you *know*?" That came out inquisitorial, though she had meant to invite a confidence. Daniel Orton was fat and religious. Frederica both did and didn't want to imagine what it could be like to love Daniel Orton.

"How does one ever?" She sat up, flushed and shiny and looked vaguely about. "I went to bed with him."

"And was that exciting?" enquired Frederica, in a voice that startlingly combined the lubricious and the acid.

"It was a revelation," said Stephanie with dignity. She heard her ordinary Cambridge voice fall squat on the cushioned silences of Calverley's gossipry, looked up, and met, not a friendly curious nod from a college friend, but the greedy, strained, overpainted foxy face of Frederica, which expressed a horrified glee mixed with an overpowering fury.

"And will you," she cried hoarsely, "have orange blossom and veils, will you make me a bridesmaid in a pretty hat and scatter rose-petals in your path from a dear little basket and will you promise to obey, or are you marrying a *modern* clergyman . . .?"

"I can't see why you are like this."

Frederica could not see herself. Boundless unreasoning malice possessed her.

"I wish I hadn't told you."

"I'm jolly pleased for you. Honestly I am."

"Yes. Well," said Stephanie. She stood up and pushed two half-crowns across the table. She had walked away before Frederica had time to frame her next sentence.

Frederica sat fiddling with the coins. She had behaved frightfully and felt frightful.

When they were little girls, in the war, they had played at being grown-ups, a different game from playing house, more limited in what it imitated, with rules they had never quite understood. They had dressed up in Winifred's cast-offs, an old black velvet evening gown, a flounced crêpe with scarlet poppies and brilliant cornflowers spattered on it, satin pumps, petticoats, torn fringed shawls, hats, silk flowers, pheasant feathers. They had carried a sequinned purse on a tarnished chain and a patent poche, and had made imitation powder compacts from Elastoplast tins, cigarettes from rolled paper, lipsticks from waxed crayons jammed into cardboard tubes. It had been a game designed to discover what its own subject-matter really was, and in this had signally failed. They had pranced and paraded, had endlessly prepared themselves for events they failed to bring about. The game came to be played, necessarily, in imaginary waiting rooms – vestibules, foyers, ladies' cloakrooms at dance halls or hotels, places where, according to their meagre knowledge of the worlds of film and the novel, significant adult events, events not confined to kitchen or bedroom, took place. Neither of them considered acting a man, so their encounters were always with thin air, with which Frederica held terse, abortive dance-hall dialogues and from which Stephanie ordered unavailable luxuries, cream, grapes, oranges and lemons, fresh butter and little iced cakes. This game always began by offering a sense of the tantalising, the forbidden, the arcane, and ended in frustration and boredom.

Now Frederica snapped her handbag once or twice, as she had done then, peered at its contents, fat Burgundy lipstick, Max Factor solid powder, as though conjuring them, wondered why she had been, why she still felt, so venomous. Stephanie had stolen a march on her and simultaneously corrupted the vision of getting out of semi-detached Blesford and Calverley to a more real and necessary world. If Stephanie, having tasted freedom, could settle for domestic bliss with a fat curate, defeat was horribly possible. Anybody at any moment could become enslaved by a cooker, a set of Pyrex dishes with snowflake crystals stamped black on negligée pink, a personal teapot. It had its secret attractions, that, as one recognised from a reading of *Good Wives* or *The Rainbow*, to be enclosed with a transfigured man and transfigured possessions in a private place. But mostly, and in Blesford, it was horrible.

She thought of Alexander. Stephanie's apparent defection from the love of Alexander made him seem more insubstantial and further away. How would he live now? When he was rich and famous as he would be, and deeply concerned with art, as he already was? Her imagination boggled and failed as it had in those early games. He would listen to the

Four Quartets. And set out to observe rehearsals of his plays, which she
could imagine, and attend literary cocktail parties which she could not.
The essence was talk not tea-pots and she could not imagine the talk. It
would not be like Potter talk, it would be like writing, not ponderously
about writing.

There would also be sex. Stephanie had found out about that. They
had never discussed Stephanie's sex life or even whether she had one,
and Frederica was now troubled to imagine that it was, and had been,
matter of fact. This enraged her, at least as much as the surrender to
bourgeois solidities. At both ends of the scale, style and fact, she was
wandering in an imaginary vestibule. That Stephanie had abandoned the
chaste, fantastic hope of Alexander for solid flesh made the hope of
Alexander either impossible or more concrete. "I went to bed with
him." "It was a revelation." Somebody, some time presumably would,
or did, go to bed with Alexander. So logically one should either want
that, or call a daydream a daydream. "This is flesh and blood, sir." It was
extremely likely that he had never noticed, and never would notice, that.
But he too, like Daniel Orton and unlike Mr Rochester, was flesh and
blood. And so . . .

She decided that her frightful behaviour to Stephanie must be
expiated. She would spend some of her T. S. Eliot fund on an appropriate wooden spoon or rolling pin. She pocketed Stephanie's change,
from the coffee, and set off for the Household Basement.

Wallish and Jones, that total emporium, was as old a part of her way
of life as the black velvet game, or older. When she was a tiny child she
had been brought there year after year at Christmas, to see Father
Christmas in his Fairy Palace, or, alternatively, Father Christmas in his
Underground Grotto. One of her earliest memories was of her first
hydrogen-filled balloon, pearly and ebullient on a silver wire, which had
been handed to her by the bearded old man himself, from his throne winking with tinsel and fairy lights, in the glass-green depths of the Grotto.
She had held it ten minutes before it exploded in the jaws of the dark-
varnished, piston-armed, heavy doors of the ladies' lavatory. She had
heard her own voice wailing in the grimy tiled area behind the lavatory
windows, an imprisoned soul in torment, echoing and re-echoing. She
had been consoled, they told her, though this she could not remember,
by pink ice-cream in the Chattery, then, before it was done up, tiled
in green and gold with lace doileys and bentwood chairs, almost
austere.

The war had been bad for the verisimilitude, the glamour, of both
Palace and Grotto, the one inhabited by clusters of starry fairies, the
other by diamond-studded, shovelling, barrow-trundling gnomes. The

lights winking and twinkling on battlements, stalagmites and stalactites, the shimmering cascades of silvery-dry water had become a little shivery and creaky. Papier-mâché encrusted rocks, or pinnacles on which tiny Gothic windows entrancingly shone, had, like the gnomes' hose and the fairies' tulle, the cobwebs in the caverns and the banners in the Castle, become a little threadbare and grubby. Balloons, being rubber, vanished. The true brilliance of the Land of Faery was succeeded by the specious glamour of the discovered theatrical illusion, the back of the grotto was exposed as something akin to the flats one walked knowledgeably behind on the stage-set. The venerable silver-bearded mage who had handed her that first shimmering, fragile translucent ball, had been succeeded by an ambivalent old-young cotton-woolly, grease-painted smiler who had held her on his knee in the Fairy Palace, uttered a lubricious chuckle, rubbed his prickly crimson cheek on her face, patted her hot and lingering on her small bottom, and had given her a curious object like a jet turd, or rubber lump of coal, which had turned out to be a liquorice-sherbert fountain, from which you sucked a lot of bright yellow sparkling powder, which dyed your tongue and teeth mustard-colour.

Even so, there it had been, an annual festival, an annual assurance of the power of the imagination, spreading the spun web of its shining influence far beyond itself, over the whole contents of those heaped floors, counters, racks of material goods. Sprinkling serviceable stockings with snail-trails of silver thread, bobbing up in glass balls, crimson, green and gold amongst the Pyrex dishes, dangling in lines of celluloid and netting gnomes and fairies on black cotton from the whizzing and clanking machinery that shot canisters of money around overhead.

In those early days some mechanical genius had made it possible for you to ascend to the Fairy Palace, or descend to the Grotto in wobbling little chariots, piloted by gnomes and fays, chariots swan-shaped or dragon-shaped, which were winched along what must have been the service escalator and then vanished with a swoop and a clatter, above, or below, as the case was. Frederica had loved that, as she loved ghost trains and helter skelters, the whisking away under a mysterious arch into another place, shiny with artifice. Now she stood sourly on the silvery turning, gliding steps of the main escalator, and was slowly swallowed, erect, into the depths. Past racks of dresses and frou-frous of stiffened net, down past chairs and radiograms and three-piece suites and tables, mahogany, walnut, oak, laid with china, Wedgwood, Minton, Coalport, cut glass and the new Dartington glass with crystal tears enclosed in stocky stems. Down past the Bedding, where someone had built, round the escalator, a radiating series of alternative bedrooms, like segments of an orange, offering, as it were, endless variations on the Idea of a Chair, or of a Bed, low divan with careless striped spread, high quilted scallop shell with glazed chintz valences, utility pale wood with white candlewick, vanitory units in white and gilt, carpets with flowers, with shaggy white fur, with the ubiquitous sperm and matchstick geometry, nut-brown, rose-pink, acid yellow. Each of these roomlets had windows in hardboard and cellophane, under curtains matching the bedspread, gathered net, looking out on a bright dark blue paper sky and a few artificial stars, in the windowless inner dome of the centre of Wallish and Jones. Down past the ground floor, a mart of little things, a Vanity Fair of notions and necessities, novelties, and eye-catchers, to the Household Basement, where segmented kitchens, bright with imitation daylight and abbreviated vistas on to painted pathways and paper floral borders, succeeded the segmented bedrooms. Frederica stepped off the escalator. She glowered into the little kitchens and was not tempted to cross their thresholds, or try their ingenious folding stools or spidery-legged bar-chairs. She passed them by, dismal scarlet and clinical white, ice-blue and jiggy Formica imitating marble chips, made in the days before plastic colours acquired clarity, when they did not know what they were but were only uneasy imitations of other things, and when, furthermore, good taste required that scarlet be muddled and muted before it was an acceptable brightener.

Amongst the gadgets she had hoped to find something cheap and real and ingenious, a tool with an elegant functional shape, or an exotic appliance – a garlic press, a well-shaped spatula, a corkscrew, something inessential but showing goodwill, admitting the *fact* of Stephanie's domestic intentions. But in practice she could not bring herself to touch, or take, any of these either. An inveterate lover of depths, she suddenly developed claustrophobia, and made again for the upper air.

The haberdashery had always been a favourite haunt. They had come here in their early days for lace collars for party dresses, ribbons for hair, tape, elastic, buttons and press-studs. Frederica in 1953 was disposed to see these visits as tedious rituals, although she saw that it might be possible to see them otherwise, with a kind of Dickensian nostalgia for the details of a vanished life, which was, in fact, how in 1973 she came to see them. But today she was depressed too, by papers of pins and packets of needles. She wandered towards the frankly frivolous area of this department, where sleek velvety headless black-amoor busts were draped with gilt and glassy chains, where hooped ear-rings hung from leafless ebony-coloured trees, where monstrous champagne glasses were piled high with solid plastic bubbles, wine-coloured mixed with gold and silver and pearl. Here the counters were festooned with mists of rainbow-splayed chiffon scarves, amongst which blossomed dahlias, roses, asters, peonies, poppies, in silk, or paper, or the new true-to-life plastic, with gold and silver leaves of tin-foil and tinkling aluminium. Wandering through these notions she came unawares on a struggling circle of people, beyond whom was the whirling glass circle of the revolving door, and saw that she had reached the display of bridal veils. Grimly she stopped to survey it. In the centre was a circular kiosk, with a harassed plump girl revolving jerkily within it. Round her, on layers of glass shelving, supported on fragile chrome bars, rose little pronged gilded stands on which were balanced or suspended the wreaths and haloes. Waxen orange blossom, papery silver laurel leaves, velvet bows, glass-studded tiaras, waxy conglobated simulated pears in little clusters on wire stalks, all with their suspended froths of tulle, with those networks of sharp, geometrical lines the random folds take on. Some were by now distinctly grubby, and some were fresh and snowy.

Around the central figure a kind of rugger-scrum of brides-to-be were easing and squeezing their hips. Outside was cold and wet: inside was hot: steam rose from tweed and gabardine and fur-lined bootees. A larger ring of attendant mothers, grandmothers, aunts and sisters stood like seconds in an enclosure around the working throng, and clutched umbrellas, hats, and damp parcels. It was possible for the girls to get their heads to the counter, and to stretch their necks in the direction of the many stalked and circular mirrors that stood on the counter among the veiling. It was almost impossible for them to make space for their bodies to follow. They bent their trunks acutely forward, their bottoms wedged, elongated themselves unnaturally and obliquely, and reached, clutched, wavered, at the crowns above. When they had reached these, and lowered them onto their damp hair, they had to keep up a steady shoving and wriggling of their lower parts, in order not to lose their balance. Some, having peered in the mirrors, twisted their torsos to display a framed face to the attendant relatives, tilting, nervously clutching, sometimes, as though in a wind. Frederica watched, fascinated. Inside the frames of veiling, over the bulky, too solid bodies, the faces changed. There was an occasional smirk of embarrassment, or grimace of distaste, but most of these faces, revealed with a classical gesture of a hot damp hand suddenly taking on a produced, shy grace, composed themselves into a remote and reverential expression, round faces, horsy faces, prim faces, anaemic faces, faces with steel-rimmed glasses, all with parted lips and eyes stretched in a kind of ritual amazement at an as yet unachieved new self, new world. Frederica thought it was touching and absurd, and looked at their legs, stumping, thumping, jostling on the muddy floor.

After a moment she laughed aloud, and went back to the Notions for a silly present for Stephanie.

In the end she bought two silly things, a pair of swansdown and white kid slippers in a kind of transparent casket with a pink bow on it, and a belt, one of those chain-mesh belts, somewhere between a dog-lead and armour, that were then so fashionable, where you hooked one end into a link of the chain and let the rest dangle like an imitation châtelaine. Or fetter. This took up the whole of her *Four Quartets* fund but satisfied her. Stephanie could save the slippers for her honeymoon, they would be a sign that Frederica sympathised with the whole enterprise. A revelation. As for the belt, she had chosen it on the very good principle that it was what she would have liked herself, as a random gift.

After that she inserted herself into the whirling glass door, described a neat half-circle, took a deep breath of fresh air, which made her feel giddy, and strode away down the grey and rainy street.

20. *Paterfamilias*

It was a rule of Alexander's not to enter the houses, or homes, of married women with whom he was in love. It was, he believed, good neither for them nor for him. Either they did not like their houses or homes and were therefore irritable and distracted, or else they did, secretly, like them, and wanted to consecrate either house or lover by bringing him into it. There was a third possibility, which he had never encountered, but feared, that one woman, one day, would require him to join in the ritual destruction of house or home, to take hatchet and blowlamp to it, and make love in the wreck of the drawing-room curtains. Once or twice it had come perilously near that. He preferred to be the man outside.

He had had a good Easter. He had written to Jennifer how he missed her in all places, walking through his parents' hotel, peering through numbered doors at anonymous bed after anonymous bed, striding, alas alone, over chalk downs or prowling along the tide-line on Weymouth sands. His parents had an endless series of brown Edwardian basement kitchens and sculleries, sparsely furnished, with ill-fitting glazed doors and gusty coconut matting. There they sat amongst monstrous cans of tomato soup and boxes of dehydrated onion, turning the pages of the *Daily Telegraph* and listening to the radio. Captain and Mrs Wedderburn were both proprietors and staff, planning comings, goings and shoppings, sorting soiled sheets and damaged crocks. Alexander did not

write to Jennifer about this. "My parents are well and happy and glad
to see me," he wrote, though they had barely found time to address him.
He wrote elegant letters also to Crowe, about the intense pleasures of
solitary walks and no boys. Crowe's replies, full of enthusiasm for the
summer ahead, he carried with Jenny's in his pockets.

When he got back Jenny's spirits seemed low, and her manner almost
fractious. He was not sure whether she was distressed because he had
been away, or angry that she was forced to stay put. They met once on
the Castle Mound and realised they were being overlooked by the
apparently disembodied, grinning face of the girl in a snood, who
materialised in a bramble bush. "Like the Cheshire cat," said Alexander,
but Jenny said fiercely that that was no joke, she was now a perpetual
Alice peering through tiny keyholes into inaccessible gardens, she
wanted a bit of mundane reality. Thank you.

So Alexander found himself calling on her for tea, having carefully
arranged to be expected down the road at the Potters in the evening.
Bill Potter was not speaking to Geoffrey Parry since they had quarrelled
about Thomas Mann, who was, Bill said, an otiose charlatan. Parry said
they could agree to differ. Bill said no self-respecting intellect could
carry on like that. Parry said Bill did not read German. Bill said that in
this case that didn't matter. Parry said Bill was insular, and Bill said that
was ignorant abuse. Parry told Jennifer, who was not listening, that
irascibility and immoderation need not be infectious. He had not spoken
to Bill since.

Jennifer had baked a special cake for Alexander, and made special tea.
She rubbed her face ecstatically against his when he came through the
door, and small Thomas, on her arm, gave a proprietary pull at the flesh
of her cheek. She took Alexander on a guided tour which he had not
asked for. He was troubled to realise that she attributed to him the
lover's intense curiosity to know every detail of the hidden life of the
beloved, pink-blossomed lavatory, nursery with Beatrix Potter frieze
and cheery sub-Miro mobile, bedroom with Swedish furniture and tweed
curtains. In the bedroom he felt like a voyeur, a dirty intruder. Jennifer
moaned softly and took his hand. Small Thomas, propped on her hip,
moaned too. She put the child on the bed and sat down herself on its
edge. Alexander went on standing. Thomas whickered and tugged at her
clothes: she gave him a little push and he burst into tears. She picked
him up, twisting him expertly and not ungently, hung him head down
over one shoulder, where he could not see, and returned abruptly
downstairs.

They took tea, both jumpy, both aching with something that was
neither desire nor the opposite. Thomas, in his high chair, stared at

Alexander with glass-blue eyes. Alexander sipped tea from roseate china and thought: she would have let me, with him peering from the other side of the bed. Jenny cut bread and Marmite soldiers for Thomas, who cast them on the floor. She turned his chair away to the window. "Look at the trees and the blue sky and the sun, Thomas." Thomas gulped and churked and twisted back to continue his gaze at Alexander. Alexander felt he should address him, and held out an uneasy finger which was taken in a wary, buttery grip. "He likes you," she said. "Oh dear." She wiped a few tears, gathered up Thomas and seated him on Alexander's knee, allowing one of her own hands to linger electrically in his crotch as she did so. She sniffed and stood back to contemplate them.

Thomas was small, hot and solid. Thomas's little hand rested on his arm. Thomas smelled both very washed and very grubby, soap and urine, witch-hazel, Marmite and jam. Thomas was human, would be a man, stared steadily, critically, gloomily. After a moment he jack-knifed, agitated his whole body like a jelly or jumping bean, and nearly plunged to the floor. She snatched him up, twisted him into blank reverse over a shoulder, kissed him, squeezed him into silence.

"He would *love* you, Alexander."

"I must go to the Potters." He stood up and brushed his clothes.

"I love you."

"I love you. I can't bear to be in this house like this. It's no good. You must get a whole day off and come out in my car. I have *got* the car."

"I can't."

"You must. Use your ingenuity."

"My cunt hurts." Blushing.

"It will. So do I. I can't bear any more of this."

He got out, and went to the Potters.

Frederica let him in. As she opened the door she warned him in a stage-whisper. "There's a monster row brewing in this house. I should say it'll blow up about now. Everybody's been foul for days."

"Perhaps I should go home."

"Oh *no*," said Frederica, and closed him in.

They were all there. Something was wrong with the lighting: it was unusually cold and dim. Bill asked if Alexander would like sherry, poured a little for the two of them, and then, as an afterthought, a small dose for Winifred. No one but Frederica showed any impulse to speech: Frederica rattled on to Alexander about Mrs Parry, and her performance in *The Lady's Not for Burning*, from which it was only a short step to Frederica's own determination to be a professional actress, not sit in a house and let her talents, such as they were, fust in her unused, by God. Since she had had Lodge's letter offering her the part of Elizabeth before her coronation she had been, apart from the contretemps in the Chattery, in glory, and had taken to decorating her conversation with oaths and expletives, not exactly archaic, but obviously modern versions of Elizabeth's. This was very trying. Alexander tried to damp her enthusiasm with statistics about the number of unemployed female members of Equity. Bill said she would go to University and get a good degree, like Stephanie, and then she would be equipped to choose a profession.

"Like Stephanie," said Frederica jeering.

"Like Stephanie," said Bill. "Though you show surprisingly little sign of Stephanie's self-discipline, or respect for truth, I must say."

"I suppose Stephanie's done what you want, then, Stephanie's career is O.K. by you?"

"She could do better. She will do better. This place is only a stage."

"You don't know anything about Stephanie, or what she means to do. You don't know what she wants, or what any of us want. You don't know what you've done to us."

"Oh, Frederica," said Stephanie. She began to redden. Alexander looked at her with interest. He thought that Frederica had predicted a row with such certainty because she intended to provoke it.

"I know that Stephanie wants too little. I tell her frequently she's wasting herself in that place. You would agree I'm sure, Alexander."

Alexander was saved from replying by Winifred, who said, without thinking rapidly enough of the consequences of speech, since she was put out by Frederica, "That isn't it. Something's wrong – Stephanie?"

"Nothing is wrong. Nothing at all. The truth is, I am engaged to be married. I didn't want to talk about it yet."

For some reason she was addressing Alexander. She looked unhappy. Bill said, "And to whom, if I may ask, since I must ask, since I have no inkling, are you engaged to be married?"

Still addressing Alexander, she said, "To Daniel Orton."

"And who is Daniel Orton?"

It was impossible, Alexander decided, to work out whether this question arose from genuine ignorance or heavy irony. It was answered by Frederica.

"He's the curate. The one who comes, you know, who came about kittens."

"No," said Bill.

"My felicitations," said Alexander, weakly.

"You must be out of your mind."

"I want to marry him. I've thought about it. So has he. It's something you're supposed to think about for yourself."

"Piffle."

"Daddy, please don't *start*. Please don't. I do mean what I say. It is my life. Please don't."

"Your life. And what the hell do you think that will be, married to the curate? Chat and hassocks and Brownies and Mothers and Fayres. You're totally unfitted for that sort of non-existence. Like a race-horse in a milk-float. You'll go crazy in a week if you aren't, as I said, already. And he must be mad, or totally without imagination, to expect it of you. Not that he looks as though imagination's his strong point."

"Daddy –"

"And then there's his faith, such as it is, in these latter days. I take it you don't share that, you haven't gone as far as *that* –"

"No, but –"

"No but?"

"His work, his *work* is good, I respect his work."

"It isn't *your* work, you fool, it doesn't require your gifts, and it does require things you haven't got. The man can't have thought at all. His Vicar'll never permit it. My God, Stephanie, you aren't going to tell me you can honestly want to go and join an institution with St Paul's views on women, and views, no doubt, about breeding and the sanctity of recurrent parturition. You'll become a cow. A cow and a slave and a tweedy tea-pourer. You can't."

"I wish you would stop it. You are making a thing of Daniel. You have no right to do that."

Bill turned histrionically to Alexander.

"I am at fault. I am at fault, I must be. I have failed somewhere. All my children lack guts, they lack real guts and persistence. They creep and sidle away from the real challenges. My son is a moony fool, and my daughter wants to marry a lie and a totem and bury her one talent –"

"You are at fault," said Frederica. "You are at fault because you do what you're doing now. You make it impossible for us to do what you want us to do because you make it seem totally repulsive by the way you go on. I should think she's marrying the curate just to spite you, just to shut up your voice grinding on and on so sure what's right and good . . ."

"Frederica be quiet," said Winifred. "And Bill. Be quiet. You are doing irreparable damage."

"I'm trying to *stop* irreparable damage, you lunatic. Do you want the girl to marry a fat curate?"

"No. I don't. But I don't think it matters, what we want. It's her decision, and I shall stand by her."

"You'll get no thanks. She's intent on flouting us."

"No," said Stephanie chilly. "Whatever you – and Frederica – think –

it's nothing to do with you. I love Daniel. It wasn't an easy thing. And you are making it all much worse. But you won't change anything. So please, don't go on."

Bill gathered up a tall pile of books topped by an ashtray and flung them at her. She bent sideways. The books landed, fluttering and thudding, around her: the ashtray hit a small lamp, which exploded, scattering glass and a smell of burning. Stephanie picked up two books. Her hands were shaking. Alexander saw that there was a crusty thin line of foam at Bill's mouth-corners. He averted his eyes and said, "I think you shouldn't say any more. And I feel it isn't right for me to be here. And Stephanie is very distressed."

"Very distressed," said Bill. "Very distressed. And so she should be and so am I. Very distressed. All right. I won't say any more. I shan't mention this topic again, ever. You may do what you like, of course, but whatever it is, I want no part in it, so you will kindly not bother me with it ever again."

He glared round the room, nodded curtly at Alexander, and slammed himself out. Winifred, her face expressionless, went after him.

"I told you it would be awful," said Frederica.

"You didn't help," said Stephanie.

"I tried," said Frederica.

"Hardly," said Alexander.

Stephanie had wrapped her arms round herself and was shivering. Alexander went over to her.

"Are you all right?"

"Probably. I feel sick."

"You shouldn't try so hard to be reasonable."

"We were brought up to be reasonable."

"Hardly," said Alexander.

"Oh yes we were. To believe in reason and humanity and personal relations and tolerance. You can reinforce any precept with any technique. I shall never feel the same for him after this."

Her voice was thin and small. Alexander had a nasty moment's doubt as to whether it was Bill or Daniel she would never feel the same for. Frederica declared robustly, "He'll come round. He does."

"And if he does I shall have been through all this for nothing. I shall be expected to pretend it doesn't really matter. That's what he does to us, what he always does, so we are in the wrong to mind what he says, because he explains he didn't exactly mean it. So you become guilty of letting ugly words go sour in your head because they've been unsaid."

"You can't afford to mind what's absurd."

"No." Very coldly.

"Stephanie – go and talk to Daniel. Now. As soon as you can."

"Daniel? I can't tell him about this. That would be *terrible*. I can't . . ."

"It's his business," said Alexander, gently. Stephanie began to cry in great panicky gulps.

"I can't *remember* him. I can't remember him properly. It's not as though I hadn't had my own – debates with myself – about those things – the Church –"

"But Daniel's there," said Alexander, "and real." He put his arms round her and she smelled the fragrance of Old Spice. She could not say that his own unreality, in that sense, and his presence now, exacerbated her uncertainties. She clung to him and wept and he stroked her hair, over and over.

Frederica sat unremarked on the sofa. She felt shaken and invigorated. Their lives had been punctuated by such gales of rage. This was by no means the first broken lamp. They lived by a myth of normality, an image of closed family safeties and certainties. But there were rips and interstices through which the cold blasts howled, had always howled and would howl. That had its exhilarating aspect. Howls, grimaces, naked unreason were not, as the Potter ethic and aesthetic said, temporary aberrations. They were the stuff of things. If you knew they were there you could act, truly. She uncurled, patted Stephanie, who winced, on the shoulder, and went out.

"The trouble is," said Stephanie, "I feel unfit to live."

"Nonsense."

"No, truly. He makes me feel like that. I don't think it's a sensible thing to feel, I just do."

"You placate him like Jehovah. That's no good."

"Isn't it?"

"No, because it makes it worse. For him, too."

"I should be dead. I want *not to be*."

"You want to marry Daniel Orton."

Having said this, he kissed her, drily and gently, on the mouth. She dropped her head on his shoulder, and so they sat, for some time. She could not remember Daniel, it was true.

21. *The Traveller in Dolls*

Frederica offered her gifts, with a flourish and an apology, to Stephanie. Stephanie thanked her, and said she really need not have bothered. Stephanie was clever enough, Frederica considered, to know how hurtful such remarks about not bothering can be. She tried to make allowances for stress, but thought Stephanie should have recognised that she was under considerable strain herself.

She was suffering from a generalised wrath, inspired by a kind of illicit sex-film, blurry and full of hiatuses, which ran constantly in her head and elsewhere. Daniel, however fat, had become monstrously interesting: willy-nilly Frederica's imagination lifted the clerical shirt and rolled down the clerical trousers, measured the weight of the mountain belly or fleetingly saw the gleeful prancing of Stephanie's soft white and his craggy and hirsute black. She exposed herself to the air, which was not penetrating but encased her in claustrophobic heat. She snarled at everyone, postured and boasted, and elicited a response only from the mirror. Winifred suggested that she go for a good long walk and get some fresh air. This released Frederica like a spring: she took the bus to Calverley, from where she intended to take a further bus onto the North Yorkshire Moors, and tramp.

Behind Calverley Minster, in which she wandered for a rapid fifteen minutes, was the bus yard. Frederica mounted a brown bus that was going to Goathland and Whitby, and settled back against the window, hoping vaguely for the sense of disembodiment a good journey can confer. A man came and sat beside her. She ritually rose, subsided, indicating concession of space, drawing in her skirt. Her neighbour immediately swelled to fill the space. The bus drew away, out of Calverley. She glanced quickly at the man. He wore a hairy, reddish-brown suit, inside which he was very solid. The square hand on the knee next to her wore a gold signet ring. She looked out of the window.

Outside Calverley, the bus began to climb. Frederica, loosed from grumble and heat, began to think. She thought about Racine. They were doing *Phèdre* for A Level. Miss Plaskett, the French teacher, set them to write endless character analyses: they had done Phèdre, Hippolyte, Aricie, Oenone but not yet Thésée. A Level took that form. Somehow what they were doing made Racine seem exactly like Shakespeare and Shakespeare exactly like Shaw – last term she had done Joan, Dunois, Cauchon, de Stogumber in exactly the same way. One was required to discuss the function of the characters in the plot, and on top of that, like cream on a trifle, what extra individuality they had, what intrinsic nature, unique and separate. The other thing they did, which made Shakespeare like Racine, but not like Shaw (who was indeed rather recalcitrant to the good, professional A Level candidate), was trace recurrent images. Blood and babies in *Macbeth*, blood and light and dark in *Phèdre*. This made both Shakespeare and Racine seem very like Alexander Wedderburn. (Shaw was more difficult. If you did not repeat his own polemical points you had almost nothing left to say. If you were any good, it was most unsatisfactory, repeating someone else's, even the author's, remarks about what his play was about. He had made that kind of commentary redundant. There must be some other kind, but she was damned if she knew what it was.)

Whereas what struck one, meeting Shakespeare and Racine, was the difference, in the whole frame of the work. There ought to be a way of describing the difference. Compare and contrast Phèdre and Cleopatra as portrayals of passionate women. No, no. It was not really to do with the unities either, which felt like a red herring.

It was to do with the Alexandrine. You had to think differently, the actual form of your thought was different, if you thought in closed couplets, further divided by a rocking caesura, and if you thought in French, in a limited vocabulary.

Ce n'est plus une ardeur dans mes veines cachée.
C'est Vénus toute eutière à sa proie attachée.

Four segments of a proposition, balanced, *balanced*, even in this most extreme statement, and think of the effect of emphasising cachée and attachée by the rhyme. Did one *see* Venus toute entière? She had without thinking always seen a formless crouching thing, dropped from a branch, claws extended, involved in the struggling body like Stubbs's lion and horse. The outer ripping up the inner. But the verse form separated the clutcher from the clutched whilst linking them inexorably. Something like that. Now if one wrote, Frederica thought, on the thought processes of the Alexandrine – one might get somewhere – see how *argued* comparatively the images were, not fluent as in Shakespeare. She grinned a grin of pure pleasure, sitting staring out at what was by now a distinctly moorland landscape, the road bordered by uneven banks and expanses of wiry grass and trembling cotton grass, the earth humping and folding and cracking away to the horizon in granite and heather and bracken plots.

The man next to her encroached. It was usually true that the person on her own side took up an unfair proportion of the seat. This man's large bottom was warm on hers. His forearm overlapped her space. When the bus swung round a corner he put out a hand, clasped her knee, righted himself, and said,

"Sorry. Bit unsteady."

"Not at all."

"Going far?"

"Goathland."

"You live there?"

"No, no."

"Sightseeing?"

"A day out."

"Likewise. Got a day to spare, thought I'd view the wilds. On your own?"

"Yes."

"Likewise."

Economical, Frederica thought. He relaxed into silence again. His bottom grew larger and closer. His lapel nudged her breast. His breathing was noticeable. She put her face on the window and studied the landscape. Last year's browns, faded biscuit bracken, old heather, on this year's raw earth and coming greens. There was art without landscape, before it, maybe after it. Racine for instance, would have had no interest in shades of bracken, and Mondrian, whom she had just discovered, almost certainly had none either. If you lived up here, you supposed landscape was of the essence, you had a Brontesque sense of using it to think and perceive with but at the same time it was in the way. You could neither see it nor through it, it was thickened with too many associations. Momentarily she envisaged an imaginary London flat, possibly Alexander's, smooth pale woods, much white, closed curtains, soft light, artificial shapes, squared, rounded, streamlined, touches of cream and gold. She grinned again, which again aroused speech in her neighbour.

"Got any tips about what to do in this place?"

"No. They say it's very pretty."

"They do. Might take a stroll, stretch the old legs, eh? Funny, me taking a trip on my day off, seeing I travel by way of business. I've been all up and down this county this week. Huddersfield, Wakefield, Bradford, York, Calverley. Off to Harrogate Toy Fair. I'm in the toy trade. You'd think I'd want to keep still on my day off, but I find I'm restless."

Frederica nodded cautiously. The man said, with a surprise flare of irritability, "You get lonely travelling. It's hard to keep up house and family, if you've got to travel. I pour money into that home, I pour it, you'd not believe, but I get no benefit of it, unless you count the pleasure of knowing they're better off than they'd otherwise be. Nothing personal. You can't expect to be part of things, like if you came home regular for your tea. I sometimes feel I'm resented, if I turn up, making trouble, like, so I don't, if I can help it, any more, I don't put myself out dashing around, straining myself, I send a nice postcard and stay put, take a little trip or two like this, see a thing or two, chat to people. I find it's more pleasant in the long run, less disillusioning."

"Yes," said Frederica, who never came to know who inhabited that home, parents, wife or children. "My sister's getting married. So we've got chaos."

"I bet, I bet," said the brown man, with huge sympathetic force.

When they got to Goathland the coach stopped outside a pub. It was cold: on the irregular village green geese walked, and moorland sheep trailed, munched, glowered, trotted away. Frederica's companion said, "Buy you a drink." She thought of saying no, but wanted to see inside a pub, where she had never been. Asked what she would drink, she said "whisky", which she had had for colds, with honey, and felt was more appropriate to the place where they were than sherry, or gin and lime. The man bought her two whiskies, and talked to her about dolls.

"Now you wouldn't think it, but the Huns make much sweeter dolls than what we do. Real pretty little faces, soft hair, ever so natural, ever so delicate. Our own average doll's a real hard-faced little thing, with cheeks like red marbles and rattly eyes like little stones, and they don't stop them clattering when you tip them. Surprising the kids like most of them at all, with their blood-red sweetie pie mouths and cutie expressions, which make you a bit sick if you really look at them, which I don't, of course, in the run of things, my job being to sell the product. Mind you, kids'll love anything, I often think they don't really see what they're cuddling at all, any old rag, or clothes-peg, or rubber contraption'd do most kids if they'd decided on it to cuddle. I've noticed that. But if you're in a position to make comparisons you get a sort of sense of the ideal. I'd really like to see a natural doll, you know, a soft one, with real wrinkles like babies have, one that drank and wet and all that, with those useless little legs real babies have. I could design one but the trade wouldn't touch it, much too ugly, no hair, all that bulgy tummy, they wouldn't contemplate it. Pity that. Pity about little boy dolls too. Just permissible if black or Dutch, costumes on over nice smooth nothings. I wonder if the kids ever ask where the little cockle or winkle or widdler or whatjumcallit they see on self and brothers is. We wasn't made to be so bashful, it persists throughout life. More whisky? No harm in accuracy, wouldn't you say? But if I tried it, I'd be prosecuted."

"I'm sure. I had a nice rubber doll. Her name was Angelica. But her stomach perished. Her vest melted into it. It was horrible."

"Too hot, I expect you got her. Talcum powder helps, with rubber. Now take hair. Take hair. The Huns are better at hair, too. They've got a much better range of colours – quite realistic – our stuff's all raven black or platinum blonde or occasionally auburn, if you can call it that. Henna'd I'd say. But the Huns make quite natural looking hair and space the tufts better, not in regimented rows as you might expect of them, but natural like, all over the head, some of them real pretty, as I said. It destroys your faith in Made in Britain, it does really, and I don't want to have to praise the Huns, I assure you. Not me. I've seen too much. Though mind you, not the Huns, nor the British or anyone else could get hair so lovely and soft and unusual as yours is. Such a marvellous shade, really unique, if you don't mind the remark."

"Thank you," said Frederica, with irrelevant dignity.

"Not at all. Now, I was in the occupying forces in Germany and I can tell you artistic dolls is the last thing you'd want to think Germans could do. Lampshades of human skin, more like, and walking skeletons, same as what we saw when we marched in to liberate those Polish death camps. I tell you what reminded me of them; I went in the Minster and there was those figures of corpses and skeletons those old bishops used to keep on the bottom shelf, of their tombs, to remind themselves. Think of a host of those twittering at you, and smelling something awful when you came in. Turn your stomach and your nerves for good that would. You couldn't think they were human, tho' they were what you'd come for. More whisky? No. How about a bit of a walk round?"

Under the table his ankle hooked hers, wrinkled sock on nylon stocking. She felt that the rules of some game she didn't know were being strictly if eccentrically observed. So much drink, so much talk, a ration of each, and then,

"What's your name?"

"Freda. Freda Plaskett."

"Unusual. Mine's Ed. Edward really, of course, I prefer Edward, but Ed I always get."

"Ed."

"Shall we go?"

They walked through the centre of Goathland, down a road that became a track, scrambled over a little beck, and took a few steps into the real country. It became clear that Ed meant to go no further. He enquired whether Frederica felt it would be too cold to have a sit down. She said no. He produced a macintosh and laid it out under a somewhat Wordsworthian thorn bush. Frederica sat stiffly on the edge of it, telling herself that there were certain things that when she knew them would not bother her in the same way any more. She had read *Lady Chatterley*, true, and *The Rainbow* too, and *Women in Love*, but it cannot be said that she expected a revelation from the traveller in dolls. She wished her ignorance, part of it, to be dispelled. She wished to become knowledgeable. She wished to be able to pinpoint the sources of her discontent.

Ed propped himself, rather clumsily, on one elbow beside her, and looked up at her face. She did not meet his eye. Throughout the whole proceedings, she did not really consider his face. Its general outline was heavy-jowled and clean-shaven. He had short, bristly brown hair.

"Comfy?" he enquired.

"More or less."

"Better if you relax a bit and lie down."

She lay down.

"Good girl," he said, and humped his body over to hers. He threw one leg over hers and applied his face to her face, kissing, pecking, with hot, firm, dry lips, every bit of it, brow, cheeks, closed eyelids, chin, lips. He had a kind of daemonic proficiency, he had entered upon the performance of a routine technique. After a certain time spent on this dry kissing he began to apply himself simply to her mouth, nipping it, with lips, with teeth, rubbing it sideways, finally pushing it open with his tongue, which seemed monstrously huge, round and swollen, breathing nicotine, beer and tea. Their teeth clashed and jarred. Frederica tried to twist away, which increased his activity, he clamped her close with one arm and lifted the weight of his body onto hers. She felt his hard front pressing on her, rubbing, rubbing, and her own tongue, curled back in retreat, relaxed momentarily and brushed his, which caused her to quiver with anxiety, revulsion, and the persistent and appalling anonymous curiosity. Perhaps he was a sex maniac. She should have thought.

At this point he ran his hand up her leg, inside her skirt, as far as her thick school knickers. These he began to rub as efficiently as he was rubbing her face. Frederica wanted to twist away in embarrassment or revulsion. I shall go mad, she thought, I have got to know and I can't stand it. It doesn't matter how you get to know, it has got not to matter. She tried to close her legs, to say no, but her mouth was occupied, her pelvis weighted, and the busy hand was slowly moving round to the inside of her knickers which was, to her intense embarrassment, becoming hot and wet. It was strange: the more she disliked the whole business, the more a kind of automatic greed in her body took over, so that it rose of its own accord to meet, to invite the intrusive fingers so that when finally, he thrust two of them into her she twisted in anguish on them, convulsed by something, and tears started to her eyes. She imagined those working fingers, blunt, unknown, nicotine stained, not too clean, and went wild with contrary passions, biting back at the biting mouth, arching her body, flinging up an arm to beat at or caress the wiry hair which turned out to be, in fact, baby-soft and giving. Her dress was thrown up and her legs were both cold and wet. It occurred to her to wonder what if she were to want to pee, and this thought stilled her. Ed then took her hand and guided it gently to his fly front. Frederica let it stay there, uncertainly, for a moment or two over his suit, and then removed it, after a momentary vague pressure for politeness sake. She did not know what she was expected to do, and did not want to do it. She went suddenly, largely involuntarily, limp. When Ed picked up her hand again she removed it fairly firmly and turned away her face. He sat up abruptly and could be seen carefully wiping his hand on his handkerchief. Frederica pulled her legs together over the hot, scratched, throbbing feeling and considered him. She had no means of telling, no precedent, whether this was an expected outcome, a monstrous frustration, a signal for a new onslaught. In fact, staring out at the impassive moorland, Ed began again to talk.

"Some of the chaps and me, in the Army, before the German bit, we used to visit the brothels in Cairo. They had shows, you know, as well as the usual, and the unusual I expect you might call it. Some of it wasn't much cop, you can see enough of the same thing and I've never been one for boots and such. But there were things you don't see every day. Like the place where they had this girl, and they used to hang this donkey over her, in a pretty tough net, suspended from the ceiling. She'd work it up, like, the ass, lie under it and work it up, with her hands and her mouth and all she'd got, a real active girl. It had this great tool, fair bursting through the net, and it would get properly worked up, but it couldn't come at her, because of the net. They had to have it tied up, like, or it could have done her a lot of damage, torn her up, split her apart, and its hooves plunging about and her twisting and turning. That was something, that was."

He stopped talking, as abruptly as he'd started. Frederica could think of nothing to say. They sat side by side, both with a slightly puzzled frown. He said,

"We'd best be getting back to the village. Could take the next bus to the coast."

"I think – I'll stay here, and just walk about."

They sat a bit longer.

"Well," said Ed. "I'll be off. If you would get off my macintosh."

Frederica stood up in a hurry, whilst he gathered up the macintosh, brushed it meticulously, hung it over his arm, gave her a taciturn nod, and set off back up the track.

She did not, in fact, walk very far: only a little way onto the moor and then, rather aimlessly, back onto the track again. The desire to stride out had quite left her: so had her strip-film. She did not by any means know all that was necessary but it was undoubtedly true that she knew considerably more than when she had set out. She walked along the track, and came across a very clean, silvery car, parked in a gateway.

It seemed familiar, and then was certainly recognised. She walked up to it, put her face against the front window, and peered in.

The front seats were empty. In the back seat, Alexander was spread ungracefully, one knee trailing off the seat, over some vanished and un-identified woman. His jacket and trousers were on, his waistline lumpish and knotted under the flaring corduroy coat-skirts. The beautiful hair hung smooth and soft over his face and onto the woman's, brushing her, obscuring him. Frederica froze, and stared. She continued, mesmerised, possessed by curiosity, to peer in; Alexander, alerted by something, raised his face, flushed and delicately shining, and met her eyes.

The framed face of Frederica Potter, in the midst of the Goathland moors, was much worse than the Cheshire cat apparition of the girl in the snood on the Castle Mound. She had repaired her make-up after the episode with Ed, and the face Alexander saw had a certain puppet-like garishness, as was then fashionable, arched, gilded eyelids, gleaming wine-dark mouth, pale-powdered mask around them. Large gilded rings depended from the ears, under the red hair. Her expression, as Alex-ander read it, was eager and cruel. For what felt like a very long moment they held each other's eye, silently. Then Alexander decided confusedly that if he ducked, that was, if he dropped his face again over Jennifer, who was he hoped protected by his own body from Frederica's scrutiny, Frederica might not identify Jennifer, and might perhaps, ignored, go away. She was no hallucination, her breath misted his windscreen. He curled himself, with as dignified a motion as was possible, around Jenny, and waited, listening to his breathing. He wished, for all sorts of reasons, aesthetic and muscular, that they had got out of the car. But Jenny complained of the cold.

Installed again in the bus, Frederica was surprised to see Ed mounting its step. She was more surprised when he came and sat down beside her and pulled out a fat black notebook. Before the bus got moving, he told her, business-like, he would just like to take down her name and address. In case he ever came her way, which was likely enough, with the travelling. Frederica reiterated Miss Plaskett's surname and recited a fictitious address, composed of the number of Jennifer's house with the name of Daniel's street, and a telephone number composed of half the school's number added to half the doctor's. This fictive tissue of true facts had a plausibility pure invention could not have had: she was rather proud of it: though unable to understand why Ed should have shown any interest in having it. He wrote it down, slowly and patiently, breathing heavily, and spoke to her no more between Goathland and Calverley, though occasionally on corners his bottom squashed hers in the old way.

She thought, hard. Her day had been bitty, but full of things: Stephanie, Calverley Minster, Racine, the moorland, Ed, Alexander. Taken together, as they undoubtedly could be, these things had alarming aspects. If, for instance, you took the bad pictures of Daniel, and related them to *Vénus toute entière*, and that to Ed, and Ed's hot swollen tongue to the donkey's hot swollen tool, and those to Alexander, and if, for aesthetic elaboration you pressed, in a military sense, the Cathy-Heathcliff aspects of moorland, the crude Freudian view of the upthrust of the spire of Calverley Minster, you had what could be called an organic image that was, there was no question, extremely depressing, if undoubtedly powerful.

But, if you kept them separate. If you kept them separate, in many ways you saw them more truly.

Racine, for instance, was important because of the Alexandrine. *Vénus toute entière* was simply an example, not a particularly good one in fact, which she happened to have chosen because everyone knew it by heart, you could remember it easily on a bus bumping over a moor.

The moor, to continue, was nothing to do with Cathy-Heathcliff unless she chose. What she had seen was that last year's bracken was pale biscuit colour, and that at a distance the haze of biscuit over the uncurling green seemed striped.

Ed was nobody. She had let him do that because he was nobody. She had not seen his face and if that had been accident it was now design, she would not look at his face. He had his function. Beyond it, she had stopped him off.

The donkey was nothing to do with anything but she now knew about it. It was, in itself, interesting.

As for Alexander. She knew perfectly well who Jenny was, having recognised the colouring of those parts of her that stuck out. She ought to have been put out, but was not. The feeling she had, on seeing Alexander, was one of power. Knowledge was power, as long as one did not muck it up by confusing one piece of knowledge with another and trying to ingest it and turn it all into blood and feelings. She knew now what was what, who did what to whom, and what Ed did to her, and Alexander to Jennifer were useful knowledge but different things from what she would do to Alexander, or he to her, when the time came. It now seemed possible that there was a time, which would or could come.

One could let all these facts and things lie alongside each other like laminations, not like growing cells. This laminated knowledge produced a powerful sense of freedom, truthfulness and even selflessness, since the earlier organic and sexual linking by analogy was undoubtedly selfish. It was she, not Daniel, Alexander, Racine, Ed, the Cairo donkey, Emily Brontë and the architects of Calverley Minster who had linked these creatures to each other out of her own necessity. The whole problem of selfishness and selflessness was odd, since seeing things either separate or linked felt like an exercise of power, which she had been most ambiguously, by her father, taught to eschew theoretically and pursue in practice.

She sensed that the idea of lamination could provide both a model of conduct and an aesthetic that might suit herself and prove fruitful. It would, she decided, as in the event it did, take years to work out the implications.

She returned to the Alexandrine, as the part easiest to concentrate on, least likely to stir up all the others. It seemed that there was some very simple way in which it was clear to her that Racine's play was *good* – hard, strong, finished, durable – in a region in which she was very much less sure about *Astraea*. Now, how did one come to recognise that sort of goodness, and how did one check one's judgment? Could that be measured in the structure of the lines of verse?

It was probably a good thing for her at seventeen that she had no knowledge of Coleridge's ideas of the origin of metre. By the time she acquired this piece of information, she was equipped to laminate it, too.

22. *Much Ado*

Winifred came to Stephanie's room one night, an unusual step for her, who assumed that Stephanie, like herself, preferred things unstated and undiscussed. She said that she had come to the conclusion that she herself must invite Daniel to the house, if Stephanie wished it, and welcome him. As for Bill, she went on, when Stephanie did not answer, he would come round, Stephanie knew that, he always did. Stephanie replied that she doubted this. A man like Daniel, Winifred hoped, would respect another man's passionately held beliefs. Stephanie said dully that she doubted this too. Daniel was not a tolerant man, was capable of considerable anger. Winifred showed agitation, and asked if she could sit down. She did not want Stephanie, she said, to marry an angry man. She had tried to make them all a happy home, to give and take, to make allowances; it had cost her. She sat on the end of the bed, in her dressing gown, and said,

"He left me on my honeymoon."

Stephanie stared.

"I've never talked about it to anyone. We went to Stratford-on-Avon and he walked out of the theatre bar in the interval. We were watching *Much Ado*, and I felt so happy, those love scenes are so real – I do love nothing in the world so well as you, is not that strange – so in the interval I told him what I'd done. I felt such accord with him, but it was the play."

"What had you done?"

"Oh yes. I wrote to his parents to tell them we were married and happy. I hoped they might get in touch then, or even come to the wedding."

"But they didn't?"

"No. He was right and I was wrong. Potters are rigid and stubborn."

"Yes," said Stephanie, and thought, she is not a Potter. But I am. I am.

"Anyway, when I said this he began to scream and shout in the bar, as he does. That was the first time. I didn't know he . . . I said, please be quiet, and he said, if it's like that, I'll go where you can't hear me. He rushed out. He took the little car we had. He was gone for two days."

"What did you do?"

"Oh, I tried to sit in my seat, but I couldn't. So I went back to the hotel, and waited. You know, about waiting, you set yourself a limit, before you'll start worrying, an hour, six hours, a day, two days. Two days and two nights in a hotel, with no money and no one. I daren't go far away. Little walks, in case he came back and rushed off again, not finding me waiting. Sometimes I sat in the garden at New Place. I hate those smells now, that garden, ladslove, artemisia, so sour. The weather was lovely, and dog roses too, very pretty. I thought of going home but I was humiliated."

"Was he ill?"

"I wondered. I'd got it in my head to call the police, but it was such a worry, and on one's honeymoon, a difficult time. Then he came back. He said he'd been to Malvern, and walked. So he took me there, too, and we stayed up at the British Camp, and were happy, the happiest time in my life, possibly. Why did I tell you that? Oh yes – I was saying – he does come round, you see."

"You said you didn't want me to marry an angry man."

"No, I don't."

"What did he say when he came back?"

"Oh, he burst into the dining room – I was eating an omelette – I daren't eat anything else, with no money, and I was afraid I'd have a huge bill. And he began to shout how his behaviour was insufferable, and the more he stayed away the more he daren't come back. So we went upstairs – and he said – he was crying – he didn't think he could ever calm down, not really. He shouldn't have married, he said. So I – calmed him down – and said we would work out a way of getting on. And we have."

"I'm glad it ended happily."

"Oh, Stephanie. Don't sound like that. It produced you. I didn't come to tell you that. I came to ask Daniel to lunch. Would he come?"

Daniel did come. Winifred took trouble over the lunch. She made a cheese soufflé, roasted a chicken, put together a fresh fruit salad and splashed in a miniature bottle of Cointreau. She enjoyed the soufflé-making, with a limited nostalgia for pre-war plenty. It was her daughters, children of austerity, who would later go in for authentic, gluttonous cookery with butter and wine and roasted spices. Winifred believed in convenience foods as she believed in labour-saving devices. She remembered baking days in the past, raised pies and kneading dough, as she remembered galvanised wash-tubs, copper ponches and monstrously strutting hand-wringers, chores you were glad to be shot of. She bought wine, for Daniel, and got out damask napkins and cut-glass goblets. She was determined that he should feel both feasted and at his ease.

He crashed into the hall and slammed the front door so violently that the sherry-glasses in the sitting-room tinkled on their tray. He cried out "Hullo, hullo", and admired things too loud, too soon and too much. He was over-confident; he had assumed that he could deal with the social flow of a lunch-party since he spent his life not unsuccessfully battering his way through awkward gatherings. He had exercised his usual sense of priorities and told himself that what Bill and Winifred thought or felt should not, must not, and therefore would not, alter what was between him and Stephanie. This made, as he was to discover, insufficient allowance for what Stephanie thought and felt about them.

He drank several glasses of sherry, very fast. He refused to recognise difficulty. He filled the frequent silences, too rapidly, with comical parish anecdotes and nervously forceful clerical laughter. The anecdotes were mostly bluffly and humbly slanted against himself. He admired the soufflé, which he greatly enjoyed, so vigorously that Winifred felt like some intractable slattern being congratulated by a caseworker on having, at long last, produced an acceptable Spotted Dick. Stephanie said almost nothing.

After lunch they drank coffee out of tiny lustre cups. No one had mentioned marriage. Daniel described to Winifred Stephanie's success with Malcolm Haydock and Winifred was moved as he had meant her to be. She said she knew little of his work, and Daniel, remarking that the left hand was often better not knowing what the right hand did, went into it, perhaps offering credentials, in a professional way. Winifred asked if his profession made it harder and Daniel burst into an account of the funny ideas people had about clergymen, ending up, unfortunately for him, on the subject of clerical sex. Stephanie was already constrained: she had been moved when he told her about the railway-carriage ostracism in Felicity's room but disliked the comic oratorical flourishes he gave to it for her mother. She loved his harsh and practical work, but hated to hear him root out, for her mother, the sloppy abstract words, "spontaneous," "personal," "caring," "tenderness," which made it sound muffled and facile. He began to assure them with booming jollity that clergymen were really just like other men, more or less, as regarded sex, that very few held high views about renouncing birth control, or low views about self-denial, or even sacramental views about Beautiful Unions which entailed a lot of bedroom prayerwork. He became aware of a constraint between the women, and saw Stephanie's face over her coffee, a cool rejecting mask.

"My God," he said to her. "I'm sorry. I was just going on about things I've gone on about before, in other places, in silly contexts. Not to you. I oughtn't to talk like that to you."

Although this was what she thought, she was worse embarrassed to hear him say it.

"Don't be silly," she said.

Winifred took up her courage. "I don't think you should criticise Daniel. There are difficulties – about this marriage – and this is one of them. I am glad you spoke out."

Daniel continued to stare frowning at Stephanie, who did not meet his eye.

There was a further succession of crashes in the hall. The coffee cups rattled. Bill's head came round the door.

"Ah. Am I interrupting? Please tell me if I am, and I'll go." No one spoke.

"Clearly I am interrupting. I'll take myself off."

He made no move. Daniel stood up and extended a hand.

"Good afternoon."

"Thank you," said Bill. He did not take Daniel's hand. The women were still as stones. "Courting my daughter?"

"I hope I've finished with the courting."

"I take it you've been told I think it's potty."

"I'm sorry about that."

"I refuse my consent."

Daniel opened his mouth. Bill rushed on.

"I know I've no *legal* force. But morally, morally I stick. I can't countenance something so patently doomed."

"That's not morality. That's arrogance."

"As for the vulgarity of surreptitious get-togethers . . ."

"I'll go now," said Daniel. "That's best. I've no wish to stay where I'm not welcome. I hope Stephanie will marry me soon. It strikes me she'll be better off wi' me."

Bill skipped dramatically across his path and held out his arms, barring the door.

"You've nothing to offer her. You're nothing to do with what she is."

"That's for her to say." Daniel was very angry, and the anger was fuelled by his awareness of his own previous ineptitudes, and Stephanie's prolonged silence. "I don't like to see you torment her. You presume too much on her love for you. What you do is downright cruel, that's the word, and it's lucky for you she's so very strong. But I'm not sure it's lucky for her. You put it all on her. It's got very little to do with her really. And now will you let me get past."

"Pastoral!" Bill remarked, weak and jeering. He dropped his arms, however, and collapsed into conciliation, with the characteristic suddenness that so disoriented and cheated his family.

"Please don't go. They all know I don't mean most of what I say. Good heavens, I'd – I'd *kill* myself if I thought for a moment anyone *believed* what I say. I huff and puff, I can't deny, but there's smoke and no flames, you ask them, no one's singed. You can't go, we've discussed nothing. Now, Stephanie, you must know we'll stand by you, you are our first-born."

"It isn't a question of standing by," said Stephanie. "I'm not in disgrace, nor am I pregnant."

Daniel sat down. The women were still stony. Bill surveyed them all and said, "Perhaps we should have a glass of – what have I got? – I see you have had sherry and wine is heady. What have I got? Will you have whisky?"

"Yes please."

"Stephanie, please fetch a little jug of water for Mr Orton's whisky. Now Mr Orton I cannot have you supposing I don't love my daughter. All families have their own ways, you know, and if I am volatile and inflammatory in expressing my love, I am at fault, but I am understood. We are a very close family and very alike, and it is *that*, Mr Orton, that leads me still to question whether you have fully thought out how Stephanie will deal with your – faith."

"We have talked about that."

"I suppose you well may have. And your Vicar? I can't imagine he feels great enthusiasm –"

"He's fond of Stephanie," said Daniel, concealing from Bill as he had from Stephanie Mr Ellenby's tortuous anxieties and his own grim stand. "He wants to see her. But he thinks – if she agrees – that it's our business in the end."

A look of passionate distaste played around Bill's pointed face.

"I suppose you can hardly plan to carry out this project for some considerable time."

Better to marry than burn, said Daniel to himself, and said carefully to Bill, as Stephanie returned with the water, that he hoped on the contrary to marry as soon as the banns could be called. That he had been promised a council house on the Arkwright Estate where he felt he should, professionally, be, and which was possible to afford. Bill's slender white hands went to his chest in mock palpitations, he gasped ostentatiously and said, "I see you are a fast worker. I underestimated you. You'll find yourself alienated in that modern desert. I've tried to teach there. It's an asphalt desert, with no sense of community, no cultural roots no . . . In Yorkshire we say Our Nellie, Our Ernie, Our cat, Our Dog, Our Street. But in that place it's *The* Estate, and *the* everything else down. They hate it. Prowling kids and regularly sawn-off cherry-trees. I've been there."

"So've I. It's not that different from where I come from."

"I see. Well, you may be right to want to go there. But I think you should wait some considerable time before taking my daughter."

"I want her now."

Bill poured whisky and chatted on, mostly affably, about the deficiencies of the Estate. The women did not join in. Daniel was aware of their reserve, but nevertheless felt he was managing, he was getting on, the thin end of the wedge was quivering in the aperture. He decided to leave before he outstayed his welcome.

At the door Bill said, "It's all been most instructive, our discussion, I've learned a lot." He contracted his face with chill venom. "But nevertheless, Christianity died in the nineteenth century, my friend. It began to die long before, and achieved it in the third quarter of the nineteenth century. What you think you feel now is an amputated limb that incorporeally wiggles."

"You've said that before. I shan't try and change your mind."

"You couldn't."

"I have a mind of my own, however."

"Not much of one," said Bill, and shut the door in his face.

23. Comus

A few days later Matthew Crowe appeared to Frederica out of the gloom of early evening from behind Pallas Athene in the Blesford Ride Cloisters. He seemed to be delighted to see her, trotted portly up and clasped her hands.

"Dear girl, an unexpected pleasure in these *dismal* surroundings. I have just been to see Alexander, who was surly and unwelcoming. Were you on the same errand?"

"I went to see my father. Also surly and unwelcoming."

"What a *rejecting* institution. My worthy forebear. All this catholic atheist religiosity. Hideous, truly. Look at them. No one smiling except ever-so-sweet Jesus. Athene with the muscles of a coal-heaver and a mouth like Lizzie Siddall. Pop-eye Shakespeare with no calves and drooping garters. Let us go away from them."

"Yes please," said Frederica, who cherished in fact a childhood affection for the hefty Pantheon. They fell into step.

"Working hard?"

"I suppose so. The idea of the play unsettles me. But I can usually work no matter what."

"A great gift."

"Only I get so restless."

"You will always be restless. It's in your blood. Shall I drive you back to my house for a nice relaxing drink? How about that?"

Frederica resisted only ultimate temptations. Crowe conducted her into the Bentley, which gleamed in the school drive. Relaxing into an almost indecently comfortable seat Frederica had a momentary, very distinct perception of what it would be like to want to be a vandal, to bring a heavy knife and rip and shred all this smooth, soft-smelling leather. This startled and then interested her; she folded her hands in her lap as Crowe accelerated and then accelerated, sweeping smooth and monstrous past fields and patches of moor and dry stone walls as though they were floating ribbons of grey, brown, olive and buff.

At Long Royston Crowe walked her through the dark, silent, partially sheeted halls. Light caught the apple breasts and buxom knees of Venus and Diana on the plasterwork, highlit Actaeon's white corse. Elizabeth-Virgo-Astraea was picked out by a tiny spotlight that sallied a little way into upper darkness and was blunted. It was all stone-cold and gusty: Crowe trotted and Frederica dashed: they followed corridors and came to the hot, bright little study. In the stone hearth here a wood-fire flickered.

Crowe offered her a deep, high-winged leather chair and what seemed an inordinately large glass of brown sherry, glinting reddish gold in the firelight. He held a plate of salted nuts, of which she greedily took a fistful, her usual practice in case her host should forget to offer them again. At this, he laughed. She need not have worried: he was an attentive host and filled her glass frequently and assiduously.

He talked to her about herself. His talk was fluttering and caressing, a titillation with feathery praise, a curiosity as warm and rich as the sherry, about her ambitions and intentions. He told her she had "presence" and that presence was a gift, not to be learned, and went with "drive", which she also had, and would make her always fascinating to some men, if not to all. A characteristic of 1953 in Frederica's life was to be an extraordinary preponderance of encounters with people ready, indeed eager, to offer her summarising definitions of herself which fell, almost all, between the triple stools of aphoristic wisdom, clique banality, and the straight pass. Crowe's remarks fell on her irritable consciousness like the rhythmic strokes of a hairbrush on hair: she sat up, preened her mind and body, smiled graciously and downed another glass of sherry.

Crowe said, "Of course I have no particular gifts. I only care for gifts in others. This tends to make one a bit bitchy, I will freely admit, people have so much to live up to, in the eyes of anyone who's invested, as it were, in them. That's a veiled warning I'm sure you'll ignore, as it's all you really can do with it. Power fascinates me."

"Power's what you have."

"Not in the way you have, my dear. A heritage I hold in trust for the culture. Yours is in the blood."

He invited her over to the desk, where he showed her a miniature of Johanna Seale, a frowning, bejewelled beauty, cut off below the forced-up breasts under brown velvet. He put two small plump hands about her waist and remarked that power even created electricity in certain people. She was undeniably prickly, it was most interesting. He drew her proficiently into his lap in the desk chair.

Frederica was startled, simply because she had assumed Crowe was an old man. She had the vague idea that at his age (and she was entirely uncertain about what his age precisely was) men were frequently reduced to talk instead of action. She thus felt she was performing some kindly, even condescending act, out of her total youth and vigour, to cast back demurely suggestive glances at his most piercing sallies. Demureness was in fact incompatible with her foxy hauteur, but she had not yet worked this out, and thus invested her glances with a lewd, hinting quality which was not intentional. Grasped, she realised immediately that Crowe was neither senile nor awkward. He patted, poked and fingered with automatic sureness. She sat rather uncomfortably on his lap. Proficient he may have been but he was also little: her legs, her torso, stuck out in ways she felt must be gawky and unaesthetic. She tried to smile, but it was not easy, as she was developing a crick in her neck from trying to keep her head on a convenient level for Crowe, whose love-making was as chatty and verbal as Ed's had been taciturn.

The chat took the form of a running commentary on her parts as though she was a work of art, or a beauty queen. After each item of the inventory, Crowe applied his fingers and lips to the part just enumerated, tickling, twisting, nipping, brushing, as seemed appropriate. Her eyes, he declared, should be bigger and darker, but there was nothing to be done about that, though he was against heavy pencillings around them, the remnants of which he wiped away with a licked handkerchief. Her hair, which he fanned his hands in, needed a good conditioner and a good thinning, *never* lacquer, maybe a Titian rinse to modify the ginger – but it was springy, energetic hair, he said, twisting it playfully round several fingers and snuffing it with his snub nose. He loved her cheek-bones. He pecked at them like a dry, soft, warm bird. Her mouth had great character: she must vary its downdroop and never, *never*, as he could well see she had, apply lipstick beyond the true periphery. He did a bit more scrubbing to the offending remnants, which left her feeling rubbed and glowing, then he bent, warm and dry, and enclosed her lips in his. He smelled of sherry and wood smoke. She saw the glistening moon-round of his tonsure, ruddy in the firelight. She wished she looked less like Worzel Gummidge with stiffly protruding unbendable arms and legs. Crowe put one little hand into her shirt and began to rotate the nipple between finger and thumb. This was a distinctly unpleasant sensation but she felt powerless to stop him. She hoped her underwear was clean, which it frequently wasn't, very. Crowe said, "Oh, like new hard little apples, what a delight, as firm as the rest of you, my dear girl." She stared out of the window, which was uncurtained because Crowe loved to see his cypresses, yews and junipers fade slowly into the thickening night, because he liked to smell gillyflowers and night-scented stocks and to watch the white moon sail over his box hedges, over the white Apollo and Diana poised over the walk which led to the sunken garden. In and against this window, as Alexander had seen her own face at Goathland framed in his windscreen, Frederica now saw a disembodied face, white, staring, with flowing hair and horrified aspect. It was Alexander, whose lovely hands materialised for a moment on the glass beside his face, as though mutely pleading, before the vision wavered and receded, the gravel scrunched and there was a knock at the door.

Crowe called, "Come in," without letting go of Frederica. Indeed, he tightened his grip on her groin with one arm and removed his other hand only from inside her shirt to the same position outside. Frederica stared like a monstrous defiant puppet at Alexander, who said, "You *did* ask me to a drink. You *did* say, walk round the terrace and walk in."

"I did. But you were so reluctant to leave your grubby exercise books that I assumed you would not materialise. And Frederica was as eager for a drink as I was. So here we were, dallying until you came."

He tipped Frederica neatly off his knee, patted her bottom, and poured sherry for Alexander. Frederica hiccoughed and held out her own glass, which he refilled. Alexander creased his brow. Crowe smiled over them both, benign and rubicund, his silvery fringe of hair floating slightly in the draught to his chimney. He threw wood chips in his fire and sparks raced and streamed upwards, green, silver, blue.

> Thrice toss these oaken ashes in the air
> Thrice sit thou mute in this enchanted chair;
> And thrice three times tie up this true love's knot
> And murmur soft, she will, or she will not.

"*Comus*," said Frederica.

"No, no," said Alexander, teacherly. "Campion."

"You were confused by the enchanted chair," said Crowe mischievously, brandishing the decanter.

"The chair in *Comus* is most repellent," said Frederica.

"Most," said Crowe. "This marble venom'd seat/Smeared with gums of glutinous heat/I touch with moist palms, chaste and cold."

"Obscene," said Frederica, flushed and meaningful. Alexander looked at her coldly and sat down. He waited for someone to speak. No one did. After a time Frederica announced that she must be going. Crowe said surely not, and Alexander said he would give her a lift. She looked, he thought, positively drunk. Crowe said, ring your mother and say you'll be home late, and relax, and Alexander said he was really quite happy to give her a lift. He ought to be getting back anyway. At this, Crowe laughed inordinately and asked Frederica if she was sure she could get up out of her chair.

They walked, all three, along the terrace, and then through dark grassy alleys, smelling of rosemary and box. They had a brief view of a fountain between yews, bubbling in the moonlight. Frederica felt quite sick with sherry, excitement, aesthetic surfeit and financial greed.

"Such a pleasure," said Crowe, closing her into the silver car. "Come again."

"Please."

Alexander said his thank you, and drove off with a jerk. He said, "What were you doing?"

"Nothing much."

"Do your family know you're here?"

"I doubt it. Why does it matter to you?"

"As a friend of the family."

"Oh, as that." She hiccuped. "It's my life. I don't see why you should interfere." She hiccuped again, and added, "Particularly, particularly since I *don't* interfere in your life." She leaned back and closed her eyes.

"That's different."

"Maybe. In any case, I don't, do I?"

"No. As far as I know, you don't."

She lolled, rolling loosely, as he turned corners. He was annoyed by her. He had been very shocked to see her perched on Crowe's diminutive lap. She was in the way of his evening with Crowe; and he was embarrassed by the imagination of intimacies of Crowe's, or hers, he hadn't known about; and he had felt prudish, and something else, on seeing the shadowed round in her shirt, palped by Crowe's fingers.

"Frederica –"

"M'm."

"You're very young –"

"I know. I'm getting older as fast as I can. If I keep it up I shall be quite worthy of consideration quite soon."

"You should be careful. You have a lot to lose."

"What? What have I to lose, that I would not willingly part withal."

She began to laugh in a tiresome way, rolling her head from shoulder to shoulder.

"Added to which, you're drunk."

"Probably. I've no idea at all how much I've had. He's deft."

"You are a revolting child."

"Not a child," she said, leering up at him, making the same mistake about demureness.

"It is my duty to fill you with coffee, but I will *not* take you to my room."

"No. Most unwise. The Coffee Bar's open."

"My God."

"I don't care about the coffee."

"You had better have it."

So Alexander took her to the winking ultramarine depths, where they consumed boiling froth and sour coffee.

"Are you the Elder Brother? Or the Attendant Spirit?"

"What?"

"Well, you got me out of that chair like one of those. Only I'd drunk the cup and chewed up lots of peanuts. I don't believe in turning down things you may never get offered any more."

"You are too young to know what anyone is doing. You don't . . ."

"Don't I? My sister goes to bed with the curate. Imagine that." Alexander tried very hard, and failed, not to be interested in this information.

"I shouldn't have thought so."

"No, you wouldn't. But I *know*. I know all sorts of things . . . But I don't want to be a bridesmaid in primrose poplin like a Flower Fairy of the Spring. I suppose I don't know enough. Not about a lot of things. I know something about the Alexandrine."

Alexander took this as a silly oblique reference to his own affairs, which it was not. Frederica had never even thought of connecting the verse form and her beloved's name. It was an attempt, unrecognised and unrewarded, to wrench the conversation away from sex and back to the intellect. In practice, Alexander took it as a signal to get her back home at all costs: abruptly and authoritatively he pulled her, giggling, off her chair and up the spiral stairs, propping her with both arms as she teetered, catching her once under both breasts which to his horror produced a flicker of sexual excitement in him. He hustled her into the car, drove to Masters' Row, and pushed her out into the road where she stood, as she had landed, idiotically still like a child playing statues. Alexander rolled down the window and hissed, "Go home."

"You are mean."

"No, I'm not. *Go home.*"

Lights went on in the Potter hall. Alexander drove off in a hurry, trusting, craven, that she would at best not betray him, and at worst not blame him for what he was not responsible for. He had little confidence in this as discretion did not seem to be one of her strong points.

24. Malcolm Haydock

Daniel went round to the Haydocks' on Stephanie's "day". It had somehow become impossible to see her at Masters' Row or in the Vicarage. As he strode up the concrete path he heard a muffled din.

She opened the door to him, her hair all over, her eyes wild.

"Quick, shut the door."

"What's he up to?" Daniel abandoned his prepared speech on their immediate future. "You look grey and tattered."

"I am grey and tattered. He's washing. He's got everything in the bath and the tap pouring out scalding water. I can't cope. Neither of us seems to keep still the way we did."

"Hang on." Daniel mounted the stairs, two at a time. He stood in the bathroom door and confronted Malcolm Haydock, if that could be called confrontation in which one party shows no awareness of the other's presence.

In the bath, soaking and steaming were: Mrs Haydock's floral eiderdown, a knotted mass of underwear, pink and black, an octopus of suspenders and straps, several pairs of shoes, a spilt Meccano, a floating army of little grey inch-high soldiers, a dissolving jar of bright pink bath crystals, and the hoover. Malcolm Haydock was singing, endlessly, like a hurdy-gurdy, the tune, "How *much* is that doggie in the window".

Daniel hoisted out the hoover and stood it, soggy and steaming, in a corner. He addressed Malcolm with grave courtesy.

"That could damage you. Or anyone, it could damage, if it got plugged in as wet as that. And I'll have the eiderdown, my lad. Feathers don't take too well to water."

He hauled, bear-like, and piled it into the washbasin, soaking the front of his shirt and trousers in the process. Malcolm Haydock retreated in a shambling manner and sat down with his cheek against the lavatory pillar. He began to make a deadly even, shrill squealing noise, on one note. His eyes rolled up and round and down.

"I'll have your mam's woollies. Because of shrinkage, you see. And I'll have the shoes, or they'll perish. I don't see why you shouldn't go on with all this nylon stuff, though, now it's wet anyway, Malcolm. You may as well wash it properly, I reckon."

He held out a sopping handful of petticoats and suspender belts. Malcolm flung his head round and round on his neck. Daniel hung the garments over the edge of the bath and summoned Stephanie.

"Have you got anything we could squeeze this lot out in? It's a right mess. The colours are running." He turned back to Malcolm.

"We mean well. We're not just out to thwart you. I don't see why you shouldn't wash things, if you want to. It just depends *what* things."

Malcolm Haydock emitted, like a radio signal, the information that he was not there, that no one was there, nothing. Stephanie appeared, lugging up the staircase a galvanised bath into which working jointly against Malcolm's most piercing train whistle noise they managed to hump and slither the sodden eiderdown. For quite a long time they worked, silently, fiercely, together wringing, squeezing, rubbing, stretching, hanging. Daniel brought the hoover down to the kitchen, wiped what could be wiped, and stood it on a newspaper. Water trickled from its works. He then peeped into the bathroom again. Malcolm was standing in the bath, one hand trailing a kite-tail of nylon underwear, the other, one would have thought painfully, twisting his own pink cheek round and round. His shoes and socks were on, and submerged. He was making another noise with Daniel slowly realised was an uncannily efficient imitation of a hoover perpetually choking on a regurgitated hairpin.

They went and sat on the edge of Mrs Haydock's unmade bed, in earshot of the bathroom, but out of sight. They slithered on an oyster art-silk coverlet, which Daniel angrily screwed out of the way. He put one wet black arm round her shoulder. She said,

"I'm glad you came. Please don't go. Unless you must."

"That's the first thing you've said *to* me, since . . . for weeks – since the explosion."

"I know. I'm sorry."

"Sorry isn't enough. We've got to shift all this. We've got to get banns called, now, and get married, now, and stop this nonsense. I know they've all got it in their heads that we'd be wise to go in for a *long* engagement – th' Vicar's bleating about it, as well as your Dad. But that's just got to be stopped. Either we get married, or we don't."

"We can't, before the end of term."

"We can. We can do what we will. There's no cash for honeymoons and such nonsense in any case. You can go on with your teaching. But you can't go on just drifting away like this, and going grey. I won't stand for it."

"Daniel!"

"What?"

"Has he got the Hoover?"

"The Hoover? I put it . . . No, no, no, it's him, he thinks he *is* a hoover. Listen, I'll listen to him, if you'll listen to me. What can we gain by waiting?"

"He – Daddy – might come round. You – might decide it wasn't a good thing. I might feel less dead."

"I doubt all that. I doubt that very much. That's what worries me. He wants you to think he *might* come round, so he stays this side of absolutely intolerable, but he won't. And as for you, you are making yourself ill, and I'm damned if I'll let you go on. I want you the way you were that day, alive, love, not grey. I've seen it. I want it back."

"Oh, Daniel. Maybe it's all your own, the energy. Maybe you did it all. Maybe I've had the life knocked out of me before I was old enough to know."

"No. That's not true. I *know*. If I have to drag you into Church . . ."

She put her face on his wet shoulder. It was as though he was steaming from his own internal heat. She rested. She told him, "I went to see the Vicar, like you said. He likes me. I'm a fraud."

"Told you he would. Doesn't see anything can be much wrong with someone who likes George Herbert and has lovely manners. You aren't the Enemy. That's me."

"That's ludicrous."

25. Good Wives

Daniel set to work to bring his marriage about. He had little help from Stephanie, who simply acquiesced patiently to everything he suggested. Daniel was wildly angry with her and also sorry for her, sensing that she doubted everything, including himself and herself. This simply made him work faster, since he had only his own energies to rely on. He had a battle with the Vicar about the banns, and another about his intention to live on the Arkwright Estate. The Vicar talked about the position the Church had to keep up, about the way in which social workers resented encroachment on their preserves. Daniel shouted, loudly, about what Christ had said, done and enjoined on his followers. He knew that the Vicar was physically distressed by his own noisiness, that if he roared the Vicar would do almost anything to have him go away and be quiet. He roared. He roared, too, about the banns, about which he was secretly convinced that the Vicar might have a stronger case than he would admit openly. But he was a man of will. In the second week of May Mr Ellenby, with a nervous glance across the choir at his frowning assistant, called the banns for the first time. Stephanie Jane Potter, spinster, also of this parish, was not, Mr Ellenby noticed, present on this occasion. The congregation shuffled. Daniel glowered at them.

He had, he found, one ally. Winifred suddenly rose up, like an ageing Valkyrie, and set about constructing a wedding. During late April and May Bill's behaviour was uneasy and lurking. He stayed long hours in the school and longer hours with his WEA students in pubs in mining villages. He brought home surprise gifts, mostly books, mostly for Stephanie, and stood sharp-mouthed and moist-eyed waiting for a gratitude that became difficult to express. In the month of May he gave his daughter: *The Confessions of a Justified Sinner*, Carey's translation of the *Divina Commedia*, Wittgenstein's *Tractatus Logico-Philosophicus*, and T. S. Eliot's *Notes towards a Definition of Culture* which she already owned, and so passed on to Frederica. Stephanie told Daniel that it was impossible to tell if these were furtive wedding-gifts, or contributions to the Christian-humanist debate in her warring soul. Daniel said he had no idea what most of them were, and did she think he ought to read them. No, no of course not, said Stephanie, and relapsed into her grey silence.

Winifred, growing rapidly in political cunning, asked Bill flatly one evening whether he was, or was not, positively against wedding arrangements being made. Bill shouted out that he had told her once that he did not care what anyone did as long as no one tried to involve or consult him, and could she not see that he was working. He waited for her anxious rephrasing of her request. It did not come.

Winifred then visited Mrs Ellenby, and after Mrs Ellenby Mrs Thone, wife of the Headmaster. Mrs Ellenby's feelings about Daniel Orton were at best lukewarm. She considered him extravagant with electricity, a spiritual nosey-parker and an unreliable attender of bazaars. But she liked Stephanie, as everyone did, disapproved of Bill, and was passionately interested in the ceremony of weddings. Winifred exposed the family differences with what she hoped was a tactful mixture of personal distress, sympathy for her daughter, and tolerant acceptance of her husband's eccentricities. Mrs Ellenby was touched, and mildly flattered. She agreed to receive wedding presents and messages, as far as possible, so that the Potter house could be kept quiet. She suggested a dressmaker, a baker and a printer. She offered to attend personally to the Church flowers and to invite Daniel's mother to stay in the Vicarage.

Mrs Thone was more formidable. In Winifred's early days at the school Mrs Thone had made overtures of friendship, invitations to coffee, to dinner, of which Winifred accepted a bare minimum, and which she felt unable to reciprocate, since Bill was contemptuous about the Headmaster and Winifred feared, hardly admitting it even to herself, that if she had the Thones frequently round in the evenings Bill would engineer some monstrous rudeness which would make her tenuous social life completely non-existent.

Monica Thone looked more like a headmaster than her husband: she wore grey tweed suits and expensive silk shirts: her hair was short and salt-and-pepper coloured: she had read Greats at Oxford. The Thones' only son had one day in 1947 fallen from a low bench in a playground, hit his head and died instantly, aged ten. The boys at the school were afraid of Mrs Thone: they said she had a witchy stare. She strode up and down the school grounds, stood in for sick teachers, and taught a curious class in English Comic Writing at Calverley Prison, where she was apparently popular.

She received Winifred coolly, and Winifred found it hard to open a conversation. They sat in Mrs Thone's chill drawing-room, two stiff, grim, tall Englishwomen, unable to drop their English shields of cautious silence. Winifred thought: I could weep, I could fling myself about. How she would hate that. She said neutrally, "I need your help."

"How can I help you?"

"It is my husband. I shall have to explain . . . my husband . . ."

"Are you quite sure . . ." murmured Mrs Thone.

Winifred, more decisively, said she was indeed sure. She offered an excellent and unemotional précis of the events so far and explained that the wedding must take place and soon, and that Bill must not be troubled, or involved.

"And what can I do?"

"I don't like to talk about Bill. He would hate it so."

"According to my husband, he is a difficult genius."

"If you are married to him," said Winifred, "you notice the difficulty more than the genius."

"My husband says he is invaluable. And often intolerable."

"Exactly."

They smiled, very briefly, together.

"I wondered if you – if your husband – if the school – might help with a wedding reception. To be truthful I can't even be sure Bill will *come*. I want her to have things done properly. All the proper things. Here, he couldn't . . . object . . . or derange . . ."

"I do see. Forgive me," said Mrs Thone delicately, "but will you be all right, in the circumstances, for money?"

"We have a joint account. I shall use it."

Mrs Thone began to laugh.

"I must admit, I should take some pleasure in fixing that without telling him, though I shouldn't say so. I don't see why we shouldn't use the Masters' Garden, weather permitting. I don't see why – for the daughter of a long-established colleague – we shouldn't use the kitchen staff and crockery and glasses. I don't think I shall bother Basil with it much. He's scared stiff – between you and me – of your husband's tantrums. I shall simply inform him it's being done – that *I* am doing it – and that there's no need at all for him to mention it to Bill. It'll leak through of course."

"I'm relying on Bill to pretend not to take any notice."

"He might not."

"He might do . . . such things and so on. But with luck he can't stop a whole wedding."

"Your daughter seems a good, calm sort of girl. Is the young man a solid young man?"

Solid, yes, said Winifred. And like a steamroller. Didn't admit obstacles. Winifred, Mrs Thone said, showed more similarity to a steamroller than might have been expected. Would she – and any available Potters – and the ferocious curate – care to come and watch her television on Coronation Day? All the boys had a holiday, of course, but there were always one or two with no home to go to, whom she would ask, and a few staff. Winifred felt both obliged, and pleased, to accept this invitation.

Daniel and Stephanie had now a wedding date, June 21st, and an invitation to the Coronation (on television). Winifred got out her treadle machine and began a yellow poplin dress for Frederica. Mrs Ellenby's dressmaker measured Stephanie. Invitations were despatched, even to unknown Potters. Stephanie wrote briefly and delicately to Mrs Orton, suggesting a visit. She received a floral postcard, depicting a huge silver jar of dahlias on a burnished table, on the back of which Mrs Orton had written, no, don't come, it would be too much upset for all concerned, my health is NOT UP to MUCH, but I'll be there on the day don't worry, thanks for writing and all the best. Daniel said she was a lazy old so and so and always had been. He added gloomily that she'd irritate Mrs Ellenby proper, but what must be must be. Stephanie found nothing to say about that, either.

26. Owger's Howe

Lucas Simmonds said they would plot a Mental Map of the part of the earth on which they were. The biosphere was to be drawn up into the noussphere, where it was to be fulfilled and completed, so that change and decay should no longer corrupt or impede its full shining. This was to be aided by their instrumentation. Led by their, particularly of course by Marcus's, intuitions, they would perform experiments, or rites, which were strictly different names for the same thing, in those Places of Power they could certainly locate in the area surrounding Calverley. Their proceedings must be both biological and mental, because they, partaking of both worlds like amphibia, linked both worlds. The night's meditation would reveal the *locus* of the next day's experiment.

To assist the work he hung like mandalas in his room Ordnance Survey maps of the North York moors, photographs of Whitby Abbey, a marine pothole known as Jacob's Ladder, Calverley Minster's rose window, standing stones and geometrical earthworks on Fylingdales moor. He extended his eclectic reading to books on Fairy Mythology and druids. He told Marcus there were places which traditionally and for good reasons had been felt to be meeting places between the earthly and the unearthly, umbilici of the earth, hilltops and caverns, and there they would go. They would go in a scientific spirit and write up, neatly, their observations and conclusions. They would collect physically as well as mentally specimens, talismans, significant creatures. It was a scientific field trip combined with a spiritual pilgrimage, healthy fresh air, combined with mental gymnastics whose modes Marcus had not yet grasped. Any coincidence, analogy, concatenation, of dream and object, act and vision were pounced and worked on. Everything bristled with possible significance.

Marcus, over-alert and tremulous, nevertheless enjoyed these exercises more than the rest of the discipline. Lucas had begun to record and exploit his waking visions, that endless train of detailed shape-shifting images he saw when idle, or betwixt asleep and awake. The spider-web in various forms, grey ropes and glassy fibres, hyacinth, iris, gentian blue, recurred frequently. Or cloth, unfurled and undulating, decorated with spangles and paisley coils, faces and hands, on and amongst the layers of tissue. Once he saw a long procession of creatures, reptilian, rhinoceroid, elephantine, marching on bleeding feet over ice and snow against a line of stunted bushes whose leaves and twigs he could draw but not recognise. Once a face in a helmet rose and would not go, though he opened and closed his eyes, though smoke flew across it, though its outer peripheries temporarily transmuted themselves into conger eels or layered black wing-feathers. Perhaps because Lucas talked of them he began to see flowers, anemones rising and uncurling like serpents into cups of crimson, sapphire and purple, branches of blossom snapping into light and taking flight into a black sky. (The vision of the bleeding creatures in the snow was almost the only one with a pale sky.) He saw sap rising in transparent reeded stems, clear green flowing light up to gold cups, and white throats, crimson-spotted, and trailing swirling speedwell-blue florets. Lucas said he was seeing the inner Forms of the Biosphere, flowers as they had been, or would be, or innerly meant to be. Lucas told him that Goethe had *seen* the Urpflanze, the Typical Plant, revealed in existing plants, though it did not grow in Nature. So maybe Marcus saw the species-pattern, the Plan of creatures as he had seen the mathematical Forms. He himself had recently been led to wonder whether the numerous fairytales about ointments which, rubbed on your eyes, caused you to see tiny species, moving invisible creatures under hills, in streams, even in market-squares, were to do with vision peculiarly attuned to the creation of species-patterns of microscopic or yet-uncreated life. Blake had drawn the ghost of a flea and had declared that if the gates of perception were cleansed man would see everything as it was, infinite. Imagine, Lucas cried lyrically, waving a crocus under Marcus's nose, imagine being able to *perceive* the infinity of this creature, the matter and force that have flowed in and out of it through all time, the power that as we see it at this moment holds it in this pure and complex form . . .

Marcus could not follow Lucas's excited analogical leaps. He did see the crocus, the fine lines and channels on its sheen, the deepening gold, the almost transparent flower-flesh. He was in a perpetual daze of focused visions and things, real things, studied and learned with a hallucinatory closeness that was so like the visions that the memory-images of both ran into each other. This was bearable because it had the firm purpose of Lucas's sense of direction.

They covered their chosen ground in Lucas's car, which was black and low and shining. Inside it Marcus was initially tormented by geometry. The way in which the sides of the road, the white lines, converged, were swallowed and vanished, filled him with the plughole and graph paper alarm. Trees and horizon were converted by speed to converging geometry: tall trees bowed and danced towards the windscreen in car-constructed lines. Lucas drove very fast, hissing between his teeth as he leaned extravagantly round corners. Marcus said he was afraid of speed and parallax. Lucas said this was good for vision. In the old days, did Marcus know, they suspended witches in sacks from the boughs of trees and gave them a good shove. In there, detached from time, space and the body, they were aware of other dimensions and saw visions. There was no earthly reason why sports cars shouldn't have the same effect on moderns, at least passengers. He should empty his mind and stop fussing. Marcus said he was afraid of that. Lucas said he, Lucas, was there, wasn't he, he could bring Marcus back from any temporary displacement of consciousness to hedgerow or white line. Thus encouraged Marcus began to enjoy speed. Disembodied he saw the overarching heaven and mapped the moorland as a series of turning concentric globes. He was carsick once and once only. Lucas said carsickness was a failure of the will, a failure of control in the solar plexus. He said he, Lucas, *didn't wish* Marcus to be sick in his car. It was distracting and the smell lingered. He gave Marcus a barleysugar. Marcus was not sick again.

One Spring Sunday they visited the Dropping Well at Knaresborough

and a second powerful place, a long barrow on a tumulus known as
Owger's Howe.

Lucas had read up on Mother Shipton who had once lived in a cave-
house by the Dropping Well. This person he told Marcus must have had
considerable Mental Power since she had foretold tidal waves in the
Thames, the Plague of London, Wolsey's death, the dissolution of the
monasteries, the defeat of the Armada, the length of Elizabeth's reign,
and the execution of Charles I. She had power over nature: she threw her
staff in a fire and retrieved it unharmed. She had predicted many of the
advances of our own time.

> Around the world thoughts shall fly
> In the twinkling of an eye,
> Through hills men shall ride
> And no horse or ass by their side
> Under water man shall walk
> Shall ride, shall sleep, shall talk,
> In the air man shall be seen
> In black, in white, in green . . .

Lucas thought it might well be that such persons were in touch with the
motions of earth's magnetic fields. Marcus had no views, but listened.

It was grey when they came to Knaresborough. They proceeded, a
usual pair of tourists, man and boy, along the river walk beside the Nidd,
under the overhanging cliff, to which the spring-water, full, Lucas
explained, of fine particles of nitrous earth, dropped through a pipe over
what was now a stone fall of solidified streamlets, droplets, ferns, roots
of trees and plants, bulging and sagging, to the shallow stone basin of
the Well. In the early nineteenth century the conduct of the guardians
of the Well had aroused serious aesthetic objections in lovers of the
picturesque. Lucas had borrowed an old guide book from Calverley
library. "The top of the cliff," he read to Marcus, "with all its vegetation,
has been naturally encrusted with carbonate of lime, which drops over in
a continuous stony mantle. Beneath this the guardians of the spring have
suspended dead birds and animals, branches of trees, old hats, stockings
and shoes and various matters equally absurd which become 'petrified'
under the dropping and are carried off as 'objects de vertu' by the
curious, chiefly visitors from Harrogate."

When Marcus and Lucas came there, there were indeed, suspended on
strings, partially encrusted gloves and socks, a bowler hat, green around
the still unswallowed band, over which the stony crust was slowly
advancing. Lucas stood and watched Marcus eagerly as Marcus gravely
considered the heterogeneous petrifying objects under the heavy, slow

drops. There was a whole birdsnest, layered straw, smoothed feathers, clutch of tiny eggs, slowly becoming stony and durable. Marcus stared at this for a long time. There was also a book, its pages sealed by congealing lime, its title obscured already forever. There was something sinister about this uniform, permanent transmutation. If one broke off a stone bough, a stone fern frond, would there now be, inside, even a dark thread of what had once been alive?

"I don't like it. I wonder why people put things in."

"Curiosity about change of substance. Curiosity about curios. It's like *real* sculpture, if you see what I mean."

Marcus stared at the pathetic dangling stone socks, every weighted crease fixed.

"It's all dead. I can't see why it's so fascinating." But he was fascinated.

"You have to put your hand in. And wish. And let the water dry naturally on your hand."

"Why?"

"It's the customary rite. An invocation perhaps. A contact. We should put our hands in."

Marcus had no wish to do so.

"Touch, smell, taste, hear, see," said Lucas. "Rocks and stones and trees. This is where the lithosphere touches the biosphere. A point of entry and exit as I see it. We need to know."

He took off his jacket and rather solemnly and portentously rolled up his sleeve. Marcus discarded his blazer, opened his cuff, and rolled up his own sleeve. Side by side they extended their arms and hands into the frigid fall and pool. It bit. It burned cold.

"Concentrate," said Lucas, without specifying on what. Marcus fixed his eye on the limed nest. Addled liquid sealed in a stony shell. He looked away and was struck by a cluster of contorted stone bootlaces. For what might people require household objects stiffened into stone? He pulled out his dripping arm and hand which tingled and crimsoned. Beside it Lucas's forearm, rosy and freckled, trembled slightly.

"Did you wish?"

"I can't think of anything to wish for."

"Open your mind to the future."

"I can't like this place."

"It has an aura."

"It is cold and wet. And tripperish." The water was still freezing on his hand. He would be there for ever. If his hand was not stony it would crackle with ice.

"We must leave something of our own. To maintain contact. A terminal as it were. Have you got anything?"

Marcus poked with his left hand in his blazer pocket. His right hand flamed and tingled. He found a pen, some pennies, a handkerchief, some string. Lucas turned these over and decided on the handkerchief, which had Marcus's nametape stitched neatly to it. Marcus said he might need to use it, it was cold. Lucas said he had several and would lend one. He placed Marcus's handkerchief and his own pencil together under the drip.

"Part of us. Part of the Well. A link."

"I'm hungry."

"The pencil and the handkerchief should solidify together." Lucas added rather plaintively, "It's the pencil I wrote it down with, what you saw. It's partaken in large areas of the experiment. It should make a powerful terminal."

Marcus had a brief vision of a stone wire appended to a stone pencil humming stony notes, and a distant crystal set. Lucas peered like an anxious dog into his face. Signs of scepticism, or boredom in his generally well-impressed colleague always filled him with alarm. He made further proselytising efforts.

"You know, Mother Shipton lived in a house cut out of the rock. Like the Sibyl at Cumae, and the Pythian priestess. A striking coincidence. And *they* were known to be at the entries to the other world, umbilical points . . . *known*. It did seem likely you might be aware of . . . some field of force . . . or something."

"No. Everything seems solid and heavy and oppressive. I want to go."

"What form does the oppression take?"

Marcus, tracing aimless figures on the still air with blotchy damp fingers, turned a stony face on Lucas and for the first time exploited his knowledge of his own dubious authority.

"It takes the form of knowing we ought to get away from here fast. This place is against us staying. It doesn't like us moving."

For a moment his mind's eye saw turning corridors of polished smooth blue-veined stone, inviting inwards. He ignored this. He repeated, "It's against us."

"But you see no more."

"No."

Lucas shrugged himself into his coat.

"We'll go then. We should take something."

In a nearby wood they found what Lucas said were some very satisfactory flowers, late winter aconites, dog's mercury, hartstongue, the only true indigenous fern with undivided leaves. Lucas showed signs of wanting to offer these, green-ruffed gold, creeping hairy foetid spurge with tiny green flowers, to the Dropping Well for preservation. Marcus said they were not going back there. Lucas acceded meekly. Marcus said with cunning, "Tell me about Owger's Howe," and Lucas brightened, and said it was on a moor south of Calverley near a place called the Obtrush Yat, or Gate, and was an imposing tumulus with door pillars and a threshold which had a long tradition of propitiatory rituals and sightings to do with it, special knockings and bowls of milk put out at certain times of year, ring-dancings and lights from inside at midnight, a vanished shepherd and dog who were believed to have entered Fairyland through those stone gates and never returned. It might take a couple of hours' driving but it would be a good place. He had brought a picnic. Before they set out he read to Marcus an account by one William of Newbridge of a countryman in the Province of the Deiri (i.e. Yorkshire) who heard from a barrow "the voices of people singing and as it were joyfully feasting. He wondered who they could be that were breaking in that place, by their merriment, the silence of the dead night, and he wished to examine into the matter more closely. Seeing a door open in the side of the barrow he went up to it and looked in; and there he beheld a large and luminous house full of people, women as well as men, who were reclining at a solemn banquet and, as it were, raising their cups to a tall and excellently fair couple who appeared, from the woman's wreath and fantastic garb, to be newly wedded. One of the attendants standing at the door gave him a cup. It contained a clear, red liquid, something like wine. He took it but would not drink, and casting the contents secretly upon the grass, was struck with terror on seeing that the ground flamed and smouldered where the drops had fallen. At this, still tightly grasping the vessel, he took to horse, and fled; the people of the place, making a shrill buzzing, pursued him with all speed, but he came safe to the town, and there gave the cup into the keeping of the Curate. Once the cup was out of his hands he could neither see his pursuers nor hear their shrill outcry, although his horse was maddened seemingly, and could never again be comfortable or quiet. The vessel, made of an unknown material, indescribable in colour and extraordinary in form, was kept in the Church a many years; and they could not come in at it; though he who held the cup could hear their wailing and singing and threatening sometimes on the wind."

Marcus asked what Owger meant, and Lucas said it was believed by some to be a corruption of Ogier le Danois, a Danish paladin who had gone into Fairyland for several centuries but had been promised release in time of great need – like Arthur and Merlin and other aeonic sleepers under stones and within hills. Others insisted Owger was just a local goblin, who took the offered milk and occasionally bothered cattle and sheep with his pranks.

The Howe was reached by a grassy track running steeply up a hillside of fields so clotted with bracken, heather and thistles that it was hard not to see them as invaded by moor. The barrow, high and distinctive, stood on the top of a raised circular mound surrounded itself by vestigial terraces, or furrows in the crust of the earth which, Lucas waggishly assured Marcus, beaming brightly at him as they tramped upwards, bearing canvas holdalls of picnic and specimen jars of fauna and flora, *which* were generally believed to be the marks of the dying wreathings and constrictions of a loathly worm or dragon which had secured itself to that tump for its last battle. Marcus, somewhat breathless, did not ask why Lucas was so sure that the idea of Worms was comically fictive whilst the ideas of little or good or green folk or people in barrows and mounds, or angels in cathedrals, or Mothers who sensed magnetic shifts centuries ahead, were somehow wrong-headed descriptions of actual forces. No doubt all would be made clearer, in so far as Marcus chose to seek clarity. He preferred, in fact, a certain area of cloudiness, as to the naming and categorising of things. His capacity for belief in particular propositions was no greater than it had ever been. Plans and patterns there might be; biospheres and lithospheres and entelechies were no more than evocative words.

The terminals and focal objects Lucas was scattering about the surface of Yorkshire he treated with a mixture of scepticism and fear. They were almost certainly not what Lucas said they were. But what they were doing was instigating all sorts of tuggings, and urgings, and pricklings and singings and expansions and contractions in him which were connected with fields of force in which he did perforce believe, and which resembled things that were most respectably taught in schools, electricity, X-rays, magnetism. An electric charge could pick up a mouse or a sheep, or a man, and shake it till it chattered, singe and char it to a calcined clod. Something had gone through him when he saw the light, and something related went through and through him now, and shook him, so that without Lucas he might well, he considered, have been wiped clear of mind like a washed slate, or clear of body, like something set in a vacuum.

They made a sort of camp near the earthed and closed mouth of the barrow. Lucas, who tended to treat Marcus as a kind of human dowsing twig, or divining rod, or maybe, Marcus grimly thought, exposed on this hummock top surrounded by blackish clouds, as a lightning conductor, now plucked at his blazer elbow and asked if he had any sense of the nature of the place, any awareness of anything there. Marcus said, rather irritably, "Let go of me, I can't think if you touch me," and wandered away along the side of the hummock, trying dutifully to empty his mind. He reiterated hopefully that he was hungry. Lucas replied, equally irritably, that they should do their work on *empty* stomachs, that was well known. Look at the Eucharist. When their work was done, they could have their picnic, of which there was a lot, and very good too. He giggled. Marcus went on walking, listening to earth and air, sniffing, staring. The tumulus was old, and silent. Inside, there was earth, and dust, and earthy, dusty particles of air. Things grew on it. Things here were mingled: out of earth, grass, and thistles, out of bones, earth: water ran through it all, and came out, and fed things, and evaporated. He put a hand on the grassy flank of the thing: it had its own warmth. He went down, and found a blue flower. He called to Lucas, "Here's a blue one. I've found a blue one. A lovely blue." Lucas trotted up, smartly, and became very excited. The blue flowers rose on fluted tall cups on smooth stalks, an inch or so high. Their leaves were in a little rosette at the base of the stalk.

"Don't pick it," Lucas cried. "It's rare. Up here, very rare, very rare indeed. That's a spring gentian. You get them up here very infrequently – there are more in the Burren, but no one could say they weren't rare. It's a sign. Here, where it is, we must carry out the experiment. Wait, I'll bring the aconites. And maybe milk. Shall we pour milk, a kind of libation? The country people did."

Marcus sat on the grass and considered the rare gentian. Lucas came and laid the other plants, aconite and wood mercury and fern round the gentian. He poured a small glass beaker of milk from the thermos, and set it beside the flower. After thought, he crossed some of the stems of some of the flowers. He said to Marcus, "I'll also have one of your pennies. And with one of mine, we shall have an offering. You took coins to the underworld. And I'm sure I've read somewhere that gentians are torches of the dead."

The blue flower had a very airy outdoor look. Marcus said, "I don't think we ought to try to call up the dead." "No, no, not that. We want a way in, a way through, to another dimension. I only mean a light to see by. Now, how? What did they do, the wise old ones in such places? They danced. They danced fast enough to make the cosmos dance with them, part of them, till they could see the dance of particles . . . That's why dervishes whirl, to free the mind, to have power over the solid parts –"

Marcus dropped his straw-coloured head. He said, "I can't whirl like a dervish." He stared at the little circle of flowers. It looked silly. It looked glittering and significant. Lucas crossed his wrists and held out his hands.

"If we hold hands – crossed – over this spot. Then do you see, we shall form your intersecting pattern – and if this *is* a Place of Power, we are over another intersection – of two realms – we shall align ourselves with the powers of this place –"

"Owger –"

"That's a name. You might as well say, grass, gentian, dog mercury, aconite, earth, air, water . . ."

"I feel a fool."

"Please *try*. Please at least *try*, after all this trouble."

Marcus held out his hands, bony and long, and they were clasped in Lucas's thick square ones. It was the first time they had deliberately prolonged any contact by touch since the experiment began. Marcus, limp, was gripped: Lucas gripped.

"Lean back. Clear your mind utterly. *Now* . . ."

The grip tightened and then strained. Their feet moved fast and faster. The heavy sky swung and swooped: the hill lurched and hovered; their feet tamped, stamped, shuffled, and whirled: Marcus heard his own voice nervously and wildly laughing: Lucas was making a strange hooting; in their ears the air became a high-pitched shrill singing. They went faster: now and then, in the middle of the spinning cocoon of his vision, whipping lines of grey and brown and gold and green and flesh, Marcus saw the blue point of the flower. From outside, had anyone been there to see, they looked less like whirling dervishes than school-children who spin in playgrounds in such tense figures of eight in order to disorient themselves, to laugh, scream, stumble, stop and see the school, iron railings, goal-posts, wheel solemnly past.

They spun themselves out of laughter into a panting silence. The rhythm of their feet became delicately automatic. What happened then had the inconclusiveness of much reported occult experience. Neither of them remembered the end of the spinning. Both certainly woke, at different ends of the barrow, both having the impression that they had been sleeping heavily. Marcus opened his eyes to blackness on the cold hillside, so for what seemed a very long time he thought it was night and could not remember where he was. He stared into the black, which took on the aspect of a tunnel when he saw a white disk which grew and shimmered towards him, opaque and milky until, when he could no longer see round the circumference, he saw undifferentiated paleness as he had seen undifferentiated dark. Then, bit by bit, as in lifting fog, he saw his surroundings: the ridged hillock, the poor fields, the barrow-mouth, the standing stone gate, against which he was propped. He stood up, and went uncertainly back to where they had gone round. The gentian was still there. The beaker was empty. There was a half-crown, possibly spun out of someone's pocket, on the flowers. From the opposite end of the barrow Lucas staggered. Marcus's ears, or the air, or just possibly the tumulus, made a shrill singing sound in his head. Lucas put his hands on Marcus's shoulders: Marcus solemnly reciprocated: they stood, heads down, breathing heavily. They bent down and picked up the beaker, and the half-crown, which Lucas pocketed.

They had the picnic some miles away. Salty beef sandwiches, a thermos of tomato soup, apples and cheese and heavy fruitcake were very strengthening. Marcus, looking back as they opened the car door, had seen a thick twisted column of different-coloured light, amber maybe, compared to the slate-grey of the sky, which rose like boys' books' depictions of waterspout or hurricane, or like the rooted bole of a transparent, measureless tree, up and up over the tump, sending threads of seeking, aery root down between cleft and stone, along ridge and under ledge. He did not at that time tell Lucas about this. He did not want Lucas either to have, or to be unable to find, words for what they had done. After a moment or two of frantic chewing he noticed that besides beef he could smell fear, in Lucas, in the tiny car. So he said mildly, "I don't think we should talk about this, now, maybe ever." Lucas's round sweaty face came up from his sandwich. Marcus said, "I *know* we shouldn't talk." He hoped he was making it better for Lucas. If not, there was nothing he could do.

When they got home, they realised that neither of them had checked the period of blackness on his watch.

27. *Coronation*

Before June 2 that year most of the people collected in Mrs Thone's drawing room had never seen a television broadcast. Amongst these were all the members of the Potter family, Felicity Wells, the Parrys and Lucas Simmonds, who was very excited, and had told Marcus that both Coronation and television might provide fruitful experiences of the transmission of power. There were six little boys there, some of whose parents owned sets, and the Ellenbys, who were sophisticated, having visited various parishioners who had not turned the thing off whilst offering tea or sherry to the Vicar. There was also Alexander, who had hoped to be invited to Long Royston by Crowe, and had not been. In the middle of the morning Mrs Thone answered the doorbell and found on the step Edmund Wilkie and a strange girl. He had heard, Wilkie said blandly, that she was keeping open house. This was Caroline. He wondered if

they might call. All the streets of Calverley and Blesford were emptied
of their folk and desolate: it was like a death or a disaster: they needed
people. They were up for Crowe's jollifications that night but found
themselves a little previous. He came past Mrs Thone into the hall,
pulling his girl by the waist, dropping a lengthy scarf and a globular
crash helmet on Mrs Thone's oak chest. Mrs Thone ushered him in. He
had been a thorn in Dr Thone's flesh. He had broken every rule; he had
created emotional, intellectual and moral factions whilst adhering to no
one but himself. He had conspicuously claimed that his conspicuous
success was in spite of, and not because of, the efforts of Dr Thone and
the community. Basil Thone nevertheless felt a not uncommon perverse
affection, not for Wilkie's intellect, which he mistrusted, but for the
pure difficulty he presented. Like many teachers he was compelled to
love the most complex problem, not the ninety and nine. Like many
prodigal sons, Wilkie returned from time to time, to re-establish, to
flaunt, to exact and to reject this unreasonable liking. It was not shared
by Bill Potter. Bill admired Wilkie's mind, despised his posturing,
argued his morals on their merits and did not much care what happened
to him. This was largely because he had little time for psychology as a
part of the cultural hierarchy. So when Wilkie came into Mrs Thone's
rose and silver room, Dr Thone, rosy-faced himself, with a silver flow
of hair the boys believed, without evidence, to be a toupée, rose to greet
him joyfully. Bill grunted, and settled deeper into his chair. Wilkie, still
clutching his girl, flashed happy nods of greeting at his acquaintance:
Bill, Alexander, Stephanie, Frederica, Geoffrey Parry. He raised his
voice above the orotundities of Richard Dimbleby, and told them that
this was Caroline. Caroline was dark and thin, with the urchin hair and
prominent slender bones then fashionable, a skipping walk and little
ballet-like slippers which made her ankles seem tiny and her calves
curving.

"Look," said Frederica, "the Queen's coming out."

"What a farce really," said Wilkie's girl.

Miss Wells made a distressed little noise.

"Sit down," said Alexander repressively to Wilkie, "do."

In those days, neither the public nor the private mores that went with
the intrusive camera-eye and the obtrusive screen were established. The
official BBC report on the coverage of the Coronation enquired of itself,
"Might there not be something unseemly in the chance that a viewer
could watch this solemn and significant service with a cup of tea at his
elbow? – there were very real doubts . . ." Most of the Press was
democratically statistically ecstatic. "The Coronation brings the tiny
screen into its own, turns it into a window on Westminster for

125,000,000 people ... All these millions from Hamburg to Hollywood will see her coach jingle through rejoicing London *this very day* ... 800 microphones are ready for 140 broadcasters to tell the world Elizabeth is crowned. But today is television's day. For it is television, reaching out to the Queen's subjects, which will give a new truth to the Recognition of the Monarch on her Coronation Day ... 'And the Queen, standing up by King Edward's Chair, shall turn and shew herself unto the People ...' "

They called it the tiny screen and they called the Queen, repeatedly, delightedly, a tiny figure, exclaiming also repeatedly, how erect and undaunted she was, however exhausted by the long ceremony and the weight of all those robes and the exceedingly heavy crown. Diminutives and superlatives proliferated as they stared at the flickering grey and white shadows, sparking shoots of light off metal and gems, a matt and twinkling tiny doll, half an inch, an inch, two inches, a face maybe eight inches across, grave or graciously beaming, a black and white smiling image of pleated linen and cloth of gold and shimmering embroideries in mother-of-pearl shades – pink, green, rose, amethyst, yellow, gold, silver, white, embroidered bands of golden crystal, graduated diamonds and pearls. Crisping black waved locks and a mouth black with presumably red lipstick since an unslicked mouth in those days was naked. Squared postage-stamp-sized, envelope-sized, columns of pin-headed marching men, soft tapestry-stitch flowerbeds of dotty undifferentiated faces and hats in crowds after crowd, the same and not the same, gun-carriages, tiny coroneted breeched peers, windows, choirboys, regalia, greyly swirling, with Dimbleby's thick rolling voice informing, and crashes of psalm and anthem accompanying all this flow, formation, dissipation, reformation.

What did they truly make of it? The Press used blandly lyrical, spasmodically archaic, uneasily hortative words about a New Elizabethan Age.

"The bright promise of tomorrow is of a second Elizabethan age when the expanding resources of science, industry and art may be mobilised to ease every man's burden and produce new opportunities of life and leisure.

"Yet these are the years when the first atomic clouds have drifted between us and the sun. If anything at all is plain it is that many a generation will be robbed of its future unless there can be established a settled peace ..."

Winston Churchill's rhetoric had its own note of archaising certainty, heavy with worn and inherited rhythms.

"Let it not be thought that the age of chivalry belongs to the past.

Here, at the summit of our world-wide community, is the lady whom we respect, because she is our Queen, and whom we love because she is herself. Gracious and noble are words familiar to us all in courtly phrasing. Tonight they have a new ring in them because we know that they are true about the gleaming figure whom Providence has brought to us in times when the present is hard and the future is veiled."

Dubiety intruded oddly into affirmations of promise and significance. The *Daily Express*, in an imperial Leader, quoted sonorously and incongruously

> The glories of our blood and State
> Are shadows, not substantial things,

glossing this gloomy thought with the explanation that they were shadows, that was, unless commoners and Queen dedicated themselves to "high aims" and pursued these with "tenacious purpose".

The *News Chronicle*, on Everest, wavered between uneasy blasts of acclaim and contortions of verbal and moral embarrassment. It also produced an irrelevantly uncertain piece of great English verse, this time Browning:

> Ah, but a man's reach should exceed his grasp
> Or, what's a heaven for?

It was lyrical about "the cold, beautiful, cruel, desirable peak of the Earth, beyond man's grasp – decade after decade". It was not quite prepared, although it flirted cloudily with the concept, to say that the Coronation and conquest of Everest indicated the coming of the new Imperium, Heaven on Earth, Golden Age, Cleopolis or any such conjunction of temporal imperfection and eternal satisfaction. Instead, it ruminated:

"These islands are fluttering with flags; and now another flag flutters half a world away, on the pinnacle of the earth. It is the same emblem.

"What is it in this news that must stir the deep pride of a nation? It is the sense that all is possible: it is the elation of the knowledge that the age of Elizabeth II is opening dramatically and magnificently. Let them scoff who will, but there is a quality about this news that lifts it higher than the headlines it makes.

"An earlier age would have called it a Sign. Being unsure what that can mean, we are inclined in this age to be embarrassed by any such extravagance of language."

In 1973 Frederica saw Alexander, on an adult education programme on the television, give a lecture on changing style in public communications, illustrated with words and pictures culled, like these extracts, from the events of June 2 1953. Alexander analysed shrewdly, Frederica thought, the flimsy vocabulary, the trumped-up, wilfully glistening sentiments which juxtaposed words now no longer permissible, like gleaming, drifting, visionary, jingling, glittering *et caetera*, Churchill's courtly phrasing, itself already vapid, with the new awkward tech-nologico-Benthamite pieties about the "resources" of science, industry and art, these three, "mobilised" to ease every man's burden to produce new "opportunities" of life and "leisure". If the easing of burdens, Alexander said, ran back in unbroken rhetorical lines through Bunyan to Christ, morally weighty, heavy with dead resonance, "resources", "mobilising", "leisure" were hopefully vague new abstractions to conjure, with their own jargon, their own telling redeployment of words with old useful meanings smaller and more precise. The truth was, Alexander said in 1973, invoking some abstractions of his own, and of that time, the huge misguided nostalgic effort of archaism had been a true shadow of blood and state, a real fantasy and trick of fame. The truth was and had been that the party was and had been over. He ended his programme, predictably, with Low's impressive cartoon, broken Union Jacks, limp dolls, deflated and burst balloons, empty glasses, blank screen. The new language and the old, he said, and their uneasy marriage, were vacant, as events had proved.

Frederica, in 1973, thought he oversimplified. What he said was part of the media's pervasive receding narcissism, mirror on mirror mirrored and their peripheries endlessly commented on by commentators. In 1953 Alexander tried to write, to discourse, in verse, about history and truth. In 1973 he criticised, in prose, modes of communication. There were other truths. There had been, Frederica considered, some sort of inno-cence about the rejoicing at that time (when she was a sharp but un-observant seventeen). There was no duplicity, only a truly aimless and thwarted nostalgia, about the pious enthusiasms of the commentators. And the people had simply hoped, because the time was after the effort of war and the rigour of austerity, and the hope, despite the spasmodic construction of pleasure gardens and festival halls, had had, alas, like Hamlet's despair, no objective correlative. But they had been naturally lyrical. Their lyricism had turned out to be wandering and threadbare, but nothing had replaced or succeeded it. After the threadbare lyric had come threadbare "satire", a sluggish and ponderous anti-rhetoric, a laboured passion for deflating almost anything. Low had been tough, but much of what followed was only shrill.

She did not think this at the time, in 1953. Then she largely agreed with Wilkie's girl's "What a farce!", sensing immediately that this was the "right" response. It was what contemporary people would say and

feel about these events. "Contemporary" was in those days synonymous
with "modern" as it had not been before and is not now (1977). Contemporary was what she wanted, then, to be, and she was quite clever
enough to see that the Coronation was not only not the inauguration of
a new era, it was not even a contemporary event. A year later, when
Lucky Jim came out, Frederica wept with hysterical glee over Jim
Dixon's bludgeoning animosity towards Merrie England, although she
was, also, quite shrewd enough to see that Amis and Dixon would have
shared her ambivalence about Matthew Crowe's public festivities that
evening. Crowe was rich enough to pay real musicians to play real
Elizabethan music in real Elizabethan gardens, and real jazz for variety,
whilst people in real silk clothes drank rather a lot of real drink,
champagne or Newcastle Brown Ale. Money was real to the contemporary mockers, and as the glittering coach rolled the real Queen in her
cloth of gold garments into the courtyards of Buckingham Palace, the
Age of Affluence, pound in pocket and man-made fibrous fancy dress
brightly shining, bubbled up over the edge of Amis's glass of vintage
wine, or whisky, was photographed for the Colour Supplement, clothed
itself in silver PVC buskins and plastic union jacks and addressed itself
to the production and definition of Beautiful People.

True Paradise, Proust said, is always Paradise Lost. Only when
Frederica was old enough to equate the tenuous pastel hopes of 1953
with her own almost-adult knowledge that everything was a new
beginning, that reality for her was the future, did she come to feel
nostalgia for what at the time she diagnosed boldly as blear illusion. In a
Proustian way too, as she acquired age, she came to associate her
obsession with the *Four Quartets* with the Coronation, with the Coronation's gestures towards England, history and continuity. It had tried
and failed to be now and England. There had been other worse failures.
In the sense in which all attempts are by definition not failures, since now
is now, and the Queen was, whatever the People made of it, crowned, it
was now, and England. Then.

As for the others, they had their thoughts. The Ellenbys were
delighted and reassured, as though the whole world wore, briefly and
significantly, a Sunday aspect. Felicity Wells was in a state of cultural
ecstasy, seeing the vaults of the Abbey, imitating the inhuman perspec-
tives of the reaches of Heaven, and the Queen's little white human face
over her emblematically embroidered robes, as a promise of renovation.
Eliot had said, and she remembered, that the "English unbeliever con-
formed to the practices of Christianity on the occasions of birth, death,
and the first venture in matrimony . . ." Now a whole Nation was con-
forming to an ancient national Christian rite. It was a true Renaissance.

Daniel and Stephanie noticed very little. Stephanie watched Bill and Daniel watched Stephanie, and Bill watched the television, apparently taking a childlike and unexpected pleasure in its mechanics. Jennifer Parry watched Alexander, and Geoffrey watched Thomas, who was strapped into a little chair on the floor. Mrs Thone was little moved. Her interest in the future, and her real interest in the outside world, had ceased with her son. Once she had understood exactly that between a good breakfast and an end of break bell a boy could run, fall, smash, twitch, stop moving forever and begin to decay, she understood also that nothing could be undone, no air raid, no death camp, no monstrous genesis, and that the important thing about herself was that she had not much time and it did not matter greatly what she did with it. In lieu of caring, since she had unfortunately a good deal of vitality which this understanding had not diminished, she had developed a sharp and pointless pride in the keeping up of appearances. The Coronation was an appearance that was at least being pretty well kept up. (Winifred's efforts on Stephanie's behalf were another: therefore the invitation.) The dead king was buried and his daughter was his future. For her his going was simply another landmark, a further indication that her own real life, including any future she might have cared for, was in the past. She served sausage rolls and squash to the little boys. She liked to have them in the house. She found it quite proper that they could not or would not look her in the eye. If they knew her thoughts, they should be unable to.

Alexander's preoccupation with the past made him highly critical of the present. He was excessively irritated by Richard Dimbleby who chose to emphasise his encomium of Elizabeth II with sharp disparagement of Elizabeth I.

"Once again the fortunes of England are low, but in the character of the Queen how much greater is the advantage with which the second Elizabethan era begins. Her character is well known to all; it is the product of a happy childhood, based on the highest ethical and Christian principles, and serene in the knowledge of family love and unity.

"By contrast, the first Elizabeth, with the lusty imperious Henry VIII as her father and the scheming Anne Boleyn for mother, was not perhaps without some qualifications for the title 'the daughter of the devil' which the Spanish ambassador bestowed upon her. In mitigation she could offer evidence of a childhood that would make most of the twentieth-century's broken homes to which young criminals' delinquencies are so often attributed seem highly respectable. This grim childhood fostered the development of her wiles and cunning . . ." Alexander's feelings about the "young wife and mother" cried up by Dimbleby were luke-warm at best. The young wife and mother, moreover, was on record as disliking her predecessor for having been cruel to her ancestor, Mary Queen of Scots. Alexander brooded about the neo-Freudian social pieties implicit in Dimbleby's panegyric, and then became gloomy as he thought that his own play, too, presented neo-Freudian pieties about what drove the original Gloriana. He had not really dealt with government: only with family life. Of Elizabeth I's Coronation a contemporary had said, "In pompous ceremonies a secret of government doth much consist." Elizabeth had "spontaneously" addressed the people in the City on the way to her Coronation: Alexander had stitched these words into the patchwork of his play.

"And whereas your request is that I should continue your good Lady and Queen, be ye assured that I will be as good to you as ever queen was to her people. No will in me can lack, neither do I trust that there lack any power. And persuade yourselves that for the safety and quietness of you all I will not spare, if need be, to spend my blood. God thank you all." "If it moved a marvellous shout and rejoicing it is nothing to be marvelled at, since both the heartiness thereof was so wonderful, and the words so jointly knit."

No, Alexander thought, that day, it is very apparent that we lack both heartiness and words jointly knit. Years later, before his successful lecture on the commentaries, he had written a parodic screenplay around the Coronation, trying to capture his sense of it as an attempt on style in a time of no style, a watery bright nostalgia created in weak, meandering, failing rhythms that were still moving, had surely some kind of unintentional dying fall. No producer could be got to be interested in it. It lacked, they said with bland tactlessness, topicality and bite.

Lucas had told Marcus that millions of mental energies would be concentrated on this one place, on this one event. Marcus must attempt to hook on or tune in to these forces. Real electrical connections were making invisible powers produce visible signs and symbols, the anointing with oil and the operations of the cathode rays. He spoke of flowing and combing and bands. Marcus had a confused impression that their efforts of attention were directed towards weaving a smooth flow of new forms with the aid of the ministrations of Princes and Bishops, Lords spiritual and temporal. Lucas sat at the other side of the room from Marcus, who was with the other boys on dove grey velvet stools in the front row. Lucas had said better keep the work unnoticed. Now and then Marcus felt the swivelling of his friend's intermittent lighthouse glare of concentration on himself.

Most of the time his dutiful staring produced nothing but a geometrical vision of the glass surface, swanning with dots, pothooks, worms, pillules, blotches, rhythmic ticking and twitching. However, at the moment of the Queen's anointing, to which Lucas had adjured him to pay particular attention, he suddenly managed to focus the image as an image, the shiny grey cloth of gold put off, to see the tiny woman with fifteen yards of pleated white linen folded over her substantial breast, sitting in the clumsy ancient chair, hand on hand, as his own sweating hands were. The picture now flicked, flicked and flicked, as he saw it, so that the frames rose and rose again from underneath themselves, feet over head over feet over head, therefore two-dimensional.

Maybe Lucas had hoped he would see the dove descending, or, as one clairvoyant had, the pillared feet and knees of the Angel of the Abbey rising glassy and huge through the fabric of the roof.

What happened was closer to the spreading. For a moment Marcus's fingers plucked at white linen chill on his shoulders and breast. Mrs Thone's placid cool room humped and shuddered. Marcus stood up, muttering incoherently, and blundered towards the television, which immediately abandoned the representation of the human body for a representation of waves of wires vibrating in a blizzard. People told him to sit down. He wandered away a step or two and as he stepped away so the screen, still crackling, returned to the transmission of its images. Lucas Simmonds rose to his feet. So did Daniel. Lucas, seeing Daniel, sat down again, looking frightened and angry. Marcus rotated slowly. Daniel gripped his arm; it was observable that once Daniel's body was between the boy and the instrument the crackling ceased and Her Majesty stabilised and beamed again. Marcus, in pain, considered biting Daniel, whom he could not see for haze, but who was, he felt, enveloping him like a boa constrictor. Daniel, after a look at his face, gave his elbow a violent pinch, the least conspicuous shock he could administer, and said to Stephanie on the sofa, "Shove up, make room for him over here." Between their two warm bodies Marcus sagged and shivered. Daniel gave him another pinch, almost vicious, which caused him to snap closed his hanging mouth. Then he shut his eyes, too, and rested against the dry black heat which seemed to move from Daniel to Stephanie, making a circuit that kept him from whatever other forces moved in the room.

Stephanie, roused momentarily from the too-placid lethargy that was her defence against Bill's crackling, remembered that worry about Marcus had sent her to Daniel in the first place, and that she, they, had forgotten Marcus in their own troubles. She had been sleeping like the dead, so as not to think, a gift she shared with her brother. She did not know whether or not he was still weeping at night. She glanced briefly at Lucas Simmonds. He wore a pleased and conciliatory grin, boyish, pillar-box red under the curls, and tears stood in his eye-corners. When he saw her looking at him he gave a series of rigid, presumably affable little nods, put his hands under his buttocks and sat on them, giving the impression that he was exercising some form of difficult self-control.

The processions wound on. Dimbleby remarked on the superb English gift for ceremonial, several times. So many men moving as one, so many hearts beating as one. Frederica observed that she hated being moved in the mass, that the thing she really feared was great groups of people moving around like one animal. This seemed to inspire Edmund Wilkie to make a speech. At one point during the proceedings when the London streets were jetty with rain, he had put on a pair of pink goggles, through which he now smiled out at them, saying that he had met a most interesting psychoanalyst called Winnicott who had some really riveting ideas about the unconscious drives behind democracy. All human beings, Wilkie said, according to Winnicott, were possessed by an unconscious fear of Woman, which made it very difficult for individual women, naturally, to get or handle social or political power. Rulers were surrogate parents, and both men and women wouldn't accept women in this position because in their subconscious jungles lurked monstrous and overpowering Fantasy Women. According to Winnicott this explained the terrible cruelty to women found in most cultures. People were afraid of Woman because they had all, once, in the beginning, been totally dependent on Her, and had had to establish their individuality by denying this dependence. Dictators, according to this Winnicott, dealt with the terror of Woman by claiming to encompass her and act for her. This was why they demanded not only obedience, but Love. This may be why Frederica was so afraid of group emotion, love or hate.

Everyone furtively searched his or her unconscious, in so far as it could be said to be accessible, for a fear of Woman, and, it must be related, duly found it. Bill Potter told Wilkie that the whole thing sounded like codswallop to him, ludicrously pat, and Frederica said well, then, what about the Queen and all this affection we're demonstrating?

Ah, said Wilkie, the Crown was O.K. because it was hereditary and at the top of a chain of symbolic parentage, as the first Elizabeth had cleverly known. The Commons were the parents of the people, and the Lords of the Commons, and the Monarch of the Lords. If the Monarch could manage to believe in God then the chain extended conveniently to infinity and was quite safe and stable. Thus, said Wilkie, Winnicott demonstrates, that the myths of the Dying God and the Eternal Monarch are still at work in our own culture at this juncture. The Queen protects us from the fear of Woman because she is a good, distant, unthreatening parent, and so we have our democratic monarchy.

Bill said that he was sick and tired of having everything brought back to sex and the family. Wilkie said he did agree, but in our time we had to be Freudian, we had no option, and universal psychological tropisms always looked wrong dragged into the light of day where they were not meant to be, since one resisted and repressed them, or they would not be what they were. That, said Bill, was the trouble with psychoanalysis: it was a closed circle: any disagreement was simply ascribed to resistance, which reinforced the original point. In the eyes of the believers. That was the nature of belief. He preferred not to tangle with it. And if Wilkie wanted to know what he thought, he thought the real danger to individuals came not from Women but from this bland little, simple little, universal little screen. Which would clearly do away with reading, talk, communal play, craft and life.

Wilkie said it might not do that, but that if they had seen the experiments he had seen with subliminal suggestions – giving a man a raging thirst with a series of invisibly rapid frames of a glass of iced water in the middle of a film about something quite different – they would be afraid of what a Hitler could do with pictures of leering Jews strangling starving kids. But the thing was here to stay, and he personally intended to involve himself in it, because it was where the centre of energy was, in our culture, and you either used it, or sat on your bottom and watched it. This dictum at least Frederica and Alexander took to heart and remembered, though Wilkie appeared on this occasion possibly foppish and of no account, with his round pink eyes and a captiously sprouting bit of beard he was trying to grow for Ralegh.

Years later, after his play and his play's aftermath, after his abortive screenplay and his severe lecture, Alexander was visited by total recall of the Coronation day on an evening when he was employed to write 500 words about a very different television occasion, the grilling of the female Jan Morris by Robin Day, and a team of women, psychological, feminist, fierce, friendly. During this exercise film was shown of the beautiful young James Morris leaning out over the shining white reaches of that conquered virginal peak that was not a Sign, and gleefully proclaiming its submission. Here in person was a sign, Alexander thought, if a hard sign to interpret, female by sex, male by gender, undergoing a positively Attic self-mutilation to become an analogue of the first Elizabeth's emblem, the renewed Phoenix, the alchemical *mysterium coniunctionis*, Hermes and Aphrodite, mother and father, like Spenser's Ovidian Nature. He thought of the occult myth that the first Elizabeth was a man, or a woman with male characteristics. The reign of the second had, it turned out, been ushered in by Hermes on a mountain who became Aphrodite and enjoyed having her bottom anachronistically slapped by taxi-drivers in Bath. Robin Day trapped and teased this ambivalent but dignified figure with unexpected images of her, or his, earlier incarnation. It was a long way from Richard Dimbleby's orotund homage to the Young Woman.

Alexander spent an unduly long time trying to write a riddling metaphysical witty meditation on Ms Morris and Mr Day, and gave up, out of considerations of courtesy, taste, and legality. What he published was, ironically, an almost Dimblebyesque tribute to Ms Morris's leggy poise and husky civility.

In his drawer he kept a dozen Spenserian stanzas about nature, genius, and the square world of glass which perhaps only Frederica would entirely have understood. And he had no intention of ever showing them to her.

28. On the Interpretation of Dreams

Three or four times before in her life Stephanie had had dreams which were heavy and bright, different in kind from other dreams, visions and conundrums admonishing and enchanting. This latest dream was both fascinating and insulting, as though it had been done to her.

She went along a long white beach. The sea was far out, sluggish waves rolling over silently on distant sand. She was not hot, or cold, but chilly. She was aware that she did not want to be where she was.

She went slowly. She was held up by some inertia in the nature of things, as though the world was exhausted. Things appeared bleached, though some had hints of possible colour palely vanishing as in an over-exposed negative. The sand was transparent ash-silver, filmed with a yellow stain. The pearly cliffs were smeared in places with a ghostly flesh colour. The sky was white with creamy streaks like folds in cartridge paper. The water was milky and the distant rocks were white like stranded dry sea-skeletons.

The silent horse and rider came from the cliffs, contained in their own wind, which troubled the many layers of clothing in which they were wound. The horse, pounding along under fluttering scalloped trappings, stretched a soft white muzzle through a white hood. Its ears were back: its mouth foamed: under its muffling its eyes couldn't be seen. The rider was cocooned in goldish and whitish veilings, flapping and whipping behind her, bunched in her fists on her breast, together with the loop of scalloped reins and some indistinct wrapped object. The face, still in the moving cloths, was bone-white.

She watched them scud away towards the water and went on, with difficulty. The beach was almost airless now they had taken their disturbance with them. She had to look for something in or under the rocks. She was confident she would remember what it was when she got there. And then the confidence drained away and she knew she had overestimated herself. Her head was empty.

Behind her the pony slopped wearily back along the edge of the sea, which had crept up, rapid and shining, crested now and swaying vigorously, close to her.

She put out a hand and caught the rein. The touch of warm flesh, the soft, barely furred horse-lips, the wrinkling nose, was a shock. She let go. The creature drew up, head hanging. It was not so wild and bright after all – rather heavy, barrel-like, hairy-fetlocked. The rider sagged in the saddle. She felt a weight of responsibility; she must get them moving again at all costs. And she was gripped by that ancient, primal feeling of being in a story one has no desire either to share or to see out.

She looked up at the knot of cloths and fingers on the rider's breast, and enquired whether it would not be best to go on? The rider, hunched, did not speak, but exuded panic. The primal storyteller communicated to her that the urn must be buried, that the world was drowning. At this she slapped the pony's solid haunch and it started forward and trotted away in the water.

She looked behind and saw the high glittering wash of water, collected so rapidly in the bay, sweeping towards her.

She began to run, getting nowhere, and smoothly the fleet waters moved after her.

In dreams, if what pursues comes up with what is pursued, the story merely begins somewhere else some other way, failing awakening.

She scrabbled with wet hands under the cliffs near the rocks, weeping a little, far too hot now, making a hole with slithering spangled wet at the bottom, into which its walls perpetually caved and slipped. Elbow deep she tunnelled down, until she reached a rusty iron pipe mouth and a ring of white froth appeared on the dark smooth surface in her hole. She sat on her heels and surveyed her work. This was not the urn, this was sewage, and should be covered up. The urn should not be hidden but multiplied. She was digging in the wrong place. Everything was wrong. She would be punished.

She ran on the rocks. The wish not to be part of this story was stronger, but she was dutiful. Here were shelves of rock on which, as in a druggist's shop, were ranged rows of alabaster urns, jars and vases, certainly multiplied, corked and lidded, rising through fronds of cushioned bladderwrack and those sleek swollen squares with spiked corners laid by dogfish and called mermaid's purses. She could not touch these containers, all similar, none identical. She sat down on a heap of that seaweed which is like tough old unbleached linen, its living texture seeming woven, its scalloped edges reminiscent in little of the horse's trappings. The air had a milky, misty whiteness and was closing in. She had lost the urn that had contained all there was to be saved, although the rocks bristled with other lidded jars containing who knew what ashes or unguents. She should have kept still. She had left undone something essential. She could never walk back over the hissing acres of bladderwrack. The white water was rising, sucking and soughing up the bony cold rocks.

She woke in terror and found her face wet and slippery with tears and her bladder bursting.

When she came back from the lavatory it was impossible to slip back into sleep, which was one reason why she was able to fix and remember the dream with such clarity. Such dreams in any case, in her experience, continued into waking and reason. It was just after dawn, pale violet-grey. She drew her quilt round her shoulders and sat up to apply her mind to the matter.

Ends of verses curled and coiled in vacancy, like clues of thread, like shining ends of flying gossamer. Which is death to hide. Tender curving lines of creamy spray. Cold pastoral. The fleet waters of a drowning world. Thou silent form dost tease us out of thought . . . Behind these stalked the high forms of high language, ghostly grammatical skeletons of forgotten periods, inchoate remembered cadences and unheard melodies with continuing lines of singing rhythms. She could have wept because they were bleached and vanished, all the same blank whiteness.

There were other emotions involved. One was plain wrath at what had been made willy-nilly of a real, complex and vigorous memory. The roaring wind and blown sea, the local precision and true drama of the day at Filey had been in this dream, without her will, unified, internalised, drained and stilled. High art, modernist shored fragments of allusive high art, pickings, flotsam and jetsam of a foundering culture, had been made of it, but she had not made it. She had called up this impotent ghost of English poetry, but could offer it no blood to make it utter.

It was also a ghastly Freudian joke, working with the reductive simplicity, the obtrusive meanings, of its animated picture-language. Delicately, fastidiously, she sorted out the fronds as it were of this psychoanalytic growth.

Item: bladderwrack was, to an habitual sufferer from post-coital cystitis, a peculiarly painful pun.

Item: the womb-tomb-urn complex was intellectually insulting in its simplicity, and heavily reinforced by seaweeds and holes. One would have to hint, allude, obscure what, in a real dream, apprehended as a real event, sensuous object or motive for action, reduced one to wet tears, frenzy and terror.

Item: digging frantically in order to locate or maybe bury the one precious urn, she had created a deep, bloody wet hole and discovered in it a rusty, frothy parody of the male organ. The associations called up by this were peculiarly nauseating because of the presence, on the real beach, of real rusty, frothy sewage pipes and real blood-coloured clay.

She was also appalled by, indeed she almost succeeded in not noticing, an association she only too neatly made, between rings of froth on the sand and the traces of white round her father's pinched, enraged hole of a mouth.

Then there was the didactic message. As though dictated by some bookish pythoness from an English *sortes Virgilianae*. "Which is death to hide" was Milton, talking about literature and the loss of it, talking about blindness, cross-referring his own inertia to the terrible story of the unfaithful servant who cravenly buried the one talent instead of multiplying it. There was the Grecian Urn. Thou still unravished bride of chastity. The non-sensuous sensuality in the mind. Urne buriall. Monumental alabaster. Smooth as monumental alabaster. That was surely far-fetched, dragged from too remote a text. Association looped irrelevances together. White, pale, cold, urn, horse, sky, sea.

The horse had antecedents, of which death on a pale horse was a remote and uncertain avatar. There was an archaic palfrey she couldn't place, instinct with fear, and some other very precise literary image of a rider hurrying to bury a treasure. This she waited blankly for, conjuring it, with the phrase "fleet waters of a drowning world", with a kind of contrary after-image of her dream, a humped and trundling dark steed on a reach of black sand, not white, William Wordsworth's dreamed dromedary.

She called up various other verbal quirks – from *Moby-Dick* and *The Idea of Order at Key West*, from *Dover Beach* and the Tennysonian last battles in the mist. But the didactic centre, she knew, was with Milton and Wordsworth and the urn burial. She got down her old Cambridge *Prelude*. Wordsworth's dream occurred in the middle of that unsatisfactory Book V, entitled *Books*. In this dream, the rider, neither Arab nor Don Quixote, was fleeing the ultimate flood to bury a stone and a shell, which were, in the dream, an impassioned Ode and Euclid's elements, language and geometry.

Stephanie read. Some passions are the regular subjects of fiction and some, though certainly passions, are more recondite and impossible to describe. A passion for reading is somewhere in the middle: it can be hinted but not told out, since to describe an impassioned reading of *Books* would take many more pages than *Books* itself and be an anti-climax. Nor is it possible like Borges' poet, to incorporate *Books* into this text, though its fear of the drowning of books and its determination to give a fictive substance to a figure seen in a dream might lend a kind of Wordsworthian force to the narrative. In Wordsworth's dream and Stephanie's the undifferentiated narrator made clear the nature of the events. It is not so easy to describe a careful, conscious reading as an event. What Stephanie found in *Books* was a superfluous fear, a fear of drowning, of loss, of dark powers, ambivalent about whether it was life or the imagination that was the destroyer, or where these two became one, where, if at all, the undifferentiated narrator tells a solid tale. What she thought she thought, weeping a little, consciously and decorously, was that she should not marry, she had lost, or buried, a world in agreeing to marry, she should go back to Cambridge and write a thesis on Wordsworth's fear of drowning books. Then she thought this was ludicrous and laughed hysterically. Then she thought she herself was afraid of being in the same place as her attention, body and imagination at once, and that Daniel would require this of her, and there would be no place for urn or landscape in their own terms. But if it was death to hide them, it was, it surely was, death to immure oneself with them. She had no answer, so would do what came easiest, what was already well-fixed, and marry. She turned back to the beginning of the book and began wildly to read it all, as though her self depended on it.

29. *Wedding*

The Coronation commentaries lavished superlatives on the English genius for ceremonial. The events which constituted the Potter wedding were characterised by muddle, ill-temper, and aspersions on the church service. Bill waited until the arrangements were near completion and then announced that of course they must understand he would not countenance the thing by going into any church. Just in case they had supposed he was going to give his daughter away. Winifred said no, of course, dear, and went away and co-opted Alexander. Like many acquiescent people she was over-decisive when wrought up to it: she neglected to ask Stephanie about this: Stephanie was embarrassed: by then Alexander, who liked ceremonies, had accepted most gracefully.

There was a general feeling that the bride was somewhat unresponsive to events. She had her own sourish thoughts about ceremony. Like most little girls she had played ritually, pruriently, narcissistically, at "my wedding". Like most citizens she craned to peer into white-ribboned cars to see The Bride pass briefly, some unrecognisable typist, duchess, riding-instructor, schoolmistress whom she would neither see nor recognise again. Primitive societies had ceremonies for circumcision, puberty, hunting, shooting, fishing, birth, marriage and death. Bodies were decorated with knobs, scars, blisters, paint, leaves, flowers and feathers. People marched in the Queen's wake with slashed cheeks under English hats and helmets. It was habitual. Her distaste for the Church enactment was to do, as was her family's, with Daniel's presumed belief in the real efficacy of the ceremony. No God for Stephanie stared down from the rood-beam, nor would touch the ring with true magic, nor knit up handclasp or eyebeams. Nevertheless there she would be, murmuring Cranmer's prose in a cloud of white veiling. Her thoughts flirted persistently with blasphemies and indelicacies. There was the brute reality of the friend whose new husband, after an ill-judged wedding journey from Keswick to Dover, had put on his pyjamas in the hotel bedroom and had, whilst his bride struggled in the lavatory with a slippery and intransigent Dutch cap, ritually removed the trousers again and sunk, bare buttocks and striped torso, into a snoring torpor on the counterpane, from which he could by no means be waked. Everyone insisted in telling Stephanie such tales. She was glad that both actually and metaphorically it was at least certain that no one could hang her own marital sheets out of the ill-fitting council house window.

Leaving home she had always imagined against a background of thick domestic life and closing family ranks. When the wedding day began the house in Masters' Row had a stripped, windswept look and there was one large gap in the ranks. Breakfast was very early, and all the women came down bundled in dressing-gowns, unkempt. Bill was not there, nor, it was subsequently discovered, anywhere in the house. On Stephanie's plate was a brown envelope. In it was a cheque, made out to Stephanie Potter, for £250. This made everybody feel very uncomfortable.

"She won't be Potter by the time she pays that in," said Frederica obviously.

"I expect the Bank is used to that," said Stephanie. Marcus, in flannels and aertex shirt, slid quietly into his chair.

"Where do you think he's gone?" said Frederica. No one answered. Stephanie pushed away an unchipped egg. Winifred poured tea.

THE VIRGIN IN THE GARDEN

"Do you think he'll come to any of it?" said Frederica. No one answered that, either.

There was a long silence. Frederica said, "Oh well, if nobody's got any bright conversation, I think I'll go and have a nice bath."

Winifred roused herself.

"Now wait a minute, don't just dash off, this has to be thought about. It's *Stephanie's* bath that counts, we must think about that, and the boiler, and make a careful schedule, time things . . ."

"Oh, Mummy, don't be silly, anyone can go whenever they want, we've all got nothing to do and there's huge deserts of time between now and then because you would insist on doing everything yesterday so now we must all sit and bite our nails for an eternity today, just in case the boiler blows, or the bouquets don't come and we have to cycle to Blesford and back, or . . ."

"I get no thanks for trying to organise things smoothly," said Winifred, tight-lipped. "You all seem to suppose arrangements just make themselves."

"No, no, that's just what we *don't* suppose. We are complaining of oppressive fixing of hours of boring waiting . . ."

"I don't care when I have my bath," said Stephanie. Winifred, catching her tone, looked at her anxiously. She made an effort. "That is, I go very pink, bright pink, so I must have my bath in time to fade again before . . ."

"The blushing bride," said Frederica.

"Shut *up*," said Marcus, surprisingly. Everyone turned to stare at him. He got up and went upstairs, into the bathroom.

"Well," said Frederica, "I shall go after Stephanie, and then I can have a good soak and a good sing and put myself in fettle."

"No one," said Winifred, "has time to *soak*, dear."

This was not true. Frederica was right, there was too much waste time. A florist's van came with flowers, Mrs Thone telephoned to say the catering was in hand, Bill stayed away, and nothing else happened. The three women trailed round the house in dressing-gowns, making unnecessary cups of Nescafé, glancing casually out of the windows. The house was full of piles of parcels and temporary spaces where a chair, or a clock, had gone to furnish the maisonette. Frederica knew they should all have been laughing or crying together but Winifred and Stephanie were silent and closed and her clumsy jokes seemed like monstrous acts of aggression or vulgarity, so after a time she did indeed close herself in the bathroom, where she sang with gloomy glee "No Coward Soul is Mine", "Abide With Me", and Feste's cold little song from *Twelfth Night*. After Winifred had nervously ejected Frederica, Stephanie took a brisk bath – she did not want to look at her body – and wandered, pink, damp, slightly curly-haired into her own bedroom, where she sat on the bed and waited until she could decently begin to get dressed – a time which was still some hours away.

The room, always bare, was now denuded. Her books, her mantelpiece things, the stool, the bedside table, had been carried down to Askham Buildings. The wardrobe contained only clothes she had grown out of, worn out or rejected. In a nervous attempt to occupy herself she had stripped the bed and folded the blankets, on which she now sat, quietly, not recognising the place, which she could not leave, because it had already gone away. She envied Frederica, who always wanted something – who had indeed carried off a few of the things that had been left, a tapestry cushion, a hair-pin tray, a print of Botticelli's Primavera whose blank space on the wall was a paler green than the rest, making it all look dusty. She thought of her childhood, and it was nothing to do with her. She thought of Daniel, and decided not to. She thought of Wordsworth, and felt a momentary relief. Winifred knocked at the door and appeared, wearing, under the dressing-gown, a gleaming new corselet. She was carrying yet another cup of Nescafé.

"Do you feel all right, dear?"

"I'm not ill."

Winifred looked round the room. "It all looks a bit stripped. I thought we might make a study here, for him. I'm sorry he's being like this."

"Not your fault. Not unexpected, really."

"It's your day. And he's trying to spoil it."

Stephanie saw she was weeping.

"I wanted it to be right, for you, a real family wedding, for you . . ."

"It will be."

They looked at each other with mirrored despairing patience. Winifred's hands were tucked in her dressing-gown cuffs, wrapped round her body, for comfort. Stephanie thought, a woman, a house, "a real family . . ." Did she want to make a "home" for Daniel? What did she want? Frederica burst in, clothed in the yellow poplin, her hair tied back with a long chocolate ribbon. She said,

"Get a move on. I can see Alexander walking across Far Field looking absolutely all pearly grey, and a top hat, imagine the beauty, and here you all are in your underthings. Things are starting. May I borrow that new lipstick you bought, Steph, that softy one. Mine are all altogether too strong for this buttery colour, you need subtlety, and you wouldn't want a tarty bridesmaid, would you? You wouldn't lend me a bit of your greeny eyeshadow too, would you?"

Stephanie mutely indicated her chest of drawers and watched Frederica

briskly apply her pristine wedding makeup to her own face. She was
ashamed of the feeling that the things were hers, should have been used
by her; like a small child on its birthday, not a grown woman, she told
herself, watching Frederica spit expertly on her mascara and twist her
mascara brush on the sandy lashes. The green eyeshadow looked rather
nice on Frederica.

"There – all done in a jiffy. Now I can let Alexander in whilst you
beautify yourself. Mummy's been pressing your folds out. I'll go and
get The Dress, shall I?"

"I suppose so."

Frederica gave her a long, greedy, proprietary look and flared out
again, rustling net petticoats and crisp cotton skirt. After a moment, she
came back with the white, sagging plastic bag containing the dress and
hung it in the door.

"If you need a tirewoman, shout. He's coming up the garden path, I'll
open the door, I hope he doesn't think this yellow is juvenile . . ."

Left alone, she moved the naked bulb of her bedside lamp nearer to
her mirror – the shade had also been taken down to Askham Buildings.
In the theatrical glare this produced she made up her own face, rapidly,
minimally, stepped out of her dressing-gown, stared at her naked breasts
for a cool angry moment, and began on a whirlwind hooking and
zipping. She brushed too fiercely at her hair, so that protesting damp bits
of it whipped into unintentional tight spirals, and then, as ruthlessly as
she could, she poked and pinned and squashed the little white wired cap
and the clouds of tulle onto her head. It was all a nonsense. One, two,
she tapped her heels into white kid slippers and stalked out, skirts
rustling, onto the landing. In the hall Frederica was making little rushes
in search of a lost glove and Winifred, military in glossy navy blue, was
struggling with a pleated linen hem. A car-driver stood by the door.
Stephanie stood on the stairs.

"Oh, you're there. Oh, good. You look lovely. Alexander's in the
sitting room with the flowers. If he – if your father – comes back – tell
him – oh, I don't know – tell him – but don't on any account wait,
whatever you do. Don't wait. Is my back hair all right? Do I look silly?"

"Lovely, you look."

"Not that it matters, anyway. Perhaps it will be just as well if he
doesn't put in an appearance. My dear – I will see you in the church."

"I hope so," said Stephanie, still on the stairs. Frederica spun past,
gesturing with a handful of cornflowers and white rosebuds.

"I tell you one thing, Alexander's much the most handsome . . ."

"I feel a fool," said Stephanie.

"You will," said Frederica, in a thoughtlessly soothing voice, and rushed out to her carriage. Stiffly, Stephanie went into the sitting room.

Alexander rose most gracefully, smoke-grey, pearl-grey, oyster-grey, from the sofa, gave her a half-bow and said, "Ah, let me look at you, let me see." She stood stony in the doorway. He gestured with a hand. "Please, walk towards me. I am so honoured to have been asked. Could you put your head up a little. Take longer steps. Forgive me. That's lovely."

Flustered, she nearly tripped over the trailing flex of the iron. She caught up a pointed trail of veiling, bent awkwardly down, rustling and white, to disconnect the plug.

"Let me," said Alexander.

"Fires can start that way."

"We have avoided a fire." He put the iron onto the bookshelf. He put the ironing board behind the sofa. The room was a graceless chaos: Frederica's discarded dressing-gown on the carpet, dirty coffee cups on mantelpiece and table, trails of packing shavings. In the middle of this, Alexander took her hands.

"Lovely dress."

"I feel silly."

"Why?" He was excited: he felt a pronounced distaste for the domestic mess. He would never have advocated the wearing of bright red jackets and white tight trousers on the buttocks: but a woman in a white veil, a long, wide skirt and a sash caught his attention in a way a woman in an apron – off-stage – never would. He repeated, "Why? Use your sense of occasion. Step out." He studied her with a practised eye. Some of the seams were puckered: a hook and eye at the waist were sewn askew: her rigorous dressing had depressed the waistline of the dress below the line of the sash; there was something wrong with her head. He gripped her hands, briefly, and said,

"If I may – I could just fix your sash. Give the veiling a tweak? May I?"

She nodded, speechless.

"You look so lovely." His hands were busy round her waist, pulling, pleating, tucking. "Have you any of those tiny gold pins? There's a stitch here." She shifted brusquely, with the immediately suppressed impatience of those who are required to keep still and be touched by helpers. The hands stopped for a moment, hard, on her waist. She began to inhabit the dress. She lifted her shoulders. "Little gold pins," said Alexander's beautiful voice, amused, deprecating, insistent.

"Oh, little gold pins. By my bedroom mirror. I'll go."

"No, no, keep still, I'll go."

She stood like a white pillar, hearing him, Alexander, prowling in her bare box of a room, swinging downstairs. He took her in his hands again, turning, bending, delicately inserting a pin here, tugging a fold there. He retied the sash, running his hands down her ribs, one over her buttocks, suggesting, somehow, the stance that would hang the dress. He turned her to face him. Abstractedly, he pulled at her collar, peering into the chaste V neck. He put a hand under her chin, turned up her face.

"Have we time? I could do something with that hairline. Your pretty little cap is all asymmetrical. Stephanie, you are deliberately torturing yourself with those ferocious grips and pins. You are a beautiful girl, all soft curves and rounded lines. You can't *drag* your hairline, love, it won't do. May I?"

"Do I have any choice?"

"You know I know better."

"I know you know better."

He had the pins out in a few seconds, produced a shining new comb from a breast-pocket, soothed, curved, resited the little cap, pinned it down. One or two sore and burning places she had made on her own scalp glowed and vanished. She breathed deeply. He stepped back to look at her, stepped close again and studied her face. She wondered if he was going to offer to apply fresh make-up, too, but he simply nodded appreciatively, touched her cheek with a gentle finger, tucked a curl behind her ear.

"I am enjoying this," said Alexander. "I am so glad to have been invited. I shall get your flowers."

He strode away and returned with the wired cascade of white and gold, roses and stephanotis, freesias and orange blossom, the heads bitten in their metal stems, the surface dense, crisp, scented.

"I shan't know how to hold it."

"I shall show you."

He handed the thing to her. She held it awkwardly, protruding, dangling, heavy.

"No, you must clasp it – *not* down there – at waist level, and tuck your elbows in. Above your sash."

It looked so light and airy, and was so rigidly wired.

"Like a chastity belt," she said vaguely.

"The way you were holding it, it would have been easier to give it a grosser name," said Alexander, and they both laughed. "Now, you mustn't stand, frozen, you must step out lightly. Take long strides, from the hip, *move* that skirt. Try it."

She stepped out. His hands, his eyes, defined her body. She was briefly pleased with it. The doorbell rang. The driver of the car had returned from the church for this last cargo. Together they went out into the little hall. Cream paint, flowered walls, telephone table, coat hooks, hardboard bannister case. She remembered the sites of unbuilt homes, marked out with corner bricks, strips of wood, concrete. A house takes up so little earth – a few of these floating white strides and you had covered it, end to end. A child playing out of doors could skip a minute and move over living room and kitchen, step quickly beyond the equivalent of the inhabited space. In some way this perception was linked with the disturbing idea of Alexander, in her stripped bedroom, rifling her dressing table for little gold pins, where she had so often daydreamed him into a finished box of a home, curtained and carpeted against the night and cold. It was all struts, and padding and muffling, a house. She tightened a little white-gloved hand on Alexander's arm. He bent and kissed her mouth, and then lifted the veiling and covered her face with it. Neatly, pacing together, they went down the garden-path and into the ribboned car.

The next stage was briefly endless. They sat silently in the car and small knots of people stared, even waved, from street-corners, as to a princess passing. She picked her white way across uneven churchyard stones, Alexander's hand under an elbow. In the porch a man with a camera crouched and grinned, gestured and begged her to smile and smile again. Muffled in white, she turned her head this way and that. A black verger beckoned her into the dark, and there was Frederica, yellow and peering, with glittering eyes. Between porch and church was a black velvet curtain, up against which the verger led her, so that she stared into it whilst Frederica and Alexander twitched at the veiling and shook out the flow of skirts. The verger said that when the organ sounded he would whip back the curtain and give a vicious shove to that sticky door. She should mind that old step down, a bride had measured her length only the other week and been spliced with smashed glasses and a beautiful black eye. Frederica curvetted like a restrained procession of one. Alexander arranged her arm over his: there was a wheezing and winding of bellows and then suddenly music. The verger pulled the curtain, Alexander negotiated the step, Frederica paced after. The Vicar, in rehearsal, had urged her to give Daniel a big smile. He loomed under the bright brass lectern eagle. She met his eye, briefly, vaguely. He had his concentrated frown.

The congregation swayed like a windy garden, tilting helmeted and floral heads to see the bride. They judged the dress, they were caught in the throat, they remembered their own moment, or looked forward to it, they divested the woman of her clothes in their mind's eyes, they speculated about what she knew and did not know. She was their dubious innocence, their experience, come, coming or to come. Under a

Peter Pan cap of overlapping mauve grey petals Felicity Wells's withered cheeks were wet. Alexander wondered why people should be so watery at weddings. He himself felt a certain satisfaction at his handiwork. He stepped forward to give this woman to be married to this man, and admired the effectiveness of his underpinning.

They stood before Mr Ellenby, their backs towards him, one white, one black, one airy and foaming, one dark, thick, slightly shining. They were both very solid. Stephanie's dress was plain, no lace, no floss, nun-like under the falling triangle of veiling. But she had big round breasts under the bodice, and grand hips emphasised by the reasonably small circle of the waist. A child-bearing body, Alexander thought, sharing the general impression. He was moved by the exchange of vows, the old clear words, the uncompromising rhythms. Daniel spoke gruffly and Stephanie spoke clear and low. Mr Ellenby was solicitous, rather than clerically hooting. He had given great thought to the few words he felt bound to speak, on this occasion. He had read over and abandoned his usual remarks on the duties and delights of true Christian marriage, in favour of something new, vaguely literary in honour of the bride, and yet firmly reminding the bridegroom, he trusted, of those other vows he had embraced. With what he hoped was a graceful kind of tact Mr Ellenby proceeded from Spenser's epithalamium and Milton's celebration of the nuptial bliss of Adam and Eve to the biblical unions mentioned in the marriage service, including that primitive, first one. Eve was flesh of Adam's flesh and bone of Adam's bone. Man and wife was one flesh. The marriage service explicitly likened this union to the coming together of God and Man in the union of Christ and his Spouse, the Church. "So ought men to love their wives as their own bodies," St Paul said, and his saying was incorporated in the prayer book, "He that loveth his wife loveth himself: for no man ever yet hated his own flesh, but nourisheth and cherisheth it, even as the Lord the Church: for we are members of his body, of his flesh, and of his bones." Daniel when he was ordained had been enlisted to serve and protect the Church and Congregation who were the Spouse and Body of Christ. "They two shall be one flesh," St Paul went on. "This is a great mystery; but I speak concerning Christ and the Church." In a truly English way no one looked at anyone's face during this exhortation. Descending his winding stair to the earth again Mr Ellenby reflected on Daniel's impenetrable reception of his private remarks on St Peter, "himself a married man" according to Cranmer, whose pithy advice on the conversion of a pagan spouse was also included in the marriage service. "Even if any obey not the Word they may without the Word be gained by the conversion of the wives." Or husbands, he had said to Daniel, who had said yes, bluntly, and no more.

Mr Ellenby sometimes suspected that Daniel himself was more than half pagan. The girl, whom he liked, was paradoxically more capable of understanding the drift of his, or St Paul's, parabolic analogies than his grim curate. She had sat in his study and talked wisely of Herbert's *Temple*. She had the essence of the matter in her, must have. In some further divine paradoxical way, her chaste conversation might indeed Christianise her uncouth partner. So much must be prayed for. He looked benignly upon that veiled white head, which harboured briefly savage thoughts about the essential shiftiness of argument by analogy. He blessed the couple, gracefully.

Marcus, at the back of the church, rested his face on the cold pillar from behind which Stephanie had overlooked Easter. At moments during the ceremony he consulted his watch: synchronicity was of the essence. He could see the rare old paintings above the arches. He could see the backs of Stephanie and Daniel. He could smell the strong smells of stephanotis, stone and wax in that place. He partly heard the vicar. He looked idly at the faded stains of charcoal, ochre, yellow and red, white and streaked cobalt. Ramping serpent, protesting Eve, recumbent Infant, dolorous Mother, Christ on the Tree, Christ in Wrath and Glory, the gaping, toothed Mouth of Hell. He yawned himself: nervous tension always made him sleepy. He checked his little dial again. Lately, since they had submitted to the apparent aimlessness of the proceedings, he and Lucas had had some startling successes with the transmission of very detailed mental pictures. In ten minutes or so he must make himself into a receiver, an antenna, an aerial. And after that, a transmitter. This was now done briefly and simply. Feet together, hands together, eyes closed, mind cleared, eyes opened, unfocused. Then the figure was called up and held, and held, geometric and pure. After a time the image rose, through and athwart it, an after-image on the screen of the mind's eye, a projection. If possible, it was noted with pencil and paper. If not, committed to memory.

They had had no success with the transmission of words, nor with the transference of thoughts. Lucas felt that this was a failing. They should be able to communicate thoughts. Marcus himself had trouble about the definition of thoughts, in so far as these differed from words. A thought to Lucas might be said to be a truth about the biosphere, or the nature of consciousness, or the mental Plan for the evolution of the Species. Marcus asked how such a thought could be formulated for transmission, or, even more, apprehended. Lucas protested that what they did achieve was so pointless, so almost wilfully redundant. What use was a detail of a flowered counterpane in the Calverley Local Arts Centre? Or the Piranesi-like grilles and winches, transmitted by Marcus and clearly received and sketched by Lucas, of the interior of Winifred Potter's toasting-machine, stripped and partly dismantled for repair? Marcus had discovered, since the events of the Dropping Well and Owger's Howe that he had a certain authority over Lucas that he took a cool, limited pleasure in exercising. The truth was that, message or no message, the things received were to him, in their limitations, manageable and pleasant. They were without the endless extension which so terrified him in the geometry which in its inhuman clarity also so consoled him: they were without the stammering, stumping thick wordy mess of human theory with which Lucas sometimes seemed to be positively belabouring his mind. They were shared yet separate, a detailed achievement yet point-less. He liked them the way they were. He therefore said to Lucas that he thought they were meant, that the meaning would be revealed as long as neither of them did anything to disturb the process. They had after all discovered that what they transmitted must come to them at random, for success must not be deliberately selected for didactic or "testing" reasons, must, as it were, almost be noted slyly and sideways, rather than stared out of countenance. This was so true that Lucas was forced to concede that they must go on as they were. He came up, a little later, with the hypothesis that they were being trained to remember, when their time came, some mental blueprint so precise, novel and intricate that an unprepared mind would be able neither to plot nor to recognise it. Marcus was partly pleased by this idea. Some such extreme, required precision, taking him over totally, would relieve him of many of his present anxieties. He still carried a dumb doubt as to the possibility of naming any of these things at all.

He didn't altogether like the idea of transmitting things in the Church. Lucas's identification of places of power had been sure enough, whatever qualifications one might want to make about what he did with this knowledge. The pillars and arms of stone had their own geometrical singing, which he could seize and see as a strong three-dimensional structure of interlocking lines and proportions, enclosing a space and a knot of intersections and yet also flowing away, doors, roofs, aisles, lines of arch-openings, into infinity. An infinite box is alarming. Then the field of flowery heads was a field of force that could powerfully intensify, he would guess, or distort, any message. Who knew, he thought, hearing and not hearing Mr Ellenby promulgating St Paul, *what* could get through. "O God, who by thy mighty power hast made all things of nothing," said the Vicar, "who also (after other things set in order) didst appoint, that out of man (created after thine own image and similitude) Woman should take her beginning . . ."

The minute hand reached the appointed stroke. Marcus gathered and excluded his body, looked into the dark and saw the swimming figure, in its no-space. Quiet deepened down. He waited.

He saw grasses. At first, briefly, he saw what he identified as the flower of lords and ladies, pointed pale green hood bowed over the purplish-brown spadix. This was replaced by the brilliantly clear grasses, a substantial handful of them, folded in some large green leaf, hanging their seeded ears out and low. They were varied kinds: fescues, rye grass, couch grass, meadow grass, hair grass, silky bent and quaking grass. They were silver-green, green-gold, pale and glassy, clear, new elm-leaf green and darker, bitter marshy-green. Fine lines down their stems glistened like stretched hairs: their finely swollen joints were glossy and shiny. If he had walked across a meadow, over a moor, by a river, he would have trodden down thousands. Here they seemed almost impossible in their intricacy and difference one from another. Also beautiful. Marcus was not one for beauty: he had early given that up as a value, in his imaginary mudscape: he had been frequently told to identify it, and had looked the other way. He did not now use the word to himself – in any case, he was occupied simply with seeing – but the pleasure that accompanied the seeing was an intense recognition of something satisfactory in colour, variety, form. Once or twice what Lucas had sent him had taken this particular form of a variety of related natural objects – eggs, vertebrae, stones and shells. On all occasions it had had this overplus of intense aesthetic pleasure. He did not know, indeed, he did not ask, if the feeling had been transmitted with the grasses, if it was Lucas's or his own. As he watched, the grasses faded and for a time a strange transparent glassy shade of them hovered and trembled, each tube now defined as a translucent colourless cylinder by the light of its circumference, each seed, each sharp husk or falling spikelet revealed in its implicated, minute combing of particles. If one did not count such things, one frequently, Marcus frequently, remembered a large amount of exact numbers – of grasses, of ears, even of spikelets. Lucas would have preserved the grasses themselves for a check.

When the inner eye was emptied the primary geometry recurred, known, rather than seen – that is, Marcus sensed its shape rather as if he had heard it, or known it in the way one knows a chair one is about to occupy, or an obstacle one must avoid in the dark. He could have made it materialise, ropes or planes of looped fibre or tracery or light, but chose not, and cast about for something to send back through its funnel. His look lit on hell mouth on the opposite wall. He had started to scan and map and absorb it before the flicker of doubt about the propriety of the subject, and by then it had chosen itself. It yawned energetically, a squared oval, red and deep and cracking between strongly curving portcullis tusks. Above it dragon nostrils flared and smoked and round black eyes bulged and stared. Around the lower jaws a crowd of black matchstick demons capered with curling tails and hooked pitchforks: between the teeth, in diminishing clouds, tiny figures flew like chaff, or lay baled, waiting the push. Marcus's eidetic vision composed itself to include what it had not previously remarked: clouds of insect-like creatures somewhat realistically swarming over ears and nostrils as though the thing were a cow recumbent in a summer field: hairy ears pricked above the gateway: black bristles on ochre skin like slashes of infantile rain. It was a bit obvious, but even so, it would serve: Lucas was not to know which of the famous paintings he might select, even if he might have them, in general, in mind. Having fixed outlines and details Marcus went on staring and ceased attending, became blank and blanker, a way of work he had found peculiarly effective but had to recover from. So it was this time. When, suddenly, the pull between himself and fading hell mouth was relaxed he felt the church chill and heavy: its goings-on, which he had excluded, became oppressive.

They were singing "Teach me my God and King", which Stephanie had chosen because it was by Herbert. Marcus turned his attention to the bride and groom, feeling his hand and cheek clammy on the now warmish stone.

He tried to make geometrical sense – a strong design – out of the fine, crisped, overlying triangles in the slopes of that veiling. His eye was always peculiarly attracted by transparencies over transparencies. But no sense could be made: the thing produced the random frustration of certain car or bus numbers he hated to travel with, near-weak, vague numbers, neither prime nor particularly variable, but with one or at most two possible threads of relation to tighten. It was a senseless cocoon. In retrospect an analogous dissatisfaction struck him about the crossings of the lines of the visionary grasses. They would not *go*. He did not in any way have it in him to do a little mental rearrangement, a little design of his own, using this material, to get it right. As it was, so he saw it. He began to be uncomfortable between this vague web and the very much overdesigned web of the church's geometry, closed to convey openness, heavy to suggest lightness. He stared glumly at Daniel's wide black back and was suddenly affected by it as he had been at the Coronation. Black absorbed light and did not reflect it. Black gave out radiant heat: it was dark and warm. The lines of energy, the fuzz of forces went into that solid flesh and ceased, coiled and rested, or so it seemed. He looked flatly at Daniel's unbowed, unmoving shoulder-blades, humped a little below the cloth. He stopped thinking. He felt hungry. He yawned. He

struggled inside his best suit and good shoes and got up to follow the
family to the vestry.

In the vestry they all nestled and chattered. Alexander approached his
charge and said, "A kiss for the bride." Daniel said, "Me first," turned
back the veil, and kissed her firmly. The vestry was small and stony with
one little high window, heavily leaded. Marcus thought he might go out
again, to make breathing-space. Winifred wiped up some tears, when
Daniel kissed Stephanie.

They signed the register, scratching and spidery. Daniel Thomas
Orton. Stephanie Jane Potter. Morley Evans Parker. Alexander Miles
Michael Wedderburn.

Stephanie found Daniel's Mum looking up at her. Mrs Orton hooked
a little hand over the white arm and said confidentially, in a chesty
whisper, "I do like to hear folk speak up. I suppose our Daniel gets lots
of practice. But you spoke up lovely."

Stephanie stared down. "I get lots of practice too, in my job."

"Aye, I expect you would. I were that shy at my own wedding, I
couldn't get up more than a whisper, me throat were so dry, and I were
all shaky. But you were cool as a cucumber."

"It doesn't all seem quite real yet," said Stephanie, conventionally and
truthfully. She didn't want to be touched: she would have been glad to
be able to shake the clutching little fingers off her arm. They were
covered with spotted grey transparent nylon, through which the flesh
took on strange tinges of brick, and brown, and bluish-purple.

"Aye, well it'll dawn on you gradual," said Daniel's Mum, with a
certain grim satisfaction. "You can't expect to tek it in all at once, like."
She gave a peremptory little tug on Stephanie's arm, preluding a
confidence, and Stephanie bowed her head over her. She had discovered
– indeed, it was the only thing she did know about her – that Daniel's
Mum saw life through a stream of endlessly dredgeable, endlessly
self-referring anecdotes.

"T'other night I dreamed I were young again, I war young Clarrie
Rawlings, and there was Barry Tammadge – a young man as I used to be
friendly wi' – and we were walking out, and he were pressing me, like
– and I were saying, well, I don't know, and, it might be, and, we'll have
to see, won't we, and all the while I knew there was some reason I
couldn't, *you* know, something I'd gone and forgotten like. And when I
woke up I cast about and it were a good five minutes, must have been,
before it came to me I were a married woman. And widowed, and Dan's
Dad buried these thirteen years.

"I were married in 1922 and there it was all gone out of my head.
Funny, that. It were so natural to be young and courting, as though all

the rest hadn't gone by, as though I'd never taken me wedding right in, though Brian *is* gone, and has been all these years. Sometimes I look at me own hands and I think, whose are those then, old woman's? But there it is. E'd have liked to see our Dan married, Dad would. We did have doubts as to whether he'd make it, him being so religious, which is inclined to put people off, and so fat into th' bargain, which naturally made him shy, like. But he's a good lad, in his way, I will say for him, and his Dad'd have been right proud to see him so well set up."

Stephanie continued to lean foolishly over this new mother, unable to think of a word in answer to these confidences. She was rescued by Mr Ellenby who was forming his reverse bridal procession. He coiled the trail of incongruous pairs: bride and groom, Morley Parker and Frederica, Alexander and Winifred, Marcus and Daniel's Mum, round the vestry table, signalled the organ, and got them going out again.

Daniel smiled around the church. He felt more that it was his, on this one progress as bridegroom, than he did proceeding towards his vicarious handshakes on ordinary days. He felt like a conqueror. He had brought it off. Against odds. His wife paced beside him in her drooping garments. He himself strode out jauntily, almost springing. He turned his head this way and that, surveying the flock, grinning a little with a primitive huge pleasure in the fact that they were there, and as they were, in their Sunday best, all different, portly and willowy, grey and gleaming, greedy and melancholy. They were all right, they were in the right place. He gave them private nods and happy acknowledgments. He saw Mrs Thone, sitting very still, her hands folded in her twilled silk lap, her face set and stony under a brimmed dark hat. He registered this stillness, dropped his smile, gave her a brief, harsh look that showed he had seen her, and went on to smile with unabated delight at the becks and bobs of the school matron behind her.

They came out onto the doorstep where they stood for some time, in twos, threes, groups, for the photographers. During this time Daniel said to Stephanie,

"I heard my Mum telling you what was what."

"She seemed to think one didn't believe one was really married until — until one was dead — or something."

"Depends who you are. I doubt she exactly wanted to know. I reckon it'll take us a bit of time to know what's hit us. But not that long, I hope. At any rate, I'm enjoying this so far."

"Are you?"

"Of course I am. We're getting on fine. It's all great fun."

She took his hand and looked up at him, and all the cameras appropriately clicked.

Daniel included his Mum in his pleasure in the present solidity of the people around him. He had not, oddly, felt either alarmed or embarrassed to hear her discussing his fatness and churchiness with Stephanie. More a great, rash, comic glee. He was here, and married as he chose to be, and she was his mother. His little mother, with her thick humped pad of flesh across her upper back, with her small body now shapelessly squared above her narrow, bowed legs and thickened ankles. He was amused by the structure of her face, tremulous, greying, spattered with brown skin-stains, petulant with vanished prettiness like a ghost in the pout of the mouth and the pleat of the eye-corners. She wore on her head a kind of shiny, squashy bowl of unreal violet straw with a bundle of plaster holly-berries, cloth cornflowers, limp marguerites and bristling emerald feathers. Under this her thinning hair was permed into rigorous little coils; he remembered when she had had soft golden curls, much prized, hair that in her generation had led her to be labelled "a beauty" before she had any choice in the matter. She was hung about in a square crêpe dress with large purple and white flowers on, a modesty front of fluted lace, a rusty black winter coat. He did not like her. But with some quite other part of him he was simply delighted that she was there, just as she was, and that he knew it. He was even delighted that he knew that, and how, the grey coils had been gold.

30. Masters' Garden

Alexander found himself alone outside the church, waiting for the white ribboned car to come back for him. He felt happy and English. Bells sounded their clear, limited, recurrent jargon, notes tumbling over each other and caught up. The grass between the graves, thick with daisies, was soft and silent. He was a man who made detours to be alone in such places, green and still and stony, a man who felt reverent in porches, a man moved by stones, mossed over, rain-pitted, sooty, leaning displaced on railings and walls. Churchyards made more of Alexander. He drifted off down a path under dark flowering yews. Tennyson had written that yew trees, the males anyway, standing separate, smoked with pollen if you struck them. Idly, curiously, Alexander gave one of them a random blow and saw that it was indeed so, a living smoke did indeed go up into the still summer air, spin a little, and settle on his sleek morning suit. Someone, bystander, gardener, delayed wedding-guest, was loitering at the far end of the graveyard. Alexander picked his way delicately, with long pale grey legs, over two yellowing, newly-turfed hummocks. The air was so thick and slow he could not have called out.

The man wore a crumpled summer suit in an intense colour which Alexander thought of as electric blue, without knowing what kind of blue electricity might truly be. Over this he wore an elderly, deep-crowned panama. He was squatting against a Victorian tombstone-slab, poking with a sharp stick at the encrustations of moss over the lettering. As Alexander came nearer he did not look up. His shoes were muddy brown veldtschoen.

"Bill," said Alexander, wondering if he should really have tiptoed mutely back the way he had come.

"I trust it is finished," said Bill, still jabbing at the stone. "It took an unconscionable long time. I take it there was no hitch."

"No."

"Flattish strains of jubilation crept by me across the graves from time to time, whilst I was prowling around. I thought this was as near as I should decently get." He rattled his stick in the holes of an imitation marble flower holder, which contained some browned dahlias and stiffening cornflowers. He read out his handiwork.

> "Peace, perfect peace with loved ones far away
> In Jesus' bosom we are safe and they.

Ambiguous, don't you think, and not totally coherent. I suppose I even hoped someone might rise up mightily and proclaim a cause or just impediment. But I gather no such luck?"

"No," said Alexander. Bill rocked back squat on his heels and gestured up at him with his implement.

"I suppose you think I'm overdoing it. I suppose you think blood should call. I suppose you think I should have given up my profound beliefs and gone in there. I don't suppose you see that I *could* not, I simply could not."

"I haven't said so."

"English mollysoft politeness before anything else. Sheep. At least I take it seriously."

"It was very moving," said Alexander, leaning gracefully against a newish marble stone, to prevent green staining on his nacreous sleeve. "I was moved."

"You would be. Anything moves you. I saw you, batting trees. 'Thy gloom is kindled at the tips And passes into gloom again.' Remember that, in your clouds of fruitful smoke, or whatever. Gloom, gloom. That's what I see."

"Bill, they were very happy."

"Like sheep, sheep, temporary sheep. I wanted something real for her."

Alexander could almost hear the hissing and spurt of his wrath. He was reminded of his perpetual image of Bill Potter as a fire smouldering in the inwards of a straw stack. He felt a vague responsibility to douse this one, and did not know how. He said, "I don't see why you should mind quite so much."

Bill turned sharply. "You don't? You think I exaggerate? You think I'm putting it on."

"No, no," said Alexander soothingly.

"I wanted something *real* for her."

Nettled, Alexander said, "Daniel is a real man. By any standards, I'd say."

"Would you? Now that's where I doubt, I do genuinely doubt, if it's possible. In that world. Embalmed zombies. Christ. No one's interested in that aspect of it, they think I've no manners, he's a nice enough chappie according to his lights, serious and so on. It's not a question of manners. The English panacea, good form. Good form, dead form. No, no. It's a question of *life*. And that's not in there." He flung a crumpled hot arm in the direction of the church and nearly over-balanced.

"You think I should extend a loving hand and dance at the wedding?"

Alexander was not at all sure what he thought about this. All he could say, however, was, "Yes, of course."

"I don't want to."

Alexander looked at him gravely.

"However, you have persuaded me. I will come with you. You were going there, I take it?"

"Oh yes," said Alexander.

They got into the car together, and there was another delay whilst Bill instructed the driver to furl and stow away his white ribbons. "*Most* unsuitable," he said to Alexander, leaning back on the grey cushions and pushing the panama almost down to the bridge of his nose. "We are neither virgins, nor cakes, nor festive. Certainly not *festive*. Lambs to the slaughter, you might say, but we'll go quietly without bows, I think."

The Masters' Garden had elements of the ultimate garden in *Alice*, with its locked door in the high wall. Like everyone else Bill and Alexander made their way down the steep alley from the school and peered in. It was a rectangular walled plot: Alexander was perennially irritated by the limited imagination apparent in its layout. On the far wall was a kind of raised embankment with a paved ridge: at one end of this was a mock orange bush and at the other a waterless weeping willow. Here he had staged *The Lady's Not for Burning*; from behind these inadequate bushy brakes he had sprung in scarlet tights and black jerkin. Today trestle-tables, hung with much-laundered school damask, were balanced on the paving stones. On those were a cold buffet, two worn urns of coffee and tea, and a two-tiered, doric-pillared, blue-white cake. Alexander would have planted lavenders and lings, thymes and rosemarys, espalier peaches and pears. There should have been clematis and briar roses tumbling over the gate. But the uniform beds round the plot of grass were laid out in tidy rows of scarlet salvia, blue lobelia, white alyssum, in patriotic streaks, with two or three clumps of crudely brilliant petunias. Alexander disliked puce, and the more clamant purples. Along the margins of the hoed earth trotted school waitresses with foaming bottles and flat glasses.

Bill peered furtively round the door and then made a little dash in. Alexander was at a loss; he enquired if he should find Winifred, or Daniel and Stephanie. Bill said no, no, he was simply putting in an appearance, and an appearance, simply, was all he wanted to put in. He would creep about the peripheries, Alexander need not bother. Alexander did bother. He attracted a waitress, with a tray.

"That's right," said Bill. "Have one of my drinks, do. I do foot the bill. They are determined to confine my activities to that useful function. Very wise, no doubt. Which of us is going to make the speech as Bride's Father or Close Friend of the Family? Have you prepared a few notes? I hoped you'd have gone so far. I shall leave it all in your capable hands. I detest speech-making. I shall enjoy listening to you deputising for me. It will amuse me. Now you go and mingle and I'll go and wander up and down. *Please* don't worry about me." He swallowed a glass of wine, took another, and hurried away, his hat dangling now on the back of his head, looking distinctly tripperish.

"Hell," said Alexander, and discovered Frederica, standing near the mock orange. He was almost pleased to see her.

"I found your father in the churchyard."

"So I see. I expect he'd got all there was to get out of *not* being around, so now he's going to try being around. You should have locked him in the vestry or something."

"I don't quite understand if he wants to make a speech."

"Well, he will, if he does, and he won't, if that would be worse, and there's nothing to do about that. If I were you I'd keep out of his way and drink rather a lot."

Alexander found another waitress to refill both their glasses. Stephanie could be seen, somewhat plumply flowing between the guests.

"I hope nothing spoils it for her. She seems so happy."

"Do you think so?" sharply.

"Don't you?"

"How do you tell? I know *he's* being awful, but basically he's got a point. What's in that world, for her?"

"I like Daniel."

"Oh, I like Daniel, I suppose. Daniel's O.K. In some ways. But I don't see how she can think she knows him."

"Maybe knowledge, as such, isn't necessary to love."

"Love," said Frederica. "Love. She was in love with you until just a few weeks ago, as far as *love* goes. And then this."

Alexander involuntarily turned to stare at the bride, now bending again over Daniel's little Mum, holding the veil from her face with a self-consciously ringed hand. She looked suddenly very secret and interesting. He remembered spanning her waist that morning. Frederica watched him watch Stephanie. He said, "That's nonsense. She really barely knows me . . ."

"You've just said yourself knowledge isn't necessary. She thought hard enough, anyway. You were a great topic of conversation. And speculation. And passion. If thinking had had anything to do with knowing you'd be scanned through and through."

Alexander felt stupid and, as she had meant him to, uneasy. Frederica said, "You were a beautiful hopeless passion. She's very shy. And you didn't notice."

"No. I didn't, I must say."

"You wouldn't," said Frederica, with great finality. Alexander was needled by her manner, which had become very faintly patronising towards the end of this exchange. He had a quick-come, quick-gone mental flash of the two of them, earnestly, head to head one evening, talking him out of shape. He drew himself up and together and looked down on Frederica. She gave a little grin.

"Anyway, it settled something for me," she said.

"What did?"

"That service. I can't do it. I couldn't ever go through that myself. All very well, with my body I thee worship, but St Paul I can't stomach. I was struck by how mad I was getting. I don't want to be loved because a man loves his own body, that's ridiculous. And all this about Christ and the Spouse. Can you see *any* point in that? This is a great mystery, but I speak concerning Christ and the Church. And all this about submission like the body to the head. It's horrible. It's degrading."

"You must have some historical . . ."

"I have, I have, but I've also got a respect for words and up with those *I will not personally put.* Saying 'obey' is the least of it. I even *might* obey, but I'm not having those analogies said over my body, dead or living."

"You are very vehement."

"I know. I surprise myself. Let's talk about something else."

Stephanie moved amongst the guests, thanking people for things. Her gift of recall came into its own: she could see each salad bowl, teaspoon and towel, and frame appropriately detailed gratitude. Suddenly, at a distance, she caught sight of her father, in his horrid clothes, peering between Daniel's youth club boys. She waved. He ostentatiously pretended not to see. She took a few steps and waved again. He began to dodge away towards the gate, behind bushes and clusters of people. Unthinking, she caught up loops of white dress in her fists and began to run, scudding across the grass, bundled and floating. The sun suddenly flowed out from behind a racing cloud. People laughed as she passed them, as though some primitive festal act was taking place. Bill dodged back behind the tump on which the tables were. Stephanie, her face stiff with alarm, took a leap up the tump, and dashed down, veiling floating up, hanging a moment, sinking lightly.

"Stop," she said. Bill stopped, and faced her, but said nothing. Then he began to inch away again. Involuntarily, she said, "Oh, don't go."

"I'm not officially here. I'm only putting in an appearance."

"Please don't go."

"I can't say I feel very welcome. I can't say I feel exactly at home."

"We were very glad of the cheque."

"I do what I *can* do."

"It was very generous."

"I wouldn't like to be ungenerous."

"Well, please stay, come and see Mother . . . Daniel . . . now you've . . ."

"I only wanted to see what had been done with my resources."

Even he looked alarmed then, at the ungraciousness he achieved with this last sentence. He scrubbed with his veldtschoen in the gravel path. He had a wooden look, a marionette jerked by clumsy powers. She thought she might step forward and kiss him, and was prevented by a very clear mental image of him pushing her fiercely over in the grass and dodging away again.

"Oh, why are you like this?"

"I feel," he said. "I feel . . ."

Daniel came over the hump and stepped heavily down. Bill jerked to life, staring shiftily as though confronted by a policeman about to make an arrest.

"Glad to see you," said Daniel, briefly.

"I'm sure," said Bill. "I was just off. I only just looked in, just to . . . I'm not really here. I'll go."

"You are here," said Daniel. "We see you. They want to cut the cake. Will you come?"

"I have no part in this."

Daniel felt murderous. He wanted to take up Bill Potter and grind his head, panama and all, into the gravel. He received a hot gust of impotent passion from the figure in the path: if it had been to do with himself, he would have left him there. He said, "Please come. We want you to come."

Bill opened and closed his mouth like a nutcracker. Daniel said: "Stephanie," and began to walk steadily back up the hill. He would have taken her hand, but he sensed that the proprietary gesture would have puffed wind into the flames. She turned to Bill, her face crumpling.

"You are my first-born," said Bill, emotionally, fiercely, with self-directed sorrow. "After all."

"Please," she said dutifully, "Please."

Together they ascended the hummock, and together the three of them stood by the cake, between the hissing urns. From that small eminence Bill peered at the coalescing half-moon of guests with a cross between rage and hobgoblin glee.

"Don't mind me," he said to Alexander, who was there, glass in hand, to propose the toast, "I am not really here, I am just looking in. I look forward to hearing your few words. Don't let me delay them."

Alexander spoke briefly and gracefully. Inhibited by Bill's presence he stumbled over the reasons for his own participation in this ceremony. He spoke a few words of admiration for Daniel's work, and a few about Stephanie's wisdom and beauty. He compared the bride to a white rose. He raised his glass, pale gold liquid slanting in it, and felt the pleasurable trouble stirred by the confidences Frederica had imposed on him. He quoted Spenser's epithalamium, clear and florid. This in its turn moved in him his Tennysonian passion of the past, the sense of other moments of vanished perfection, or translation. He spoke of the pleasurable conjunction of tears and laughter. He asked everyone to drink to the happy couple.

The form was for Daniel to reply. He had indeed eased a postcard of notes from a breast-pocket. But Bill Potter stepped out between the urns, hat and shoulders back, slewing the blue trousers round on his hips, to announce his intention of adding just a word or two to what his colleague had very eloquently said. He was not, as they might know, officially there at all, but a few words of unofficial good will might just be acceptable. He referred to his colleague's white rose. He said it was hard for him to believe that this vision of delight was his daughter who seemed to himself hardly out of the days of sticky fingers, uncertain elastic, and grubby serge knickers. He waited for laughter. He described his little girl trotting off to school under a tucked-up blazer and a battered satchel. He quoted her school reports, interpreting these. "A valuable member of the community" meant an orthodox slave-driving prefect – well, she would need that, where she was going. "Undoubtedly gifted when her interest could be engaged" meant pig-headed, frequently lazy, but with a head on her shoulders. Well, that head had got her to Cambridge. In due course she had swopped the serge knickers, sugared petticoats, and the devoted inky slaves for a string of besotted, indistinguishably solemn young men who were given to "just dropping in" at Blesford Ride on their way from Bristol to Cambridge, or some equally circuitous trip. (He thought she had found time to put in an appearance or two at the Library.) He had never managed to identify one young man before he had been replaced by the next. And now there was Daniel – for whom it could at the least be said that he was identifiable, by indubitable signs. He trusted Daniel would be happy. He hoped it was hardly necessary to warn him that the child was mother to the woman, and that whatever Daniel's Church might say about obedience, he had personally found his daughter to be rather an irresistible force on matters where her excellent mind was fixed. But then, there was evidence that Daniel was an immovable object. He wished them happy, he was sure.

It was generally felt that Bill had acquitted himself with great good humour.

Daniel pulled out his postcard and thanked everybody, on the gallop, Winifred, Ellenbys, Thones, Alexander, Frederica, and Bill, woodenly, for his words of goodwill, using Bill's own phrase. He managed to do this without any reference to himself or to his wife. He then retreated.

Alexander felt a sharp blow in the lower part of his shoulder blade. It was the ubiquitous Frederica. She hissed at him: "I almost thought he was going to say she has deceived her father and may thee, didn't you? Honestly, what an exhibition. That was all lies you know. She was *never* grubby, not Stephanie, and her knickers always fitted, and the boyfriends, if there were any, never came here, for very obvious reasons. That settles it. If ever I marry, he's coming nowhere near, it'll be secret, secular and miles away from Yorkshire. I liked what you said. Even the Spenser, though I prefer Donne. Go to where the Bishop staies, To make you one his way, which divers waies, Must bee effected. Don't you like all that grammatical *layering* he goes in for? I like things separate that are."

Alexander reflected that what this dreadful girl had somehow managed, by sheer persistence, was to impose on him a tone of long and accepted confidentiality, which he was too well-mannered to break.

Moreover, it would be quite hard to acknowledge it enough to break it without somehow exacerbating it. And further still, what she said had its interest.

"Really not true?" he enquired, looking behind, to see if he was overheard.

"Not a word of it. You can see, it's just a string of the sort of cliché anyone who knows her at all would know she most wouldn't want."

"I wish I could have stopped him coming."

"You must admit, it has its awful drama."

The pillared cake was dismantled and cut. The flowers, bride's and bridesmaid's, lay by its crumbling ruins in the sun. They were a little limp and bruised, now: the vices of wire showed. People began to nudge the couple into going away. They left on foot, through the wicket gate, down the steep path to Far Field and Masters' Row, where they were to change. Since they were going nowhere, since there was no money for a honeymoon, the guests waved at the garden gate: only the family, and Daniel's Mum, went down with them. Alexander went too, but at the railway bridge he stopped, and decided to turn back. He was nobody's father, bridegroom, or relation. He was not necessary, and he had had enough.

So he stood and watched them, strung out under the sun, bustling, trotting, strolling across Far Field, past the Bilge Pond, out under the goal posts, on the other side. Black Daniel, white Stephanie, thin gold skipping Frederica, Winifred, her dark helmeted head down and weary, Bill winding across the field in sinuous loops, deflecting people, little Mrs Orton making a rolling effort with jutting shoulders and quavering head. Marcus, last, tall and stick-like in his dark suit, his straw-smooth hair neatly brushed. Frederica looked round for Alexander, and he waved, pointed behind him, indicating his intentions unequivocally. He remembered how he had stood in this place, the day his play was accepted, had seen that none of this, none of these people, nothing of this world, was now necessarily either related to him or limiting for him, and that therefore he had found them interesting. Today he had been with them too long, too close. He had almost become part of them, and almost lost interest. As they lessened across the playing field, entering like mannikins in at the garden gate, he breathed deep, grew, became substantial. He remembered other places: an Oxford garden, a terrace at Grasse, Dorset chalk heights, the Bois de Boulogne. No, for all the incidental pleasures of white roses and yew pollen and Cranmer's prose, a man might do more, so much more, than settle for the repetitive rectangles of Masters' Row. He remembered the unmysterious woman's mess in the bride's bare box of a room that morning, and he remembered the moment when he had looked through Jennifer's pretty printed bedroom curtains at a very small square patch of blue sky. He would get out. He was almost sure he would make arrangements to leave after his play, come what may. Across the field a small yellow figure pranced and fluttered something white. He took off his silk hat, swept it finally to and fro, settled it back on his head, and turned back up the lane.

31 · Honeymoon

Daniel had imagined darkness, but it was high summer and the light went on and on. Morley Parker drove them from Masters' Row to Askham Buildings, along scaled-down crescents and artisans' terraces of back-to-backs, grimly compact, slate-roofed, coal-smoke rising. There were six Buildings, laid out in two three-sided rectangles around what the Plan had shown as two grassy courts with blossoming trees. These areas were in fact churned clay and cracking concrete paths, heavy clods, caterpillar-tracked, sprouting plantains, willowherb, yarrow and sowthistle. Their flat was on the ground floor at the back; the ground floor flats had back-gardens, small patches of turned and clotted subsoil, surrounded by wire netting, concrete posts, little creaking metal gates. People upstairs had concrete balconies with iron railings and networks of clothes-line. From the kitchenette you saw a black rubber tyre, hanging on a knotted rope from a kind of scaffold, and a hawthorn tree, an old one, twisted, scored, black-barked, and at that moment bright and airy with green leaf. It was older than the Buildings. It had been spared when the bulldozers roared in to prepare the site.

Mrs Ellenby had prepared a cold supper for them, so they would have nothing to do – a chicken, a salad in a cut-glass bowl under a plate and a damp tea-towel, a fruit salad in another covered bowl, a bottle of hock. There were some bridge rolls and a new crusty cob, a tin of Lyons coffee, a packet of tea, two bottles of milk, a Camembert and a piece of Edam. There was also a large bunch of flame-coloured gladioli in a glass tube on a lace mat on the table, and a note, saying that beetroot was in a separate saucer in case it discoloured the hardboiled eggs, and that Mrs Ellenby hoped they would have a jolly good rest and a delightful time in their new home. They stood together and took all this in, blinking a little. The gardens, Far Field, had been very bright and staring, and the little flat, with its small, heavily-netted windows, was dim and close. Stephanie disliked net curtains, but even she admitted their necessary impenetrability, here. The walls were very thin, and she caught herself moving cautiously in case anyone noticed she was there.

It was about seven o'clock. Daniel, considering his home and, side-long, his wife, wondered if he should have arranged to have supper, with a number of people, out. She stood quietly, looking around, not at him.

"What shall we do?" he said.

"We could sit down and eat all this food."

"Aye."

"Or open the packets on the sofa."

"Aye."

"But I don't feel very hungry, not after so many toasted morsels and cakes and wine."

"No."

He realised he must have thought they would simply walk into the bedroom, pull the curtains, tear off all the tidy clothes they had just put on, and fall into the bed. He saw it would not be like that. She had gone away from him and was aimlessly turning things over on the kitchen dresser, new canisters, scissors, lemon-squeezer. She said, handling the scissors as though they were some unrecognisable engine whose nature she was required to guess blindfold, "What I do want is to take my shoes off. Just to take my shoes off."

He pondered the tone of the word "just". He picked it up.

"Why don't you? We need a rest. Just a rest. I feel done in," he said untruthfully. She bent down, at this, and eased off her shoes. Without the stiletto heels she looked dumpy and middle-aged in the squarish linen suit and circular hat she had Gone Away in.

"You could take your hat off, as well," said Daniel, staring at her with interest. She still did not look at him. She did take off the hat, revealing the shining, tidy yellow rolls of her hair. Daniel thought it was, or had been, longer. If you pulled it, would it float out, or spring back, like a metal coil, or was there simply less? In a week, or a month, he would know her hair. The thought gave him a great and simple pleasure. She walked through to the bedroom, carrying hat and shoes, and Daniel followed her. She left dark, elegant, damp footprints on the linoleum. These stirred him. In the bedroom she put the hat on the chest of drawers, and the shoes beside the bed and came out again, quickly, Daniel still padding after her. She sat down on the sofa and held her feet up to the air, wriggling toes and ankles.

Everything seemed terrible to her, terrible, dark and final. All these new implements, the unaccustomed net and lace, the solidity of Daniel's things, all over, big worn black shoes in the wardrobe, huge dressing-gown bellying from the bedroom door, prayer-book on the chest, next to the male hairbrush, with coarse black hairs in it. She looked up and about, for airholes in the box. Around and above different wirelesses jangled and crooned different tunes. Outside feet thudded and voices suddenly shrilled:

> Our Gloria is a fool
> Like a donkey on a stool
> When the stool began to crack
> All the fleas ran down her back.

Stephanie's face twitched in and out of a brief smile. The song was repeated. It was repeated again. And again. She wished Daniel would stop looking at her. It left her nowhere to rest her eyes.

"Why don't you lie down?" he suggested. "Close your eyes. Have a nap." He wanted to say, I won't touch you, but that offended some sense he had of the proprieties of a wedding day. "Go on," he said, making his voice deliberately inert. He could see her thinking. She said, "All right," in a toneless voice. She stood up and went into the bedroom. In there, there was just room for the bed, a chair, the chest, a little rug. He watched her slide off her skirt, her shirt, her jacket. He went round her and closed the curtains. She got quickly into the bed, extended herself, in slip and stockings, stole one glance at Daniel and closed her eyes. After a moment he took off some of his own clothes and lay down carefully beside her. She was screwed up, eyelids, mouth, little fists on the pillow by her cheek, even the stockinged feet. He gave a large, deliberate sigh, kissed her briefly on the brow, clasped his hands under his head, and stared darkly at the shadowed ceiling. To his subsequent surprise, he slept.

They woke, after an indeterminate time, when it was dark, a dusty summer dark. They had moved together on the new bed, in a dip created by Daniel's weight. He felt her struggle vaguely to raise herself, and he put out a heavy arm and pinned her down. "Here," he said. "Here I am." She turned her head sideways, between his pillow and hers, and he could see her shining eyes staring quietly in the dark. "Come on," he said. "Don't be afraid." Lovers' talk stands on a fine edge between babbling folly and wholly explicit plainness, depending simply on whether it is heard as it is said, or not. He could not tell, at all, if she was listening. "I love you," he said hopefully. She made a small sound. Her lips, he thought, moved. "Hmm?" said Daniel. "I love you," she said in a little voice. He had no idea what she meant by it. He pulled at some of her straps. She did not resist. Awkwardly, in silence, accompanied by jingling piano above his head, and Glenn Miller a few feet beyond the bed-foot, conscious of his weight on her small if buxom frame, and on the new bedsprings, which twanged. Daniel consummated his marriage. There was a moment during this time, when his face was on hers, cheek on cheek, brow on brow, heavy skull on skull, through soft skin and softer flesh. He thought: skulls separate people. In this one sense, I could say, they would say, I lose myself in her. But in that bone box, she thinks and thinks, as I think in mine, things the other won't hear, can't hear, though we go on like this for sixty years. What does she think I *am*? He had no idea. He had no idea what she was. Alone in the vicarage, he had had an idea, he had addressed a clear enough figure of her, who laughed, and answered, sitting on his bed, in his chair, swinging imaginary legs. He opened his eyes in a hurry to see the outside of her face and not the red and black inside of his own head, dark and flaming. He saw closed lashes, damp frowning brow, precisely tight lips, a series of signs, indicating closure. All the same, he thought, I am *here*. I am here whatever she thinks. This was as near as he got to triumph.

After this, she became astonishingly lively, as though she now again understood the social forms that obtained. She sat up briskly.

"Maybe we should eat Mrs Ellenby's supper."

"We don't have to."

"Well, it was nice of her, it'll be on my mind, just lying around . . ."

"I thought you weren't hungry."

"I am, I am now, horribly hungry."

"Well, if that's so, obviously we'll eat it."

So they washed, and dressed, and sat across the table from each other and ate the chicken, and the two salads, green and fruit, and drank some of the wine. During this meal she chattered. He had never known her to chatter, but now she ran on fluently with a public social intimacy quite different from her usual lazy or thoughtful silences. She made sprightly remarks about the wedding, hats, mannerisms, awkward moments, the capacious urns and the frosted tier of cake they had in a tin in the kitchen, the disposition of their books and pictures, the view from the kitchen window, the cupboard that always stuck, the need to replace the awful overhead light-fitting with something milder and more welcoming. She arranged stones from the maraschino cherries in the fruit salad round her plate, even counting these with nursery jingles and ancient magical rhymes. One for silver, two for gold . . . He said yes, and no, even made a blundering attempt to join in, since he had a parish capacity to plump out the surfaces of a battered cushion of gossip, but he felt obscurely he was being treated as a woman, fed kitchen chit-chat as pabulum, denied and neutralised.

He had not been a member of a family. He had no experience of, no gift for, that kind of communication that consists of the conversion into matter-of-language of all the bare and self-sufficient matter-of-fact of a day endured. He had heard it going on, but he hadn't time for it, he preferred, and encountered, extremity. He had never really heard the anonymous recuperating voice that speaks on and on over lunch and of an evening, telling what is known or will be forgotten. Saying, half-a-dozen eggs, when I distinctly said a dozen, too bad really, a very lovely shade of rose-pink, rather like that blouse of yours, not the one you had on last Saturday but that one I haven't seen for six months, with the embroidery, gas *is* better than electricity, I always swear by it, you can turn it up and down so economically though the surfaces are *much* more difficult to clean, I tried very hard to get silverside but all they had was brisket, what you're eating, actually, a bit fatty, I think you'll agree, but there was really no choice, so I put in a few extra peppercorns, nice bits tend to be tastier on brisket even if it is fattier, or may be *because* it is . . .

She ran on. Why should she *tell* him, damn it, the gladioli were red, and red wasn't a colour she cared for, when he could see they were red and had known for months that she didn't like it? A clutter of talk derealised and still emphasised a clutter of things. He didn't exactly think that out: he was hazed: he chewed his chicken. She still spoke brightly. What she touched with words was for her defused and neutral-ised; acceptable. She moved verbally round inside the confines of the flat, appropriating, in this primitive way, a mirror she didn't want by declaring it to be the right size to make the little lobby look larger, coming to terms with the bathroom tiles, in that windowless tiny room, with words like cucumber and avocado, with the voiced hope that their shrieking could be muted if one had matching bath-mat and curtains in a much deeper version of the same shade. He had no recollection of the bathroom tiles. He said he was sure she was right. She pushed cherry pits and grape pips nervously round the rim of her fruit-dish with a spoon. The fruit salad had been heady with some dark and potent wine in the syrup. She asked him was it sherry or port, and he said he was sure he didn't know, the Mothers' Union madeira at a guess, not the altar wine at any rate, that was very thin and acid. Quite a kick, it had, she said. That too, he didn't need telling.

She washed up, with a kind of formality, and he helped her. She wrung out a number of cloths, and polished the draining board, whilst he watched her. She made some coffee and he drank a little. She went in and out of bathroom and bedroom, doing things he couldn't identify and took no interest in. As she touched the circumference of the flat it became tolerable to her: as she touched it, it closed in on him. He thought of the streets, out there. He got up, after a time, and went into the kitchen, where he stood in the dark, staring out. Two lights, a midsummer moon and a sodium cube on a concrete pole lit the sleek cut surfaces of the clods of clay, making it glitter like motionless waves on a thick, still sea. The hawthorn trunk and the coil of black tyre were sooty-dark, but the surface of the hawthorn leaves was dappled and patched with moony white and stained with acid orange. He pushed his hands down into his pockets, pushed his shoulders up, settled into silence.

In the end she came up quietly behind him.

"Daniel –"

"Hmn."

"What are you doing, in the dark?"

"I don't know." Loudly. " *I don't know*." It was a declaration.

"I thought you were sure you did."

She put a hand on his arm, which he shrugged away. She stepped back, and stood very still. After a time, she said, "You were the one, you were the only one, who knew what he was doing."

He didn't answer: she saw him indistinctly, a big black mass against a black window-pane. She remembered his sudden burst of wrath in the Vicarage. That day in Miss Wells's room. He had done it all, it was all his doing. She took hold of his arm again, and pulled herself up on her toes and kissed his hard cheek. He jerked his face away: she felt his anger, crackling on his skin. She tried to kiss him again, making a little cajoling noise, which she did not mean, which was neither here nor there, since by now he had her attention, except that it roused him to fury. He turned round and grabbed for her, cracking her in his arms, twisting at her hair and grinding her face under his. They stumbled back through the flat into the bedroom. He remembered now, the first time he saw her, he had wanted to break her. He caught her a kind of blow across the shoulders. She subsided. He thought again, I am *here*.

Later he said, I am hurting you, and she cried angrily, no, no, no, you are not. Later still he was lost, and opened his eyes to see her sitting, naked, staring at him, both faces running with tears and sweat, both heads of hair soaked. His face was too stretched and tired to smile. Hers had a rigid, mask-like look that, he imagined, mirrored his own. He touched her hot breast, and nodded at her. She put a hand over his.

Later again he woke, and woke her, and made love to her for a long time, quietly. If he did not know who she was, this was desirable, they were both in the same place, that was all. They were anonymous, it was dark, he did not know what either of them felt, but he felt it. Now there was no extraneous music.

As for her, she had the thought, in words, that this was truly the only

time in her life when her attention had all been gathered in one place –
body, mind, and whatever dreams or makes images. Then the images
took over. She had always a very vague imagining of the inner spaces of
her body, dark interior flesh, black-red, red-black, flexible and shifting,
larger than she imagined herself from outside, with no kind of graspable
perspective, no apparent limits. If Daniel defined these spaces by moving
amongst their shape-shifting chambers and blind vistas, they neither
contained nor were contained by this definition. This inner world had its
own clear landscape. It grew with precise assurance, light out of dark,
sapphire rising in the black-red, wandering in rooted caverns, glassy blue
running water between carved channels of basalt, and coming out into
fields of flowers, light green stalks, airy leaves, bright flowers moving
and dancing in wavering tossing lines to the blown grass of a cliff over a
pale bright strand beyond which shone the pale bright sea. They have
their own lights, Virgil said of his underworld, and this too, however
bright, with the clarity of more than a summer's day, was seen in its own
light, knowing it was seen against dark, had risen out of dark, was in the
warm dark. It was seen, not with the memory's eye for recollection or
recognition, but with the blind boy's vision, and the light came off it,
was in it, shone through flower stalk and running water, in the rippling
heads of the flowers and corn, a sunless sea brimming with its own
shining, white blowing sand with a night sky just beyond vision. She
was this world and walked in it, strayed lingering and rapid between the
line of leaves and the line of sand and the line of the fine water, the line
perpetually glittering and falling, perpetually renewed.

32. *Saturnalia*

The Long Royston gardens filled with voices and bodies, gilded palanquins and floodlights with serpentining wires. The bedrooms, the upper rabbit-runs where once armies of servants had slept invisible, were now inhabited by actors, technicians, property people and hangers-on. Coaches and charabancs carrying crowds, orchestras, dancers and ultimately audiences rolled in from Calverley, York, Scarborough and points north, south, west and east as far as the sea. These battalions were summoned by Matthew Crowe, who charted their movements in time and space on ordnance survey maps and calendars in the Great Hall. He was a wizard with brilliant multi-coloured tacks. He made rehearsal charts in different coloured inks, emerald, ultramarine, vermilion, on spreads of graph paper. He showed people through the intricacies of these with a school-masterly ferule borrowed by Alexander from Blesford Ride. He pointed paths also through his own domain: pleasure garden, winter garden, herb garden, water garden, Ancient Maze, called Roman, but much older. He had had it surveyed from a helicopter and made new with sand and little box hedges.

Hampers of paper roses and crates of bill-hooks and rapiers arrived in delivery vans to be stored in stables and disused sculleries. Beer came early in large quantities and champagne in lesser ones. Sounds and strange airs arose from hidden plots and copses. From the rose garden a counter-tenor offered repeatedly the assurance that here dwelt no serpents, no devouring bears. In the kitchen garden a Spanish accent struggled with tongue-twisting anathematising sibilants. Nymphs and shepherds danced in perspiring circles on the lawns beyond the ha-ha.

Crowe told Marina Yeo, who was sleeping under the moony coverlids under Cynthia descending, that the affair was taking on the proportions of one of the Virgin Queen's State Progresses. Miss Yeo, staring regally at him over champagne on his terrace in the golden evening said she assumed that was how he meant it to be. Crowe admitted to liking Occasions. "Fireworks come tomorrow. I shall go out with a bang not a whimper before the students ramp and tramp all over my lawns. I like to see a lot of people in one place doing what I call Art, not what they call Life." Miss Yeo pointed out that no one who came ever seemed to go away, and indeed that was a characteristic of that hectic yet lucid July and August. The sun shone, and those who were rehearsing rehearsed,

and those who were not somehow stayed there, picnicking on grass and
stone steps, shifting scenes, knocking in nails, sleeping, looking on,
quarrelling, drinking, making love.

Alexander came one afternoon to a winter garden from which somewhat perfunctory laughter and squealing could be heard. Nothing could
be seen from outside the hedges, which were tightly glossy against
winter winds. At their narrow entrance was a stone putto on a Doric
plinth, and leaning against this, one brown arm encompassing the rough
grey buttocks, was Edmund Wilkie, in sky-blue aertex shirt and sky-blue
glasses over fluted and clinging white shorts. He smiled at Alexander and
said, "Genius at the gate of the garden," which Alexander momentarily
took for a compliment of sorts, until it occurred to him that Wilkie was
probably referring to himself.

Wilkie went on, "Ben is having trouble educing any form out of those
three, I can tell you. That girl wants her bottom slapping or pinching.
Maybe I should do it. Or you should."

"There isn't much of it," said Alexander, taking up, as it were, the
position of contrary voyeur on the other side of the garden gate. "And I
don't feel any urge to pinch what there is."

"No?" said Wilkie. "Not for Art's sake?"

"No," said Alexander. It was almost impossible, watching Wilkie's
plump Hilliard parody, not to strike some pose himself. Consciousness of
this drove him to a disagreeable Guard-like rigidity, and to the reflection
that Wilkie's own bottom would, in ten years or so, be approaching the
steatopygous. He noticed that Wilkie's soft fingers were caressing the
hard little stone penis and balls of the putto. He turned his attention to
the goings-on in the garden.

Elizabeth's first big scene, Alexander's first big scene, Frederica's first
big scene, was the one where the Princess ran hither and thither in the
orchard, pursued by that amorous and politic satyr, Thomas Seymour,
and her stepmother, Catherine Parr, who together cut her garments,
laughing hugely, into a hundred fragments. Alexander had, he hoped,
used this scene delicately to intimate the contrarieties of his heroine's
sexuality as he saw it: the ferocious flirtatiousness, the paralysing fear,
the desire for power, the sense of solitude. In this scene the Princess
spoke out a panic which was, in the play, frequently recalled but never
overtly repeated, since she had intelligently decided not to repeat it. In
this rehearsal none of Alexander's words had so far been audible. Lodge
was trying to teach his actors, who were slow learners, to scream and
laugh and run. Thomas Seymour was played by a rather brutal local
librarian called Sidney Gorman, who bore, like Frederica, a considerable
physical resemblance to his prototype. Katherine Parr looked more like

the Wife of Bath than like that Puritanical and sadly passionate queen. She was a barrister's wife and had played motherly bodies in local dramatics for years.

"*Run*," said Lodge. "*Run*, for Godsake as if you meant it."

There was a minor fountain in the middle of the winter garden, trickling out of a reversed conch held up by a coiled mermaid with a sly little smile. Frederica set off round this, followed by Gorman, followed by Joanne Plummer. She tried a rather desperate toss of her head, and put one hand gawkily and most unnaturally on her hip. She stopped theatrically to look provocatively back at her pursuers who were very close, and heavily prevented themselves from falling over her. Lodge shouted "*No!*" He said, "You were very sexy in a funny way in audition. What's happened to it?" Gorman, rubbing a shin he had banged on the rim of the fountain, looked ostentatiously as though he found that hard to believe. Wilkie said to Alexander, "It's when she's talking she's sexy. I've noticed." Frederica said to Lodge, "Can't I repeat my speech?"

She was desperately distressed by her inability to move. Subject to contrary tugs of arrogance and childish subservience she had simultaneously assumed that she could walk into rehearsals and assert her natural superiority as an actress, a queen, and that she was supposed to be pliable, neutral material for an impresario to blow breath into, to bring to life in what form he desired. She did not know, now, whether to show off, or to take marionette-steps as they were dictated. She hated Lodge for not telling her how to run, and felt humiliated that he could not see she did not, naturally, know. Gorman and Joanne Plummer she did not take into account. Physically she disliked them both and showed it in a way quite apparent to Lodge, who was used to having to deal with such chemical motions. It was also apparent to Wilkie, whom it amused. She did not meet the eyes of Gorman and Plummer, when they spoke, which was partly in character, and partly destructive, since it made everyone's performance clumsier and more uncertain.

"Repeat a bit if you like. Take it from Tom Seymour's bit about flames and cream. Try and remember you're *trying out* the royal flirtation game – you're scared it won't work. Remember what Marina does with that teasing note in the big masque scene. Try and get a gawky parody of that. Marina's got the tone of that dead right. And when he makes a lunge at you, *run*. Run, look back, run. Remember part of you wants to be caught. Let him bring you down, though, *don't* bring yourself down. O.K.? Mind the pond. No duckweed called for. What I want is a real romp. This scene's the *real thing*, see, – it's got formalised into a kind of weaving, dancing chase by the big masque scene. But you three have got to tangle and *romp*. See?"

Frederica was quite intelligent enough to see what was required. She was simply not bodily inventive enough to do anything about it. Lodge's voice purred and threatened together. Many actresses, including Marina Yeo, were stirred in nipples and vagina by such sheathed threats. Frederica was chilly, intellectually anxious. Gorman took her by the shoulders and began again. "See, little lioness, little prickling rose . . ." His breath smelled heftily of beer and pickled onions. She wrinkled her aquiline nose. Her thin breast swelled, not with excitement, but with pain and inadequacy.

"Don't you think we'd improve it if we stopped lurking and went to swell the audience?" said Wilkie.

"We'd make it much worse."

"Nonsense. You bring out the vestigial peacock in that painfully virginal creature."

"I didn't *ask* Ben to cast her."

"Non sequitur. You know she knows what you want. And you know she wants so much to do what you want." He gave a final flick to the putto's little stone bubbles. "Come, Sir, be useful."

They sat on a stone bench, at some distance from Lodge, who seemed gloomy. Frederica, edgier, spoke a few lines vigorously, tripping over words and recovering her dignity fiercely with a dramatic tension that could have been deliberate good acting, and could have been consciousness of Alexander. Lodge sat up. Gorman made a half-hearted unctuous pounce. Lodge rose from his bench with a roar. Wilkie just audibly sniggered. Frederica, flaming with embarrassment, the red and white rose quartered in her face, fell over the rim of the fountain and began to bleed profusely at the ankle. Lodge required a clean hanky of the company at large and the cleanest was, inevitably, provided by Alexander. Alexander knelt to tie this neatly round the thin, dusty leg.

"I can't move, I'm no good. I'm letting you down."

"You'll learn."

"You don't really think so. You never did. You were dead right." Alexander wiped his blood-stained fingers ruefully on his pristine handkerchief.

"I did think so," he lied. "I do think so. Would you find it easier if you had a real long skirt on?" He had often found in school productions that this helped with boys.

"It might."

"It could be fixed. Shall I try?"

She sniffed away a tear, at his kindness, at her humiliation. Alexander spoke to Lodge, who spoke to someone, who produced a kind of papery stiffened under-petticoat, and, after some debate, armed Joanne Plummer with the wardrobe-mistress's cutting-out shears. Alexander helped, with nappy pins, to attach the floating paper to the games shirt Frederica was wearing. Lodge took them through the scene again. During it several actors from the next scene to be rehearsed, which included the Masque, wandered in. These included Jennifer, and Matthew Crowe, who had contrived to be cast as Francis Bacon in a furred velvet gown.

This time the scene went better. Wrath, Alexander's touch, a half-glimpse of Jenny's bare brown shoulder and newly-washed hair brought considerable life to Frederica's riddling invitations and rebuffs. The petticoats gave her something to do with her redundant hands. Joanne Plummer of her own accord laid a restraining hand on the girl's scrawny shoulder, and Frederica winced royally and convincingly, addressing herself in mock rebuke to the empty air somewhere between Sid Gorman and Alexander Wedderburn. "I am not used to be so used," she said, and the voice had at last the combination of dry impatience and involuntary lewdness that had kindled Lodge at the auditions. Gorman was provoked to genuine aggression; he brought the girl down, rather heavily, with a kind of rugger tackle, and Joanne Plummer, excited by the shears which she brandished above her head began to laugh and snip and laugh and snip with real hysteria, waving the scissors in the air between slashes, whilst Gorman tore with some deliberation at the paper between Frederica's legs. Shreds and floating scraps of white paper, like fallen petals, settled on pond and lawn: Frederica wriggled free, clutching her own skirt against her crotch and chanting, rudely, nervously, cleverly as Alexander had intended, the old woman's cry from the ancient ballad. "Lawks a' mussy on me, this is none of I." The audience applauded. Wilkie said to Alexander, "Do you see the final state as a body-stocking or a layer of petticoat?" And Alexander said, taking seriously what was to him a serious question, "I want her hair down and a few shreds of cotton-something between a whore and a nymph – a bit of whalebone – a few flowers stuck on by Seymour –" "Lady Chatterley," said Wilkie. "Rubbish," said Alexander. "The flowers is a nice touch anyway," said Wilkie.

The next scene, not chronologically, but to be rehearsed, was the big Masque scene. This came at the end of Act II of the play. It might at this point be useful briefly to indicate the structure of Alexander's play, both as he had devised it, and as Lodge now elaborated it.

Each of the three acts was prefaced by a meditative dialogue between Ralegh and Spenser, sitting spotlit on the dark terrace, playing chess as it might be, gossiping, in verse, on practical things of permanent import, such as the fitting out of ships, Guinea cannibals, the brutishness and total unreason of the Irish peasantry: or on speculative matters to do with moons and vision, optic tubes and whether reddened or obliquely elongated eyes saw reddened or obliquely elongated worlds, a matter on which Ralegh, following Pliny, had written his treatise, *The Sceptic*. They gossiped also a little about the Queen, real queen and eternal empress, the Ocean's Cynthia, Faerie's Gloriana, Drayton's, and Plato's, Idea.

Act I contained Mary Tudor, the imprisonment of Elizabeth, the Accession. Act II encompassed danger and the Golden Age: the Armada, the death of Mary Stuart, the marriage bargains. Its finale was the court Masque, the descent of Astraea the Just Virgin, last of the immortals to leave the earth at the opening of the brutish Iron Age, first to return and usher in the new Age of Gold. *Redit et virgo, redeunt Saturnia regna.* As Virgil hath it. Act III observed the Queen's decline, the Essex rebellion and marshy triumphs of the rude Irish. It lingered on the interview with the archivist in the tower, to whom she had said "I am Richard II, know ye not that?" *King Lear* got in here, echoed and slyly quoted, often only in the casual incorporation of powerful nouns: samphire, the nightmare and her ninefold, germens and moulds, the tight button, the feather and mirror of the promised end, or image of that horror. Sometimes Alexander thought he should have taken these out. Frequently Lodge did take them out, shaving and planing things Alexander believed to be natural growths, sprung unbidden in his mind, a sacred grove. Lodge said whatever their provenance they would be seen as vulgar and ostentatious curlicues, glued on.

Each act had a solitary prisoner: Elizabeth, Mary Stuart, the degenerate and undignified Essex. The epilogue was Ralegh's, also imprisoned in the Tower, with fifteen years of confinement, the terrible voyage to the Orinoco and the *History of the World* before him. The sage and serious Spenser was then dead, his castle of Kilcolman burned by the savages along with various lost volumes, it was presumed, of the endless *Faerie Queene*, and himself buried, destitute, next to Chaucer in Westminster Abbey, by Essex. At the putting-out of that light, in Alexander's play, the shadows began to lengthen and grow cold.

The imprisoned speakers alternated with populous romps and ceremonies, richly elaborated by Lodge. Against this dance were set various black messengers from the outside world, telling of the hanging, drawing and quartering of Lopez on his gibbet, of the dignified and ridiculous death of the bewigged Queen of Scots, of Essex's horrible lonely progress through the City. Alexander's messengers were he hoped like the crucial Messengers of Greek tragedy and spoke what he hoped was particularly well-fleshed and full-blooded verse. Lodge kept cutting them down. He said they detracted from the action. Alexander said on the contrary they *were* the action, they were to work in poetry on the audience's imagination whilst the silver and golden maskers wove their labyrinth of pleasure and virtue, and the poets sat on the steps of the terrace. Lodge said audiences would get shifty and restive on cold evenings no matter how well provided with blankets and thermoses and really things must be kept moving. Alexander, said Lodge, was imagining endless balmy clear evenings with the moon high in the sky and stars floating but he himself had seen too much outdoor drama to fall for that. Secretly he thought Alexander's play was a little like Frederica Potter's body – clever and static. They needed a bit of pushing around and limbering up.

The *Astraea* masque, Alexander's box in box play in play, coincided then with the report of the death of the other Queen, giving its vision of golden world, completed circles, eternal harvest, a grim counter-point. Lodge had wanted to let down Astraea and her maidens on gold wires, but this proved impracticable. Their formal dance, as court masques did, nevertheless involved the whole court finally, including Ralegh, Spenser, Bess Throckmorton, an anti-masque of schoolboy satyrs with horns and fur, culminating in an orderly-disorderly Saturnalia and the famous swisser-swatter dialogue, straight from Aubrey in its pristine glory. Wilkie-Ralegh was an elegant Dionysos. Marina Yeo, high-enthroned and jewel-encrusted, sat like a still point until at last she too was induced to dance, high and disposedly.

Astraea and her maidens were played by Anthea Warburton and the lovely girls who had caused Frederica's earlier despair: they had almost non-speaking visionary parts. Anthea had a face like a Botticelli Venus, a Beauty Queen's body, and a dignified manner. She could carry a sheaf of corn at various classical angles, all of them lovely. She could wave her white arms, or incline her heavy harvest-coloured head, and cause audiences, and Lodge, to smile involuntarily because it was so rightly done. The attendant bevy of graces and young maids-in-waiting had an atmosphere of female wholesomeness, innocence, readiness and wonder at the glamour of the actors which became an increasingly crucial part of the Bacchanalian atmosphere which developed. They giggled over sandwiches preserved in helmets, developed crushes on the great, Max Baron, Crispin Reed, Roger Braithwaite, Bob Grundy, neither knowing nor not knowing what effect their sweet and silly intensities were having.

From this bevy Frederica, by virtue of her part, and more of her nature, found herself excluded. She could not giggle. No one in a flood of sudden tears turned to her for help. Nobody confided to her that she had become possessed of one of Braithwaite's handkerchiefs with initials on. She was quickly known to be soppy about Alexander Wedderburn but this was felt somehow to be a folly, an aberration, even, she surmised darkly, pathetic. The kind of rage the Bevy's soft twitterings induced in her plays its part in what follows of this story.

The Bevy also had an effect on Jennifer. She had applied her intelligence to the problem of her love and decided that this summer Alexander should hear nothing of the washing-machine and see nothing of small Thomas. This required considerable planning, since both Thomas and the washing-machine were certainly still there. She dealt with them at night, she borrowed friends of the Bevy to baby-mind. She went to Calverley, had her hair dressed, and bought sundresses and whirling skirts. Today she was in peach-coloured poplin with ribbon-straps; she sat more or less with the Bevy, looking younger, less wan and less brisk. This touched Alexander, who went and sat at her feet. He was followed by Wilkie, who assured Jenny that he was greatly looking forward to their contribution to the dance.

Lodge disposed the Bevy in fair attitudes at one end of the terrace, the boy-satyrs in convenient shrubs, and the nuclear court rising in the centre, from step to step to throne. The girls danced forward, strowing imaginary garlands. The boys leaped, acrobatically pumping little legs. Lodge walked lords and ladies into the pattern, pacing deliberately over ground where they would scamper and skip. There was no music; the Consort had not yet come to rehearsals. Frederica sat with Alexander; there was now no reason why she shouldn't go home, except that she feared to miss something. "Ah, bonny sweet Robin . . ." said Marina Yeo to Max Baron. "*Now*, Wilkie," said Lodge. Wilkie pushed Jenny against a rocky stone pillar – "It should be a tree," said Alexander, leaning forward – and thrust a plump knee into the blown peach folds of her dress. "Nay, Sir Walter, nay sweet Sir Walter," cried Jenny with conviction. Wilkie applied his face to Jenny's breast above the frilled edges of the sundress. She flushed, and stumbled convincingly in her lines. "Smashing," said Lodge. "Our best days are shadows," said Marina Yeo, "my Robin, and our gestures, the same and the same, stiffen a little, though always new."

"Alexander," said Frederica, "why do actresses always trill words so? Why can't they just speak clearly?"

"Hush," said Alexander.

"Bonny sweet Robin," said Frederica, in a thrilling parody.

"Hush."

Wilkie's knee was deeper, his arm gripped. "Swisser swatter," said Jenny. "Stop," said Lodge. "Not embarrassment, a kind of manic screech, if you can see your way to it, love."

"A kind of orgasm," said Wilkie.

"It is certainly very funny if the timing's right," said Frederica to

Alexander, who did not answer. Wilkie took hold of Jenny's naked parts and seemed to whisper fiercely in her ear. This time the sweet Sir Walter had a sawing-quavering edge, and the swisser swatter could certainly be called a manic screech. Lodge clapped, Wilkie kissed Jenny, Alexander crossly hushed Frederica and the Queen rose in virgin wrath before the whole party dissolved in laughter.

Later that afternoon the first note of the bottle-chorus, which was to reach such glorious and hideous proportions, was heard. Edmund Wilkie, who had emptied a bottle of beer, blew a meditative note across its neck, a soughing, hooting, owlish music which sounded surprisingly loud off stone and treetrunks. He tried again, and picked up one of the beats of the dance-steps. Alexander laughed, and blew across a fuller bottle from the other side of the terrace. Crowe magisterially waved his ferule and the two fluted and huffed their way through a kind of melody. Lodge bowed to them, called "Encore", and returned to the dance. In later days Wilkie made an octave of bottles, and then an orchestra, combining champagne, cider, large and small beer and whisky, enrolling tappers as well as blowers, chipping, singing, sighing. Later still there was a time when musical discord fell away into wild cacophony and mindless drumming. But now Alexander stood on the terrace nodding at Wilkie and tapping his foot; Anthea tossed mane and wrists; Thomas Poole, having found a full bottle of Guinness and drunk most of it in a long swallow, was hooting too, and the duet was a trio. The Bevy was giggling. At the end of the figure Alexander danced Jenny along the terrace and into the Great Hall: the Bevy followed: Frederica, unmusical and ungainly, was left to Crowe, who tucked his rod under one arm in a military way, offered her the other, and led her in.

Crowe gave them drinks. Max Baron sat on a table and lectured the Bevy on the secret of *Hamlet*, in which he had played a much-remarked Claudius. Alexander and Jenny sat in a window together. "What on earth was that creature *saying* to you?" said Alexander. Wilkie was presenting, with both hands and considerable drama, a large cup of wine to Marina Yeo. "He only *said*, wait till I get my hand in. Only a joke." "He was a repellent little boy." "He's not a little boy now. And not repellent. But you don't have to take him quite seriously." She was flushed and happy: it was playtime again: Alexander squeezed her hand.

"So I *knew*," said Max Baron to the Bevy, "I simply *knew* that Claudius had seduced Ophelia before the action began. It makes sense of it all. The fact that he's the centre of corruption, it's to *him* she's singing all that stuff about virginity . . ."

Anthea Warburton, surprising Frederica badly, suddenly sang in a clear, cold soprano,

> Then up he rose and doff'd his clothes
> And dupped the chamber door
> Let in the maid that out a maid
> Never departed more."

There was a moment's pure silence, then the Bevy giggled in unison. "Exactly," said Max Baron. "And she sings it to him, to the *King*, in the *flower scene* – it's the last casual betrayal of poor Hamlet . . ."

"Who isn't there," said gruff Frederica.

"That's not the point. The *point is* that something is rotten, and *Claudius* . . ."

"I don't think that can be right," said Frederica.

"I *knew*, when she came up with those flowers, that *he* knew, that *Claudius* knew, that *I* knew . . . she should be played as a young-old minx who knows it's his fault, she's his *creature* . . ."

"I think that's brilliant," said Anthea Warburton.

"Nonsense," said Frederica, having meant to mutter it, hearing it clear as a bell in her father's voice.

"It's a fascinating theory," said silky Crowe at her elbow.

"No, it's nonsense. He was a better playwright than that. If he'd meant it to be that it'd have been clear enough. Laertes thinks *Hamlet* may have stolen his way into her favours. But all this just can't be so."

"I don't see why not. I tell you, I *knew*."

"What you *knew*," said Frederica, painstakingly, accurately and unforgivably, "was your own feelings." Ignoring Crowe she turned to Alexander. "Alexander. Alexander – he *was* a better playwright . . ."

Alexander, his arm easily round Jenny, let Frederica largely down. "It's the most riddling of all texts," he said, his voice dying away to a murmur. He was annoyed with himself, and then thought, I am not a school-master now, and tightened his arm round his love.

Crowe said to Frederica, "You haven't a drink."

"No."

"You want one."

"Have you ever known me refuse one?" She said that badly. Her face was hot, hot. Crowe gave her a cold glass and said, "Come, I have something to show you."

So she was back in his inner room again, and he was showing her drawings for masquers, horned men and frondy women, and his pudgy little hands were round her waist.

"Cross-patch, stick-like girl. Bend, bend."

The room was mostly dark. A strip-light over the Marsyas, a confined bright circle of desk-light.

"All the same, he was wrong, he was simply wrong, he was reading it *wrong*."

"Yes of course, but what does it matter?" He had brought the cold bottle as well as the glasses. "Sit down, look at my Inigo Jones . . ."

She walked away and sat down. He came padding after, cherub-red face, silvery tonsure, tiny paunch. "I could make you into a real woman, Frederica."

"More to the point to make me a real virgin princess. I've got to be good, since it's no good being clever, and I've got no skills like singing and dancing, and to be truthful I'm too uninformed to see what's special about your pictures, except they're old, people are always *showing me things*, and I'm simply too ignorant to know why the things inspire whatever they do inspire. And when I do say what I do know I get hooted at."

"Dear girl, *dear* girl, I only want you to remember in ten years you saw such things – my line drawings, my bleeding Marsyas, my ripe Hyacinth, I want you to remember, you stand for who must remember. Have more wine. You may be unappreciative now, but you will remember clearly. When I am dead or senile."

"Nonsense."

"Having said nonsense so recently in such clarion tones in such a good cause, don't lie now. How old do you think I am?"

"I have no idea."

"Old?"

"Compared to me."

"Ah, well, yes." He sat on the edge of her chair. He put his hand in her dress and began to pinch her breasts. "Not old enough to be necessarily repulsive?"

"No." Though he was, or that particular activity was, repulsive, then.

"But not compelling like Alexander Wedderburn."

"I've loved him all my life. Or almost. You know."

"I don't know. In spite of his other – preoccupations."

"That's not serious."

"You speak with such appalling certainty. Do you –" twisting her breast almost sharply now – "know what *is* serious, with him?"

She began to say that she imagined she knew, meaning that she herself would be, when the time came, when she got there, which had not yet, it was true, come about, and then, sensing danger, she closed her mouth. She began again to say that his play was, and again closed her mouth, as though she was exposing something vulnerable in Alexander, which was ridiculous, since Crowe must know, better than she did, what Alexander's play meant to Alexander. She turned up a silent fierce face to

Crowe, who gave her a nip, and then something of a bite, on the lips. He was now definitely hurting, as well as fondling, her breasts. She wondered if she should perhaps bite him back. She went on talking.

"It's no use, I'm not cultured, I just know a bit more literature than most girls my age."

"Tell me."

"Well I know *Phèdre* and *Le Misanthrope* and *Vol de Nuit* and *Hamlet* and *The Tempest* and *Paradise Lost* IX and X and Keats (1820) and *Wuthering Heights* and *Kubla Khan* and Goethe's lyrics, a selection, and *Tonio Kröger* and *Aus dem Leben eines Taugenichts*, and I will know *Persuasion* and something by Kleist because those are my A Level set texts. Oh, and some Ovid and Tacitus and *Aeneid VI*. And I've read," she added, as Crowe inserted a hand under her skirt and nipped far in with sharp nails and she thought grimly of Ed and Goathland, "I've read *Lady Chatterley* and all the other Lawrence Daddy insists on. But I can tell you," she said, glowering up at the gouts of blood in the woven muscles of the Marsyas, "all that's no help with *your* culture, with what you keep showing me."

"Like hard little apples," said Crowe, "and soft little fish-roes. You're a nice creature, a hard and soft creature, and you will know, if you don't now, that *Aeneid VI* and *The Tempest* and *Phèdre* and *Tonio Kröger* are directly to do with what I show you, and if you are using words at all accurately when you say you 'know' these things, you are doomed to have no hope except to take in everything else as well. Shall I drive you home, or make Alexander take you as an awkward third with Mrs Parry? Which will induce you to come and sit on my knee again, and show me a little more while I show you a little more?"

"Alexander, please."

"You won't be popular."

"I've got used to that."

"Do you think you'll get what you want?"

"I don't know. That doesn't seem to be the point."

"I admire your single-mindedness."

"It's all I've got."

"Not quite. Apples, fish-roes, a minimal basis of culture. But I don't think you'll find what you want is what you want when you get it. There's a hairbrush in my bog, and a mirror. I'll trot off and do your bidding."

Jenny was happy. Lodge was congratulatory and Alexander was attentive and Wilkie was just sufficiently flirtatious. She thought, not about Thomas, but about symbols of the fact of Thomas; her front door, an unwashed Peter Rabbit dish, daylight on closed cotton curtains. She hated closed curtains, but you had to do it to babies. Crowe came up, and told Alexander that Frederica had had too much to drink and he had promised her Alexander would take her home. Alexander said he had other plans. Crowe said they could wait. Jenny said it was of no importance. Her tone was so different from her late sharpnesses that he gave her a quick hug and was bathed in warmth and ease, a feeling that persisted when Crowe returned with a slightly hectic Frederica. An intimacy is often intensified by the presence of an excluded third. It was so on this occasion. Jenny sat beside him; thigh and shoulder and lingering fingers touched. Frederica was jounced in the back, in solitary dumps. As they rolled over Crowe's cattle grids she remembered her vision of humped figures on this back seat at Goathland, and Alexander simultaneously remembered her bedizened face peering in at the glass he was now looking out of. He swerved dangerously under a cedar. Jenny laughed. Frederica said, "Gosh, look where you're going." Alexander said, "For God's sake, shut up, Frederica."

33. Annunciation

Stephanie stood in the telephone box in the middle of the circling caterpillar tracks on the sea of mud at Askham Buildings, trying to make a call. It was hot. The box smelled of stale tobacco, evaporated urine, warmed metal. The children bounced and slouched round the black tyres on their scaffolds. The directories were coverless and puffy, with a patina of grey-brown grease. She stood in her column of foul air, fastidiously reading a number from a folded scrap of white paper. Daniel watched from their window. A figure rosy and white between scarlet bars, bending an ear, turning a finger, pushing button A.

The connection clicked. Her knees trembled. "This is Mrs Orton. You said if I rang about now you might know something."

"I'll get him to speak to you. A moment, please."

Clicks. Humming wire. Humming waiting mind.

"Ah yes, Mrs Orton." A booming, authoritative voice. "I am happy to tell you the results are positive." Happy was not a good word: he sounded more like a judge than a bringer of good tidings. "You'd better come and see me as soon as possible. You'll need to make some arrangements, fix up a bed and so-on . . . Mrs Orton, are you there?"

"Oh yes."

"Did you hear what I said?"

"Yes. I did."

The voice hunted a phrase, asked quite smoothly, "Was this news unexpected?"

"Yes."

"Now you must not be silly, Mrs Orton, you must come and see me and make plans. You've not got only yourself to consider."

"I know."

"Then I'll make you an appointment. Which day would suit you?"

Paper crackled over wire, the appointment was made, the receiver cradled. She continued to stand in the box, staring at its one opaque wall. She folded her arms round her belly.

She tried to think. She was wholly dazed by Daniel, his weight, his warmth, his being, whether he was there or not. This had not prevented her from doing other things. She had taught successfully to the end of term, and was now reading *The Prelude* minutely and with delight in the evenings, despite gang battles on the stairs, shrilling bells, chronic radios, breaking glass. It was all lit by Daniel, as though the clarity of reading was his gift, or a gift of sex, to whom, or to which, the moment he returned from church or home or hospital she gave her entire attention. He was so strong, so ingenious, so much there. She must have known that he was like that, or she could never have done something so contrary to what she believed she cared about. Like many intellectuals she was possessed by amazed delight at having done something instinctive and right. She had thought with her body, must have, and was being rewarded with pure pleasure, of a kind she vaguely believed most people were never privileged to know.

She thought she remembered the moment of conception. Sunlit and glassy, like waterglass, and she compelled drowsily to listen to her internal dispositions, cells shifting, like yeast in dough, so that she caught her breath. They had not meant this to happen. Probably she thought, still motionless and cradling her belly, with the secret smile that belonged to past plains of pleasure, there had simply been too much of Daniel for flesh or blood or any rubber device to withstand. She thought she was sorry. This must be the beginning of the end of extravagance, and she had never before been, or wanted to be, extravagant. Clustered implanted cells would perhaps, like rubber, not withstand extravagant energy. It was strange how rapidly one developed an instinct to protect this unwanted thing. But there it was. Her senses quickened by Daniel she took note of it. Ten minutes, in her case, was apparently long enough.

Money would be a problem. Daniel was so sure what he wanted, and had not said he wanted children. Some men, she knew, listened to heart-beats through belly-walls and some resented intruders. What should she say to Daniel?

He came across the mud, dog-collared and hulking, and tapped on the glass. She stared out at him. He opened the door.

"Well," he said. "The Annunciation."

"How did you know?"

"Well, you look like all those pictures of the Virgin at her desk, and just as stunned as if you'd seen an angel. No, no, it's the arms. All women do that, hug themselves like that, you can always tell. Then their hair goes awful." He touched the bright gold and grinned blackly at her. "You can't be quite shattered, we did stretch a point and cut a corner here and there. It can't have been a bolt from the blue. Steph?"

"I was worrying what you would feel."

"I feel clever. Most people can do it if they try, most people feel clever, I feel clever. Won't you come out of there?"

"Daniel, it's not clever, it's a mistake, it's an awful problem –"

"I know. But I reckon we'll cope, won't we? It's very interesting. You look quite different."

"I feel quite different."

"Well, there you are. Ten minutes, and we're quite changed. Do come in."

They went in. Daniel kept looking at her as though she must be transfigured. Possibly because she felt indeed transfigured this struck her as wildly funny. She began to laugh. Daniel roared with laughter. All the same, she thought, it's an end, things have changed, we have changed, we haven't understood that. But they couldn't stop laughing.

34. The Dragon at Whitby

The extraordinary success of the experiments in transmission carried out during the Orton-Potter wedding seemed to galvanise Lucas Simmonds into a new and different phase of activity. The experiments had been successful beyond doubt: the laboratory beaker of grasses seen by Marcus in St Bartholomew's Church was observably standing on Lucas's workbench. Lucas had made a drawing of a lipped and fanged mouth, surrounded by a cloud of flying particles, which was recognisably a crude adumbration of the St Bartholomew Gate of Hell. He had even put in a kind of jagged halo of red pencil, so certain was he that the colour was of some importance. What they had achieved, Lucas declared, pink and beaming, was irrefutable proof that they could both receive and transmit complex images and messages. Now they must, they absolutely must, establish contact with the outside intelligences who were waiting. There was, in his own mind, no doubt that this would be done, and very shortly. A little contemplation, a little research, would produce an appropriate technique. He had every confidence, every confidence. He laughed, loudly, out of an apparent superflux of physical energy.

Marcus, unjudging but curious, remarked Lucas's behaviour during the following few days. He seemed to have become possessed of an almost daemonic health and vigour; he strode up and down to explain a point, instead of sitting, he made endless little journeys to fetch this and that; he walked on the edge of running speed habitually through the cloisters. His ruddy cheeks shone like apples but he was observably growing trimmer, even thinner, about the waist and down the thighs. His flannels hung baggier, and he bunched clumps of them from time to time in clenched fists. Some of his hesitance before his disciple had vanished – he no longer looked at Marcus for pointers of direction with the dog-like, questing look he used to deploy. He seemed to be getting messages of his own, about which he was cheerily, busily secretive. He looked for signs, straws in the wind, coincidences, and found them. He became excited by the interrelatedness of volumes grabbed at random from the library shelves and seemed to be consuming vast tracts of written works: Freud, Frazer, Jung, the records of the Society for Psychic Research, Gerard's Herbal, J. W. Dunne, Gerald Heard. He used all these, the Red Guide to the North Yorkshire Moors, the Bible, his field guides of British flora and fauna, Mother Shipton, indifferently as a kind of eclectic universal *sortes Virgilianae*. Puns, or multiple uses of words, greatly excited him. He lectured Marcus incomprehensibly for a long time on the meanings of the word Mercury, mythical, chemical, alchemical and botanical: they had found creeping dog's mercury at Knaresborough, there was meaning in that. He made a sally into hermetic doctrines and hermetic seals on vacuum jars and the alchemical hermaphrodite who was the human symbol of the perfected Work, spiritualised matter, the *lumen novum*, the Stone.

Marcus sat and listened to all this, letting most of it pass over his mind without trying to grasp it. It confirmed his mistrust of words, when he thought about it, which he did with the use of a rather peaceable mental image of a globe, scored, pierced, and netted with lines meeting and diverging at poles and centre: all such languages could be made to head at breakneck speed towards coincidence and coherence, if that was what you set out to do with them. Marcus thought: to say "the light was too much for me" is to speak a different language, in which he doesn't seem to be interested. He stared out of the laboratory window at the small white sun, painfully glittering, and thought that the relation between the light, which bothered him, and his own perceptual equipment, and that mass of flaring gas and matter, and any other intelligence, might not at all be so seamlessly interrelated as all this pretty but reductive word-work made it. But he was not uncontent: Lucas had, at least temporarily, stopped attempting to use Marcus's hypnagogic visions for divination, and thus he was getting more sleep. And the word-work, even more the bodily cheerfulness, of his friend, consoled and protected him if he did not think.

It was a curious coincidence between his readings in Jung's *Psychology and Alchemy* and the description of Whitby Abbey in the Red Guide which led Lucas to select the ruins of the Abbey as the site for their experiment. He chose Whitby partly because it was the place in which Caedmon the illiterate cowherd had been visited by an Angel who had enabled him to sing an English *Song of Creation*. More tenuously, he was much taken by the myth, recorded in the Red Guide, and supported by a quotation from Sir Walter Scott's *Marmion*, about the gifts of the founder of the Abbey, the ferocious St Hilda.

> They told how, in their convent cell
> A Saxon princess once did dwell
> The lovely Edelfled;
> And how of thousand snakes, each one
> Was changed into a coil of stone
> When holy Hilda prayed;
> Themselves, within their holy bound
> Their stony folds had often found;
> They told, how sea-fowls' pinions fail
> As over Whitby's towers they sail,
> And sinking down, with fluttering faint
> They do their homage to the saint.

They thought, of course, he told Marcus, that the ammonites were petrified snakes, made stones by Hilda's holiness. But the truth is different – the ammonites are early records of the *true* history of creation, and the secret meaning of the petrified snake, its *real* relation to holiness, is to be found in Jung's account, in *Psychology and Alchemy*, of Mercurius – as a dragon. He read out a whole page to Marcus, with mounting excitement:

"The dragon symbolises the vision and experience of the alchemist as he works in his laboratory and 'theorizes'. The dragon in itself is a *monstrum* – a symbol combining the chthonic principle of the serpent

and the aerial principle of the bird. It is . . . a variant of Mercurius.
But Mercurius is the divine winged Hermes manifest in matter, the
god of revelation, lord of thought and sovereign psychopomp.
The fluid metal, *argentum vivum*, 'living silver', quicksilver – was
the wonderful substance that perfectly expressed his nature: that which
glistens and animates within. When the alchemist speaks of Mercurius,
on the face of it he means quicksilver, but inwardly he means the
world-creating spirit concealed or imprisoned in matter. Time
and again the alchemists reiterate that the *opus* proceeds from
the one and leads back to the one, that it is a sort of circle
like the dragon biting its own tail. For this reason the *opus* was
often called *circulare* (circular) or else *rota* (the wheel). Mercurius stands
at the beginning and end of the work: he is the *prima materia*, the
caput corvi, the *nigredo*: as dragon he devours himself and as dragon he
dies, to rise again as the *lapis*. He is the play of colours in the *cauda
pavonis* and the division into four elements. He is the hermaphrodite
that was in the beginning, that splits into the traditional brother-sister
duality and is reunited in the *coniunctio*, to appear once again at the end
in the radiant form of the *lumen novum*, the stone. He is metallic yet
liquid, matter yet spirit, cold yet fiery, poison and yet healing draught
– a symbol uniting all opposites."

Lucas was of the opinion, he said, that Scott's passage contained more
wisdom than he knew, traces of a powerful but corrupted primitive or
occult symbol in the combination of serpent and failing pinions precisely
at Whitby Abbey, because *together* bird and snake made the finished
circle, tail-in-its-mouth dragon, a meeting of earth and air which was just
what he and Marcus wanted, was it not, the raising of the earth to the
fluid state of light, less actualised than the earth, and they could add the
other of the four old elements, too, fire and water, if they were very
clever, yes and quicksilver and the piece of vegetable mercury, the dog's
mercury. The place was no longer in doubt: the exact experiment or rite,
depending on your terminology, still needed thought.

There was a boy, a chess player, once, who revealed that his gift
consisted partly in a clear inner vision of potential moves of each piece as
objects with flashing or moving tails of coloured light: he saw a live
possible pattern of potential moves and selected them according to
which ones made the pattern strongest, the tensions greatest. His
mistakes were made when he selected not the toughest, but the most
beautiful lines of light. Something like this took place in Marcus's mind,
listening to Lucas's chattering switchboard of crossed lines of reference.
The spider-web had its beauty, but it was tenuous, tenuous. Marcus did

not mind this: there *was* a pattern, even if it was one composed of dotted lines of intermittent flashes. It was not his place to comment on the exiguous nature of the invisible threads. Maybe in these realms everyone's inner spider web had its own necessary and different thickness and tension anyway. Maybe Lucas's was like woven steel.

They set off, then, for Whitby, in the sportscar, side by side, one hot and sunny Sunday. In the boot were baskets, two of them, one containing a large picnic and one containing various pieces of equipment packed by Lucas secretly and wrapped in various white napkins and handkerchiefs and silk scarves. He wore a red and white spotted silk handkerchief himself, jauntily at the open throat of his white shirt, under a navy blue college blazer. Marcus had his usual aertex shirt and a school blazer, which had a turret woven on the pocket in gilt thread with the motto "ad caelum hinc". No Latin master had ever quite liked this, which had been written by Crowe's ancestor: the turret, which was said to represent the building itself as a tower of strength, was known in the staffroom as the Tower of Babel, or the Leaning Tower.

They drove south and east, over the moors, reasonably quietly, dropping down high hills eventually towards the coast road along the cliffs, taking a loop round the Goathland moors, along the road where Frederica, her thigh and breast rudely pushed by the solid Ed, had brooded on the Alexandrine, so as to approach the Abbey itself, on foot, from the cliffs to the south, avoiding the town altogether.

On the top of the cliffs the weather was what it was meant to be, as Lucas put it to Marcus, blue and deep and empty with a high sun and a light wind from shore to sea. They walked to the Abbey through fields thick with buttercups, cow parsley, speedwell, brushing them with white and yellow dust. The naked unsupporting arches were white against this weather and the stone trunks seemed weightless and visual only, as Lucas again remarked, though they were cold to touch in the shadows. He was put out to find trippers wandering along the bare choirs, or stepping from designed empty space to empty space: somehow, Marcus gathered, he had expected to be alone at an altar, or where an altar had been, and little girls singing and running, old men with knapsacks, stumping booted motorcyclists dangling goggles from gloved hands, disconcerted him. He and Marcus stood as trim as reserve players on a visiting cricket team, gripping their tidy baskets, and stared at the site, the looped and windowed walls through which the seawind ran, the ancient stone paving surrounded by cliff grass. Marcus remembered the oppressive geometry of the enclosure of St Bartholomew's and took pleasure in finishing and extending these broken sweeps and rhythms in his mind's eye. The sunlight danced on seawater swell and polished

stone and blades of grass and buttercup-enamel. Little streams of it ran,
like visible convection currents, in eddying circles everywhere between
ground and sky, sprinklings and shoots and trailings of brightness.
Lucas Simmonds stepped with military or processional precision round
the bounds of the building, as he might have marked out a rough cricket
stump or football pitch on Far Field, stepping and turning where the
white lines would follow. He carried the mysterious basket. Marcus, the
acolyte, stepped after, with thermos and bottle, bakelite beakers, bread,
meat, apples, sweets and wine.

And why should they not, after all, said Lucas in an urgent whisper, do
what they had to do as well alone in a simple field as here, where there
was so much interference. He gestured at the little girls, who were
mopping and mowing and chanting about Tom Tiddler's Ground, as
though they were so much materialised static. Marcus said irreverently
that they might after all accidentally light on the site of Caedmon's
cow-byre, which was where the Angel had actually come, and Lucas said
quite seriously that the grass must have been the grass which Caedmon's
cows pastured on, that was so. Not the *exact* grass, said Marcus. Not so
different, said Lucas, giving his flapping trouser leg a hoist, shifting his
basket from one hot hand to the other. They set off again, along the
cliff-edge, past the weather-hut and its rough garden. After a time, they
found an ideal patch of ground sheltered enough to support not the
wiry cliff grass and blown scabious and sea holly but a dense yellow
thicket of buttercups hazed with the lace of the cowparsley. In such
richness of tall grasses and various pollens Marcus wondered briefly
about the asthma, took an experimental breath, sneezed pollen, but felt
no machinery of constriction or seizure moving inside him, only a hot
dazed sense of vegetable too much. He heard an echo of the little girls –
"We are on Tom Tiddler's ground, *Picking* up gold and si-ilver" and
remembered a hymn they had sung when he was little. Daisies are our
silver, buttercups our gold. This is all the treasure we can have – or –
hold. Lucas took out a tartan rug from the basket and laid it on the grass,
where it stood suspended and prickling, air running under it. Now we
begin, said Lucas. On empty stomachs, as at Owger's Howe.

Despite Owger's Howe, Marcus did not exactly expect anything to
happen. Somehow, in his mind, the human precision and over-deter-
mination of Lucas's planning made it less likely that anything would. He
was a little afraid, but his fear was of being made to do something
ludicrous or unbalanced. Lucas took out some of the contents of his
basket, laid a large white napkin on the rug, and laid on the napkin: a
fossilised ammonite, a bunch of dried grass in tissue paper, a cellophane
packet of pressed flowers, a corked test-tube with a ball of quicksilver in

it, some circles of smoked glass, a large circular magnifying glass, a hand-kerchief. There was also an implement resembling a surgical scalpel.

Lucas explained. The object of the exercise was to make contact with the noussphere, was it not, and this was hampered, as sages in all times had known, by man's own too great actualisation as a physical entity. Thus, it seemed, to transmute Life into Spirit meant to consume matter into pure being. It seemed likely that that, symbolically and in part actually, was what the old burned offerings had been meant to achieve. He, Lucas, had also been struck, very struck, during Marcus's description of the photisms and the figure of the crossed cones, if he might speak so, by Marcus's recurrent references to a burning glass, which he took in retrospect to have been a Sign. So he proposed, in short, to make a burned offering, by means of a burning glass, releasing Matter into Light and Energy by communicating the energy of the Sun who was the source of our earthly light and heat. He had decided to offer, of course, those grasses which had already been a Sign, and the dog's mercury and aconites and gentian of the vicinity of the Dropping Well – to be made into, not Stone, but Light, the Lumen Novum, another Sign. He had also brought with him an ammonite, which was a stony symbol of Creation and the Work (though he was afraid it came from Portland Bill, not Whitby – but it was a good one, one he had been given as a boy) – as he was saying, an ammonite as a symbol of the perfected Work, and some mercury to represent spirit imprisoned in matter, in a corked tube, and there should clearly be flesh as well as grass, to complete the burned offering, especially if one considered that Abel served God flesh and Cain served him fruit of the ground and the Lord only had respect unto Abel and his offering. He thought the flesh should be their own. He had thought of bringing worms or something but really it should be their own, didn't Marcus think? Marcus, his mind jumping from Cain and Abel to Abraham and Isaac looked rapidly over the shining buttercups for signs of life other than himself but could see only butterflies in the distance, brimstone and small blue. The hair of their head and drops of blood should be enough, Lucas said, he had brought a knife. Did Marcus think anything else was necessary?

Marcus stared at the buttercups and the tartan wool of the rug, and listened to the sighing of the subsiding grasses under the rug, and said no. Unless, something from here, from this place exactly. Caedmon's cow-byre. He smiled palely. Lucas pointed out that Caedmon and Abel were both herdsmen, and Marcus said there were no cows. There was *milk*, Lucas said, in the thermos, and they could gather some plant from the field and put them together, an excellent plan.

They hunted in the hedgerow for a suitable plant to offer: the yellow

was somehow too pervasive to be considered. It was Marcus who found
something unusual, a tallish plant, with small fierce blue, pink-tinged,
trumpeted florets. The leaf was darkish and had prickles on it. Lucas,
called to inspect it, said it was viper's bugloss, and would do very well,
another transmutable snake or dragon plant. He pulled it up by the roots
and laid it, in a sprinkling of earth, beside the other grasses, the gentian,
the mercury.

Then he picked up the little dissecting knife. "Put your hand out," he
said to Marcus. "I want to squeeze three drops of blood – or so – three
drops would be good – onto this handkerchief. From each of us,
mingled." Marcus jerked involuntarily back. "It's sterile," Lucas
assured him, putting out his own hand. "I assure you it's sterile."
Marcus imagined the same little triangular blade turning back the lined
wormskin from the rolling flesh. He hung his hand limply. Lucas
gripped it, turned it palm to the sun, pounced, and made a little slit on the
ball of the thumb. Blood spurted and dripped. Considerably more than
the regulation three drops. Lucas laughed immoderately and pushed the
blade down into his own forefinger. His blood ran onto Marcus's, onto
the white cloth. There was a patch of irregular red circular splashes.
Lucas raised his hand and sliced away one of the springing curls from his
own forehead, and then, for a moment, cupped Marcus's head in a
bloodstained hand and sheared a wisp of the limp, haylike hair. He
twisted the hairs together, and put the flat little clump on top of the
blood. After some thought, he put the ammonite under the handkerchief, under the grasses. It would be unrealistic, he said, to expect the
sun's energy to consume an ammonite. But it could be communicated to
it, could transform it in some way, no doubt. Now, didn't Marcus think,
they should dance as they had at Owger's Howe, in the successful figure
they had made on that occasion. He held out his hand, gripped Marcus's,
blood smearing blood and drew him to his feet. He gave him a piece of
smoked glass. "To look through. To look directly. To catch any
indication of change, or intent, or . . ."

They spun. Marcus felt silly, sick, dizzy, unreal, outside himself.
Their feet rose, crashed on buttercups, fell and thumped earth. When
they stopped, the flowers were swirling in concentric circles of butter
and cream, and the lines of green on the tartan rug were serpentining like
the sea. Lucas raised his smoked glass, stared up into the blue at the gold
flourisher, gold guinea, flaring helium, bowed solemnly and sat down
on the tassels of the rug. Marcus quickly imitated these movements.
Lucas raised the magnifying glass. He said, "Do you think we should
address Them in any way."

"No."

"No, neither do I. Words sound silly. I think we should hold hands."

So they sat, holding hands, and Lucas raised the glass circle, catching the prism of light for a moment and reflecting it on the napkin, and then held it steady.

It was hard to see whether there was a white flame, or only molten air: it was very steady: no tongues licked: only what was laid out was eaten away, shrivelled and charred black. The transmitted grasses flew into fine ash, a shadow that held shape and then trembled into dust, and with them the gentian. The cellophane containing the dog's mercury flared gold and platinum for a moment, went treacly and then black, and then nothing. The hair, over the blood, crisped, squirmed, settled and was blackly gone, and the blood under it with it. The viper's bugloss hissed, boiled, curled up: most startling, the glass tube containing the mercury gave a creaking cry, shattered, and released a multitude of separated silvery droplets that ran through threads of charred cloth into burned earth. On the napkin, a charred circle, a black hole, spread silently, eating away the glare, briefly gold where the black advanced. There was a smell, animal and vegetable, of protesting, consumed matter. Over the hump of the ammonite the cloth flaked into darkness and fell in shreds, leaving a black and juicy tracery on the stone coils. Marcus stared: he remembered the earlier experience: this was concrete evidence of the power a lens could concentrate: flame or hot air it danced white, white, thick transparent white: a nothing into which if you put your finger you would most painfully be included.

Hold the glass, Lucas said, hold the glass steady and watch. I'm going to finish it off with a libation of milk and wine. He fiddled in Marcus's basket, poured a little milk from a bottle into a tin lid, struggled briefly with a corkscrew and a bottle of Nuits St Georges. He splashed wine into the charred circle, where it steamed, flamed, smelled and went out. The milk in the tin lid contracted to wax-dark, then brownish traces and bubbles, producing a particularly nasty tortured smell which Marcus remembered from schooldays when he was five or six and the boys had clustered round the school stove, spitting bubbles of their ⅓-pint milk rations through straws onto the cast-iron surface. Lucas added a further drenching of wine, a reasonable puddle, on which charred fragments floated and which the earth supped up slowly.

Marcus put down the burning glass, which was truly burning to touch. He looked around him at air not molten, and down at the blackened sun-shaped patch which was the end result of their acts. It had been an extraordinary demonstration of the power of forces one normally had to take no account of. Lucas's face and hair were sodden with sweat.

"Now what?" said Marcus.

"Now we sit and wait. We have made our cry, we have indicated what we want. Now we wait."

Marcus watched the light move softly over the buttercups and wondered: what had they indicated that they wanted? To be consumed hotly and vanish? To become invisible? Black scraps and brimstone butterflies eddied and settled. They waited. The still afternoon went on.

"Have some wine," said Lucas. He poured. After a time he said, "Have some more wine." Marcus, unused to alcohol, drank thirstily. Lucas, erect, as though waiting for a touch of flame on the brow, or a voice from the blue vault, sipped angrily from a bakelite mug. He offered Marcus a beef sandwich and an apple, which Marcus accepted. He ate nothing himself. After two good beakers of wine Marcus lay down with his head on the rug and folded his arms over his face, making darkness. The light that had purposefully invaded him on the Far Field was conspicuous by its absence. Here was the sun, a burning glass, too much intention, a headache. After a moment, Lucas's body was lowered next to his. The old questing voice said, "What next?"

"Oh, wait." Thickly, into the crease of his elbow.

"Wait for what?"

"How should I know? You started this."

After some more time, his friend said, meekly, "I'm sorry."

"You don't have to apologise to *me*. I didn't think the heavens would open. We did really burn up some things, though, it was extraordinary."

"Not extraordinary. Simple."

Marcus realised that he had been reinvested with his dubious authority. He became angry.

"You *saw* what happened to all those things. You did. Now you ought to know what I'm so scared of, you ought to go carefully. I'm scared of my brains boiling in my head like the viper's bugloss. You don't seem to see that there is a simple real thing there that one could be really scared of. You ought to be scared, not put out, you haven't *thought*. Do you want to be melted into a column of hot air and scattered on the sea by convection, do you, or made into ashes like the lovely grasses? Do you want to be nothing, do you? How near do you want to get? I don't think you know what it might be like. I know. What you made was at least an illustration of what I'm scared of, but you'd never let me say it was terrible, you kept saying it was glorious. What do you want it to do? How do you know, if it took any notice of you, if it's intelligent, that you could stand its attention? No, keep out of the way, keep still, that's all we can do."

There was a long silence. Then Lucas said simply, "I am so unhappy."

Marcus turned his face away, and then, with darkened eyes, held out his cut hand to Lucas, who took it, and hotly held it. Their bodies moved closer together. There was a strange clicking: Marcus became aware that Lucas's teeth were chattering. He rolled over and put a tight arm over his friend's shoulder, clutching the hot flannel. He smelled sweat, and panic. He scrabbled at Lucas's body, like one keeping someone from dying of cold with his own warmth. The dull little voice said:

"I am so unhappy. I have nothing, no friends, nothing I do is real. And every now and then I almost see something, almost – and then there's a disaster."

"You have me," said Marcus, trembling himself with unaccustomed gentleness.

"I am no good to you. You live in the real world. I go in and out of a phantasmagoria. I ought to know, I ought to keep watch, when I get thinner, it's a Sign. I ought to protect you, you are in my care, not . . ."

"No. You've changed my life. And, Sir – what we saw was real, the grasses and the picture, that hasn't gone, and maybe this is only taking its time to work, and there was Owger's Howe – you did a lot – a lot – a lot was real – *is* real –"

He did not want this closed world to go. Lucas Simmonds was his protection from the importunity of the infinite.

"I am not pure. That's what it is. Partly. Of the earth, earthy, though it smells and I hate the smell, I hate the whole messy business. I hate my body, I hate bodies, I hate hot and heavy . . . You are pure. One recognises it when one sees it. You are a clean being, you see cleanly. You are . . ."

Marcus did not want to know what he was. He edged closer, pulling at the blazer, and the weight of flesh under it. He said, as one might to a child, "Hush, keep still, it doesn't matter. Something did happen, you've got to keep still. You've got me, I'm here." And when had his own presence been a help or a consolation to anyone, ever, he thought, not re-membering the days of his youth, or the moments shared with Winifred, speechless and closed, in the maternity hospital. He said, as she might then have said to him, a woman with a restless, struggling child, "Keep still, keep still, it doesn't matter." And quite suddenly Lucas Simmonds dropped into a flushed sleep, his wet mouth slightly open, his face turned towards Marcus, who lifted his head slightly and glimpsed the glitter of sweat along the cleft of the nose, the little balls of it gleaming amongst the hairs of the eyebrows. He held onto Lucas's hand, and closed his own eyes, and slept, heavily and blackly, as though unconsciousness was what was most deeply to be desired.

When they woke, they disentangled arms and legs in silence and, backs turned one to another, gathered up their things, the blanket from the crushed grass, the apple core, the knife, packed and set out walking.

Marcus felt terrible. Indigo circles, like after-images of the sun, danced before him in triads and circling spires across the cliff grass, hovered over the fall to the water, hung in the sky. Lucas said nothing and went very fast so that Marcus had to stretch his legs and trot to keep up with him.

The glossy black-beetle car, parked on a grass verge, was very hot, outside and in, a little furnace, throwing off a haze of visible heat like a jellyfish skirt swaying in cool water might be, undulating. Lucas flung the baskets into the rudimentary back seat and got rapidly into the front, slamming the door and winding down the glass. Marcus followed him, running his hand round his neck inside the shirt. They added their blazers to the pile in the back. Marcus looked at Lucas who leaned back in his seat, staring not at the boy, but through the windscreen. Heat coiled about them.

Lucas said, "There are a lot of things I should say, things you should know, things I haven't mentioned."

"No, no . . ." deprecating. "It doesn't matter."

"How can you know that? There are things about me you should know, perhaps – though I've hoped this wasn't all primarily a *personal* matter, I've hoped so. But I have cheated you in a way, there are things that happen – to me – you might feel you had a right to know about, if they happened again. I'll tell you, I will tell you, in good time. No one can be blamed for being afraid of being transformed, translated or incarcerated, as has happened, in the past, I have to admit. It began with the destroyer. In the Pacific, when I was serving on that destroyer. There was some trouble, with aerials and messages, there too, and a Tribunal, I was called before a Tribunal, and then in a white cell for a long time – They told me then, you must never have children, you must never contemplate having children, you can transmit . . . I had the idea they had me electronically tracked to see if I was going in for – activity – on that front, to make sure there were no children. Maybe all that was an illusion. They were all white and the rooms were white, might have been anywhere, on the destroyer, outside time and space, I believed various things at various times as to the precise location of the events, and only really came to when I was somewhere in Greenwich which was certainly not where I began. Maybe I flew. Maybe they flew me. Maybe time stopped. Nobody told me. They didn't think, I expect, that I was fit, in a fit state, that is, to take information in, but I didn't stop thinking on that account, by no means, I formed hypotheses as to my whereabouts. I think, I'm not sure, I know I *thought* they had electrodes in my lobes, and in my . . . To make sure . . . Maybe they did. They can do such things. You'd be surprised if I told you some of the things I saw them do, before . . . before I left.

"I told you, they wanted me to teach sex instruction at that school, as an extension of human biology, but I said no, no, no, you must get a good lady from some Welfare in a hat to do that, or some wholesome smiley girl; I leave the Undying Worm alone, in my condition, nice hermaphroditic anonymous earthworms are as far as I go, convenient creatures with few problems, at least as they are made apparent to the human eye. I do amphibians and rabbits, but man that great amphibium I leave alone and hope very much we may so evolve that the whole issue becomes redundant, I tell them, or not, depending on who I think is listening, and *how* they are listening, naturally. There are ways to eternal life that aren't available to the higher organisms, you know, even Freud said so. He said death was bound up with our sexual method of perpetuating ourselves. Once the cells of the body have become divided into *soma* and germ-plasm, he said, an unlimited duration of individual life would become a quite pointless luxury. A quite pointless luxury. When this differentiation had been made in multicellular organisms death became possible and expedient. The *soma* dies, the protista remain immortal. The undying seed. But they told me, you must never contemplate ... I said that. Another thing, Freud said, was that reproduction didn't begin only when death did. Oh no. It's a primal characteristic of living matter, like growth. Life has been continuous from its first beginning upon earth. There's a mystery. It's only the individual higher organism that's sexually divided and dies. Not the biosphere on the one hand. Nor the hermaphrodite hydra on the other, that divides and divides and becomes more examples of the same form, somewhere between vegetable and animal.

"There was a book I was led to read recently, an odd old book of Heard's, not one of the ones about the evidences of God, a book called *Narcissus: An Anatomy of Clothes*. I liked that because it saw the clothes we wear as our way of modifying our anatomy – corsets and razors – and later, chemistry and pharmacy, control of the pituitary gland, the removal of unwanted hair – Heard sees it all as an evolutionary move to reduce the *mass* of our bodies. That's very interesting, I thought. He said that houses and wardrobes and tool chests were ways of laying aside fur and nails and teeth. He said scientific diet would in due course rid us of our clumsy distillery of intestinal coils. He said that we should grow to be like Wells's Martians, tentacled brains in machines, only we would not find that repellent but beautiful, a man without his machine would revolt us then, as a man without his clothes disgusts respectable ladies now, or the sight of the lovely brain without its covering of hair and skin still revolts us irrationally. He said we should become swarms of bright little clockwork organisms like watch cases, with tiny opalescent bodies at the heart of the springs. It fitted into the Jung in my mind – about Mercurius and the *prima materia* – because he said we could get back to where we began – an idea imprisoned in matter –

"You said out there, did I want to be nothing. Like the grasses, you said. Well, yes, I do and I don't. Do you read much poetry?"

Marcus said no, he did not. He added that he had been allergic to poetry, which had lain about his house all his life, like so much dust or pollen, all over, and he now considered himself desensitised. To this remarkable and illuminating confession Lucas did not listen, or barely, since he was going on to explain that he had also recently been led to read a considerable amount of poetry and particularly the works of Andrew Marvell who had seemed to understand about the desire to be without the limitations of sex and the troubles of flesh. He had written a very lovely poem called *The Garden* in which he spoke of Annihilating all that's made To a green thought in a green shade. My vegetable love, Lucas said, broodingly and apparently irrelevantly. After a further gap, he said, "I wish I could simply teach botany, I wish it were possible to stick at a green thought." After another silence he added, "I'm not a homosexual you know, I'm not anything."

"It wouldn't matter," said Marcus, embarking on a protestation, or assurance he couldn't finish. He had not followed the narrative of Lucas's speech; he was struggling with his own fears, shadowily bodied forth in Lucas's half-formed memories of actuality; but more powerfully, he felt moved by gentleness. Lucas had fed and lectured and admired him: something was owed in return. He wanted to offer consolation, and had not the wisdom to know how or why to console. So, like so many of us, he offered himself instead.

"Sir, Lucas, *I* care. I do care. There is me. Can't I do anything?"

Lucas turned on him a face red with sun and shame.

"You could touch me. Just touch. Contact."

Slow Marcus again held out his hand. Lucas took it in his own, which seemed puffed and clumsy, and after a moment laid both their hands on his own lap. They sat, silently, not looking at each other, staring out through the windscreen. Lucas moved their two hands closely into his crotch. Marcus jerked involuntarily and Lucas gripped tighter.

"*Never* say," he said, pleading, pedantic, breathing with difficulty, "*never* say, it was all only sex. But if only you could . . . no more than touch, I assure you."

He fumbled desperately with his strained fastenings and suddenly, hot, straight and silky, the penis sprang into view. Marcus pulled back: Lucas gripped, and gripped.

"I know I shouldn't," said Lucas. "But if only you could, if you could bring yourself – just to touch – I should be connected . . .''

Marcus looked sideways, his way, and out of pity, embarrassment, honour, complicity, put out his thin, pale hand and laid it limply on the burning thing, neither clutching nor caressing. "Ah," said Lucas, "ah," and the hard root flowered extravagantly and wetly and wilted slowly in the same moment, leaving Marcus's hand full. "Ah," said Lucas again, shuddering in the driving seat. "I didn't mean that. I'm sorry. It was a failure of the will."

They could not look at each other.

"It doesn't matter," Marcus said in an undertone. "It doesn't matter, Lucas."

But it did matter. For a moment he himself had stirred in sympathy, and then Lucas had been convulsed and he was where he had always been, alone, out of touch, separate. He wiped his fingers on his handkerchief, his own trousers, anything.

"It does matter," Lucas said. "It's a disaster. It's the beginning of the end." He said this in a quiet, dogmatic way, buttoning himself as he said it, and waited for an answer. Marcus could think of none. Lucas then inserted the key, started the car with a jerk, without looking at his passenger, reversed off the grass and set off down the road.

What followed, the drive over the moors, was a nightmare. Marcus, before he stopped thinking at all, thought it should not have been possible to drive so fast. Air and heather and dry stone walls whipped past: corners screamed and sickened: parallax wavered, spun in like a cocoon, centred between his eyes, which he closed. He tried to speak and his mouth was dry: they leaped hills and floated or plummeted into air pockets: cross-roads went past with the slamming sound of gates or trees unregarded and unrespected. Marcus got down on his knees after a time and buried his face in his seat, stealing only one glance up at the set, stony figure of his friend, his rosy face staring impassively under its sunny curls over the wheel into empty space. Do you want to kill us, Marcus wanted to say, and could not speak, nor repeat, do you want to be nothing, either. Marcus crouched, stared, lost consciousness, gained it to see the sky whirling and closed his eyes again.

35. *Queen and Huntress*

The night of the dress rehearsal came. And this is our last chance, said Lodge, haranguing principals and extras from the Royal footstool on the terrace gravel, whilst in the trees one green bottle enquired, musical and most melancholy, who, who? This is our last chance to put it all together, to get the magic right, and we have so nearly made it. He waved his arms, intoning, uncharacteristically, with the musical slither and bell of the true actor, charming, cajoling, minatory, and they all, in wigs and furred gowns, in hoops and bulging trunk-hose, sighed and laughed and gathered up their skirts and their courage.

Frederica sat on a rug next to Edmund Wilkie, under an arc light hung in a tree. Wilkie, in black velvet rayed with seed pearls, the living image of the cloaked Portrait Gallery Ralegh, was doing tiny fine sums on graph paper with a pencil. He had several sheets of such paper, covered with diagrams of test-tubes, tall and fat bottles, demi-johns; also with odd traced diagrams of cosmic serpents traversing the heavenly spheres, Apollo with a pot of flowers, the Graces. Over the last weeks he had expended considerable ingenuity on making the Bottle Chorus, scientifically, into a fine art. He measured columns of air over columns of water, mapped velocities and frequencies of sounds and airs as they echoed round cavernous glass globes or whistled in slender glass tubes. He had assembled a consort of more or less reliable boys from the fauns of the anti-masque, whom he rehearsed, in spare moments, in the great hall. Now these clutched to their doublets mathematically labelled bottles, diamantine, amber, emerald: wine, beer, pop. They could, when Wilkie gave the sign, render *Giles Farnaby his Toye*, *When the Saints Come Marching In*, Dowland and Campion's *Paradise*, the *Foggy, Foggy Dew*, with embellishments and intensified din devised by Wilkie himself. That man of many parts was now writing, he said, the true music of the spheres, according to a scheme to be found in the *Practica Musica* (1496) of Gafurius, who had drawn a series of correspondences between Doric, Lydian, Phrygian and Mixolydian modes, the planets in the heavens, and the muses. Wilkie told Marina Yeo that he would create a true Apollonian order from a Dionysiac cacophony – and all so that he could stand on the terrace and cry out, "The music of the spheres, list, my Marina!"

"How can that be," asked Frederica sceptical, "when nobody *knows* you've been fixing all these planetary octaves and transcendental notes?"

"You know. Marina knows. The bottle boys know, I've told them. They twitter and giggle, but they know. Anyway, people will intuit an order if an order is there, even if they can't name it or the principles it's derived from."

It was difficult to know how seriously he took himself. Certainly he did like order, a plurality of perceptual orders, he was a fixer and orchestrator.

"They won't," said Frederica. "They won't intuit anything, and I won't, either, however much you inform me, because I'm tone-deaf."

This information appeared to give Wilkie great pleasure. "You are? How splendid. You bear out a theory I have about flatness of speaking-tone in the tone-deaf. That explains why you're so good at sounding stony." He mimicked a line or two of her rendering of Alexander's Tower speech. He was very accurate. "Flat," he said. "Flat in semi-tones, and shifting key inconsequentially. Like sweet bells jangled out of tune and harsh. Like a peacock. We can't all sing the music of the spheres. Now *you*, my dear Marina, something tells me *you* have nearly perfect pitch."

"I had once," said Marina Yeo, above them, propping skirts vast as empire on two gilt ballroom chairs. "It's not been quite so good lately."

"It decays with age," said Wilkie with gusto. "But slowly, if surely, you'll be glad to hear. Shall I write you a song, Marina, to sing to my spherical bottle music, will you sing with my choir invisible? You can listen, Frederica, darling, but you won't hear. 'Such sober certainty of waking bliss.' As Huxley once said, so accurate a description of good music. What *do* you do without it?"

"I meditate," said Frederica with asperity, "and frequently wish it would stop."

Wilkie gave her a plump puckish grin, since Lodge had reached the end of his peroration, pointed his flimsy poniard at the bottle players who puffed out their cheeks like Botticelli's Zephyr and embarked on *Rule Britannia*.

"What we need is *drums*. You'd hear those, girl, the deaf hear those. Hissings and heartbeats both. Now, what *sort* of drums, for the music of the spheres? Did you know, sweet ladies, that the iambic pentameter embodies, as it were, the number of heartbeats between a breath taken in and the same breath sighed out? Shakespeare's verse is human time. But for spherical music you need a drum-beat set on some inhuman measure, a non-anthropomorphic tic-tac, a water-clock, an astronomical pulsing . . ."

"Shut up, Wilkie," said Lodge. "I want to begin. Clear-off, non-beginners, or sit still and shut up and be audience. Wilkie, *do* shut up, and come and do your Prologue. Quiet please. Lights, please."

And in every tree, like shining golden fruits, lights sprang warm and round and clear on the green. It was late afternoon, grey and dark blue, not darkness. Total dark was due to fall in the final Act, where Lodge, inspired by the York Mystery Plays of 1951, when the real sun had set, bloody and huge, behind the impersonated, crucified Christ and the ruined Abbey with board additions, had used nightfall to emphasize the dying rays of Gloriana. Wilkie twitched his mantle, gave a skip on to the terrace, and sauntered over to Thomas Poole/Spenser, to begin his Prologue.

Jenny, late because of settling fretful Thomas, ran up and down the old kitchens, which housed the women's dressing-rooms, begging someone to hook her at the back. In a stone scullery she found Alexander. Who said he would hook her himself. They were both reminded of their first embrace in the Music Hole under the school stage. Alexander pushed his hands inside the pliant whalebone, round the soft breasts. Oh, the rows of little hooks. "Did Crowe suggest . . .?" She laughed. "He suggested. He's an old Pandar, a Lord of Misrule. I said yes, of course, I said yes."

Crowe had offered food, drink and beds to whoever wanted them that night and to Jenny expressly. Geoffrey had said he did not at all see why she couldn't get back to Blesford. He would fetch her. He must mind Thomas, she had said. She did not report this altercation to Alexander.

"And if I stay, if I stay tonight, will you, will we . . .?"

"Of course."

"And it will be all right?"

"Of course."

His voice sounded saccharine in his ears. He was by no means as sure as he sounded. He remembered Stephanie Potter's little gold pins and cloud of veiling. He wondered why anyone should wish to paddle with fingertips in the hollows of another body. He wanted a clean white empty room and silence. He wanted no liquor and no dancing.

"Jenny, I must go, I'm nervous about this thing, I must bugger off. I'll see you after."

"Of course," she said, with her new deliberate assurance. "After. Kiss me."

He touched her red mouth, brushed her stiff, light ruff. She looked as he had designed, tiny and birdlike in floral skirts and gauzy sleeves. What he felt could not have been nostalgia for the drawing-board, nor yet for the dummy on which the dress had been built in summer afternoons in the sewing rooms of Blesford Girls Grammar.

There was now a semi-circle of seats suspended on scaffolding on Crowe's great lawn, somewhat reminiscent of the stands that had lined the late Coronation route. Alexander did not join Lodge, Crowe and the rest. He sat on one end, high up in tree shadows, listening to Spenser and Ralegh bandying words, his own, their own, to unseen melodies in the bushes.

He remembered his first ideas. A renaissance of language, florid and rich and muscular. The untouchable complete man-woman under whalebone. A laboured metaphor, grasped too early in the writing, blood out of stone. Pure invisible colours, red and white, green and gold.

And then all the hard work towards complexity and solid incarnation, all the incorporated stuff of fact. Diplomacy, cloaks and daggers, mead, seeds, pearls, neo-Platonic mythography, muckenders, bum-rolls, verjuice and penny royal, *Polyolbion*, the *Faerie Queene*, butchery in Holland and running wet Irish bogs. Giddiness of words and things. If he wrote: "cup" – the word contained all he knew of sack, and household stuffe, Circe, *Comus*, gifts presented on royal progresses. Roses and slaughter, the red and white rose quartered in her face, funest butchery as in the case of Dr Lopez whose grimly detailed death had been so chastely curtailed and adumbrated by Benjamin Lodge.

He had known, because of his earlier play, of the limiting sense of solidity that came with the incarnation of the idea. This one was worse, as he had seen it so sharp as he wrote, in some stereopticon or inner camera obscura, bright with colour and feature. Often one gained from what actors, directors, brought to the airy spaces left in the text for them, a new vision, something undesigned and unexpected. So far, with this, this had not happened. His creatures had acquired local habitations and names: Max Baron, Marina Yeo, Thomas Poole, Edmund Wilkie, Jenny and most confusing, Frederica Potter. It was hard not to resent as brute embodiments what these actors saw as their original interpretations. Marina Yeo was given to speaking of her "creation" of a role. Maybe he had left them too little to create or render. What he had made was so dense: thick, like all good fifties verse drama, with witty imagery, which meant jostling suns and moons and swans and gossamer and flowers and stones, and again thick with the specificity of the visual imagination of a playwright who designed his own costumes, chestnut and twilight velvets, packed radiant pleats and gilded stitchery of which actuality could only be a shadowy representation.

And Lodge had worked steadily away from this fleshed complexity to the bare bones of primitive obsession: sex, dancing, death; death, dancing, sex. Lodge rewrote lines – many lines – at the behest of players who found them awkward or undignified to say. Marina Yeo was a persistent offender. Alexander knew they could be spoken, had heard them clear and flowing in the theatre of his head.

And deeper than his sense of some dilapidation of his imagined gorgeous palace ran the sense that he had meant to state his passion for the past, to provide pipes, timbrels, wild ecstasy, Tempe, and the Vale of Arcady. What they had made was not immortals stalking under Hesperidean boughs but sex in sundresses, sandwiches in gilded papier-mâché helmets, the extravagances of Edmund Wilkie's Bottle Chorus.

The Prologue passed. Lodge cut another line, one of Ralegh's, not Alexander's, about the fickleness of the chill planet. The late afternoon sun displayed the cavorting and scissor-waving in Catherine Parr's orchard. Alexander watched the satisfactory slow fluttering descent of the shredded particles of the girl's skirt onto her spread naked legs. Her body was rigid with exactly the right combination of wrath, ungiving solitude, excitement. She knew, he thought, what she was doing, all right. Her red hair was furiously unfurled on daisies and turf. Alexander felt a stab of plain, urgent desire. He told himself it was for his play, for his character. Frederica stood, laughed shrilly, barked out, "Lawks-a-mussy on me, this is none of I," roared an oath, fled. There was a spatter of applause, from which she derived considerable satisfaction.

It was only when, in the last week of rehearsal, Lodge told Frederica that he believed her performance had "come together" that she wholly took in how dubious he had been about its doing so. She had, despite bodily panic, persisted in the easy and comfortable assumption that what she did was likely, without very much effort, to be better than what anyone else could do anyway. That was true with school work. It was true with reading aloud in class, in her view, because her grammar was stronger and her vocabulary larger than anyone else's. She told herself she understood this play. And that understanding must show.

What saved her performance, however, was not understanding but unpopularity. She wasn't liked at school, but believed she didn't mind that. She didn't like her coevals. But here, amongst artists and wits and what she innocently thought of as Bohemians she had expected to come into her own. Maybe her definition of her "own" had been inadequate. The real actors laughed at and with the Bevy, rumpled them in bushes and made them little gifts. They made adoring noises and obeisances at Marina Yeo. When Frederica spoke, they looked, usually, irritated. They giggled at her devotion to Alexander, but not with her, not as they giggled communally about Anthea's crush on Thomas Poole, that sober and secretive man, pearly-crowned gleaming heads swaying together. She had no manner of addressing them, although her imaginative life had been full of sophisticated laughter, and companionable allusive jokes such as they, certainly, shared. She was saved from despair, as she was frequently to be saved in later life, by pure competitive rage, an ugly but effective emotion. They might not like her: all right, but they must admire her.

She would do it with will. She asked advice of Crowe and Wilkie. She waved her arms and legs in front of the mirror until they no longer looked statuesque, stick-like, or purely foolish. She performed grimly for some monstrous, infallible, inexorable inner Frederica. Because the part was what it was this largely worked.

It is an irony possibly worth recording, in this context, that whilst Alexander, perhaps because he had imagined an unreal and vanished world too intensely, perhaps more simply because he was already too old, his memory too long and full, his visions or hopes of glory formed some ten or twenty years before 1953 – whilst Alexander was never able in retrospect to see this high moment of his career as any kind of archetypal golden age, Frederica was easily able to do so. Again this may have been purely a function of age. At seventeen the world was all before her, unspotted, whatever it might become, whatever it was already doomed to be. Disembarrassed, in the sixties, of the awkwardness of being seventeen, a virgin, and snubbed, she was able to fill her memory theatre with a brightly solid scene which she polished and gilded as it receded, burnishing the image of Marina Yeo's genius, after Marina Yeo's slow and painful death from throat cancer, seeing the Bevy, as they developed into housewives, gym mistresses, social workers, boutique assistants, an alcoholic and another dead actress, as having been indeed golden girls, with a golden bloom still on them, seeing the lawns, the avenues, the lanterns in the branches and the light winking on half-obscured singing bottles, in the still eternal light through which we see the infinite unchanging vistas we make, from the height of one year old, out of suburban gardens or municipal parks in summer, endless grassy horizons and alleys which we always hope to revisit, rediscover, inhabit in real life, whatever that is.

The first Act ended on the tower speech. Wilkie's mimicry of her tone-deaf intonation had strengthened a suspicion she'd formed after a suggestion he'd dropped, earlier, that this play was in fact a backsliding from Alexander's true line in metaphysical puppetry, like *The Buskers*. She wondered if her speech were not dangerously pretty. She wondered how to excise the rhapsodic note from this very wordy renunciation of biology. She cut out the wheeling steps Lodge had instructed her in, stood blunt and heavy, was sardonic about the sealed fountain, gave a convulsive giggle and cut it all short. "I will not bleed." Lodge shouted crossly "Never mind", as she walked off. Alexander, who had begun by resenting her tampering with his stresses, ended by suspecting that his speech tripped too easily off the tongue, and that she was dealing with it for him. He decided to come down and reassure her.

Lodge harangued them like a football-team in the dressing-room, told them they were dragging atrociously and would be there till dawn, and asked Frederica pointedly if she'd got muscle-bound. That word always made her think abstractedly of Blake's marmoreal eidola whose long thongs, slivers and lumps of flesh were indeed precisely bindings. She said no, it had just seemed all right to her that way, did it matter? I thought I'd got you on the move, said Lodge, and you backslid. Kindly run up and down in future.

Alexander slid into the seat beside her, Alexander's Old Spice smell brushed her nostrils, Alexander's soft-modulated voice murmured no, surely not muscle-bound, but with her nerves chained up in alabaster and she a statue, or as Daphne was, root-bound, that fled Apollo. Was that how it looked, Frederica enquired, and added, there was something wrong, somewhere, there was something. He said he was afraid it was his verse. She nodded, and continued to puzzle her mind about sweetness and grammar.

Even before the embarrassment or disaster there was something frenetic and uncontrolled about Act II. People were underacting and overacting, roaring out sage counsels as though they were news of an imminent day of doom, reacting to the production of the death warrant of Mary Queen of Scots as though they had been offered a tepid cup of tea. The maskers could not co-ordinate their movements: Wilkie corpsed the Bevy by striking a posture as the Fairy Queen armed with Astraea's gilded sword, and the little boys of the anti-masque swarmed over the stage and each other like the inhabitants of a disturbed ant-hill. Alexander and Frederica sat on the scaffolding, both of them now supernumerary, and watched Lodge cuffing tiny demons or dragging the sauntering men and maidens into artistic groups, out of which they then again automatically strayed. Someone shattered a beer bottle on a stone baluster as the strains of heavenly harmony sang out raggedly for the third time. Jenny's big moment came, the swisser-swatter episode, and as Wilkie, imperturbably lively, moved in on her and began his expert fumbling, a new noise added to the sawed strings, bubbling lute, hooting bottles, muffled shrieks and giggles of Bess Throckmorton under siege. It made itself heard in the distance round the corner of the building, a rattle and squeak as of a child driving an iron hoop irregularly over gravel, a regular, rapid, marching crunch of feet. Between posed Astraea and furred Baron Verulam, driving furiously onto the terrace and excruciatingly in need of oiling, came a swaying perambulator, and behind the perambulator, Geoffrey Parry. He halted in the gold light directed on to the tiered Bevy, peered owlishly through horn-rimmed glasses for his wife in the shadows, and advanced on her, wearing, above his heathery tweed and folded flannels, an unnatural rational smile.

"I have had enough," he said pleasantly, taking Wilkie's hand and plucking it abstractedly out of Jenny's bosom. "I have done more than my share, and now enough. You can come home or take your baby. I have work to do. I am supposed to be a scholar. I will not sing Hush-a-bye baby or Ten green bottles one more time. You must come home or make other arrangements. Do I make myself clear?"

"You are making a fool of yourself," said Jenny. "I can't come, it's the dress rehearsal, it's obvious. You can't . . ."

"Oh yes I can." Rage is always partly comic. Frederica gave a snort of laughter. Several little boys giggled in the undergrowth. Geoffrey Parry stripped the blankets from the perambulator and pulled out his son Thomas, who roared. Geoffrey's face was scarlet. Thomas's face was scarlet. "He does this all the time," said Geoffrey. Thomas wriggled and howled. "Are you coming, or not?"

"Obviously not," said Jenny, staring from Crowe to Wilkie to the uninterested beautiful gaze of Anthea Warburton. She did not look at Alexander. Crowe and Wilkie were smiling broadly, with what she interpreted as male malice.

"Right," said Geoffrey, pleasantly. "O.K." He gave Thomas a little toss and then threw him, hard and neatly, across the stage at Jenny's breast, to which she clasped him, hugger-mugger, winded and staggering. Thomas fought for breath and roared more crimson. Geoffrey considered the perambulator. He considered the terrace and the cast. He gave the perambulator a fierce precise kick towards the top of the terrace steps where it teetered, rocking on its springs, before descending jerkily and falling on its side on the lawn. A bottle, several Heinz cans, a bundle of nappies and a teddy bear rolled out.

"Well, that's that," said Geoffrey. "Now I can get on with some work. You'll be better with Mummy, won't you, Tom?" he finished sweetly, viciously, in a voice no one had imagined he could muster. He walked away, into the dark of the corner of the house, and after a time they heard his car starting up.

Shrilling and twittering and booming of actors began. Jenny's breast heaved with the onset of tears. Lodge beckoned wardrobe ladies and asked them to try and take the child. Frederica said abstractedly to Alexander, "It would seem more sensible never to marry." "Yes," said Alexander, thinking that these events had brought him himself considerably nearer marriage than he had thought to be. He looked briefly at Frederica, who was watching him with intent amusement, and then, because he was a gentleman, after all, and Jenny was in pain, he uncurled

his long legs and went over to comfort her. Jenny turned fiercely on him
and sobbed out that it was all all right now, it would really be no trouble,
everybody could get back to work, Thomas knew Alexander, he would
be all right with Alexander, Alexander could hold the baby.

Alexander dandled Thomas through Act III, having offered him to
Frederica, who simply said she did not like babies, thank you. He had a
dismal sense that honour required this of him, though on the one or two
occasions when he met Thomas's furious stare he felt a compulsion to
push him under the scaffolding and take off alone in his car for Calverley
and points north. Frederica sat next to him, studying him. She was
uncharacteristically silent, which made him wonder, for the first time in
their relationship, what she was thinking. Thomas disrupted Marina
Yeo's silent dying with odd squawks and obscure liquid noises. The dark
descended: the poet Spenser had vanished to his obscure death: black,
flamboyant, and preparing for his long fall and incarceration, Wilkie
delivered his epilogue. Jenny came, then, and took the child in her arms,
where he renewed his screams of rage: Lodge began his judicial sum-
ming-up: serious drinking began. There was dancing, to bottle chorus,
gramophone and Tudor consort, on lawns and terraces. There was
kedgeree in quantities and hide and seek in the bushes. Jenny said she
had got to talk to Alexander. Frederica, realising that no one would be
giving Jenny or herself a lift back to Blesford, went to ask Crowe if she
could, after all, stay the night. Crowe said she could not only stay, but
sleep in one of the great bedchambers, if she wanted to. Wilkie turned
up at Frederica's elbow and said *do* stay, do stay and dance, do have fun.
   Some time much later that night, when Jenny had temporarily
vanished to settle Thomas in his pram, Alexander found himself walking
with Frederica and Wilkie along moonlit grassy paths in the old herb
garden. Wilkie had Frederica by the arm; their steps were silent; the
twanging and jangling sounded far away. They could smell rosemary,
and thyme, and camomile. Alexander thought he must soon turn round,
and go back to Jenny, who had a little wooden maid's-room in a high
attic. He was a little hazy with drink, but seemed to see clearly that the so
much imagined moment was upon him. He found himself wondering
about Frederica. What would she do? He remembered her hot, pink and
firelit on Crowe's lap, he took a look at Wilkie's plump body walking in
step with hers. Perhaps he ought to have returned her to Bill Potter. She
wasn't his business. Pale grey foxgloves stood up by the gate of the herb
garden: Wilkie said, if you go out here and turn sharp right down this
little alley there's a fantastic bit of scented shrubbery which might be nice
at this time of night. They followed him amongst a maze of high clipped

hedges, deeper into dark and silence. Alexander thought, it would be pleasant, more than pleasant, just to sit still here all night amongst the pungent leaves and soundless grasses. He saw a naked white foot, protruding from behind some bays and was uncertain for a moment whether it was flesh or stone. Turning the corner the three of them found themselves staring down on two interlaced and skimpily clad bodies, a pile of rumpled cloth, a glinting champagne bottle.

What Frederica took in, before she took in the rhythmic movement of white female thighs and darker white male buttocks, was the upturned face of the woman, or girl, who was Anthea Warburton. It was a face as blank with violent, mindless abandon as on stage it was blank with regular, untouchable loveliness: the blonde hair streaked black with wet under the bleaching moon, the huge eyes glittering and empty, the mouth a black, soundless cry of extreme pleasure or pain. The man's body, half-seen through a shirt, hung poised and straining, wet falling down blond hair over hidden eyes. It was Alexander who realised that this intent creature was his bland, civilised, secret friend, Thomas Poole, who lectured so quietly on the moral world of *Mansfield Park*, making meditative gestures with a stumpy tobacco-pipe, and then went home to a round happy wife and three bouncing children. He felt that it was obscene not that he, but that Frederica, should see this. He put out a hand to draw her back: when he touched that bony shoulder she winced furiously, looked at him for a moment with an expression that he could only translate as contempt or hatred, pulled away and began to run back down the alley. The sound of her departure disturbed Poole and Anthea, who drew defensively together, and looked up at the remaining spectators. Poole picked up his glasses from the grass, wiped them on his shirt-tail and stared, sternly, at Alexander. Anthea's lovely face settled slowly back into its schoolgirl softnesses. They were all silent. Alexander bowed, and withdrew. Wilkie gave a little skip and came after him. Poole and Anthea remained, sitting on the grass, naked white legs extended, shoulder against shoulder, heavy heads drooping against each other.

"I didn't know," said Wilkie, "that it had got that far, did you? I thought they were both just dreamers, quite happy to stand and stare."

Alexander had not thought at all. He was profoundly disturbed.

"Some strong enchantment," said Wilkie, dreamily. "If I'd've thought you could have got that out of that girl I'd've had a go myself. But she seemed so static. Not muscle-bound, like our vanished friend. Static and slumberous. Ah well, we all make mistakes. Don't you think you should go after Frederica? She seemed quite upset."

"She should have gone home," said Alexander with some violence. "And anyway, I'm not responsible for her. I've got other things to do."

"I suppose old Poole has lots of chances to practise on all those dreary students," said Wilkie chattily.

"Oh, Wilkie, shut up, do."

"Perhaps I'll have a go at Frederica."

"Do whatever you like, it's none of my business, just leave me alone."

"Do you mean that?"

"No. She's a baby." Anthea Warburton's face rose before his imagination. "Or else I'm getting old. She seems a baby to me. So ought you, but you don't."

"Perhaps you'd better get back to your real baby," said Wilkie, silkily. Alexander strode away. Wilkie laughed, plucked himself a sprig of rosemary and went back towards the music.

Alexander made his way up to what had been the servants' floor. Here large dormitories had been divided into a warren of little cubicles with wooden partitions and whitewashed ceilings into which, in later years, privileged students of the new University would be packed. Jenny had been allotted a little room, under the eaves on the corner of the building, near a tiny pantry with a gas-ring in which she had warmed milk, tinned Liver-and-rice Dinner, and prune and apple custard for a distracted and smeary Thomas. Thomas's detachable pram had been lugged from its wheels and rested on the floor of the room: Jenny was sitting by this, patting her son's back, in an attempt to allay his suspicions, and get him to sleep.

Alexander knocked: Jenny jerked nervously up, let him in, and hastened back to the pram, which was already convulsively heaving and jerking. A woman with a wrathful and sleepless baby is the compulsive puppet of strings of tiny sounds, rattles, scrapes, pace of breathing, the no-sound of intent listening on the part of the invisible non-sleeper. Alexander sensed none of these: he came into the little room and said, gallantly and reverberatingly, "Well, I made it."

"Sh," said Jenny.

"Something very strange happened in the garden, just now –"

"Oh do shut up," hissed Jenny, desperate, every muscle rigid. Alexander obligingly hushed, and wandered over to the window. Thomas could be heard, by Jenny, listening to every step. There was a wooden window seat under the dormer slope: Alexander sat on this and peered down through silver and black boughs into the garden. He saw people passing. Lodge and Crowe, with glowing red cigar-tips. Thomas Poole and Anthea Warburton, brushed and blonde and pristine.

"Darling –" he said.

"Sh. If I don't get him off, now, I can't, we can't . . . he won't ever settle."

"Shall I go away and come back later?" said Alexander, mildly ruffled. He had been bracing himself for passion of some kind: nervous tears or reckless abandon, he couldn't gauge which – but not for this pure, absorbed irritability. His suggestion made Jenny more irritable. She said no, if he would just be quiet a minute in a sensible way, Thomas would drop off, for certain, whereas if he kept coming in and out and banging the door like that, they might well be at it all night. She then reapplied her attention to Thomas. She had discovered that a *very* sleepy baby will sometimes capitulate if forcibly restrained from moving. But this is a nice problem, as one less sleepy can be rendered furious by the same treatment. She put pressure on Thomas's bottom and the small of his back: he stiffened and relaxed, and after a moment the tone of his breathing changed. His hot wet face went into the cot sheet: his mouth opened. She rose stiffly, and looked uncertainly at Alexander. Alexander had been keeping himself in temper by remembering the painful pleasures of his early longing for her. He remembered the moment in the wind on the car-seat at Goathland, and suddenly saw again Frederica's staring face on the glass. No, not that. He half expected her to rise on the air and put her sharp nose to this high window.

"Well," he said to Jenny, "here we are. After all."

She tried to laugh, and almost wept. She came and sat beside him on the window seat. He had meant to go out and procure a bottle of wine. He now felt he would be berated if he left the room again. So he began, in a rather matter-of-fact way, to undo Jenny's buttons. When she, reciprocally, started on his shirt, he was put out to have to stifle an impulse to push her hand away.

They reached a point when Jenny was clothed in bra and suspenders and nylon pants and Alexander still in trousers and stocking feet. Jenny pulled away from him and went to put out the bedside lamp; Alexander said, softly courteous, "I wanted to *see* you." She was crying gently. She said, "No you don't, I've gone all soft and pulled, I've got lines on me." "I want to see those, then," said Alexander, who did not. "I want to see *you*."

"Really?" said Jenny, and cast off the last clothes, pulled out her hairpins and padded back to him, swaying on naked feet. "Really, don't you mind?" "I love you," said Alexander, doggedly. She sat down again beside him, head drooping, round soft breasts falling very slightly against her body from skin less than tense, less than wholly elastic. She had little silver lines criss-crossing round the nipples and when he looked, there they were, like rippling fish, pale eels, round her belly and thighs. "I'm not very new, I'm used," said Jenny, and Alexander bent his head and brushed his lips along the silver lines with a kind of protective despair. She must be loved, he thought, she must, and he stroked her spine gently, and her still solid sun-brown knees.

"Let's go to bed," said Jenny, so Alexander stood up at last and let down his trousers and went white and long to lock the door, whilst her head spun with his casual beauty and terror lest he wake Thomas.

"How marvellous that it should be in this house, after all," said Alexander, in a preoccupied voice, coming back. Jenny, also preoccupied, said as he slid into the sheets, beside her,

"I can't stay with Geoffrey after this you know, I can't live a lie."

Alexander's penis, whose rudimentary snail-stirrings had been troubling him with their inadequacy, wilted at this into a totally quiescent rose. He lay beside her, running his fingers abstractedly along the stretch-lines in the dark of her groin. After some time she put her hand on his genitals which retreated, soft, soft, soft. She gave an inexpert little tug, and he gave some snort of protest. He said, "It somehow seems awkward with him in the room."

"And after so long," she said. "Never mind. Just keep still. I can't believe I'm here, and it's you."

He had a vision of the still herb-garden, moonlit and silent inside its clipped hedges. He had a vision of Thomas Poole's falling hair, and the wet glitter of his working body. He put a hopeful hand between Jenny's legs and she jerked with a tense pleasure that alarmed him.

"I'm sorry, Jenny."

"Don't be. It'll be all right."

"I've waited too long."

"I don't know enough," she said, acknowledging embarrassment. "Kiss me, just hold me and kiss me."

He kissed her. He moved his body hopefully against hers. He meant very well. Thomas, hearing in his sleep these desultory shifts and dispositions, twisted his tiny body with total competence and could be seen peering with large dark eyes at their nakedness, a domed head raised over the pram-side, wobbling with intent interest. He opened his mouth to wail. He shrieked. Jenny was up in a flash, and had caught him to her naked breast which he clutched with tiny plump fingers, twisting crossly where Alexander had sketched his distant concern. They sat on the bed together, and after a time, for sheer fatigue, lay down together, the hot cross tiny body clamped to Jenny's, the fat little feet somewhere on Alexander's collar-bone. "If I hold him a bit," said Jenny, "he'll go to sleep, he always does." Alexander nodded, always polite, and turned his face to the wall. It was, out of a profound desire for unconsciousness, Alexander who went to sleep first.

Frederica was in a passion. Everything in the emotional life must have a first time, and for her that year had already provided almost too many and was to provide more: family shifts, sex, art, culture, success, failure, madness, despair, the fear of death. Some of these vicarious. As well as more recondite, perdurable first things: the old voice murmuring about beginnings and ends out of the walnut cabinet, the Sunne Rising, *Troilus and Cressida*, *The Duchess of Malfi*, Racine and Rilke. How can one, in middle age, truly imagine meeting such forms for the first time? How can the young truly imagine the forms this new acquaintance will impose, limiting and extending, on the lifelong set of the mind?

Such imaginative incapacity also occurs with sex and identity. The dull, furious days of the past weeks had become Frederica's first experience of willed solitude. Mirrored Frederica had desired and admired only Frederica. Before that had been the prurient turmoil over Daniel and Stephanie. Before that again, she had wanted to know Alexander. As some women might desire unknown actors at first, and through them Benedick or Berowne or Hamlet, and through them a dead playwright. After Goathland there were indications that that kind of want was inadequate. Ed, Jenny, Crowe, Wilkie, had not let her love any Benedick or Mr Rochester. They had fleshed Alexander. Lodge, Elizabeth, and anxiety about pretty verses had unfleshed him again, perfectionism and intellectual snobbery combining against him. Now the flashing white vision of Thomas Poole and Anthea-Astraea had stirred to life that unassuaged greed. If Anthea, a schoolgirl, could . . . then Frederica, a more powerful schoolgirl, *must* . . . If the gentle Poole could be induced . . .

She did not know then, that as an ageing woman walking along a London street she could almost with certainty tell herself: I have come to the end of desire. I should like to live alone. Or that, shaken by desire at forty, she could know with a very comfortable despair that desire will always fail, and still shake. At seventeen it was virginity that was, like the grasshopper, a burden. It caused Frederica Potter to drink a good deal of red wine and two brandies and go in search of someone to relieve her of it.

Temporarily, as he took care to inform her, with what she only later recognised as courtesy, she found Wilkie.

"I can give you a little time, my dear, later I have an *appointment*."

"I wasn't looking for you."

"No, no, I know, but I will have to do, he has other things to do, just now."

Frederica gulped wine. *"Why?"* she got out.

"Isn't it obvious? A lovely woman, sympathy, a long – and hopeless – love."

"I don't see it. She doesn't *love* him."

"Not as you would? Now what you should be bothering about is whether he loves her. If you ask me does she love him as much as you would, I should say, considerably more. If you asked me, does he love her, I'd say, he's scared. Which he enjoys. He likes to be scared stiff, if you'll excuse the joke. And there you have, if you'd the wit to see it, distinctly the advantage. Because you could be naked terror. And poor dear Jenny scares him not with severity but with suburbia, the dread of our generation, the teacup, the nappy, the pelmet, the flowery stair carpet, the click of the latch of the diminutive garden-gate."

"I come from suburbia."

"You come from haunts of doiley and teacosy, I know, so do I, I've eaten crumpets with your Dad. But you're no more staying there than I am, and our Virgin Queen ought to be able to see that, poor timid thing, if he looked. Stop caring. Any woman can get any man, if she's dogged enough and doesn't love him too much. But women are daft. They won't use their heads."

"Stop it, Wilkie. I don't feel like you going cleverly on. I feel sick. Because of all this wine, and him creeping off with her, and me talking to you about love and love and love, and nothing happens."

Wilkie went Shakespearean. He asked what was love, and answered himself there was no such thing, nor honour either. He was very unsatisfactory to listen to. He must, he said, love her and leave her, he did, as he'd said, have an appointment. He told her just to make certain of her lift back to Blesford, swept her a bow, and sauntered off. It seemed inevitable, in the pattern of this garden state, that he should be replaced by Crowe, who gave her a third glass of brandy, expressed concern about the dark lines under her eyes, and asked if she would like to sleep in the Sun room, since Marina had already installed herself under the Moon.

Her head was going round with alcohol, aesthetic effort and love. She said she would go to bed, and followed Crowe, who chose to provide her with a candle in a glass and pewter holder, along dark corridors. The lighting in the Sun room, he said, was for display, not for reading in bed by. She might find a candle a comfort. Behind a carved panel in the Sun room he had a concealed dimmer switch which threw theatrical beams of light onto the terra cotta Hyacinth and Apollo on the ceiling, hazy patches of cold red in a tall gloom. The curtains were slatted blinds that kept light off the hangings. Odd knobs of plaster and gilded threads of tapestry in the candlelight showed writhings and excesses picked out from the half-dark. Crowe put the candle on a marble-topped table, turned down the coverlid with a finicking gesture and implored her not to smoke. He opened a panelled door behind which was a mahogany lavatory and a huge wash basin with brass taps.

"Inserted by my granddad. For the Assize judges, who slept here. I shall leave you to your toilette. Do you require a nightshirt?"

"No." She was half-surprised when Crowe, rapidly enough, went away.

She got into the bed in cotton pants and poplin blouse, having discarded the boned bra she wore for the play, which had dug various raw red pits in her. It was the only time she had slept, or tried to sleep, under a canopy: the spangled cressets and broidered suns hung round her head and glittered in the candlelight. Apollo, Zephyr, Hyacinth, the puddle of blood and the crimson flower were too high to be seen with any exactness and were further obscured by hangings. She discovered that the room was rising and falling at her, like waves of the sea, like Keats's long carpets on the gusty floor. She fixed her eyes on the candle, which had its own rhythm of rising and falling, the flame bellying mitred and double in the draught. The mattress rose smoothly to a central whale-backed bulge on which she could not settle. Moreover, she had no wish to be sick in this ancient bed. She sighed, wrapped her thin arms round her breast, sat up, and stared at the candle.

There was an iron creaking sound, and red light increased and wavered on the white Apollonian frieze and the peopled red desert on the ceiling. She craned out past her curtain to peer at this, but turning her head upwards made her feel ill, so she swayed back to the vertical. Crowe came through a door, lapped now in a crimson and gold brocaded dressing-gown, with scarlet embroidered velvet slippers, a fat bottle, and a platter of fruit in his hands.

"I thought you might be hungry. A dormitory feast."

He poured a glass of champagne, which she knew she must not drink, and sat down uninvited on the side of the bed. It was, after all, his bed.

"You weren't asleep?"

"No."

"And all alone. Have some grapes. You don't mind a visit? I'm sure you don't."

"I'm rather drunk," said Frederica hopefully.

"I imagined you were. It might even improve your appreciation of my lighting effects. I can do sunrise and sunset, the blaze of noon and a rather inadequate twilight, which I thought might amuse you. An indoor sun at dead of night. Shine here to us and thou art everywhere."

He skipped off the bed and operated switch-handles. The desert was flooded with gold and amber. He returned. Frederica noticed that under the robe he wore nothing. She ate a grape, then two grapes, and spat the pips into the candlestick.

"May I look at you?" He was not really asking. He took off her shirt and she sat still, stiffly upright. He turned back the covers and plucked at her pants. "Off," he said, not so nicely. She wriggled them off. Her face was stony. Crowe stared at her, throat, breasts, little hard belly, gingery thicket, long thin legs.

"Have another grape. Are you a virgin?"

"Yes." She was caught in some madness of minimal courtesy. It was his bed, his house, his initiative, his game.

"That's a nuisance."

"I can't always be," said Frederica crossly, remembering Anthea. In the abstract, virginity was a very simple nuisance.

"I could teach you a lot."

"Do I want to know?"

"Oh, I think so. I think so."

She did want to know. She wanted not to be ignorant. But his face, rubicund if sunny, surrounded with its mock-tonsure of wisps of white hair was, as it set intent, faintly ridiculous, and Frederica found it hard to tolerate the ridiculous.

"Lie down," said Crowe. She did as she was told. He stroked her from top to bottom, gently: she shut her eyes, which increased the whirling of the room, but cut out his silly shining face. He poked amongst her hairs and damp places: she remembered Ed: her body arched up of its own accord: she remembered the coherent rhythm of white bodies under dark bushes. Crowe dabbled. He bent his head and brushed her prickling skin with mouth and eyes and teeth and camel-brush lashes. Her senses flickered from unfocused desire to highly focused irritation, fast and frequently. He pulled sharply between her legs, hurting her. He kissed where he had hurt, causing such mixed local delight, total embarrassment and drunken sickness that she jerked away involuntarily like a whiplash. "Keep still," he said. He was taking his gown off. She sat up and took in his lower half, raw-specked crimson with a blue undertone, like the flesh-tints on the ceiling, and the angry red tip of his engine. He lay beside her and bit bruise-marks into her neck. All his movements were neat and fierce. He tried to pull apart her thighs, which she twisted automatically together, like roots.

"It won't hurt. It won't hurt, or not much, only a *nice* sort of pain, the sort you really like, that puts an edge on . . ."

She might have dreamily or politely or nervously allowed him to go on if he had kept silent. But the tone of "a *nice* sort of pain" made her whiplash again: one thin knee cracked up against his double chin.

"Don't jerk," he said crossly, rubbing this, but she had stopped taking orders. She wriggled away and stared with cold judgement at his white Silenus-paunch and rosy appendages on the sheets.

"I am going to the lav," she said, rolling off the whale-back and springing up like a cat.

"Of course," he said, suave again, but the honeyed voice came incongruous from that cherry-face and circling tired white flesh. Frederica stalked away, under the hectic glare of the murderous sunny desert, and locked herself with a flourish into the mahogany room. Here, sitting on the lavatory, she acknowledged herself flummoxed. She would not go out again: and could not stay there. She gathered up a large white bathtowel and tied it toga-like round her body. At that moment she heard a voice: not Crowe's: saying incongruously "Here's rosemary for remembrance" and answered by a low melodious laugh. It occurred to her that what she had taken for a cupboard door in the bathroom might well enter some adjoining apartment. Even though this seemed to be inhabited, it might provide an escape route preferable to the way back to where the fierce jolly little satyr lay sprawled, ready to bite and hurt. She tried the door, which opened. Soundless, barefoot, she stepped through.

Naked, on the high bed under Cynthia descending, arranged in a straining parody of Rodin's Baiser, were Marina Yeo and a man who, when he spoke, Frederica knew to be Wilkie.

"I brought you chamomile, my dear, as well as rosemary, and eyebright, and lemon thyme, and bergamot, to strew on your pillow."

"No rue?"

"No rue. It causes terrible allergies. We don't want to lie together covered in prickly heat and unsightly blotches."

Marina laughed again. Wilkie murmured something inaudible. The theatrical voice said, "Ah, but I am an old woman, a tired old woman, age can wither me, and has . . ."

"Age has made you more fragile and wiser, and you know it. I love old women. Truly I do. As long as they want loving."

"You are an indiscriminate young man."

"No, no. I'm very discriminating. Just insatiable. Like you. I recognised it immediately in you. Admit it."

The actress laughed in her throat. "When I am a *little* older, only a very *little* older, it won't be safe to admit that, even to myself, dear."

"But tonight – to me –"

"Ah, Wilkie," she said, with a marvellously modulated break in her voice, "love me tonight, love me –"

"You're crying real tears."

"I can produce them to order."

"You needn't cry to me. I'll be so nice to you, so very nice, all night, my most beautiful old woman, and you'll show me things I never thought of – because you're the best . . ."

"You are a cuddly, insinuating little . . ." said Marina, and chuckled, and then, to Frederica's dazed relief, the statuesque arrangement entwined itself more closely and fell back against the pillow, and speech was reduced to little questing moans and murmurs. Frederica judged that now, if ever, was the moment for her démarche. Clutching her towel she strode from door to door, past the foot of the bed, across the light through the uncurtained window. As she passed the loaded bed she turned involuntarily to have a good look at it, and found Wilkie's expressionless brown eyes staring, over the buried and twisting actress, straight at her. She nodded severely at him, in some kind of mad ritual of greeting. A grin flashed across his face – slowly, elaborately, he winked, and bent his head again to his business, as though keeping Marina's eyes closed with kisses until Frederica had got round the door.

She went quickly along the long galleries, in moonlight and dark, stopping for a moment under the iconographical representation of Elizabeth with the cornucopia. She shifted the knot in the towel over her own shoulder, which pulled like Scotland over Polyolbion's, and made a sketchy obeisance to the squat figure. She herself had no river, no cornucopia, no golden fruit. She had also better get rid of the toga. She progressed downwards, into the great kitchens, and clothed herself in some layers of the paper petticoats she used for the orchard scene, and a torn muslin blouse worn by one of the crowd. She covered this with a green stuff cloak. She considered walking barefoot back to Blesford in this gear, and decided against it. She went out into the gardens.

Rounding the terrace, she stared up at the windows of the servants' lofts. Somewhere up there Alexander was . . . She should have stayed with Crowe; if she had let him go on, she would have taken some definite step, made a purposeful move in whatever game she was playing. She was afraid of Crowe. She began to run.

She ended up in the little winter-garden with the fountain, where the nymph still smiled slyly though no water slid over her fingers or thighs. Frederica sat crosslegged on the grass, much in the attitude of the Polyolbion icon, and considered the iron-grey hedges, the moon, the water. At first she looked about aimlessly, for a long ten minutes, and then the thing formed itself as a kind of trumped-up vigil, none the less real for its deliberation, which lasted a considerable time. Dawn came up, and through gaps in the hedge edges of moorland could be seen, where night had earlier not differentiated the surrounding bowl. On the terrace someone sounded a clashing breakfast gong. On the moors, a sheep made a thin, dry bleat. Frederica stood up, still, and went back.

A huge communal breakfast had been provided for those who were able to eat: kedgeree, sausages, toast and marmalade, urns of coffee and tea. Crowe sat at the head of the table in the Great Hall, presiding, genial and dapper, with Marina Yeo at his side. Frederica, whom he ignored, did not sit down. She observed Alexander and Jenny making their way through on to the terrace, each supporting one side of Thomas's baby-carriage. Remembering what Wilkie had said, she plunged at them eagerly, driving the skeleton wheels along the gravel.

"Are you looking for these? Are you going back to Blesford? May I have a lift?"

Sleeplessness and solitude had made her clear and sharp. They were blurred and puffy with anxiety. Alexander looked sheepishly at Jenny and said he didn't exactly know: Jenny said briskly that of course that was the sensible thing, and could he concentrate on holding his end steady whilst she clipped the struts together. Frederica studied Alexander for signs of bliss. His mouth had a droop, a different slackness, but she was not prepared to ascribe it to bliss.

Wilkie, plump, sleek, smelling freshly of soap, appeared with trays of sausages and dishes of kedgeree. He winked at Frederica, and looked her up and down.

"No shoes?"

"I mislaid them."

"Maybe I could retrieve them for you."

"*No*," she said, with unnecessary violence, and saw their drowsed stare flicker with curiosity.

Alexander drove away with Frederica firmly in the back.

"I'll drop you," he said, on the outskirts of Blesford, "and then Mrs Parry and Thomas."

"Easier the other way round. I can help decant Thomas."

"We don't need help."

"I've lost my handbag as well. With my keys in it. I can't get in at this hour if I don't ring the bell. I'll be slaughtered. You'll be doing me a favour if you let me hang around."

"You seem to have lost everything, overnight."

"Yes," said Frederica, simply.

Jenny said tartly that she thought it would be *very much* better if she and Thomas were disposed of before Frederica. Alexander puzzled himself sleepily with permutations of motives for this suggestion: these ranged from hoodwinking Geoffrey into supposing Frederica an integral member of the party, to rage with himself for his erotic inadequacies (though Jenny had expressed gentle understanding of these), to jealousy and pique that he hadn't strong-mindedly got rid of Frederica at the outset. He made another weak protest and was further talked down by Jenny, who seemed to be in some irrational female mood of vengeful self-sacrifice. In the event, it was the strangely draped Frederica who helped Jenny and Thomas up the garden path, juggling ebulliently with wheels and superfluous Heinz jars. Alexander knew he should have managed to assert continuing concern over Geoffrey's probable mood, to offer refuge and consultation when they were, as they would be, needed. He was ashamed at his relief that this wasn't possible.

When Frederica came back he exerted himself to open the back door of the car for her. She got in meekly enough, and then said, "Would you mind just driving me up to the school and back, or just anywhere, while I think things out? I seem to have got rather into difficulties."

"You do," he said, more knowingly than he felt. He thought it would be injudicious to question or lecture her, though he felt some compulsion to do both. He was, in addition, not very eager to go back into his own room and start thinking out his own position. He started the car and drove off, obediently. After a few moments, in a crackling and rustling of paper skirts she began to climb over into the front seat.

"Get down."

"Why?"

"It's not safe. And I don't want you."

"Why don't you?"

She landed beside him in a tangle of arms and legs, wriggled and got upright. He drove slowly on. After a moment she put an unequivocal hand on his knee.

"Frederica, this has got to stop. You're making both of us ridiculous."

"I don't care about that."

"Well, I do."

He pulled up. They were now, by some accident of his habits, in the mouth of the old concrete drive leading to the OTC Nissen huts and the Castle Mound. From high elms came an absurdly uproarious dawn-chorus of birdsong. The terrible girl flung herself furiously on him, and clutched thin fingers tightly in the hair behind his neck. For what seemed a very long time he struggled uselessly to free himself: she was very strong. Finally he managed to break her grip, and pushed her back into her seat, holding her hands down into her lap. He was panting. She had scratched his ear, and drawn blood.

"This is not my idea. I don't want this, Frederica."

"Are you quite sure?"

"I ought to know."

"Well, I expect I've thought about it more than you have," she said, as though this explained her indubitably superior insight. He looked at her: dangling, uncombed red hair, blue-shadowed chalky face, creased bow, cross stare. She was a parody of the virgin in the garden.

"What on earth were you doing all night?"

"Various things, some nice, some nasty. Mostly nasty, I must say. I seem to have become an involuntary voyeur, among other things. I suppose I can be said to have learned something. What were you?"

"Nothing I should choose to tell you."

"No, well, none of all that's really important now. I wish I hadn't lost my clothes, though. I thought all this paper was the least like pinching things, which I couldn't bring myself to do. I mean, it's expendable. I had a very moral upbringing. About stealing and things like that. And bourgeois, of course, about losing clothes."

Alexander laughed briefly, half-excited, despite himself, at her cavalier dismissal of his unsuccessful night of passion, half-amused at her accurate deployment of the Potter morality, which might well take no cognisance of possible losses more considerable than clothes. He then said gloomily, "I feel vaguely that I ought to stop you or something. I mean, I feel responsible for your antics. God knows why."

"No, that's exactly it. You aren't responsible, not in that sense, of course not. I wouldn't have it, anyway. I'm responsible, and that's how it'll be. The only thing is, I do love you."

"O God," said Alexander. Some demon of politeness, or sense of occasion, or temporary truth, or female will drove him to add, "I suppose I love you too."

He was a man of words. Once those were said, they took hold of him. He saw with a kind of haggard horror that those were, now, true, that he had made them true. That perhaps, though unfortunately not certainly, it was only leaving them unsaid that had kept him so coolly secure from them.

"Not," he added miserably, compounding the offence, "that that's any good, or can make any difference, to either of us, you do see. It's impossible."

But she was already sitting astraddle his knees, pressing her face against his. She gripped and clutched and wriggled. He gave her a little slap on the papery folds and saw for a moment the torn scraps floating and falling on the forked creature in the summer air. His flesh was indubitably not unresponsive. She was even more impossible than Jenny had ever been.

"Stop that, you intolerable creature, keep still. I don't seduce children."

"I'm not a child. And I don't need seducing."

"You are a child to me. And you are a virgin."

Alexander's long, dismayed, gentle face spoke closer to her than she had ever imagined it would truly come.

"No, no, I'm not, I'm not," crowed Frederica, in a paroxysm of daring. After all, she thought, remembering Ed's fingers and Crowe's teeth, it was pure accident that she was still technically intact.

Alexander felt the world shift round him. "You're not?" he said, and "Oh, God," again. He kissed her, then, with some fury, tearing unintentionally at the paper skirts. It was she who pulled away, staring at him with more of a peremptory challenge than the soggy devotion he had feared. She was growing up, had grown up, fast. He felt some curiosity about the time and place of her defloration.

"In my day," he said, "we were, anyway girls of your age were more innocent. Or had less opportunity."

"This *is* your day," she retorted, adding, like the old gaffer demonstrating to Henry James that circumlocution did not coincide with circumvention, at least as far as the High Street of Windsor was concerned, "You're in it." They listened in silence together to the furious jargoning of the birds.

"And I can't do with any more complications. You're quite intelligent enough to have noticed that I've got problems as it is."

"I've thought about that, too. I've decided that that's nothing to do with me. I'm not a problem, anyway. I only want you to see me, to treat me as someone."

"I shall have to do that. But I don't think it is all you want."

"It's what I'll settle for, for now."

He fell upon her again, and rumpled her considerably. He had no idea what either of them wanted. He thought he would leave it to her. He was obscurely pleased and alarmed when she suddenly shifted her weight and fell heavily asleep, her hair spread innocently over his thighs. He held her, staring at the trees and the Nissen huts, whilst the birds sang on and on. He thought ruefully of previous meditations on the inviolable voice, as they ran up and down their simple, chattering scales.

"Damn," he said, "oh damn," and pulled at the thin shoulders to stop her slipping away from him. "Oh damn."

36. Interludes in Two Towers

Marcus walked the biology corridors, past corals and bones and fossils. Term was now over: the boys had all gone home except one or two stray foreigners. The place had lost its thick smell of grubby clothing and smelt stale and empty and disinfected. He went up and down there a lot now, under Lucas's tower. Since the drive back from Whitby, it had been unclear whether the great experiment was continuing or not – or, if it was, who was in charge of it. At the time of the drive itself Marcus had supposed he would die: crouched with his face in the leather seat, on the floor of the car, his skeleton jarring and his flesh juddering, he had dropped into dark and had been physically shocked to find himself, let alone Lucas and the vehicle, stationary and steaming in the school car-park. He had somehow tumbled out onto the gravel and lain there, curled up and still. Lucas had walked off mechanically towards the building, leaving doors gaping and not looking back at his passenger, who had after a while stood up, locked up tidily, and put Lucas's car-keys into Lucas's pigeonhole at the bottom of his spiral stair. Sunspots revolved before his face during this time. He had supposed it likely that Lucas would never again acknowledge his existence, recognising without thinking, and without previous experience, a state of sexual extremity in his friend that would make this the only possible course of action. He didn't ask whether he himself wanted to recognise Lucas, or to continue with the experiment. He considered himself committed: and responsible for Lucas. He had made that plain by putting out his hand, and more so by leaving it there. Again on the edges of thought he was aware that if he consulted his own sexual feelings they would be somewhere in the area between mild distaste and violent disgust. But this was, or should be, a matter of no importance besides the responsibility and commitment he felt, the first, the unique experience of these things in his curiously null life. He had involuntarily, nevertheless, received enough moral training to recognise these at least for what they were.

In fact Lucas had subsequently steered a lurching and veering course between acknowledging and ignoring the events of Whitby, acknowledging and ignoring the experiment and the relationship. A few days after the return, Marcus had felt compelled, he who habitually initiated nothing, to knock on Lucas's door. Lucas had called cheerily enough "Come in" but on seeing Marcus had sat in his arm-chair staring at the wall in a fixed and rigid silence until the boy had gently closed the door and stolen away again. He had not been able to find anything to say, and had understood that in any case Lucas was physically preventing himself from hearing anything.

Two days later, they had met, not entirely accidentally, in the Cloisters. Lucas had said, "Oh, hullo, it's you, is it, come up and have some crumpets," and had cooked for Marcus an archetypal schoolroom tea, which he accompanied with a smiling, avuncular discussion of Marcus's academic progress, as though his A-level candidature was the most striking, most profoundly interesting characteristic of his visitor. Twice after that, clothed in his white garments, he had walked past Marcus as though Marcus was insubstantial: on a third occasion he had said "Oh *there* you are," as though the boy had been absent, or dilatory, and had drawn him conspiratorially into the laboratory where he explained that they were certainly being watched, and indeed visited, by outsiders, beings, of whose nature and precise intent he was uncertain, but that when this was revealed the experiment would enter a new phase which he had almost resolved upon. On a fourth occasion he had proposed a drive to the field of the 1000 cairns at Fylingdales in Yorkshire, where there was bound to be a considerable concentration of radiant power. Marcus realised that he would be wholly afraid of entering that car again: and that, if he were invited, he would do so. He began to wonder if there was any action he could take with regard to Lucas, whose moods were no indication of the validity or otherwise of his theories: better men than either of them had, as Lucas had lucidly pointed out at the beginning of the enterprise, cracked under the kind of strains they were imposing on themselves. He could think of none at that time, and so began his patrolling of the corridors, to keep an eye on things, as he put it, with deliberate vagueness, to himself.

One day as he walked towards the Bilge Lab door he saw about three feet in front of him at eye level in the interior dark a burning and glowing orange-red circle, moving along, also, towards the door. The thing was solid and gave the impression of being distinctly opaque and spherical, without the obvious immaterial quality of simple after-images. Marcus blinked, and glanced away from it to the tiled floor behind him: the thing climbed down leisurely, diminishing in size, not in brightness, and followed him along the ground. He went on: the thing, being related to his eye-movements, must be some optical illusion, and yet, when he looked back for it, there it was, tracking from side to side of the corridor with what appeared to be enough independence of movement to suggest at least purposes of its own. He pushed at the swing door which was not, though it should have been, locked, and went in. The thing followed him, changing in the evening sunlight to a vivid kingfisher blue: it lay glowing on a bench for a long time, diminishing, still very slowly, in size, and then changing to a narrowing, still solid crescent. The last fine curve of it persisted for some time more, and then where it had been, Marcus saw, as it were, its shadow, perceived again circular, smoky, and finally at last clearly a function only of his own vision. Marcus had seen things before: apart from trouble with light, or Lucas's transmissions: but this thing had a perceptual difference. It was as much *there* as the jars or books it had rested beside. Hallucinations, he had thought, had always a perceptual insecurity you could locate. This didn't. It was admittedly, as far as he could tell, pointless. It was, on the other hand, immensely sensually pleasing, more almost than anything else he could think of, although orange had never been a colour he liked, seeming brash and violent: his preferred perceptions had always been in the range of lavender, blue and green. This flaming was beyond orange.

In the early days of the experiment Marcus would have been anxious to describe this thing to Lucas, in order to neutralize or incorporate it. Now he felt distinctly reluctant. The thing was as it was, and he wished simply to have seen it, not to be forced to discuss or contemplate it. It went with another recent phenomenon about which he had also more or less decided not to tell Lucas. This was a recurrent dream – only since Whitby – in which he simply was, timelessly, in the garden of mathematical forms which he had lost by attempting to describe them to his father. The garden had darkened: the sky and the measurable vegetation were a rippling mussel-blue: there were no lights in that sky and no horizon, but placed here and there in satisfactory radiating lines and clusters were the forms, cones, pyramids, spirals and aerial networks of spun paleness which were an order and a source of order. The cones and pyramids were like polished marble, it might have been said by anyone interested in similes, which Marcus was not, but they had a life, or at least an energy, contained in them which precluded any chill to the sheen. *In* this garden Marcus was not exactly: rather, he was coextensive with it, his mind its true survey. Maybe for that reason, maybe for others, he did not want Lucas, or anyone, to come into it or know of it. It was the blueness and paleness of this place which made him recognise how startling was the flaming concentration of what he automatically alluded to, in his mind, as "that indoor sun".

When he came into the laboratory he expected both to find it empty, and to find Lucas there though he could not imagine what he might be doing. He was in fact at the sinks, white-coated, sleeves rolled up, wearing onion-brown rubber gloves that gave his hands a look of mortified flesh. Marcus came on gingerly. Lucas said, without turning round, "Is anyone there?"

"It's me."

"I've been waiting for you," said Lucas in an accusing voice as though this meeting was pre-arranged and Marcus was late for it.

"I'm sorry."

"I'm trying to put my house in order. Before anything happens."

Marcus took a few steps forward. There was a strong smell of formalin, with an undertone of sickly sweetness. Lucas was transferring handfuls of dead batrachians from a basin to a tall jar: the dull mottled flesh slithered and flapped. In another basin floated various severed parts and undulating pale internal organs. A case of dissecting instruments was open on the bench beside him. Lucas gave Marcus a friendly patronising grin, pointed at the dish and said with determined jocularity, "If you were superstitious enough to want to read the future from these entrails you'd find it pretty thin and grey, I'm afraid. Do you have any idea why people in the old days ever thought entrails were a particularly good guide to events in the outside world? Did they think chickens and goats were microcosms? You might read your own future from your own entrails if you could get at them, and make a lot of sense, but of course you can't. Or from your genes and chromosomes which can't be revealed with the crude machinery at our disposal."

"No," said Marcus, cautiously. He snuffed the dead smell. Lucas meditatively tried the edge of his little triangular knife on the ball of his rubbery thumb. He gestured at a whitely coiling jar of worms.

"As for them, their insides are too simple and similar for augury. The lowly worm. The lowly necessary worm. I'm collecting them up for the Lower IV. Worms have many uses, of which being dissected by the Lower IV is not the most important. Still, there are a great many worms on the surface of the earth, and I do want to leave everything in good order before . . ."

"Before what?" said Marcus, daring and troubled.

"Before what is going to happen. Something will happen shortly. There have been indubitable signs already. I'll tell you about them. For instance I knew you would come today."

This may well have been true, but the gleaming authority with which he had invested his earlier declarations that things were prefigured seemed to be lacking. Lucas looked grey, the bright curls limp, the brows and chin clammy and glistening. Marcus wanted to walk out again, and knew he must not.

"Will you come upstairs? We must now be prepared for any eventuality, good or evil. I've had signs that I've let forces in – that there is conflict – in the outer spheres possibly – my fault, my failure – a *fault* in the coherent surface – from which great gains or great losses could issue.

Please come up. You must be in possession of the facts, in case –
before –"

Marcus said he would come up. Lucas rubbed his squeaking palms
together and slopped another handful of small corpses into his jar.
Marcus stared round, remembering the day the light had driven him
here, the beginning. He looked at heaped bones and bottled embryonic
forms, and then across at the hanging images of Man and Woman.
Something about these was odd. Marcus realised that small patches had
been sliced very precisely from each body where the genitals had been
depicted, including, in the case of the interior views, the internal organs
of reproduction, the seminal vesicles, fallopian tubes, the whole frilled,
winding or bulging apparatus. As far as he could see these the resulting
apertures were exact squares, windows on a blank, unsunned, unfaded
wall. He looked across at Lucas, not doubting for a moment that this
trimming was his work. Lucas was now rolling up the cloth case of
dissecting instruments, which he popped into his white pocket. He
shelved his damp jars. He beckoned to Marcus.

In Lucas's tower room Marcus stood awkwardly in the door whilst
Lucas investigated, at random, cushions and curtain rails, remarking
darkly that wires were always on the cards now, it had been done before,
he had certainly been wired before, and it was only sensible to be on the
lookout. There had been incredibly fine work with wires on that
destroyer in the Pacific. Had Marcus thought about the paradox implicit
even in that simple factual phrase, the destroyer in the Pacific? The ocean
was pacific and the man-made vessel, even if it said it was on a peace-
keeping mission, was a destroyer. Lately he had had a series of encounters, indeed near-collisions, with a curious van which was labelled
Sun Ray Blinds Whitby and was certainly a sign. It had a curious symbol
on its side, a sphere divided by a wavy line, which was a crude attempt
at the Yin and the Yang, the ocean of light moving above the ocean of
darkness. Some of that light they had concentrated at Whitby with the
burning-glass and blood and wine, no question, but he was inclined to
think that then they had not gone far enough, not offered enough, and
that later they had been punished for this by his own failure of tact, or
taste. Marcus must be aware that tact or taste were curious ambivalent
words too, Marcus must have wondered why these sensual words were
applied to matters of judgments which often bore no relation to sensuality. The terrible anthropomorphic universe again. To be avoided at all
costs. Possibly one way was to crash out of it with sexual magic or rites
he should have said but that was accompanied with such dangers, and
deceptions and dubious advantages . . . where was he? Oh yes, the van,
the van. It jumped at him out of side roads or stood across his path in

Blesford. It was driven by a creature who was clearly not of this world, a demon in angelic form, with a leathery sort of skin and a mop of clearly unreal golden curls on its head. It grinned and grinned but also sometimes threatened distinctly, and made various beckoning or exorcising gestures, also unfortunately ambivalent, which he, Lucas, found hard to read. And there had been a milk-bottle full of blood he had found outside the lab, which certainly had some meaning, had been put there by some visitant for some reason. And there were the watchers. Faces, for instance, at these windows, yes these, so high up this tower, staring in, taking their time, grinning and grinning, making sure he knew he was under surveillance. If you drew the curtains they were to be seen mopping and mowing at the foot of the stairs. And the breathing. You would hear breathing in the room, as though the tower stood near the lung-tip of the universe, if it were anthropomorphic, which of course it was not.

All this was delivered in what Marcus could only think of as a threatening manner, accompanied by punctuating blows on Lucas's desk surface for heavy emphasis. Marcus felt accused of provoking or manipulating these manifestations himself. He said to himself, in his mind: he is mad. This was terrifying, not because he was afraid that Lucas-as-madman would act dangerously, or damage him, but because of what it did to the pattern of preceding events. He, Marcus, had been afraid he was mad: had been offered a reasoned explanation of the phenomena that tormented him by the super-sane Lucas: had shared with Lucas experiences, the transmission of images for instance, which suggested that they were at least on the same wavelength (oh those wires), and working with mental events mostly unacknowledged. If Lucas was mad, he, Marcus, was on his own with the things which had initially been almost too much for him, the geometry of water in plug-holes, the terror of staircases, the spreading, the fields of light. If Lucas was not quite mad, then it was at least a tenable hypothesis that they had aroused angry outside forces of some indeterminate nature. Marcus had always felt an abstract scepticism about the names and histories Lucas chose to ascribe to things seen or sensed; even if this masked, to some extent, a readiness to be credulous because he had no names and histories of his own. Angels or demons these were not, precisely; they were experienced as cones and winds and spirals of light, as magnetism and heart-hammer. It didn't mean they weren't there.

And, if Lucas was mad, he was responsible. Responsible that was, for Lucas, because he had agreed to be his friend. And responsible perhaps also for the events that had led to the madness, what with his photisms and hypnagogic vision.

"What are you going to do, Sir?" he asked, neutrally, respectfully. Lucas dropped into the arm-chair at one side of the fire.

"I called you up," he said, producing another effortless *double-entendre*, "I called you up, because I have a very important communication to share with you."

"Thank you."

Lucas sat in brooding silence, apparently attempting to recollect what the communication had been. He slapped his hands vigorously on his thighs, and cried out,

"We should have been more extreme."

Then, in another voice, he said, "Do you know, there are men in the prisons, a great many men in His Majesty's, or I should now say Her Majesty's, prisons, some of whom, in my view, can't strictly be called criminals, although many certainly can, old men who expose themselves, flash out from behind bushes at silly little girls, or abuse, on commons and open land, what they'd do better to hide – a great many such men, who beg, who cry out, for hormones or even more drastic treatment, for surgical interference, and are denied. They would not have been in all times and cultures. Frazer tells a lot about the priests of the old gods, Adonis and Thammaz and Atthis, which makes it sufficiently clear that they cut themselves voluntarily and joyfully . . . If fasting and celibacy and austerity produce new and different knowledge, why not the knife, I sometimes think, though that is not what I called you up to say."

Marcus could smell fear, rank over sportsclothes and cocoa in the close little room. He said, "Maybe we should just give up. Maybe this is too much for us."

"I shouldn't like to think that. All good things are dangerous. I think we should follow the signs, the leadings we have, even into disaster, if necessary."

Marcus waited politely to be told where the leadings led.

"On Fylingdales Moor, as I told you, there are over 1000 small stone cairns. Over 1000. One of the things I've found out in my reading is that the very early gods – and goddesses, Aphrodite for instance – were just pillars or cairns or cones of stone. I think that was a system of calling down power, a field of force, of terminals. They are – ah – *touchstones*," he said, smiling with a touch of his ancient brightness over this last revelatory *double-entendre*. "We should go there. I suppose the dark forces will have it ringed. We could be burned to a cinder. But if not, we could go there."

"How?" Marcus breathed.

"I'll drive you. In a day or week or two. We need to purge ourselves – eat no blood and nothing after sundown – to make our bodies less accessible to the eaters, to the bloody-minded. I expect it will become quite clear when we must go. I expect you will see that, if I don't. Won't you?"

Marcus nodded, painfully. He looked at the window, but no faces stared in, only sunlight. He looked at Lucas, whose hands were weaving his flannel lap. He remembered his secret garden of forms and felt pure rage that Lucas should have connected gods and electricity to cairns or cones of stone. The connection impressed him, of course; but not enough for him to share what he had no doubt was his own knowledge, sure and certain, that their thoughts had again overlaid each other, that each in his method, or system of signs, had seen what the other had seen. Lucas was a fumbler, there was no doubt of it, mucking up the purity, the cleanness of what he, Marcus, knew, with all this *stuff* about ancient gods and demons and bodies, human or hydra. And Lucas was dangerous: demons or no demons, it was to Marcus clear that if they got in that car together again and anything happened, they were likely to end up dead. He did not have to specify what kind of "thing" had to "happen" – sexual, religious or mathematical, its end would be the same, cinders, whether caused by demonic intervention, burning petrol, or light from heaven centred by some metaphysical burning glass on them. He also knew that although he would not tell Lucas about the mathematical Forms and their return he would, if asked or commanded, get into that car, whatever forebodings he might feel. He owed him that. He owed his perspicuity that, whatever filtered through sweaty smells and buzzing wires of guardians on destroyers. He thought he must now, at last, speak to someone else, and made a decision.

In the other tower Alexander sat at his desk on which he had laid out the *Times Educational Supplement* and a pile of application forms he had acquired. An application form is neither a passport to another place or another way of life, nor is it an examination paper: it has a reassuringly vacant, routine appearance, like the census, or an opinion poll. He could fill in details of his qualifications and views for the BBC, in London or Manchester, for an ancient school or a modern training college, strong on drama, without overstepping the threshold of imagining or desiring any of these places. He knew, indeed, he would be foolish to come to any decisions about his life until the play was opened and closed, as Crowe said. This knowledge simply helped to make the forms appear neutral, and papery. He remembered, as a man with a hangover might, the events of the night and the early morning, winced, and drew the BBC forms towards him. Wedderburn, he wrote. Alexander Miles Michael. A peculiarly resonant and militant array of names for one as passive as he was, he had always thought them, and he considered the anomaly again as he filled the little boxes, date of birth, places of education, parentage, nationality and publications, conducting a retreat with his only weapon, the pen, and hoping that it was a strategic withdrawal and not a rout. Maybe only a feint was necessary. He did not have to send these things off. Perhaps it would be enough, for the time being, to assure himself of the possibility.

He considered his own erotic oddities and embarrassments. What he liked, he believed, was nearer what most men liked than they would be prepared to admit. He liked the imaginary relish. He liked imagined contact with real women, and real contact with imaginary women. He liked his delicious solitude, certainly, and intended to let no one invade it. But also – and this was odder, if still not *very* odd, surely – he liked fear. Not excessive fear. He had no fantasies of ripping flesh, piercing heels or whirling knouts and could not, even by the usual process of extending the fantasies he did have, reach any real imaginative apprehension of what it might be like to desire these things. But the ripple of apprehension, the prickle of hairs on the skin, the sense of panic flight through crashing undergrowth and under whipping foliage, the alertness of scent and sight bestowed by a flicker of real fear, this he repeatedly provoked. Embarrassment and humiliation afforded him no joy and so his relationships had been transitory, since he terminated them when embarrassment and humiliation supervened, which they always did. But he liked, his desires were most immediately stirred by, minatory and ferocious women, when they were angry. He had never, even as a very little boy, had any trouble with Keats's line about "When thy mistress some rich anger shows". This recondite pleasure seemed to him entirely natural.

So far, so good. He had fallen in love with Jennifer because she had admonished him, indeed, knocked him down, in the music-hole during *The Lady's Not for Burning.* He had taken his customary pleasure in appeasing her wrath and converting its energies to those of desire. He was still afraid of her, it was true, but he had realised, when his flesh had retreated before her need, and she had been so understanding and so gentle, that the fear had changed its nature. He was afraid now of her love, not her wrath, of Thomas and being shut in a house, not of any savage and unsubdued quality in the woman. Whereas in the case of Frederica Potter some roughly antithetical process had taken place. He had found her attachment to him humiliating and embarrassing, had been afraid of its stifling domestic implications, had seen her as some childish nuisance, dragging Bill's suburban proprieties behind her.

He had no exact idea when this had changed. Partly, it had changed through the princess in the play, who represented his desire for fear of

344   THE VIRGIN IN THE GARDEN

minatory women, but also, being a self-portrait, shared it, and not only
it, but his own secretly acknowledged delicious solitude, which was both
escape, energy and power. She knew how to be stony, did that girl, how
to display fear and rage and grace. He was afraid of her knowledge. He
was afraid of her. When she had clutched and scratched at him, he had
been most happily afraid. He looked at the submissive, lovely lines of the
white marble back of the Danaïde, on his chimney-breast, and began to
fill the forms in, rather fast. He had no intention of becoming any further
embroiled with Bill Potter or his family. Or, he realised more sadly, with
Geoffrey and Thomas Parry and the rifts in their household. He would,
when his play was over, pack all these things, stone, harlequins, books,
in his trunk, and drive away, to Weymouth and points south. He would
leave, for Jennifer, a very large potted plant – he thought about it – a bay
tree in a wooden tub, a white rose out of Nicholas Hilliard, and some
book or other, some appropriate book, not *The Ocean to Cynthia* of which
anyway there was no decent edition, but some book he would think of.
As for the terrible girl, he would count himself lucky and she would
trouble his dreams – but there was advantage in that – she would forget,
very quickly, because of her energies, which were restless and incessant,
she would scrabble at someone else's hair. He would not, because of her,
keep in touch with Bill, but he would keep in touch with Crowe, he
would maybe even visit, after a decent interval, before Long Royston
was handed over to the academics.

He filled in the rest of the BBC script department form and embarked
on the BBC educational programmes form. His handwriting calmed him.
It was a little like Elizabeth's own elegant and businesslike Italic.
Running footsteps sounded on the stairway. His door was unceremoniously pushed open. He imagined an apparition of Frederica-as-huntress
and had the ludicrous idea that a man was cornered in the top of a tower,
as though egress would have been more possible from a room situated
somewhere else. This caused him to smile to himself, in a way which
seemed to annoy his visitor, who was, in fact, Jennifer.

"I had to see you," said Jennifer. "There is only you."

"Should you be here?" said Alexander, weakly. He had always
managed to stop women from visiting his room. This was one way in
which he, and his reputation at least for discretion, had survived so long.

"Everyone has gone demented. And I should have thought this, and
everything else, was so public by now that it hardly arose whether I
should be here or not."

"I suppose not," said Alexander, equally weakly. He began to shuffle
scripts over his application forms. Jennifer took off, and threw down,
her macintosh and headsquare.

"It's all right when I see you," she said, "it all falls into place again. Honestly, you can't imagine what it's like in that house. I wish you wouldn't grin conspiratorially to yourself. Nothing's funny. Geoffrey's smashed a lot of things, the dinner service, the Spode, imagine it, *Geoffrey*, who never hurt anything or noticed anyone or anything, or I shouldn't have . . . or maybe I shouldn't . . . anyway. And he won't speak, except to Thomas, and he addresses Thomas in an awful false mournful voice. I wouldn't have thought him *capable* of it, honestly."

"Was it wise to come out?"

"What *do* you mean? I can't stay in, not with things like that. I can't. I had to see you. Though you don't seem overjoyed to see me."

"I can't be overjoyed when you are so alarmed. I get alarmed myself."

She was silent for a few moments, striding up and down and rearranging things, the Wedgwood bowls with their fleeing forms and forest boughs, the stone cairn. She breathed in, dramatically.

"I'm all right here. See, I'm all right, now. What were you doing?"

She came over and sat on the arm of his chair. He curved a sad arm round her bottom. She scrutinised his papers, a habit he disliked in anyone, and pulled out the end of the application form.

"Alexander Miles Michael. How lovely, what lovely names. What are you doing? Alexander, *what are you doing?* You aren't getting another job."

"Only thinking about it."

She pulled, with customary efficiency, at the stack of papers and uncovered the remaining forms.

"Five other jobs. You must be desperate, even if only in your thoughts."

"Well," he said carefully, "there does seem to be some sort of crisis. At least in my thoughts. Doesn't there?"

"You must have sent for these long before last night."

"There was a crisis long before last night."

"Because of me."

"And Thomas," said Alexander, truthfully. The fact of Thomas alarmed him genuinely.

"Thomas? Thomas. Were you going to leave us?"

"I was only thinking."

"You could take us. I'd come. I love you. You could really go, and we'd come, and start again, properly."

"Jenny, my dear . . ."

"You wouldn't leave me?"

"No, no. I wasn't going. I love you, Jenny."

"But you *could* go, and take us, it would change everything, it'd be truthful, and open, and hopeful . . ."

"What about Thomas?"

"He *loves* you. He's little. He'd come."

"Jenny. If I were Thomas, I'd, I mean, he has his own life."

"I could leave Thomas. That is, I don't want to, I don't want to leave Thomas, but what is there left for him or me as things are?"

"A lot, maybe. How can we know, just now, as things are now? Jenny, love, let's get through this play. It means a lot to me. And you are so good in it, if you will try to be – even if I've ruined things, at least partly . . ."

"No, don't say that. *You* haven't. Between you and me things are all right, we're *all right*, my darling, I came to prove that."

"What?"

"It would have been all right for you without Thomas. What you've just said makes me quite sure about that. I knew you'd brood, I knew you'd suffer, I came because I *know*, if we try now it will be all right, we owe ourselves that."

"Jenny – this is a boys' school – my room – in the middle of the morning."

"You can't be pernickety about *everything*. I should have overridden you long ago. It isn't as though that usually happened to you." Sharply. "Is it?"

"No," he said truthfully.

"Well, then." Her skirt slid to the ground. She kicked out a leg and unfastened her suspenders. She was naked beside his desk, naked under the Danaïde, naked in his narrow bachelor bed. He undressed, politely, without haste, and climbed in. He could not. If he could have done, he would have, he told himself grimly, not to prolong the embarrassment, to get it over, now. But he could not. He turned his face to the wall. Jenny, crimson to the curve of her breasts, suddenly collapsed into noisy weeping. Alexander was appalled by her pain and humiliation. He picked her up and cradled her in his arms, murmuring, "Don't take on, ah, don't," wondering, even then, where he had got an idiom like that, northern and not his own, and tracking it down wryly a few moments later to Lady Chatterley's lover. Jenny went on and on crying, accelerating in speed and sound. He sensed that she found it the only possible thing to do, did not know what to say, or how to touch him.

"Don't take on, love, it's only not the moment, we are both so jangled and have had no sleep and I feel nervous here, now . . . It's really of no significance, it will be all right, when . . ."

"When. *When?* Oh, I meant so well, and have made it so much worse, blundering in, displaying myself, all cocky . . ."

"An unfortunate word."

"Alexander, don't laugh."

"Why not? What else can we do? You had better laugh, too. For now. I assure you, it will be all right . . ."

"*When?*"

"When we have decent time and space."

"Then you will take us, me, away."

"I don't know. I can't think."

"Honestly. I can't see how you can honestly mean anything else."

"Well, in that case," said Alexander, placatory, "I must mean that, mustn't I?"

She smiled a watery smile and began to cry again, more quietly. He held her. She stroked his persistently limp member, and his flanks, in a nervous manner, as though he might explode, or recoil. He was patient. She said, "You are so white, you are so lovely, you have such an untouched, unused look, I love to see you."

"Well, you can do that," he said, and something in his voice must have alarmed or embarrassed her for she sprang up and began to dress again, hastily. He dressed himself, before she could change her mind, and saw her out, before she could offer to stay. He even made himself appear deliberately more hangdog than he felt. For the time being he was quite happy to have ascribed to him a psychic anguish he didn't feel. It seemed to put her in a tolerant and uncertain frame of mind that was the best he could decently hope for.

He went back, feeling hot and a little sticky, to his forms, and filled out another one. This took ten minutes or so, after which he again heard running feet on the stair, and the door was again pushed open. He assumed it was Jenny come back for something forgotten or some further urgent admonition. This time it was Frederica.

"I had to see you," said Frederica, "there is only you."

His blood raced. "I can't say the same," he said, "unfortunately."

"No, I know," she said, "I've been lurking. In the tomatoes. Luckily I had a book. And it's quite sunny out there. So I dozed in the tomatoes and read little bits of this book. Tomatoes have a terrible smell, they smell like powdered hot metal and something else, maybe sulphur, is it, it's a smell that *comes at* you and attacks your metabolism, or that's what I think, this morning, having had no sleep and feeling kind of scraped and over-sensitive to everything. But the sun was as nice as the tomatoes were sinister, and I'm a bit better read than I was when I set out, for what that's worth."

"What are you better read in?"

"Well, I'm having another go at *Women in Love*. I was suddenly afraid I might be Gudrun. I mean, I saw the house as an awful trap, like the red-brick Brangwen house in that book, and Daddy was really beastly to me, and I thought of how Steph and I used to talk about you, and thought Steph was Ursula, and then I got really put out because that only left Gudrun, and I don't want to have to be her."

"You could always read someone else."

"True. True. I love Lawrence and I hate him, I believe him and I reject him totally, all at the same time all the time. It's wearing. Maybe it was just the title. I mean, I wanted to read a book called that. What else shall I read then? You give me something, something different."

"What do you like best?"

"Best of all, at the moment, I like Racine."

He thought about Racine and about *Women in Love*, and about Frederica Potter, and could make only one connection.

"Vénus toute entière à sa proie attachée."

"No, not *that*, the awful balance of the ineluctable. Let me tell you my clever thought about the Alexandrine, which I couldn't get in my A level script, or hardly, because the questions were so circumscribed. I'm *breaking* with knowledge about Racine I shall never tell anyone, and after a time I shan't know it. That's terrible."

"You will," he said. "Tell me about the Alexandrine."

He was a good teacher, not, like Bill, because he charismatically communicated passion and a sense of importance, but because he could listen, he could ask the next question, he could hear a train of thought. He made a space of time in which Frederica could tell him about the Alexandrine. He sat, with the warmth of Jenny's crimsoned flesh fading from his arms and belly, and looked at this girl, who had always roared and rumbled at him, vacillating between the Lawrentian hyperbolic and the Just William bathetic, and she told him, cleanly and neatly, quoting at length and with increasing calm and order, about the structure of one Alexandrine, and then two, and then strings of them, from *Mithridate* to *Athalie*, from *Britannicus*'s heavy ironies to the flame in the blood in *Phèdre*. She sat neatly and on a hard chair, and he thought she had a good ear, a very good ear, and then remembered she was a muscle-bound actress, and smiled to himself, at which she said, as though she had heard his thought,

"I love it because it's all so chill and precise on the page, it's so *lucid*, and yet I can't imagine it being acted without extravagant gestures and a kind of roaring noise that would quite ruin its symmetry. I can't imagine anyone acting it who didn't just stand still and occasionally sweep an arm up and down, or drop his head in his hands. Do you think so?"

"That seems right."

"I love you."

It followed so naturally, the whole explanation had been a love-offering, so made and so received, he reflected.

"I love you," he said, as simply as he could, wanting her somehow to know that her cautious and tentative, then fluent and abstract and impassioned words had moved him as another woman, rosy and naked in his hearth, had not. The inviolable voice with a vengeance. No, not that, only how rare it was to offer anyone a thought. He had always been told she was very clever and taken it on trust: she had told him so herself often enough.

"I love you because you are very clever," he elaborated, to show her that he now knew it.

"I love you because you can write."

"Are those good reasons?"

"Well, novels would say not. People in novels don't love each other because they can both see that Racine is – is what he is. Like maths, really, only I can't do maths, I was going to say sensual but it *isn't*, or at least, the sensual pleasure is geometry, not sex. Actually, I don't know much about sex, I shouldn't talk. What was I saying? Oh yes, if we were in a novel it would be most suspect and doomed to sit here drily discussing metre."

"If we were in a novel they'd cut this dialogue because of artifice. You can have sex, in a novel, but not Racine's metre, however impassioned you may be about it. Pound said poetry was a sort of inspired mathematics, which gives one equations not for abstract triangles and spheres but for human emotions. Wordsworth said metre and sex were all functions of the flow of the blood, you know, and the 'grand elementary principle of pleasure in which we live and move and have our being'. We can hear each other's blood running, Frederica, in a sort of inspired mathematics, in incantations precise and arcane."

"How lovely."

"Yes. I shall give you a book that isn't *Women in Love*. I shall give you my messy Everyman *Silver Poets of the 16th Century* because it's got the *Ocean to Cynthia* in it, printed all wrong and spelt very oddly, but you must read that ebb and flow."

"I shall always keep it," she said, mocking and serious, parodic and truthful. They sat and stared at each other.

"People in Lawrence's novels," she began again, "love each other because of their unspeakable selves, their loins of darkness and starlike separateness and all that. They hector and gabble but they don't *talk*, though he does, Lawrence does. He loved language, he lied in a way when he indicated all those values 'beyond' or 'under' it. I like language, why can't one love in language. Racine's people speak the unspeakable. That's odd, I was going to say he had a very *small* language, but so did Lawrence, of that kind, and both of them indicate forms of what isn't speech, and yet one is as clear and precise and formal about what it isn't as the other is yelping and muttering and . . . oh, I don't know. I do love the bit with the rings, and the venison pasty, and the rabbit, I think. One reason I like Racine so much is that Daddy doesn't. He doesn't understand French. I think he thinks it's chilly and immoral. Perhaps I'll read French and German. He can't do his cultural value-judgements so well on what isn't English.

"I'm sorry, Alexander, I'm so drunk with you, and not sleeping, and now seeing you, and having this talk, I can't shut up, I run on, I don't imagine one can be happy for more than a day or two at a time, so I feel I must make the most of it."

"You say Bill was beastly. What exactly happened?"

"He said I was a messy slut," said Frederica with considerable verbal satisfaction, "and he bashed me, and he tore a lot of those paper skirts, which I said weren't my property. I said I didn't like his language as well, and that my affairs were my own, and he said not if he knew it, and I hit him. With a proper fist, clenched, in his eye. It's all swollen up. He sent me to bed, so I went, and dozed a bit, and then when I heard him going to the lav I got out and ran here."

"That can't be a true account."

"Well, no. It's tidied up, and presents me in a flattering and resourceful light, and it's considerably abridged, for which you ought to be very grateful. It was a pretty mucky episode. Nothing was said about you, if that's bothering you."

"It was, a little."

"Don't let it. His mind works slowly, he's still so busy resenting Daniel that I truly think he only minds him, and my having got dirty and lost some property he'd paid for. I told him I'd get it back."

"Did that comfort him?"

"He didn't believe me."

"I can't, I can't get in a mess with him, and your family and you at your age. It's like seducing pupils, Frederica. It isn't done."

"Isn't it? That's not what Wilkie says. I should have thought – I don't know, the High School's no paradigm of anything, it's dead-and-alive, *I* should have thought it was a primary instinct, subverting that relationship. A *possible* variant of the Oedipus thing, I mean, not actually forbidden in any primeval way, only school rules, which we all know are there to be broken. I wish I *was* your pupil. We could have a lovely time. Like Eloise and Abelard."

"I don't call that a lovely time."

"Ah, that was their day, as we were saying. This is our day. We're in it. Even my daddy doesn't wield a butcher's knife."

"You are horribly reassuring."

"Well, I've got to say something. And it's true." She stood up, and came and sat where Jennifer had sat on his chair arm. Her eye flickered over the application forms. If they meant anything to her she gave no sign of it. She touched his hair and needles ran through his veins.

"Won't you make love to me?"

"I don't know if I can. It seems dishonest. To various people. Including you. And me, I think."

"I can see that. I think it doesn't matter. Between you and me, here and now."

Here and now, at seventeen, was what she was, he said to himself. She had no real life yet, stretching before and after, pulling at her with old causes and effects, duties and sapping failures. She was pristine – well, almost. And for that reason, his intellect told him, vulnerable. What he did to her, or didn't do, could change all her life. She didn't *look* as though that was true, his body observed, his common sense endorsed. She looked tough and self-contained and simply eager to be doing.

"Hold me, anyway."

"It isn't that I don't *want* you."

"No. Just scruples. All right. There's lots of time. Just hold me a little. Without obligation."

He lifted her down into his swelling lap, and held her. They sat very still. In the forest of his mind the undergrowth crashed furiously; he was in a car rushing down a steep slope, careering out of control. He screamed shrilly and silently, in his head, with vertiginous pleasure like the child he had been on the Big Dipper, and the relentless literary tic-tac told him, not out of his childhood but sighing in German accent out of *The Waste Land*, to hold on tight, there were no clean or private phrases, but it didn't matter, there were no doubt no private or star-separate schoolgirls to hold on your knee, if the truth were known. And *Lolita* still unwritten. He held on, tight. She barked with wild laughter. If she had urged him on, he could and would have taken her. But she did not. She was afraid of possible bloodshed, in fact, and of being discovered in a lie, and was rapidly calculating that some more extended, leisurely, uninterrupted occasion would certainly do better. Also, if she respected his scruples, she thought, they would, like most scruples, come to seem a nuisance to him, in time. If you respect a scruple for a day or

two, Frederica informed herself wisely, you get to feel you've done your
duty to it, and to hope circumstances, or necessity, will remove it. Also,
she had her own reluctance. Racine was one thing, but the claws and
beak of Matthew Crowe, and further back the plucking fat fingers of Ed
were another. She didn't want to rise in revolt against the impossible,
the achieved Alexander. Not when, she thought, caressing his lovely
winged shoulder-blades under his shirt, she had come so unexpectedly
far.

Alexander's final visitor knocked. When he was asked in, his version of
the initiating sentence was also more tentative. He said, "I'm afraid I had
to come to see you. There was only you I could think of to ask, you see."
    Alexander very rarely thought of Marcus when he was not, as now,
confronted with him. Since the Ophelia he had concluded there was
something "wrong with" the boy, which he had ascribed easily and
glibly to the obtrusive difficulties of his parentage and social position.
His sense of this was complicated by the fact that he still called up this
boy's face and voice when he thought of Ophelia, and worse still,
Ophelia immediately came to mind when he saw the boy, blank, straw-
pale, bony and fragile. When he did think about Marcus, as he rapidly
tried to do now, he decided that their few meetings had all consisted of
choked attempts by Marcus to tell him, or show him, something. He
wanted to discourage this, out of an English feeling that endemic
hysteria was best kept at bay, out of a personal disquiet about meddling
in spheres of influence so directly ruled over by Bill Potter. This materiali-
sation of Bill's son, desperately polite, breathing fear, was in some way a
judgment on him for what Bill would certainly have seen as "interference" with Bill's daughter.
    "Sit down," he said nervously.
    Marcus sat on the uncomfortable edge of a hard chair, and stared
round. He took in the room, pale clear harlequin walls, the harlequin
poster for the Buskers, the Picasso acrobats in their pink-grey desert, the
Boy with his roses, the glossy Danaïde, the stone cairn below it. He
liked the concatenation of the ovoids of alabaster and the irregular dark
glossy and chalky rounds and planes of the chalk and flints; he liked the
lines of both these against the rounds and rectangles of the Danaïde's
white haunches and black limits. The place had some proper balance
between space and bodies in space. It made him, temporarily, feel safer.
    He too remembered Ophelia. He averted his eyes from the dangerous
Boy because of his heavy garland. The *Hamlet* episode had made
Alexander a possible if not an ideal confidant or confessor simply
because he had then been the Director, and had been accustomed to

direct Marcus's doings and movements. Indeed he had possibly allowed Lucas to behave as he did because he had got used to the idea of a Director of some kind. Nobody else, except his father, had taken the trouble to tell him how to behave.

Marcus's silent mapping took time, during which Alexander became more nervous.

"Won't you tell me why you're here?"

Marcus jumped.

"I don't know where to start. It won't sound sensible. That is, it will sound mad. I think it is mad. Probably, anyway. Almost certainly."

"What is mad? Or who is?"

"Sir, the thing is, the real thing, I am afraid of what may happen to Mr Simmonds. I am afraid of what he may do."

Alexander had given almost no thought to Lucas Simmonds, whose normality was unremarkable, even banal, whose staffroom conversation was a carefully achieved flow of corporate trivia. Alexander called to mind that smiling face. That look of cricket and the healthy outdoors. A second-rank character from a detective novel by a lady writer, sound in dress and opinion. Not obtrusive enough for Wodehouse. Not talked about in his absence.

"Sir, he says there are watchers at his window. He says, sir, he is wired. I mean, him and his room, electronically. I think he is going to drive that car too fast."

Marcus had decided to attempt a minimum of the most credible facts, simply to attract attention to his friend's plight. He looked up hopefully. Alexander's elegant brow was creased profoundly in puzzlement. He added more facts.

"He says his mind was destroyed by some destroyers on a destroyer. Also bits of his biomorphic equipment possibly, he says. He saw a milk-bottle full of blood. He has cut holes with scissors in the pictures of Man and Woman in the Bilge Lab. I think he has cut up some frogs."

"That's his job."

"It depends how."

Alexander tried to think. His mind was, or had been, running on women's bodies, on recesses of flesh and the singing of blood and mind. Milk-bottles and frogs dubiously cut up were beyond his competence.

"Well, what do you deduce from all this?"

"Sir, I don't know. He thinks I know things I don't. I don't understand as much as he thinks I do."

"How do you come to be expected to understand at all?"

"Sir, he's my friend."

This was a truthful, desperate and generous answer. It was also devious, in that it avoided certain things Marcus did not think he could bring himself to talk about, if he could get away without it, those queer competences of his own on account of which friendship had been required, and bestowed. Alexander took it as devious in another sense. "Friend" was not an entirely innocent word in Blesford Ride School. Indeed, it was a word best avoided, in cases of simple friendship. Alexander had never heard of "friends" being attributed to either Marcus Potter or Lucas Simmonds. But there was a lot he did not hear. Alexander stared at the boy, whose white face round his glasses bore a certain resemblance to his sister's chalky pallor, but whose eyes and hair and expression had a vanishing colourlessness. He glanced involuntarily at the insolent Boy, so very different, on the wall, and shuddered delicately. If Frederica was not a frangible virgin this creature surely was, and the unfortunate Simmonds had been playing with fire, with something unstable and explosive. A wash of irrelevant sympathy for his hypothetical Simmonds flowed over him. Boys were terrible. He asked, in a more threatening way than he meant, "Why do you want to come and tell me about all that?"

"I said, sir, because I'm afraid of what might happen. I mean, we nearly got killed, both of us, last time."

"Last time?"

"Last time we went out – on a – well, on a sort of trip together, we did, he called them field-trips, sort of days out – with a purpose – I don't want to talk about that, I – he really nearly killed us, driving back. He says speed's out of the body."

Marcus was no good with words. His dull voice failed entirely to convey the horror of that vertiginous career over moor and hillside. Indeed, his tone could be read, and was disastrously read, as querulous.

"So you feel the relationship is now too dangerous?"

"Well, no, or rather, yes, it is, but that wasn't what I came about. I'm afraid of what he may *do*."

"I'm still very unclear about what he has actually done," said Alexander, delicate, faintly hostile. "Tell me."

Marcus tried. He found it hard. He couldn't say, when it came to it, the words God, or religious, or light, and though he managed in a circumlocutory manner to speak of the "experiment", and of minor aspects of it, like hypnagogic imagery, the curious result of his bowdlerisation to protect the unspeakable was that the account he did offer was very much more one of a "personal relationship" than he meant it to be. Alexander listened for clues. The skills and dangers of being a good confidant are closely allied. Both consist of hearing what is said and listening at the same time for what is not said, of appearing to have understood something with a host of probable meanings, so that the flow of confidence will not diminish and the confider will in the end offer the one lucidly separate meaning. Alexander was usually a good confidant, partly because he was a reluctant and lazy one, which meant that he avoided the danger of treating other people's confidences as his private property. He should also have been a good confidant because he had a cool, professional dramatic interest in the unfolding of stories, but this was weak in him: he preferred stories old, intricate and finished. But in this case he listened badly. He had had no sleep and was flustered by sex and Jenny and Frederica. He heard Marcus's fumbling words and patterned them. Marcus talked about "the thing" and "the affair" in order not to name names, and Alexander slotted these words into available patterning places. Marcus talked about "interference" meaning geometry, radio waves, or disturbing Lucas's concentration, and Alexander read the murmurs biologically and deduced that Marcus had been interfered with. He began to ask Marcus more direct questions about what Lucas had "done to" him. He would in many ways rather not have known, but felt it to be his distasteful duty to let Marcus speak, if Marcus would, which he was doing, but so obliquely that the going was appallingly heavy. Marcus was now murmuring something incomprehensible about Hell Mouth. It was clear to Alexander that both man and boy were riddled with Calvinist guilt. He tried the direct approach.

"But how much physical contact was there?"

Marcus began to explain that there was none, a general truth even if not entirely exact, remembered Whitby and became incandescent.

"You are ashamed," said Alexander.

"Well, he was," said Marcus. "That isn't the important bit."

"One always wants to think that the important bit isn't really what it is," said Alexander kindly. He felt an irrational irritation with this pale boy, an irrational conviction that he had led the unfortunate Simmonds on, into agonies of frustration and impotent conscience.

Marcus, for his part, began to feel that this conversation was taking on an uncanny similarity to the conversation when Lucas had become aggressive, Germanic and interrogatory about whether he played with himself. He said, angrily for him,

"It wasn't sex. I mean. It wasn't. Not . . ." He had tears in his pale eyes and blood coursing in flat skeins under his thin-skinned face and neck.

"I know you need badly to say that, you feel damaged and corrupted by this experience, that's apparent. I can see you are holding certain things back, things you haven't said, can't bring yourself to say . . ."

"Not *those* things."

"Of course not. If you say not. I don't want to pry."

"You don't understand."

"How can I understand what you do not say? I think I have a fair inkling, though, of the general dimensions of the affair. I take it you now find it too much for you – because you are repelled or disgusted, because your friend is behaving in a funny way –"

"That isn't the point. I'm afraid of what he may *do*."

"What could he do?"

Marcus cast about. He had failed entirely to make Alexander imagine Lucas. He said slowly, "He says we have to go to the field of the 1000 cairns at Fylingdales Moor. I know if we go we'll be killed. I know."

Five or six long tears ran slowly down the expressionless face.

"I shouldn't think you will," said Alexander, heartily for Alexander. "But in any case, there's a simple answer. You mustn't go. You must simply tell him that the thing's at an end–that you feel it is all potentially dangerous and destructive. As you do." He did not think it possible, or proper, to lecture Marcus Potter on the motor car as a symbol of sexual potency, although his literary mind was constructing a series of powerful images of fear of destructive energies, Simmonds's and Potter's.

"He needs me."

"He can't *really* need anyone he's distressing as much as he's distressing you. People are surprisingly resilient. It's no good thinking yourself indispensable – almost none of us are, we only need to think so. If you can't look after yourself, Marcus Potter, you can't look after anyone."

Glib, this last lot, some of it untrue, but it was what people needed and wanted to hear, was it not? One could not say it to oneself, but ah, to others, there was a certain virtue, a certain innocence –

"But what will he *do*?"

"Someone must speak to him. I'll try to see about that. Is that what you came for? And you must go home, and tell your father *something* – as little as possible – get sent on a holiday. Stay with an aunt."

"I have no aunts. It isn't a good idea to talk to my father."

Alexander might have offered. But how can you say to a man, "Someone is messing around with your 16-year-old son," when your own hand is hardly out of his 17-year-old daughter's skirts, your own nose still aware of her hot, dry skin?

"I only want an *eye* on him."

"I'll keep an eye."

"Really?"

"Really."

He would ask him about cricket in hall. He would bump into him accidentally in the cloisters. He would make sure. He added, "Just forget, just put the burden off your mind."

It was easy, he thought, for some.

37. The First Night

Whatever Alexander might, on reflection, have decided to do about his three visitors was pre-empted, to some extent, by the opening of his play, which fell on that same early August evening. When he had earlier and frequently foresuffered this occasion he had concentrated on the success or failure of the work. He had not, as Stephanie had not when imagining an abstract Wedding, considered the distractions of flesh, conscience and simple social inconvenience which would then torment him – although it might be argued that he should have known, who had prophesied with uncanny accuracy to Jenny in their days in the dirty goldengrove on Castle Mound, just how much of a saturnalia any such prolonged work was likely to become. As he took his seat on the elevated half-moon of steel and boards he was preoccupied with how much that was private was about to become public, from his arcane knowledge of the Virgin Queen, to his attempt on florid verse, to his sins of omission and commission over the last few days. Now, of course, as the audience climbed and creaked more or less orderly onto the scaffold, the actors were no longer interested in his views. There was this composite, impersonal creature to please, placate, win over.

All traces of the previous night's misrule had been swept away by men with brooms, baskets and spiked staves. The terrace gravel was smooth and raked, with no glint of broken glass. The lawns were mown and enamelled. Laurel, yew and high pines had been clipped where clambering boys had left dangling twigs and broken branches: the soft, opaque rounds of Hesperidean light were strung orderly among them, ready to glow when dark thickened. Palanquins, wheeled turrets, thrones and battlements were ranged behind the house. The consort whistled and scraped invisible in the sunken garden. This first audience was massive, and differently composed from others there would be. Local dignitaries in golden chains of office, the Bishop in gaiters and purple vest, flanked by rural deans, the already designated Vice-Chancellor and Faculty Deans of the university to be, the men from the Treasury and the Arts Council, the local Viscount and his showjumping daughters, industrialists and the Press. There were local ladies who had stitched and collected bangles, the friends and relations of the cast, some people who had simply bought tickets. In the penultimate category was Geoffrey Parry, who had brought his son Thomas, alleging that it wasn't possible to find a baby-sitter for a child in so strung-up a state, and the Potter family. Amongst the genuine members of the audience were Lucas Simmonds, whose presence was unforeseen and undesired by the two people who might have felt any interest in it, and Ed, the traveller in dolls.

Charabancs had set out from various points and were converging on Long Royston. You could buy tickets for *Astraea or the Virgin Queen* which included the coach fare from Calverley, Scarborough, Durham or York. You could buy holidays at a chain of hotels in northern resorts, or village pubs, which included a performance of the play, with optional transport from Manchester, Edinburgh, Birmingham and London. Crowe was in some ways as good a businessman as his great-grandfather. The success of this enterprise made him wonder if he wouldn't have done better out of Cultural Trips and Events than out of giving Long Royston to the University. But if he was enterprising he was only intermittently energetic and had no wish to expend much of that energy on tourism. The coaches rolled into an inner courtyard, where they deposited their passengers, who could purchase tea and buns, or beer, or gin, at the Buttery, before wandering along walks and grassy alleys to the wooden half-O.

It was at this put-down place that Frederica, blanching, observed Ed, making his way plump down the steps, staring proprietorially around. She shivered. She saw Ed as a kind of de Flores or Banquo's ghost, a walking misdeed who would rise up to humiliate her. She drew back from the kitchen window and bumped into Wilkie, who said, "Seen something nasty?"

"A man I know. Well, sort of."

Ed pottered towards the Buttery.

"Come to watch you perform?"

"Good God no, he doesn't know I'm me, I mean, he doesn't know I'm in it."

Wilkie stroked her. He stroked everybody. It was not easy to be offended. "How's the passion for the Virgin Queen?"

Before Wilkie, Frederica had been innocent of that use of the word queen, and innocent of such thoughts about Alexander. But her first instinct, characteristically, had been not to appear naive or slow on the uptake. So she said knowledgeably that she didn't think that was quite the right way of putting it, that she *positively* knew that wasn't so, in fact.

"Aha," said Wilkie.

"Aha," said Frederica, torn between the desire to keep her dealings with Alexander quiet, and the desire to make them quite real for herself by discussing them. Like Alexander, she was a verbal creature: like the Bevy, she would have liked, if people had liked her well enough to talk to her, to gossip and tell tales of experience and triumph.

"You took my advice."

"In a manner of speaking."

"And now you're all glowing."

"Well, sort of."

"I'm *dying* of curiosity, my dear."

"I can't talk . . ."

"Of course." Wilkie's attention was deflected. "Look, Frederica. Harold Hobson. Ivor Brown. Carsful of critics. Transfigure your life overnight, if you're lucky. And mine. And his too, of course. Do you in your heart of hearts think it's a *good* play, darling?"

Frederica caught an intonation she didn't like, equivocated, played for time.

"Do you?" she said.

"I think there's a pretty fair chance it'll be a raving success. I don't think all this verse drama thing will really catch on, in the end, though. It's like the Coronation gewgaws and the awful garments of the ladies-in-waiting, a kind of no-style harking back, without the sharpness of parody."

"That was the point, he said. Real modern verse, *not* parody, *not* doctrinaire modern realism."

"Very laudable. Do you think he's done it?"

"Do you?"

"You're remarkably evasive, for a hectoring bluestocking. But I don't suppose I'll wreck your performance if I say no, I don't. Avoiding parody means he's been left with involuntary echoes – softy slurry – of things old and not so old, the filleted orthodoxy, Eliot and Fry, no blood, no bones, no guts."

"That's not fair. But it's a recognisable description."

"Good girl. Furthermore, he's not resolved the old Post-romantic problem of how to make the interior monologue dramatic. It's as static as hell – like Eliot, like Fry. Nothing happens. And when you come to think of it, that's a monstrous negative achievement, because by any account, plenty did. *Because* of the nineteenth-century failures I think verse is a lost hope. You could do it in prose like Brecht or a sort of grand guignol eloquent pastiche. But verse and psychological realism – the worst possible combination – both are *out*."

"You can't say anything's *out*, just like that. A form is as good as the writer who chooses it."

"I must not believe you. How old are you? Seventeen. Come and tell me, when you find that some forms are historically possible and some aren't. When you decide to be a lady novelist, and get set to write a long novel by Proust out of George Eliot, and it won't get up and walk, its words decay and real people turn out to be hectic puppets."

"I won't be a lady novelist."

"Congratulations."

"Perhaps you could do it like Racine –"

Wilkie did not answer this. Frederica suspected him of not having read Racine – he was not omniscient – and of being, like herself, someone who would not admit ignorance. She respected that, in a way. She respected Wilkie's iconoclastic asperity, partly because it was a tone of the times, recognisably modern, but partly also because he did seem to care about precise definitions of real thoughts. All the same, she walked away. If she was to say Alexander's speeches, it was no help to brood about slurry echoes. Judgment was not the matter in hand. It was curious that she didn't feel – as she certainly didn't – that Wilkie was either making, or inducing her to make, any personal attack on Alexander. What he said had a fashionable bitchy note, but he was not a bitch.

Alexander observed the critics. They had on the whole agreed kindly to see potential in *The Buskers*. They came more massed and apparent to *Astraea* because they had transported themselves in self-administered cohorts. He then saw the Potters. Bill had for some reason sent tickets to Daniel and Stephanie and instructed them that the family would all attend. Alexander, who had decided that it would be intolerable to sit this through next to Lodge, or even the wardrobe mistress, was alone in a high corner. He realised that the chain of Potters was ascending vertically towards him. Daniel, cumbrous and rapid, reached him first. The planking swayed under his weight. Trailing last, Marcus looked up, cast his eyes down and stumbled, earning a growl from Bill, who was wearing an open-necked flannel shirt. Alexander, like much of this audience, was in a dinner jacket.

"Do you mind us?" said Daniel.

"No. No."

"You might. You might want to be on your own. Not that I've got power to shift this bunch."

"You could sit down and be a bulwark."

"Aye. I'll put my wife between us, though, and keep them off her."

Stephanie sat down next to Alexander. The rosy poplin was tight across her breasts. She was wrapped in a green silk shawl, with a trailing

fringe. She had insisted that no one at all should know about the baby,
since Bill would roar, Winifred fuss, and everyone, especially Frederica,
would conclude it had been conceived out of wedlock. This was hard on
Daniel, who was obsessively interested in every small bodily change,
and would naturally have been loudly solicitous. Alexander considered
her with affection.

"Are you all right?"

"If I don't get vertigo."

"You won't, once it starts."

"If you do," said Daniel, "we'll move. Maybe we should move
anyway."

"No, hush. I'm all right."

Marcus looked straw-green, as though the mention of vertigo had set
him off. Alexander saw below them the little row of Blesford Ride
masters, all in dinner jackets, some with wives. The Thones, Geoffrey
Parry dandling Thomas, Lucas Simmonds, with a scrubbed face, newly
washed fluffy curls, and an expression of benignant ordinariness. Not
having heard his views either on the theatre or on Renaissance anthropocentricity Alexander did not share Marcus's alarm at his presence.
Indeed he found his doggedly cheery expression reassuring after Bill's
glare and Daniel's concealed turbulence.

The music struck up. Like a giant flock of birds settling for the night the
audience rattled, clattered, preened, smoothed and was still on its
multiple perch. Thomas Poole and Edmund Wilkie sauntered in, one
from each end of the terrace, met, handclasped and began to speak.
Gently they parodied the aesthetic Shepherds and looked back to the
mellow Ovidian age of gold. Wilkie was an actor who was never exactly
good until the performance was under way. Now it was apparent that he
was going to be very good: wry, affectionate, sad, witty, explosive.
Alexander sat back with a sigh.

Stephanie had not come expecting much. She felt perpetually queasy
now: her world seemed narrowed to her own biology. She observed her
own actions with a lazy, impersonal curiosity. She noticed, for instance,
that she had trouble to conclude a sentence, written, spoken, or simply
thought. The moment she had even a hazily shaped idea of what she
meant to say, or might have said, that seemed enough, and she let the
words trail away into blank and silence. Today her thoughts hadn't got
as far as a real play and herself watching it. She had solved practical
problems, to do with getting there on time and providing a suitably
shapeless overgarment. She had scanned emotional problems: Daniel's
solicitude, Bill's likely quarrel with Daniel and devastating assessment of

Alexander's work, the need to give Frederica moral support. She had not precisely conceived sitting through the action of a real imagined play.

She was thus startled by its density and energy as she might not have been if she had come with preconceptions, or sharp to criticise. She was not a judging nature: she took in *Astraea* with the complete scanning attention she gave to childhood trays of guessing-objects, poems, and now Daniel. She had a feeling that she occasionally had with certain "fortunate" works of art that what was before her was getting away with, realising, what should by the laws of art then obtaining, have been impossible. Alexander's play contained the possibility of being a thing of shreds and patches, a robe of verbal tatting, a pageant limp with sensibility where it should have been harsh with political necessity. Later all these things were to be said. But Stephanie saw what Alexander and Lodge had meant people to see.

She saw the young Elizabeth sit white and stump-like outside Traitor's Gate and refuse to go in: she saw the dying Elizabeth sit white and stump-like in a nightgown on a cushion placed felicitously on the identical patch of terrace and refuse to lie down and die. She saw the intervening white vision of Astraea and the palely fluttering Graces weave circles under dark eternal forest boughs and golden fruits of light. She saw patterns and broken patterns: Ralegh superbly spinning terrestrial and celestial globes in sunlit audience with a youngish queen: Ralegh incarcerated in the Epilogue, spinning the same globes in his dark tower. Catherine Parr offered apples to the young girl in the orchard, Virgo-Astraea in courtly masque offered golden apples to painted Gloriana, Robert Cecil coaxed the old queen to mumble just a small bite. She saw the symmetry of the girl spreadeagled on the grass in the warm sun, and the old woman laid out in the gathered dark as the ladies-in-waiting pulled the folds of her nightgown, after her death-struggle, into marmoreal flutings, and in the sunken garden the rebec mourned reedily. She noticed that the tableau revealed when the actors assembled for the curtain call with the young Princess staring at the statuesque old Queen on her plinth, and Astraea conjuring her into movement with her sword, was a muted parody of the resurrection of Hermione in *A Winter's Tale*. She said as much, in her drowsed voice, to Alexander, who was pleased, who pointed out that he had been playing with themes of rebirth and renaissance and the Last Plays all through, though Lodge had intended Botticelli's Primavera, and Stephanie said yes, she had seen, it worked, there was a weight of language . . . her voice fell away. He touched her hand in gratitude.

"Frederica was marvellous," she said.

"I thought so."

"Well everyone was. But I thought she rose to the occasion more than . . ."

"Yes, she did. She does."

"The audience has gone mad."

"It does seem to have." He said, "Will you come backstage? To see Frederica? I must get out and go down there."

The audience was rhythmically stamping and tossing. The Bottle Chorus had assembled invisibly and was irrepressibly and not quite accurately bubbling out the Music of the Spheres, to which part of the audience was singing, like a football crowd, like a heavenly choir, in a Hollywood Spectacular or Milton's empyrean. Alexander escorted Stephanie around the bowing and chanting multitude to the pandemonium of the dressing rooms. He was carried along by waves of sound, and wanted to touch Frederica. Visions beset him of glimpsed thighs, delicately bony wrists.

Frederica was staring into the mirror, greasing her skin. Her face shone, with grease, with tears, with heat, with passion. He looked over her shoulder and into her eyes.

"I've brought Stephanie. I can't stop. I must see Marina."

"I know."

She stared unblinking, the moppet of wool motionless in her hand, the black eyes glittering.

"O God, Frederica. I'll talk to you later. There are things I've got to do. I can't concentrate."

"Of course. I'll lurk. I'm a good lurker. You know that."

Stephanie came up. If the currents of sexual rage singed her she gave no sign of it, merely fumbled peacefully inside the green shawl.

"You were marvellous, Frederica. I never stopped to remember it was you."

"That's praise." Frederica turned wickedly to Alexander. "And you. After all the trouble I've been, did you stop to think I was me? Did you notice *me*?"

"In some ways, not at all. In others, all the time." He bent down to kiss her in an ostentatiously casual way. His knees knocked.

"Go and talk to the old Queen, go on, you can always come and talk to me."

Frederica was learning fast. There is a tic-tac, in the early stages of passion, griping constrictions and furious energies, which can, with most agreeable pain, be controlled and exacerbated by, for instance, dismissing the beloved before he leaves voluntarily. He walked away through a congratulating throng towards the old actress. Frederica turned hectically to Stephanie.

"He loves me."

"Yes. I see. Of course. He does."

She folded her hands round her thick waist in her green fringes and considered. The two sisters watched Jenny put out a hand from her dressing-stool and speak urgently to Alexander, who leaned over to kiss her, too, with a gracefully anxious stoop. He took her clutching hand from his dress-shirt front and laid it gently on the crimsoning skin between her ruff and stomacher. Jenny grasped his hand and held it there, over hers. Frederica stared, assessing, and then began to brush the curls out of her piled-up hair.

"What will happen?" said Stephanie, standing in the middle of an electric field of charge and countercharge. "You can't crash down whole lives."

"I can. I will. I'm free to do what I choose."

"You can't. You're an official child."

"You know I'm not a child. I want . . . I want, I want, I want."

"I want you to be happy."

"There are more ways of being happy than living in a council flat and making pots of tea for old bags. Anyway, happy isn't the point. The point is, it's *real*, it's alive, it's happened."

"Frederica, people will get hurt."

"That's their look-out."

"You will get hurt."

"And if I do, I can stand that."

Alexander peered over Marina Yeo's shoulder, into the black mirror between white bulbs. She too was greasy, wiping away death-pallor and blue-black hooded eyes, as well as some, if not all, of the furrows which mapped her brow and jawline.

"Isn't it bad luck," she asked, "to *loom* in people's looking-glasses, from behind?"

"I haven't heard that one. I only came to say you were a miracle."

"Well, don't pat your own eyebrows, Narcissus, get out of my light. I've got eyes in my head, and I can see that the mirror on the wall doesn't tell you that I'm the fairest of them all. Does it? The mortal moon hath her eclipse endured. Mind now, dear boy, whilst I see if these lines are fixed or scrubbable. So you were satisfied, were you?"

"I was thrilled and enchanted and so moved – you made the end magic."

"You're no good at the compliments."

"Well, if you know that, you know when I mean what I say."

She laughed, and stretched her soft kid-leather mouth this way and that.

"She was right not to want a mirror. Can you say that Kipling poem, Alexander darling?"

" 'Backwards and forwards and sideways did she pass,
Making up her mind to face the cruel looking glass'

That one?"

"Something like. Ah well, it's only a property, at my age, a face. Not yourself, you know. My face is my fortune, my living, but not me. Now go away, and when I've put a new one on, for the press, you can come and take my arm. I think we shall do all right. It was a good enough crowd, didn't you think?"

"It loved you." He kissed her hand, bowed to the haggard face in the glass and got himself out.

Upstairs in the Great Hall public and actors and everyone else were milling around. Alexander proceeded in brief, much-complimented stages towards Crowe and Lodge. He saw Geoffrey and Thomas and veered away from them, grateful to find himself pushed up against Thomas Poole who was, from grease paint or fatigue or lack of oxygen, rather grey under the spotlights cast up over his head onto the nymphs of Diana and their stiff burden.

"Thomas. Thank you. So *very* good."

"Congratulations, on a success. I've been talking to the local press and the chap from the *Manchester Guardian* and they're wildly enthusiastic. Listen – you're my friend – I've *got* to talk to you. About what you saw the other evening."

"Don't think about it. I saw nothing."

"Hell, no, you saw. I don't mind. Or anyway, I don't mind much. I just can't think . . . I can't go on. Alexander – I must tell someone. I am most horribly in love with this – this *child* – and . . ."

"Are you sure you want to tell me?"

Thomas stood, square, blond-headed, mild, and said, "If you don't mind."

"Is it not just a midsummer night's dream?"

"I don't know that I ever even thought it could be that. In any case, it can't now. The thing is, she is, she is pregnant. She thinks. I don't know how I can live without her, but I have got sense to see she can and should live without me – I mean, look at her, I'm not anyone, just a second-rate teacher of teachers, whilst she . . . in a year or two . . . now, I can make her happy or could . . . And then this."

"Thomas . . . what do you want me to do?"

"I don't know. Nothing. Listen. You're discreet, and reasonably wise.

I had to say it, to see if I could stand up and say it in an ordinary voice. I see I can. Did you see her, down there? I daren't go near her."

"She was lovely in the play."

"Virgo-Astraea. She wasn't, you know. Wasn't a virgin. I wouldn't have touched her, but she told me – made it clear – that she knew what she was doing. Used to fuck her cousin madly in copses and barns when they were supposed to be hunting, she says."

"And Elinor . . ." Elinor was Thomas Poole's wife.

"She's here, somewhere. I must shut up, go find her. I suppose I should find a doctor. It's not the sort of problem I've ever . . . Elinor. For the last three years we've had a bedful of kids more often than not, the great bed of Ware, and I'm not complaining about that, I love it, I love them, Elinor and all my little things – you should see them. Only this is. This is. This is so much *worse*, Alexander, that I can hardly realise they exist, most of the time. I'm sane enough to know it can't last, not like this – but that's absolutely as far as my famous level head will get me. God, that girl – she has me doing things I'd've thought were puerile and degrading – lying about getting the car repaired, inventing examiners' meetings, touching her up on the top of country buses. Things I couldn't bring myself to say out loud – that *are* puerile and degrading. And lovely. I know you've got problems of your own – do you have trouble with your dignity? I'm not being pompous, I need my dignity. Partly that was what she liked about me. Now I'm an incompetent panting loon.

"I suppose I ought to go and get a doctor, oughtn't I? But I can't stand the thought – I mean, that's my child, that would be – and she's only a kid herself, in that school with its clean little portico and portress, like a nunnery."

Alexander was prevented from replying to this entirely uncharacteristic outburst, by Marcus Potter, who came up with his look of staring absence more than usually pronounced. He opened and closed his mouth silently at Alexander, who felt that Fate was screwing him down with an excessive number of ludicrous parallels and analogies.

"Speak up, boy," he said almost nastily to Marcus, whilst trying to reply to Thomas Poole's desperate stare with a look of deprecating, useless understanding.

"Sir, I'm sorry. Sir, please come."

"What is it now?"

"Sir, my father has got into a quarrel with the Bishop. A horrible quarrel, that is, a quarrel about horrible things. And he – Mr Simmonds, sir – is there too, and seems to think – well, seems to be very excited and think they're particularly going on about him. I'm afraid."

"If you think I am going willingly to interpose in any quarrel between your father and the Bishop . . ." Alexander began, adding peevishly, "tonight of all nights . . ."

Huge tears stood brimming in Marcus Potter's pale eyes. Thomas Poole, a gentle man, said, "Never mind, Marcus, I was harassing Mr Wedderburn with my own less urgent problems. Just as unforgivable, in the middle of his triumph. Come on, Alexander, you can afford to be magnanimous and even you must see the immediate need to separate Bill Potter and the Bishop."

He nudged Alexander, who saw, over Marcus's shoulder, the fretful face of small Thomas Parry in his father's arms.

"Ah," said Geoffrey, with heavy meaning. "There's Alexander. Come on, Thomas, you *like* Alexander. I'm told you like Alexander very much indeed. Wave to Alexander."

Alexander strolled hastily off with Marcus. Thomas Poole said in a rapid undertone, "Just as well, you see. Not that I don't feel dreadfully for poor old Parry, make no mistake. Why can't we all live quietly? You're a lucky man, you have no ties. Make none. Poor old Parry. Women are so ruthless. What a banal thing to say. I don't mean Elinor, of course. For Christ's sake, Alexander, stop me talking."

The Bishop, the Ellenbys, the Ortons, the Potters, Miss Wells and several minor clergy were gathered towards one end of the Hall, holding glasses of champagne and shouting. By the time Marcus brought Alexander there they were shouting quite loudly about a concatenation of matters loosely ranging from pain through dismemberment, execution, crucifixion, disembowelling, regeneration and back to pain. Also present were Lucas Simmonds, who was also shouting, and Edmund Wilkie who was not, but was proffering a great deal of psycho-somatic information about pain-thresholds and the body-image to those capable of taking it in. As Alexander came tentatively nearer, Bill Potter seemed to be declaring in a barely controlled scream that the Bishop was a bloody butcher, the Bishop, flushed wine-coloured, but lucid, was apparently lecturing Lucas Simmonds on the necessity of suffering, and Simmonds was wringing his hands round and round and making agitated remarks about excising corruption. Wilkie was still clothed in the black velvet of his Tower vigil although he had resumed his roseate goggles: Felicity Wells was stiff in her grass-green train, bum-roll, ruff and farthingale. Frederica was not there, but Stephanie was, drooping heavily graceful and pensive next to Daniel, like the early Venus of the Primavera.

The conversation had not begun in this way. Miss Wells had tugged

THE VIRGIN IN THE GARDEN

Stephanie along with the Ellenbys to meet the dear Bishop. The Bishop, a tall, saturnine, handsomish man with a flow of white-flecked black hair, a trim figure and an intelligent look, had complimented Stephanie on what he had heard of her excellent work with Youth, Young Wives, the housebound and disabled. Stephanie, who had made a considered decision to help Daniel flat out in those areas of his work where no doctrinal conflict could be said to arise, would, in fact, have accepted this compliment gracefully had her father not been skipping from side to side behind her like a flyweight boxer preparing to land a body-blow on the smooth, very slightly convex purple silk front of the Bishop.

The Bishop, seeing Bill, had attempted, spreading automatically flowing oil on the choppy waters, to make a few observations about this flowering of their common cultural heritage, the sense of true communion imparted by the rising-up of all the folk, as exemplified by churches, schools and Bill's excellent adult education classes, in this sustained, jointly achieved work of art. Bill had said that the Bishop could speak for himself. For his own part, he had no faith that much of our culture, including, he might say, the Church, either could or should be revivified. Let them lie down and die decently, *he* said, he said. And moreover he was afraid he had to make it clear that he had certainly no faith in this sort of play, which he went on to categorise as nostalgia for something that never was, a *charming*, airy dream of a time which was in fact nasty, brutish, and bloody. A despotic police state, controlled by spies, torturers and executioners, whom he noticed we hadn't been shown. It was in this way that what Marcus had so accurately categorised as a "horrible argument" had been embarked upon.

Miss Wells had shrilled nervously that the hanging, drawing and quartering of Dr Lopez had in fact been reported, if briefly: Wilkie had volunteered that the original description, very gruesome, had been cut; the martyrdom of Campion had been touched on; Lucas Simmonds had asked, with a disproportionate intensity, whether pain and suffering were qualitatively different in those harsher days, either for men to watch or men to undergo. One of those curious compulsive conversations about what man is capable of doing to man had at this point erupted: the Bishop had called to witness the slaughtered saints of Foxe's *Book of Martyrs* and Bonhoeffer's concentration camp: Lucas Simmonds had recounted some tales of what he had been told, when on a Destroyer in the Pacific, the Japanese did to recalcitrant p.o.w.s. Wilkie remarked that useful work had been done on the relation between where a man felt pain and where the stimulus was applied: also on the reaction which, when the whole body is filled with pain, makes a man able to detach his consciousness, stand outside his body and watch the pain take its course. Lucas was very interested in this and pressed Wilkie for more information about the psychological machinery that made such things possible. The Bishop, at this point, remarked that there were things worse than pain and the fear of pain, death and the fear of death. There were ignorance and evil. He himself had been chaplain at Bentham Gaol some years ago and had always refused to allow those of what he referred to as "his" prisoners who were hanged to go to the drop with their minds clouded or stupefied by morphine, lest they should lose the real chance, face to face with extremity, of repentance or conversion. He was, indeed, on these grounds, in favour of the retention of capital punishment.

It was at this point that Bill Potter had begun to roar. He had called the Bishop bloody, arrogant and perverted. Marcus went to fetch Alexander. The Bishop, bland, wine-dark, and hard, continued to listen and to convey the belief that his opponents were naive and superficial, had not taken into account the true nature or real consequences of his own position.

When Alexander, Thomas Poole and Marcus arrived, Bill was graphically describing the degrading terrors to be experienced in condemned cells. To this the Bishop replied quietly, and as far as he went, truthfully, that Bill had no first-hand experience of such matters, that he himself had been witness of, sharer of, moments of great beauty and glory in these unlikely circumstances. Bill cried out that this was the more shame. Stephanie was in tears. Lucas was talking about our blind modern squeamishness, in support of the Bishop, who seemed to find his support distasteful. "If thine eye offend thee, cast it out," Lucas cried. "Or a leg, or an arm, or anything else."

Wilkie said to Alexander, "This began with a discussion of the exaggerated charm of your portrayal of the Tudor State." Bill turned on Alexander and said they were now on matters infinitely more important than *that*, and returned to demolishing the Bishop with statistics of innocent Sheriffs who had gone white and insane overnight because of duty. The Bishop said that great faith and strength were indeed requisite, and Lucas, his words falling muddily over each other, into incoherence said that the first man was of the earth, earthy, and needed to be wholly, however painfully, done away with, so that the immortal corn should spring, which caused the Bishop to click his tongue loudly and audibly and caused Bill to begin to roar about the repugnant, savage and bloodthirsty nature of Christianity, which worshipped a smashed body and a crushed self. He then turned on Daniel and said he must be mad to expect him to condone his daughter's marriage into this thwart, disnatured sect. Lucas said that a crushed body liberated a glorious soul, the Bishop said firmly that he was not sure that some of Mr Simmonds's – was it – Mr Simmonds's responses were quite healthy, that he was not advocating an *obsession* with pain or dissolution by any means, only a healthy acceptance of it, at which point Lucas Simmonds, drooping, wet with perspiration, became poppy-crimson with agitation, and Daniel spoke. He spoke first to Bill, saying that he expected nothing of him, except trouble, and second to the Bishop to say briefly and flatly that he believed that what he, the Bishop, had just been arguing was wicked, cruel and unjustifiable.

It was immediately clear that Daniel was angrier than anyone else: that he could barely speak for wrath. He added that no one had given him a good reason yet for coldly killing anyone, let alone involving anyone else in the killing, and that he was now taking his wife home. Bill was somehow silenced by this hefty and unexpected, indeed probably unwelcome support. Daniel put his arm round his wife and led her away without looking back: Mr Ellenby told the Bishop that Daniel was a rough diamond: the Bishop said, chill, that Daniel might in courtesy have waited for a reply. Lucas Simmonds suddenly ran out of the Hall: Alexander saw the Parrys, now all three, making their inexorable way to his rowdy corner. He thought he must speak to Marcus: or to Lucas: the chap was definitely odd, no question, he looked all swollen and shrunken out of shape, somehow, and was surrounded by some almost tangible electric fug of anxiety, or terror. He said, "I'm sure what I said was right. You can't afford to stay involved in whatever . . ."

"Someone has got to *help* him," said Marcus.

Alexander considered the Bishop, who now looked distinctly irate, and Bill, who was now sulking. He thought of drawing Marcus after Lucas, which would have avoided Bishop, Bill, Parrys and Thomas Poole's insoluble and terrifying mirror-problem, but was pre-empted. Floating like Gods from machines from the end of the Hall came Crowe and his three Elizabeths, Marina, Frederica, Anthea, smiling and beckoning. Crowe, still got up as Baron Verulam, brandished his long staff like Comus stilling his rabble, or his mother, Circe, dismissing the swine to their swill.

"Alexander – this is your night, my dear – the Press is wild with delight – you must come and meet – you are positively howled for, dear boy – they *die* to meet you – good evening, Bishop, a triumph, I'm sure you agree, such a marvellous corporate effort – come away, Alexander, excuse me I *must* drag him off – help me ladies – good evening Jenny darling, you were *lovely*, the *Yorkshire Post* has promised a special mention, Bess Throckmorton by sweet Sir Walter so rudely forced – so *convincing* – and you of course you bad clever lordling, your name is made too – now come away, please excuse us, good night, Bill, I'm glad you managed to get here. Alexander, come away, come away."

Marcus went out on the terrace in search of Lucas. He found him standing close to the royal palanquin, breathing fast and smiling unnaturally. He could not think why Lucas should have come to this scene at all unless out of some need, fanatical or pathetic, to keep an eye on Marcus himself.

"Sir. Are you all right? You looked . . ."

Lucas answered testily that he was quite all right, quite all right, more than all right. They were simply caught up in the flow of very big movements of force. They had a part to play. They had to be sure what it was. They were required to set off for Fylingdales on Friday.

"Sir, I can't. I can't come any more. I'm afraid."

Naturally he was afraid, retorted the flushed cherub, even more irritably, clattering a fist on the flimsy gilded panels of the palanquin. He couldn't expect to displace real powers and not be afraid, that wasn't reasonable. There was every likelihood that they would freeze on Friday, or fry, or vanish in pure energy with nothing left of them but shadows like the men of Hiroshima after the lightburst. This prospect seemed to afford him some furious pleasure. We always knew what we risked, he pointed out, sweetly reasonable. Didn't we?

Marcus said no, he had not known. And that now . . . now . . . he wasn't sure they hadn't made the whole thing up.

"And the transmissions? The levitation at Owger's Howe? Your photisms? Did we make those up?"

"No. Well, no. But maybe those – were not – what you – what we – thought."

"We don't *know* what they were. There is only one way to find out."

"No. I'm afraid."

"But you are the seer."

"I'm not sure. I daren't. You've got to let me off."

"You aren't – disgusted by me?"

Marcus began to cry. Lucas glared stonily at his tears. He repeated his question.

"No. I've told you that. I'm scared. I told you."

"Then I must go alone. Alone, I shall almost certainly fail. But there is no alternative."

Marcus begged him weakly to give up. Lucas sneered. He said, "All right. Go away. It's too late to retreat but you can delude yourself if you choose. What you fear is everywhere, and will do what it will do where it chooses."

Marcus, weeping, and not entirely truthfully, cried out that it was of

Lucas that he was afraid most of all, "of you, of you, of you." At this
Lucas suddenly struck hard at his face, cutting the corner of his mouth,
told him to leave him alone, then, and hurtled away down the terrace.
Marcus sat down by the palanquin, holding his stinging head in his hands
and sobbing. People wandering past him thought he was drunk,
considerately stepped round him, and left him alone.

Two of the people who ran past Marcus late that night were Alexander
and Frederica. Both were in flight; Alexander from the Parrys, who had
taken their eyes off him to quarrel over who should change Thomas's
stinking nappy, Frederica from the traveller in dolls, who had raised his
arm, snapped his fingers and started to shove his way towards her
through the crowd. He was not invited, but almost anybody could have,
and had, effected an entry. One might discuss Ed with Wilkie, but not
with Alexander, to whom she had simply said she absolutely must get
out. He had agreed it seemed a good idea, and so they had run, hearing
behind them faint ironic cheering and public laughter. In the dark,
hearing her breathing and leaping, he felt close to her. In the garden
with the fountain it was different. They stood awkwardly in the circle of
each other's arms, and both distinctly felt the other to be bony and
ungiving. Both were visited by a revisionary white coiling of Anthea
Warburton's fine solid buttocks and calves. He could not tumble
Frederica Potter under a bush. As for Frederica, she could not initiate
such tumbling. So they stood entwined, hardening already into familiar
attitudes like children playing statues. She chattered at him, recalling
gross compliments, stage mishaps, faux pas. He willed her into a more
desirable silence, into which she presently fell. He put a finger on her
cold lips.

"Well, what shall we do?"

No answer.

"Perhaps we should agree to forget all this?"

No answer.

"No good can come of it."

"I want it."

"It can be so little."

"I don't care. I want *you*."

"But what can we do?"

She did not know. Bed, marriage, communion of souls, a perpetual
continuing of this delightful crisis.

"Just let it go on. I love you."

She said that with a threatening imperative that melted him. Somewhere at the back of his consciousness was the knowledge that she would

deal for herself with any consequences. Her face was frowning, colourless and cold. She was the bitch-goddess in the grove, his own creation, or evocation, she was the untouchable girl, safe to want because she could not be had. He got hold of her; she twisted and tugged, rousing him to a grabbing that was not part of his usual repertory. She laughed and laughed aloud in the garden, lewd and innocent, in charge, and he knew that however he protested he was caught, pure curiosity would lead him on.

For the three following weeks they were both so entrammelled by each other and by success that his identification of her as the bitch-goddess took on a new irony. The newspapers were floridly ecstatic, in the manner of the day. The enterprise was a cultural triumph. Alexander was the most hopeful new star in the dramaturgical firmament since Shaw. Homage was done to Lodge and Marina Yeo. Wilkie and Frederica attracted a disproportionate quantity of attention, it was felt by the rest of the cast. Frederica found her own face, specked with newsprint, glowering proudly under a floral coronet in the *Yorkshire Post* and *Manchester Guardian*. Portly ladies and anxious young men from women's magazines and local newspapers made appointments to discuss the phenomenal success of an amateur local schoolgirl. She told them she wanted to be a great actress like Marina Yeo. She told them she was waiting for her A level results "with considerable trepidation". She said her family was literary. She gave her views on Elizabeth's virginity. She acted herself acting herself.

Alexander went to Manchester and talked on the radio about the renaissance of verse drama. He was asked, for large sums of money, to write on history, verse, and Women in periodicals academic, in the know, and vulgar, and tried to do so. He was approached about a London production of *Astraea* – with some changes, and an all-professional cast. None of all this, for which they had waited, seemed quite real to either of them, because their powers of concentration and enjoyment were so sapped by plain desire. Bill – "disgustingly", Frederica said with considerable satisfaction – came round. He carried in his breast pocket a sheaf of newspaper cuttings, with pictures of his thin daughter sitting on a stone, beating a fist on a stone wall, lying spread-eagled on the ground.

The rest of the cast were more hostile to Frederica than they had been, and used words like "insufferable" and "vain" about her, not with entire justice. She was, it was true, drunk with the whole business. She walked through hot cow parsley and laughed to herself at the memory of her face in the Blesford photographer's window, but the pleasure was so intertwined with a narcissistic preening of the body at long last desired by Alexander that her worst social fault was a dazed absent-mindedness that those who chose took as insult. Alexander praised her to the Press and his praise was printed. "A highly intelligent performance," Wilkie read out to her, in the gardens at Long Royston. "So sensitive to the verse, he says. You did it."

"I *am* intelligent."

"We all know that ad nauseam. How are you proceeding on other fronts? Are you bedded? Is there poison in your coffee?"

The affair, or whatever it was, had become horribly public before it had defined itself. The cast, with one of those corporate twists of judgment and curiosity of which close groups are capable, had chosen to admire, in principle, Frederica's pertinacity in "getting" her reluctant man, whilst continuing to dislike her for the inconsiderate and single-minded nature of her pursuit, as well as for hogging the publicity. (Wilkie, better organised, already known as an oddity, a polymath, a "genius" with his own file already in the BBC News Information stacks, was already juggling several agents and conducting his own skilful self-advertisement, without attracting dislike or hatred.) The cast had, however, capriciously decided to despise Alexander for capitulating to so blatant a sexual campaign. They did not show this too much: his play was great, and so was the reflected glory. But they were full of unobtrusive little attentions to Jennifer Parry: little boys wormed their way through bushes trailing Alexander and Frederica across any lawn over which they chose to walk together: Elizabethan courtiers leaned out of mullioned windows to stare and even snigger when the two attempted to sit down together on a bench.

Alexander was too bewildered to be more than peripherally aware of all this. Frederica, somewhat stoically used to being disliked for being top in exams, managed to put up with being disliked for the newspapers in a solid enough way, although she was temperamentally unable to make any deprecating or conciliating noises. The sexual attention was harder to cope with, and she suffered from it, without being able to deploy any pleas for sympathy, or interesting confidences. She became more self-sufficient with success. She would show the lot of them. Except Alexander. Even he was exposed to reprimands for cravenness which he partly gloomily enjoyed. It was clear that this could not go on, in its nature, very long. Something must shift, happen, change things. It was not at all clear what this might be.

38. St Bartholomew

August 24th, which was St Bartholomew's Day, and Frederica Potter's birthday, was, by a nice coincidence, the day on which Frederica's A level results came in the post. It was the Monday of the last week of the Play. Stephanie went into the church, which was St Bartholomew's church, early that morning to do the flowers for him: flowers were another thing she had found she could gracefully, as a curate's wife, do. She had tried to find out about St Bartholomew, but it turned out that he was a saint about whom very little was known, and that little, bloody. He was an Apostle who had travelled through Asia Minor, North West India and Greater Armenia, where he had been flayed alive and subsequently beheaded. His identity was uncertain: he was quite possibly in fact the same person as Nathanael, a native of Cana in Galilee of whom Christ had remarked, "Behold, an Israelite indeed in whom there is no guile." His movements were also uncertain: "India", Stephanie discovered, meant to Greeks and Latins indifferently Arabia, Ethiopia, Libya, Parthia, Persia, and the lands of the Medes. In his wanderings he resembled the Dionysos of the *Bacchae*, and also, she supposed, in being flayed and shredded and reconstituted. She had hoped briefly that Daniel's church was dedicated to a more local Bartholomew, St Bartholomew of Durham, a Benedictine native of Whitby who had spent forty-two uneventful eremite years in St Cuthbert's cell on Farne Island and had quietly died there, about 1193. But the little statue of the saint in his niche near the pulpit was identifiable only by his grasped knife, the instrument of his martyrdom. There was also, in the side-chapel, a bad blown-up reproduction of Michelangelo's depiction of the martyr descending ferociously in the Sistine clouds of judgment, brandishing his knife above his head and trailing his dead leathery integument, on which the artist's distorted face was depicted. Stephanie decided to embower, and partially to obscure, both these images in a cloud of wild cut flowers.

She was now, to a close observer, visibly pregnant, and had disguised herself in very churchwomanly clothes, a pleated green linen overall or smock, suggesting cook, gardener, or secular surplice, flat sensible shoes, secateurs in the smock pocket, and a trug of branches and blossoms over one arm. She could still balance a bicycle and drove slowly and erect along country lanes, gathering white umbellifers and marguerites, green hellebore and sprays of dogroses, drooping heads of wild oats and barley grasses, foxgloves, spotted and pale. She would have liked a splash of red, scarlet or crimson, in respect to the anonymous martyr, but poppies fall before they are picked and garden peonies – just possible – were almost certainly too much for the delicate haze of green and white and gold and pale purple she was constructing.

She had ceased some time ago to hate the church building. Alone in it, crushing wire, pouring water, twisting stems, she was happy. On this morning however, as for several previous mornings, she was not alone. Lucas Simmonds was there, in an attitude of rebarbative prayer, waiting close under a pillar and the painting of Hell Mouth. She cast a quick glance in his direction, padded suede-soft to the font, thought that he looked at death's door, that sweet peas were the answer and could be begged from Mrs Ellenby, that something must or might at least have happened to Marcus too, that Simmonds needed help but had sought silence, which it was indecorous to break.

So she worked silently, and Lucas prayed or agonised silently, until the door in the porch swung with a great disturbance of air and Frederica burst in, crashing along the aisle.

"Look," she cried, "look," looking at nothing herself, and Stephanie rose slowly from her knees and took the postcard Frederica was waving, grubby now and fuzzed, and read a list of marks so extraordinarily excellent that it was momentarily hard to credit them.

"Well," said Stephanie. "Well. Are you pleased? Happy Birthday."

Frederica leaped about the lectern, ruffled the Queen Anne's lace which gave off clouds of pollen.

"Don't, it's delicate, I've spent ages on it."

"It's pretty. What's it for? Harvest Festival?"

"No, silly. Not yet. St Bartholomew's day."

"Of course, my birthday. The day of the massacre. I massacred them, I did, I did, no one can beat me."

"Don't shout in church. People are trying to be quiet."

Frederica stared round. "Oh. Him. Steph, what does he *do* here? He gives me the creeps."

"Please have the grace to shut up. Your voice carries."

"Steph, I can do anything, I can do anything, better than anyone, I can *do* . . ."

"You can not mess up my flowers," said Stephanie, as gently as she could. You could not offer admiration or encouragement to anyone who was so wildly admiring and encouraging herself.

"Steph, an unheard-of thing, Daddy's giving a birthday *party* for me, a celebration, with champagne and strawberries, at school, in the Masters' Garden, or cloisters if wet. A lunch-time party, Saturday, the day of the last night. He's actually sent me out to invite you and Daniel

– he won't *go* to your place of course, but he sent me there. I saw Daniel, he said to come here, you were here.

"Oh, and Dad *telephoned* Alexander, which is hilariously funny from some angles. But all the same, rich. My cup runs over."

"Mind you don't slip," said Stephanie, referring perhaps to her own trug, perhaps to life. Frederica was waving her arms and giving little disconcerting jumps all over the nave. It became clear, as first Alexander, then Daniel, appeared through the porch, that Frederica had converted the church into a place of assignation and celebration. Alexander looked like a male moth, called by some chemistry of honey and musk. Daniel looked like Daniel. Frederica flashed her glorified postcard at both these newcomers. Lucas Simmonds remained on his knees by the pillar, his eyes closed. Frederica skipped, tripped over the trug, made sure Alexander caught her.

Stephanie turned her thick back to them, and went on placing Canterbury bells amongst the sprinkling grasses. Apart from the dog-roses those flowers of summer that foamed up, veiling the grim Sistine saint, smelled live but rank, greenish and corrupt, hellebore, digitalis, and the cousins of hemlock. Sweet peas were undoubtedly necessary. Daniel came and stroked her spine, his heavy hand warm where already her muscles hurt.

Potters, he thought, were cruelly unobservant. How could they miss her pallor, her thickness, her new slow purpose? Potters chattered on about 90%, 95%, marks, marks on scraps of card, marks on scripts, marks made on or in the world. Bill Potter might evade his eldest daughter's wedding, and make ludicrous what part of its ceremony he touched, but he would break a close northern habit of meanness to provide champagne for marks. Daniel despised them. His imagination was powerful enough when it came to a woman afraid of pain, a man, Daniel himself, who had watched other men love their sons, well or badly, and could therefore measure how he knew and did not know that he would love his own. But his imagination could not correlate blank black marks with an informed knowledge of the precise passion of Racine, with writing clearly, at least, about the terrors of *Hamlet* and *Lear*. Daniel did not desire to be a Bishop, and thus did not connect his own furiously directed energies with ambition, as he did connect the Potters' obsession with marks.

When Marcus came into the church, all those already present thought he was looking for them. Frederica assumed he had come about her birthday or her marks, Alexander that he was in search of advice and assistance so far not rendered, Stephanie that he was, as she was, distressed by Bill's new *démarche* in one direction, perhaps by the memory of the unfortunate attempts to stimulate and foster his own diagnosed "genius". Daniel supposed that he was in religious trouble. Lucas Simmonds, it subsequently appeared, was in no doubt that he had been called in by spiritual tones emitted by himself, moth-messages of another nature.

He stood uncertainly in the doorway, in any case, upon seeing them all there, clearly ready to turn and flee. Frederica waved her postcard at him and belled out percentages, Stephanie stepped out to touch him, Alexander side-stepped behind the lectern, Lucas Simmonds opened his eyes, rose neatly from his knees and stepped out to the altar-rail from where he turned and addressed the boy in a brusque, no-nonsense tone.

"It's taken you long enough to get the message. I knew we were safe here. I did tell you prayer and preparation would be required. I was aware there was a lot of interference and static you might say – we won't give it its name, not even here – but I didn't think they could join anything put out from here, or anyway, I took the risk, I took the risk. My God, if I may say so, I'm glad to see you. There've been batteries, I can tell you, infernal batteries. Now you've come, we shall stand."

He took cognizance of the others.

"Good morning, Vicar. Wedderburn. It seems too much to hope you are all come prepared to fight on your knees. However, good morning. Marcus!"

Marcus stood. He opened his mouth but no sound came. He tried to put out a hand, and could not, but did not imagine any demon or electrical mischievous elemental was holding it down. He snuffed the hot roadside smell of the cow-parsleys on the chilly stone. He stood. Daniel took a few steps towards him, and he staggered a little, and put out a hand, which Daniel clasped.

"Tell me what you want to do," said Daniel, carefully.

"I – don't – know."

Alexander strode up. "Do you want to go home?"

Marcus shook his straw head.

"Daniel's flat?" suggested Alexander.

Marcus nodded, his flannel knees knocking, trying to see neither Hellmouth nor the betrayed Lucas. His head was humming with messages like winged serpents coiling and uncoiling, his brain-box flashed with light, white, gold, imperial purple, his body was a thing that at any moment, just as Lucas had prophesied, might dissolve and fade, leaving not even its own wreckage behind. Daniel's flat was full of horribly real and just possibly consoling cushions and teapots and human paraphernalia, that if they were not a crushing trap, not like stone boots in Mother Shipton's Dropping Well, might just be plump and warm to hold on to. He gripped Daniel's dry, strong hand. "Take me," he said.

Daniel was perturbed about Lucas, the cure of whose soul was at least as certainly his as that of Marcus Potter, another victim, in his practical vision, of the over-valuation of marks. Souls, souls at least so peremptory as this one, were not his natural concern, though he did his best with those he had encountered. But at present the rather evanescent Marcus had a very drowning grip on his own flesh, to which he responded, and so he went with him. Alexander, feeling responsible in some useless way, and just less nervous of Marcus than of Lucas, went with them, and Frederica dashed after Alexander.

Stephanie picked up her trug, moved over to the alabaster flower-trough by the altar-rails, and said carefully to Lucas Simmonds,

"I was doing the flowers for the church, for the saint's day, St Bartholomew." There was a reek of perspiration, and sweet hair-oil, and carbolic, and sick breath coming from the man, which the over-sensitive nostrils of pregnancy flared and picked up, so that she was for a moment nauseated. English good manners are a horrible thing, Stephanie thought. I should ask him what is terrifying him, I should offer to kneel down with him, I should say Marcus is sick. I cannot. I cannot. She wandered as calmly as she could up and down collecting a green can of fresh water, casting out some dead arum lilies and carnations put in last week by Mrs Ellenby, whose style was more conventional.

"Sit down, why don't you," she said finally, vaguely, a hostess in her church. To her surprise he sat down just where he was, on the chancel steps, resting his head in his hands. She crunched chicken-wire, not looking at him. He said, in the ghost of his old cheery manner,

"Well, when is the baby?"

"Nobody knows," she said, quickly. And then, "About Easter. I mean, nobody knows because we haven't told them."

"I saw."

She did not like this idea: as though she was naked. She tried to turn it aside, lightly.

"You are a biologist. It's your subject."

"Don't say that. I hate biology."

"I never liked it myself," she said, comfortably, inanely, padding across the trough and disposing marguerites in a kind of fan from its centre. "It was the only science I could do, though. I had to have one, to be allowed to read English. I couldn't do the abstract things, maths and those. Girls are always made to do biology."

"Plants," he said. "Or stones. I don't mind. But you have to be better than me to get away from the flesh and specialise. I'm a hack. Why did you get married?"

"To have a private life," she said, truthfully, seeing Daniel's face momentarily, as it was, close. "Not that it is very private. There are so many callers."

"To have a private life." He thought. "I have no private life. I have no life. I touch no one. I ask you to believe that. There are reasons."

"And Marcus?" she said, very carefully.

"Marcus is gifted. Marcus – can see what – no one else sees. Marcus is – not like – other men."

"He would be better if he were," she said, almost sharply.

"You can say that if you like. It is not true."

He stood up, the momentary contact broken, and went back to his meditation or vigil at the pillar. She continued slowly about her work until all the receptacles, at font and pulpit, lectern and altar, were full, pallid, candid, greening. Daniel came back.

"Are you all right? Will you go to Marcus? Frederica is worse than useless and Alexander just leans about on the furniture looking frightened."

She reached up and whispered in his ear what Lucas had said.

"I'll hang around," said Daniel. "He might talk."

"I covered up your St Bartholomew with flowers."

"Very pretty," said Daniel. "Very pretty. For a girl who wouldn't have flowers at Easter."

"I didn't say he rose from the dead. I said I covered him up, him and his knife and his skin."

Daniel looked at St Bartholomew, Michelangelo's version, blued and blurred by a poor intermediary printer, patted his own belly, and said, "Well, if he rose not, he's bloody descending in wrath." He thought for a flicker of time about flaying, about how his own fat was held together by a thin tight skin, about how a man would spill out, about how muscular the cross Saint was, and then touched Stephanie's taut skin and said, "Go on, get out of here, go and see to Marcus." A body inside a body, his son.

He knelt down, for some time, waiting for Simmonds to get up, wondering if he should speak to him directly. When Simmonds rose, Daniel rose too, in a hurry, and for a moment they looked at each other across the church. Then Simmonds held up the flat of his hand at Daniel, warning him off, gave a jerky nod, in the direction of the altar, and left. Daniel went after him, as far as the churchyard, only to hear the roar of the little sports car on the quiet road outside. He came out, as Simmonds vanished in white dust.

39. Party in the Pantheon

Bill's party for Frederica, hastily conceived and hastily carried out, might have been expected to provide awkwardnesses. It was held in the Pantheon, not in the enclosed garden, since the sky was lowering. Yorkshire closeness had reasserted itself sufficiently for the party to have become a rather odd combination of tea-party and alcoholic celebration: tea and ham sandwiches and fairy cakes and strawberries were to be followed by one glass of champagne per guest, more or less, in which Frederica's health was to be drunk. The guests were mostly Bill's friends and colleagues, extra-mural lecturers, class secretaries, W.E.A. group organisers, amateur dramatic ladies and those school colleagues who were *personae gratae*. These included Mr and Mrs Thone, *ex officio*, Alexander and for some reason Geoffrey Parry who had after all, Bill decided, showed guts, even if wrong-headed guts, about Thomas Mann. Frederica said that was a repulsive mixed metaphor, and Bill, gleefully acknowledging this, said that wrong-headed guts *were* repulsive, but must, as he had said, be respected. Why the Parrys had eagerly accepted the invitation was a different problem, Frederica thought, and one which recurrently bothered her. Her initial euphoria over the exam results was wearing off, and she was beginning to realise that she was a very slow and clumsy student of human behaviour. It took her a long time to see what Daniel had seen immediately, that her party was not only her party, but Bill's revenge on Stephanie for forcing him to pay for champagne to celebrate her abandoning of her First Class career and her marriage to a stout curate. And then when Bill called Frederica in and asked her to say which of her "friends" she wished to invite to the party she began to see the awkwardnesses of broadcasting those 90 and 95%s, as well as the unwisdom of bringing together her daily world of school and home with the dream world of *Astraea*, in which it had seemed easy to be sweetly scornful of the public hum about her behaviour with, and with regard to, Alexander. She wished no such hum to penetrate Masters' Row. She began, indeed, to ask herself what she did wish. She said she wished Wilkie to be invited. Thomas Poole was coming in any case, as a respected friend of Bill's, so she suggested Anthea Warburton, whom she disliked, but felt would, for reasons of her own, behave discreetly about Alexander. She suggested Lodge, who was quiet, and Miss Wells, who was ignorant, and would be nice to Stephanie, about whom Frederica was feeling very stupid and very guilty. Her only other ally was Crowe, and she was not sure how much of an ally Crowe still was, after the episode

in the Sun Bed, which had never been mentioned. Also, Bill would not
stomach Crowe. He himself had a huge admiration for Marina Yeo, to
whom a card was accordingly despatched. Miss Yeo replied graciously,
excusing herself on grounds of age, headache, the length of the run and
the need to restore her energies for the exigencies of the Last Night.
Wilkie said to Frederica that she knew what *that* meant, didn't she, but
he promised, himself, not to be more than a little late for her bun-fight.
From old queen to young virgin, back round the circle of the years, he
said, I shall come. Have you done anything about that, yet? About what?
said Frederica, crossly. About the virginity, silly girl, said Wilkie, about
that. Frederica said no, she hadn't, and was getting into a dreadful state
about it, because of the lie she had told, and because she was surprised to
find she was scared, and because Alexander was somehow so *standoffish*,
even when he was being most loving, and so nervy, the beautiful thing,
that one couldn't talk to him about it as one could to Wilkie himself, and
so she had got herself further and further into a bog of circumstantial
lying and God knew where it would come out, or how, except that it
must, because she could not endure to go on, and burn, as she was. No
indeed, said Wilkie, thoughtfully, no indeed.

The party was one of those parties, unlike Crowe's Saturnalia, which did
not take off. At the beginning, it looked as though it might. There were
enough people talking firmly to each other about teaching, and the
success or failure of different ways of teaching poems or people, for a
certain intelligent courtesy to play for a little, in the light of which Miss
Wells's ruffled fluttering could be smoothed into smiling by some clever
remarks of Wilkie's about Herbert, in the light of which Alexander
could appear gracefully pedagogic faced with Bill's literary housewives
from Arkengarthdale, in the light of which Frederica's success could be
made smoothly to seem a civilised achievement by Thomas Poole, who
took her aside and talked to her about the language of the *Four Quartets*.
He was interested, he said, in whether the thought in the poem, the
element of doctrine, weakened or dried it out, and Frederica, turning the
needle of her attention to the nature of place and time in dry verse in a
dry culture, forgot her vision of his rounded nakedness, on dark green,
spoke as she had spoken to Alexander about Racine's rhythms, liked
him, and was grateful to him. And Poole, who was in agony, was later to
remember this conversation, as was Frederica, as something disproportionately sane and important in an insane day.

There were, however, dark and troubled spots on the academic light.
One of these was Marcus, got up in his one tidy suit, sitting stiffly on the
edge of the cloister wall and staring vacantly over the lawn. Daniel and

Stephanie had got nothing out of him except an assurance that whatever was up, was all over, and that he preferred not to talk. Alexander had told his version of Marcus's "problem" to Daniel, which had greatly relieved Alexander's impotent sense of responsibility. Daniel had thought about it, and about what Lucas had said to Stephanie, and had kept quiet. He wished more and more that he was what he thought of as a "religious", by which he meant perhaps a visionary, or a mystical, man. His existing strength would only be of use in this situation when it was completely out of hand, as far as he could see. He kept half an eye on the boy, and half on his wife.

Winifred, to whom nobody had said anything, stood as near as she dared to Marcus, watching him watch space. He had gone away somewhere, worse and further than he had always been gone. If she tried to go after him, or so she thought, he might vanish entirely. If he did not, a lifetime's or at least a marriagetime's experience had taught her that if she showed agitation Bill would come and club one or both of them with too much love or hate, would yank or drive them into some girning, daemonic clinch, to avoid which stillness and more stillness was the only resort.

Mrs Thone stood and watched Winifred chilly. Pain hardens, and great pain hardens greatly, whatever the comforters say, and suffering does not ennoble, though it may occasionally lend a certain rigid dignity of manner to the suffering frame. Winifred, to Mrs Thone, was simply a woman who had a son, and could, or would, do nothing for that son's trouble. Mrs Thone's son had died on a summer day, and in the winter Mrs Thone felt kinder to mothers of living sons who were less than wise and perfect. Today she watched bleak patches of sunlight and cloud-shadow on the school-lawn, rested a hand lightly on Pallas Athene's unnecessarily ample hips, and sipped tea, unbending.

Alexander drifted long-legged and lovely over to the group of Frederica and Thomas Poole, and attempted to congratulate her, in what he hoped was his old friend-of-the-family voice, on the amazing marks. She grinned, horribly, as she had been used to do, and for a moment he wondered what had gripped him, that he should have come to desire so precisely to slide his hand up those hot brown legs and his mouth down that thin throat, and as his imagination made the desire precise he knew that no matter what had gripped him, he was still gripped.

"We were talking quietly about Eliot," said Poole, sadly.

"Please go on," said Alexander, trying to lean away from Frederica onto the nearest stone monstrosity, who was the blind, straightforward, incorruptible highest Arthur. Anthea Warburton, in a great many layers of stiff white net petticoat under rosebudded poplin, came and touched Poole's elbow.

"Can you do something," she said, in her featureless well-bred little voice. "I feel so awfully green."

"Too much school tea," said Frederica, heartily, and took notice, too late as always, of the stiff, alarmed complicity of the two men. Green? Green. School slang. An old word. Oh, God. I have put my foot in it. She was annoyed mostly at the childishness of her remark about the tea, and then bothered by why *Alexander* should be so scared. At this point, as though by accident, Elinor Poole appeared, closely followed by Jennifer Parry, who was balancing her small son on her hip, and was followed in turn by her husband. Bill had moved towards the tables, clearly preparing to speak, and champagne corks popped.

"Well –" said Jenny, loudly, shrilly and terribly to Frederica. "When's the happy event?" Frederica looked at Anthea, looked away, smoothed her own skirt defensively down over her own flat front.

"*What* happy event?" she countered, drawing her brows together.

"The new arrival. In your family. I take it we're celebrating that, as well as your successes, aren't we? Though if I were Stephanie, I don't know, *entre nous*, that I'd have embarked on motherhood with such gay expedition. Too late to tell her, my dear, and I shall of course put a smiling face on it, but let me tell you, Frederica, for what it's worth, don't. Don't give it up, don't stop, don't turn into a cow and a mopper-upper, don't suppose that the death of the mind can be avoided by a little rushed reading between two lots of nappies and dishes, because it can't. Adultery you may find time for, but life, no, and thought, no, and don't let them –" she frowned round at Poole, Anthea, Elinor, Alexander and sad Winifred who had joined them – "don't let them tell you any different." She tugged at the fat little legs of her son, which were wound round her waist. "Get off, you little old man of the sea. Go to Daddy. You're a little old man of the sea, and the fact that you're a lovable dumpling makes it worse, not better. Are you listening to me, Frederica Potter? The real glory of this conversation – or monologue it's been so far, but I'll shut up, don't worry – is that you won't listen to me, because it's me telling you and you won't trust my motives, and you'll be right. But I'm right too, and you'll find that out, one way or another. End of speech. Oh Geoffrey, *do* take this damp creature. I shall move off and offer my best wishes to Mrs Orton. I'd like a word with you, Alexander, before the break-up of this happy occasion, if that's O.K. by you."

Alexander nodded, speechless. Frederica stared at Stephanie and wondered why she had failed to notice what was there to be seen. Elinor Poole fumbled in her handbag for a handkerchief and when Thomas put his arm round her shoulder Anthea began to make respectable little gulping noises in her throat. Geoffrey Parry took his son, and sat down on the cloister wall on the other side of Pallas Athene. The boy rested his head in the curve of the man's shoulder. Mrs Thone moved round and sat down next to them.

Frederica could not quite think where to go, and could not stay to meet her mother's eye, so wandered off towards Stephanie. The school waitresses were taking away teacups and replacing them with glasses of bubbling wine. Alexander watched Frederica's relentless back, caught Thomas Poole's tragic stare, and turned with graceful solicitude to Anthea Warburton, whom he wished the earth would open and swallow, asking her whether she felt quite well, whether he could get her a glass of water or wine, whether she would like to come further into the shade. She came, to his relief, thus making it possible for Thomas Poole to find his wife's handkerchief for her, and for Alexander to drift, temporarily he was aware, away from Jenny. Jenny, driven by some domestic female demon of wrath, then marched over to Bill, who was clearing his throat for the congratulatory speech he had prepared, with quotations from Ascham's praises of the learning of the young princess. She congratulated Bill, as she had his family, on the approaching happy event, aware herself by now, as she had not previously been, that the Potters were ignorant of Stephanie's state. Bill, half-listening, half-coughing, suddenly caught the import of what she was saying, and Winifred, hurrying uselessly up, was in time to see him meet Daniel's eye with a look of such concentrated and disproportionate loathing that she thought for a moment that he had gone truly mad, and was about to hurl bottles, or silver salvers, at his sturdy black son-in-law.

Daniel informed Stephanie that som'at was up, he was afraid.

Bill began to talk, much too fast and somewhat disjointedly, not about Roger Ascham, but about the eternity of the work of thought, or art, and about *Areopagitica*. "For Books are not absolutely dead things, but do contain a potency of life in them to be as active as that soul whose progeny they are; . . . As good almost kill a Man, as kill a good Book: who kills a man, kills a reasonable creature, Gods Image; but hee who destroyes a good Booke, kills reason it selfe, kills the Image of God, as it were in the eye. Many a man lives a burden to the Earth," Bill said, glowering furiously at Daniel, "but a good Booke is the pretious life-blood of a master-spirit . . ."

"A burden to the earth is what he certainly thinks I am," said Daniel, roundly and comfortably.

"What is he *on* about?" asked Stephanie, who had missed, in a dreamy daze, most of the earlier happenings.

"He's telling you books are better than babies," said Daniel. Bill was now roaring convolutedly about how he had always been a strong supporter of the equal education of women, and about the goodness of Alexander's play, and the education of its heroine.

"Oh God," said Stephanie. "He's found out. He's mad."

"I think he thought I could be got rid of, or something," said Daniel cheerfully, "but this makes it all a bit too solid, you could say."

"You don't need to look so *calm* about it."

"I don't see why not. It doesn't matter to me. I'll take better care of my son than he has of his."

"It might be a daughter."

"Or my daughter," said Daniel, who was no prophet.

Bill was uttering some uncannily wrathful hopes that Frederica would make a better use of her talents, her many talents, than he was afraid to say he had of such as he had been endowed with. A man's child was his future, unless he was rare or gifted enough to be a master-spirit, and so his own future . . .

There was a car starting up in the background. It came out under the archway between the towers on two wheels and cut screaming across a half-moon of the lawn. Basil Thone stepped onto the lawn in protest. Marcus Potter ran out, after it, out of some more complex urge, waving frantically but voicelessly.

"Simmonds," said Alexander to Anthea Warburton, and abandoned her unceremoniously. Marcus was still running, although Simmonds and his beetle-car, having demolished a few parterres and a fine verge, were now out of sight, leaving a screech, a hum, and a burning smell hanging in the air. Alexander began to run after Marcus. Daniel, patting Stephanie on the shoulder, began to lumber after Alexander. Bill stopped talking. Frederica bit her lip and put her head in the air.

Alexander caught Marcus some way along the road up into the moors. The boy had his head down, and was running, pathetically wambling, catching his breath in great gulps. Alexander was not in very good condition himself, but he put on a sprint and tried to gasp to the boy to stop; Marcus rolled on, paying no attention. For several minutes Alexander trotted ludicrously on beside him, saying things like ". . . do no good . . . told you better not . . . have some sense." He heard the thunder of Daniel's feet getting closer, and flung himself desperately at Marcus in a sort of rugger tackle, as though it was a matter of male pride to bring down the quarry himself and not have Daniel do it. They tumbled together on the road, and Marcus fought like an animal, who had seemed so bodiless, biting and scratching and occasionally landing a weak blow. ". . . trying to help . . ." sobbed Alexander.

"He was my *friend*," said Marcus, in the past tense, as though Lucas Simmonds was already dead.

Daniel came up, planted his feet in the dust, and stared down on them.
"Stop it," he said. "Don't be daft. There's no point at all in all this,
the man's miles away now. Come home, Marcus."

"No."

"Well, what *shall* you do, then?"

"I –" said Marcus. He fought for air. He had the thought that he might
die, there in the road. It was not a bad thought. "I –" he said again, his
lungs in spasm. His eyes rolled up and he passed out.

Daniel proved to be good at artificial respiration, which proved to be
needed. Alexander knelt uselessly in the dust, watching this efficiency,
and then, when the boy was breathing in a fluttering way, helped Daniel
to carry him slowly back to the school. Bill met them, white now and
tentative. Daniel, who had his second breath, ordered him to see that the
boy was taken up to the Nursery and a doctor found immediately.
Alexander, who had not got his second breath, clung to a pillar, air
tearing his lungs, his eyes blurring. His face was clawed and his clothes
begrimed; his lovely hair was every which way. Through hot tears he
saw Frederica striding away into the distance, furious, her party and her
dignity spoiled. The Parrys, on the other hand, were coming towards
him. He looked for Poole, but could not see him.

"If you have a moment, Alexander," said Jenny, "I want to talk to
you." She summoned up the trailing remainder of the family. "Geoffrey
can hear what I have to say, we've talked it over already."

Alexander began to envisage a scene not unlike one he had already
been put through before, where the lady assured him graciously that it
had all been a mistake, that she had really loved her husband, all this
time. Such scenes were a price he paid for the kind of delicate love-life
he led.

"I told Geoffrey what happened."

"Oh?"

"*Exactly* what happened," said Jenny, on an unnecessarily minatory
note.

"What did?" said Alexander, foolishly.

"We went to bed together. Twice. I told Geoffrey. Geoffrey is going
to divorce me for adultery."

"But –"

"As for Thomas, Geoffrey doesn't want to part with Thomas, but –"
here she became tearful, a little, "neither do I. I really don't, whatever
I've said about him. I love him. I love you. As I told Geoffrey. Geoffrey
says we must all sit down and talk it over sensibly, what happens to
Thomas."

Alexander looked helplessly at Geoffrey, willing Geoffrey to say

something for himself, or perhaps to take a swing at his own face, which
he felt would have been certainly proper and with any luck final.
Geoffrey, he saw to his horror, was amused. Geoffrey was at least partly
pleased by the way things were turning out. Geoffrey, he surmised,
already envisaged a life with an attractive *au pair* girl and long hours in
the library with Thomas Mann. He thought of saying, "Geoffrey, your
wife is untouched by me, I couldn't get my end up." Not the sort of
sentence he could utter. He thought, more Machiavellian, of assuring
Geoffrey that he loved Thomas himself, that he couldn't think of
separating Thomas from his mother, for Geoffrey, he saw, would fight
for Thomas however little he cared what Jenny now did. But such
assurances stuck in his craw. For one thing, he was by no means ready to
assure either Geoffrey or Jenny that he would take on Jenny herself.
How the hell, he thought, crossly, could she *contemplate* going off with a
chap who couldn't even get his end up?

"I told Geoffrey about all those application forms," she went on,
remorselessly. "It would be easier, of course, if you are thinking of
going."

"Geoffrey –" said Alexander.

"I've nothing to add to what Jenny's said," said Geoffrey, the
amusement broader on his face.

"There are things she hasn't told you."

"Nothing, I'm sure, that could change what I want now," said
Geoffrey Parry, who had totally lost the strained look of the pram
episode and seemed his old scholarly self.

"We'll talk again after the last night," said Jenny, kindly. "That is,
the last night of your play."

The Parrys walked away, an apparently harmonious family group,
whilst Alexander climbed slowly to his tower.

40. *Last Night*

Perhaps there had been too many parties. Perhaps there was too much
sense of threat and thunder in the air. In any event, the Last Night of the
play ended, if not with a whimper, at most with a melodious twang.
Alexander sat and watched it through with feelings compounded of such
desire and terror that he would not, earlier, have imagined this possible.
One paradoxical effect of Jenny's ultimatum, and of Frederica's party in
general, was to give a unique and savage sense of urgency to his desire to

possess, make, have, make love to, fuck Frederica Potter. None of these words were part of his usual vocabulary. He did not say to himself "deflower" because he supposed that had already been done. He also wanted for the first time, although he was usually lazily incurious in such matters, to know just when, and by whom, the defloration had been performed. Under his nose in his play? Or earlier? Outdoors or indoors? By Crowe, Wilkie, or some unknown acneous youth from Blesford Ride? God knew there were enough of them. He felt extremely sour towards Thomas Poole, who had put his end away with such signal, if inconvenient success, and he felt a distinct distaste for the fleshy and complacent Daniel Orton, whose success turned out not to have been even inconvenient. He was horrified by his own emotions during the scissor-slitting scene which took place in less light than in earlier halcyon weeks, and even under a few ominous drops of rain. The muscle-bound Frederica of the early summer wriggled and arched her pelvis, waved a sinewy ankle in the air and exposed most of her slight breast in a way he considered tiresomely excessive, and which produced an inconvenient erection. It was funny, he thought, how he had not minded Wilkie's excavations in Jenny's décolletage. It was abhorrent. He, he himself, had made a fool of him, him himself. At least, at the least he should have, in recompense, what he now knew he wanted. That bloody girl. No, not bloody. When she ran off, in her torn petticoats, he sat still and waited for her to return for her Tower speech which she did, surpassing herself, hysterical and chill. Ego flos campi. Stone women do not bleed. I will not bleed. Alexander felt his own hard intentions set like stone.

In the interval he had meant to speak to her but was waylaid by Thomas Poole, whose confidences he no longer wanted. Poole said that if only Alexander would stand being the Wedding Guest for ten minutes longer he'd be eternally grateful, and Alexander said, nastily for Alexander, that Poole had got the wrong poet, hadn't he, he was meant to be Edmund Spenser, sweet poet of sweeter married love, the great shift in sensibility in the amatory epic if C. S. Lewis was to be believed, and that if he, Alexander, was him, Poole, which thank God he was not, he'd retreat into married love *pronto*. Poole did not seem to notice Alexander's nastiness, or clumsy jocularity, but went on to explain solemnly that he had now found a doctor, through, guess who? Marina Yeo herself. Who had said that her career in the past had depended on knowing reliable doctors with reliable nursing homes, and that she considered it a public service to pass these names on. The problem remained of persuading Anthea, of getting Anthea organised, all of which was highly distasteful, and of finding the money, which on his salary was no joke. Marina Yeo moved in the best circles, gynaecological as well as in other ways.

Alexander said please draw on himself for money, as this play seemed to be making quite a lot. And as for Anthea, if she was scared, that was only to be understood . . .

Poole said no, she was not scared. She was mad about missing a projected holiday in Juan-les-Pins. And she didn't like having doctors fingering her, she said. Alexander said that could be a euphemism for worse terrors, and Poole said he wished he could think so. They both had a stiff whisky, on this.

Frederica, prowling in the bushes at the beginning of the second act, unwilling to put off the lovely dress for the last time, met Anthea, in her white diaphane, tinsel crown, and silver-dipped laces, vomiting amongst the laurels.

"Are you O.K.?"

"You can see I'm not. It comes in these awful waves. If I get it over now I can go on and wave my sword and corn-sheaf without feeling dizzy. Have I got trails of gunge on these frills?"

"Only the slightest."

Frederica licked her handkerchief and rubbed. There was a small slimy trail on the pointed end of one layer of frilling.

"I suppose you guessed I'm preggers."

"What will you do?"

"Get rid of it. I've got to convince Mummy and Daddy I've got a good reason for going up to London for a week or two. Marina will have to help."

"Why should she?"

"Well, she found the medic, and the nursing-home, and all that. She'll see it through."

"Do you feel awful?"

Anthea-Astraea stared white as marble in the thickening light at Frederica's gingery, questing face.

"I feel green. I feel green all the bloody time. I don't enjoy anything. Not sex, or champagne, or strawberries, or people clapping, or clothes either, because they don't fit, or anything at all, if you want to know. I feel really cross. I thought nice people could be trusted to take proper precautions. I shall have to look after myself better. And if you think I'm as hard as nails, Frederica Potter, ask yourself how else I could be?"

She tripped off, a light fantastic figure, to take her place in the final presentation of the Masque. Redit et virgo. Redeunt Saturnia regna. So Thomas Poole anachronistically intoned, and the corn-sheaf of fecundity and the sword of justice wavered only slightly from their statuesque immobility.

Frederica found Wilkie. She was nearly in tears. He got hold of her arm – he had just come off after his final rape of Bess Throckmorton – and said, "Hey, steady, what's up?"

"I don't know. It's Anthea. She's ill. It's upsetting."

"Not ill, preggers. Soon mended. Marina says so."

"Mended is the *wrong word*."

"I suppose so. I do agree, prevention is better than cure. Perhaps passion overtook prevention. Tut. I trust to continue to manage my own affairs better. How are yours?"

"I don't know. I can't. I'm *scared*."

"You're a cock-teaser."

"Oh, is that what it's called? I didn't know that word. No I'm not, and you know I'm not, I just don't know what to do. I lied, and now there'll be all blood, at best, and I'm ignorant about – taking care – and he doesn't know I am – and I simply don't know what to do or how to do it, and he thinks I does, do, and I'm scared."

"I'm told the blood is usually a myth."

"Is it? Well, most myths have got some sort of basis in reality, some people must bleed somewhere, sometimes, and why not me? Please stop quibbling. I'm not a cock-teaser, and I'm not like that girl, hard as nails, she said, either. I mean, I couldn't be, look at Stephanie, all creamy, you have to think of the other *possibilities*, Wilkie, like that babies are marvellous, or are people, or something. Though I can't imagine myself ever wanting one I must say. I expect Steph's was just as much a case of passion overtaking prevention, only Steph's got more guts, if that's what I mean. Either way, not a good example for me. *What am I going to do?*"

"Well –" said Wilkie, "my own plans have gone a bit wonky, to tell the truth. I'd planned a lovely two or three days' trip up the coast on the bike after this, with my girl, and now she tells me she's detained in Cambridge and won't come. Do you want to? Just for the ride?"

"I can't. What with Daddy and Mummy and Marcus and Alexander and Alexander and Alexander. You know I can't."

"Solve a lot of problems. We'd have fun."

Frederica smiled grimly. "You don't care about your cock being teased?"

"It wouldn't be. That is, no, I don't care, so it wouldn't be, and then, moreover, there's no reason for you to be scared of me, because you don't love me in this daft way, and you haven't lied to me. So it wouldn't be – teased – for that reason, either. So why don't you come? We'd have fun."

"I never know what you *want*, Wilkie."

"That's easy. I want to be the best. Everything else – people included – comes second."

"The best what at?"

"Everything. Now *that's* my real problem. That keeps me awake at nights. If you're the best at everything, how do you know what to do next? Anyway, think about the coast. I'm off, tomorrow. I'll drop by and either pick you up or kiss you goodbye."

And so the sun went down for the last time on the last scene of *Astraea* and most of the cast hid behind bushes and brakes to watch it if they could, whilst Alexander and Lodge sat up high on the scaffolding, thus seeing, what was denied that night to a lot of the audience, the single red sliver of descending sun. There had been nights when it had gone down glorious round and bloody behind house, terrace and cushion, there had been nights when the sky had been magnificently slashed with silvered crimson on peacock. Tonight heavy clouds were banking, higher and higher, making dark before the dark of night, so that the light on Marina Yeo had to be reinforced with an arclight from the house, a little lurid, contributing considerably more chiaroscuro than Elizabeth I herself would have thought proper.

There she sat, anyway, for the last time, in her white pleated night-gown on her huge cream silk cushion, under the now clearly ponderous high red wig. The yards of rayed linen worn by Elizabeth II for the simple and sacramental moment of the Coronation ceremony had contributed something to the final conception of this bed-garment, whose sheer weight might never have been guessed from the ease with which Marina, before she began seriously to die, that was, trailed it or swirled it.

There she sat, with her finger, as history, mythology and the text dictated, childishly in her mouth, and, since this was a verse drama, spoke to herself with broken eloquence on the nature of things, solitude, virginity, power, the approaching dark. The hunch-shouldered Robert Cecil came busily up and down the terrace steps. Women, reminiscent of Charmian and Iras, waited around. The cushion had corded seams and fantastic knots of cord on its four corners. The queen spoke of England, babbled of green fields, remembered irascibly that the ring with which she had been wedded to England had had to be sawn off, since her aged marriage finger was deformed. Ringman, she called that finger, remembering, somewhat improbably, another childhood rhyme. She spoke too of mutability, and in Ovidian terms of the Age of Gold, rivers of milk and perpetual ripening corn. Then she fell into silence.

Lodge jabbed Alexander's ribs.

"Best bit of pure theatre I've ever done."

Slowly, slowly, the erect squatting figure with its jewelled turreted head swayed over on to the cushion. Miss Yeo could hold an audience for an unconscionable time, in dying. The red wig rolled away, reminding those who saw visual patterns of the earlier description of the severance of Mary Queen of Scots' wig from her severed head, and the white-headed woman sank death-pale into the creamy folds of the cushion. Here she jerked, struggled and stiffened amidst her aurora of white pleating, and the ladies came lovingly and made her into her own monument, straightening clothing and limbs, replacing a crimson rose between the closed, outstretched palms of that Tudor Icon. Because of the weather and the arclight the whiteness of this scene was thrown into more relief than ever before, and the actress seemed faceless, apart from the beaked nose that had been so carefully constructed every night with putty, and would not be again. Once they had her displayed on the cushion it was possible to carry her off, which they did, white, soft and still.

"Twisted it a bit," said Lodge. "She *did* get into bed, the old bitch, at last. But what theatre."

There were subdued farewells on the terrace after the play. People's clothes were already being taken from them and put into wicker crates for Stratford and elsewhere. Wilkie for some reason was ordering a lugubrious smashing of the equipment of the Bottle Chorus. He had a place in the stable yard where all bottles were to be thrown, and whilst some of the little boys enjoyed the crash and clatter of this, some protested tearfully that they had meant to keep their very own bottle as a memento. And of what use, said Wilkie severely to these backsliders, did they suppose one note would be, without the consort? They could make any bottle, any time, sing some sort of music. No, no, the whole thing was going to be smashed now, and he himself had the blueprint and at some future date, in some future place, he promised, the Music of the Spheres should ring out again. In the interim he didn't want his concept mangling, and besides, broken glass glinted prettily. So they threw, and threw, and threw, in a splintering cacophony.

Frederica approached Crowe, who was busy, it appeared, listening to Marina giving Anthea sensible advice. She said she wished to thank him for all he had done. She said – more tentatively – that she wished to consult him about her future. He said, at his most urbane, that he would be delighted to advise about this, if she really wanted him to, and gave her a glass of something – very sweet sherry, she feared, it was, tho' this seemed unlikely. And what, asked Crowe, did she particularly require advice *about*.

Well, said Frederica, she had always wanted to be an actress. She wondered if, with these reviews – she did not say, this performance – behind her, she might try for drama school, or rep even, try and build on it. It was what she *wanted*, a career in the theatre. Did Crowe have any particular suggestions as to how to set about it? Crowe smiled, and patted her shoulder. He smiled more.

"Naturally," he said, "Lodge's advice to you would be of more use than mine, or even maybe – doubtfully – dear Alexander's. But you have asked for mine. And shall have it, dear girl. So brace yourself. In order to make a career on the stage you must first –" smooth as silk – "get a new face, and a new body. And then learn to enact something other than yourself. It may be that you can do all these things. But my advice would be to do as Daddy suggests, dabble your toes in amateur dramatics and build on those excellent A Levels, about which we've all heard *so very much*. You can't really *act*, you know. You were type-cast, and there's not many of those types around to be type-cast as. You have said – with justice – that sweet Anthea was cast for prettiness and grace, but on the *stage, in general*, Frederica, those qualities are slightly more in demand than yours. I agree it would be better if sweet Anthea's voice were less twittering, but then, we can't have everything, although the drama schools are crowded out, I believe, with damsels who combine prettiness, grace, sweet tones, and a modicum of that very special wit – not your kind – that is required in actresses."

"I see," said Frederica.

"I'm sure you do. May I congratulate you again on your excellent performance, which surpassed all expectations – even mine. An intelligent hunch, it turned out. And may I wish you luck, in Oxford, or Cambridge, or wherever it may turn out to be. Now I must go back to Anthea's absorbing little problem. Goodbye, Frederica."

There were a few tears – not many, for she was furiously proud – in the grease, as Frederica took off her make-up in the mirror for the last time. She watched Marina Yeo covertly. Marina was ugly. Might never have been beautiful. Could, she supposed, always have seemed so. What Crowe had said was because of the Sun Bed, but also meant, she had the wit to realise, and even, she had also the wit to recognise, probably true. So that was that. She watched Jenny too, who seemed hectic, but not dispirited, as she had been. She looked at her own face. Crowe was right, it was odd and nothing, a schoolmistressy face with freckles and a pointed mouth and chin. As to her breasts – tugging the whalebone away for the last time – they were hardly breasts, knobs more, and there were knobs in other places, elbows, knees, which spotlights would lovingly pick out. Alexander came up behind her.

"Take you home?"

"Take Mrs Parry."

"I expect her husband will come for her."

"He doesn't usually."

"It's the last night. Don't be scrupulous. Frederica, Frederica, *come*."

She came. She let him march her off without a backward glance, from either of them, at Jennifer. She sat beside him in the car, and cried a little.

"What is it, my love?"

"Crowe says I'm too ugly to be an actress. And I can only act myself. Get a new face, he told me. The awful thing is, he's right."

"I can't see why you should want to be an actress. Not with a mind like yours. And God knows you're not ugly."

"Not?"

"Not. Dry sexiness was what Lodge said, the first time he saw you, when I was so blind and pig-headed. He didn't say the half of it. Every inch of you is . . . you are . . . You are the only woman – ever, I swear – I've got myself in this state of extremity about. If that amuses you."

"It doesn't *amuse* me," slowly. It did frighten her. It frightened her even, in her present state, that Alexander should think, or wish, her to be capable of amusement about sexual extremity. She was an ignorant fool. She had wanted an Alexander who was ungraspable, unspeakable, closed.

"I love you, Frederica. You are ludicrously young, and we are surrounded by ghastly examples of error, and the whole thing is impossible from start to finish, and I love you."

"I have always loved you."

He drove her out of Long Royston and as they went past the gatehouse and through the ornate iron gates, it struck her that she would not come again. Not at least until the new University had changed the whole landscape unrecognisably. She had somehow imagined she would become a welcome and familiar visitor there, wandering across lawns and kitchen gardens, and stable yards. She heard behind her the faint crash of breaking glass. Fled is that music. It really was like being shut out of Paradise. The gate should have clanged shut, but did not, for there was a lot of other traffic.

Alexander drove her very fast to the Castle Mound, stopped between the

Nissen huts and grabbed her. He tore, most unlike Alexander, at her underwear, causing pain with elastic and pain with fingernails and tugged hairs.

"I must, I must," he kept saying, even now incapable of a reasonable verb. Frederica fought, as she had once fought for a response, to keep herself intact.

"Not here, not now," she kept saying. Alexander battled, but not very manfully. They had trouble, and some pain, from gears and handbrake.

"Listen – Alexander – I'll think of something, I'll come tomorrow, I promise – if you'll just take me home now, now this minute. It's all been too much. I feel dirty. Please."

"Of course."

He took her home. They agreed to meet tomorrow, maybe on the Railway Bridge by Far Field, and go for a long quiet walk, away from these places, and think out ways and means. As soon as he was gone and she was alone in her narrow bed in Masters' Row she was overcome with belated, confused desire, to hold his silk skin, smell his hair, let go . . . whatever had to be let go. She went to sleep with fists clenched in wrath and desire.

Alexander, staring sleeplessly out of his tower window at the moon on the tomato-houses, witnessed accidentally the weaving, lurching return of Lucas Simmonds, who drove back as he had gone out, except that he was chugging now slowly, over peninsulas of grass and flowers. Dispassionate and cold Alexander watched Simmonds, a tousled figure, roll more or less out of the front of the car, and proceed drunkenly towards his own tower. He did not close the car door. Alexander considered going to his assistance, and could not bring himself to do so – there was no sort of assistance he could render in case of peering demons and milkbottles of blood on doorsteps, and if Simmonds was all right a good night's sleep would do him more good, most good. The thought of Simmonds was distasteful to him, too. He could leave it till morning. That the man was not dead, but going quietly back to bed disproved some part at least of Marcus Potter's anxious theory.

41. The Bilge Pond

Next day was Sunday. Marcus woke at home, heard with relief the familiar squeeze and hiss of his own painful breath, opened heavy eyes, closed them again, and lapsed into dreamless sleep. He was ill. He was irresponsible.

Alexander, who had not slept, became ashamed of his last night's behaviour with regard to Lucas Simmonds. He also remembered that Geoffrey and Jennifer would almost certainly appear with their new plans for his future, and decided with a mixture of cravenness and courage to go out. He went across the cloister to the foot of Simmonds's tower, where a pristine, gold-topped, white bottle of milk stood in the sun, and ran lightly up the stairs. Simmonds's door was open. Alexander knocked. No one was there. Alexander went in, noticing that the bed had been slept in normally, that pyjamas were flung across the pillow, as though normally stepped out of. He smelled toast and sweat. It was no business of his to open a window. He decided to keep an eye open for Simmonds and take his walk in the direction of Frederica Potter.

Frederica had trouble in getting out because Bill was quarrelling obscurely with Winifred about Stephanie's pregnancy. Although it was clear that Winifred could in no way be held responsible for the engendering of their future grandchild, this in no way prevented Bill from berating her for it, saying loudly and frequently that all was now explained, the thing had been conceived out of wedlock, that clergymen should have principles, that he would make a public mock of Daniel Orton. Winifred, unusually for her, wept. She wept, not because of Stephanie, whom she bitterly envied, but because of Marcus, whom she loved and had failed. She did not mention Marcus to Bill in case he thought of something to do about Marcus, such as interrogate Lucas Simmonds, if that person could be found. Anything Bill might do would be worse than inertia. This thought made her weep, and Bill shout, louder. When Frederica said she was going for a walk, Bill said no she was not. Winifred said why shouldn't she, and Frederica retreated into the kitchen and out through the back door. Immediately she was out, alone, in the sun, her body became her own again, and glistened with hope and terror. She began to run, up across the Far Field, knowing that Alexander would, must, be waiting for her, as surely as she knew the grass was hard and the railway train thundering across the horizon.

A large number of people seemed to be leaning out of the window of this particular express, calling and pointing. She felt that they had recognised her famous face, and then, more plausibly, that she had, in the agitation of the moment, left off some crucial garment. She hesitated, stood, and looked about. It was in this way that Alexander, from the bridge, and Frederica from the touch line of the rugger pitch saw the figure in the Bilge Pond, male, naked, and singing aloud. They advanced slowly. As they came nearer, Frederica to the back, and Alexander to the front of the figure, they recognised Lucas Simmonds, Frederica by the curly head and a certain importunate jut of the ivory buttocks, Alexander by the contorted crimson face. Simmonds was stirring the black, soft, circular water with a long pole, which he manoeuvred with his left hand. The Bilge Pond, long unplumbed, must have been deeper than anyone supposed. At least, it came over Simmonds's plump knees, swaying and soughing. The singing was partly O come, o come, Adonai, with endlessly elongated and trilling vowels, and partly Milton's version of the 136th Psalm, which was sung in the Blesford Ride Sunday Service on an average twice a term. The lines of this were often truncated and fell away into swishing of water. There was a certain febrile anger about the way the rod beat the water when the words went, and a curious loud, genuine exultation about those words that were remembered. Simmonds's hair, on both his head and his body, was very carefully dressed with flowers, furrow weeds, cow parsley, cranesbill and cockoo-pint, birds-foot trefoil and carefully placed large moon daisies, with ears of rye grass and barley grass and trailing woven sticky skeins of goose grass.

When Alexander approached closer he saw that the right hand was holding a very sharp butcher's knife, and that there were little wounds, and quite possibly larger wounds, crisscrossed along the inside of Simmonds's thighs, which were sheeted with glistering and dulling blood.

Alexander saw that Simmonds was mad: he had never for a moment supposed he would ever see anyone so classically, so grandly, so archetypally mad. But he could neither begin to imagine his state of mind nor think what to do. He thought he ought probably to walk boldly up. He walked.

"Simmonds. Simmonds, old chap. Can I help?"

Simmonds, with a look of ferocious concentration, stared at the sun, and continued to sing. Alexander stepped to the edge of the pond. Simmonds, wading and splashing a little made a very threatening slash at him with the knife. Alexander retreated. He became conscious of Frederica and made frantic gestures to her to go away. Frederica came closer, and Simmonds turned to face her, so that she saw at last the wilting glory of his floral crown, and breastplate, and the drooping purple flowers looped in the soft bush of his pubic hair. She also saw the blood, and the knife.

"Run home," said Alexander, "there's a good girl. Run home, and find help."

"No help," intoned Simmonds. "No help."

"*Run*," said Alexander to Frederica.

She ran.

Alexander squatted on the margin of the pond, at a distance, and stared, mesmerised, at Simmonds's private parts, which were large, and though bloody, unbowed. Simmonds bowed and batted the water, and sang sweetly and trailed away into disgruntled silences. Alexander wondered agitatedly what he should do if this maniac took it into his head to run for the railway line, or to make a determined attempt to castrate himself. Simmonds circulated. Alexander decided that on the whole he preferred the back view.

Frederica burst into a family row that had become augmented by the presence of Daniel and Stephanie who had decided, somewhat despondently, to try and improve matters by apologising jointly for the conception of their child. She shouted out,

"Help, help, Lucas Simmonds is stark raving mad in the Bilge Pond and Alexander's up there and he's threatening him with a *knife*. And when I say stark, I mean *stark*. Help. Covered with flowers and things, like King Lear or Lady Chatterley's lover. Do something. They always said there are leeches in there, in that pond, it's horribly black. He looks *awful*, he keeps *singing*."

"Ambulance," said Daniel to Stephanie. "Stop shouting," said Daniel to Frederica. It was, however, too late for this admonition. Marcus appeared, pale and shaky, on the landing. Stephanie was addressing the emergency services and explaining that she wanted an ambulance in the middle of the rugger pitch – the Far Field – at Blesford Ride school. No, it was not a sporting accident, she thought police might be needed – a dangerous man with a knife . . . restraint.

"You needn't *enjoy* it," said Daniel crossly to Frederica.

"I'm not really, it's just my way of expressing myself, and I did come for help, that's the main thing, isn't it?" said Frederica, tossing her head like a maenad and glowing with drama and self-importance.

"You could have kept your bloody *voice down*," said Daniel. Frederica looked round blankly uncomprehending. Marcus crept quietly down the stairs and pulled at Daniel's sleeve.

"Are you going there? Shall I – come?"

Daniel turned his mind to this problem.

"You don't have to."

"I knew something terrible would happen. I am responsible for him. I must come."

"If you must, you must. If it makes it worse, or if I say so, you go home, you understand?"

"He isn't going," said Bill.

"It's his life," said Daniel. "You've let him live it up to just without interfering in it. Now they're in real trouble, if he feels he's got to see it through, I say he can."

"The man's a maniac."

"Maybe so am I," said Marcus, twitching very gently with pale fingers at Daniel's coat-sleeve. "Maybe – I can calm him down. He used – to do – what I told him."

"*You* do what I tell *you*," said Bill.

"Why?" said Daniel, who was as he put it to himself, proper narked with Bill on his own account, and maybe therefore not seeing clearly about Marcus.

"I've *got* to come. If anything – happens – I shall – be responsible all my life."

"Come on then," said Daniel. At this, Stephanie too pulled at Daniel's sleeve. "Should you?"

"Truth is better than imagination, and Marcus is right, this is his business. Come on."

They all trailed away up the garden path and onto the Far Field, at this, Marcus faltering between Daniel and Stephanie, Bill and Winifred wandering after, Frederica striding, subdued by the bad taste of her own noisiness, in their wake. Lucas Simmonds was still in the pond, the singing now a little raucous, and Alexander was still squatting uselessly on guard. Daniel strode up to Lucas.

"We've come to get you out."

Lucas circulated.

"Why?" said Daniel, who could have done without his open-mouthed audience, whom he found inhibiting. He genuinely wanted to know *why* Simmonds had chosen to enter this pond, in this state of floral nakedness.

Simmonds brandished the knife. Marcus ran forward.

"Sir! Sir! This is all wrong. I know I should have come, I didn't think what you thought I thought, I do believe, the photisms, the grasses, sir, we *saw*, there are scientific records – but this isn't the way."

Lucas turned, his head lowered like a bull, and glowered. Marcus stepped forward and held out his hand.

"Please come out."

Very deliberately Lucas Simmonds splashed the fine black silt of the bilge pond up in great blotches over the boy, clean shirt, grey trousers, white freckled face.

"Go away. You aren't going to be kind to me. Not you."

He beat again at the water. An ambulance could be observed humping its way over the grass at the edge of the verge.

"Who?" said Daniel, as various ambulancemen and policemen made their way up the field, with a stretcher, a straitjacket, a scarlet blanket in the hot sun. "Who?"

Lucas Simmonds looked desperately round the circle, so many Potters, fragile Alexander, stolid Daniel. He stepped out of the pond, which sucked at his feet, walked over to Stephanie, and buried his hot head on her breast. There he stood, grotesquely humped, since she was a small woman, grotesquely striped, black mud, red thighs, white body, crimson neck, and the blotches of flowers, and she put her arms round him, her stomach heaving and said, meaninglessly, "Never mind."

"I did tell you, I did tell you, I have no private life, I touch no one."

"Never mind."

"The destroyers are coming."

"No, no. A little peace."

"Don't you believe it, lady. I've been there before. There is no peace in those places, only white lights and the annihilation of reasonable time and space. I think I won't go."

He stood up weakly and waved his knife, so that the little posse of men came running at him from behind, tackled and felled him, took the knife, and bundled him into the ambulance. The door closed.

"Where will they take him?" said Marcus.

"Calverley General Hospital, I should think," said Daniel. "It's got a psychiatric ward."

"Is it all right there?"

"Not bad. There are better, and worse. He'll be quiet, there."

"He doesn't want . . ."

Back in Masters' Row, Winifred insisted that Marcus, who was wheezing horribly, should be put back to bed. Alexander stood next to Frederica, listening to Bill inveighing about the fundamental immorality of interfering with pupils. Stephanie sat down with her eyes closed. The man's skin had burned under her fingers, he had put his wet mouth on her breast, she would never be free of the pity, she wanted a bath. Bill said he would go up and have a good talk to Marcus, find out exactly what those two had been up to, make sure the boy knew that the whole foul thing was absolutely at an end. Winifred said, over her dead body – Marcus must be left alone, he must not be hectored or inquired of, he must have peace and privacy. Winifred was right, but it was because she unexpectedly won her point that it was not discovered until late afternoon that Marcus had climbed out of his bedroom window, asthma and all, and had vanished.

It took Bill and Winifred two days and a half to find their son, although it should have been simple. Bill began by asserting wildly that the boy was "all right" and "had only gone for a walk". Winifred was convinced that Marcus was, probably intentionally, dead. When Bill belatedly agreed to call in the police time was lost looking on waste ground and in rivers: Alexander drove uselessly up and down side-roads, and Wilkie was roped in by Frederica and roared up and down on his motorcycle peering into ditches and thickets. Daniel telephoned the Calverley General Hospital, who said that Marcus Potter was not there, and that neither was Lucas Simmonds, who had been examined, transferred under sedation, and admitted to Cedar Mount, a large asylum some twenty-five miles out of Calverley in the middle of the countryside, set in its own walled grounds. Daniel then telephoned Cedar Mount, which informed him that Lucas Simmonds was still under sedation and that nothing had been seen or heard of Marcus Potter.

Frederica went with Alexander. She felt odd: her attention flew off in all directions: sometimes she saw in her mind's eye the man's red nakedness and sometimes her brother's nonentity of a face, but could not connect the two. Sometimes a kind of warm fatigue slid over her, and with it desire, and she would touch Alexander's legs beside her. Sometimes, when she did this, he trembled with desire, and sometimes with irritation; he too could not focus his attention either on the extraneous disaster or on the girl, now. He had several pieces of paper in various pockets from the school secretary saying that Mrs Parry, or sometimes that Dr Parry, had phoned, but he had managed to avoid actually having to answer any of these calls. He also had two thick letters from Jenny, which he had not opened. Like Frederica, *mutatis mutandis*, his mind's eye was unpleasantly drawn back to Lucas Simmonds's exposed and scarlet parts.

As for Marcus, he walked. Daniel had been right in his instincts: only his calls had been mistimed and the hospital switchboard people ill-informed and inefficient. First Marcus had walked to Calverley, along secondary roads, lightheaded with movement and breathing more easily as he went on. He was convinced that he had himself, partly inadvertently, severed some thread that held Lucas to reality, and that with that thread, his own tenuous connection, through Lucas, to daily life, had gone. He should have gone with him to the stones and been killed, he kept thinking, though why that would have been better he was not quite sure. Anyway, he had done wrong – to do right was to stick to Lucas. He plodded along grass verges and pollen flew up and swelled his eyelids and the mucous membranes in his throat. No messages came through, but he had a horrible sense that the light was waiting to flow at him, and was inimical, if he let down some curious defences of inanity and ordinariness he had built up. As he was afraid of the light, so he had also become afraid of the house in Masters' Row, which he envisaged as a square black system of boxes inside which you wandered forever, in intolerable heat, ending at blank walls and turning.

When he got to Calverley, he was cunning. He found the hospital by finding a street plan outside the Minster, and he walked there, circuitously, round a ring road which was easy to follow but horribly long, noisy and dusty. By the time he got there he felt that he looked odd, which was dangerous, and indeed that he was odd, from emotion, hunger, hay fever, asthma and fatigue. He had no wish or capacity to eat, but hadn't eaten already for two days.

He sat on a park bench and let himself weep a little, soundlessly: this was part of the cunning, as the weeping relaxed him, and thus made it possible for him to do what he must, and produce a nice normal voice in which to request to visit Lucas Simmonds. He flapped his hands at his dusty flannels and polished his shoes with his handkerchief, with which he then tried, with indifferent success, to remove the film of dust from his glasses. He then got up and staggered about a bit until he considered he could walk briskly into the hospital, adjusted his smeared glasses on his smeared face, leant in the right direction, and set off.

He hated and feared hospitals. The smell, the echo, the bustles and languors. He plunged between swing doors into this one and addressed a porter in a squeak that settled, miraculously, into the right, polite, neutral noise.

He had to keep this up for half an hour as he was transferred from glass cage to glass cage, from porter to nurse to nurse to male nurse who knew, who told him, that Lucas Simmonds had been sent away to a place in the country. Which place? The male nurse was kind, wrote down directions on a piece of paper, drew a little road map, the scale of which was, perhaps fortunately, at that point meaningless to Marcus. Marcus nodded stiffly with gratitude, afraid that if he spoke any more some squeak or tremor might betray him.

Next, taking two days over it, expending some more cunning on sleeping in a hayfield to conserve what he ludicrously thought of as his "strength", he walked cross-country to Cedar Mount Asylum for the Insane. He did not remember much of this walk except that dust and sweat and tears caked on him like a death-mask, and that he had drunk a rather nasty puddle, which made him feel sick, just before reaching a quite passable cow-trough. He almost certainly – no one ever measured or knew – covered more miles, many more miles, than were necessary,

circling the place several times before hitting its high wall, round which
he staggered and trotted until he came to a gate, and a path, through
which he squeezed and down which he went. Cedar Mount was, like
Blesford Ride, only much bigger, Victorian Gothic, and like Blesford
Ride, in fact, endowed by Crowe's munificent liberal ancestor to be run
humanely, like the Retreat in York.

Now too tired for cunning Marcus mounted steps, clutched at a
white-overalled woman and said he had come to visit his friend, Mr
Lucas Simmonds, and was afraid he was a little late. He put the last bit in
to make his pink and panting appearance more plausible. He squeaked
and groaned, and let the asthma sound like an organ to cover his lack of
control of his voice. He had in fact grabbed the best person possible, a
kindly, possessive and officious tea-lady, who said, doubtfully, that she
thought Mr Simmonds wasn't having visitors. "Nonsense!" said
Marcus, in an amazing imitation of his father's bark. "Well," said the
tea-lady, she would see, and she plodded away down a hall, closely
followed by Marcus, and along a ward, in which old men in nightgowns,
or in cheery shirts and flannels, sat by lockers or near a long window. At
the end of this ward, the tea-lady veered away in search of a sister and
Marcus found Simmonds lying in an iron bed, staring at the ceiling, his
cherubic face vacant and flushed.

"Sir," said Marcus. "Sir. I came to see you."

Simmonds rolled his head over, and stared.

"I'm sorry I look so awful I expect. I walked."

"Where we are is uncertain."

"No it isn't, it's called Cedar Mount, it's in a quiet place, I know
where it is, I walked it."

Simmonds stared. Marcus thought: he will spit at me, he will just shut
his eyes, he will be sick or something. Simmonds stared. Then he said,
forming the words very carefully,

"Sit down."

Marcus sat down. He pulled out Simmonds's limp hand from under
the sheet and held it. It shook. He said,

"You see, I came. It was all *real*. It just went wrong. You were afraid
it might. You must tell me, but not now, not yet, when you can. What
happened."

"Oh. Nothing happened. Only – something – shameful."

"It doesn't *matter*, sir. You've got to get better."

"They'll – take bits of me away. Not the right bits. Bits of brain.
They'll . . . they damage my memory. Then – you – lose your job.
Probably that – anyway. Don't let them. Don't – go away – Marcus.
Thank you – very much – for coming."

Marcus felt that only his dusty death-mask was preventing his face from creasing into tears. He said,

"I won't go. I promise I won't go."

Simmonds said,

"Let me – whisper."

Marcus dropped his clay-face nearer the struggling mouth.

"I'm scared – but it doesn't – really matter – about me. You're – the real thing. The miracle. Don't – let them wire you. Don't. Don't let anyone – get your brain. God – wants – you."

"Or something."

"God or something." Simmonds gave a leaden smile. "Or me. You won't go."

"No. I won't go."

He didn't go, for some time, though he and Lucas fought a complex battle against ultimately insuperable odds. Both wept, both at one point screamed, Marcus tried clutching the bed when touched. Simmonds was dealt with by a needle, so that Marcus passed the last part of the vigil, after the threshing of Simmonds's body had been succeeded by torpor, watching a snoring lump. As long as no one knew who he was, incredibly, they let him sit there, occasionally coming to interrogate him as to his identity, or how he had come. He answered with polite, dusty, ghostly smiles. Daniel's third, more desperate telephone enquiry at length gave the hospital authorities some idea of what they had to deal with, and Marcus finally lifted a tired head from a glass of water – he had still refused all food – to see his parents proceeding down the ward towards him. Winifred averted her eyes from the figure in the bed. Bill said,

"Now, it's all right, now you can come home, and all this nonsense will be over, as though it hadn't happened."

Marcus began to scream. He was amazed he could make so much noise, and then amazed that he couldn't stop, and then amazed at the case the sound built round him. His father's face spoke earnestly and no voice was heard. An old man told Marcus – Marcus thought he was telling Bill, and giggled in his screaming – to shurrup. A doctor was fetched. A strong nurse was fetched. Marcus screamed and wept and was needled. Bill and Winifred talked to the doctors, and it was agreed that they and Marcus should stay there, overnight, they to watch with him, so he would feel safe when he regained consciousness. Then they could all talk over what to do. Winifred telephoned Frederica, and told her that Marcus was found, but ill, was in hospital and they with him, that they would not come home that night. Frederica would not mind being alone,

would she? She would be sure and lock the doors, she would let Daniel
know, who had found Marcus, she would be all right on her own.

Frederica said she would be quite all right.

42. *The Virgin in the Garden*

Frederica called off the search. It was easy to find Alexander, which she
had still time to be amazed by, since years had passed when she had loved
him and seen him only with a leap of the heart and inadvertently, every
two or three weeks, or at even longer intervals. Now, like a lover, he
never left her without instructions as to where he could be found, or
where a message could be left. This was terrible power, his anxiety that
she should be certain of him conferred on her a terrible power.

Wilkie was harder to find, now the play was over: during its run he
had had digs in Calverley but had as often as not slept at Long Royston,
and the Calverley digs, where Frederica had never been, had only a
phone-box in the hall, which mostly rang echoing and interminable, but
was occasionally answered by complete strangers, who did not know
who Wilkie was, or had seen him, but maybe two or three weeks ago,
not since. So she left messages for Alexander to call at likely places, and
waited for Wilkie to turn up, which he did, roaring goggled and leather-
coated up Masters' Row, like Cocteau's messengers of death from
Orphée. Frederica had not really expected that she and Alexander would
find Marcus at all: she realised, as Wilkie's head emerged from its
cavernous shell, that she had feared that Wilkie would find him, horribly
limp and mangled.

"It's O.K. He's found. He'd gone to the looney bin where that man
has been put. Two looney bins. He walked. They say he's ill himself,
they don't know how ill, they don't say if he's mad, too, or what."

"I see. Oh well, I'll get back to my plans for departure. You aren't
coming?"

"How can I? The parents have stayed with him, with Marcus, he's
under observation, I've got the house to myself. I'm in charge."

"Well, there's not really anything for you to be in charge of. A white
lie about staying with a friend would do it. Do you good, a bit of sea
air."

"Don't be silly. I can't. Come in and have a cup of coffee."

"No, thank you. I've got things to do." He began to resume gauntlets
and helmet. "I was only helping in case of distress. I'll be in touch.
Before long, before I go. Look after yourself."

He flung a leg over the saddle, revved several times very loudly, and roared off up the road, an unlikely black knight. Frederica went back into the house and walked about from room to room. She had never been alone there; the small silence and emptiness frightened her a little – but things had also begun to take on a rather pleasing combination of unreality and disposability. She put a vase she'd never liked in a kitchen cupboard, and was encouraged by this to wander back into the sitting room and dispose of the family photographs on the top of the bureau. Her own childish self and Stephanie's she stuck in a desk drawer, with a certain glee, but she lingered over baby Marcus, feeling confused by knowledge she hadn't known she had: how much Winifred loved that baby; how much she herself had hated it; how she had protected herself and Marcus from this hatred by what now struck her as an extraordinary deliberate ignorance of his nature and ways. She had simply treated him as a social element of injustice, to be indignant about. She pushed him away in a drawer too, and then added all Bill's spare pipes, pipe cleaners and ashtrays to this collection. She wished Wilkie would have come in to coffee. Never in her life had she had a place into which she could ask anybody or anything, and he had not noticed this momentous occasion, he had just said, no, and driven off.

She was about to wander rashly out into the back garden and cut roses, which Winifred did not do, when Alexander's silver car drew up smoothly outside the front door. He leaped up the front path, a hart in flight, his face averted from the direction of the Parrys' front gate, wanting not even to know if there was a twitch of a curtain or a chink of light round a door. Frederica opened the front door rather grandly.

"I've got a whole house to myself."

"Well, let me get inside it, don't stand on the step, if you don't mind. How is he? How is Marcus?"

"Oh, he's O.K. They've found him. Well, no, he isn't very good, but they have found him. He had gone off to that mental place. Daniel was right, it was just nobody knew who he was. Now he's in bed there himself, quite ill, Mummy says, she doesn't say how ill, or what sort of ill. Anyway, they've gone there to be with him, and I've got a house to myself."

She led Alexander into the sitting room of this house, and said, "Have a cup of coffee."

"Thank you very much," said Alexander, politely.

She clattered about, very busily and not very competently, with pans. Alexander followed her, and leaned on the dresser, watching her. Both of them were inhibited by the contradictory facts of the house: it was a closed, secretish place, and they were alone together in it. It was Bill

Potter's house, in which Frederica was a berated child and Alexander a junior colleague, in which rage, and domesticity, the tedious repetitive patterns of cleanliness, eating and sleeping, hung heavy in the air. They took their coffee back into the sitting room, sat down in separate chairs, and began a rather polite conversation about Marcus.

"I feel very bad," said Alexander. "He came and told me, Marcus, that that man was going mad, and I didn't take him seriously."

For some reason – which was nothing to do with what Marcus might have felt – this information made Frederica very angry.

"Why should he do that? Why should he bother you? They *are* lunatics. What did you do?"

"Well – I thought – it was all sex. I advised the boy to keep clear."

"Well, that was all right, that was sensible."

"It obviously wasn't sensible. I was confused. Because of you."

"Because of me?"

"Well, I felt I had no room to talk. Seduction of minors. Your father. All that."

"That isn't a very nice thing to say to me."

"You can't take that line. You aren't very nice."

"Not very nice?"

"Well, are you? If you were, we wouldn't be sitting here. We'd be worrying about Marcus."

"It wouldn't do any good if we did. It probably never would have, it certainly won't now."

"Tell me how he is."

"I told you. I don't know."

They drank coffee, silently, on that, thinking of the unthinkable Marcus and the even more unthinkable Lucas, whom they had, nevertheless, conjointly, seen.

The telephone rang. It was Winifred, who said that Marcus was worse, that he wouldn't or couldn't eat, was mostly unconscious, couldn't be moved. She was staying with him.

"And Daddy?"

"He says he must stay, too."

There was no rapport between Winifred and Frederica. No sympathy was offered to, or sought by, Winifred. Frederica said, "It feels a bit funny, being here on my own with nothing to do."

There was a dazed silence at the other end of the phone.

"I feel awful, there was the play, and now there's just all this disgusting mess about Marcus, and nothing. Are you still there?"

"Yes, Frederica."

"I might go away for a bit, with a schoolfriend."

"Which one?"

"Oh, Anthea. Anthea Warburton. You know, the nice girl who was in the pageant bit of the play."

"Yes. Well. I'm sorry, I can't think, I'm so worried about Marcus. Do go away."

"You don't mind?"

"No, no. I can't see what you're making such a fuss about."

"I thought you might need me, in some way."

"No," said Winifred, who felt that she might just, possibly, conserve enough calm and strength to deal with Bill and Marcus if someone would simply remove Frederica for several days.

"Well, I'm sorry I'm not needed. I'll take myself off. Or perhaps I won't. I've told Alexander and Wilkie to stop looking for him."

"Thank you."

"Has he said anything?"

He had begged to see Lucas, he had told his parents to go away, he had screamed and screamed that he would not go home.

"Nothing really," said Winifred. "He's ill."

"Oh well. How awful. So you aren't coming home?"

"No."

"You do sound rotten. Don't worry about me. If I can't cope, I'll just take myself off. I'll be sure to keep in touch."

"Thank you."

"It might come out all right," said Frederica with a touch of doubt. She was speaking to the black air. Her mother had, out of pure fatigue, put down the receiver.

"How is he?" said Alexander.

"Worse," said Frederica. "They aren't coming home."

"What's wrong with him?"

"She won't say. She won't say anything. She doesn't trust me. She only cares about him."

"You can't blame her."

"Can't I? I do. I do. I do."

"I think I'll go, now."

"No, don't. Don't. I'm sorry. I only grate on people's nerves because I don't know what to do, I don't fit in anywhere, I'm not seen, for all I flaunt myself so. I agree, that doesn't matter, beside what Marcus is going through, whatever that is, but it does to me, I've got to *be*, I can't annihilate myself."

"Stop whirling about. I'll go now. I can't sit in your mother's house, like this, and feel as I do, with all this going on."

"No, don't. Don't go. Stay with me. I'm scared in this house, by myself."

"What can I do here? I feel I've betrayed their trust once, and now I'm starting again. I feel terrible."

Frederica did not want to know that. There was something finally disastrous in confessions of doubt, or inadequacy, or guilt, from Alexander at that time in that place. It increased her dangerous sense of power, over him, over things, intolerably. She became glittering and irresponsible, in answer to this.

"It's only a place. It's only bricks and mortar and chairs and things – not your chairs, or mine, just chairs that are here, as far as we're concerned. You can touch me up in the garden at the House, or on the Mound, or here, it doesn't matter, the place doesn't matter, that's just – a matter of taste. Aesthetics. Love isn't a matter of aesthetics. *This is just a place.*"

Alexander, whose nature was profoundly aesthetic, chose to respond to this by saying that he was sorry, he saw she was really upset, he shouldn't have fussed her further. Frederica said that he mustn't go, that odd though it might seem, she was afraid of being alone in the house, she had bad thoughts. Perhaps Alexander would stay to lunch.

He stayed to lunch. They had spam, and tinned carrots, and old bread, and some vinegary beetroot out of a jar, and tea. Frederica observed that this was a very nasty meal, and Alexander agreed. Both, after the debauchery of Crowe's hospitality, were beginning to feel badly in need of a drink, which wasn't to be had, without going out which, under Jennifer's eye, they didn't want to do. After lunch they went back to the sitting room, and Alexander took hold of Frederica on the sofa. This was not a success. All their limbs were at awkward angles, and Frederica was rigid with terror. This drove her, glittering again, to say that since they had a whole house, it would be better if Alexander came upstairs.

"No," said Alexander. "Not here."

"It's only a house, it's my house, it's my room, I want you to."

They went upstairs. Alexander remembered his brief trip to Stephanie's room, on the wedding day, in search of small gold pins. He then remembered his trip round Jennifer Parry's considerably brighter and more "contemporary" version of this form of house. Why were women, even Frederica, apparently compelled to act like estate agents and proudly display the cramped comforts of brick boxes? Frederica had a glorious apprehension of which he was quite unaware, that this house would never seem to her again so dumpy and solid and indisputable. She had imagined Alexander on these stairs, entering this bedroom. She was converting the blocks of house into her own imagination. She flung open the door of her little bedroom and said, as she had never expected to, "Come in."

He was moved by its poverty: the few things, the lino, the faded prints, the piles of books, for which there was not enough shelf space. There was no dressing-table, only a square mirror over an old oak chest of drawers. In one corner of the mirror was stuck a rather blurred newspaper photograph of himself: in another was a large glossy proof of a press photograph of Frederica in the Elizabeth costume. This moved him too, though differently. Frederica, catching him looking at it, said, "I see Crowe was quite right, it was type-casting. School makes me play men, and Crowe picks me up for a chance facial resemblance. How humiliating."

"It wasn't only that. You can't carry off a part like that only on type-casting."

"I will not bleed," she said, ruminatively, and became nervous, there in broad daylight, of what might happen. Alexander, for reasons of his own, also became nervous. He sat down gingerly on the end of her bed, motioned to her to sit beside him, and said, "I keep thinking your father will come hurling in. I feel very unsafe. And in bad taste, which I do mind, actually."

"I don't see how you can afford to. The whole affair is in *terrible* taste, but there it is, and here we are, and we aren't unsafe. I think."

Alexander put his arms round her and pushed her down on the bed. He kissed her. His feeling of being overlooked became more pronounced, and so did her fear of his discovery of her ignorance. She bobbed up again, like a Kelly doll.

"This is all wrong," she said.

"Yes. I told you so."

"It seems such a waste of a lot of private space."

"Maybe tonight," said Alexander, laying a heavy hand on the now, again, pleasurably inaccessible line of her crotch. She sighed.

"I could come back much later, with a bottle of wine. When you were sure they weren't coming back."

"I could make you some dinner."

"So you could."

"With candles. In the *dark*."

"Splendid."

"Would you like that, Alexander?"

"Yes," he said. "Yes. I shall walk down, quietly in the dark, across the playing fields, and in at the back and we'll sit and have a quiet drink, and a night, a whole night –"

"And you won't mind that it is this house?"

"I want you," he said, as fiercely as he could. He thought he might
not mind the house so much, in the dark. Anyone might enter any house
in the dark, clandestinely, for love: things would look different.

After this was decided they lay together and struggled with fruitless
passion, for a little time, fully clothed, and then Alexander got up and
went away.

He drove back ruminatively to the school. This time he looked at
Jennifer's house, but it was still and eyeless on the roadside. And it did
not, he reflected, overlook the playing field, since it was too near the
end of Masters' Row. His pockets were crammed with unanswered
letters. He must, he thought, remember to empty them before tonight's
engagement. Besides Jenny's thick, still unopened envelopes he had
answers to most of the wild batch of application forms he had sent off.
Everyone seemed to want him. He was summoned for interview in
Oxford, in the Manchester BBC, in the London BBC, at the famous old
public school in Dorset. He had also unsolicited letters from drama
publishers, literary agents, a London producer, an American producer of
doubtful standing and various school and college and town and country
literary groups. He was somebody. He was mobile. He was advancing.
And all that was in his head was an image of a thickset naked man in a
pond and a ferocious schoolgirl in a cheap brick house, waiting for the
dark. It might be more sensible not to turn up: simply to pack his bags
and go. The moment he had that thought, he realised, with a wave of
weakness and heat that that was out of the question: there were things to
be settled with Frederica, here and now, before he could be his own man
again. He would settle them, in the dark. As for Geoffrey and Jenny, he
would simply write and tell them the truth, as he saw it, the whole truth,
to both of them, and the truth would release him. But not quite yet.

Frederica realised she would have to go shopping. The spam had not
done, really, once, and would certainly not do again. She realised she had
never cooked dinner for anyone, and didn't really know how. She
realised she had almost no money. It was before the days of Elizabeth
David and her ideas of what constituted a nice dinner for two were
derived from *Woman's Own* and her mother's exceedingly infrequent
practical example. Grapefruit with cherries in, and a roast duck, and
fresh fruit salad with cream? Hors d'oeuvre and steak with jacket
potatoes and salad, followed by baked bananas with rum and cream? Ice
cream? Soup with hot rolls followed by trout followed by trifle with lots
of sherry in it? She did not trust herself to roast a duck, or to choose and
cook a steak without producing something leathery and unchewable:
there wasn't any sherry or rum and she hadn't got any money to get any

with. She couldn't think what went in an hors d'oeuvre, never having had one she liked. She knew soup should be home-made, not tinned, and had no idea how to make or improvise a soup. The only bits of any of these menus she could do were the grapefruits and jacket potatoes, so she decided to get those and try to get inspiration for the main course by staring at the Blesford butcher's window. It was whilst she was doing this, gloomily, with a bag full of potatoes, grapefruit, Danish blue cheese and cream crackers, that Wilkie roared past again. Frederica went hastily into the butcher. The butcher, when asked, suggested a nice pork chop, and Frederica, who didn't know the difference between a lamb and a pork chop, or if there was a beef chop, somewhat weakly bought two, because she vaguely remembered that male characters in Dickens frequently found chops very succulent, and because indifferent chops she had had were never as nasty as the gone-wrong steaks.

When she came out again, she had almost no money for the unsolved pudding, and Wilkie was waiting for her on the pavement.

"Housekeeping?" he said, pleasantly.

Frederica glowered at him. "Trying to cook dinner for someone. But I haven't got any money."

"I could stand you a bottle of wine."

"I don't have to get that. I've got pudding problems."

Wilkie swung his helmet, and expressed great interest in the pudding problems. Frederica deployed the fruit salad, the bananas and rum, the sherry trifle. Wilkie said he didn't really think any of those were very *nice*, and he suggested a sizeable bunch of grapes and some really good chocolates, which he would lend her the cash for, if that helped. He came with her, most obligingly, selected her bunch of grapes for her, bought her the chocolates, commented adversely on her choice of cheese, insisted that she go back for a piece of real Lancashire or Wensleydale, and offered her a lift back home on the back of the bike. The shopping was strapped to the luggage rack, Frederica, her red hair blowing out, swayed breathlessly on the pillion, and they rode back to Masters' Row. This time, uninvited, Wilkie came in. He watched with interest whilst Frederica wandered round the kitchen looking for presentable plates, and candles.

"Who's coming, then?"

"Alexander. They've all gone off, to look after Marcus. Alexander's coming."

"I see. The classic supper and wine and candles and conversation and bed for two. God, you are a loon, Frederica Potter."

"What do you mean?"

"I told you he was in flight from suburbs and teacups. And here are you, all domestic and *not*, if I may say so, any good at it, preparing him a bourgeois seduction. He'll run a mile. Before or after."

"I *want* him."

"Do you? In a house? In this house?"

"It's a rather nice destructive act. Like sacrilege. He was here all morning."

"I see. And if it's a destructive act, why are you flapping about chops and Danish blue? And if he was here all morning, did you get deflowered, and if you did, why did he go away at all, and why the candles and grapefruit, girl?"

"It isn't your business."

"No, it isn't. I'll go, if you like, and leave you to your preparations. Why don't you have a bowl of roses in the middle of the table?"

"Oh, Wilkie, don't go, I'm all in a mess, I'm so *scared*, and no, it didn't happen this morning, and it should have, and now I don't see how it ever will, because if I'm not scared, he is, and vice versa."

"If he does manage to make you, here, tonight, I can tell you, that's the last you'll see of him. And if he doesn't, *you'll* never have the guts. You are in a mess, love."

"I don't see how you can be so categorical."

"O.K., I can't. It's a hunch. I have good hunches. I have a hunch you want to cry off the whole thing."

"Me? I love him. I *want* him."

"You might still have got him in the wrong time and place. It happens all the time. Love, and want, and two people the wrong age, or going in the wrong direction; look at me and Marina. I might have loved her, if I'd been born twenty years ago, or hadn't got my girl in Cambridge, or could stand being a gigolo. But as it is, I can fuck her more or less affectionately, pro tem, and that's it. She knows."

"What does she *feel*?"

"What she knows she can afford to feel. She's a wise woman, no fool."

"I feel a strong urge to throw these horrible chops at you, Edmund Wilkie."

"Better pack your nightie and get on my motorbike and let Alexander sort you out some other, better way."

Frederica put the dead chops down on the draining board.

"I told my mother I might go away with a friend for a few days."

"Ah, you did, did you? And what did she say?"

"She said, who, and I said, that nice girl, Anthea Warburton, and she said, fine."

Wilkie began to laugh. He laughed a great deal. Frederica began to laugh, somewhat hysterically. When they had stopped laughing, Wilkie said, go on, get your nightie and toothbrush, and a swimsuit and a towel.

"You don't love me, Wilkie."

"No. I love my girl. Sort of. You don't love me, either."

"That's awful."

"That's sensible. I can show you a thing or two, and then you'll be able to look after yourself. Now *I* am in the right time and place, here. Go and get your nightie."

Frederica went to get her nightie. Edmund Wilkie, a tidy-minded man in a less than wholly practical way, made a neat pyramidal pile of the dinner ingredients in the middle of the kitchen table. Frederica came back, with her things in a rucksack, and Wilkie, smiling slightly, said,

"Now, telephone your Mum, and Alexander, so you aren't flapping or brooding or changing your mind once we've gone, and we'll be off."

"I can't telephone Alexander. Not now."

"Write him a note. We'll drop it off at the school."

Frederica did as she was told. Winifred sounded unbothered by her movements and the note was delivered, by Wilkie, to the school porter, who said gloomily that it was 'ard to get in touch with Mr Wedderburn, these days. Good, said Wilkie, and went back to Frederica and the motorbike.

It was now late afternoon. Wilkie said that they would stop and buy a crash helmet for Frederica at the next big garage, and that if she didn't mind him giving her a few tips about riding motorbikes, they would get on better, safer, and faster. For instance, she was to lean forward, not sway about, hold him tightly about the waist and move with him. That would anyway be good practice. They would go out through Calverley, east across the moors, south through Goathland and down to Scarborough, where he reckoned they could be before dinner. Frederica said something awful had once happened to her at Goathland. Wilkie said in that case it would be good for her oversensitive psyche to speed through it on a bike, and that she could tell him about it, if she felt it would do her good, in Scarborough.

Frederica at first intensely enjoyed the motorbike. The crash helmet, when she acquired it, felt like a second high head, and an empty one at that. Wilkie put it on for her, laughed at her, and put on his own, pulling down the goggles, so that only his rather curvy mouth remained of a human face. The mouth was grinning. In motion, she realised that the strong wind they made, and the motor, imposed total silence on her in a flow of inhuman noise, and this she liked. She liked the peculiar intimacy and distance of this relationship with a man, too. There was Wilkie's ample bottom, and her own pushed against it, there were his strong arms, gripping and twisting, and her own clasped tight but not lovingly round his waist. There was the uncommunicative flat of his leathery back and the shiny smooth unmarked globe of the back of his helmet. His legs went up and down, now and then, and hers did not. After a while, as evening drew in, her own legs became very cold, as she had come out in a dirndl skirt, no stockings, and sandals. After more time, she became very stiff, and ached. The heather darkened and began to vanish: Frederica saw little of it, for she had her head tucked most conscientiously into Wilkie's shoulderblade and saw always and only the strip of verge, the flow of tarmac, the white line and the lighting cat's-eyes. Once they stopped at a transport café for a hot cup of Camp coffee and sat next to a wailing and juddering juke box, their limbs too stiff and their faces too set by the wind to speak or smile. There Wilkie expressed concern about her cold legs, said he had not been as clever as he should have been, and insisted on lending her a pair of bright yellow oilskin trousers, hugely too big for her, which she pulled on with stiff hands in a very smelly lavatory. There, too, she remembered Alexander, lovely, elegant and neither in her power nor feeling inadequate. She remembered the sunken garden where they had stood like statues, the eyebeams crossed from stage to scaffold at the height of their incipient shared passion. It would be all right. She had written that he was right, she was wrong, the house was impossible, she had behaved badly and was ashamed and had gone away to think things out and would assuredly be back.

The awful yellow trousers creaked and slithered as she struggled back to Wilkie, clutching them up. He grunted with laughter, and said she looked shapeless and awful, that if she wanted a nice anonymous disguise there wasn't a better one than motorbike gear that didn't fit.

When they finally drove into Scarborough her body was nevertheless frozen and set into a tense curve she wasn't sure she could come out of. Wilkie roared along the Promenade, changing gears and jerking, and out over the rail the black sea stood, with white curls appearing and disappearing in it, with lines of light from harbour wall, and further out, boats, and further out still, the point of cliff and lighthouse. Her heart lifted, as it always did when she saw the sea, no matter how, or when, and always would, she thought, being only just eighteen, and like Daniel, no prophet. Wilkie drove straight up to the Grand Hotel, and parked the bike.

"The bigger, the more anonymous, the less inquisitive, the more fun," he said. "I find. You stay out here and try and get those trousers off, or you'll never get up the steps, and I'll enquire about rooms. Or room."

He came back and said he had booked a room. He pulled off his little signet ring, and suggested she wear that, with the signet itself turned in. "It's worked before," he explained.

She followed him, hobbling, in. He had written in the register, Mr and Mrs Edmund Wilkie, Cambridge. She trailed her rucksack, feeling that she looked unlike Mrs anyone, but the porters were polite, indeed smiling, they bowed and opened lifts, and doors, and there she was, with Edmund Wilkie, in a high-ceilinged room with crimson and gold brocade curtains, a lace counterpane, a kidney-shaped dressing-table and a soft, silent carpet. There was also a large bed, with lamps on little tables and bell-pushes.

Wilkie rattled crash helmets like coconuts and made no attempt to touch her. He said she should have a hot bath, which she did, and put on some make-up so that she looked less like a runaway schoolgirl, which she did, and have dinner, with him, which she did, in a dining room red and gilt and cream with chandeliers and stiff white damask napery and heavy silver knives and forks and spoons. Wilkie laughed at her face. "This is something like," he said. "Posh, Frederica. Not posh, for the likes of us, you understand, but posh for men in Yorkshire industry having weekends off with wives or secretaries. Have what you like to eat, within reason. I'm flush. And I've got more money coming in from some broadcasting I'm lined up for."

"Broadcasting?"

"Well, yes. Two sorts. One on my funny experiment with the coloured glasses, which has produced some quite interesting results. And then I'm doing Parolles in a recording of a Marlowe Society *All's Well*. Still no clear guidance as to the future, you see. I progress on all fronts. I might quit Cambridge, though, if I can get my girl to come. There's beginning to seem no point in actually getting a degree."

They ate consommé julienne, lobster thermidor, and a pudding which was constructed of meringues and cream and sugar and ice cream and nuts to look like a swan sailing with furled wings. They drank a lot of white burgundy. Wilkie made little jokes, and urged Frederica to tell him about Goathland, but she could not, beyond saying that odd things had been said to her, a story about a donkey in a brothel. Donkeys in brothels, said Wilkie, went back to Apuleius and were staple stuff. Look at the lovely little pudding, said Frederica. Just like Elizabeth might have actually had, she thought, she said. This reminded her again of Alexander, and she fell silent.

"Don't *worry*," said Wilkie. "You left a note. He didn't want to go there, not really, you know that with absolute certainty. I'll deliver you back to him."

Alexander had not got the note. He had barely avoided Jennifer, whom he had seen at the foot of his staircase just in time to slip, himself, into the doorway of Lucas Simmonds's, where there gleamed now several bottles of milk, which no one seemed to have cancelled. He did not consider it his responsibility to do so. When he had seen Jennifer leave, he ran back to his car, which he drove up and down, at one point passing Crowe in the Bentley, which hooted peremptorily and rolled on. He got out in Blesford and bought a large bunch of cornflowers, white asters and moon-daisies. He realised that his pockets were still full of intractable letters, which he did not want to spread around his little bedroom, and that he was hot, and tousled, and should have had a wash. All the same, he did not want to go back to his tower. He put the letters in the glove compartment of his car and locked it. He stopped at a pub, drank two pints of beer, and had a wash of sorts in the men's room. He remembered he had promised wine, and purchased two bottles of Vin Rosé d'Anjou. When it was dark he drove back to the school car park and walked down, past the Masters' Garden, across the bridge, past the unruffled black Bilge Pond, towards the garden gate. His heart thumped. His breath came hard. He would do this.

Outside the gate, the blackness of the house struck him. An empty house is recognisable by senses other than sight, but he told himself he was confused, that it could not be so, that she had said repeatedly, as as though it was important, "in the dark". He smelled the cut grass of the terrible Far Field and the warm scent of Winifred's unculled roses: Virgo, Albertine, King's Ransom, Papa Meilland, Elizabeth of Glamis. He banged on the back door and the French window. He called Frederica. No answer. He stood his bottles on the sill of the French window and laid his harvest bundle of flowers beside them. He wandered, with a pretence of casualness, back to the gate and leaned on it. He peered up at bedroom windows, looking, if there had been an observer, as Stephanie had seen Lucas, like Lady Chatterley's lover. He sat on the grass, with his arms clasped boyishly round his knees. Lines of "Come into the garden, Maud" floated with ridiculous persistence through his memory. Queen lily and rose in one. The white rose weeps, she is late, she is late. I am coming, my dove, my dear. The conviction came to him that this moment was, that he himself was, ludicrous.

Time passed. He strode about, but there is not much room for striding in the back gardens of Masters' Row. He lost his temper, and kicked cornflowers and daisies all over the lawn. He said, "Bitch, bitch, I knew it," aloud to the moon. His capacity for both anger and desire had its limits. He remembered the prurient laughter of the bottle chorus and experienced a moment of uncomprehending cold like Demetrius unenchanted by Puck and Oberon. He knew that there would be a moment, very soon, when he would not even be able to understand how he had come to be waiting in that garden. If that were so, there was nothing to prevent him getting out, out of the garden, out of Blesford Ride, out of the North of England, now. It was the glare of her will that had held him, and wherever she was now, he was free. He kicked a few more cornflowers, without savagery: his storms were brief and subsided quickly. He thought of kicking the winebottles, but did not. They could sit on that sill, an offering, for anyone to make of them what anyone could. He would not be there to see. He was going. The whole episode was at an end.

43. *Seas of Blood*

In due course Wilkie took Frederica up to the bedroom, where the bedspread was now off, and the corner of the sheet turned neatly back.

"Well," he said, "we might as well get in."

After some undemonstrative washing and undressing, they got in. Wilkie walked naked towards the bed; Frederica glimpsed him, moony and plump, with sunburned hands and neck and the V of his shirt collar, and his thing, as she thought of it, red, and rigid, and curving up. She turned her face away. There was a smell of toothpaste, an inhuman little smell, and soap, and an undertow of warm bodies. Wilkie made a crinkling sound with paper and rubber, his white back towards her, his neck muscles, which she could see, stiff with concentration.

"Now," he said, "listen. I'm a scientist. I'm going to tell you how all this works, what gives women pleasure, and what gives me pleasure, and then you won't be frightened, and I shall enjoy myself, if we go along gently and carefully. O.K.?"

Frederica nodded. Wilkie sat up and, using her almost as a demonstration model in a human biology class, touched her here and there with dry, delicate fingers, telling her that here she liked to be rubbed, there she liked to be tickled, here he himself was sensitive and could be irritated or pleasured. He murmured something about the need for lubrication, and produced a small jar of vaseline with which, his back again modestly turned, he carefully anointed himself. He was courteous,

THE VIRGIN IN THE GARDEN

dogmatic and authoritative. In later life Frederica was to discover that his knowledge, both about these things in general, and about her own reactions in particular, was not as exhaustive as he might have thought, or claimed, it was. At the time she was grateful to him for seeming so matter-of fact and secure. Later, also, she came to be grateful to him for providing her with the capacity to make further discoveries with aplomb.

At first, Frederica was startled by a kind of running commentary that went on in her ear. (Wilkie did not kiss her. It was as though that was an inappropriate intimacy.) "Oh," said Wilkie, entering her with some slithery effort, "that was a big push. God, that is tight. Are you O.K.?"

"Yes," said Frederica, briefly tight-lipped.

Wilkie made a grunting noise, and pushed up and down for a time. "Is that nice?"

"Oh, yes," said Frederica, who did not find it either particularly nice or particularly nasty, more like incessant Tampax, but was glad it was happening.

After a few moments, and with more vaseline, Wilkie began to rub round and round her clitoris. This struck Frederica as a ridiculous gesture, and also as something unnecessarily intrusive, despite the presence of Wilkie, much larger, much further inside.

"Is that nice?"

"Oh, yes," said Frederica, frowning with concentration. Some vague flickers and ripples of turmoil were happening inside her, a slackening, a ventral dizziness like going down a slide very fast, like the onset of drunkenness. She suppressed all these strongly, sensing with her body, beyond the reach of her mind, that at the end of these waves of feeling was a surrender of her autonomy that she wasn't going to make.

"Put your knees up."

She put them up. Wilkie touched her breasts, which reminded her of Crowe, and murmured something about "erectile tissue", a biological phenomenon she had already decided was overvalued. He continued to pump efficiently up and down. She continued pliable enough, concentrating on not letting go. People's buttocks, thought Frederica, were ridiculous, a ridiculous mixture of wobble and muscle. She laughed.

"Happy?"

"Oh yes."

"Good. Good."

Frederica thought, with a moment of nausea, of Lawrence's descriptions of Constance Chatterley's florid spreading circles of satisfaction. What she had was vertical flickering lines of local tickling, interrupted electric messages which she hastily earthed. Wilkie stopped talking and began to go faster. Frederica stared at his face with interest. His mouth was drooping open, his eyes closed, his breath heavy. His little fat belly was hot and sweaty on hers. After a time, he went very fast indeed, suddenly gave a loud, very private groan, and dropped his head, very heavily for a moment, on her breast, looking tragic and drained. Frederica felt a kind of fluttering and wincing inside, his, or hers, she wasn't sure; there was also some pain, and a hot throb. Wilkie whipped his penis neatly and smartly out, turned over to attend to himself, and fell back on the pillows, turned away.

"Was that all right?" he said, in a fading voice, breathing heavily.

"Oh yes."

"You didn't come."

"I'm sorry." She did not quite know, despite earlier thoughts about Lady Chatterley, what he meant.

"No, no, probably my fault. We'll try again. I once took a girl to a hotel who, every time she came, would scream out like a train whistle, earsplitting, awful. People used to knock on the door to see if I was murdering her. I couldn't moderate it. Pity, really."

"It's all wet."

"Well, it will be." He sighed. "Was it painful?"

"Not much."

He seemed to be drifting into sleep. Frederica stared at the back of his hair, and reflected that she had never known him less well, or felt less close to him, than now, since they first began to talk. She had learned something. She had learned that you could do – that – in a reasonably companionable and courteous way with no invasion of your privacy, no shift in your solitude. You could sleep all night, with a strange man, and see the back only of his head, and be more self-contained than anywhere else. This was a useful thing to know. It removed the awful either/or from the condition of women as she had seen it. Either love, passion, sex and those things, or the life of the mind, ambition, solitude, the others. There was a third way: you could be alone and not alone in a bed, if you made no fuss. She too would turn away and go to sleep.

She went to sleep and was woken, after all, in a panic, by the blood. She pulled at Wilkie.

"Wilkie – please – it's *very* wet, it is."

"Hmm?"

"Please. I seem to be lying in a sea of wet."

"That's wrong," said the obliging Wilkie. "Let's have a look." He leaped out of the bed and turned back the blankets, observing that there'd certainly been blood on the durex thing, but not such a lot he'd thought it worth mentioning.

Blood was rising and puddling round Frederica, her thighs were scarlet, it was creeping in a puddle up her back. Even the collected Wilkie blanched a little at this sight, and asked if she felt faint.

"I don't think so. Just *wet*."

"Sit up."

She sat, and said she did feel faint, a little.

"Let's have a look, how fast it's coming out."

He put his head down, and said it seemed not to be gushing, or even running, very noticeably. He said he would make a pad of a bathtowel and she would sit on that, and he would deal with the bed.

"Wilkie – it's awful, it's embarrassing."

"Rubbish. Hotels are for dealing with this kind of thing. As long as you feel O.K. But I'm not sleeping in a pool of blood, there's limits to my sang-froid. I'm clearing this up. Now sit on this towel and keep still."

She watched, fascinated, whilst he removed the bloody sheet, rinsed it as far as possible in the basin, and hung it over a radiator. Then he remade the bed, with the over-sheet under and the blankets on top. Then he sponged Frederica with a flannel, and reinspected her and the towel.

"It doesn't seem to qualify as a haemorrhage," he said, with his usual cocky certainty. "Just heavy hymeneal bleeding, I'd say."

"Has this happened to you before?"

"I can't say it has, no. I wouldn't like it often, either, it's a bit alarming. And very messy. I think I'll keep off virgins. You can be my only good turn to virgins, Frederica. Now if you get cautiously back in that bed I'll wrap you up in all these towels and fix them on you and then we'll get some sleep. If it were to get worse we'd have to get a doctor, but it won't. You're just a very bleeding sort of girl."

"You are *useful*."

"Right man at right time in right place. I told you so. Poor old Frederica. No point in bringing your swimming costume if that won't stop, either. Now, concentrate on stopping the flow, mind over matter, and wake me up if you're worried."

In ten minutes he was asleep again.

44. *Returns*

Bill and Winifred returned to Blesford the next day. They brought with them Marcus, in an ambulance. Marcus was observedly thinner, and stared with extravagant terror at everything. When he saw the Masters'

Row house he flung himself about, and screamed, and tossed his arms, with an energy that it had not seemed likely he could summon up. He then fainted on the gravel. They carried him into the house and put him on the sofa. When he came round, he began again to scream and flail. A doctor was telephoned. The ambulance returned and Marcus left again. The hospital psychiatrist sent for Winifred, alone.

Frederica and Wilkie had a day on the beach: the wind came howling and icy off the North Sea: Wilkie threw a few stones, and Frederica hobbled beside him, swathed in cotton wool and bleeding, if not profusely, considerably more than she was used to. Finally she said she was sorry to be a drag, she must sit down somewhere, she felt wobbly. Wilkie took her back to the Grand Hotel, where she lay on the bed in a huddle, imagining looks of pity and curiosity on the faces of chamber-maids and porters. Wilkie went away to make a phone call and came back to say that his girl wanted him in Cambridge rather urgently, she was a bit put out not to have been able to get in touch with him, and there was a possibility of a part in a production of *The Changeling* at a student drama festival in Munich. So if she didn't mind, they ought to be getting back.

Alexander did a lot of telephoning. He was feeling buoyant. Now he was out of that garden, his success, his prospects, seemed his own. He arranged to see the BBC in Manchester, and to travel down to London, for interviews there, and then on to Oxford about the schoolmaster fellowship. He refused the interview at the school in Dorset, he had had enough of education, for the time being. He had his trunks brought out of the school basement and some tea chests from the school stores. He went to see Dr Thone, and proffered his formal resignation. He locked his door, sported his oak, put his fretwork notice to OUT and began to pack.

Daniel had a letter from Sheffield, in an unknown hand. When he opened it, he read that his mother had had a bad fall, had cracked her hip in several places and would be in hospital for some weeks, maybe months. At the end of that time it would be quite possible that she would be unable to continue to manage for herself as she had. He appeared, the hospital authorities wrote, to be her closest and indeed only relative, although she had not asked for him. He went to the station and took a train to Sheffield.

Thomas Parry developed a complex infection of the middle ear, with a raging temperature, and screamed day and night for five nights. Geoffrey and Jenny sponged him with cool flannels, tried to make him drink, sat over him.

The psychiatrist said to Winifred that the root cause of Marcus's troubles appeared to be fear of his father, and that it was most desirable that he should recuperate elsewhere, with someone understanding and less alarming, if that could be arranged. He did not want to keep him in the hospital since the place itself was doing him no good, and had unfortunate and undesirable associations with Lucas Simmonds, who was a very sick man, and best left to professional care.

Anthea Warburton set off for a fortnight's visit to the kind Marina Yeo, and a sunny holiday with friends and cousins in Juan-les-Pins.

Frederica and Wilkie drove, as stately as a motorbike can drive, back into Blesford, and roared along Masters' Row. Going in the other direction, behind the Blesford bus, was Alexander's silver Triumph. It had, as it had not had before, a roof-rack, which was tidily loaded, and roped in with a tarpaulin. Frederica saw Alexander, quite clearly, beautifully brushed, smiling, preserved and distant behind the greenish glass of the windscreen. Alexander saw Wilkie clearly enough, allowing for the insect-bulge of helmet and goggles, and saw a flicker and puff of ginger hair behind Wilkie's clinging passenger which allowed him to identify her. He looked out at the road in front of him and continued to smile, thus missing the nervous waving and leaping of Jenny Parry at her garden gate. It was not in Alexander's nature to let other people have the dénouement, or crisis, or climax, to which they might in life feel entitled, however well he knew that in art such things are necessary. His endings, like his beginnings, were solitary things. He let out the clutch and fled faster.

Wilkie put Frederica down, gathered up her helmet, strapped it to his pillion – "do for my girl," he said – and pushed up his own visor to kiss her.
  She said, "I will see you again, won't I?"
  "Probably. It's a small world. Look after yourself."
  He closed up his face, too, in plastic shields and screens, and clambered onto the bike. She stood on the pavement, and watched him roar away after Alexander. She saw Jennifer Parry on her garden path, and began to take in the implications of Alexander's roof-rack and comportment. She walked into the house and was met by a roar of rage from her father

who wanted to know where she thought she had been, why she had left such a mess in the house, with uncooked food scattered across the kitchen, and why, when he had opened the French window, wine-bottles had shattered all over the paving. And as much mess in the garden as in the kitchen, and her mother quite distracted, and all she could think of was swanning off with smart friends. Frederica was saved from answering these reproaches, which shed a little more murky light on Alexander's possible feelings and movements, by the telephone, which Bill answered. It was, he said, coming back hunched and suppressed, her mother. He told Frederica what Winifred said the psychiatrist had said about Marcus. He said he had always believed they all knew he didn't mean it – the things he sometimes did and said. Frederica said testily, her mind still on Alexander, that Marcus had clearly not known, had he, and that if he wanted to know, she thought Stephanie had not known, either, but that she, Frederica, if it comforted him, was made of tougher stuff, and did know that he wasn't going, in this crisis, to fuss about uncooked chops on the kitchen table and wine-bottles on the flower-beds. She then took in his expression and felt a twinge of pity and more than a twinge of fear. She cast about for a practical solution. There was Daniel, she said. Marcus seemed to trust Daniel. She'd noticed. Maybe Daniel and Stephanie would have Marcus until he'd pulled himself together a bit, or whatever he had to do.

Bill said gloomily that there was hardly room in that ludicrous little flat for another person, let alone two more with a baby, and that Daniel had enough on his plate. Frederica said that was one thing about Daniel, you could never say with certainty that he had enough on his plate. Bill became tense and thoughtful, and then put on his coat and rushed out to Askham Buildings.

It had turned out, as it happened, that it was to be impossible for the Ortons to stay in Askham Buildings. Daniel returned from Sheffield and said that he feared they would definitely have to house his mother. Mr Ellenby found for them a workman's cottage in a part of Blesford where the younger middle classes were doing up such dwellings into tiny first homes, and suggested Daniel get his Youth Club layabouts onto the decorating. Stephanie, after the surprise of Bill's inrush, his tears of self-accusation, his dramatic enactment of Marcus's plight and his own guilt, said to Daniel that it was as much their duty to have Marcus, if he would come, as to have Daniel's mother. Of course, said Daniel. Of course they must have Marcus. If Marcus wanted. Marcus, when Daniel went to the hospital and asked him, said he did want. It was the only thing he said at all for several days.

Autumn came and grew cold. Marcus was brought to Askham Buildings, where he slept on the sitting-room sofa until the cottage was fit for habitation. Frederica went back to Blesford Girls' Grammar and began to work for university entrance. It had rapidly become clear to her that Alexander had gone for good. She felt humiliated, but also, without the stress of his presence, of desire, of a crisis to work for or avoid, she felt self-contained. The most useful lesson of the summer, she discovered, had been that things, and people, could by her be kept separate from each other. She could lie on her bed and weep for Alexander, also for Wilkie, and even for *Astraea*, but she could then rise up neatly and discover large available reserves of energy and concentration to spend gleefully on her work. She was pleased that the simple landmark of the bleeding was, however messily, past. She was shaken and discomposed by the change in her parents. Bill had cancelled a lot of classes, and spent his time wandering up and down, restlessly, in carpet slippers. He spoke to no one, often even opening and closing his mouth silently as though physically choking back speech. Winifred spent days together in bed. Frederica worked through this, for the sake of the way out, for the sake of the books themselves. But one night, feeling the danger of emotions seeping between the laminations of her attention, she decided to go and call on Daniel and Stephanie, to see at first hand how Marcus was, what was to be hoped, or feared.

Daniel opened the door to her, did not smile, but let her in. She said brightly, "I just dropped by, to see you. It's unbearable at home. Oppressive."

Daniel could have said the same, but would not. He said, "Well, do sit down, now you're here. I'll make a cup of tea."

Stephanie and Marcus were sitting in silence on the sofa, side by side, his thin body in some strange way propped and supported by her swollen one. Stephanie nodded at Frederica, as though Marcus was a child or invalid not to be disturbed: Marcus gave no sign of having noticed her.

Since Marcus had come, the Ortons' whole life had changed. For the first two days Marcus had turned to Daniel, whimpering like a small child if he went out of sight. Stephanie had noticed that this irritated Daniel, and was dismayed. She tried to take over: sat for long hours next to Marcus in a neutral unmoving silence, as she had sat with Malcolm Haydock: it was not, indeed, so very different. One day she had offered him the information that Lucas Simmonds had been moved again and was said to be feeling calmer: Marcus had asked if Lucas had been hurt or attacked, and when assured that he had not, had offered Stephanie a version of his fears for Lucas and himself, of Lucas's smashed hopes, of the photisms, the transmissions, the light. She had not understood much of this but had thought, possibly wrongly, that what was required was not understanding but "total acceptance", and she had set with her usual conscientiousness about accepting Marcus. Animal taming came into it, as it had into her imagery about Malcolm Haydock: she had made it possible for him to lay his head in her lap for long hours and do nothing, be still. So Daniel increasingly found them when he came in from his work: he accepted her recuperative stillness, he tried not to interfere.

He went into the kitchen now, to make Frederica's cup of tea, clattered with kettles and plates, lumbered from cupboard to cupboard. After a moment, Frederica followed him out there. She hissed, "Is it like that all the time? Will he get better?"

"I don't know."

"How do you *manage*?"

"I'm not sure." Daniel gave a brief, grim smile. He did not like Frederica Potter: he would not tell her how he felt, who in any case habitually told no one. But the answer was that he barely did manage. A moral man, he was appalled by his own reactions to Marcus's presence, and to Stephanie herself. He dreamed nightly of murder. Pale innocent Marcus, slaughtering his unborn child. The child ripping Stephanie bloodily apart under his own eyes. Himself, Daniel Orton, pursuing Bill Potter across Far Field with Simmonds's carving knife. And, most terrible of all, a blanket terror of smothering: his own bulk accidentally weltering on a, on the child, some unknown damp and heavy monstrosity pressing and choking away his own life. He could not speak to, or frighten, his wife, who was pregnant, and was doing what she believed to be right. He was truly sorry for Marcus. He missed the days of laughter and heat in that little flat, which would never come again. Even on a purely practical level he could say nothing: the walls were thin, the flat was tiny, the boy was always inert but alert and nervous.

"How do you *manage*, Daniel?" Frederica repeated.

"It's got an end. There'll be more space in the cottage. He'll get over th'shock. It's to be hoped. And there'll be the baby."

He stood for a moment staring out, as he often stared, as he had stared on his honeymoon night, at the black tyre turning and returning on its gallows, at the twisted thorn and the tracked muddy sea. She stared with him.

"In our house everyone's gone passive and flabby as though energy was indecent. I work but I feel I'm attached to nothing, all in the air, loose."

"Aye."

"Whereas you seem – a bit clotted with problems."

"Oh, aye," said Daniel, staring. "In the midst of life, I am. It's the normal course of things." He had told himself that, often and often. But his powers were blunted by care: for the first time since his conversion he acknowledged the possibility of being wholly impeded from using his energies. He sensed some shadow of this care in the thin silly girl beside him.

"You'll be all right once you've got into t'university. It's just the waiting time."

"I suppose so. And you – when the baby's born."

"Aye."

"And Marcus?"

"I don't know, Frederica. He's not my kind of practical problem."

He piled up teacups and a packet of biscuits and they went back into the little box of a room. Marcus had his head against Stephanie's shoulder; he sagged like a straw man; his limp hands and legs were still. She sat, like some unnatural and ungainly Pietà, looking out over his pale hair at Daniel, with what seemed to be unseeing patience. He had unfrozen her once, and could surely do so again. He said again to Frederica, "It's a question of the waiting time – of being patient now – for all of us."

Waiting and patience, of this inactive kind, did not come easily to him. Or to Frederica, he decided, without much sympathy for her. He gave her a cup of tea and the two of them sat together in uncommunicative silence, considering the still and passive pair on the sofa. That was not an end, but since it went on for a considerable time, is as good a place to stop as any.

About the Author

A. S. BYATT has written six works of fiction — *Possession*, which won the Booker Prize and the Irish Times/Aer Lingus International Fiction Prize, as well as *Shadow of a Sun*, *The Game*, *The Virgin in the Garden*, *Still Life*, and *Sugar and Other Stories*. She has taught English and American literature at University College, London, and is a distinguished critic and reviewer. Her critical work includes *Degrees of Freedom* (a study of Iris Murdoch) and *Unruly Times: Wordsworth and Coleridge in Their Time*. Her latest book is entitled *Passions of the Mind: Selected Essays*.